T0387963

Practiceopolis

This is a graphic novel about the contemporary architectural profession, in which it acts as the protagonist in the form of an imaginary city called Practiceopolis. The novel narrates quasi-realistic stories that exaggerate the architectural everyday and the tacit, in order to make them prominent and tangible. They depict and dramatise the value conflicts between the different cultures of practising architecture and between the architectural profession and other members of the building industry as political conflicts around the future of Practiceopolis.

The book uses the metaphorical world of Practiceopolis to provoke big questions about everyday routines in the profession that practitioners may take for granted and to examine different ideologies at work among architects and other members of the construction industry. The novel ends in the tradition of dystopian worlds common in a certain strand of graphic novels.

By vividly illustrating and narrating the critical issues he interrogates, the author has created a world which any architect, student or professional, will both instantly recognise and simultaneously reject, provoking the reader to challenge themselves and the profession at large.

Yasser Megahed is Senior Lecturer at Leicester School of Architecture, De Montfort University. He holds a PhD by Design degree from the School of Architecture, Planning and Landscape, Newcastle University, as well as MSc and BArch degrees in Architecture from Cairo University. His research is focused on interrogating cultures of contemporary architectural practice through practice-based methodologies, bridging design research, professional practice research and history and theory of architecture, in addition to a special interest in the use of Design Fiction as a tool for communicating architectural ideas. Yasser worked as an associate architect at Design Office, UK, where he was one of the concept team for the £25 million refurbishment of the Armstrong Building, Newcastle University – shortlisted for the RIBA North East Award 2019. Previously he worked as a senior architect at Architecture and Urbanism Group, Cairo, where he was involved in several projects and winning architectural competitions covering different building typologies in Egypt and the Middle-East.

"This engaging book is hard to place. It is a graphic novel with serious intent: to survey and critique contemporary ways of practising architecture. At the same time, it questions the idea of practice, as it operates in both a globalised construction industry and the industry of cultural commentary. So this is a professional practice textbook. But it is also a theory book. And a satire on architects and architecture. Meanwhile, it shows how cartooning and storytelling can yield methods for architectural research. *Practiceopolis* will be of interest to architects, to students of architectural design, practice, and theory, and to anyone who wants to think about what it means to construct buildings in the twenty-first century."

– Adam Sharr, Professor of Architecture, and Head of the School of Architecture, Planning and Landscape, Newcastle University, UK

Practiceopolis
Stories from the Architectural Profession

Yasser Megahed

Routledge
Taylor & Francis Group

LONDON AND NEW YORK

First published 2021
by Routledge
2 Park Square, Milton Park, Abingdon, Oxon OX14 4RN

and by Routledge
52 Vanderbilt Avenue, New York, NY 10017

Routledge is an imprint of the Taylor & Francis Group, an informa business

Publisher's Note
This book has been prepared from camera-ready copy provided by the author.

British Library Cataloging-in-Publication Data
A catalogue record for this book is available from the British Library

Library of Congress Cataloging-in-Publication Data
Names: Megahed, Yasser, author.
Title: Practiceopolis : stories from the architectural profession / Yasser Megahed.
Description: Abingdon, Oxon ; New York, NY : Routledge, 2020. | Includes bibliographical references.
Identifiers: LCCN 2020013305 (print) | LCCN 2020013306 (ebook) | ISBN 9780367425432 (hbk) | ISBN 9780367425449 (pbk) | ISBN 9780367853341 (ebk)
Subjects: LCSH: Architectural practice--Comic books, strips, etc. | LCGFT: Graphic novels.
Classification: LCC NA1995 .M395 2020 (print) | LCC NA1995 (ebook) | DDC 720--dc23
LC record available at https://lccn.loc.gov/2020013305
LC ebook record available at https://lccn.loc.gov/2020013306

ISBN: 978-0-367-42543-2 (hbk)
ISBN: 978-0-367-42544-9 (pbk)
ISBN: 978-0-367-85334-1 (ebk)

Typeset in Times New Roman
by Yasser Megahed

CONTENTS

For my lovely daughter, Alia, whose
smile always gives me hope...

PROLOGUE

NOTES ON THE CONTEMPORARY ARCHITECTURAL PROFESSION – THE STATUS QUO

The architectural profession is multiple, rich, and diverse. Inscribed in this multiplicity are diverse cultures of practice that differ in their intellectual positions, their particular visual languages, professional vocabularies, and frames of reference where their knowledge is drawn. These cultures of practice are in an on-going struggle for economic and cultural capital within the territory of the architectural profession which nevertheless together comprise what can be described as a state of dynamic equilibrium. The term refers to a system where different parts of a composition can change freely within a fixed and steady whole.[1] This state of dynamic equilibrium, it can be argued, is what allows the architectural profession to change internally while maintaining its coherence as a field. On the other hand, processes of construction and inhabitation involve several other actors in the building industry including engineering consultants, quantity surveyors, contractors, manufacturers, project managers, real estate developers, facility and asset managers, etc. In the contemporary building industry, the role of those actors is progressively intersecting with that of the architectural profession. Consequently, with the increasing complexity of the building production process, architectural decisions started to be widely influenced by agencies outside its control and the intertwined interest of these actors.

The architectural profession seems to have a distinct position within the construction industry. This is attributed to methodological differences from its siblings in the building production process. Among these differences, architecture as a field of knowledge is distinguished by its uncomfortable position between ideas, methods, and languages deriving broadly from the historical cultures of arts and science. Vitruvius saw architecture as a science that integrates the art of building functionality and aesthetics.[2] The often-favoured image of the architect is as a humanist distinct from the engineer, imbued with the literature, arts, and architecture of the past, who would approach their work as an artist aware of science rather than as a scientist aware of art.[3] Whatever the particular position of architects and architecture may be between the two worlds of arts and science, this position lends the architectural field its varied expertise and a wide frame of reference to draw from. This has resulted in its distinctive set of values, discourses, and even terminologies which are different from those of its siblings in the industry.[4]

Broadly speaking, the base priority for the architectural field might be expressed by the term 'design' with all the connotations the term may bring, to do with creativity, visual distinction, functional suitability, aesthetics, cultural and contextual appropriateness, strategic and spatial thinking, etc.[5] The architectural profession glorifies its historic legacy as the leader of the building production process. While this leadership has come into question intellectually and contractually with the complexities of the construction process, its symbolic stature remains a pervasive idea at least among architects.[6] This symbolic stature is caricatured with the image of Howard Roark, the individualistic egoistic architect who refuses to compromise 'his' architectural vision under any circumstances. This iconic figure from Ayn Rand's novel *The Fountainhead* still – arguably – represents a common self-perception among architects of their role as leaders of the building process.[7]

On the other hand, many members of the industry have challenged this perceived role claimed for the architectural profession. Their disapproval is supported by the growing technical and technological complications of the contemporary building construction that have tended to involve a vast number of specialities in the process of design decision-making. Building production has become in the contemporary sphere a scientific and technical process that many believe should be quantitatively controlled and must be translated into risk reduction and profit according to strict codes, regulations, planning permission processes, and coordination protocols. In this view, buildings have become an asset that should be readily deliverable and profitable.[8]

This understanding of the role of the architectural profession can be found even in various professional literature and discourses. In the RIBA report: 'The Future for Architects?' (2010), Dickon Robinson (Chair of RIBA Building Futures) echoed this view. He argues that:

> *"[Architects need] to respond to the impact of a globalising economy, exploding information technology capability and cultural confusion. However in the face of a continuing erosion of traditional architectural skills to other players, the profession seems peculiarly vulnerable to a nostalgic backward glance at a bygone age in which the architect was the undisputed boss."*[9]

In this view, the architectural profession is a small part of a process which – as many actors in the industry believe – cannot be led by the limited knowledge of architects.[10] Consequently, many actors in the building industry adopt a view that architects need to comply with the values and ideologies of the industry as a whole and perform as any other consultant in the process of building production.[11] The agreement between these actors may be attributed to their mutual understanding of the superiority of what can be called 'hard' quantitative knowledge based on science, technology, and technical performance. In this context, architectural knowledge is often characterised as 'soft', subjective, artistic, and stylistic. These qualities are not understood – by many – to be as valid as quantitative knowledge in the building production process.

Architects, on the other hand, tend to perceive that there is very little understanding among developers and the wider building industry of the benefits that the architectural skill-set brings to the built environment. Architects sense that they rarely have the opportunity to deploy their diligent, painstaking, and expensive design abilities for the benefit of the construction industry.[12] They believe that the technical and technological sophistication of contemporary building processes should not substitute for conventional architectural expertise.[13] They perceive it as compromising the distinctive and exploratory nature of the process of architectural design within a culture of 'the generic' that tends to stick to the tried and tested, and the temptation to do business as usual.[14] Therefore, architects are reluctant to define their role in the way that other members of the building industry want them to. They believe that their role as designers of the building has become constrained to somehow giving the building its visual image.[15]

The Domination of a Technical-rational Ideology over the Contemporary Construction Industry

The debate outlined above is not new to the building industry. It saw many variations from the 20th century to the present contested through varying mixes of technical facts, opposing arguments, value assumptions, and conflicts of interest. An important outcome of this period, especially in the post-war era, was the domination of a new ideology in architecture – and in the building industry in general – that reflects the idea of technical and technological optimism.[16] This optimism bore witness to the flourishing of the Modernist architecture accompanied by different attempts in the building industry to seek greater levels of productivity and precision in construction.[17] The foundational values of this period were centred upon rational, functional, and practical approaches to constructing space. This period offered a new level of material efficiency, at a lower cost, with ideas about simple construction and easy maintenance.[18] This involved the use of plain materials, whose grain, patina and assembly were imagined as being expressed through a kind of structural 'honesty'. These values were manifest in buildings that are rationally planned, decoratively mute and in line with the Modernist design principles.[19] Such principles evolved later to form the ethos of the technical-rational ideology that is currently dominating the contemporary building industry and mainstream architectural practice.

The philosopher Donald Schön describes technical-rationality as the mode of practice that involves selecting technical means best suited to solve well-formed instrumental problems by applying theories and techniques derived from rational systematic scientific methods.[20] In building construction, technical-rationality can be seen in the growing conception of the understanding of the building process through notions of productivity and practicality, represented often by tangible quantitative criteria for quality control. It is generally reflected in the application of management theory and systems thinking in the building process.[21] The technical-rational mode of thinking can be traced back to the divorce between faith and reason in the Enlightenment Age that culminated in the philosophy of Positivism and the idea of progress.[22] In architecture, these intellectual changes in human thoughts were reflected through attempts to found architectural knowledge in science and mathematical reason. This was developed by architects and theorists who researched optimum rules for proportions of classic orders using scientific and experimental methods to achieve what they consider 'natural beauty'.[23]

The algebraisation of architectural theory and the tireless effort to produce a rational theory in the 17th century and early 18th century had culminated in the theories of the French architect, professor, and theorist of architecture Jean-Nicolas-Louis Durand. His writings best exemplified the transformation of theory into a self-referential instrument for the control of architectural practice in the 19th century.[24] Durand's ideas involved emptying architectural knowledge from anything lacking a clear scientific value. For him, the only way out for architecture's knowledge evolution became in efficiency and economy of operations. Accordingly, in his theory, design acted merely as a vehicle for ensuring functionality and efficiency.[25] What Durand brought to architecture was the exclusion of its knowledge to the purely rational reason, following strictly the values of Positivism philosophy. Durand's approach found similar resonance in the 20th century's tendencies towards scientising architectural knowledge best exemplified in Leslie Martin's typologies and in the categorical format of architectural data and standard books. His materialistic premise became the basis of the ethics and aesthetics of architecture of the 19th century, and it still underlies many ideological conceptions from the 20th century till now, mainly those of the contemporary technical-rational mainstream architectural practice.

The current domination of the technical-rational ethos over the building industry seems like a reaction to the complexities of the contemporary construction process that necessitates surrendering to technologies, engineers, contractors, and manufacturers.[26] This domination is also an outcome of the pressing economic requirements of the complex conditions of the globalised world.[27] With its Positivist, technical, and management roots as well as the support from the values of the global capitalist market, this ideology resulted in creating a culture of 'fear of error', obsessive precision, and risk avoidance that imbued the mainstream culture of building production. Whether the rise of the technical-rational ideology drove this culture of 'fear of error' or vice versa, together they defined the priorities of the contemporary construction industry.[28]

On the other hand, the increased currency attributed to that of the technical-rational ideology in the contemporary building process has created a pressure on the architectural profession to adopt this ideology and to yield to its imperatives.[29] There has been only faint resistance to this pressure from the architectural profession's side. This may be attributed to different reasons but mainly the multiple – however slippery to define – nature of the architectural field and its particular values. While bringing intellectual richness, the multiplicity of the architectural profession also brings disagreement about foundational issues in the field. Among these issues, I can cite, for instance, questions around why we design the way we do at a certain time; why a building from a particular period has a particular form; and whether particular forms ought to be correlated with particular tasks. The architectural field is freighted with moral questions about what are the 'true', 'right', and 'authentic' ways of practising architecture and different definitions of architectural best practice, critical practice, and rigour.[30] These rich but inconclusive issues became an obstacle for the architectural profession in coping with the dominating technical-rational values of the industry that prioritise instead definite notions of integrations, control, efficiency, productivity, and timely delivery.[31] The apparent mismatch between the special – while indefinite – values of the architectural profession and those of the building industry seems to be responsible for shaping a large part of its conflicts within the contemporary construction process. All this pressure on the architectural professions has led mainstream architectural practices to defend the profession's threatened position by trying to merge more with the dominating technical-rational ideology of the building industry.[32]

The Dynamic Equilibrium of the Contemporary Architectural Profession

The growing authority of the technical-rational ideology over the building construction process has resulted in the prevalence of a certain culture of practising architecture that sides in many ways with the technical-rational values of the broader building industry.[33] From the late 1970s, a substantial share of architectural production has become centrally sited within the corporate market. The scale of projects involved and the dependence on more complex and specialised means of production and distribution have – to an important extent – imposed the predominant conditions of corporate values over the architectural profession.[34] This new condition of architectural production has effectively led to the current status quo of the architectural profession, which is dominated by a globalised normative commercially-driven culture of practice that is often associated with the production of buildings by or for multinational corporations or which tends to echo their values.[35] This culture of practice has now become the dominant mode of practising architecture in terms of number and scale of commissions.[36]

Nonetheless, the domination of the Technical-rational Culture of practice does not mean that other cultures of practice have not survived. The complex structure of the architectural field has allowed other non-dominant modes of building production to persist and to retain a significant cultural capital. Among these cultures, what can be termed the Critical Culture of practice has maintained a prominent presence within the contemporary architectural profession. This culture of practice covers a wide range of practices that broadly promote ideas of qualitative and socio-cultural conceptions of architecture.[37] It shares many lines of inquiry found in critical theory; particularly questioning claims to truth, essentialism, and autonomy; tending to render their theories political in outlook and action.[38] The Critical Culture inclines to oppose the current situation of the profession as dominated by the Technical-rational Culture.[39] It broadly views the status quo of the profession as a space of flat indifference and stagnant incommensurability of indistinct generic space, or as Rem Koolhaas calls it: Junkspace.[40] The Critical Culture rejects the notion of an authentic way of practising architecture. It generally views that the architectural profession should be a space for diverse dialogues that enrich the profession and society at large, and as an opportunity for interdisciplinary communications between architecture and other participants of the building realm.[41]

The equilibrium made by the competition between these two prominent cultures of practice reflects an embodiment of the French social scientist Pierre Bourdieu's notion of cultural capital in the architectural field, in particular, the 'field of large-scale production' (FLP) and the much smaller 'field of restricted production' (FRP).[42] Bourdieu describes the 'field of large-scale production' (FLP) as a field in which 'less' well-educated producers responded to the demands of the popular, and largely uneducated market. On the other hand, the small 'field of restricted production' is defined as an autonomous field in which well-educated consumers shared the codes of aesthetic appreciation with well-educated producers. Both cultural fields are in a continuous struggle for acquiring the dominant position and for defining its priorities. In turn, the competition between those two fields of cultural and economic production is key for the evolution of the field and for shaping its priorities.[43]

Extending the concept beyond Bourdieu's use of the term, the social space of the architectural profession can be described by the distribution of capital between these two prominent cultures of practice: the Technical-rational and the Critical. The first is broadly dominated by economic values while the other is dominated by symbolic ones. The 'field of large-scale production' reflects the more utilitarian and commercial practices that are affluent, easy to grasp, and apply more to the economic rules of the market, namely the mainstream Technical-rational Culture of practice. On the other hand, the 'field of restricted production' (FRP) could be represented by resistant critical and explorative modes of practice, namely the Critical Culture of practice. The competition and mobility between practices under those two cultures or two fields of production could be then the significant condition influencing the dynamic equilibrium of the contemporary architectural profession.

While this binary categorisation may seem a little old fashioned by developing a dualism of the Technical-rational versus the Critical Cultures of practice, it, however, provides a useful analytical framework and a starting point to explore the complex interrelationships defining the values of the architectural profession and its relation with the building industry. This dualism, however, can be implicitly traced in various forms of architectural literature. Literature on architecture is torn between those two cultures. One is often technically and technologically based, focusing on how buildings respond to material and financial constraints and on building production as a profit- and delivery-oriented process that should be controlled and measured. The other common kind of literature on architecture is more social and humanistic, about how a building expresses a certain style, a certain period, or a certain idea of what it is to inhabit a place.[44] The first broadly carries an implicit message that the other is outdated and holds up the profession from coping with the advances in the industry. Conversely, the other accuses the first of being reductive and commercial, and encourages consumerism and banality.[45] The opposing nature of types of literature in architecture may give the impression that they are representing two different professions not variations of the same profession. While not claiming a polarised clash between the two prominent cultures of practice, their value disagreement displays some similarity to C.P. Snow's *Two Cultures*, which provoked widespread debate in the late 1950s about discord between the cultures of science and humanities.[46] Interestingly, by seeing the very different nature of literature of the two prominent cultures of practice, some similar connotations can be drawn.

In effect, the existence of disagreements between the prominent cultures of practice may be what maintains the dynamic balance of the contemporary architectural profession. Nevertheless, the increasing domination of the technical-rational ideology over the profession is leading a large segment of architectural practices to restrict themselves to the mandates of this technical and economic model that favours strategies that adopt the form of the generic and normed. The accordance of this model with the values of the different members of the industry amplified its influence on the process of decision-making in the building process and eased the approval of decisions that may not accord with traditional humanistic architectural values. This has created a supposed authority of the technical-rational world-view, allowing it the lead in deciding strategies about the future path of the profession and affecting the intellectual directions of many architectural bodies such as RIBA, AIA, etc.[47]

While appreciating the benefits of the technical-rational model of practice as a shared platform with other members of the building industry, the growing emphasis on the shared may lead to marginalising many of the particular values embedded within the architectural field of knowledge. Accordingly, while still in a condition of balance, the current dynamic equilibrium of the profession is gradually becoming contingent and liable to what the dominant mainstream technical-rational model of practice pushes the profession towards. The imperatives of this unbalance have started to be perceptible in many aspects of the architectural profession's everyday routines, discourse, and aspirations. This state of unbalance has been inflated further by the prevailing global capitalist economic values that push for a competitive atmosphere of increased production and profit, and claims a special correlation between the success of the architectural profession and the prevalence of the technical-rational model of thinking. Altogether, these factors give some clues on why the position of the architectural profession is changing in the contemporary building production process and raise questions about the future trajectory of the architectural profession.

THIS BOOK

This book comes in a moment where the value of architects has started to come into question in contemporary building construction discourse. From literature about architects losing leadership position in the industry to others arguing that architects must follow the more specialised members of the building team, the book illustrates the architects' point of view in this debate, showing one important dimension of the story of the building construction process. The book calls for understanding the territory of the architectural profession and the particular values it brings to the building industry. It argues that architectural practitioners should be more aware of the multiplicity of the intellectual structures of their profession and the imperatives of this multiplicity on its relationship with other members of the industry. By doing so, architects are no different from any other profession in their need to define their territory, their area of control, as distinct from others. This may help architects to understand and then protect their unique values and allow them to communicate productively with other actors in the building realm.

To achieve that, the book delivers a story about and from within the contemporary architectural profession, in which it acts as the protagonist in the form of the imaginary city of *Practiceopolis*. Practiceopolis is a fictive city-state, representing the contemporary architectural profession and located within the island of 'Constructopolis—the Confederation of the Building Industry', a union of states representing different members in the construction domain. By using this provocative metaphor, the cultural capital of the architectural field is 'architecturalised' through visible and tangible elements that help to investigate the dialogues between prominent cultures of practice and in general between the profession and its siblings in industry. The book narrates stories about the competition between prominent cultures of practice in the city's political scene. It also portrays how the architectural profession is not autonomous but implicated in the values and agendas of other actors in the industry with whom it cooperates. The book uses the metaphorical world of Practiceopolis to provoke big questions about everyday routines in the profession that practitioners may take for granted and to examine different ideologies at work among architects and other members of the construction industry and the largely tacit assumptions which inform them.

Practiceopolis draws on diverse literature around the nature of the architectural profession and its challenges in the building industry and within the global capitalist market. It comes across works of Dana Cuff, Robert Gutman, Paolo Tombesi, Leslie Sklair, and Rem Koolhaas on the particularities of the architectural profession and the imperative of globalism on it. In addition, it builds upon Jeremy Till's critique of architects' self-image and claims of autonomy and Flora Samuel's works on the value of the architect. The configuration of Practiceopolis builds in particular upon an interpretation of the philosopher Andrew Feenberg's stances towards technology and technical knowledge, translating them into architectural equivalents that help to map the intellectual position of the various cultures of practice operating in the contemporary architectural profession.[48]

The Graphic Novel

The book is choreographed as an architectural graphic novel – drawing from methods of storytelling, cartooning, and dialectic discourse to represent the status quo of the contemporary architectural profession and its relation with the building industry. The novel employs the extremity allowed by storytelling, cartoons, and Design Fiction[49] methodologies to illustrate and investigate a perceived division between the values of the prominent cultures of architectural practice and broadly among the members of the building construction industry. It re-stages real-world instances from the author's own construction experience into the fictional terrain of Practiceopolis. The stories relocate these instances to the imaginary city and dramatise them as conflicts between prominent cultures of practising architecture. The novel then takes these value-conflicts to Practiceopolis Parliament as a political debate around competing visions for the future of the city within the Confederation of the Building Industry—Constructopolis. The stories of Practiceopolis build a fictional reality that discusses relationships among different ideologies. They make a visual representation of how value-conflicts within the building process happen in real-life communications within the construction industry. Through the different stories in the novel, we will explore relationships, world-views, and attitudes, as well as anecdotes that capture moments in architectural practice that often go unnoticed.

The novel is critical and satirical, using parody to highlight the contradictions and misunderstandings that emerge when the somewhat incompatible world-views of diverse actors involved in building production collide. The body of the novel consists of three parts: an introduction to the City of Practiceopolis, the Atkinson Building Story, and the Debate in Practiceopolis Parliament. The first part features a journey in the social, cultural, and political structure of the city. It narrates key shifts in the canonical (Western) history of architecture through a story of a power struggle between the protagonists of different cultures of architectural practice and shows how this development resulted in making contemporary Practiceopolis and setting the rules that govern this imaginary architectural world. It describes the main areas in the city, influential sources of power, its relation with neighbour states, and other fundamental details that define what is considered the city of the architectural profession.

The second part of the novel narrates some stories from within Practiceopolis that exaggerate the architectural profession's everyday routines and tacit practices, to make them tangible and ready for deep examination. It goes in detail into one of the significant buildings in Practiceopolis that witnessed many of the historical shifts of the city and reflected the ideologies and architectural logics prevailing at these times. This part narrates a set of quasi-realistic stories that dramatise real-life architectural and extra-architectural exchanges from everyday practice. These stories are based on a series of project management meetings held during the conduct of a live architectural project in the UK (named in the novel as the Atkinson Building) in which the author was part of the concept architects team. It reflects upon the exchanges that occurred during the project's Progress and Value Engineering Meetings, highlighting the presence of multiple and different cultures of practice represented by concept architects, facility management services, engineering consultants, contractors, quantity surveyors, and a multinational project manager. This part relocates those exchanges to the imaginary city of Practiceopolis, dramatising them as political conflicts between the various cultures of practice and the members of the building industry. As a blend of auto-ethnographic observation with design and fiction, it illustrates everyday events from practice, examining through them ideologies at work among architects and other members of the construction industry.

The final part of the novel displays the confrontation between the prominent cultures of practice within Practiceopolis. Taking inspiration from C.P. Snow's *The Two Cultures* (1969) and its subsequent debates and criticisms, this part takes the value-conflict to an extreme debate that polarises the dialogue between those cultures as the thesis and antithesis of a dialectical discourse.[50] The novel ends in the tradition of dystopian worlds common in a certain strand of graphic novels with near-future speculation that extrapolates present contemporary conditions to warn against a substantial change, or even an end, to the architectural profession.

The book concludes with speculations about the future of the architectural profession. It indicates the danger of the domination of a single culture of practice over the profession and the strict attachment to its value, which could result in subsuming distinctive values of the architectural profession under the values of other actors in the industry.

PRACTICE
OPOLIS

01
THE CITY OF
PRACTICE OPOLIS

No Architects land
Practiceopolis
Constructopolis

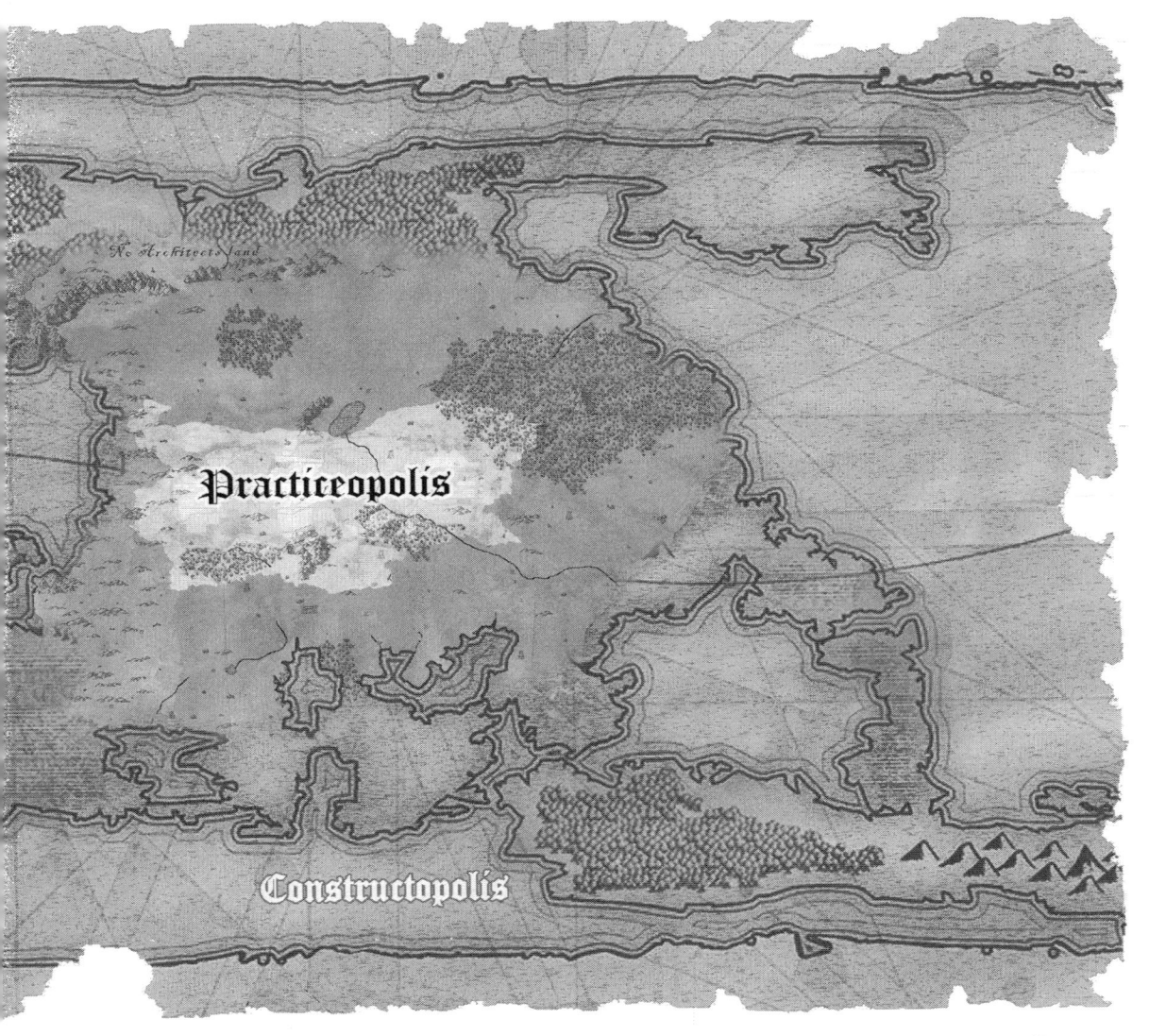

"Architecture resembles a large contemporary city, in which no overriding system pre-dominates over all the others, but, on the contrary, the inherent tensions and differences lead to alternatives and sometimes new modes of action."

Bernard Tschumi (2004: p. 15)

PRACTICEOPOLIS

In the short story: On Exactitude in Science, J. L. Borges (1975) imagined an empire where the art of cartography exceeded all limits and maps became an exact manifestation of the city. In this empire, the cartographers' guilds created a map of the empire whose size was that of the empire, and which coincided point for point with it (Borges, 1975). Inspired by this story, Practiceopolis started as a 1:1 map of the geography of the world of the architectural profession. It exists in a fictional dimension as an exaggerated version of our contemporary architectural world extracted in physically condensed form. One can find images of Practiceopolis in each city where different cultures of practice are in conversation with each other through their buildings. In any street or square in the city, one can find juxtaposed buildings that stand for different cultures of practice; each is the best evidence of the intellectual position behind its design. Practiceopolis concentrates these built conversations in one place; nonetheless, there is no place like this and perhaps could never be such a place.

Practiceopolis is a world where architecture is the centre of life, where every architectural world-view becomes tangible. In this world, all architectural ideas, concepts, theories, built outcomes become both actual and symbolic entities that together define the social, political, and economic structure of this city. In this imaginary world, architectural incidents and debates take place casually as people's 'everyday'. Conflicts of ideologies within the profession and with other members of the industry are represented metaphorically as a form of political struggle, a competition for gaining more cultural/economic and political influence among different parties. Within this struggle for power, the more dominant political positions tend to promote their ideologies to acquire greater control over decisions within the city. The opposition, on the other hand, questions these decisions and undervalues the ideologies informing them. Accordingly, doing well in Practiceopolis politics means carving out a niche in the discourse of architecture, being a topic of conversation among others, and acquiring enduring fame in the history and theory of architecture.

In Practiceopolis, buildings are the literal expression of power. They form a tangible manifestation of Pierre Bourdieu's cultural capital where buildings become the factual quality of the world, the source of pride and capital. More buildings means more power and more authority of a certain architectural ideology. The erection of a building means a political victory of a certain culture of practice over others. This means that those who build more can markedly influence the decision within the architectural territory and its foreign relations with other states of the building industry. In this sense, buildings of Practiceopolis are in continuous change according to the changes in the balance of power between its constituting cultures of practice.

In addition, capital in Practiceopolis is not only owned by individual architects, nor even only by architects. Critics, historians, schools of architecture, magazines, and publishing houses all possess varying amounts of capital. The struggle for power in the city consists of a perpetual dialectic among architects, critics, and related cultural and economic institutions through a quest for having the right to define the ruling principles of the city according to their terms.

In terms of geopolitics, Practiceopolis embraces diverse architectural communities and celebrates a democratic momentum among them. Practiceopolis is an independent city-state within a Confederation of states that form together 'Constructopolis': The Confederation of the Building Construction Industry. This Confederation includes other members of — or related to — the building industry: States of Structural Engineering, ME Engineering, Project Management, Real Estate Development, Facility Management, Asset Management, Contractors, etc. Together, Practiceopolis and Constructopolis act as a complete universe in which different stories about building production can take place. Their geography is flexible, changing to address whatever the story plot calls for. As an alternative universe, they may overlap with actual places in the real world, acknowledging these places as districts within the territory of the imaginary city and the broader confederation.

The world of Practiceopolis aims for the possibility of critically rethink the parameters of the landscape of the contemporary architectural profession and its relation with the broader industry and openly invite new futures to become possibilities.

This is the place where our story begins…

THE CITY OF ARCHITECTURE

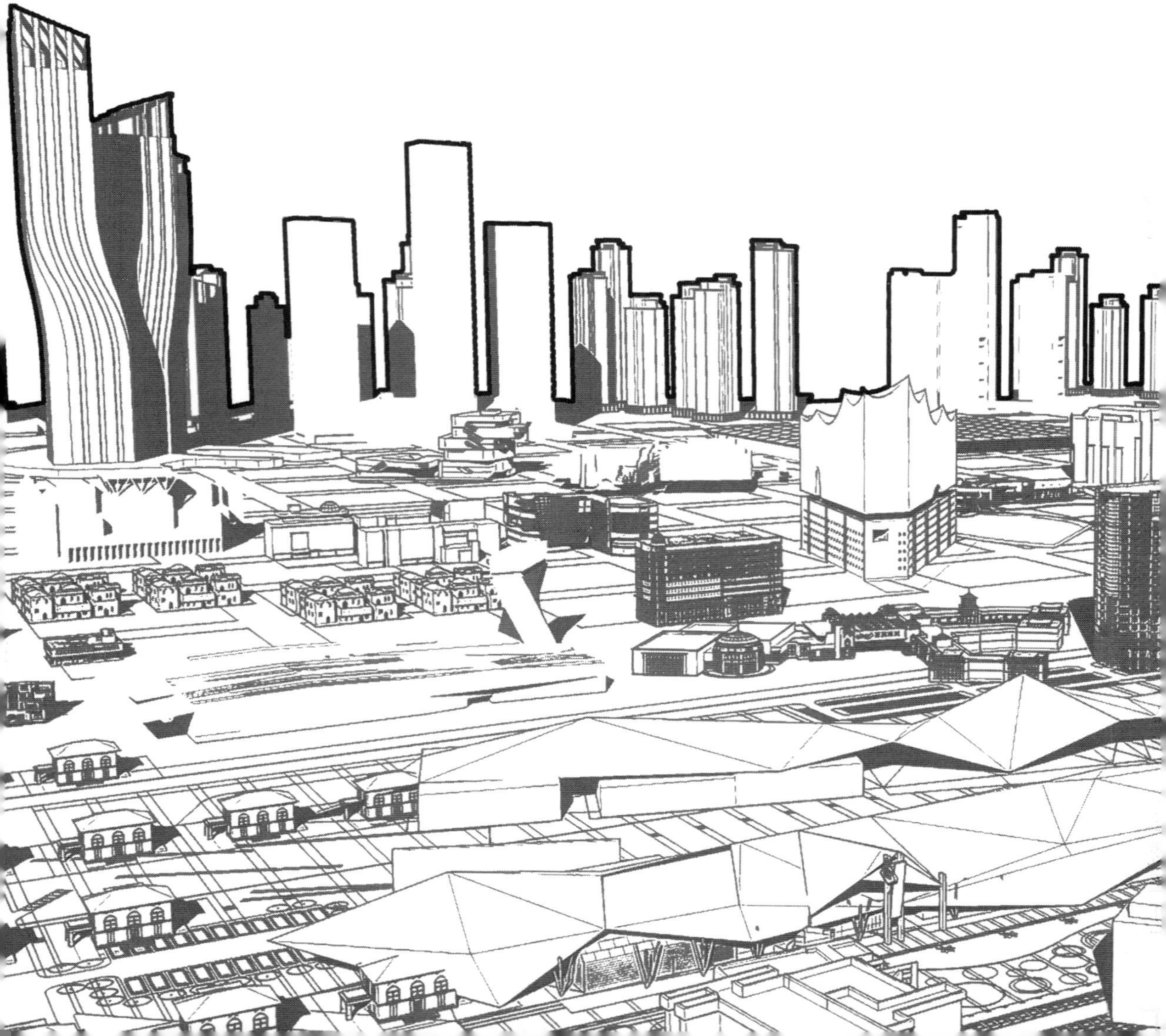

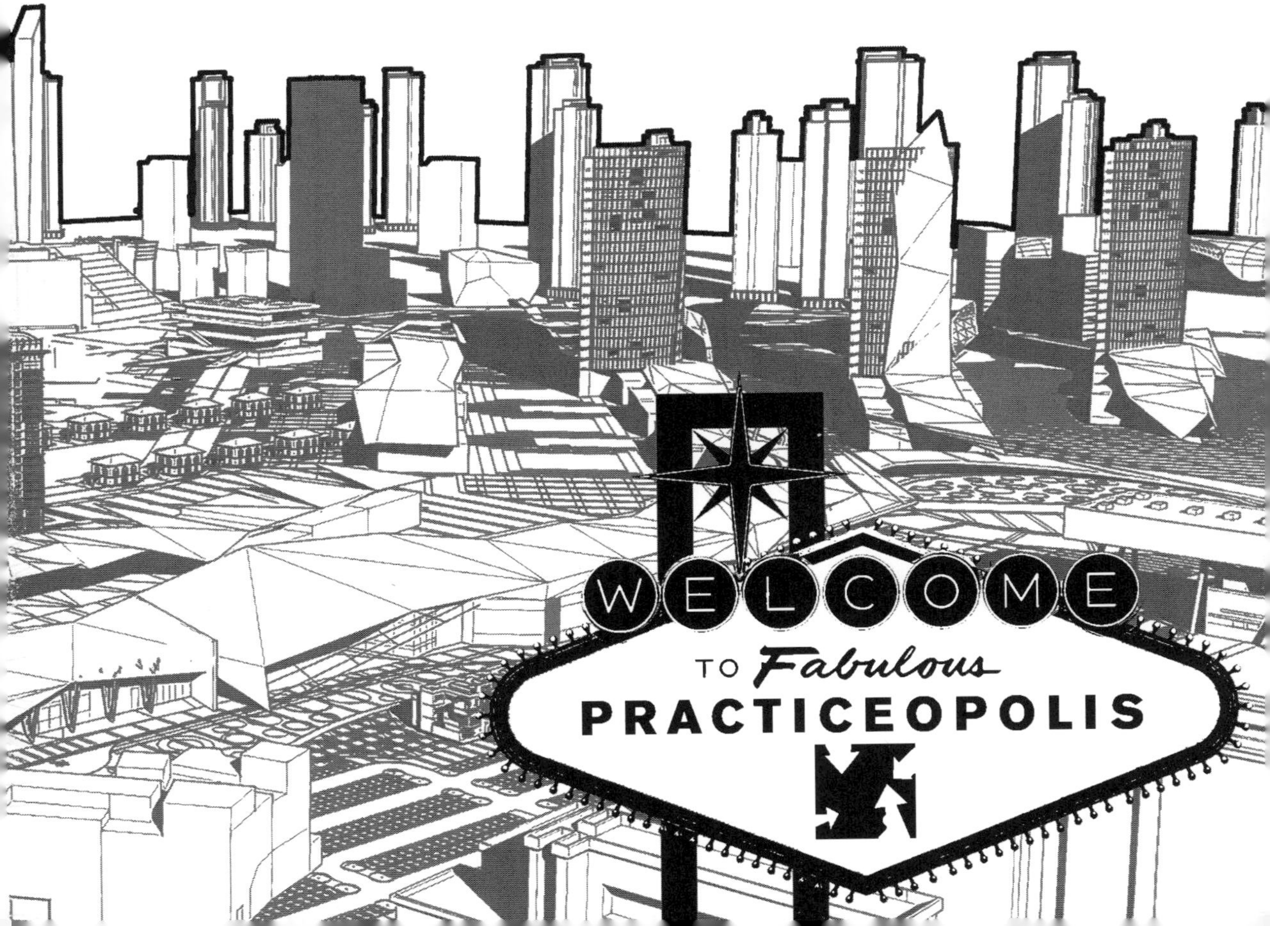
WELCOME
TO Fabulous
PRACTICEOPOLIS

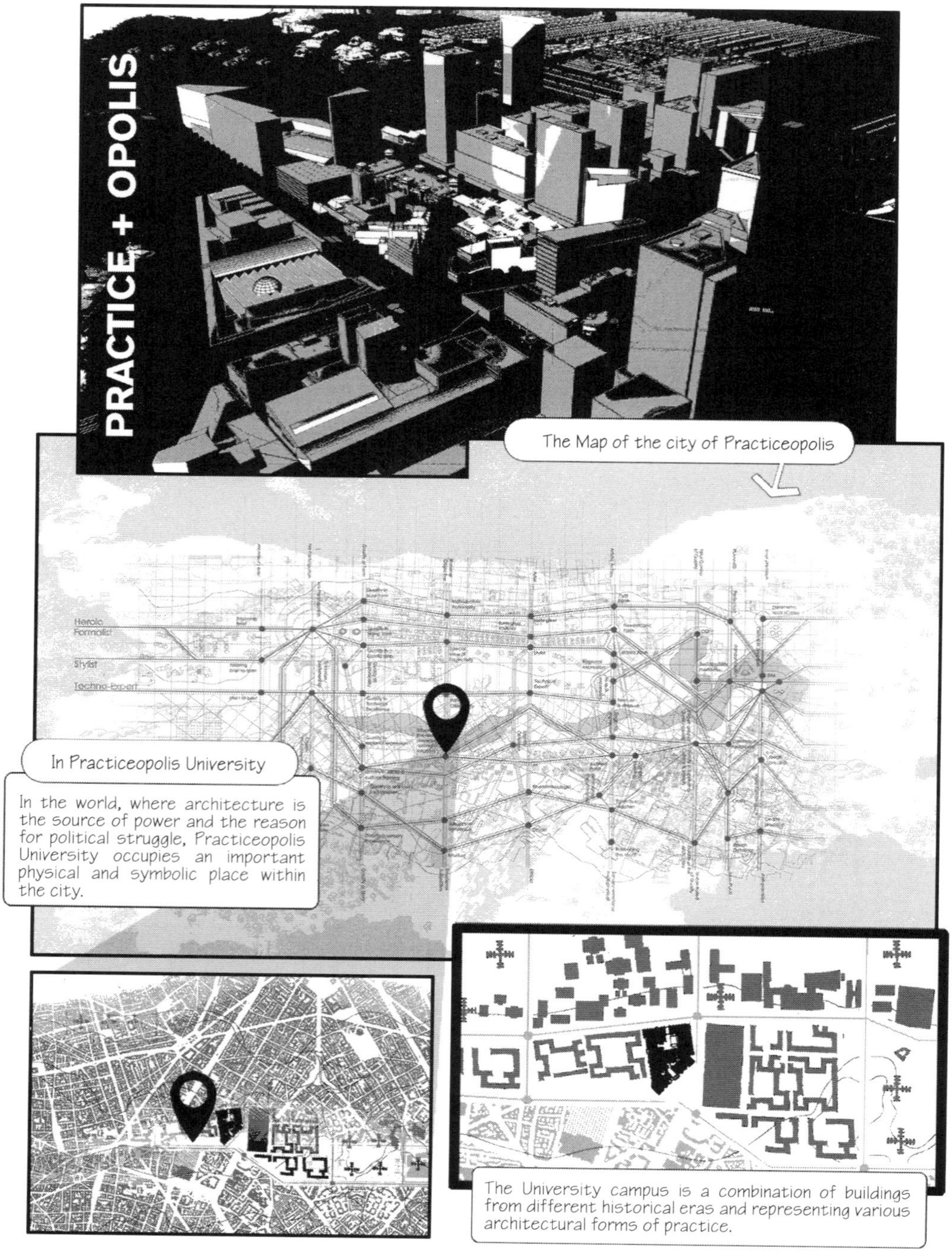
PRACTICE + OPOLIS
The Map of the city of Practiceopolis
Heroic Formalist
Stylist
Techno-Expert
In Practiceopolis University
In the world, where architecture is the source of power and the reason for political struggle, Practiceopolis University occupies an important physical and symbolic place within the city.
The University campus is a combination of buildings from different historical eras and representing various architectural forms of practice.

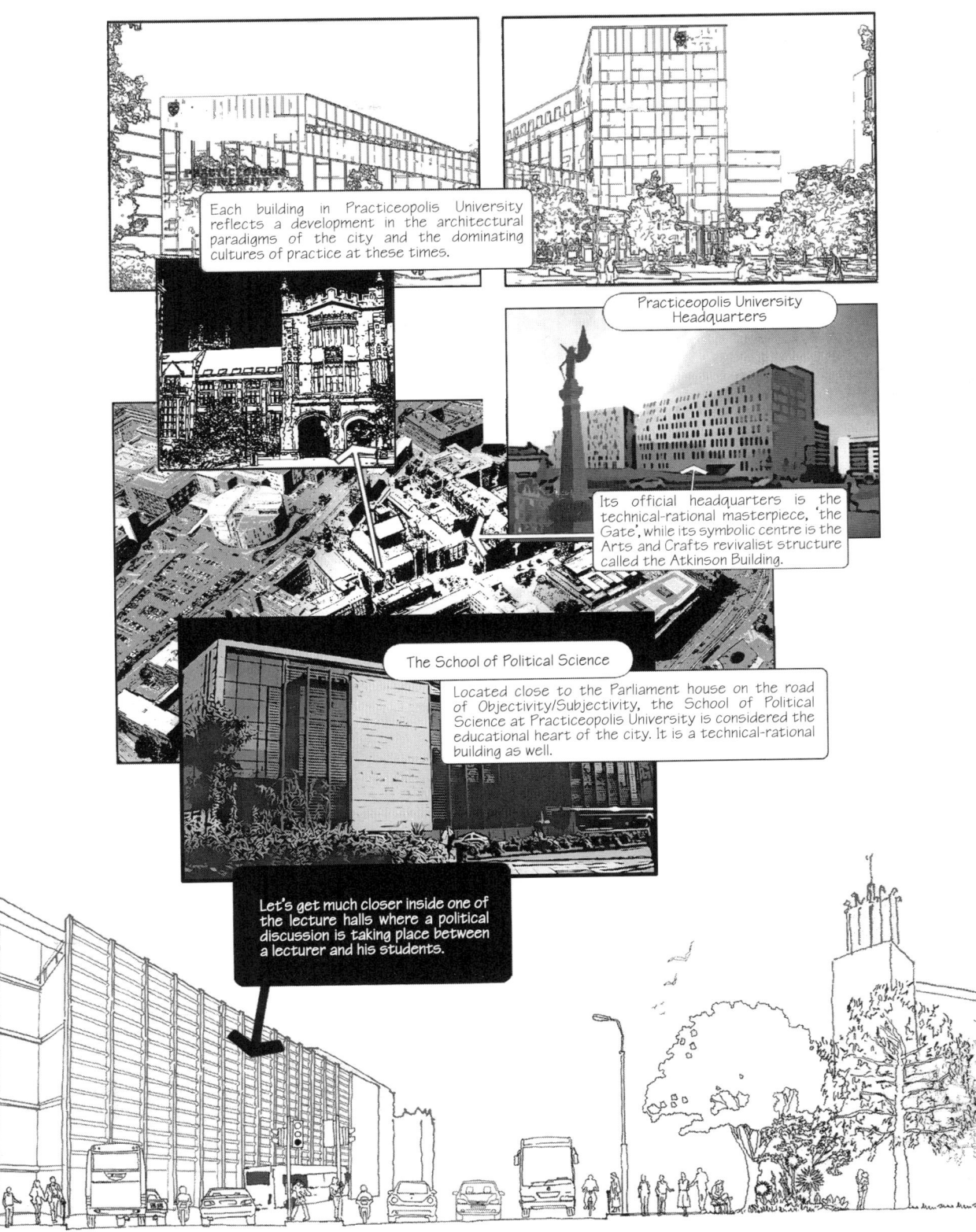

Each building in Practiceopolis University reflects a development in the architectural paradigms of the city and the dominating cultures of practice at these times.

Practiceopolis University Headquarters

Its official headquarters is the technical-rational masterpiece, 'the Gate', while its symbolic centre is the Arts and Crafts revivalist structure called the Atkinson Building.

The School of Political Science

Located close to the Parliament house on the road of Objectivity/Subjectivity, the School of Political Science at Practiceopolis University is considered the educational heart of the city. It is a technical-rational building as well.

Let's get much closer inside one of the lecture halls where a political discussion is taking place between a lecturer and his students.

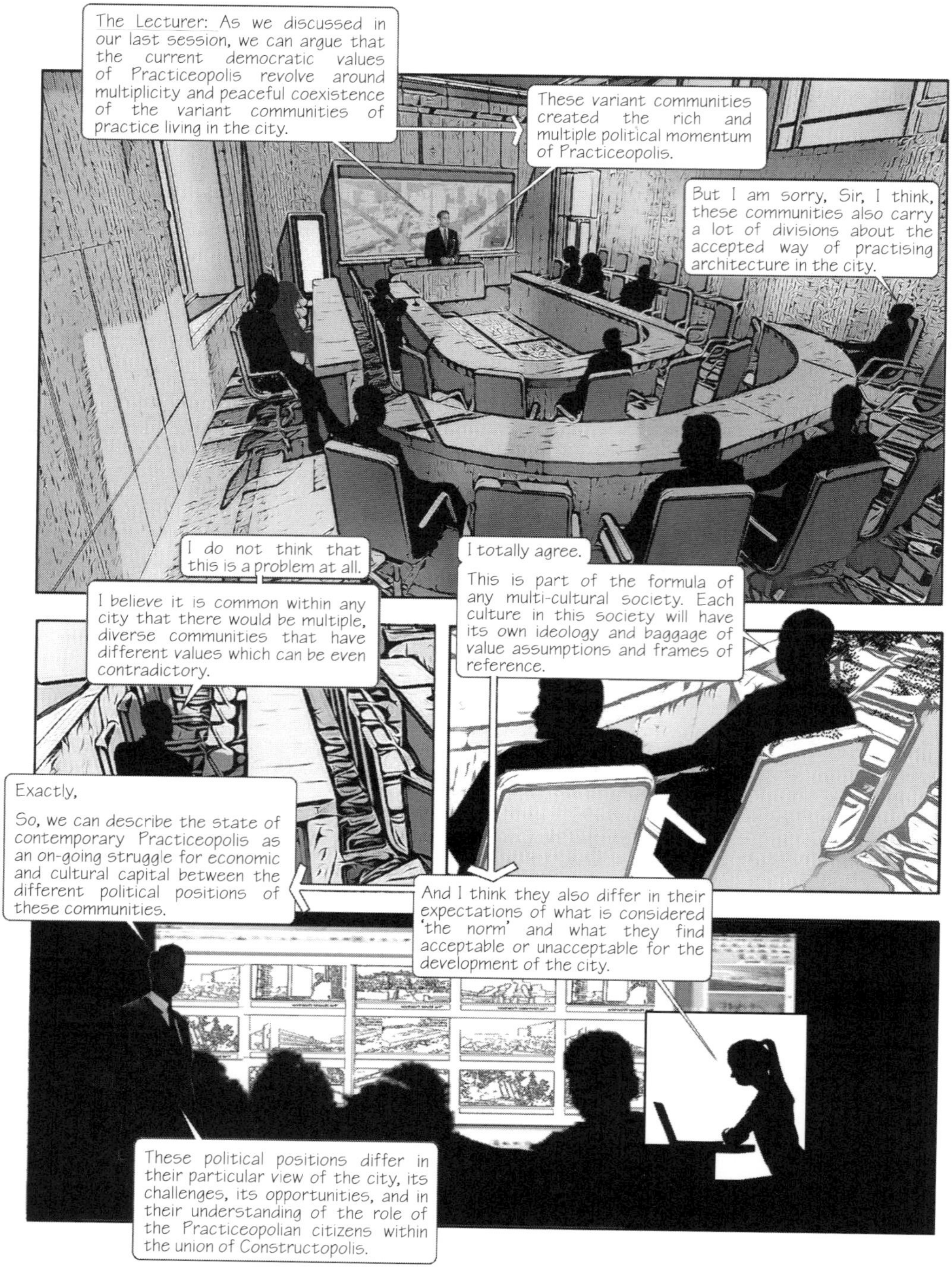
The Lecturer: As we discussed in our last session, we can argue that the current democratic values of Practiceopolis revolve around multiplicity and peaceful coexistence of the variant communities of practice living in the city.
These variant communities created the rich and multiple political momentum of Practiceopolis.
But I am sorry, Sir, I think, these communities also carry a lot of divisions about the accepted way of practising architecture in the city.
I do not think that this is a problem at all.
I believe it is common within any city that there would be multiple, diverse communities that have different values which can be even contradictory.
I totally agree.
This is part of the formula of any multi-cultural society. Each culture in this society will have its own ideology and baggage of value assumptions and frames of reference.
And I think they also differ in their expectations of what is considered 'the norm' and what they find acceptable or unacceptable for the development of the city.
Exactly,
So, we can describe the state of contemporary Practiceopolis as an on-going struggle for economic and cultural capital between the different political positions of these communities.
These political positions differ in their particular view of the city, its challenges, its opportunities, and in their understanding of the role of the Practiceopolian citizens within the union of Constructopolis.

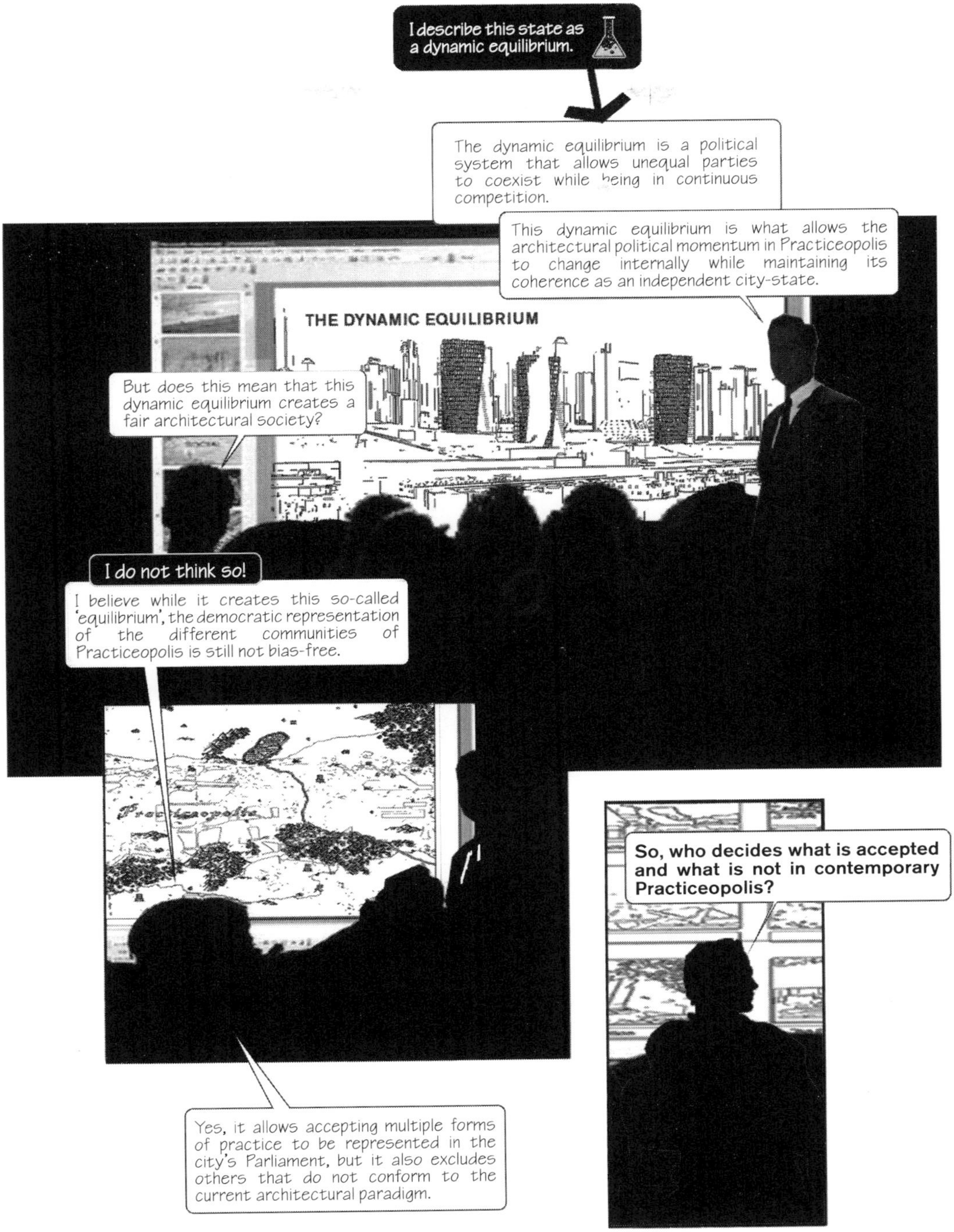
I describe this state as a dynamic equilibrium.
The dynamic equilibrium is a political system that allows unequal parties to coexist while being in continuous competition.
This dynamic equilibrium is what allows the architectural political momentum in Practiceopolis to change internally while maintaining its coherence as an independent city-state.
THE DYNAMIC EQUILIBRIUM
But does this mean that this dynamic equilibrium creates a fair architectural society?
I do not think so!
I believe while it creates this so-called 'equilibrium', the democratic representation of the different communities of Practiceopolis is still not bias-free.
Yes, it allows accepting multiple forms of practice to be represented in the city's Parliament, but it also excludes others that do not conform to the current architectural paradigm.
So, who decides what is accepted and what is not in contemporary Practiceopolis?

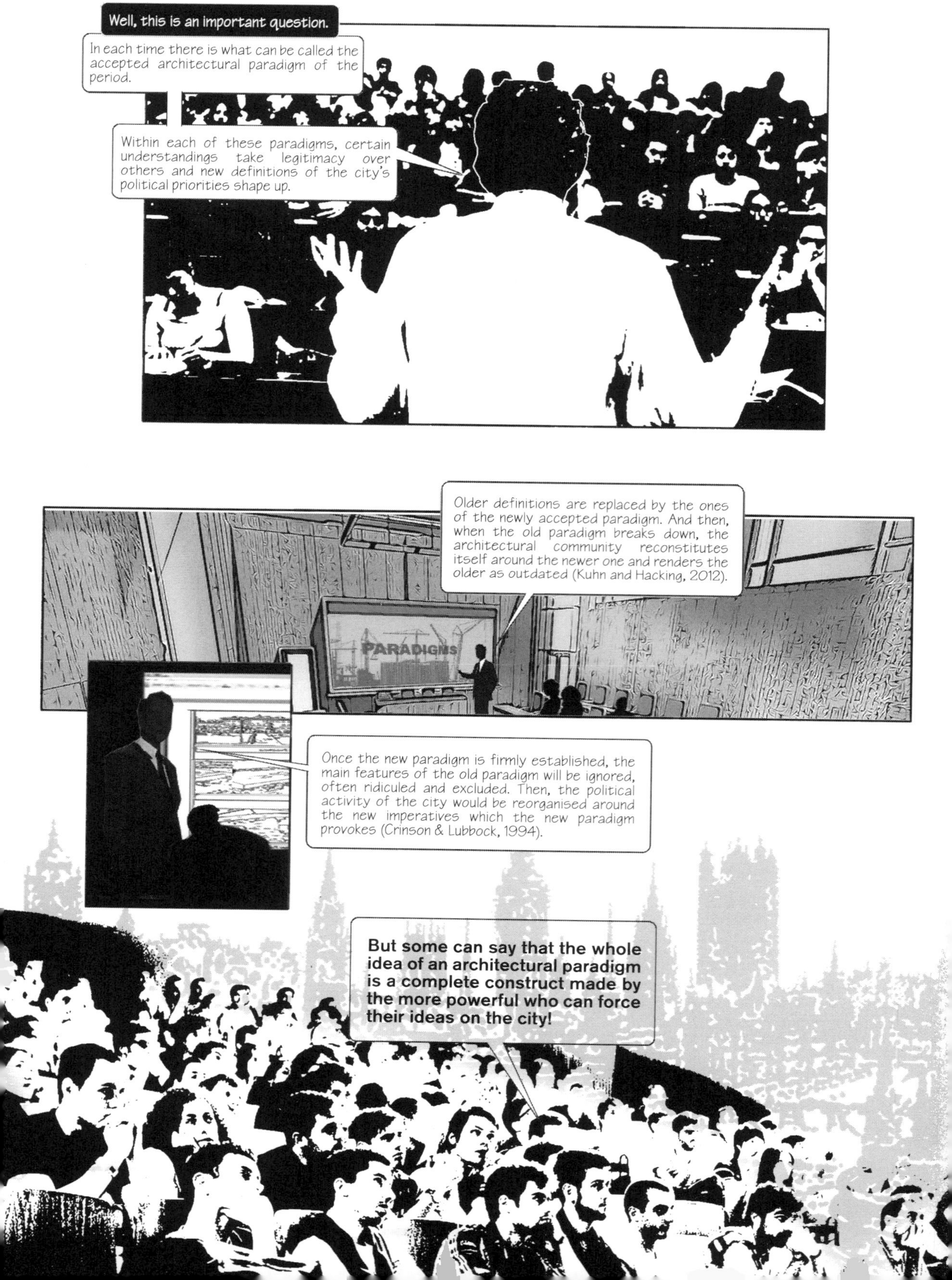
Well, this is an important question.
In each time there is what can be called the accepted architectural paradigm of the period.
Within each of these paradigms, certain understandings take legitimacy over others and new definitions of the city's political priorities shape up.
Older definitions are replaced by the ones of the newly accepted paradigm. And then, when the old paradigm breaks down, the architectural community reconstitutes itself around the newer one and renders the older as outdated (Kuhn and Hacking, 2012).
PARADIGMS
Once the new paradigm is firmly established, the main features of the old paradigm will be ignored, often ridiculed and excluded. Then, the political activity of the city would be reorganised around the new imperatives which the new paradigm provokes (Crinson & Lubbock, 1994).
But some can say that the whole idea of an architectural paradigm is a complete construct made by the more powerful who can force their ideas on the city!

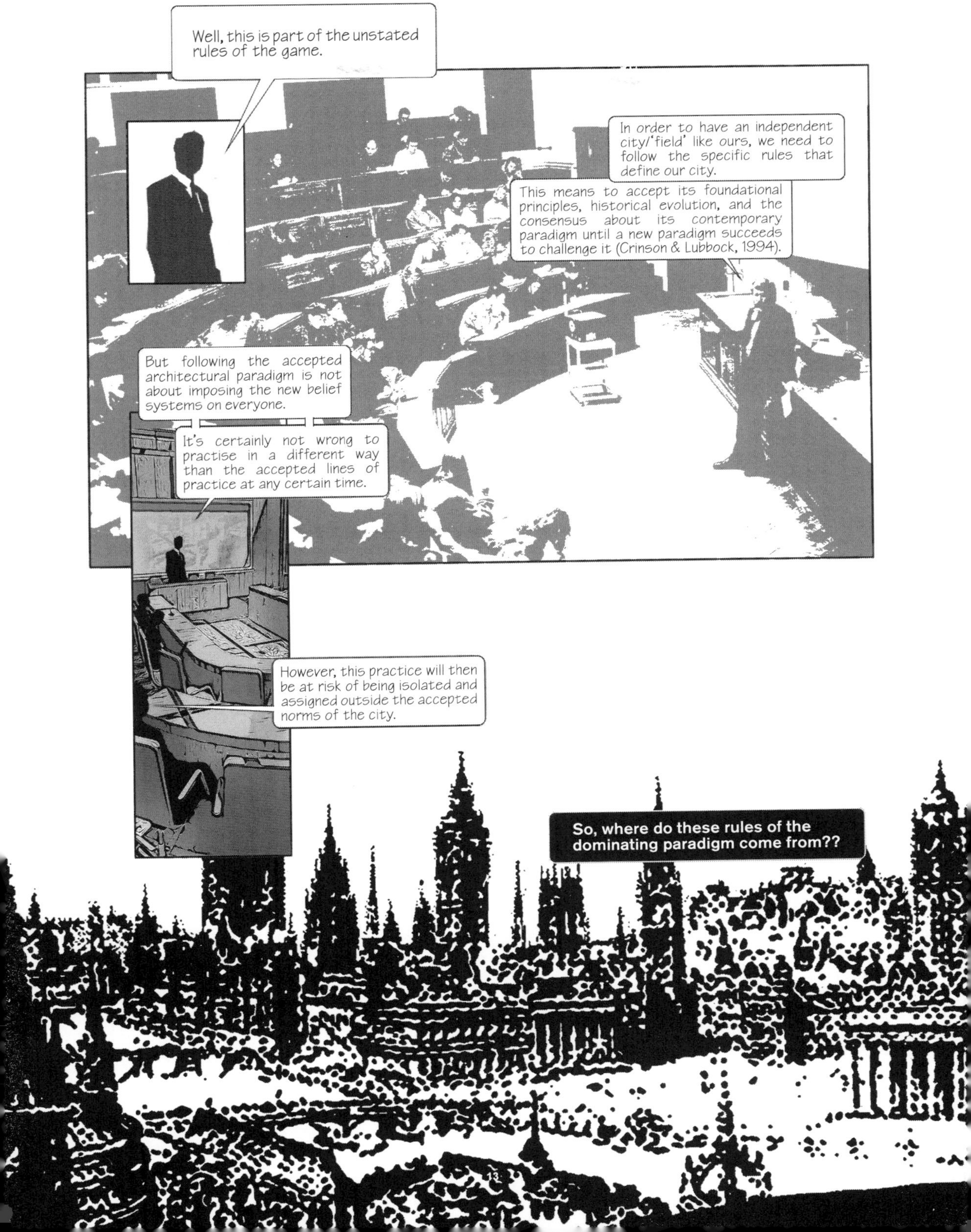
Well, this is part of the unstated rules of the game.
In order to have an independent city/'field' like ours, we need to follow the specific rules that define our city.
This means to accept its foundational principles, historical evolution, and the consensus about its contemporary paradigm until a new paradigm succeeds to challenge it (Crinson & Lubbock, 1994).
But following the accepted architectural paradigm is not about imposing the new belief systems on everyone.
It's certainly not wrong to practise in a different way than the accepted lines of practice at any certain time.
However, this practice will then be at risk of being isolated and assigned outside the accepted norms of the city.
So, where do these rules of the dominating paradigm come from??

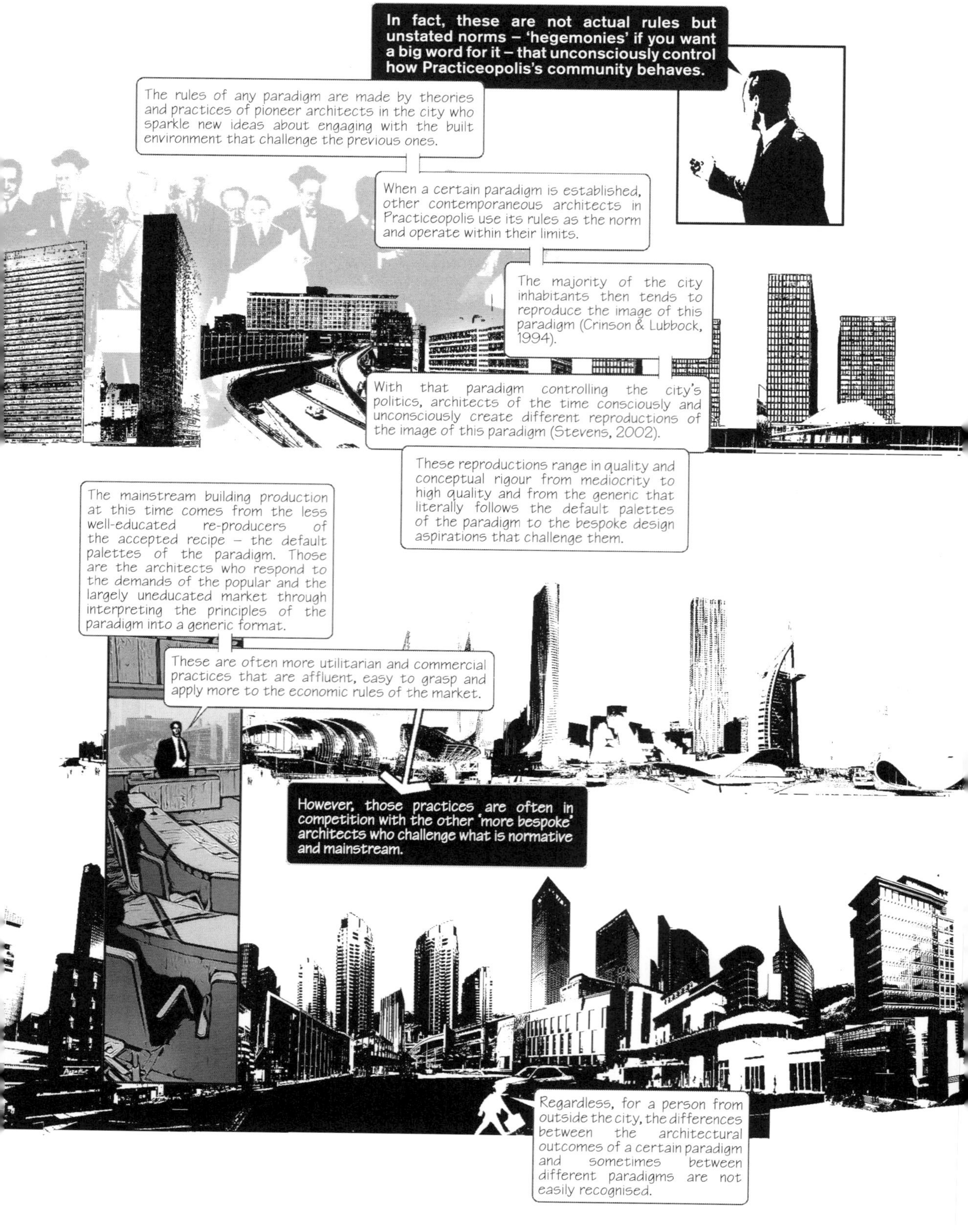
In fact, these are not actual rules but unstated norms – 'hegemonies' if you want a big word for it – that unconsciously control how Practiceopolis's community behaves.
The rules of any paradigm are made by theories and practices of pioneer architects in the city who sparkle new ideas about engaging with the built environment that challenge the previous ones.
When a certain paradigm is established, other contemporaneous architects in Practiceopolis use its rules as the norm and operate within their limits.
The majority of the city inhabitants then tends to reproduce the image of this paradigm (Crinson & Lubbock, 1994).
With that paradigm controlling the city's politics, architects of the time consciously and unconsciously create different reproductions of the image of this paradigm (Stevens, 2002).
These reproductions range in quality and conceptual rigour from mediocrity to high quality and from the generic that literally follows the default palettes of the paradigm to the bespoke design aspirations that challenge them.
The mainstream building production at this time comes from the less well-educated re-producers of the accepted recipe – the default palettes of the paradigm. Those are the architects who respond to the demands of the popular and the largely uneducated market through interpreting the principles of the paradigm into a generic format.
These are often more utilitarian and commercial practices that are affluent, easy to grasp and apply more to the economic rules of the market.
However, those practices are often in competition with the other 'more bespoke' architects who challenge what is normative and mainstream.
Regardless, for a person from outside the city, the differences between the architectural outcomes of a certain paradigm and sometimes between different paradigms are not easily recognised.

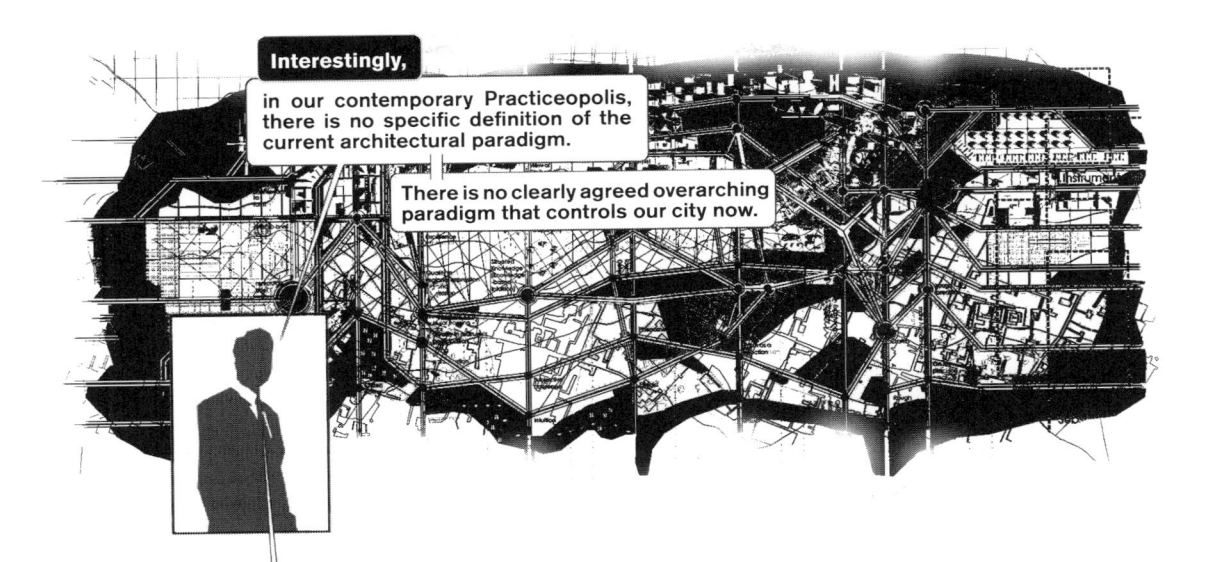

Interestingly, in our contemporary Practiceopolis, there is no specific definition of the current architectural paradigm.

There is no clearly agreed overarching paradigm that controls our city now.

Only what we can say is that multiplicity and divisions could be the clear feature of our current paradigm.

Our duty hence as Practiceopolians has become to keep trying to understand the territory of this paradigm and to question our positions and the reason why we design the way we do at the moment?

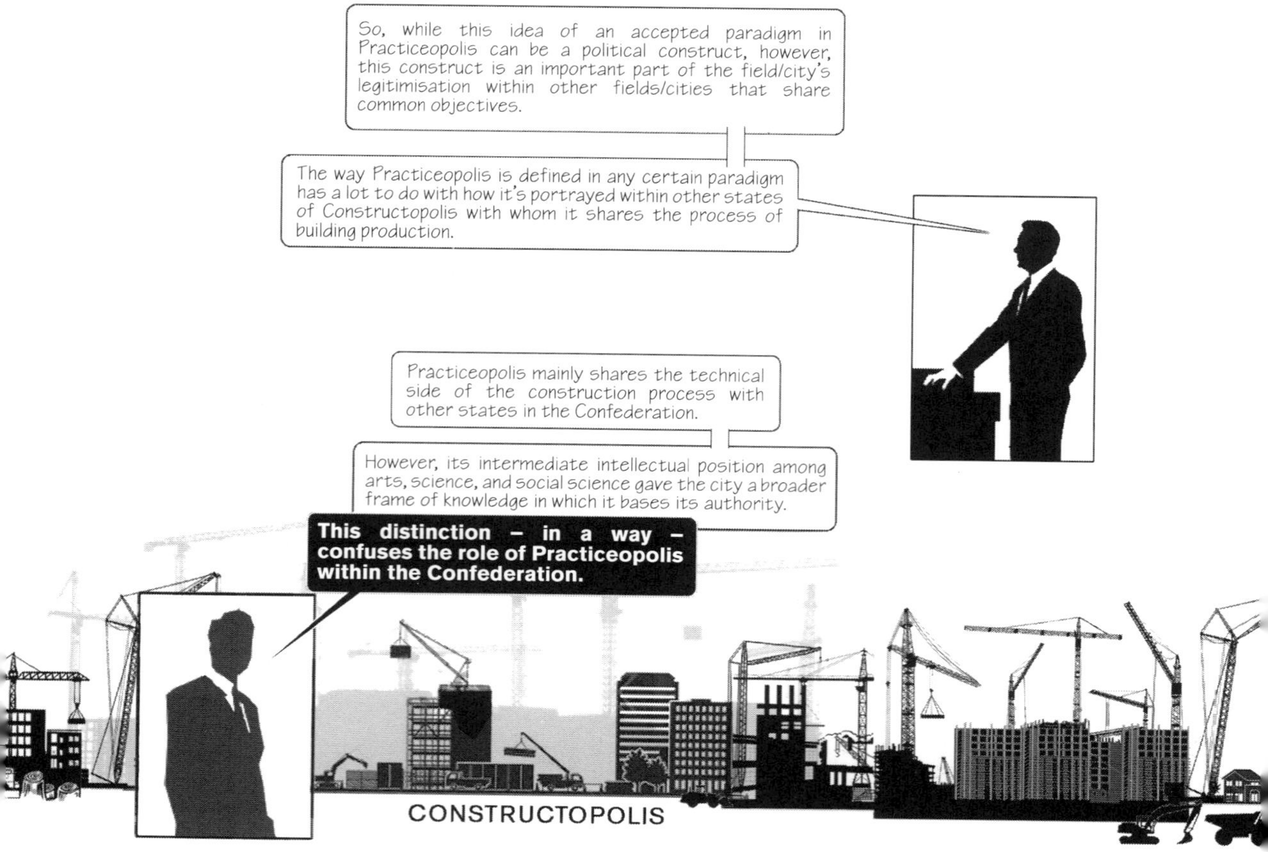
So, while this idea of an accepted paradigm in Practiceopolis can be a political construct, however, this construct is an important part of the field/city's legitimisation within other fields/cities that share common objectives.
The way Practiceopolis is defined in any certain paradigm has a lot to do with how it's portrayed within other states of Constructopolis with whom it shares the process of building production.
Practiceopolis mainly shares the technical side of the construction process with other states in the Confederation.
However, its intermediate intellectual position among arts, science, and social science gave the city a broader frame of knowledge in which it bases its authority.
This distinction – in a way – confuses the role of Practiceopolis within the Confederation.
CONSTRUCTOPOLIS

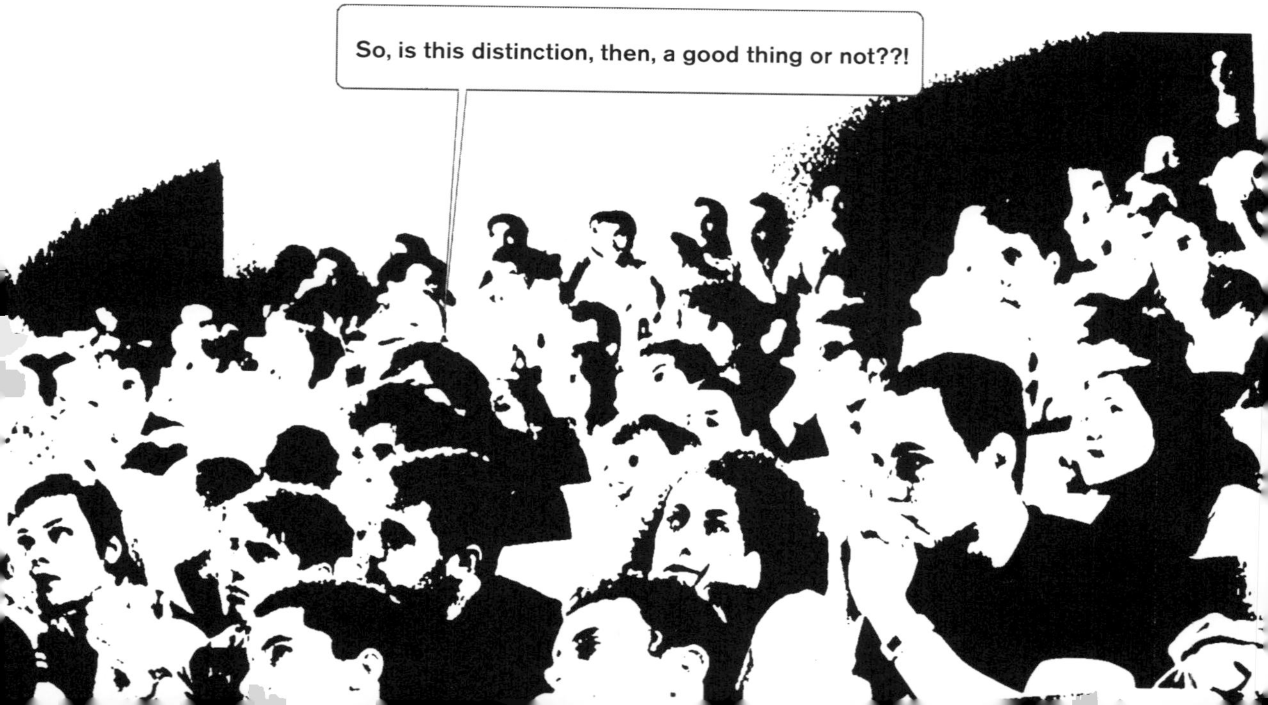
So, is this distinction, then, a good thing or not??!

> Actually, this distinction does not only confuse the definition of the specific role of Practiceopolis within the Confederation but it is also accountable for a lot of miscommunication and value-conflicts with the Confederation.

> While Practiceopolis shares its technical side of the construction process with other states in the Confederation, a large part of Practiceopolis's sources of knowledge is not shared with the rest of Constructopolis.

> This confuses Practiceopolis's role and forces it to focus on the building science or to play the aesthetics card in order to win arguments within the Confederation — a card that we are not very comfortable to only confine our identity with.

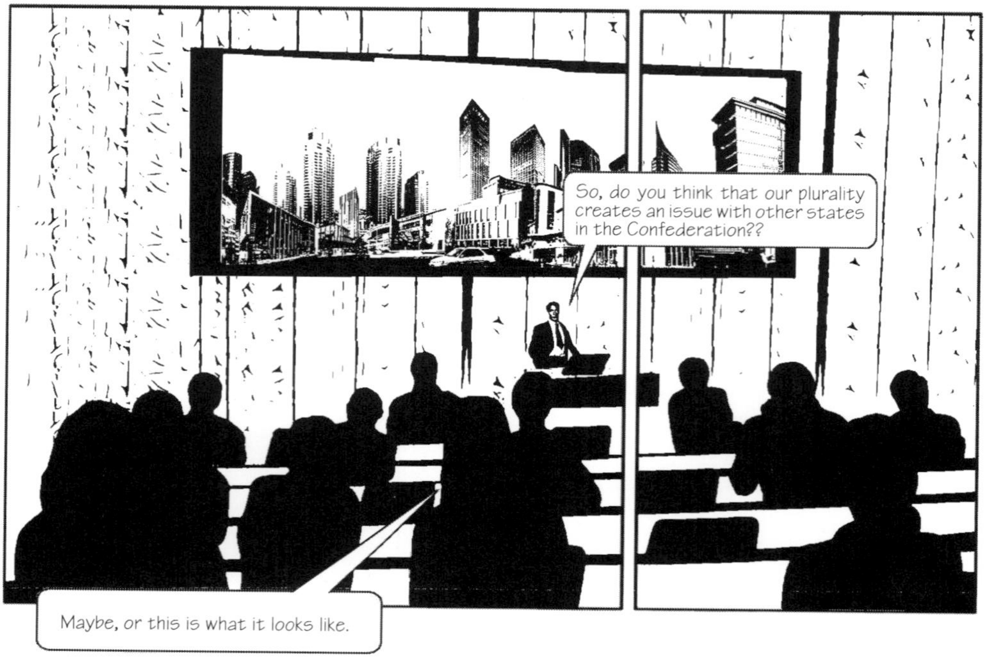
So, do you think that our plurality creates an issue with other states in the Confederation??
Maybe, or this is what it looks like.

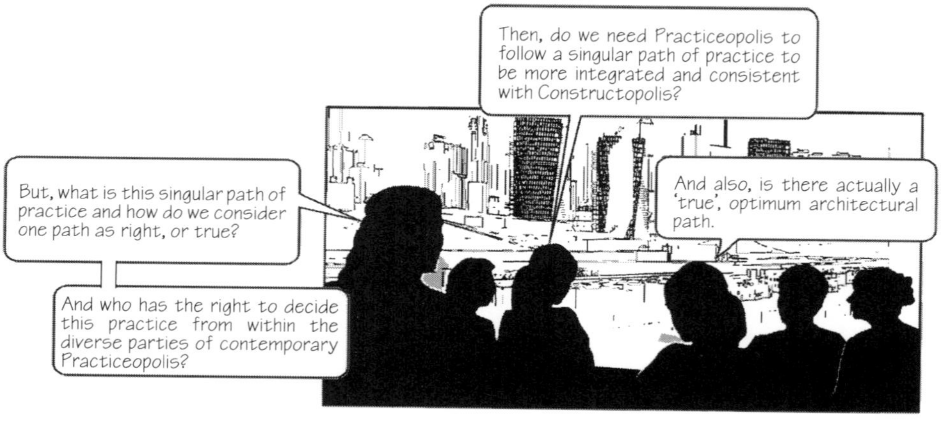
But, what is this singular path of practice and how do we consider one path as right, or true?
And who has the right to decide this practice from within the diverse parties of contemporary Practiceopolis?
Then, do we need Practiceopolis to follow a singular path of practice to be more integrated and consistent with Constructopolis?
And also, is there actually a 'true', optimum architectural path.

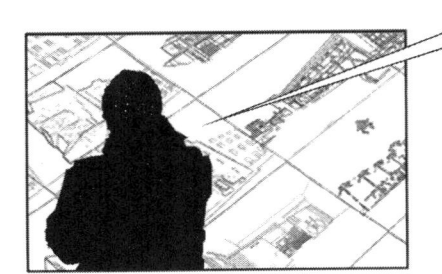

These are hard questions!!!
They have as many answers as the number of Practiceopolians!!

Each political party in Practiceopolis has its own way of answering these questions, based on its different world-view.
Precision
Detailing craftsmanship
Quality Control
Attitudes to Technology
The Visual
Heroic
Formalist
Stylist
Technical-Rational
Pragmatic
Contingent
Regionalist
Enabler
Sensory
Determinist
Instrumental
Critical Theory
Substantive
However, these are very important questions that dig into the foundations of Practiceopolis and its relation with Constructopolis.

The Map of Practice*

*The Map of Practice is the base diagram for creating the geography of the city of Practiceopolis. It derives from correlations between a set of typologies covering key aspects of the architectural field; an interpretation of Andrew Feenberg's (2012) philosophy of technology into architectural equivalents; and an identification of a series of theoretical routes of architectural practice operating within the current paradigm. In the diagram, the vertical lines stand for architectural typologies and the horizontal lines stand for alternative stances towards architectural technology and technical knowledge, and the paths of the theoretical routes of practice record the set of values that shapes their cultures of practice. Each path connects different stops on the vertical grid of the architectural typology; these stops stand for the position of each route of practice to an aspect of the architectural typologies.

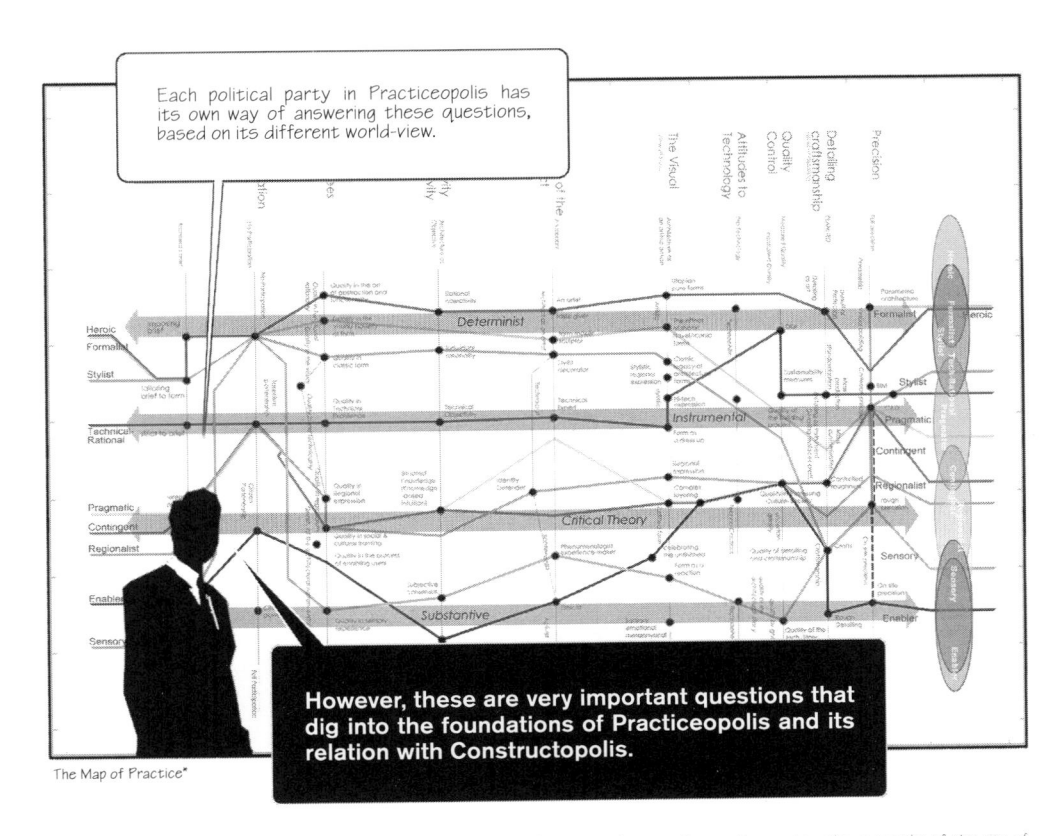

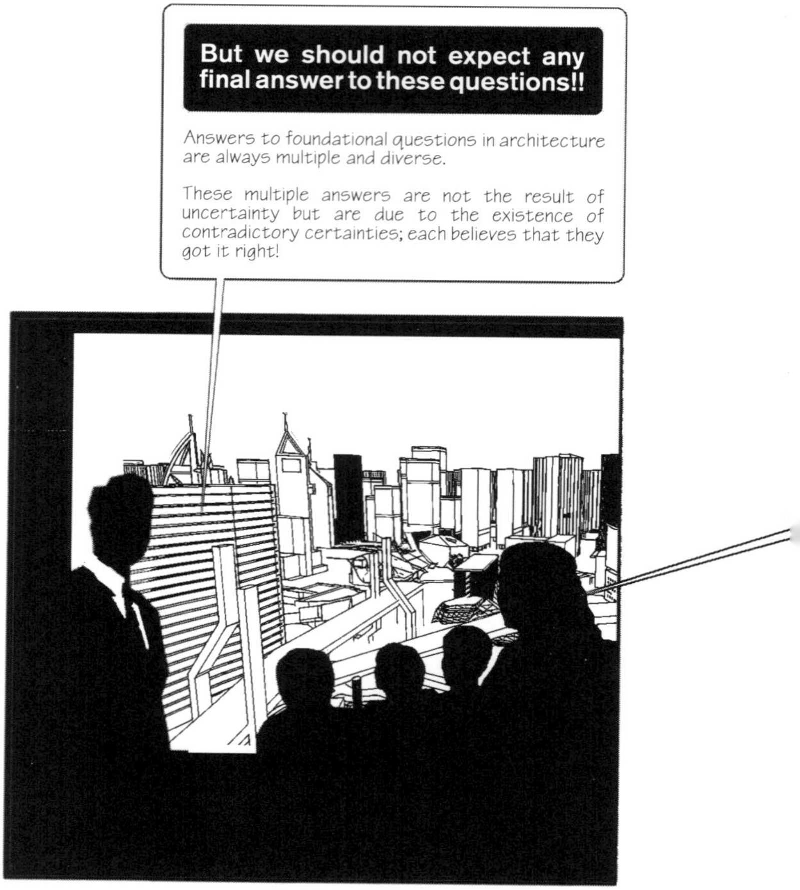
But we should not expect any final answer to these questions!!
Answers to foundational questions in architecture are always multiple and diverse.
These multiple answers are not the result of uncertainty but are due to the existence of contradictory certainties; each believes that they got it right!

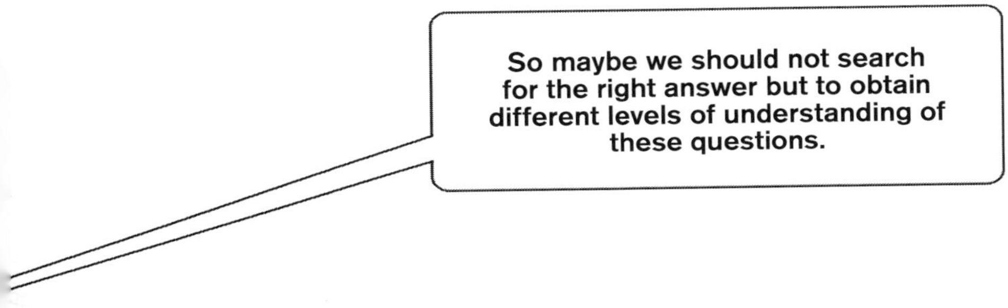
So maybe we should not search for the right answer but to obtain different levels of understanding of these questions.

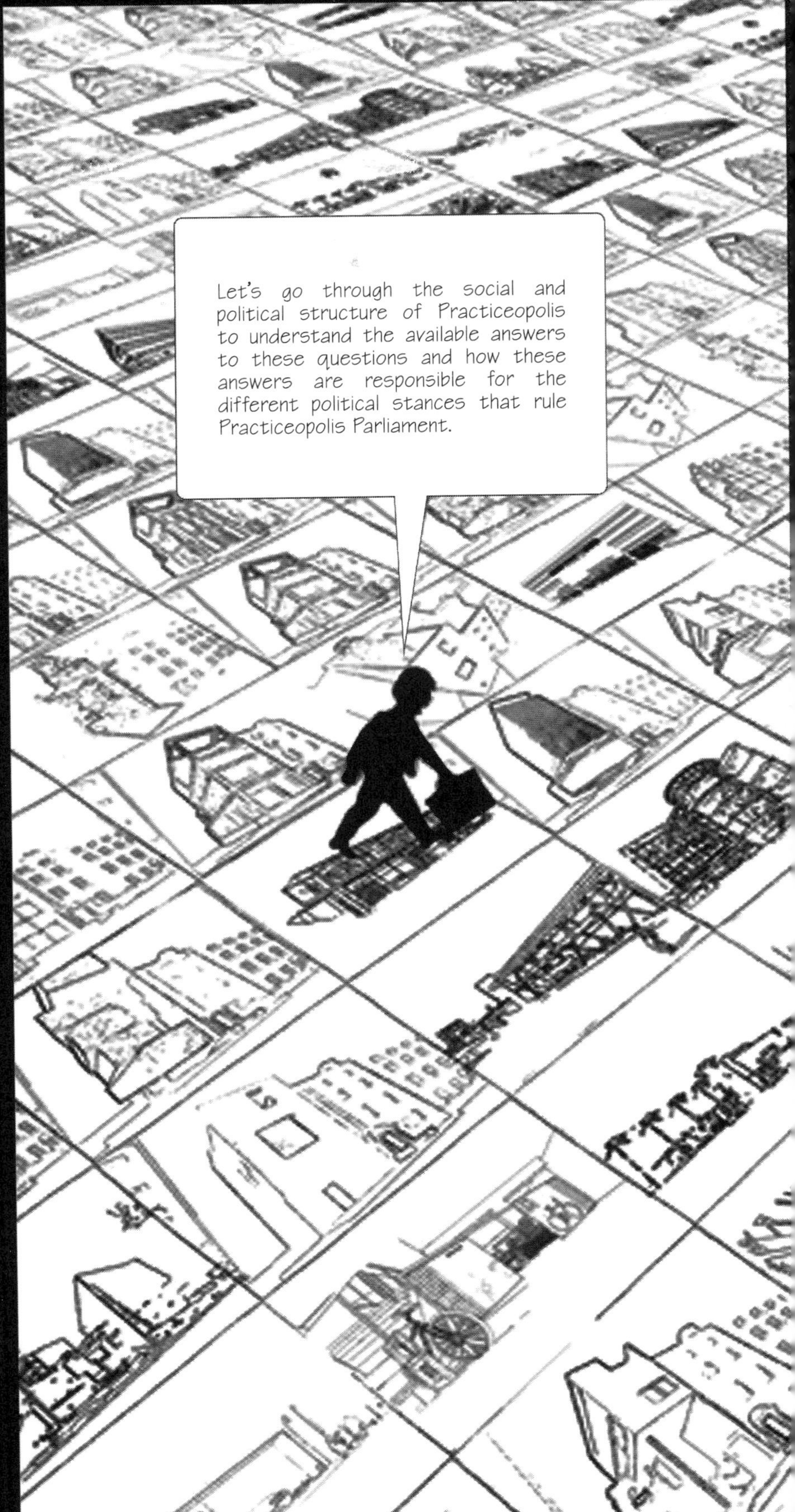
Let's go through the social and political structure of Practiceopolis to understand the available answers to these questions and how these answers are responsible for the different political stances that rule Practiceopolis Parliament.

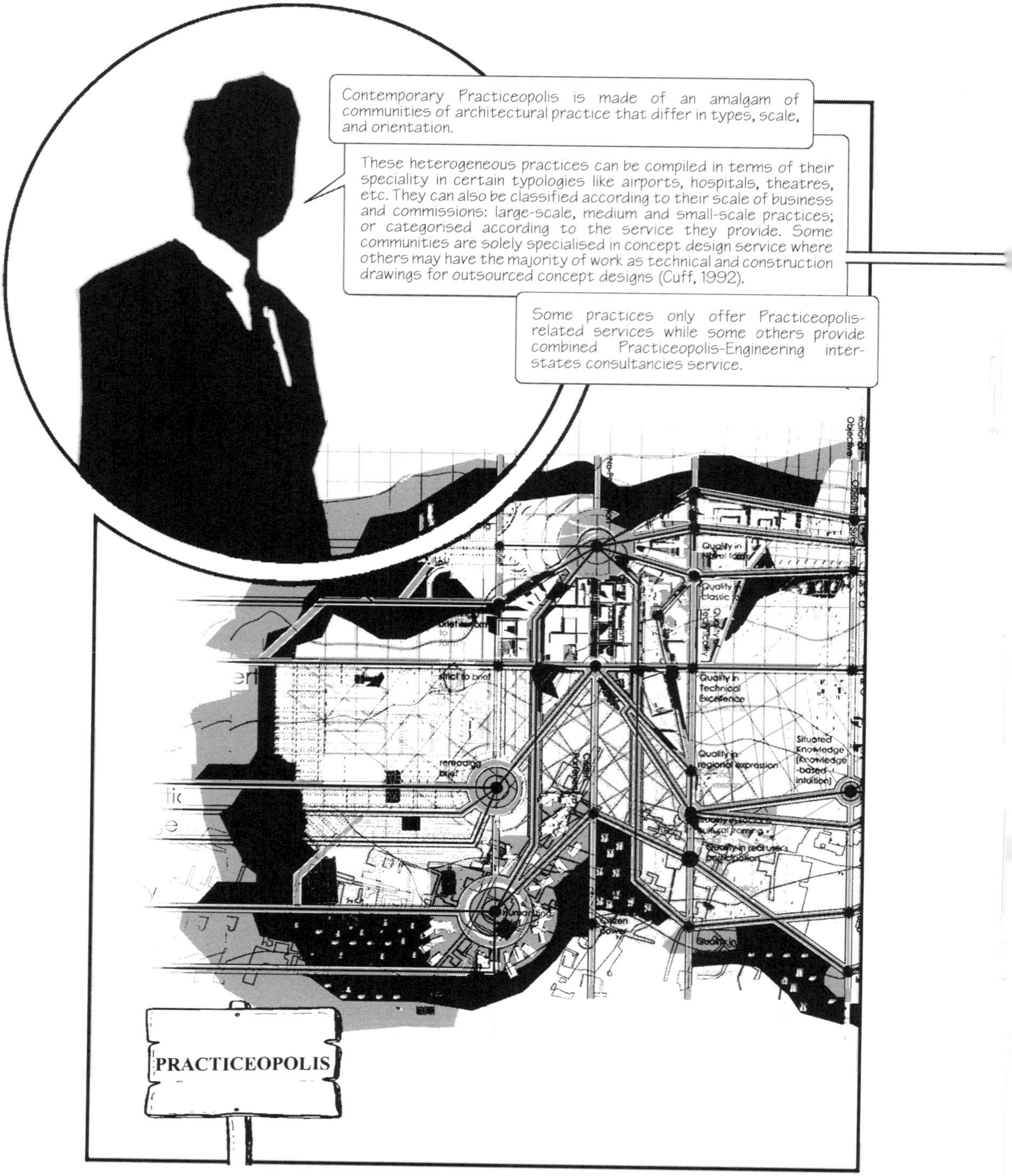
Contemporary Practiceopolis is made of an amalgam of communities of architectural practice that differ in types, scale, and orientation.
These heterogeneous practices can be compiled in terms of their speciality in certain typologies like airports, hospitals, theatres, etc. They can also be classified according to their scale of business and commissions: large-scale, medium and small-scale practices; or categorised according to the service they provide. Some communities are solely specialised in concept design service where others may have the majority of work as technical and construction drawings for outsourced concept designs (Cuff, 1992).
Some practices only offer Practiceopolis-related services while some others provide combined Practiceopolis-Engineering inter-states consultancies service.
strict to brief
Quality in Technical Excellence
Quality in regional expression
Situated Knowledge (Knowledge-based intuition)
PRACTICEOPOLIS

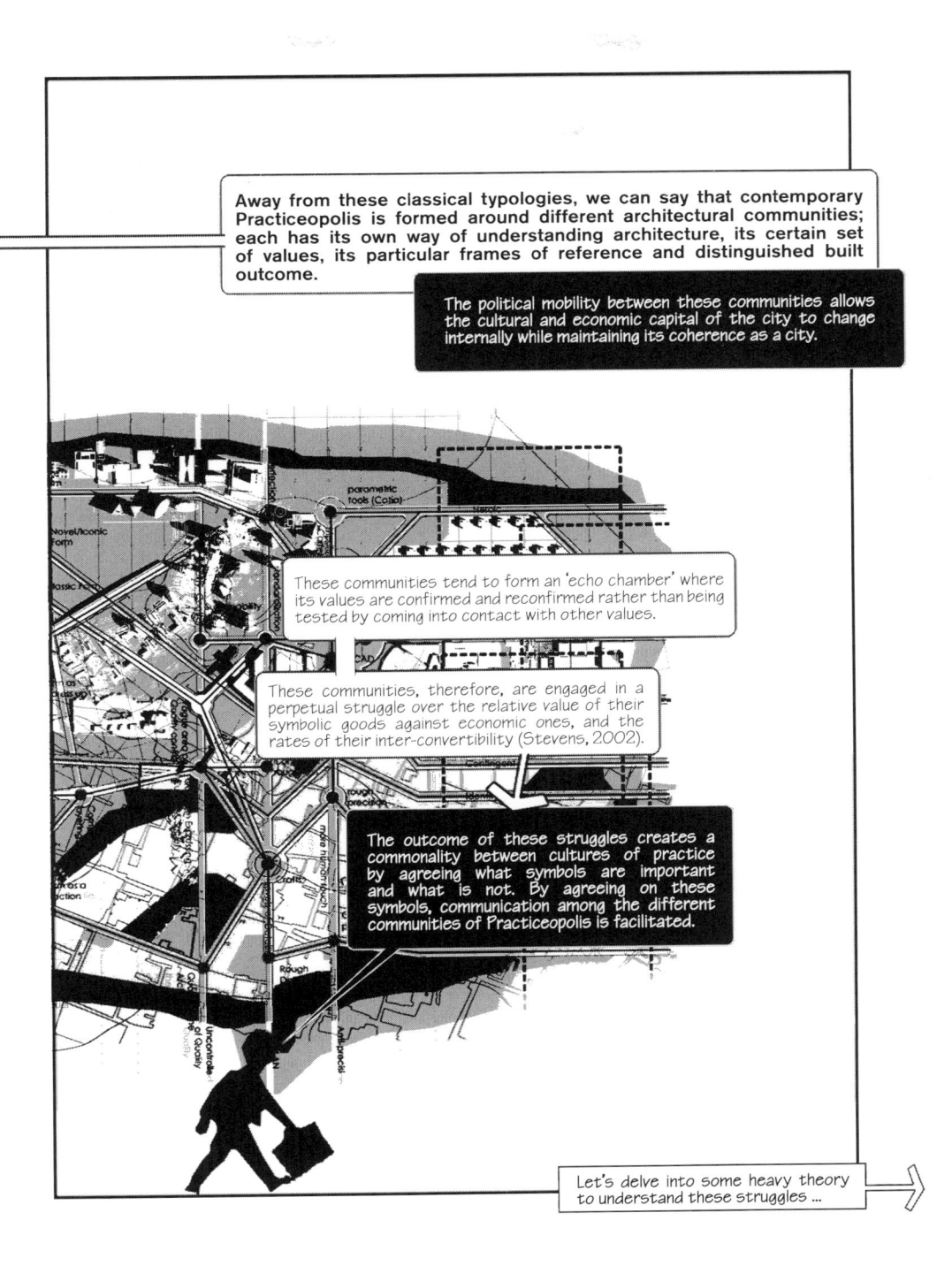

Away from these classical typologies, we can say that contemporary Practiceopolis is formed around different architectural communities; each has its own way of understanding architecture, its certain set of values, its particular frames of reference and distinguished built outcome.

The political mobility between these communities allows the cultural and economic capital of the city to change internally while maintaining its coherence as a city.

These communities tend to form an 'echo chamber' where its values are confirmed and reconfirmed rather than being tested by coming into contact with other values.

These communities, therefore, are engaged in a perpetual struggle over the relative value of their symbolic goods against economic ones, and the rates of their inter-convertibility (Stevens, 2002).

The outcome of these struggles creates a commonality between cultures of practice by agreeing what symbols are important and what is not. By agreeing on these symbols, communication among the different communities of Practiceopolis is facilitated.

Let's delve into some heavy theory to understand these struggles ...

In Practiceopolis the distribution of capital can be seen among four prominent ideologies that influence the social and cultural fabric of the city: the Determinist, the Instrumental, the Critical-theory, and the Substantive.*

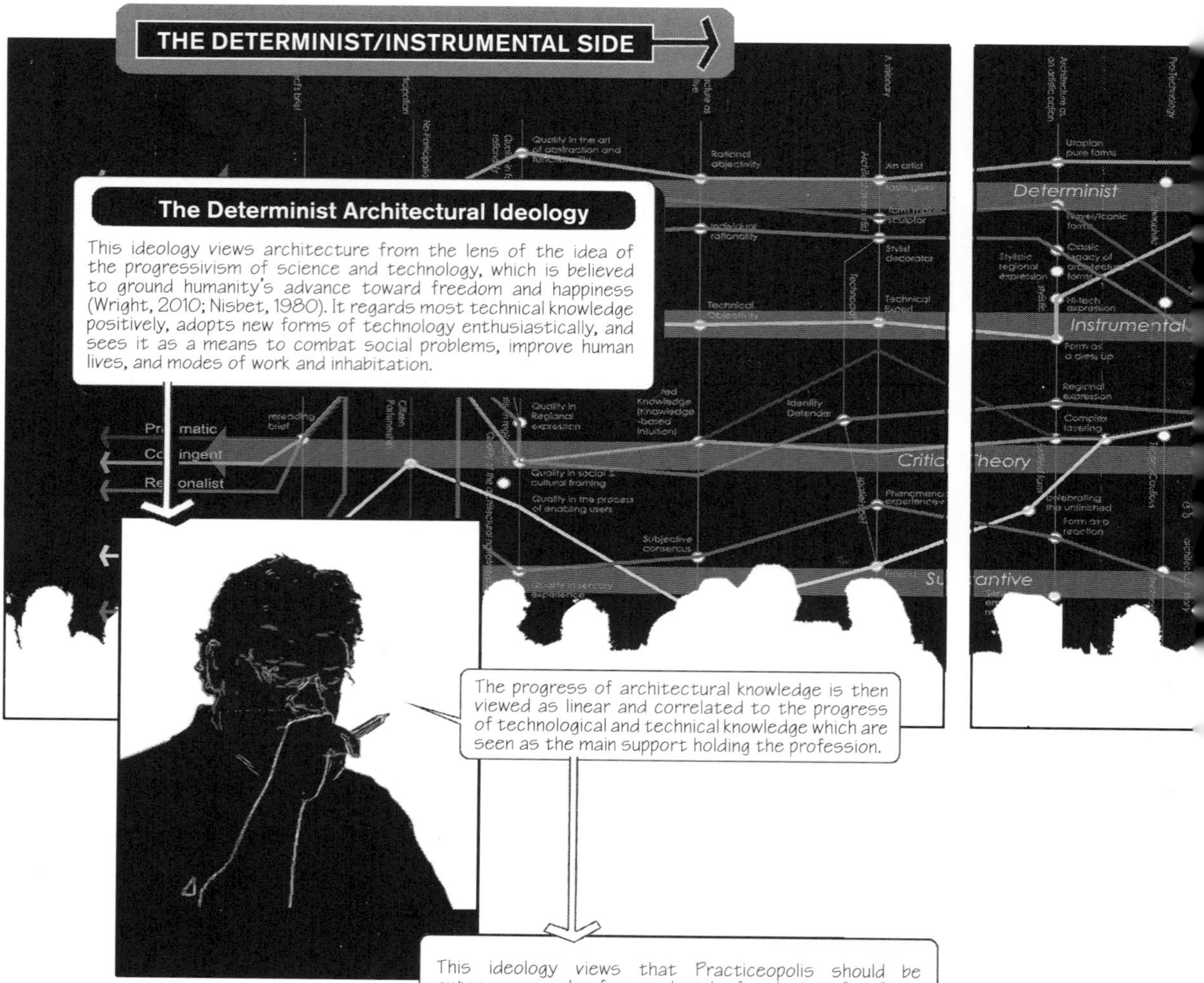
THE DETERMINIST/INSTRUMENTAL SIDE
Determinist
Instrumental
Pragmatic
Contingent
Rationalist

The Determinist Architectural Ideology

This ideology views architecture from the lens of the idea of the progressivism of science and technology, which is believed to ground humanity's advance toward freedom and happiness (Wright, 2010; Nisbet, 1980). It regards most technical knowledge positively, adopts new forms of technology enthusiastically, and sees it as a means to combat social problems, improve human lives, and modes of work and inhabitation.

The progress of architectural knowledge is then viewed as linear and correlated to the progress of technological and technical knowledge which are seen as the main support holding the profession.

This ideology views that Practiceopolis should be autonomous, value-free, and works for the benefit of the people. Therefore, Practiceopolis decisions should be made according to the higher authority of objective reason and truth. These decisions are informed by the architects' expert knowledge and therefore should be protected from inexpert interference.

In this sense, architectural technical means is neutral insofar as they merely fulfil natural societal needs. Any negative effect on people is not attributed to the architectural means used – which is neutral – but it can be because of the misuse of users. Meaning is then extrinsic to architecture. As such, architectural knowledge would resemble science and mathematics by its intrinsic independence of the social world.

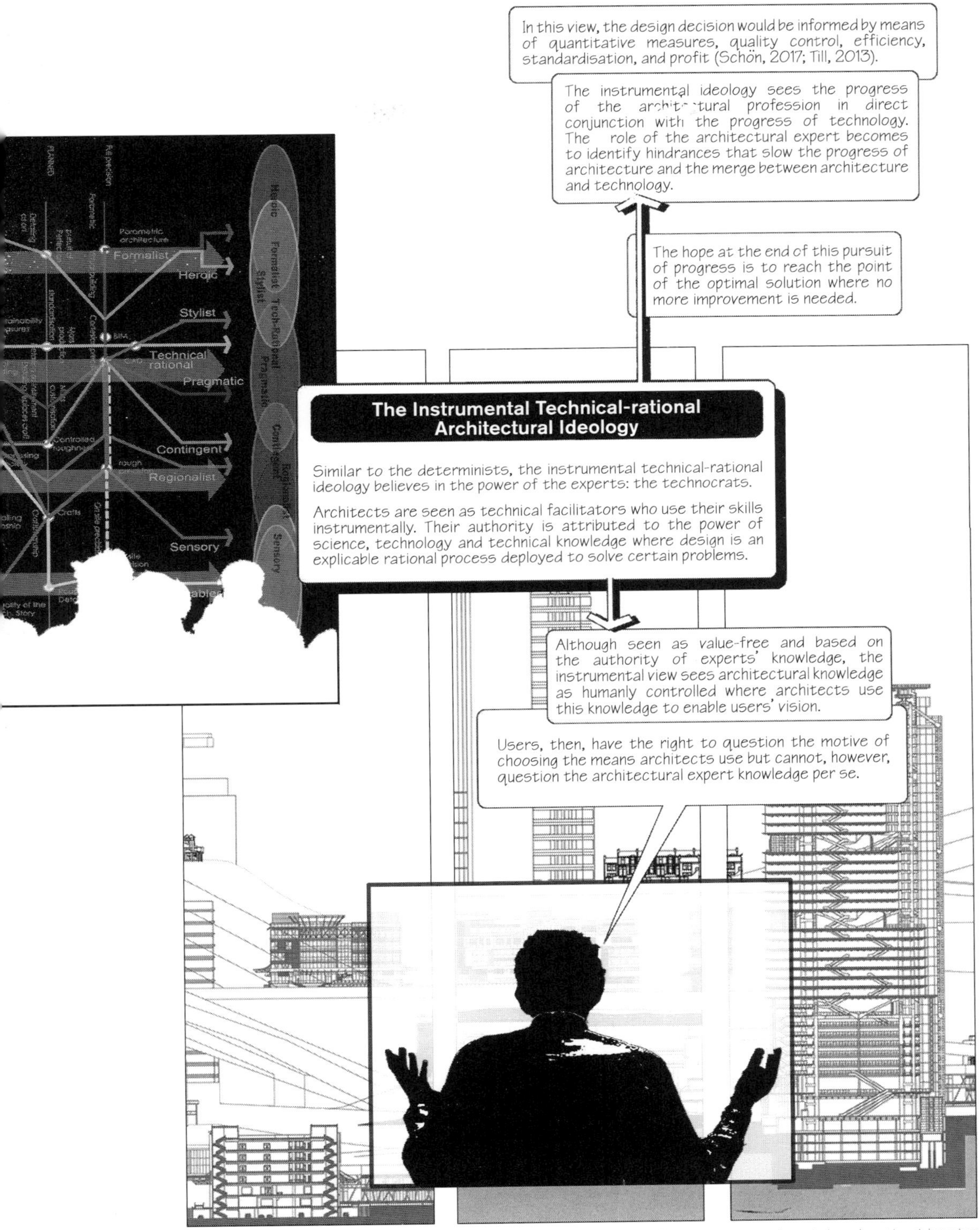
In this view, the design decision would be informed by means of quantitative measures, quality control, efficiency, standardisation, and profit (Schön, 2017; Till, 2013).
The instrumental ideology sees the progress of the architectural profession in direct conjunction with the progress of technology. The role of the architectural expert becomes to identify hindrances that slow the progress of architecture and the merge between architecture and technology.
The hope at the end of this pursuit of progress is to reach the point of the optimal solution where no more improvement is needed.
The Instrumental Technical-rational Architectural Ideology
Similar to the determinists, the instrumental technical-rational ideology believes in the power of the experts: the technocrats.
Architects are seen as technical facilitators who use their skills instrumentally. Their authority is attributed to the power of science, technology and technical knowledge where design is an explicable rational process deployed to solve certain problems.
Although seen as value-free and based on the authority of experts' knowledge, the instrumental view sees architectural knowledge as humanly controlled where architects use this knowledge to enable users' vision.
Users, then, have the right to question the motive of choosing the means architects use but cannot, however, question the architectural expert knowledge per se.
Formalist
Heroic
Stylist
Technical rational
Pragmatic
Contingent
Regionalist
Sensory

* The categorisation above is based on the philosopher Andrew Feenberg's of combination of the social critique of technology familiar from the philosophy of technology of Karl Marx, Herbert Marcuse, Martin Heidegger, and Jacques Ellul with insights taken from the empirical case studies of science and technology studies (Feenberg, 2012; Grabow, 2008).

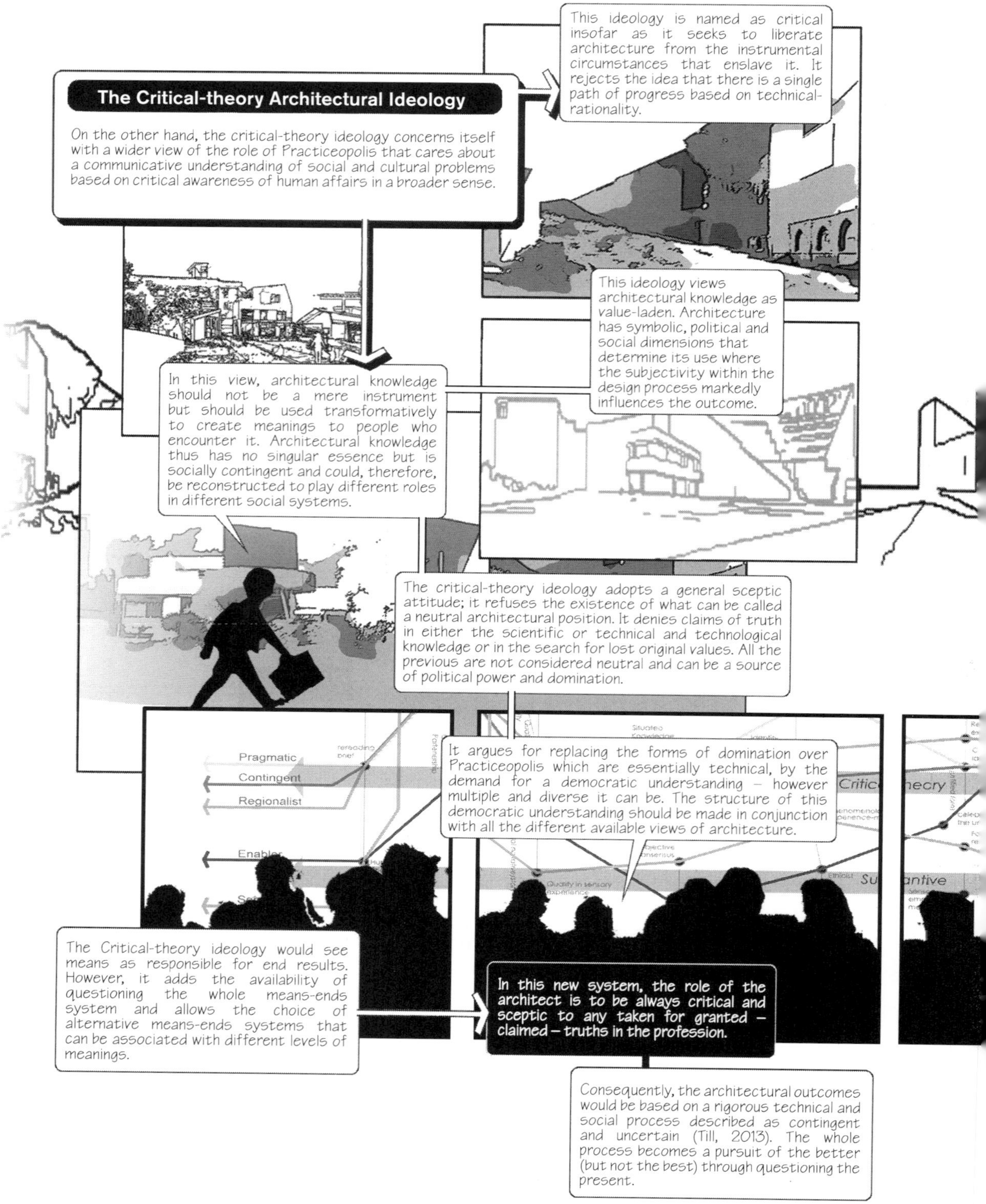
The Critical-theory Architectural Ideology
On the other hand, the critical-theory ideology concerns itself with a wider view of the role of Practiceopolis that cares about a communicative understanding of social and cultural problems based on critical awareness of human affairs in a broader sense.
This ideology is named as critical insofar as it seeks to liberate architecture from the instrumental circumstances that enslave it. It rejects the idea that there is a single path of progress based on technical-rationality.
This ideology views architectural knowledge as value-laden. Architecture has symbolic, political and social dimensions that determine its use where the subjectivity within the design process markedly influences the outcome.
In this view, architectural knowledge should not be a mere instrument but should be used transformatively to create meanings to people who encounter it. Architectural knowledge thus has no singular essence but is socially contingent and could, therefore, be reconstructed to play different roles in different social systems.
The critical-theory ideology adopts a general sceptic attitude; it refuses the existence of what can be called a neutral architectural position. It denies claims of truth in either the scientific or technical and technological knowledge or in the search for lost original values. All the previous are not considered neutral and can be a source of political power and domination.
Pragmatic
Contingent
Regionalist
It argues for replacing the forms of domination over Practiceopolis which are essentially technical, by the demand for a democratic understanding – however multiple and diverse it can be. The structure of this democratic understanding should be made in conjunction with all the different available views of architecture.
The Critical-theory ideology would see means as responsible for end results. However, it adds the availability of questioning the whole means-ends system and allows the choice of alternative means-ends systems that can be associated with different levels of meanings.
In this new system, the role of the architect is to be always critical and sceptic to any taken for granted – claimed – truths in the profession.
Consequently, the architectural outcomes would be based on a rigorous technical and social process described as contingent and uncertain (Till, 2013). The whole process becomes a pursuit of the better (but not the best) through questioning the present.

THE CRITICAL-THEORY/SUBSTANTIVE SIDE

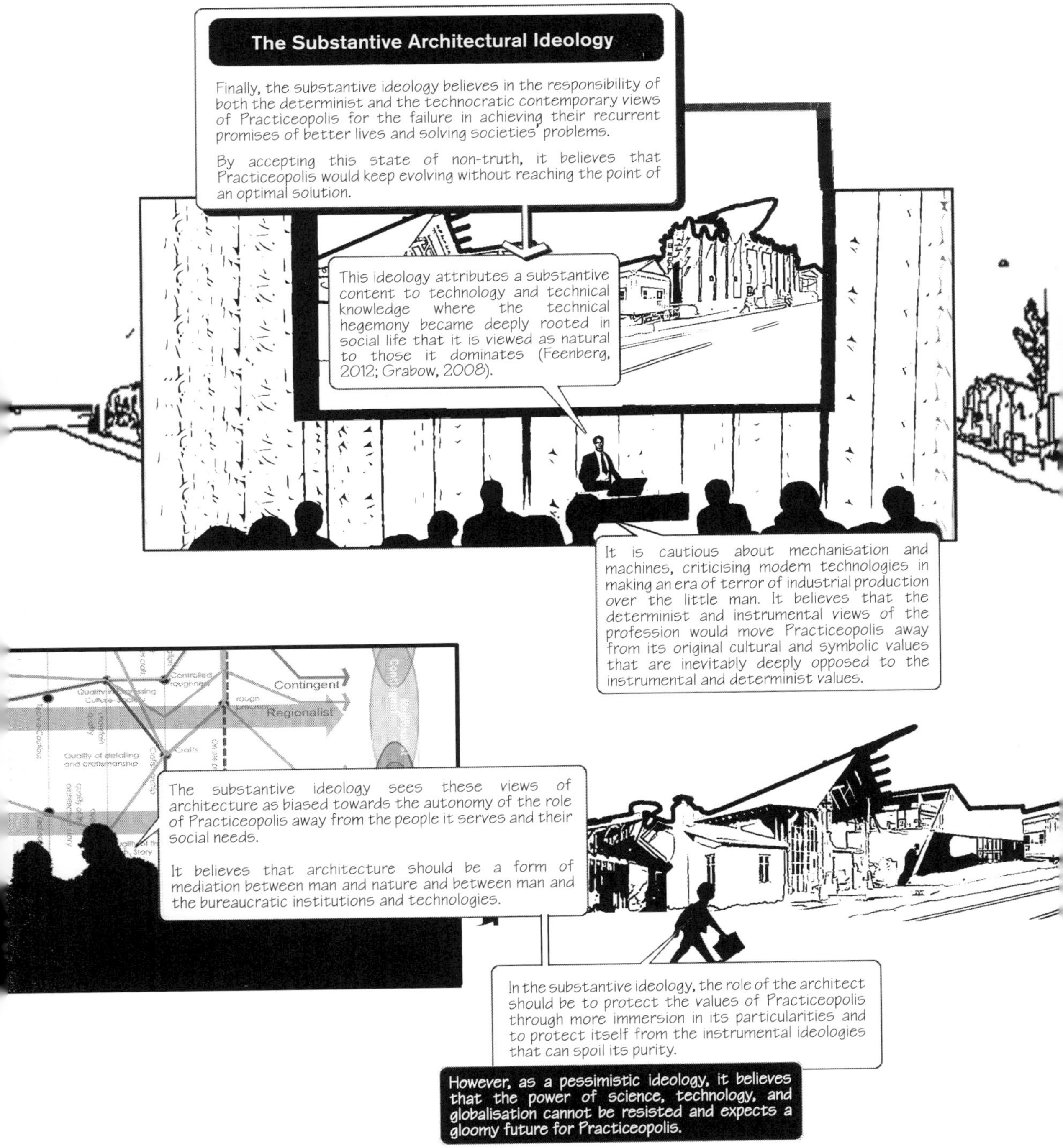
The Substantive Architectural Ideology
Finally, the substantive ideology believes in the responsibility of both the determinist and the technocratic contemporary views of Practiceopolis for the failure in achieving their recurrent promises of better lives and solving societies' problems.
By accepting this state of non-truth, it believes that Practiceopolis would keep evolving without reaching the point of an optimal solution.
This ideology attributes a substantive content to technology and technical knowledge where the technical hegemony became deeply rooted in social life that it is viewed as natural to those it dominates (Feenberg, 2012; Grabow, 2008).
It is cautious about mechanisation and machines, criticising modern technologies in making an era of terror of industrial production over the little man. It believes that the determinist and instrumental views of the profession would move Practiceopolis away from its original cultural and symbolic values that are inevitably deeply opposed to the instrumental and determinist values.
Contingent
Regionalist
Crafts
Quality of detailing and craftsmanship
The substantive ideology sees these views of architecture as biased towards the autonomy of the role of Practiceopolis away from the people it serves and their social needs.
It believes that architecture should be a form of mediation between man and nature and between man and the bureaucratic institutions and technologies.
In the substantive ideology, the role of the architect should be to protect the values of Practiceopolis through more immersion in its particularities and to protect itself from the instrumental ideologies that can spoil its purity.
However, as a pessimistic ideology, it believes that the power of science, technology, and globalisation cannot be resisted and expects a gloomy future for Practiceopolis.

Broadly speaking, the internal dynamics of contemporary Practiceopolis is shaped around this determinist/instrumental ideological side versus the critical-theory/substantive side. This ideological conflict is interpreted within the city into two prominent cultures of practice the Technical-rational and the Critical Cultures of practice.

THE TECHNICAL-RATIONAL CULTURE OF PRACTICE

The Two

The Technical-rational Culture is the dominant architectural movements in Practiceopolis in terms of publicity and number and scale of commissions.

The power of this culture and its affiliated communities help it to exert a big influence on how Practiceopolis is shaped. It adopts a position of securing the best architectural results through full collaboration and coordination between Practiceopolis and Constructopolis.

The discourse of this culture and its representing political party is so influential that it is even adopted by many architectural and building industry regulatory bodies in both Practiceopolis and Constructopolis.

The domination of this culture of practice and its accordance with the values of Constructopolis gives it the ability to claim authority over many governing aspects in Practiceopolis.

This dominance, in turn, may have induced an idea that it is the right way of practising architecture that Practiceopolis should follow.

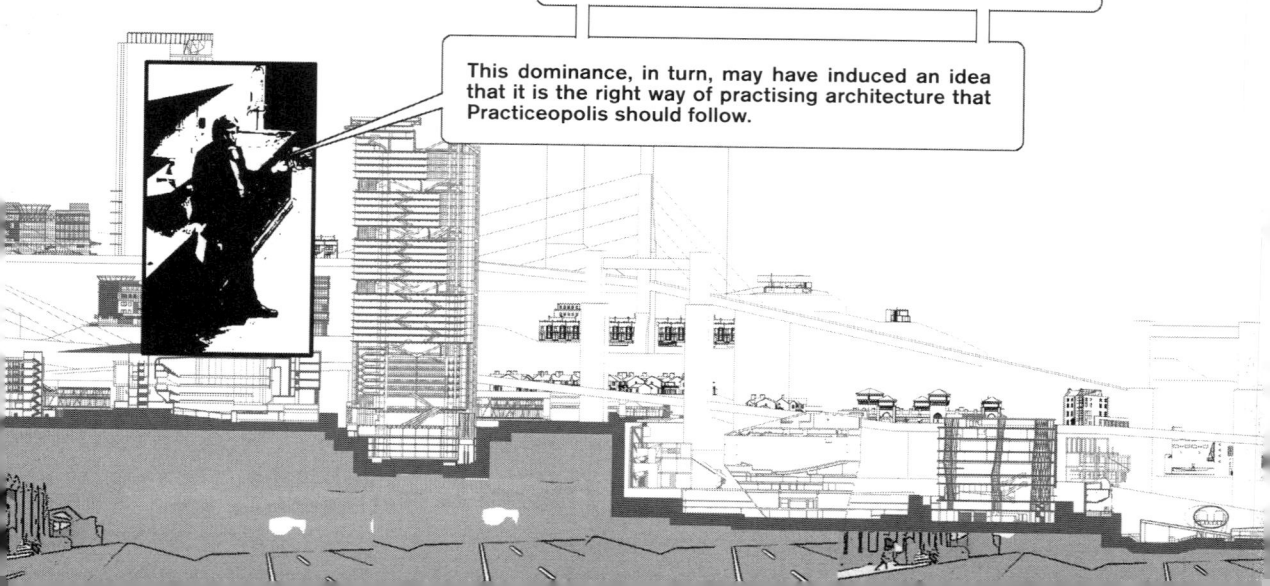

Cultures

The first is broadly dominated by the economic ideology while the other is dominated by the symbolic.

The active competition between those cultures over capital, makes up the city's political left- and right-wing parties.

THE CRITICAL CULTURE OF PRACTICE

On the other hand, the Critical Culture of practice, while not a dominant movement, maintains a prominent presence within Practiceopolis.

Its affiliated communities cover a broad range of ethos that generally embody ideas of qualitative and cultural conceptions of architecture. It shares many lines of enquiry found in critical theory; particularly questioning claims to truth, essentialism, and autonomy; tending to render their theories political in outlook and action.

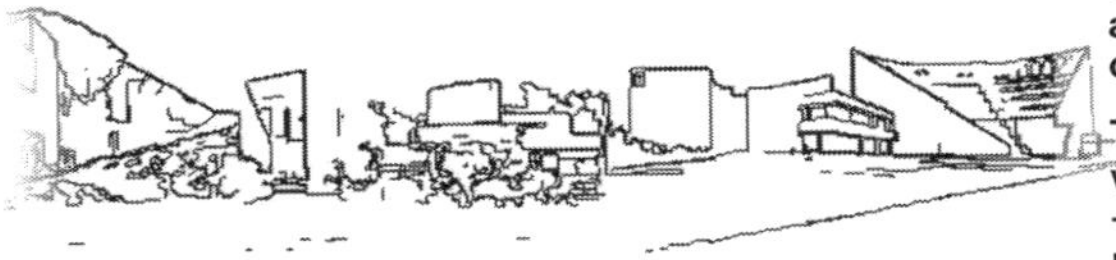

The critical political movement has discordant views against the current situation of Practiceopolis – dominated by the Technical-rational Culture of practice.

It views that the status quo of Practiceopolis became a space of flat indifference, stagnant incommensurable, and the in-distinction of architectural particular values within a zone of methodological Junkspace (Foster and Koolhaas, 2013).

The critical communities reject the notion of an authentic way of practising architecture. They often adopt a view of Practiceopolis as a space for diverse dialogues that enrich its capital, and as an opportunity for interdisciplinary discussions between Practiceopolis and other states in Constructopolis.

Yet, what may look like a tolerant view of the profession also has its own hidden biases against the technical-rational community by generally coining the instrumental communities as 'commercial' and less rigorous.

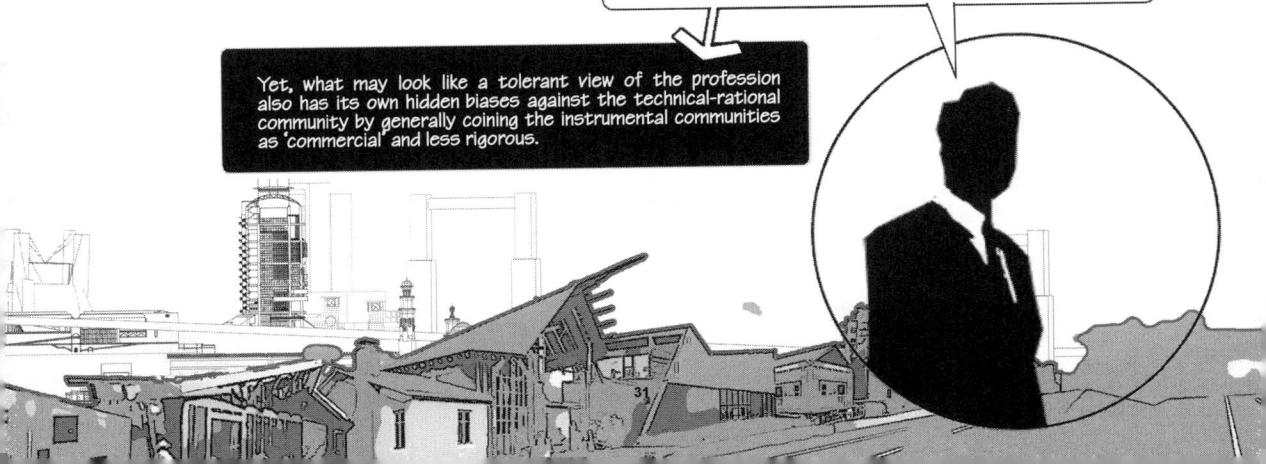

This distribution of capital in Practiceopolis and the formation of these cultures of practice and their political parties are the outcome of a long historical evolution of the city that led to its current status quo.

Let's walk through this history to know more!

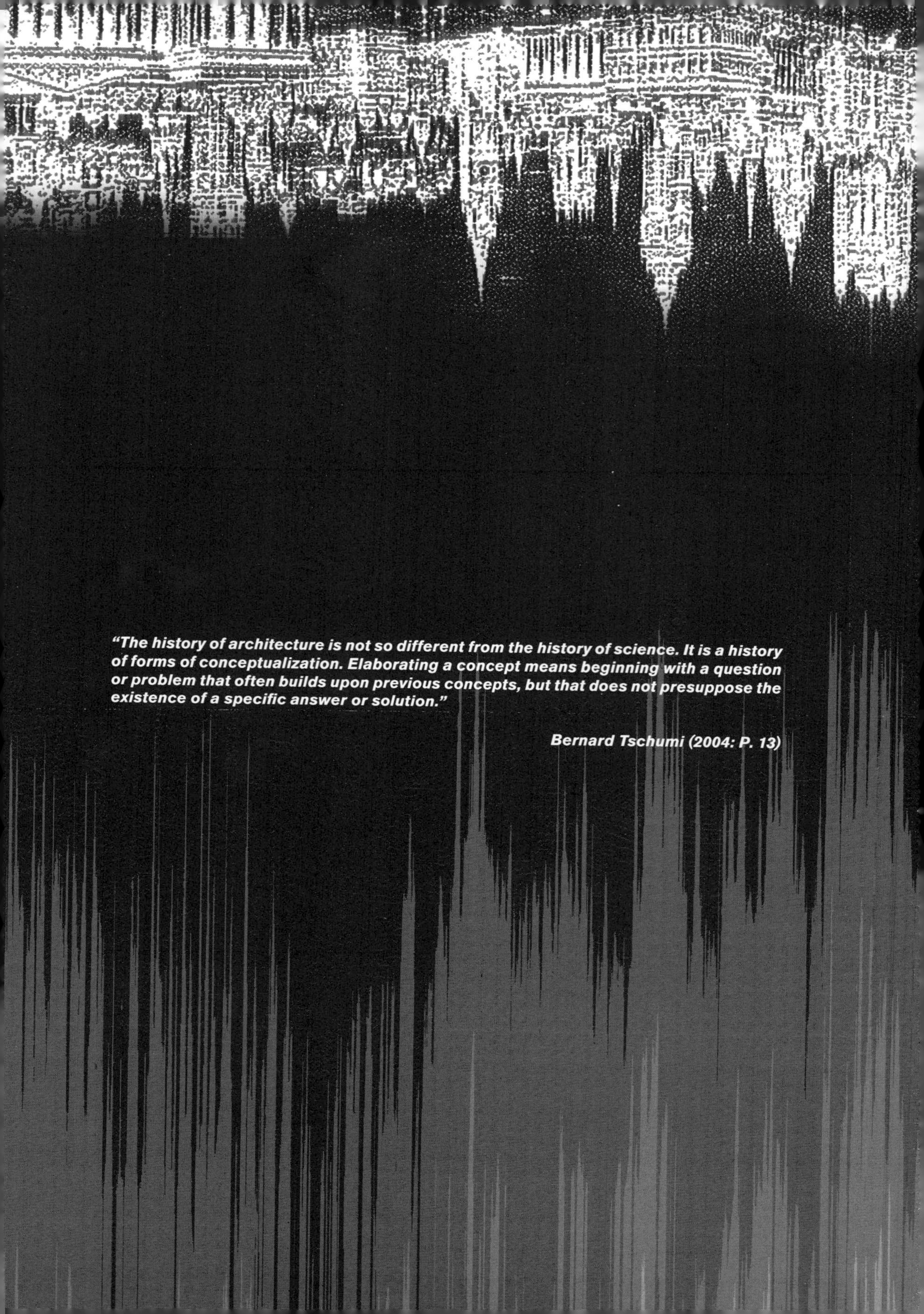

"The history of architecture is not so different from the history of science. It is a history of forms of conceptualization. Elaborating a concept means beginning with a question or problem that often builds upon previous concepts, but that does not presuppose the existence of a specific answer or solution."

Bernard Tschumi (2004: P. 13)

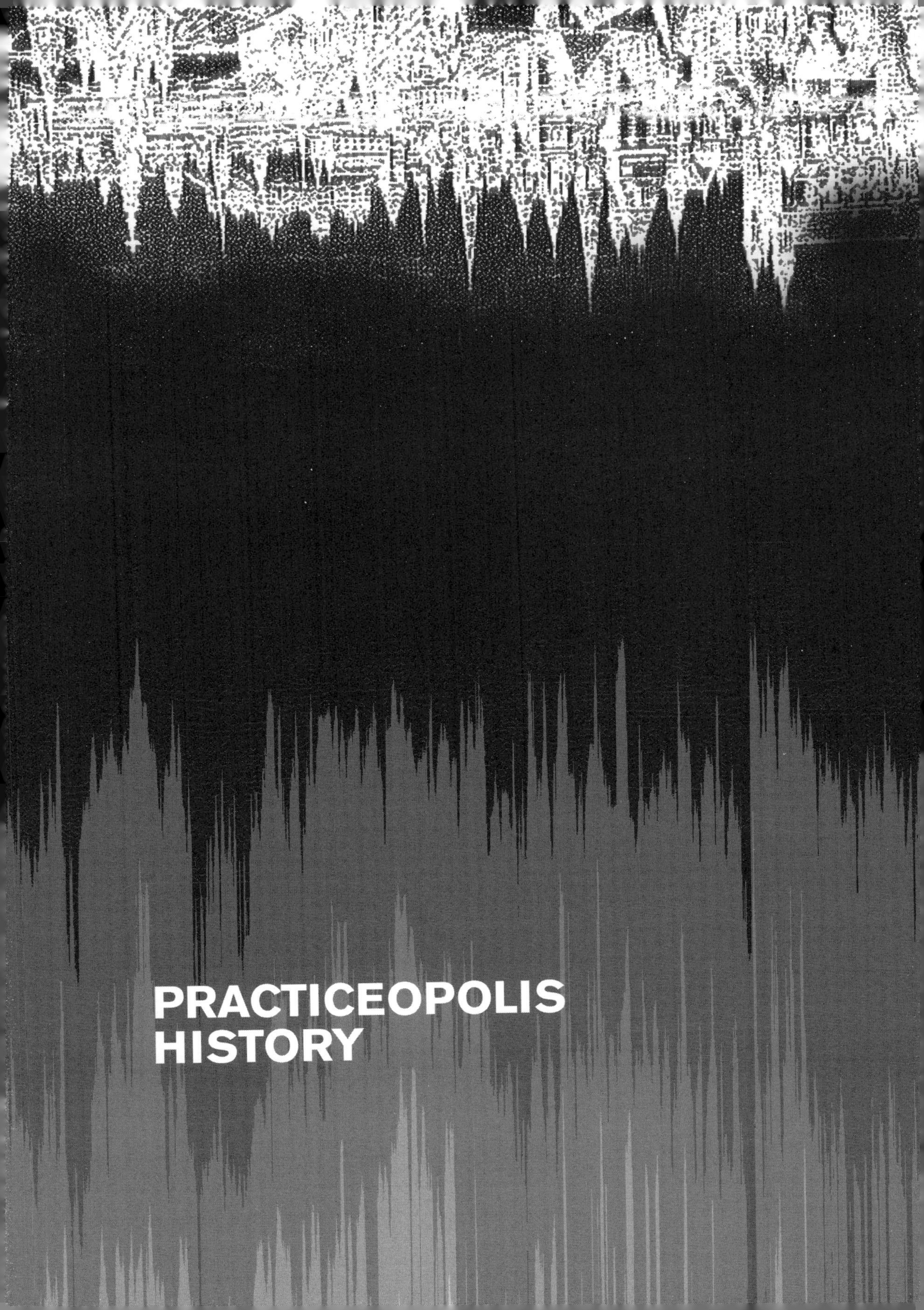

PRACTICEOPOLIS HISTORY

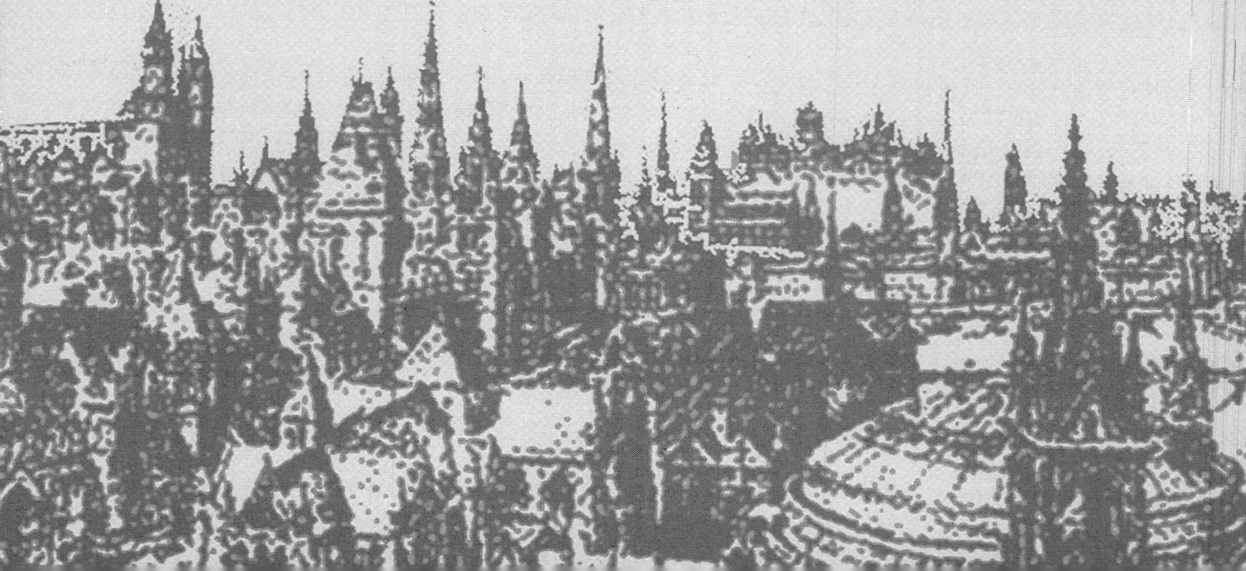

Throughout its history, varied social and political shifts changed the territory of Practiceopolis. We can describe these shifts in many ways; as a series of styles, as reflections to technological advances, or reactions to political and economic changes. The outcome of these shifts is the buildings of Practiceopolis, in which each acts as archaeological evidence of its time and the design theory behind its configuration. These design theories are the resultant of a totality of concerns integrating architecture, engineering, visual forms, building technologies, and reactions to social, economic and political changes of its time (Wagner, 1985).

The Land of Early Builders
Practiceopolis origin

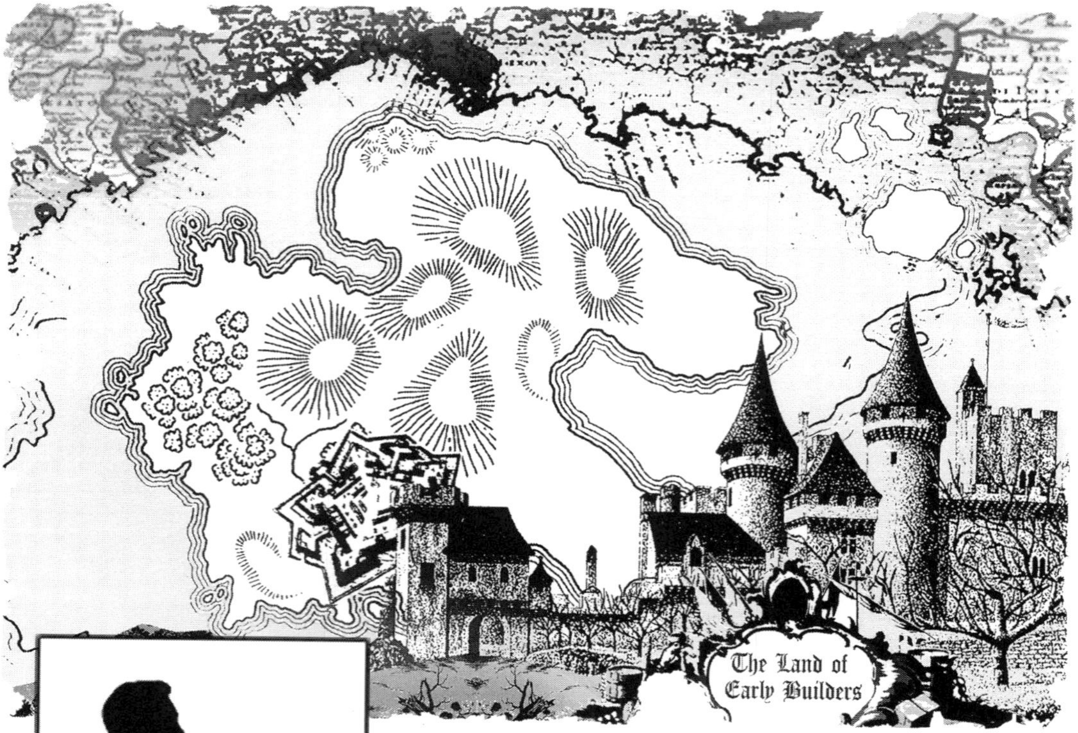
The Land of
Early Builders

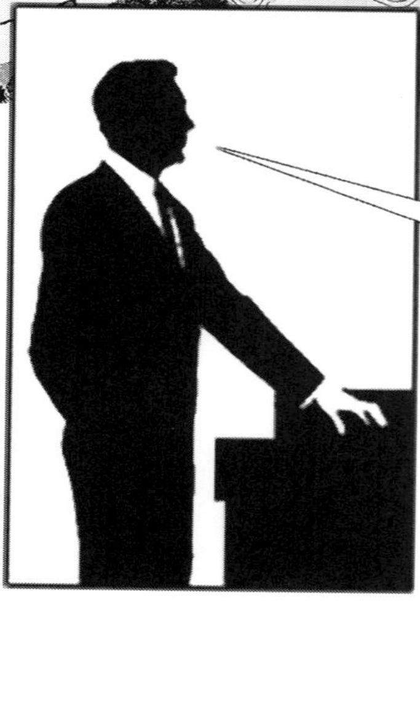
The earliest builders of old Practiceopolis wove together a mastery of design, craft and organisation to create great architecture. This was apparent in many early buildings of the old ages which still contain etching of full-scale drawings into their stone floors by the master builders to guide construction.

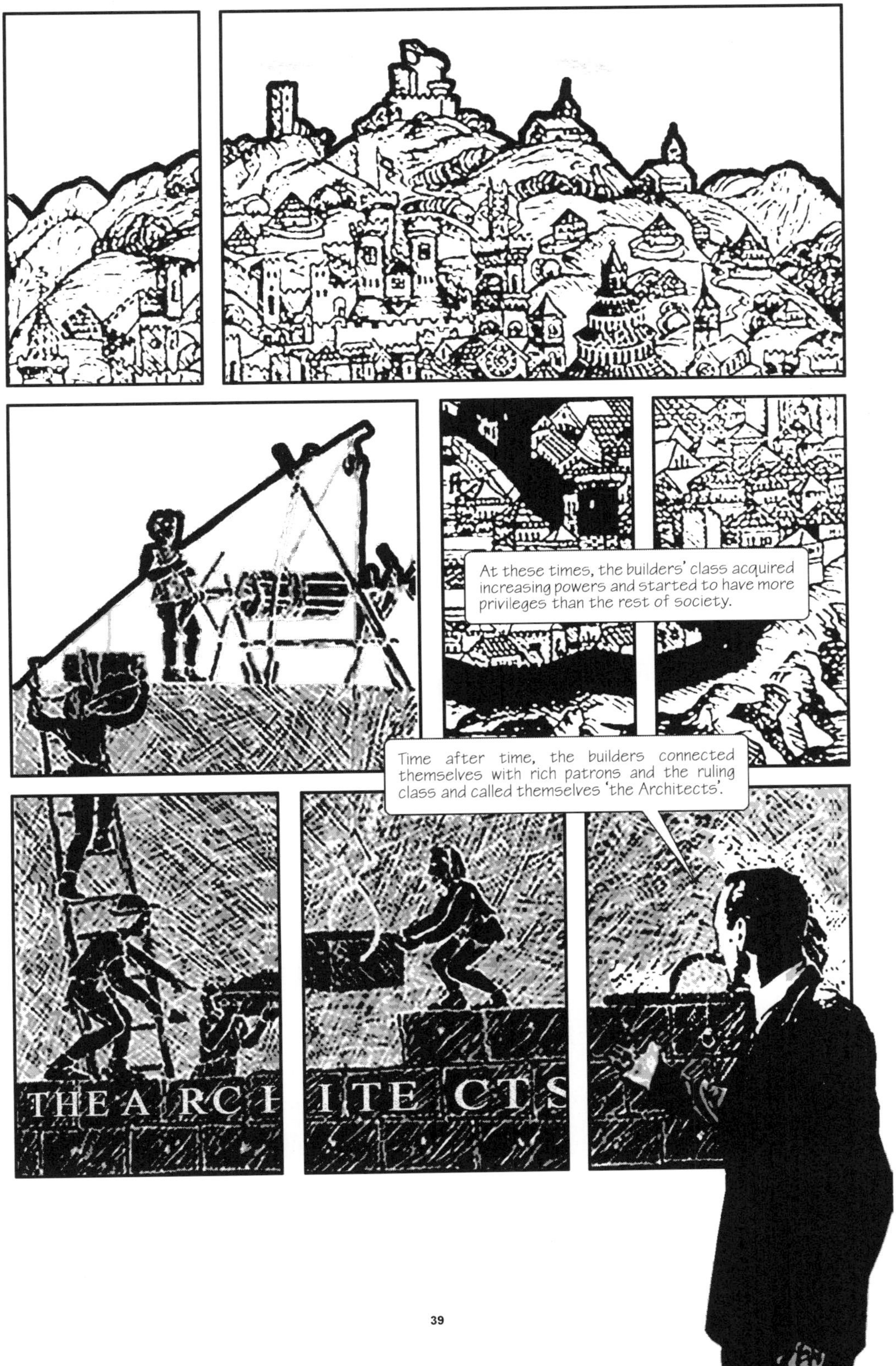
At these times, the builders' class acquired increasing powers and started to have more privileges than the rest of society.
Time after time, the builders connected themselves with rich patrons and the ruling class and called themselves 'the Architects'.
THE A RC I ITE CTS

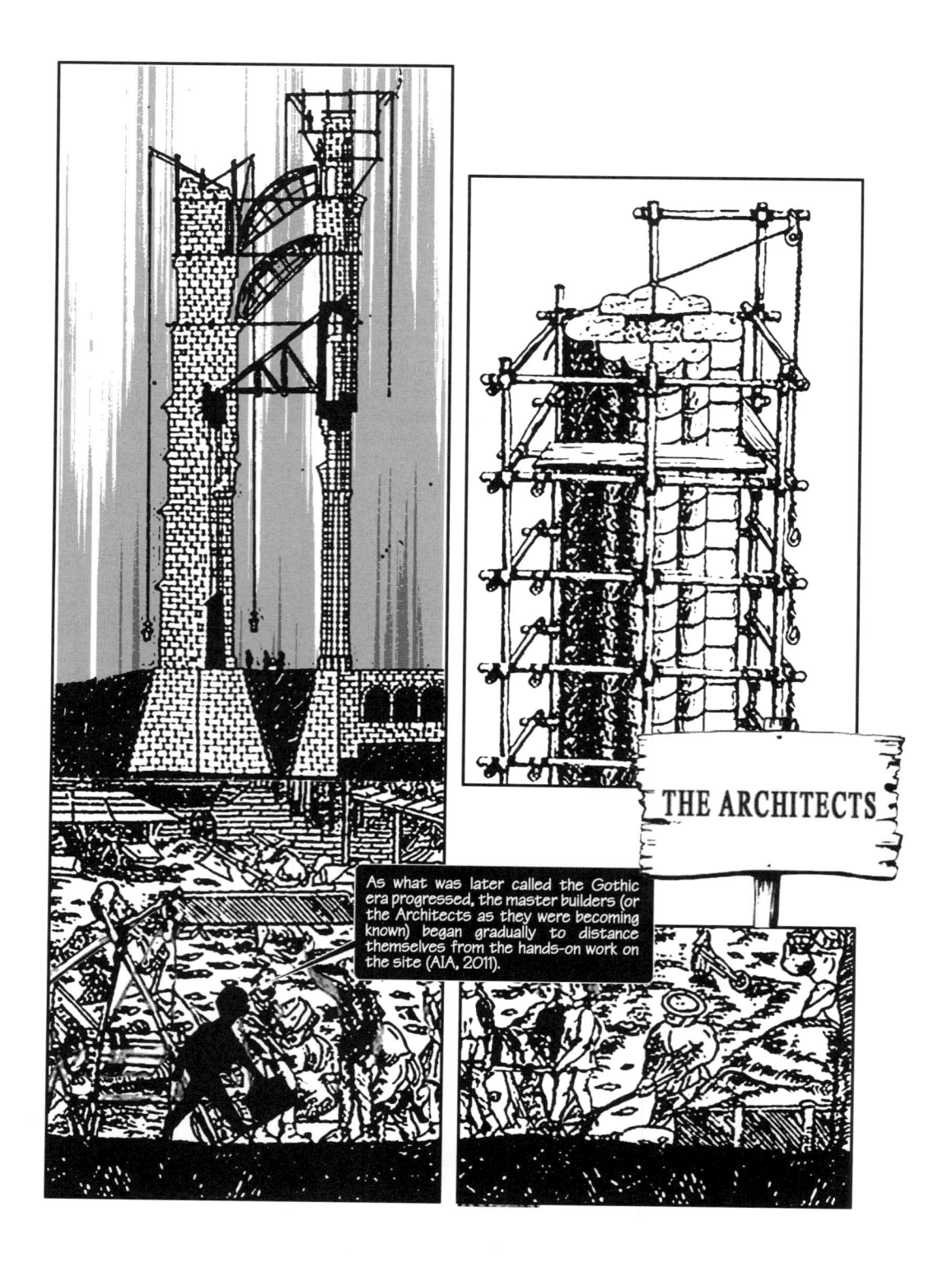

THE ARCHITECTS

As what was later called the Gothic era progressed, the master builders (or the Architects as they were becoming known) began gradually to distance themselves from the hands-on work on the site (AIA, 2011).

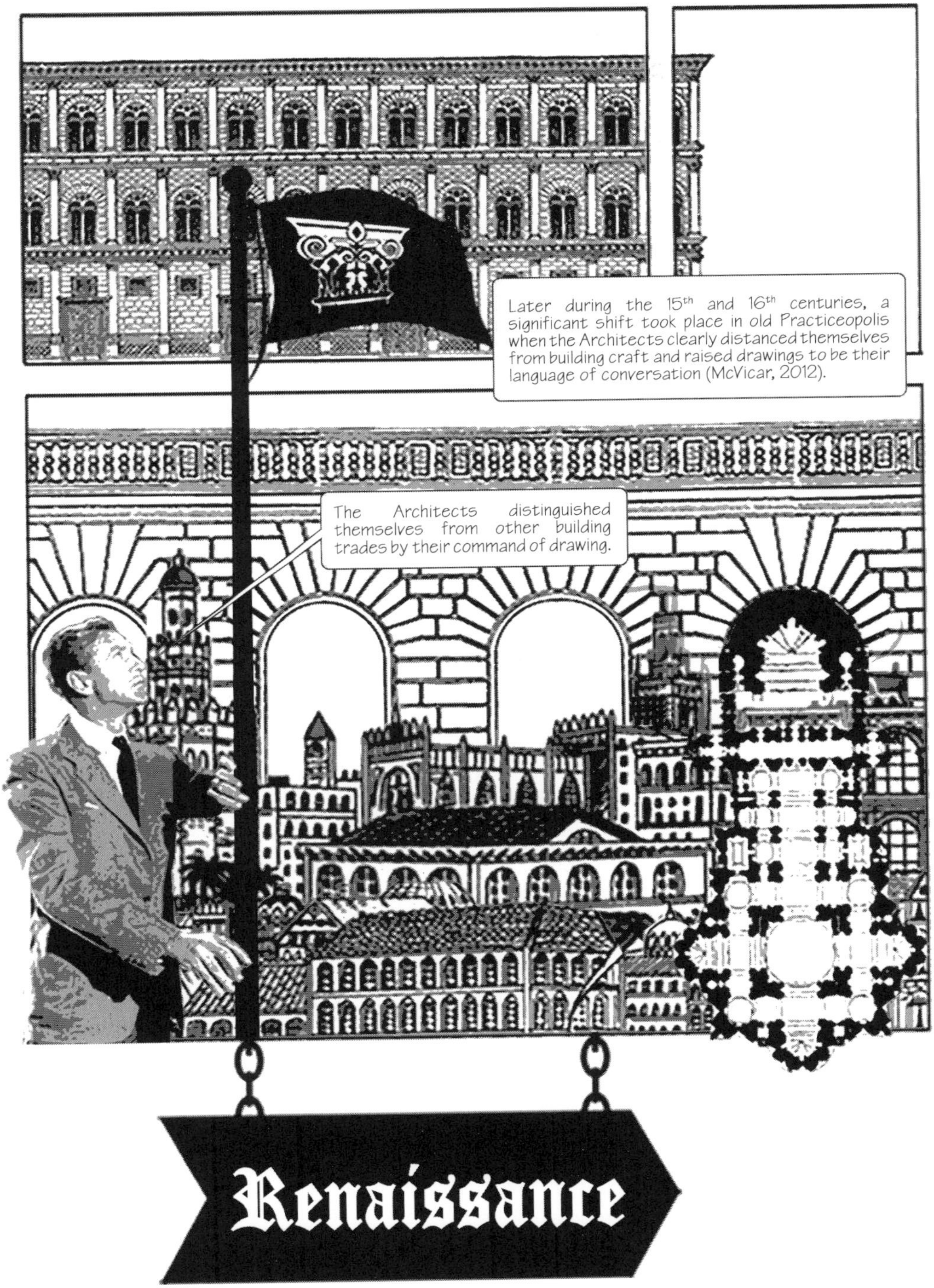
Later during the 15th and 16th centuries, a significant shift took place in old Practiceopolis when the Architects clearly distanced themselves from building craft and raised drawings to be their language of conversation (McVicar, 2012).
The Architects distinguished themselves from other building trades by their command of drawing.
Renaissance

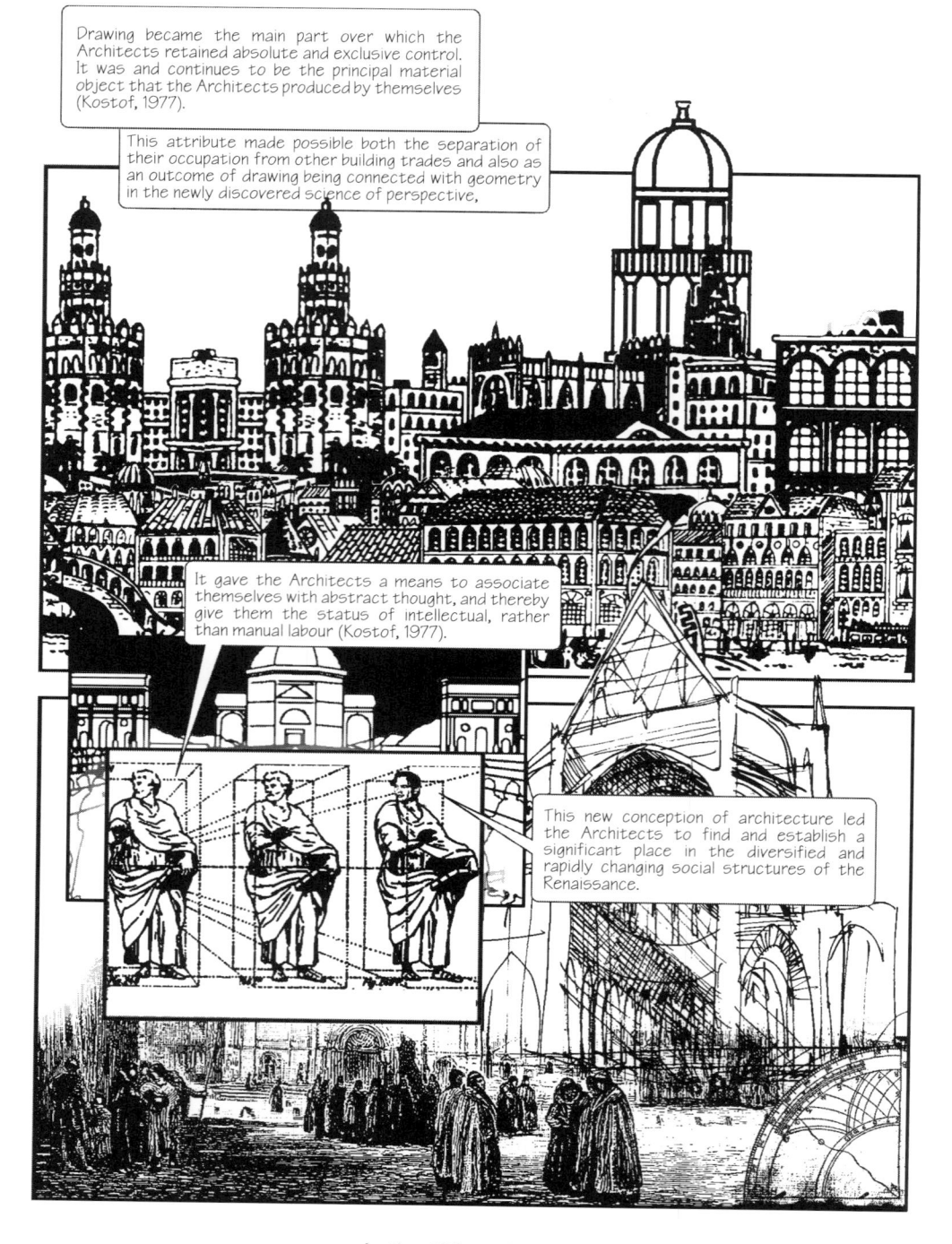

Drawing became the main part over which the Architects retained absolute and exclusive control. It was and continues to be the principal material object that the Architects produced by themselves (Kostof, 1977).

This attribute made possible both the separation of their occupation from other building trades and also as an outcome of drawing being connected with geometry in the newly discovered science of perspective,

It gave the Architects a means to associate themselves with abstract thought, and thereby give them the status of intellectual, rather than manual labour (Kostof, 1977).

This new conception of architecture led the Architects to find and establish a significant place in the diversified and rapidly changing social structures of the Renaissance.

In the 16th century, writings started to be outspokenly contrasting the architect to those who were trained for manual work and had no knowledge of the principles of architecture: e.g. master mason or master carpenter. (Kostof, 1977).

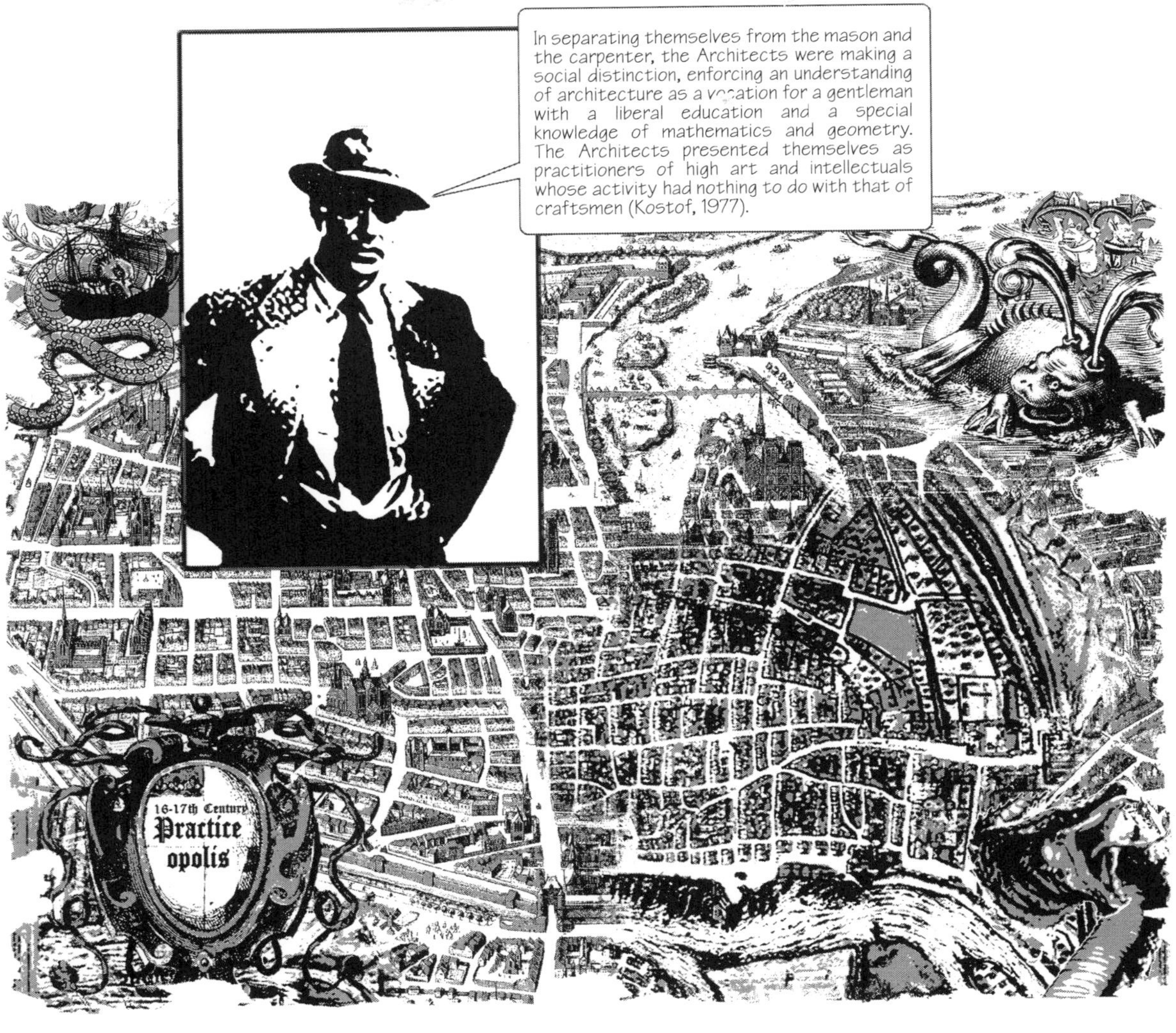
In separating themselves from the mason and the carpenter, the Architects were making a social distinction, enforcing an understanding of architecture as a vocation for a gentleman with a liberal education and a special knowledge of mathematics and geometry. The Architects presented themselves as practitioners of high art and intellectuals whose activity had nothing to do with that of craftsmen (Kostof, 1977).
16-17th Century
Practice
opolis

By the end of this era, the Architects in old Practiceopolis became a self-ruling community that had a direct connection with the sources of wealth and power.

16-17th century
Practiceopolis

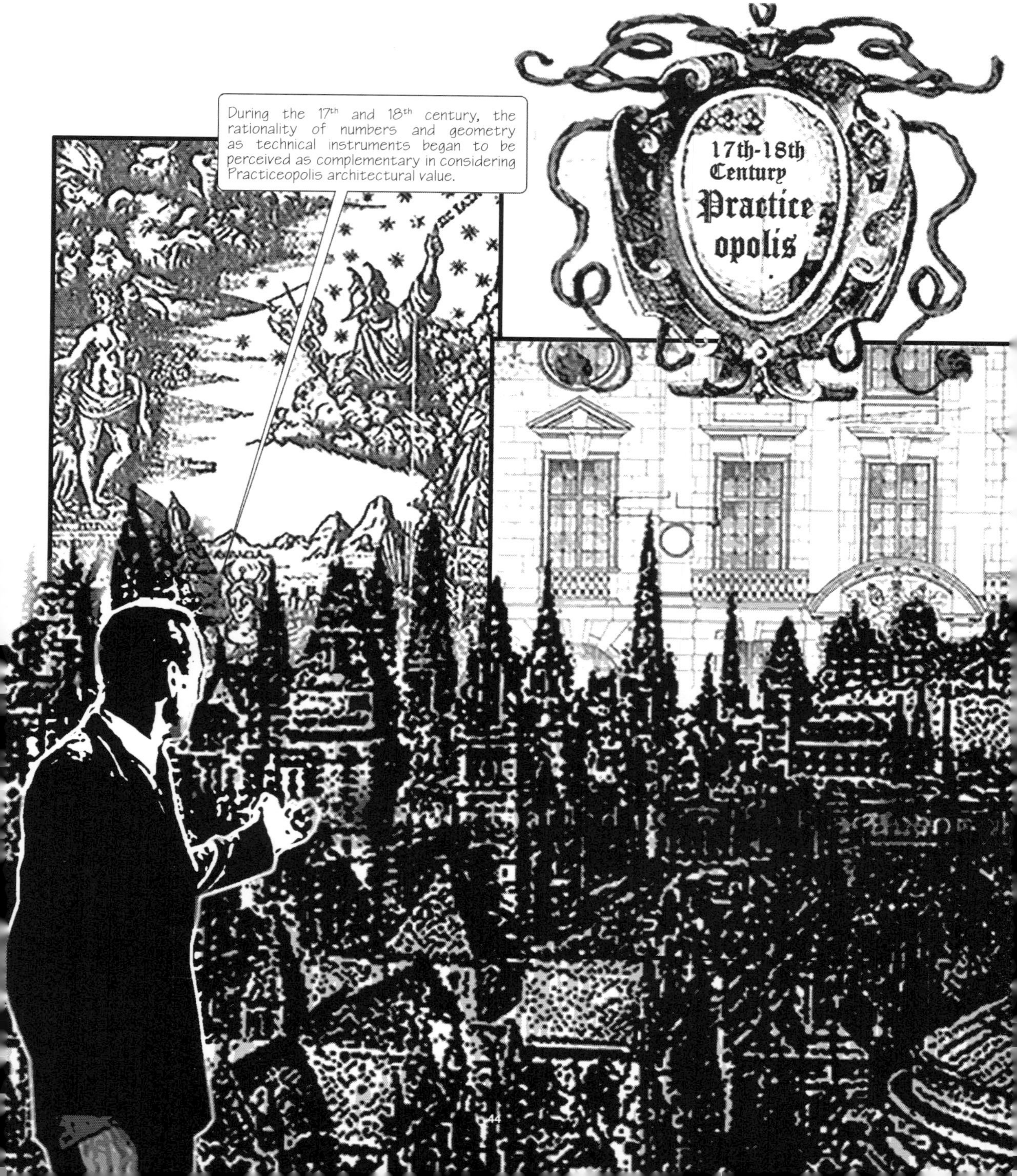
17th-18th Century Practice opolis
During the 17th and 18th century, the rationality of numbers and geometry as technical instruments began to be perceived as complementary in considering Practiceopolis architectural value.

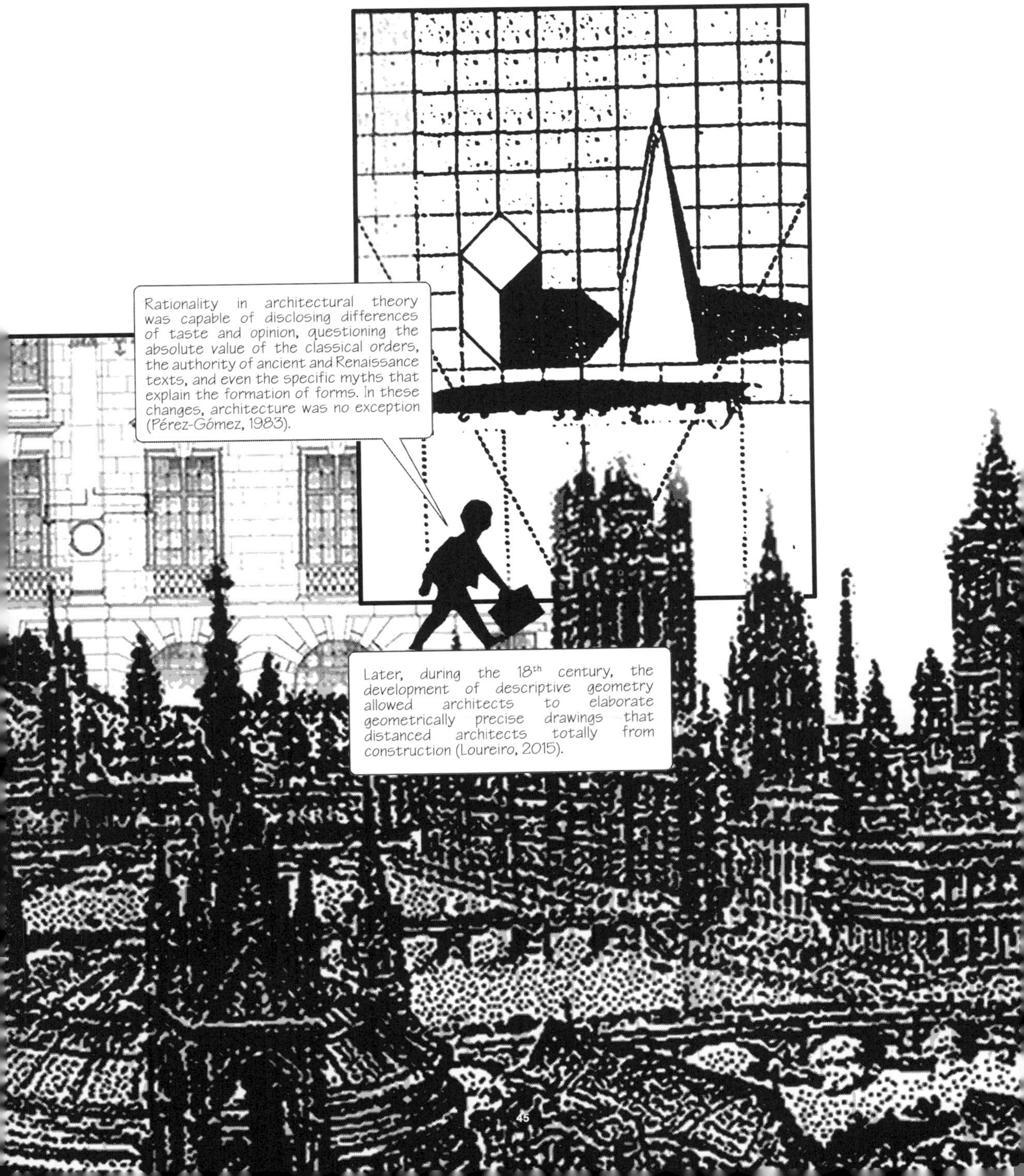
Rationality in architectural theory was capable of disclosing differences of taste and opinion, questioning the absolute value of the classical orders, the authority of ancient and Renaissance texts, and even the specific myths that explain the formation of forms. In these changes, architecture was no exception (Pérez-Gómez, 1983).
Later, during the 18th century, the development of descriptive geometry allowed architects to elaborate geometrically precise drawings that distanced architects totally from construction (Loureiro, 2015).

Around the late 18th century and the early 19th century, faith and reason were truly divorced. Scientific thought came to be seen as the only serious and legitimate interpretation of reality. Scientists and philosophers in Practiceopolis adopted the Positivism philosophy, coining all intellectual operations outside mathematical reason as illegitimate. Metaphysics was denied, Euclidean geometry was functionalised, and calculus was purged of all residual symbolic content. They condemned the subjectivity of human being as a partial perspective of the world that provides only limited access to objective reality. Reason became the only accepted way to discover absolutely certain mathematical truths. Accordingly, physical and human sciences should be combined and handled exclusively through reason. They had to be reduced to a definite truth that can be obtained through observation (Pérez-Gómez, 1983; Schön, 2017).

The Age of Enlightenment

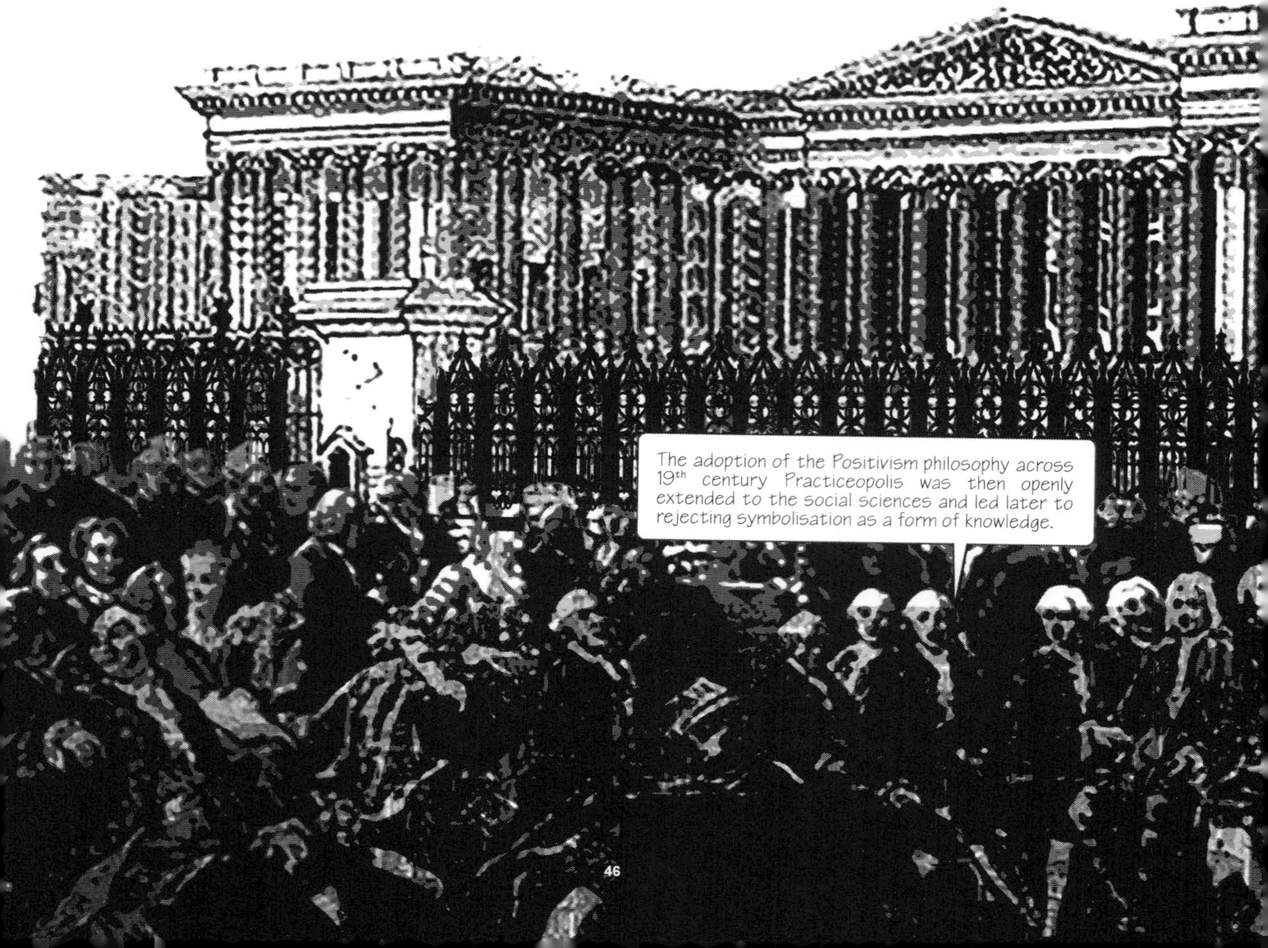
The adoption of the Positivism philosophy across 19th century Practiceopolis was then openly extended to the social sciences and led later to rejecting symbolisation as a form of knowledge.

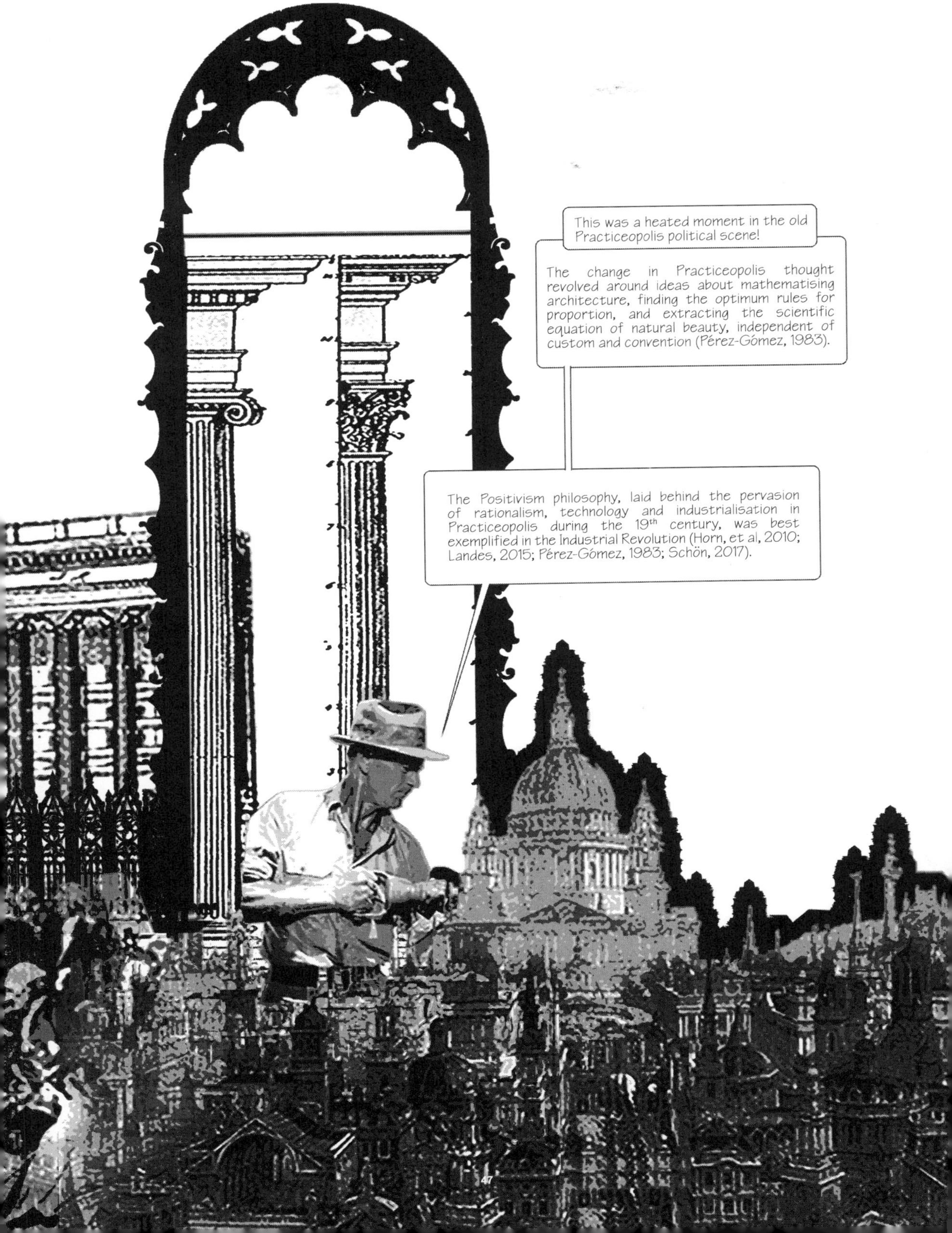
This was a heated moment in the old Practiceopolis political scene!
The change in Practiceopolis thought revolved around ideas about mathematising architecture, finding the optimum rules for proportion, and extracting the scientific equation of natural beauty, independent of custom and convention (Pérez-Gómez, 1983).
The Positivism philosophy, laid behind the pervasion of rationalism, technology and industrialisation in Practiceopolis during the 19th century, was best exemplified in the Industrial Revolution (Horn, et al, 2010; Landes, 2015; Pérez-Gómez, 1983; Schön, 2017).

Industrial Revolution
Practiceopolis

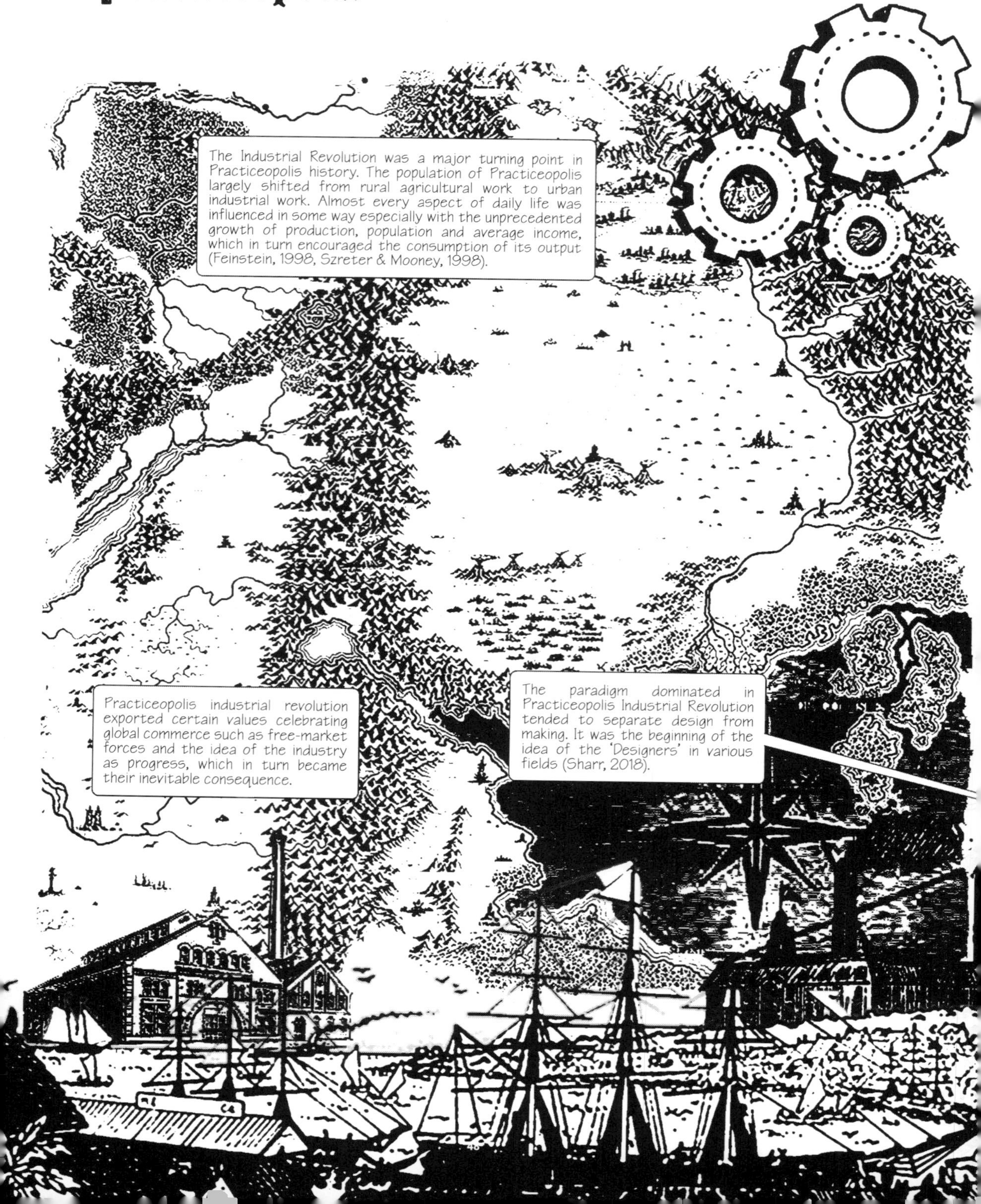
The Industrial Revolution was a major turning point in Practiceopolis history. The population of Practiceopolis largely shifted from rural agricultural work to urban industrial work. Almost every aspect of daily life was influenced in some way especially with the unprecedented growth of production, population and average income, which in turn encouraged the consumption of its output (Feinstein, 1998, Szreter & Mooney, 1998).
Practiceopolis industrial revolution exported certain values celebrating global commerce such as free-market forces and the idea of the industry as progress, which in turn became their inevitable consequence.
The paradigm dominated in Practiceopolis Industrial Revolution tended to separate design from making. It was the beginning of the idea of the 'Designers' in various fields (Sharr, 2018).

This paradigm was paralleled by the Architects continuing to redefine their role in society, moving further from their craft-based origins and forsaking the site job.

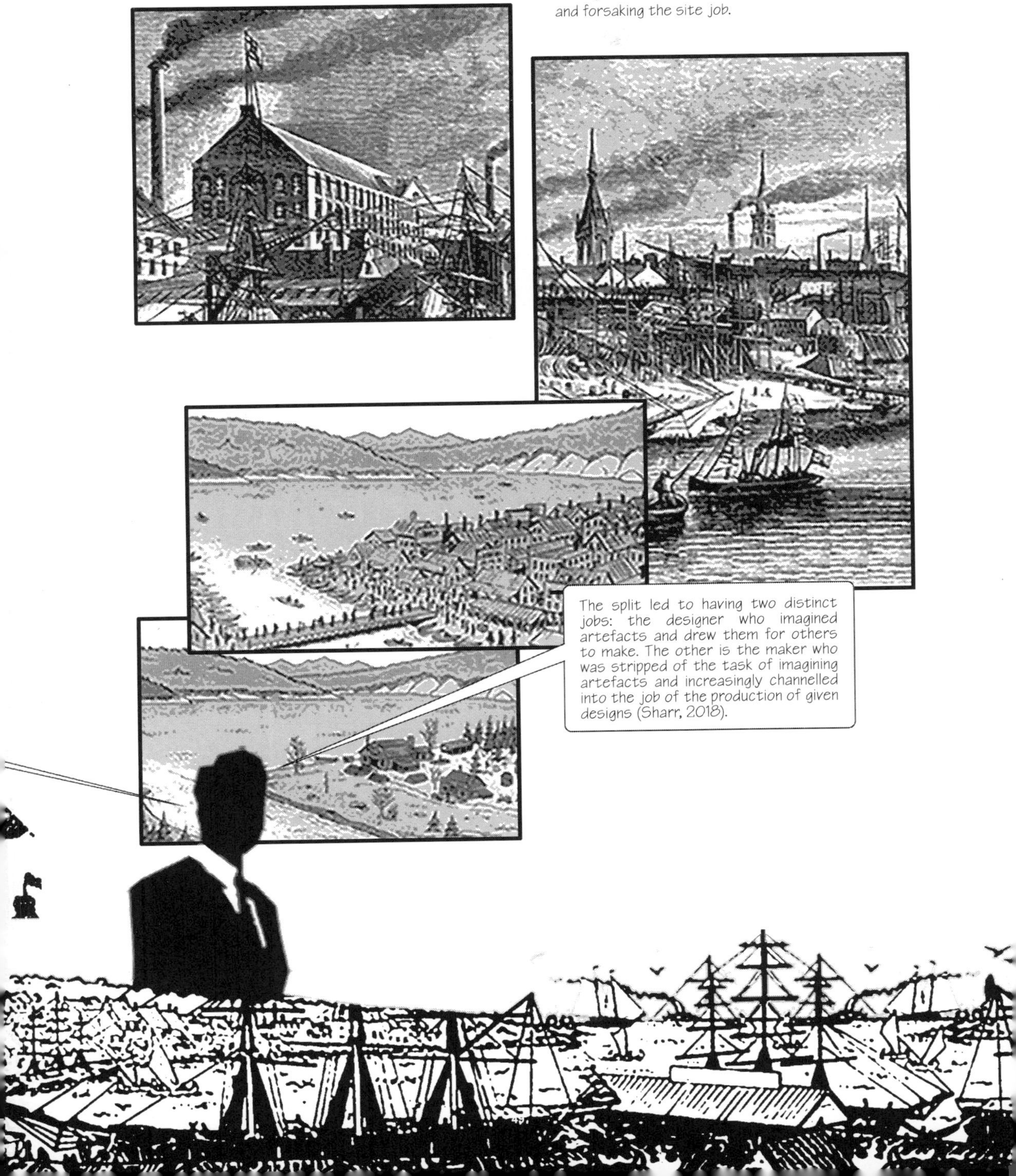
The split led to having two distinct jobs: the designer who imagined artefacts and drew them for others to make. The other is the maker who was stripped of the task of imagining artefacts and increasingly channelled into the job of the production of given designs (Sharr, 2018).

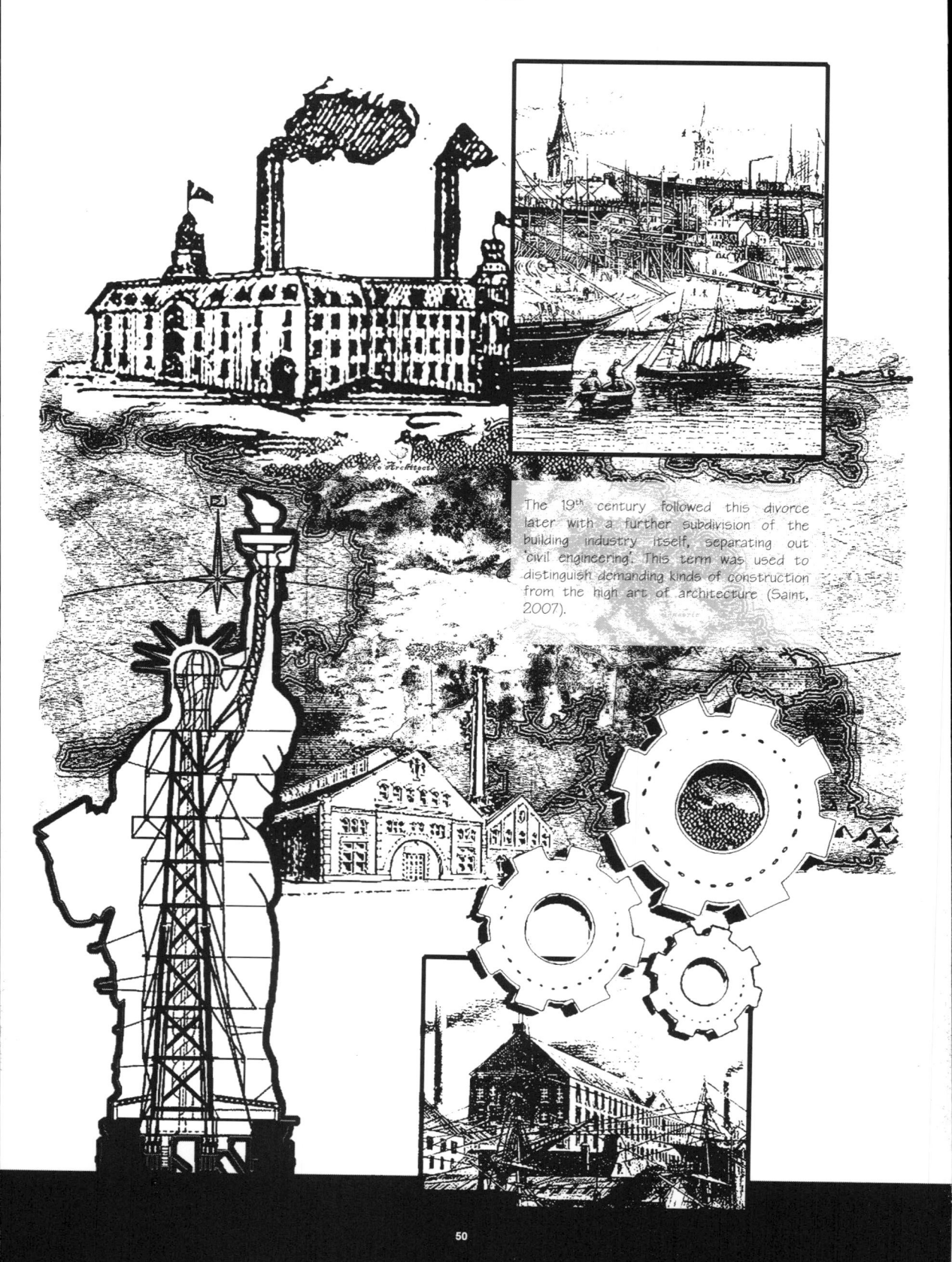

The 19th century followed this divorce later with a further subdivision of the building industry itself, separating out civil engineering. This term was used to distinguish demanding kinds of construction from the high art of architecture (Saint, 2007).

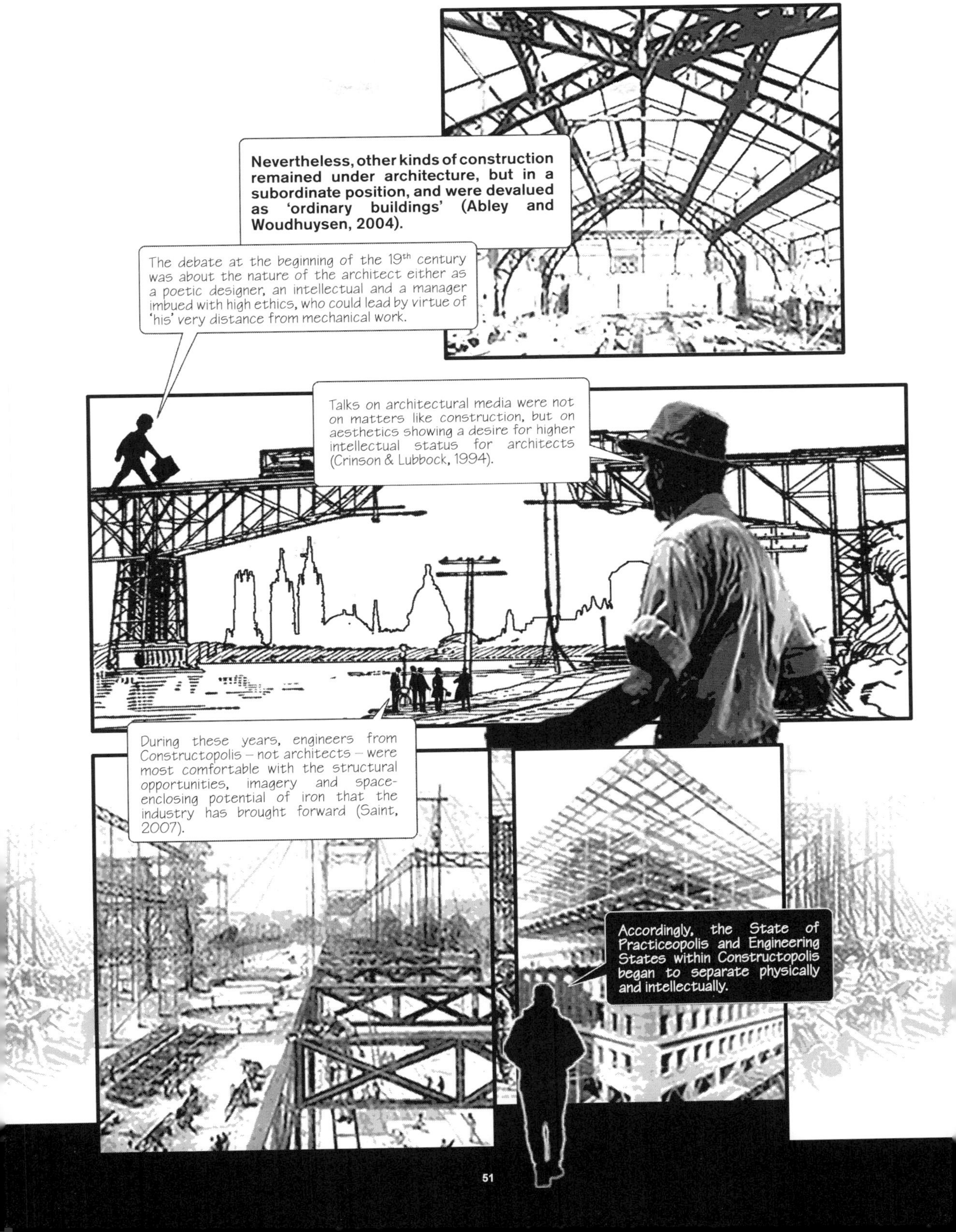
Nevertheless, other kinds of construction remained under architecture, but in a subordinate position, and were devalued as 'ordinary buildings' (Abley and Woudhuysen, 2004).
The debate at the beginning of the 19th century was about the nature of the architect either as a poetic designer, an intellectual and a manager imbued with high ethics, who could lead by virtue of 'his' very distance from mechanical work.
Talks on architectural media were not on matters like construction, but on aesthetics showing a desire for higher intellectual status for architects (Crinson & Lubbock, 1994).
During these years, engineers from Constructopolis – not architects – were most comfortable with the structural opportunities, imagery and space-enclosing potential of iron that the industry has brought forward (Saint, 2007).
Accordingly, the State of Practiceopolis and Engineering States within Constructopolis began to separate physically and intellectually.

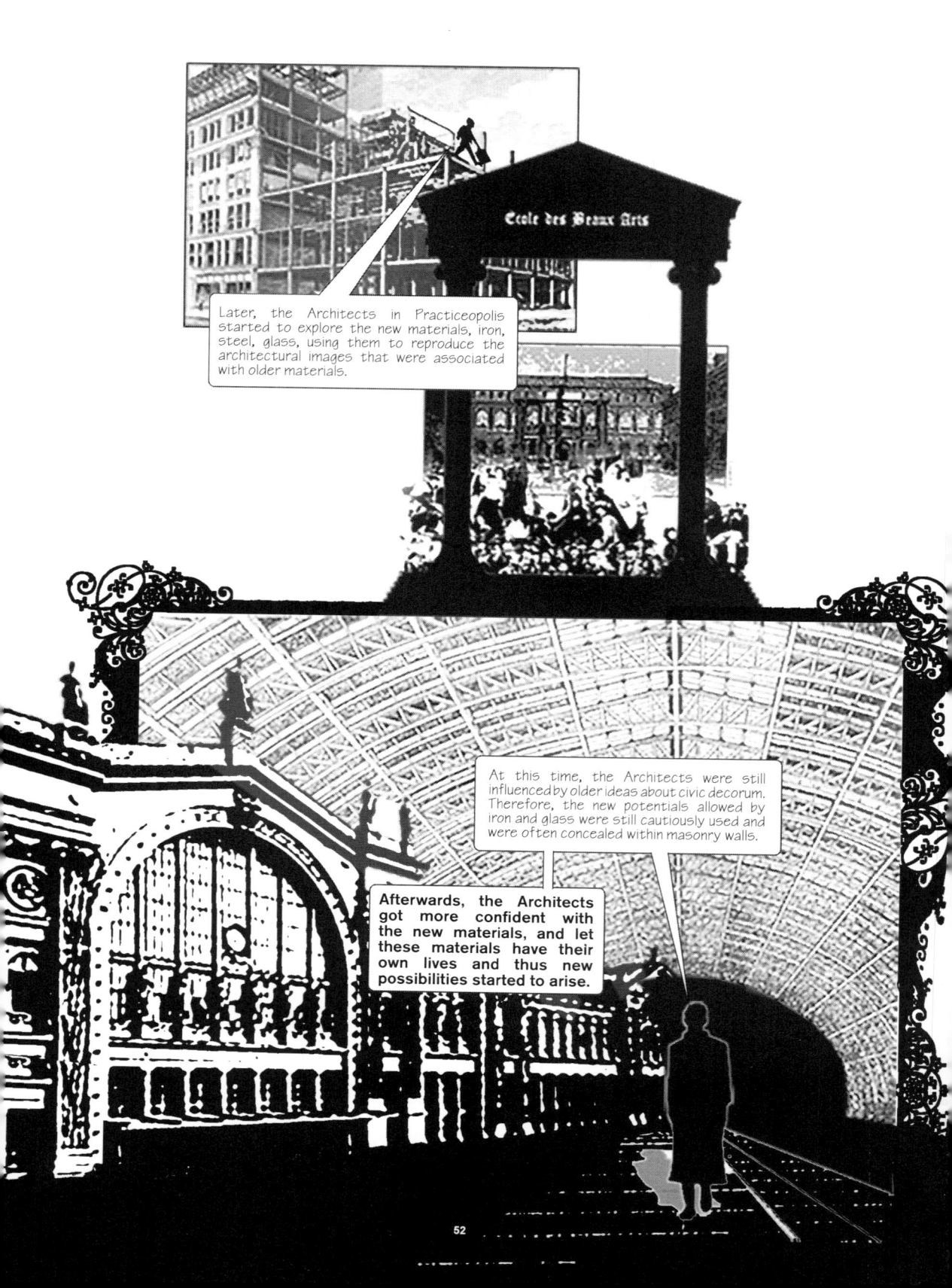

Later, the Architects in Practiceopolis started to explore the new materials, iron, steel, glass, using them to reproduce the architectural images that were associated with older materials.

At this time, the Architects were still influenced by older ideas about civic decorum. Therefore, the new potentials allowed by iron and glass were still cautiously used and were often concealed within masonry walls.

Afterwards, the Architects got more confident with the new materials, and let these materials have their own lives and thus new possibilities started to arise.

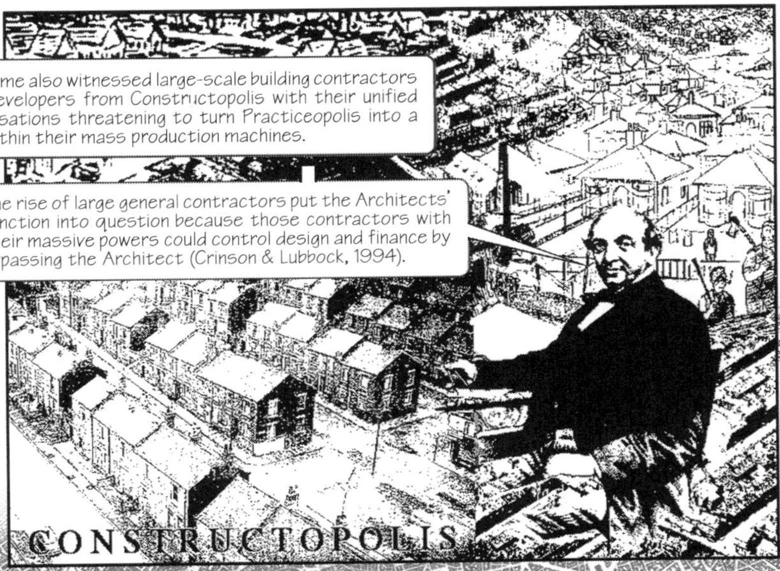
This time also witnessed large-scale building contractors and developers from Constructopolis with their unified organisations threatening to turn Practiceopolis into a cog within their mass production machines.
The rise of large general contractors put the Architects' function into question because those contractors with their massive powers could control design and finance by bypassing the Architect (Crinson & Lubbock, 1994).
CONSTRUCTOPOLIS

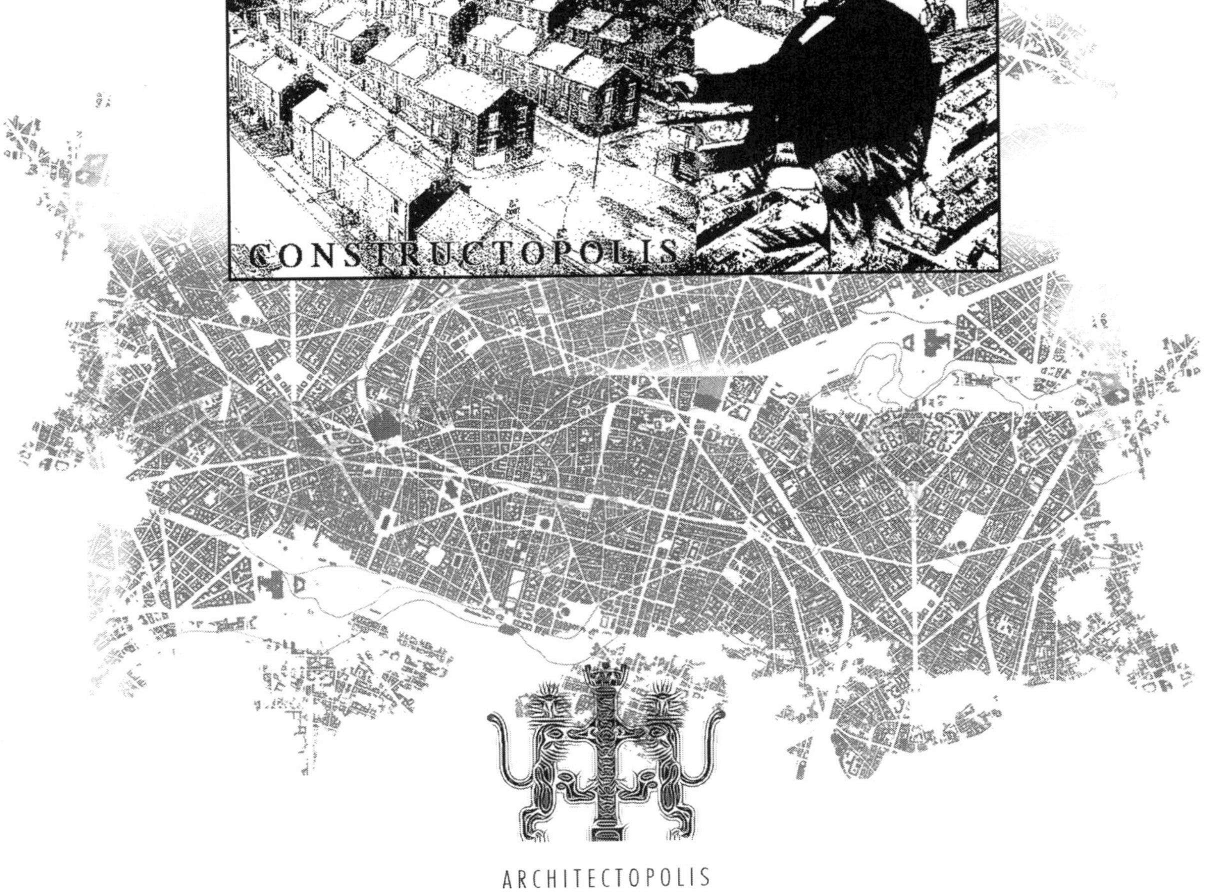
ARCHITECTOPOLIS

Therefore, old Practiceopolis started exerting significant efforts not to be swollen by giant contractors from Constructopolis.

It succeeded to make a legitimate move to protect the 'Architect' title after about a century of trials (Crinson & Lubbock, 1994).

By this time, it was informally known that the Architects were the real rulers of the city. A newer Empire was formed by the beginning of the 19th century showing the full control of the Architects over the city which was then renamed as 'Architectopolis'.

The dilemma of Style

The influence of Beaux-Arts architecture resulted in the perplexity of searching for a system of governance to rule Architectopolis from the different architectural styles available at the time.

At these times, the philosophy of the Picturesque turned this perplexity into dilemma by multiplying the range of stylistic options. Pugin, Ruskin and Viollet-le Duc and their contemporaneous architects compounded this dilemma by giving it a moral dimension.

This era was marked by a frantic search for a system of governance to rule Architectopolis from the different architectural styles available at the time.

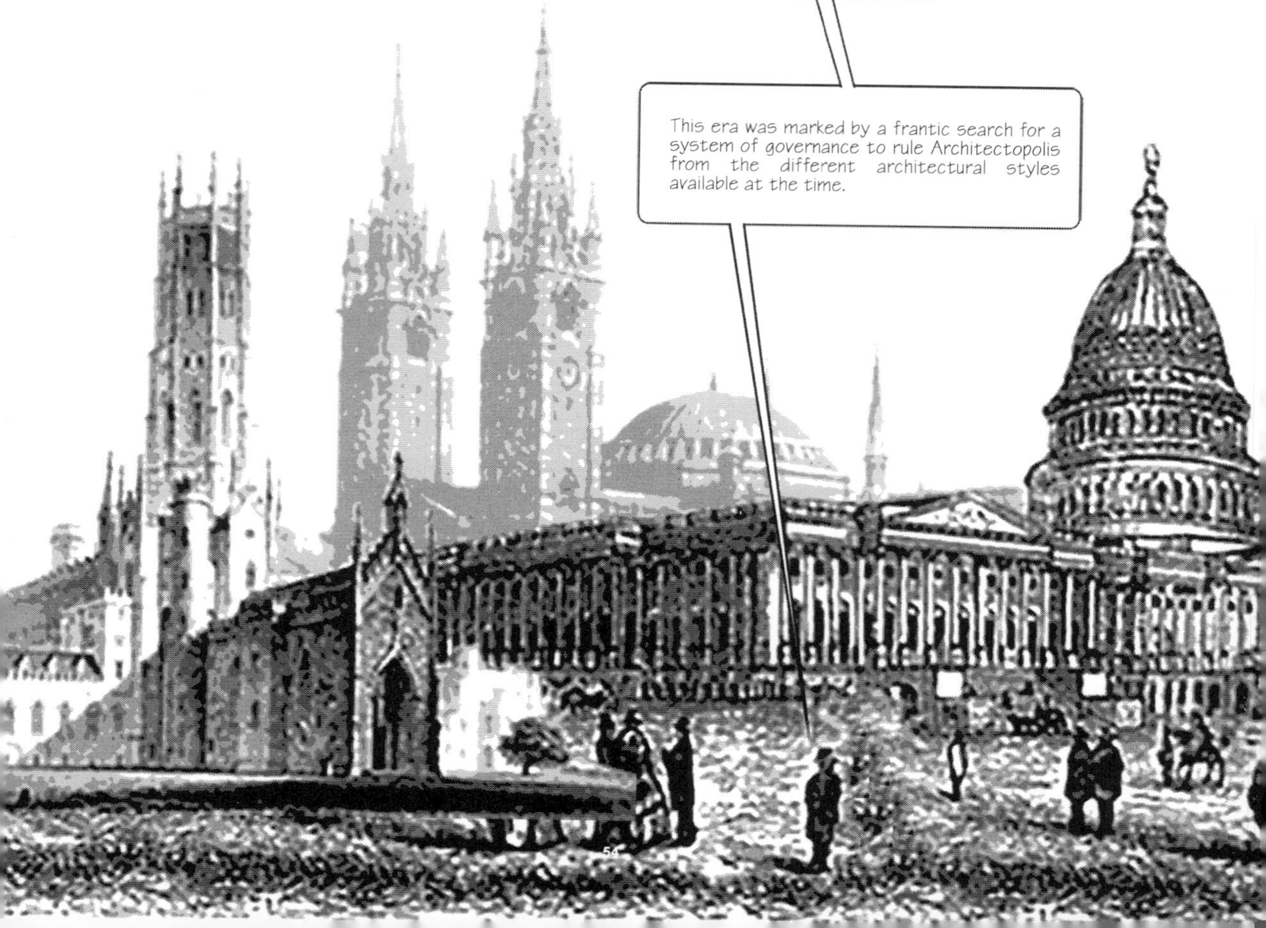

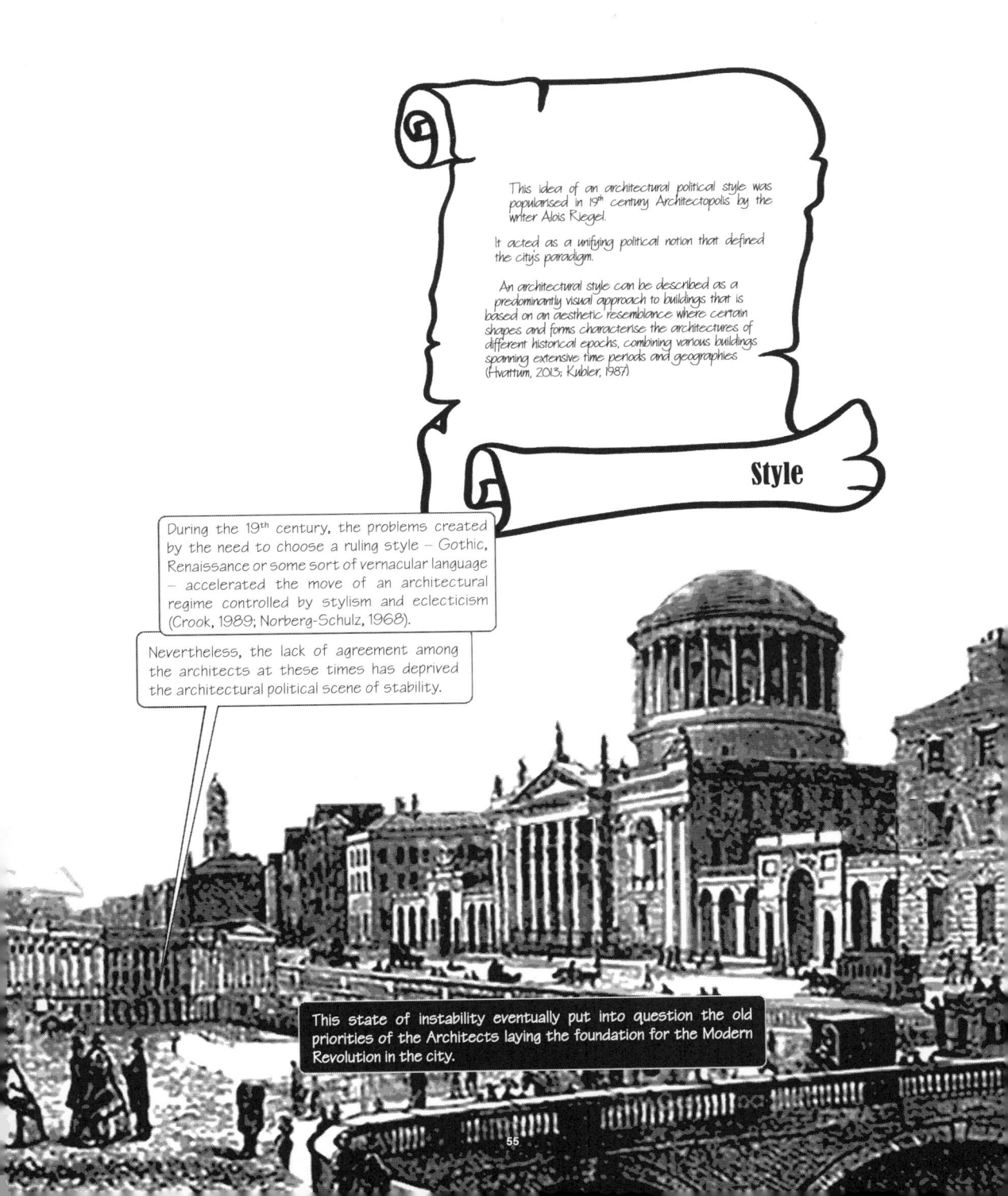

This idea of an architectural political style was popularised in 19th century Architectopolis by the writer Alois Riegel.

It acted as a unifying political notion that defined the city's paradigm.

An architectural style can be described as a predominantly visual approach to buildings that is based on an aesthetic resemblance where certain shapes and forms characterise the architectures of different historical epochs, combining various buildings spanning extensive time periods and geographies (Hvattum, 2013; Kubler, 1987)

Style

During the 19th century, the problems created by the need to choose a ruling style – Gothic, Renaissance or some sort of vernacular language – accelerated the move of an architectural regime controlled by stylism and eclecticism (Crook, 1989; Norberg-Schulz, 1968).

Nevertheless, the lack of agreement among the architects at these times has deprived the architectural political scene of stability.

This state of instability eventually put into question the old priorities of the Architects laying the foundation for the Modern Revolution in the city.

Meanwhile, some architects of Architectopolis were worried about the future of the city, not convinced about the architectural philosophies inherited from the 19th century's stylistic debates and the long extended Monarchy that ruled the city for centuries as suitable for the new conditions of modernity.

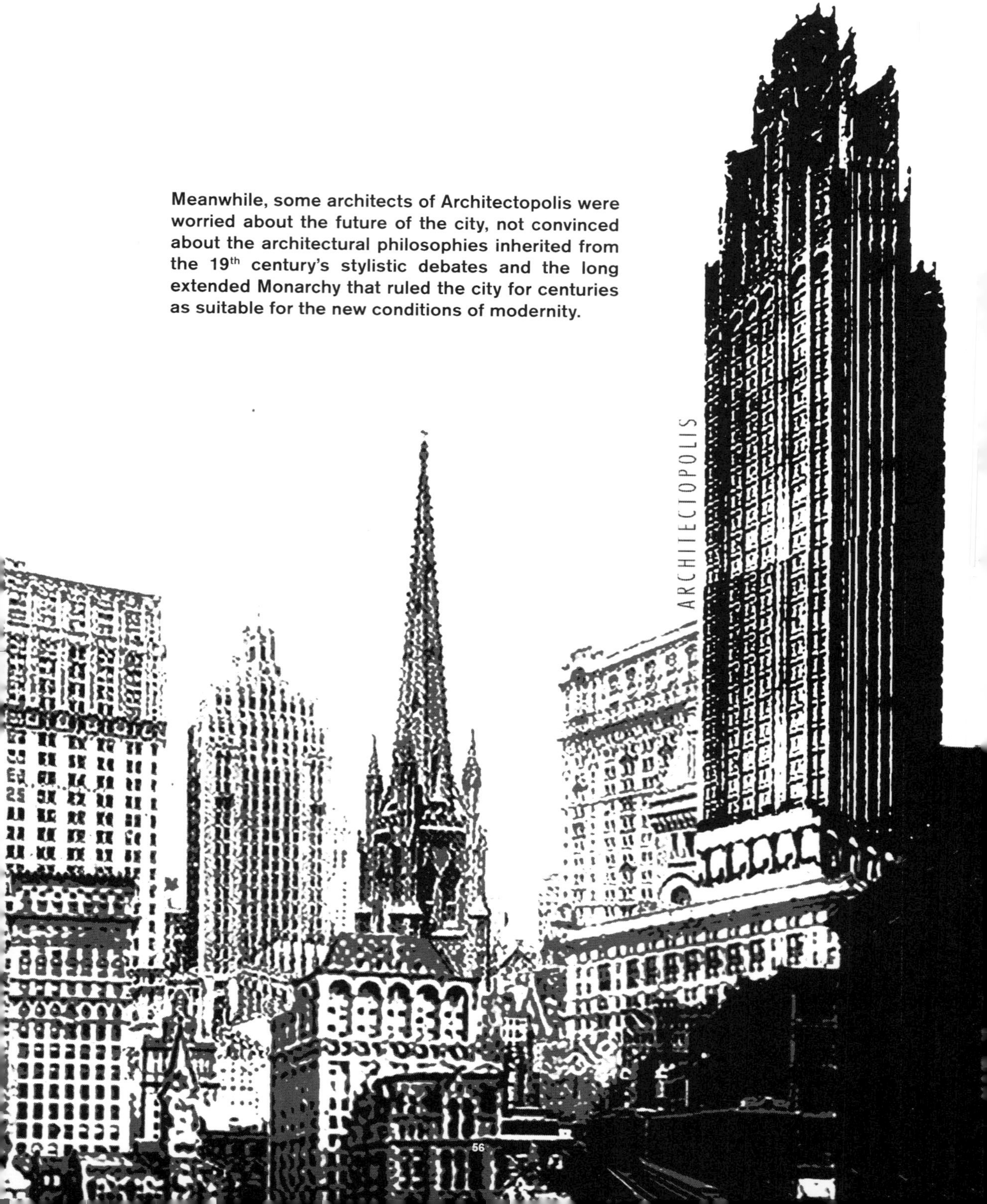
ARCHITECTOPOLIS

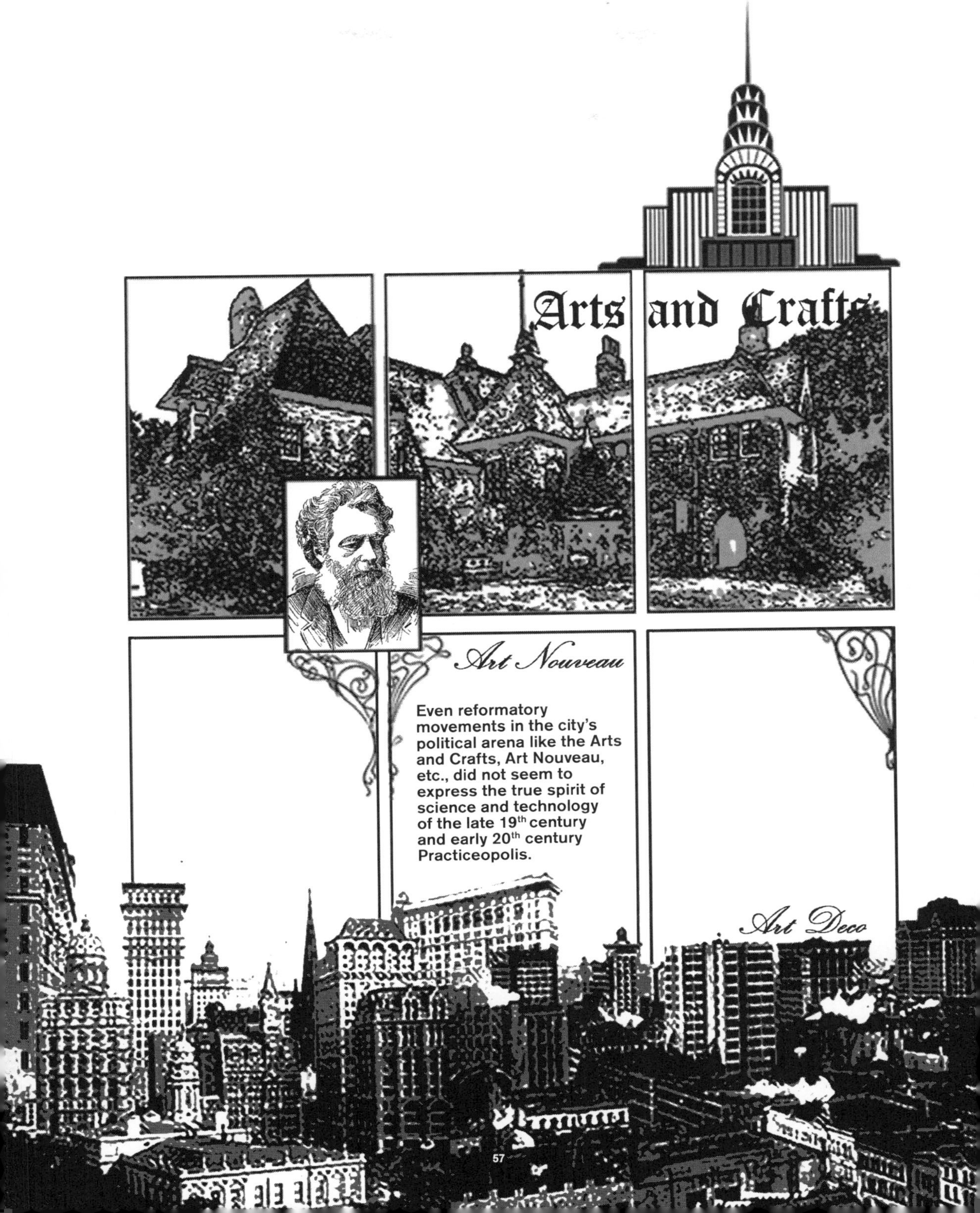
Arts and Crafts
Art Nouveau
Even reformatory movements in the city's political arena like the Arts and Crafts, Art Nouveau, etc., did not seem to express the true spirit of science and technology of the late 19th century and early 20th century Practiceopolis.
Art Deco

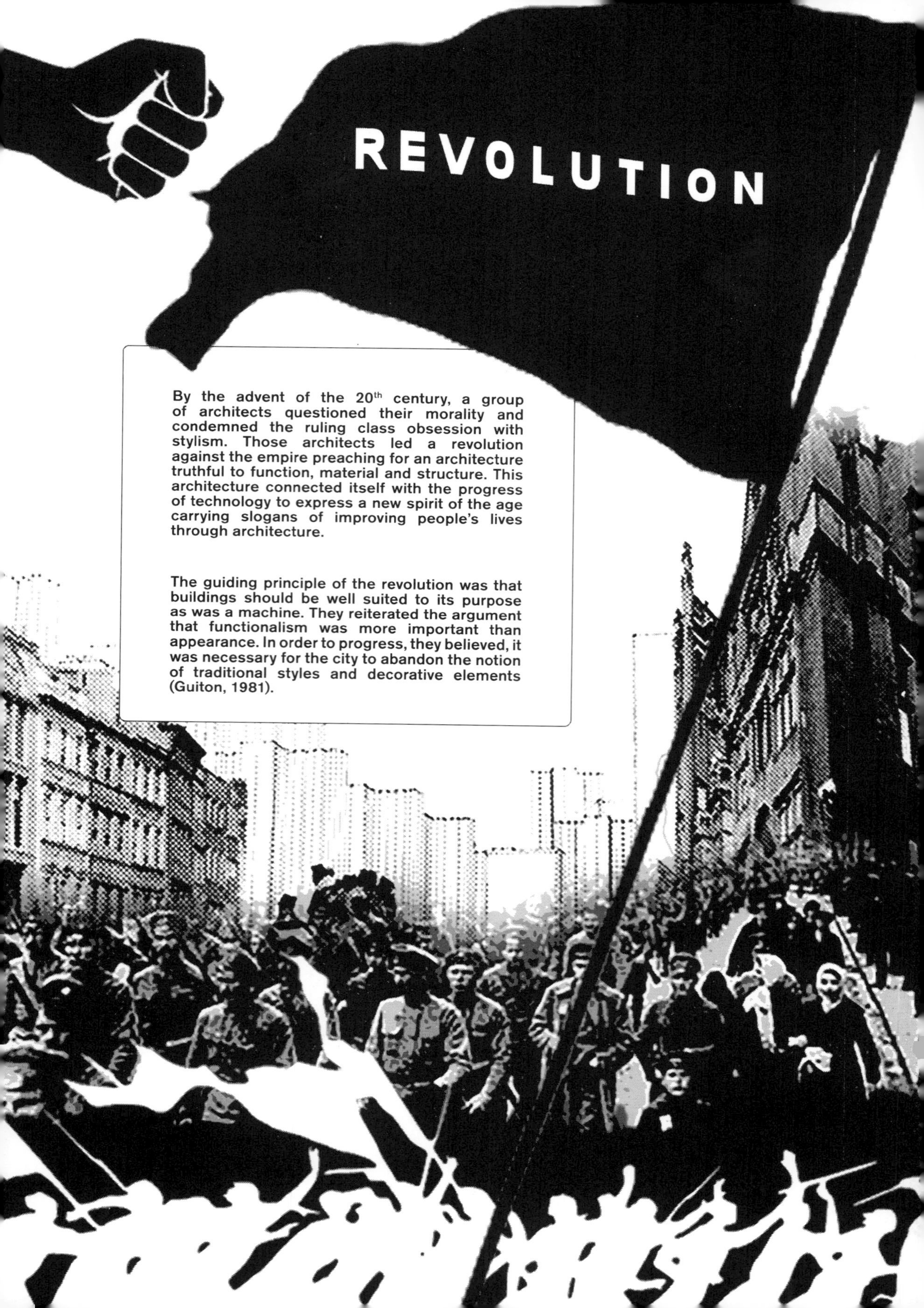

REVOLUTION

By the advent of the 20th century, a group of architects questioned their morality and condemned the ruling class obsession with stylism. Those architects led a revolution against the empire preaching for an architecture truthful to function, material and structure. This architecture connected itself with the progress of technology to express a new spirit of the age carrying slogans of improving people's lives through architecture.

The guiding principle of the revolution was that buildings should be well suited to its purpose as was a machine. They reiterated the argument that functionalism was more important than appearance. In order to progress, they believed, it was necessary for the city to abandon the notion of traditional styles and decorative elements (Guiton, 1981).

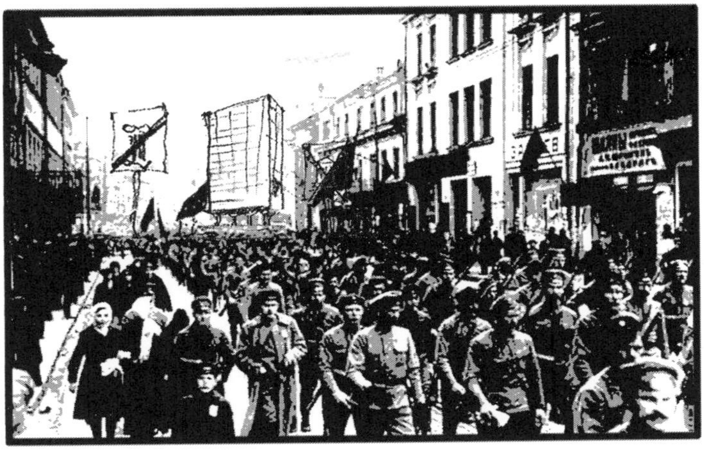

One other imperative of the revolution was the celebration of industrialisation through both design and mass production to create a type of architecture that can be repeated and refined in its newer versions.

The revolution came also with a social agenda, trying to understand the new needs for modern life, different modes of inhabitation and work that consequently would need new building typologies.

In general, the imperatives of the modernist revolution were that: materials got more honest, the honest expression of structural forces and materials, ornaments were removed, the closed plan opened, walls got whiter, linearity delivered the uniformity of mass production.

In short, things just got more and more precise.

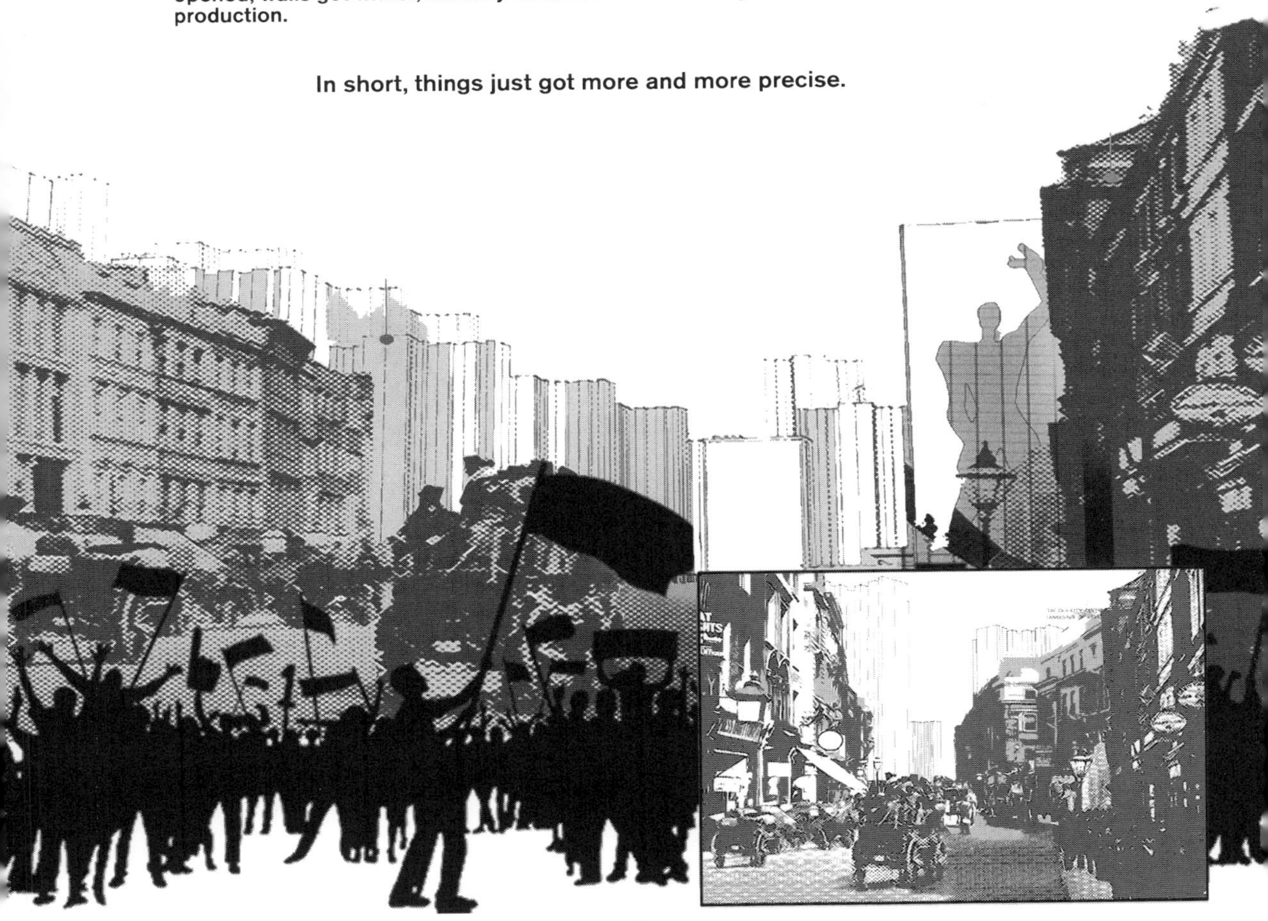

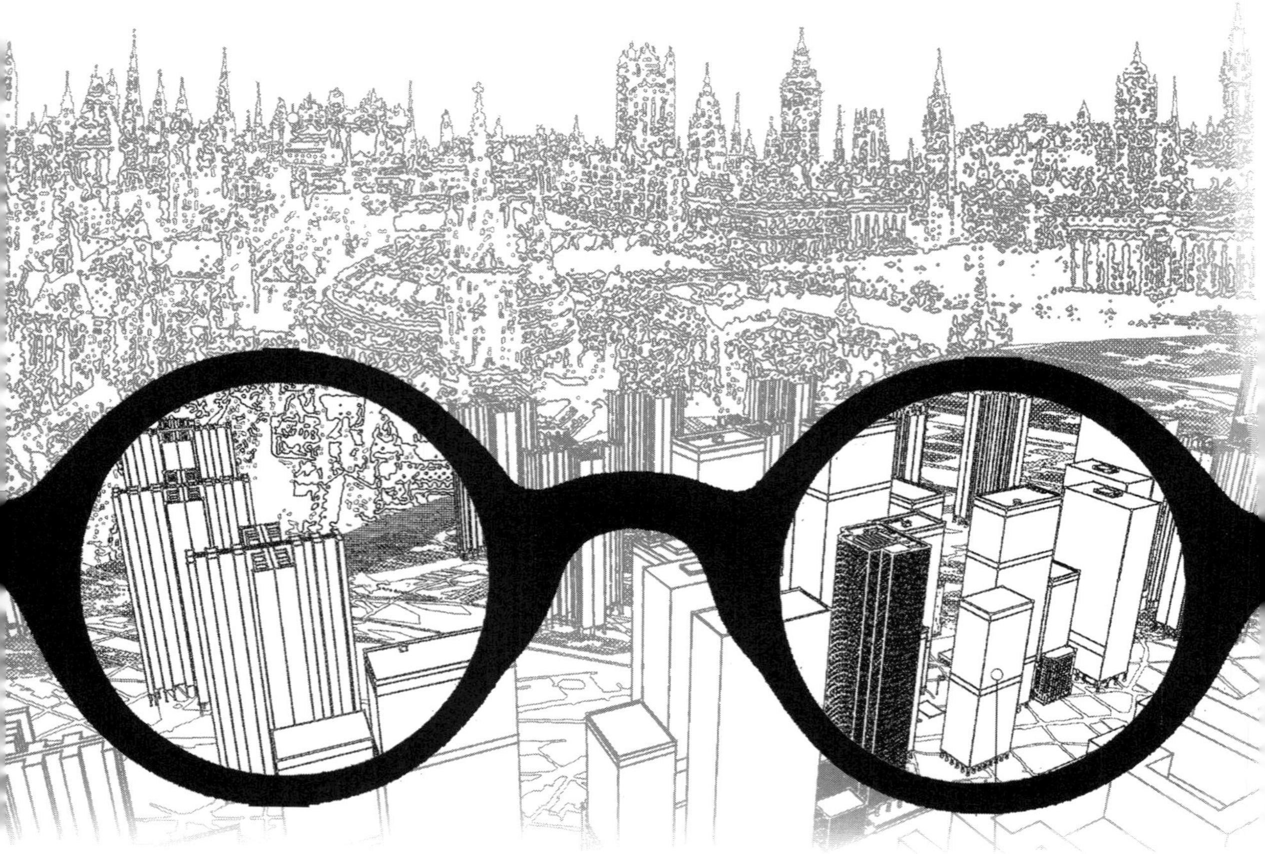

The revolutionary architects drew parallels between architecture and the 'Engineer's Aesthetic'. They argued that engineers were to be praised for their use of functionalism and mathematical order. As a consequence, the city was encouraged to emulate engineers and adopt many of their principles in order to attain harmony and logic in their new designs.

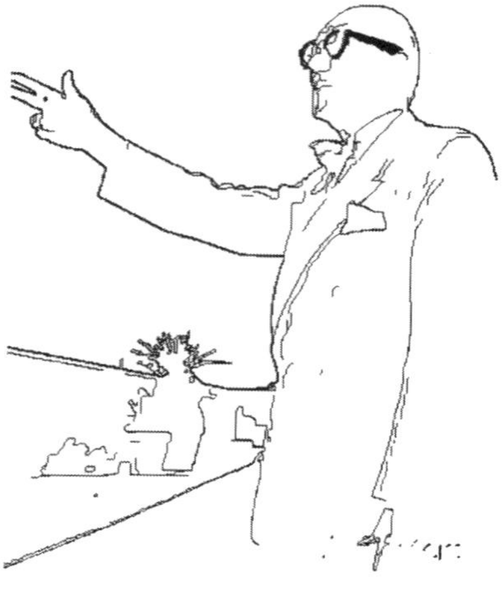

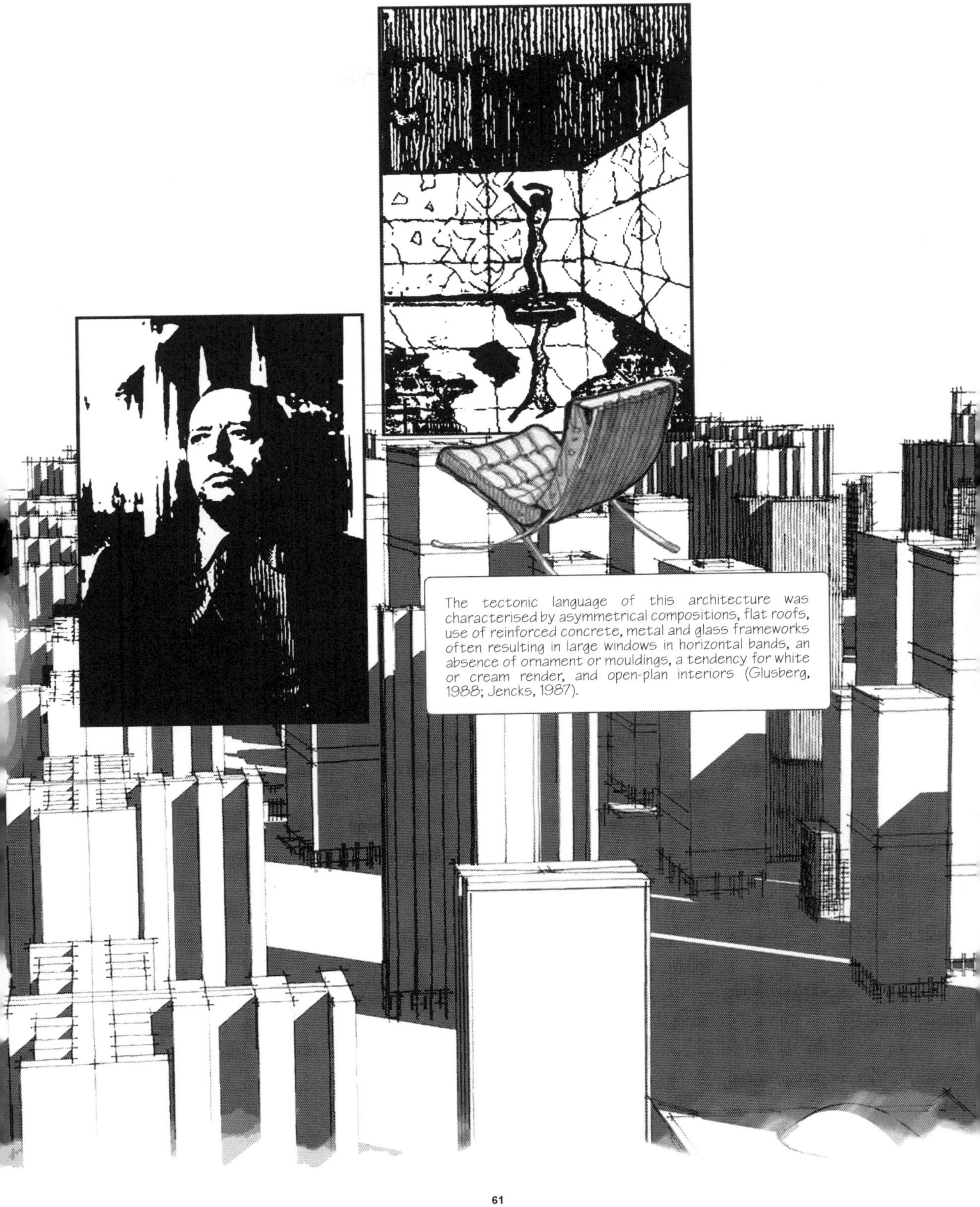
The tectonic language of this architecture was characterised by asymmetrical compositions, flat roofs, use of reinforced concrete, metal and glass frameworks often resulting in large windows in horizontal bands, an absence of ornament or mouldings, a tendency for white or cream render, and open-plan interiors (Glusberg, 1988; Jencks, 1987).

Ecole des Beaux Arts

The modernists' revolution derived a crucial political and social change in Architectopolis. It made a sharp break with the pre-existing paradigm (Beaux-arts Classicism trend). In its political discourse, style debates started to be replaced by the Bauhaus ideas of a complete break with historicism.

The activity of the architectural political community was organised around the continuing researches which the new paradigm provoked. The history of art and architecture was dropped from the political scene; instead, free experimentation with materials and forms was introduced (Norberg-Schulz, 1968).

People of Architectopolis were initiated into membership of the new architectural political discipline by studying the current paradigm of Modern Architecture (Crinson & Lubbock, 1994).

REJECTED

When the new Modern paradigm was firmly established, the main features of the old paradigm (the Beaux-arts Classicism) were ignored, often ridiculed and excluded from the serious debates of politics. Those who still believed in the old architectural monarchy suffered isolation and exclusion from the mainstream political community.

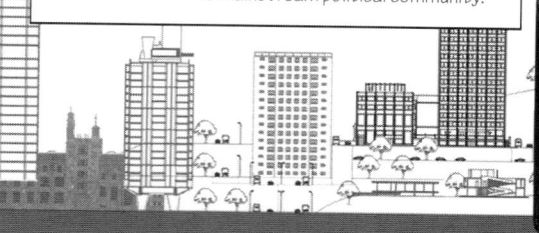

The new paradigm of Modern Architecture did not come about through gradual evolution from the former classicism paradigm but because the old paradigm simply could not follow or account for the problems which the new Modern Architecture seems to be able to solve. Recalling Thomas Kuhn's paradigmatic shifts, the old paradigm was breaking down, and when this happened, the architectural community reconstituted itself around the modernist ideas (Crinson & Lubbock, 1994; Kuhn and Hacking, 2012).

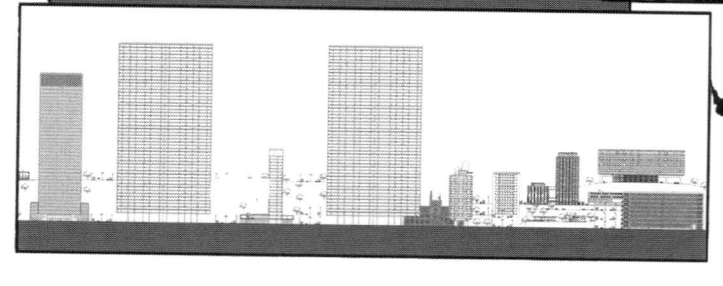

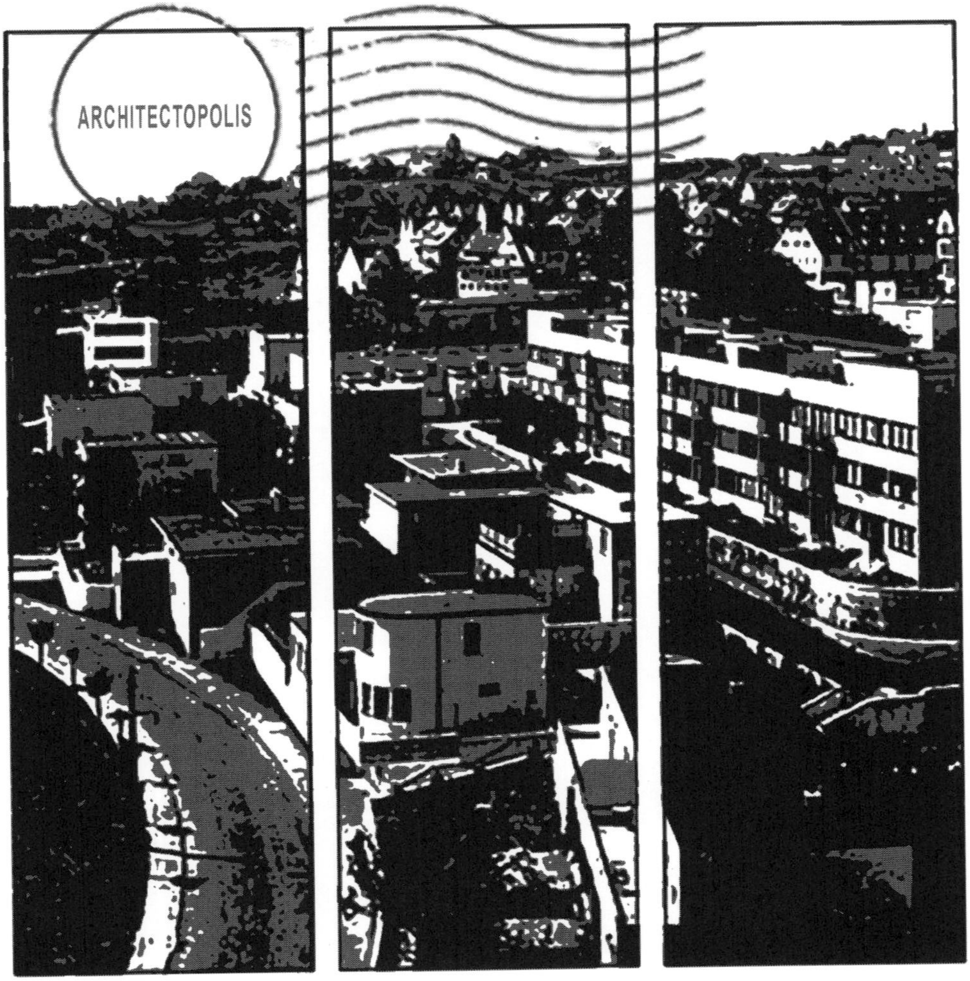
ARCHITECTOPOLIS

While the peak of modernity occurred between the late 19th and mid 20th centuries in Architectopolis, people of the city were still sceptical about the revolution. They were anxious about these new notions and feeling that the way out for Architectopolis problems may be by improving the existing ruling model.

However, things went out of hand quickly!

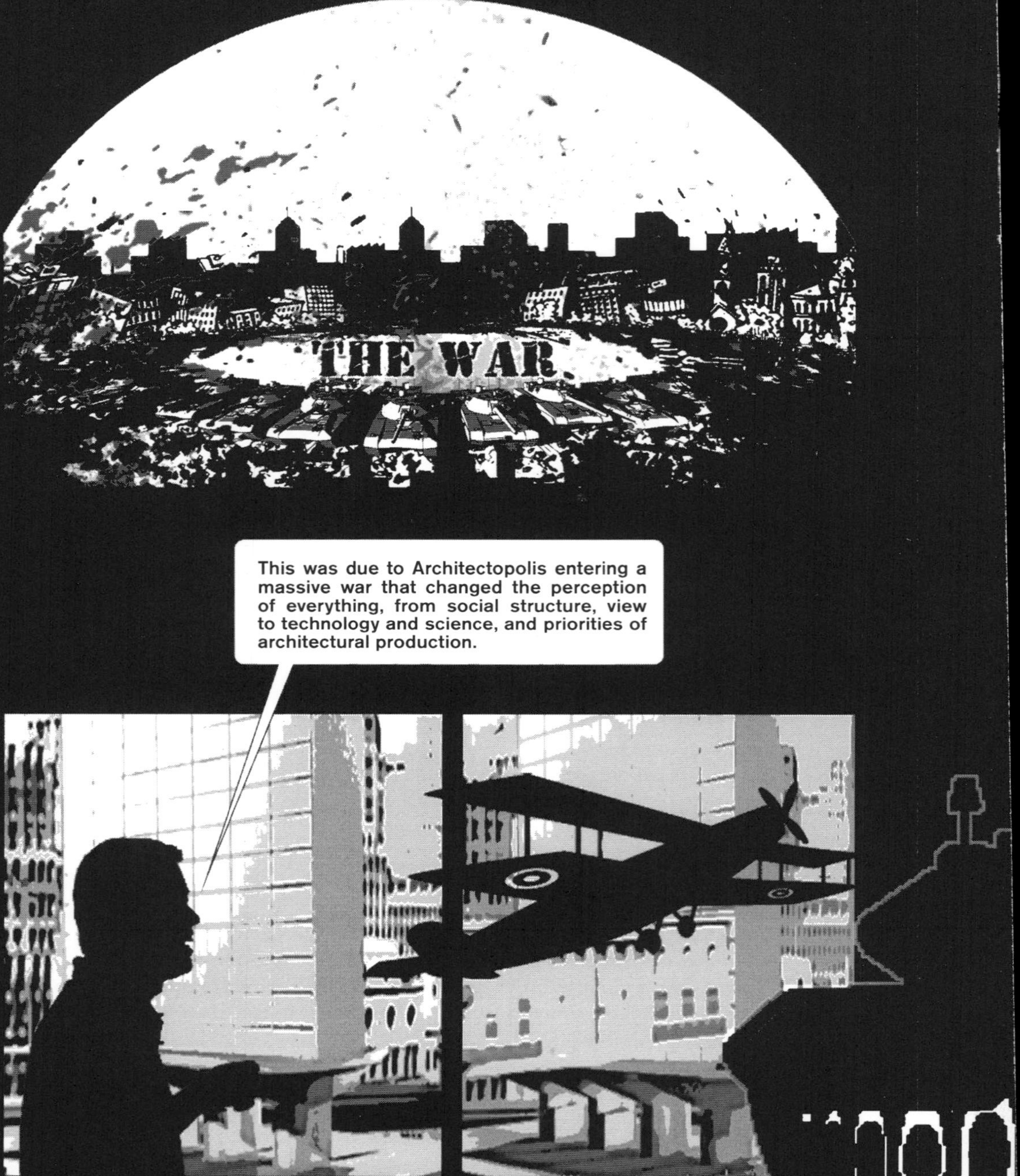
THE WAR
This was due to Architectopolis entering a massive war that changed the perception of everything, from social structure, view to technology and science, and priorities of architectural production.

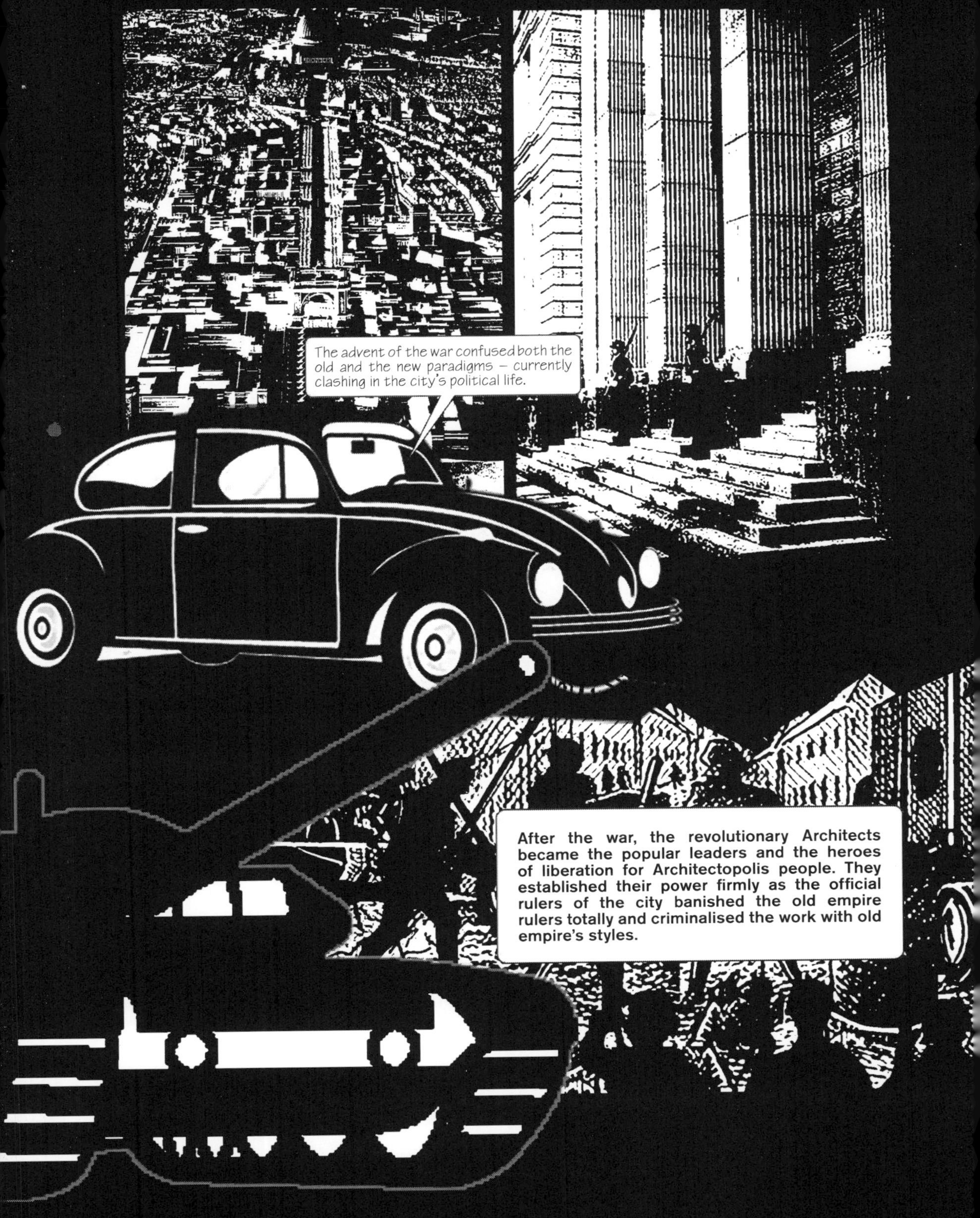
The advent of the war confused both the old and the new paradigms – currently clashing in the city's political life.
After the war, the revolutionary Architects became the popular leaders and the heroes of liberation for Architectopolis people. They established their power firmly as the official rulers of the city banished the old empire rulers totally and criminalised the work with old empire's styles.

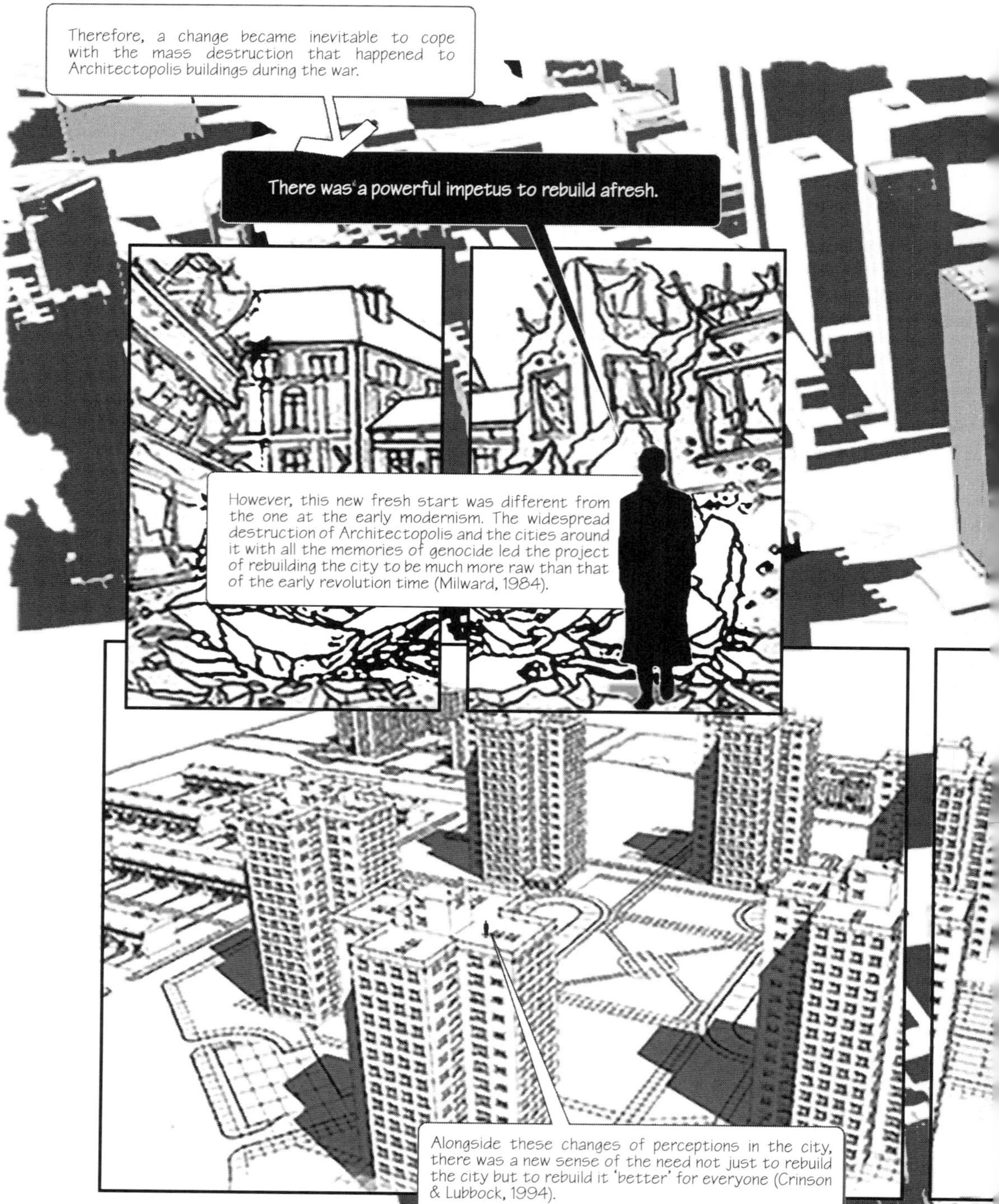
Therefore, a change became inevitable to cope with the mass destruction that happened to Architectopolis buildings during the war.
There was a powerful impetus to rebuild afresh.
However, this new fresh start was different from the one at the early modernism. The widespread destruction of Architectopolis and the cities around it with all the memories of genocide led the project of rebuilding the city to be much more raw than that of the early revolution time (Milward, 1984).
Alongside these changes of perceptions in the city, there was a new sense of the need not just to rebuild the city but to rebuild it 'better' for everyone (Crinson & Lubbock, 1994).

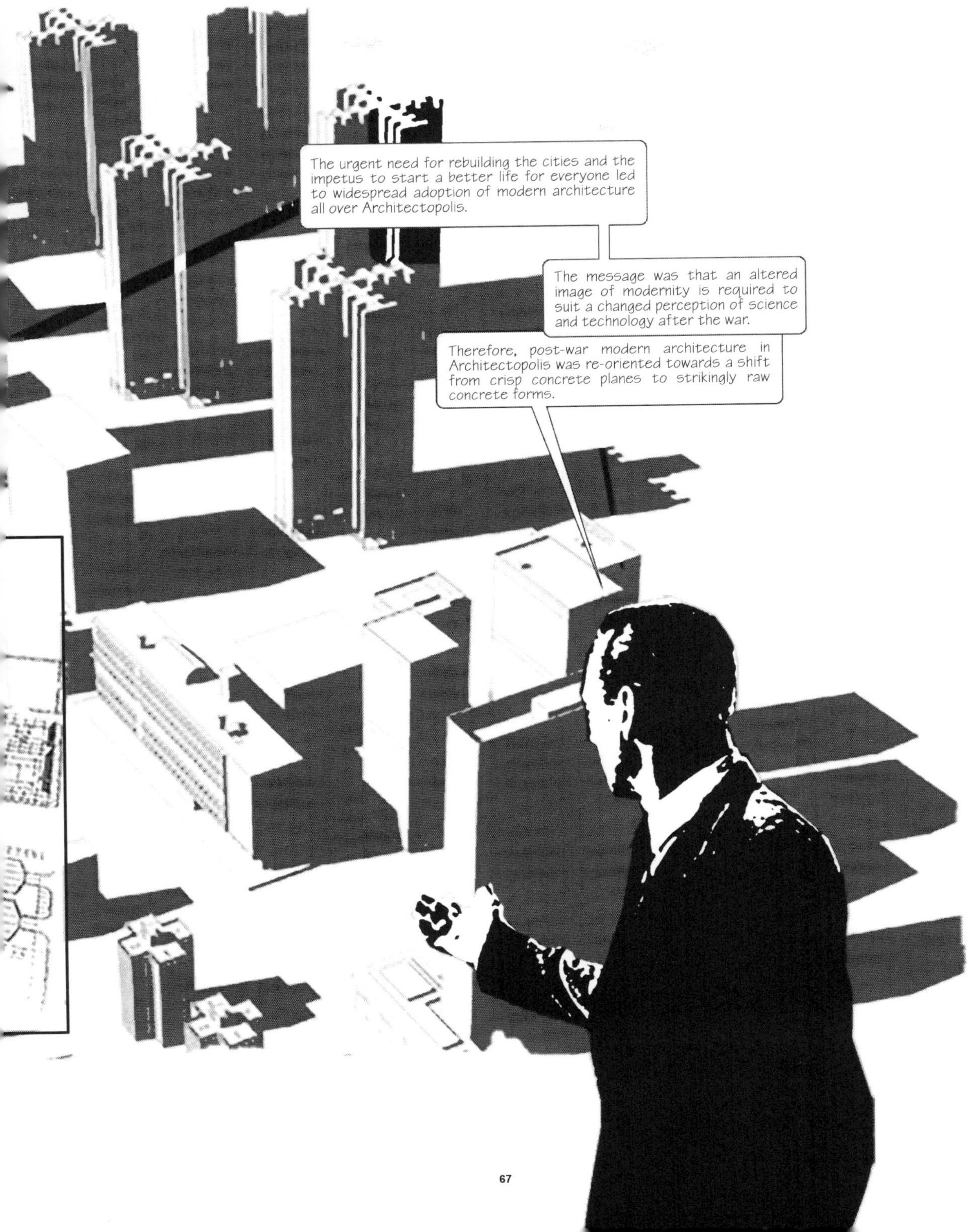
The urgent need for rebuilding the cities and the impetus to start a better life for everyone led to widespread adoption of modern architecture all over Architectopolis.
The message was that an altered image of modernity is required to suit a changed perception of science and technology after the war.
Therefore, post-war modern architecture in Architectopolis was re-oriented towards a shift from crisp concrete planes to strikingly raw concrete forms.

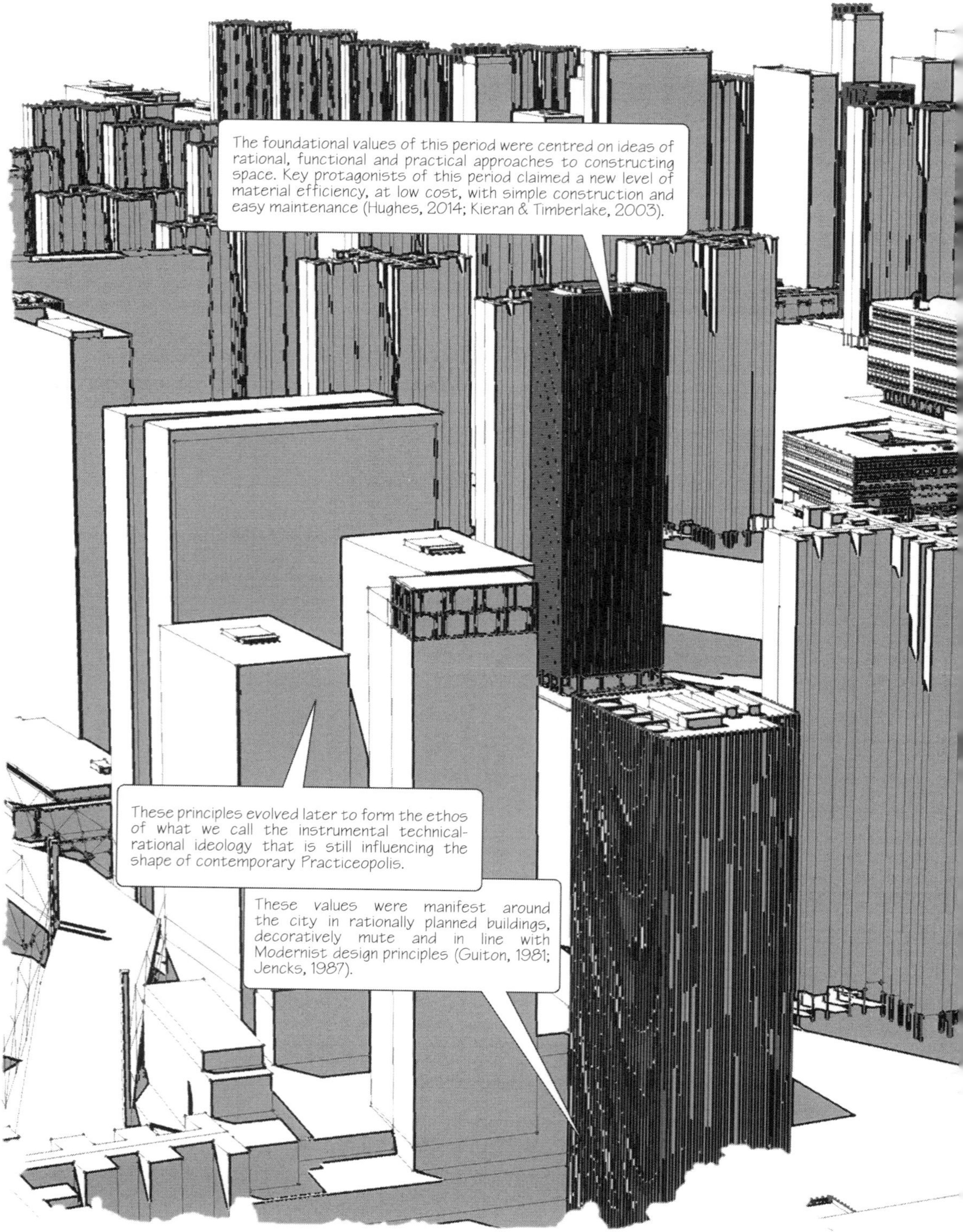
The foundational values of this period were centred on ideas of rational, functional and practical approaches to constructing space. Key protagonists of this period claimed a new level of material efficiency, at low cost, with simple construction and easy maintenance (Hughes, 2014; Kieran & Timberlake, 2003).
These principles evolved later to form the ethos of what we call the instrumental technical-rational ideology that is still influencing the shape of contemporary Practiceopolis.
These values were manifest around the city in rationally planned buildings, decoratively mute and in line with Modernist design principles (Guiton, 1981; Jencks, 1987).

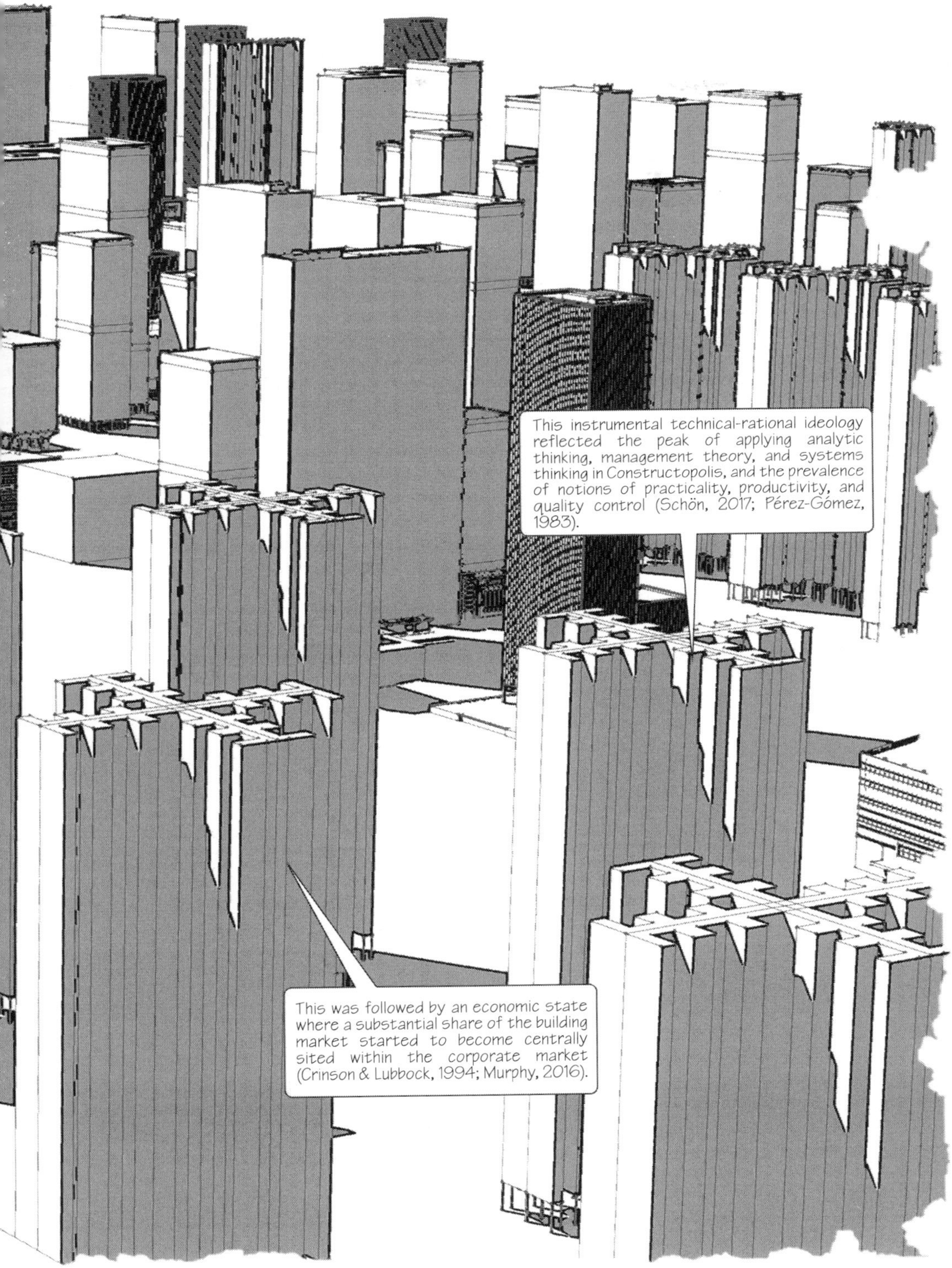
This instrumental technical-rational ideology reflected the peak of applying analytic thinking, management theory, and systems thinking in Constructopolis, and the prevalence of notions of practicality, productivity, and quality control (Schön, 2017; Pérez-Gómez, 1983).
This was followed by an economic state where a substantial share of the building market started to become centrally sited within the corporate market (Crinson & Lubbock, 1994; Murphy, 2016).

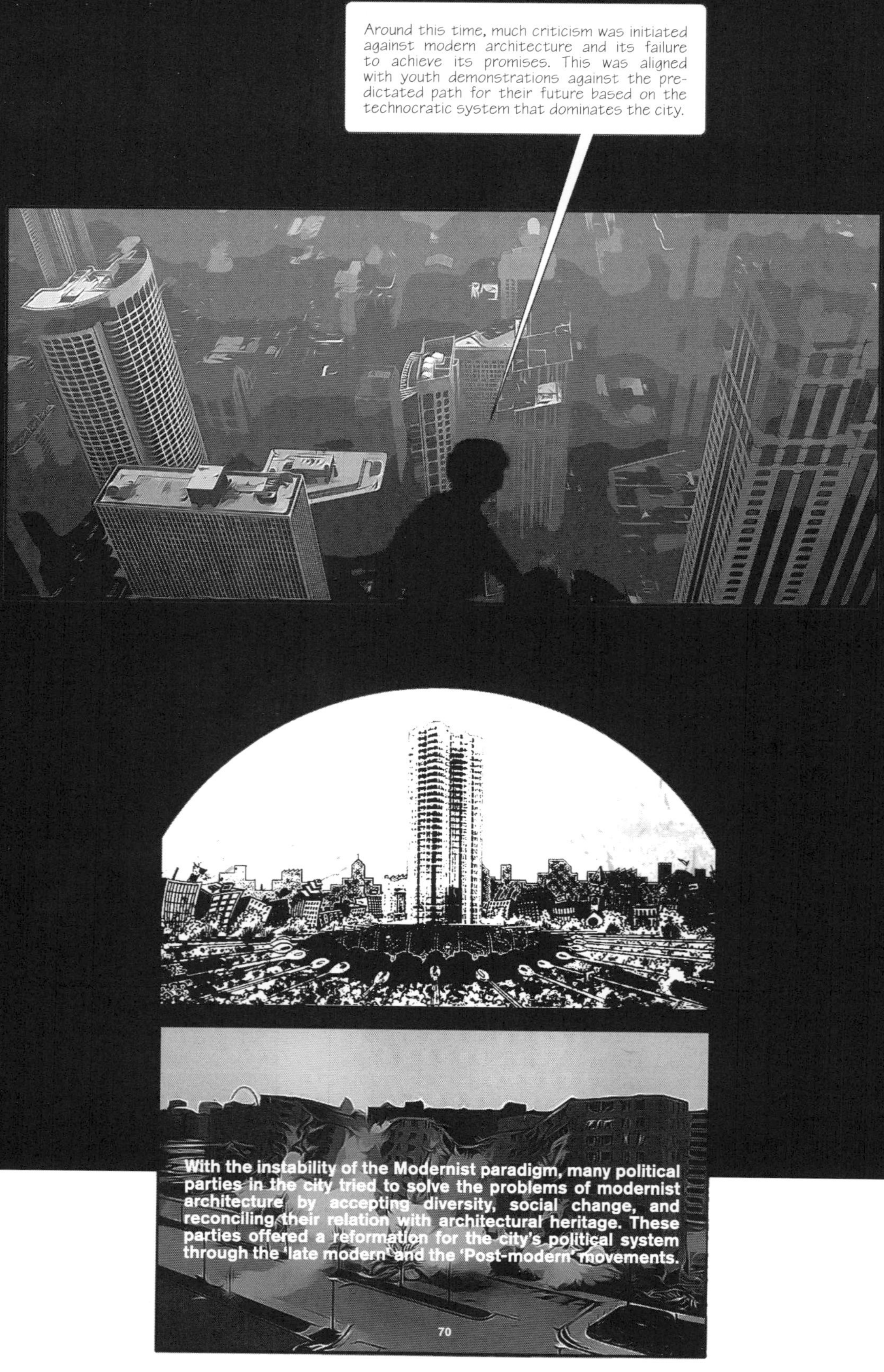
Around this time, much criticism was initiated against modern architecture and its failure to achieve its promises. This was aligned with youth demonstrations against the pre-dictated path for their future based on the technocratic system that dominates the city.
With the instability of the Modernist paradigm, many political parties in the city tried to solve the problems of modernist architecture by accepting diversity, social change, and reconciling their relation with architectural heritage. These parties offered a reformation for the city's political system through the 'late modern' and the 'Post-modern' movements.

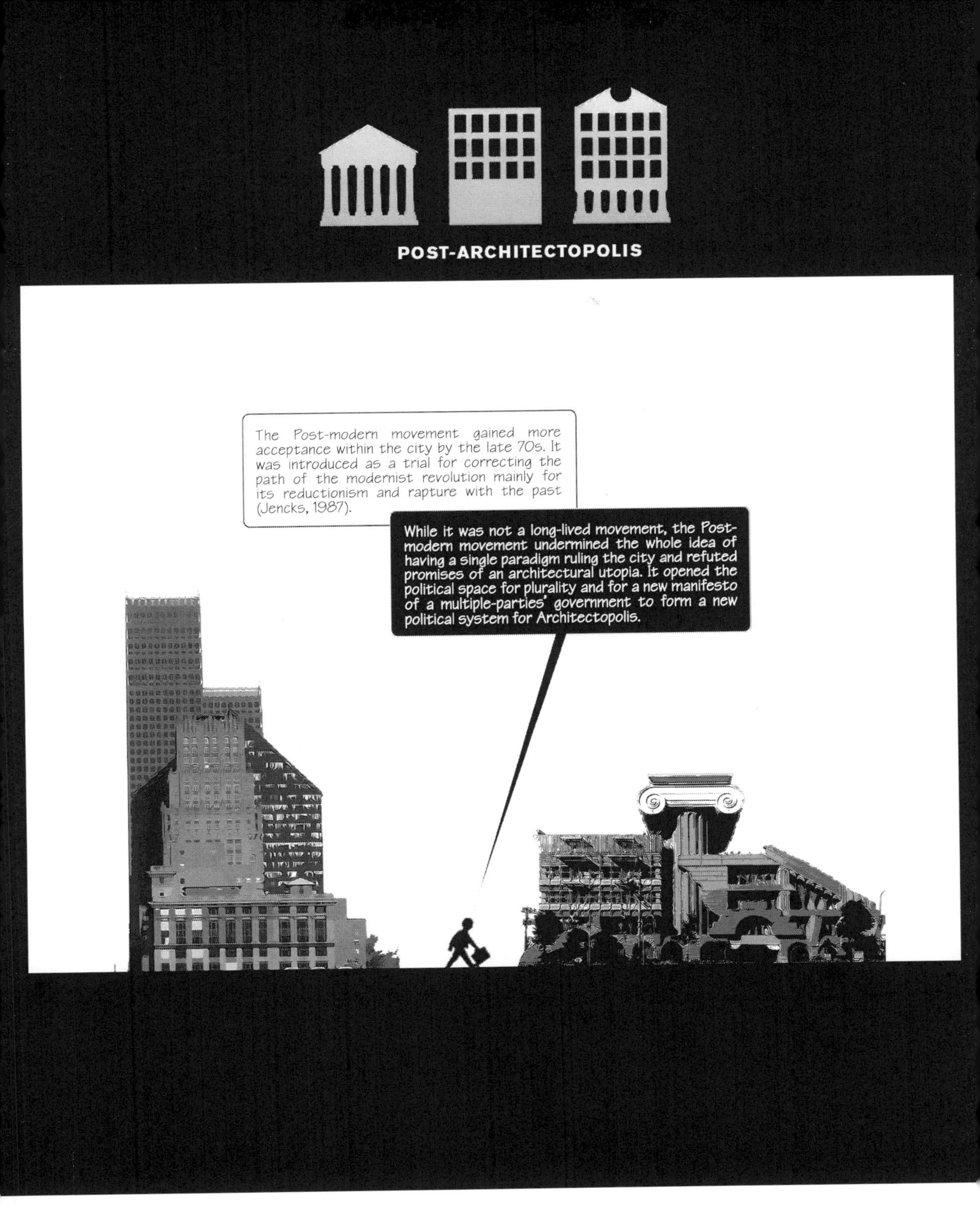
POST-ARCHITECTOPOLIS
The Post-modern movement gained more acceptance within the city by the late 70s. It was introduced as a trial for correcting the path of the modernist revolution mainly for its reductionism and rapture with the past (Jencks, 1987).
While it was not a long-lived movement, the Post-modern movement undermined the whole idea of having a single paradigm ruling the city and refuted promises of an architectural utopia. It opened the political space for plurality and for a new manifesto of a multiple-parties' government to form a new political system for Architectopolis.

THE CONTEMPORARY PARADIGM
THE STATUS QUO

Coping with the new wave towards diversity and democracy, the name of the city was changed to 'Practiceopolis', referring to its multiple architectural communities.

By mid-1980s, a new Parliament was formed to express different cultures of practice in the city. An honorary building was designed as a symbol for the new plurality era on the life of the 'Practiceopolians' where the original map of the city was kept.

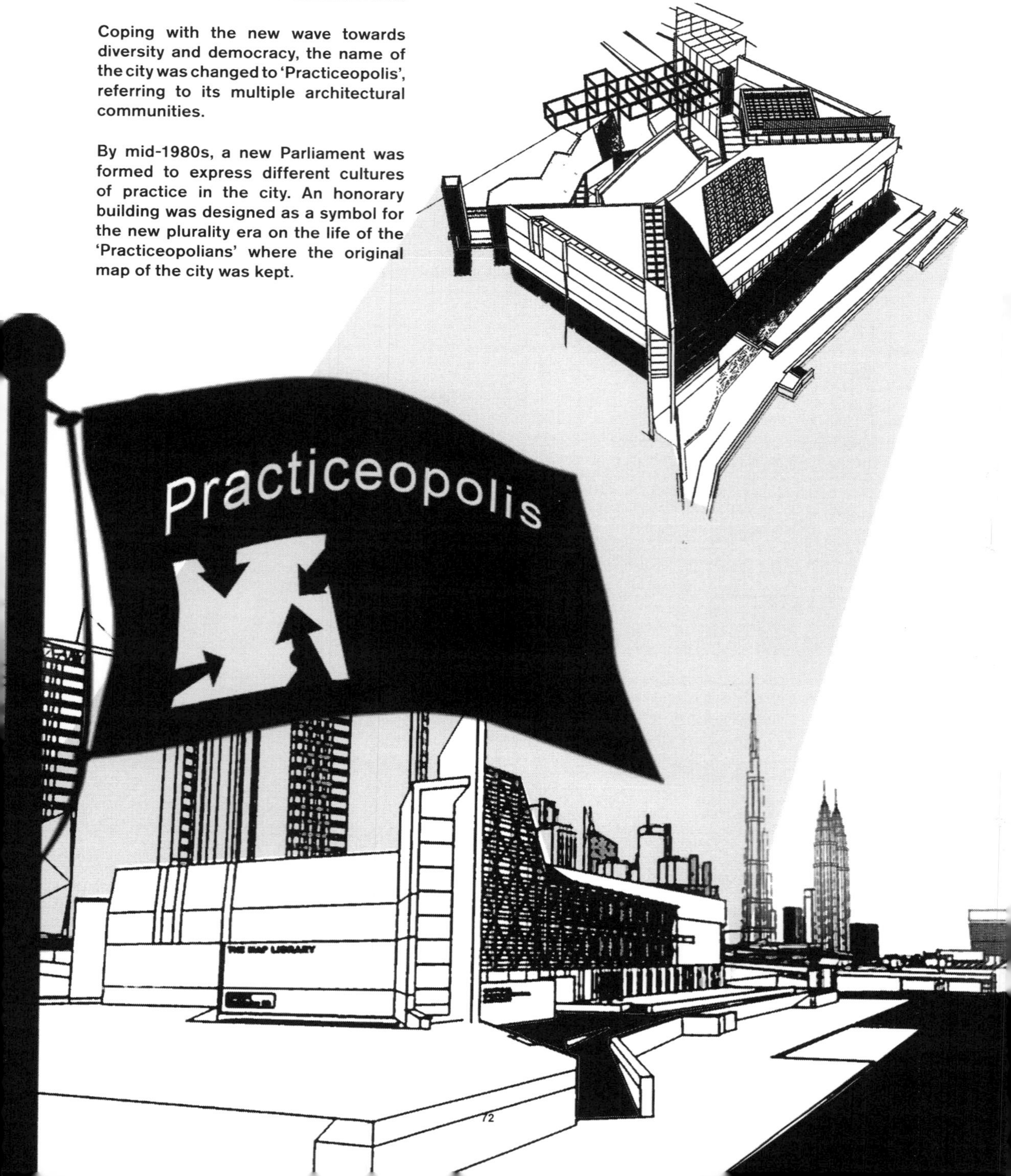
Practiceopolis
THE MAP LIBRARY

With the formation of the parliamentary government, political debates have become multiple and not confined under a singular notion of practising architecture. The different social groups that make the demographical structure of the city were represented by parties that express the views of the main cultures of practice within Practiceopolis.

Heroic

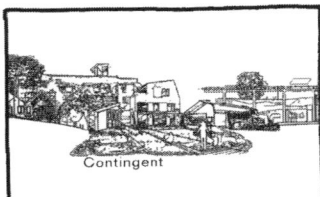

Contingent

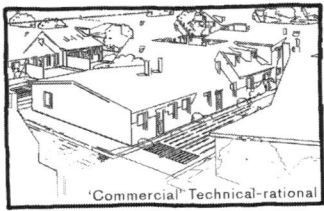

'Commercial' Technical-rational

Formalist

sensory

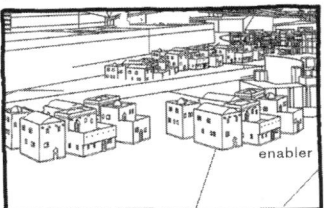

enabler

Other smaller parties were formed representing other modes of practice in the city. These parties made different coalitions under the powerful parties of the Parliament which carry close ideas about architecture to theirs.

regional

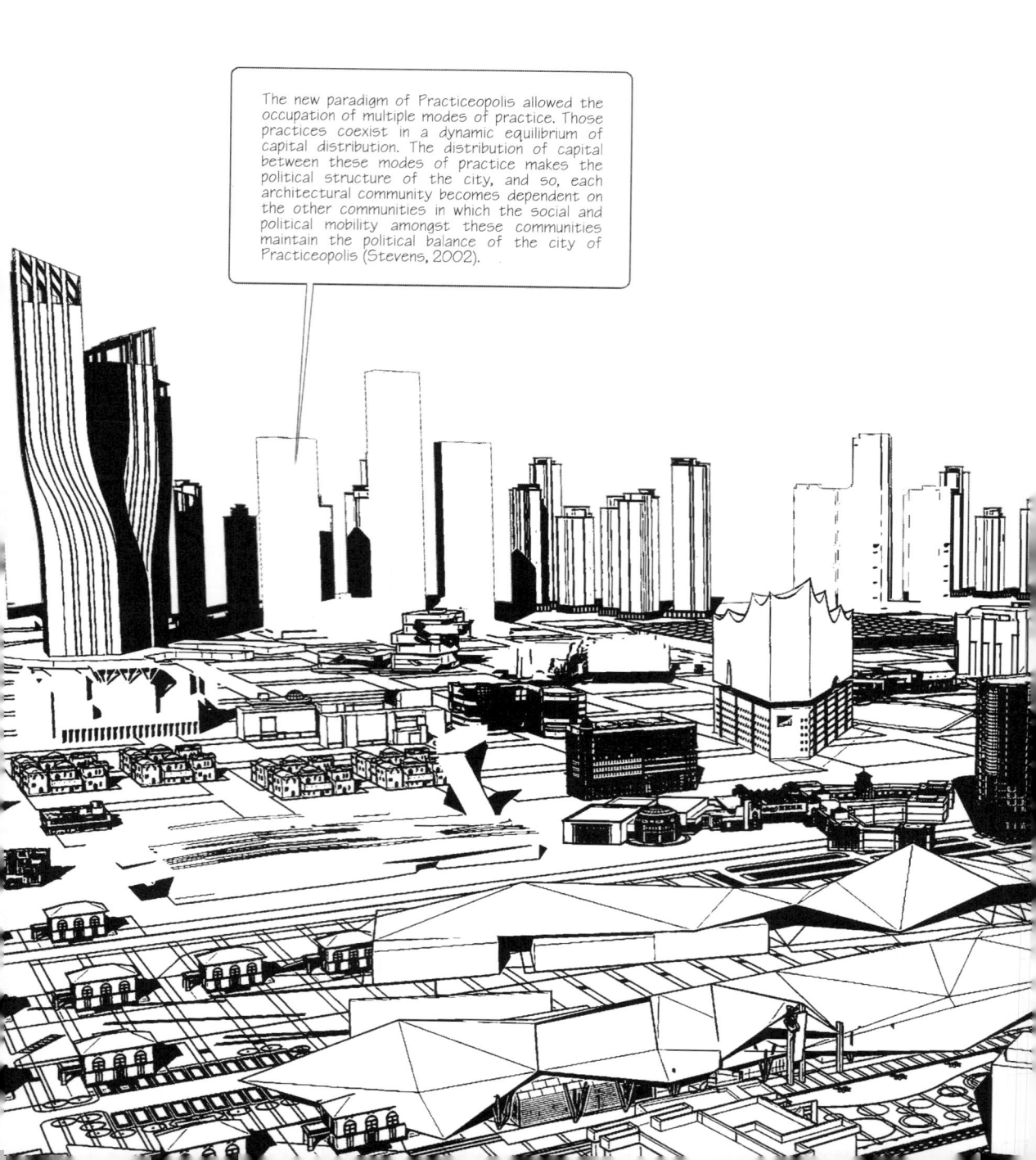

The new paradigm of Practiceopolis allowed the occupation of multiple modes of practice. Those practices coexist in a dynamic equilibrium of capital distribution. The distribution of capital between these modes of practice makes the political structure of the city, and so, each architectural community becomes dependent on the other communities in which the social and political mobility amongst these communities maintain the political balance of the city of Practiceopolis (Stevens, 2002).

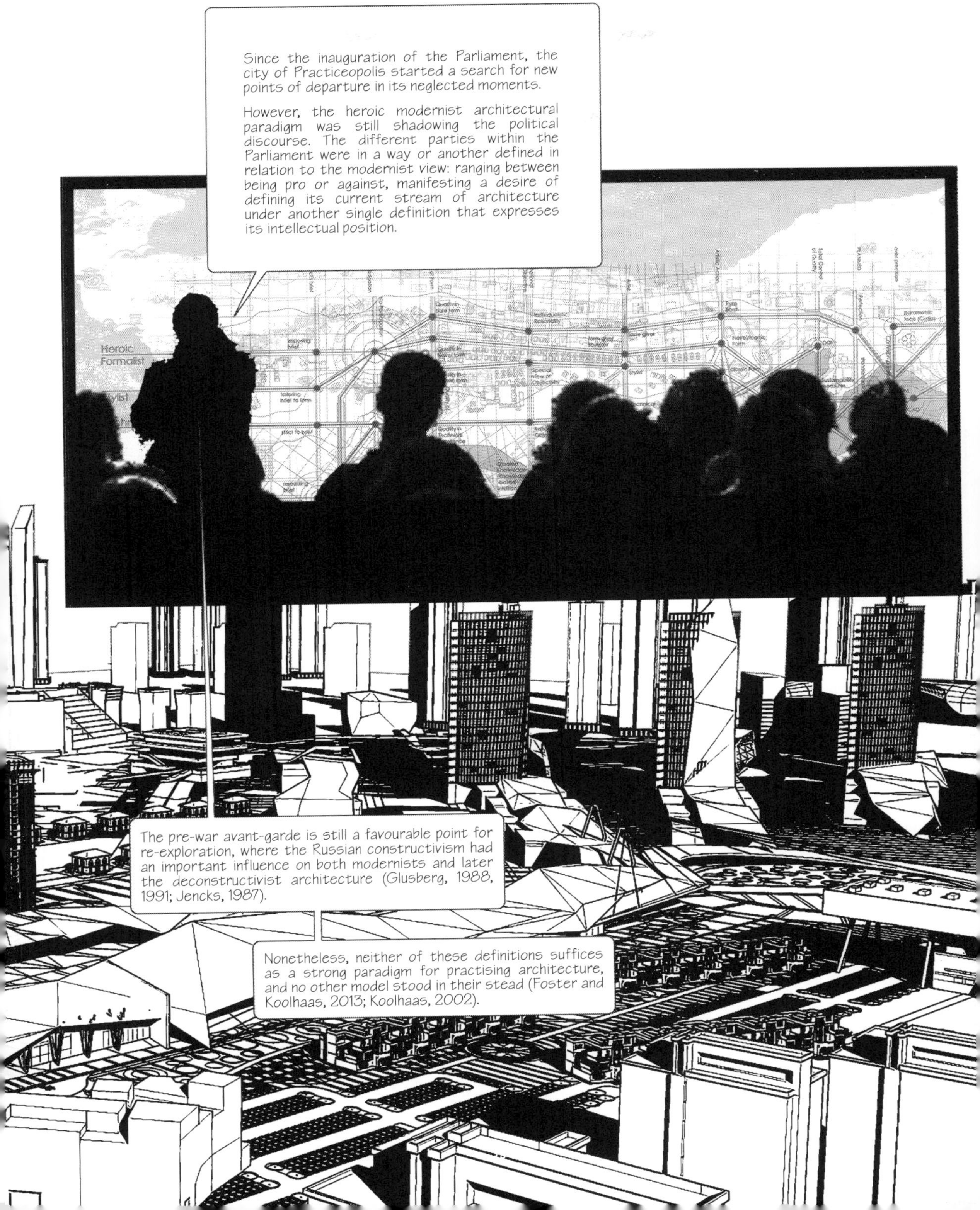
Since the inauguration of the Parliament, the city of Practiceopolis started a search for new points of departure in its neglected moments.
However, the heroic modernist architectural paradigm was still shadowing the political discourse. The different parties within the Parliament were in a way or another defined in relation to the modernist view: ranging between being pro or against, manifesting a desire of defining its current stream of architecture under another single definition that expresses its intellectual position.
Heroic Formalist
The pre-war avant-garde is still a favourable point for re-exploration, where the Russian constructivism had an important influence on both modernists and later the deconstructivist architecture (Glusberg, 1988, 1991; Jencks, 1987).
Nonetheless, neither of these definitions suffices as a strong paradigm for practising architecture, and no other model stood in their stead (Foster and Koolhaas, 2013; Koolhaas, 2002).

THE DEMOGRAPHY OF PRACTICEOPOLIS & ITS DISTRICTS

In today's Practiceopolis, the city comprises nine main communities that constitute its social demography. The Heroic Community represents the old revolutionaries of Architectopolis, a community that still has an important symbolic and cultural stature in the city. The Heroic Party forms the council of the elders in the Parliament. Most of the other parties in the Parliament in one way or another align themselves along or against the principles of this party.

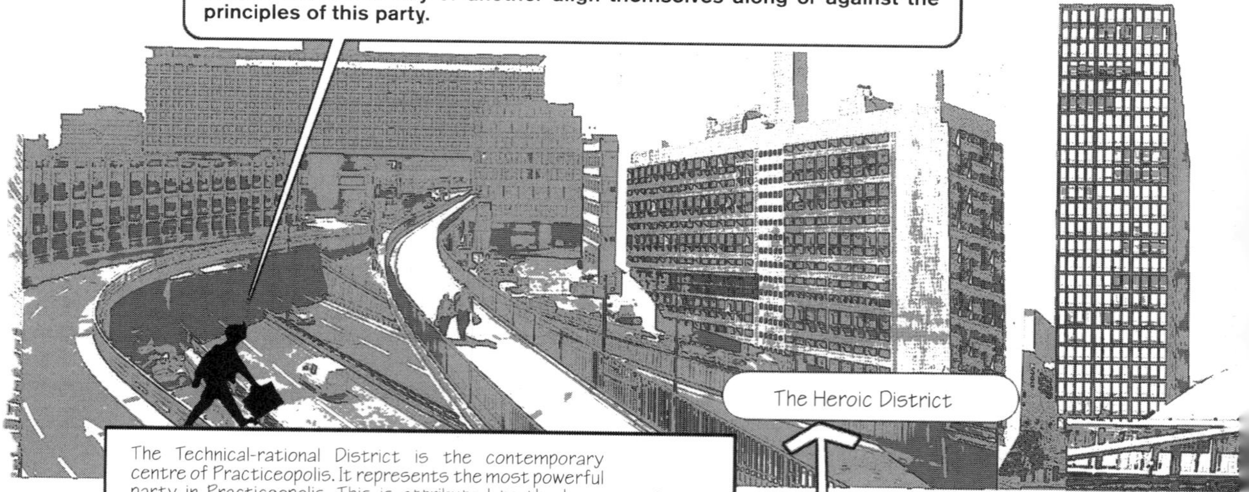
The Heroic District

The Technical-rational District is the contemporary centre of Practiceopolis. It represents the most powerful party in Practiceopolis. This is attributed to the large share of building commissions that it has around the city. The Technical-rational Party forms the government and hence controls the political and economic activity within the city.

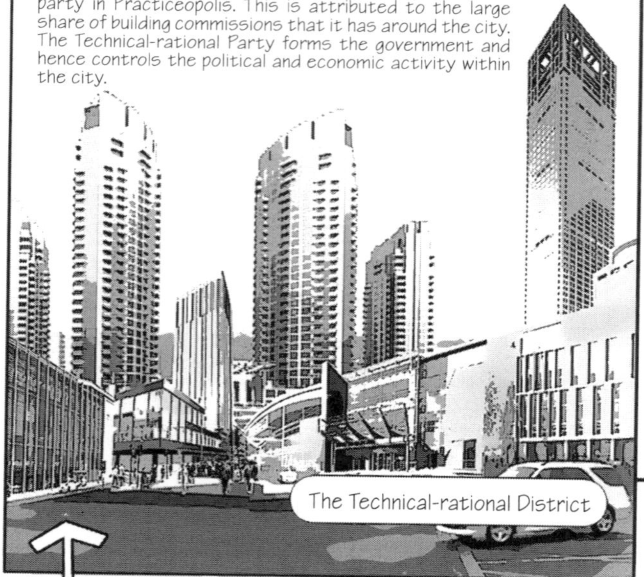
The Technical-rational District

Heroic Modernist architecture represents the shift from the style-based architecture to a new rational-based architecture expressing the condition of modernity. The significance of this practice is attributed to its sheer difference from its preceding paradigms and its deep influence on most of the other modes of practice until the present (Cohen, 1996; Crinson & Lubbock, 1994; Glusberg, 1988; Jencks, 1987).

The Heroic District was for a long time the heart of the city's political and cultural centre of gravity. The city centre of Architectopolis was known for its high-end modernist architectural character. The centre has moved later in contemporary Practiceopolis to the Technical-rational District.

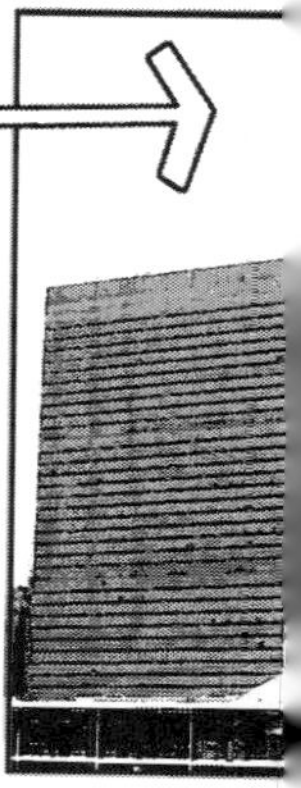

From the last quarter of the 20th century, the Technical-rational Party has increasingly become a more prevalent player in the architectural profession growing hand in hand with the increasing complication and specialisation of the building industry (Cuff, 1992, 1999; Womersley & Portman, 2002). This culture of practice can be represented by multinational architectural corporations like works of SOM, KPF, DAR, Perkins and Will, Aedas and the like.

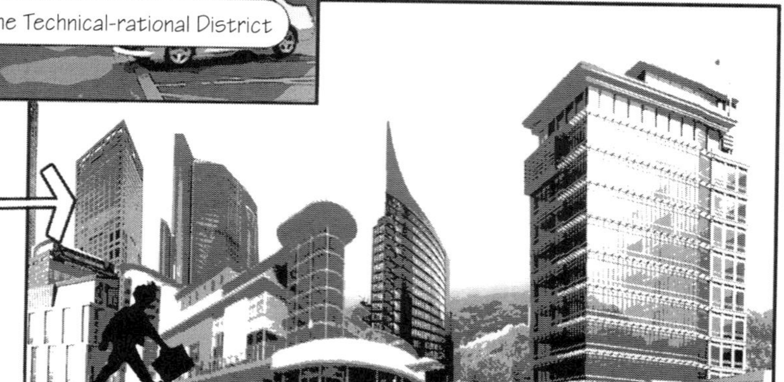

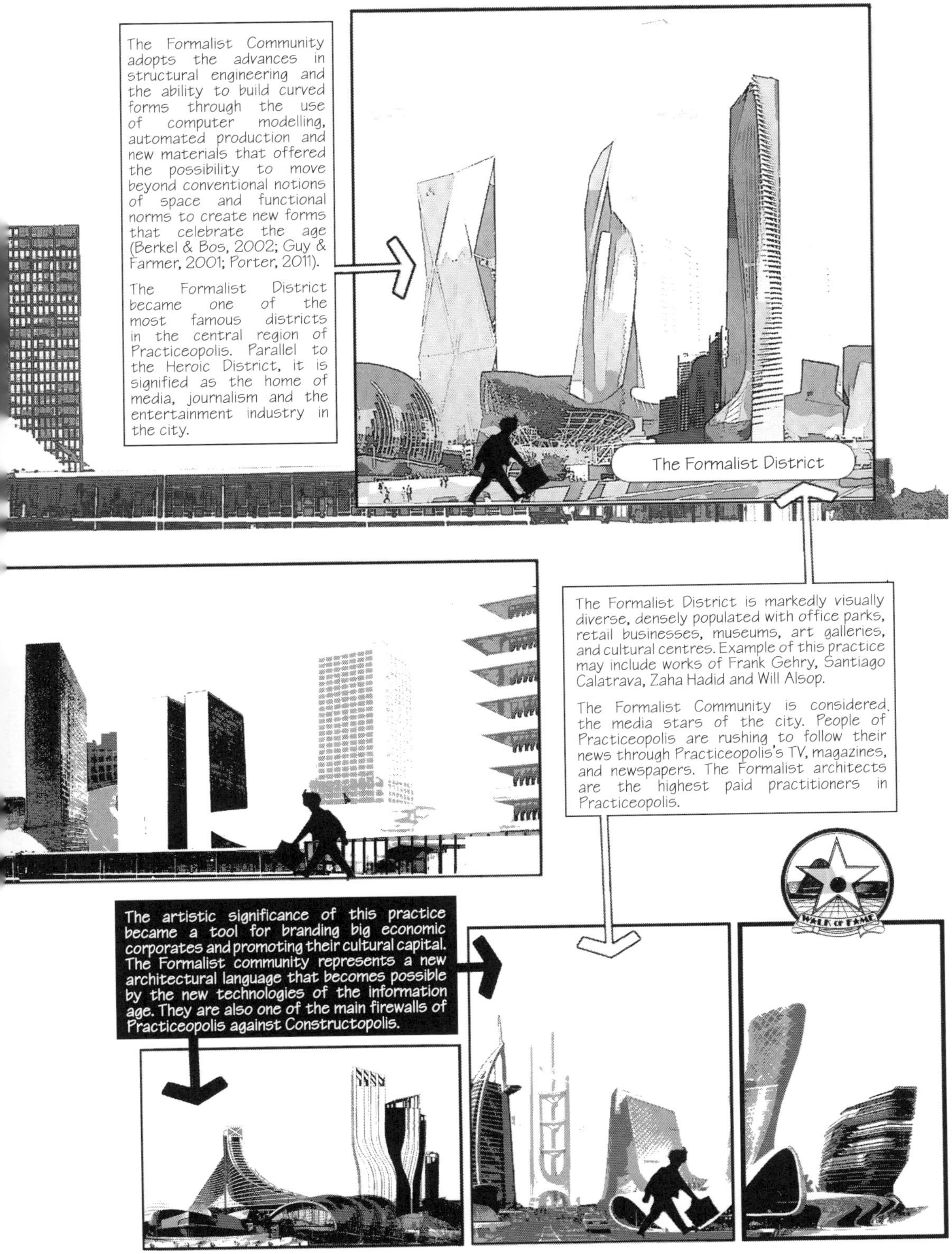
The Formalist Community adopts the advances in structural engineering and the ability to build curved forms through the use of computer modelling, automated production and new materials that offered the possibility to move beyond conventional notions of space and functional norms to create new forms that celebrate the age (Berkel & Bos, 2002; Guy & Farmer, 2001; Porter, 2011).
The Formalist District became one of the most famous districts in the central region of Practiceopolis. Parallel to the Heroic District, it is signified as the home of media, journalism and the entertainment industry in the city.
The Formalist District
The Formalist District is markedly visually diverse, densely populated with office parks, retail businesses, museums, art galleries, and cultural centres. Example of this practice may include works of Frank Gehry, Santiago Calatrava, Zaha Hadid and Will Alsop.
The Formalist Community is considered the media stars of the city. People of Practiceopolis are rushing to follow their news through Practiceopolis's TV, magazines, and newspapers. The Formalist architects are the highest paid practitioners in Practiceopolis.
WALK OF FAME
The artistic significance of this practice became a tool for branding big economic corporates and promoting their cultural capital. The Formalist community represents a new architectural language that becomes possible by the new technologies of the information age. They are also one of the main firewalls of Practiceopolis against Constructopolis.

On the other hand, the old monarchy of Practiceopolis is still symbolically represented by the Stylist district. This community adopts the idea of retrieving the continuity of architectural progress which the heroic modernists have unnaturally stopped. It is rooted in the nostalgic way of seeing the architecture of old days and the essential beauty of historic architecture (Till, 2013).

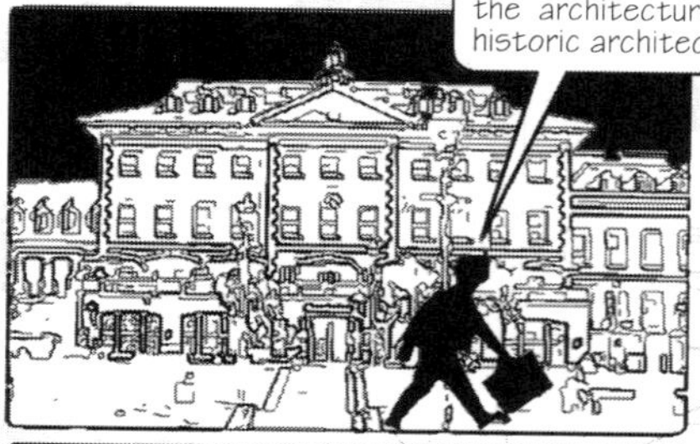

The Stylist District

This community carries a dogma of anti-Modernist architecture as being not constructive and opposite to what was done in the past. This community sees that architecture should keep its cumulative development over the huge heritage of architectural styles (Terry, 1993). They believe that the modernist revolution was a step back on the progress of architectural politics in Practiceopolis. Example of this practice can be seen in the works of Quinlan Terry, David M. Schwarz, Ramy Al-Dahan, and Duncan G. Stroik.

The Regionalist Community has a reactionary critical position to the imposition of globalised architecture which did not respond to the local culture, social values and environment. As supporting a relatively nationalist party within the Parliament, it calls for seeking back the identity of the society which was globalised and Westernised by the forces of the Modernist movement. It celebrates the re-use of built cultural archetypes, traditional construction techniques, and building typologies.

While it may share some of the outer characters of the Stylist party, however, the Regionalist party celebrates the variety of built archetypes inherent from the past, combining them with a concern for cultural continuity expressed through the re-use of traditional construction techniques, and building typologies. This community seeks the deployment of an appropriate language, based on relevant religious, social, and cultural precedents, with which to demarcate authentically a divergent identity (Frampton, 2016)

The Regionalists adopt a nostalgic architecture; however, they see nostalgia with its original meaning: a longing for something lost or out of reach by responding to the local culture, social values and environment (Guy & Farmer, 2001; Steele, 2005; 2019). It is best expressed by works of Charles Correa, Rasem Badran, Abdel-Halim Ibrahim, and Hasan Fathy.

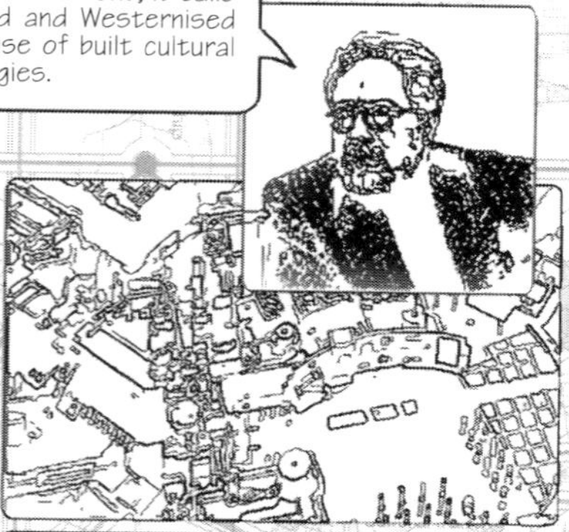

The Regionalist District

Like most practices belonging to the Critical Cultures, the Contingent party is a reformist movement that critiques the mainstream way of practice. It is a critical movement against the claimed autonomy of architects above people's lives. This community criticises the patronising position of architects as the connoisseurs or taste givers that teach people how to live. Their manifesto is that architects should declare the imperfection of their practice. They need to engage with everyday life by creating buildings to be lived in, not just objects to be seen.

The Contingent District

However, some see this social group as an anti-architectural movement that critiques the core ideas establishing Practiceopolis. Buildings with contingent qualities may include works of Sarah Wigglesworth, Samuel Mockbee, and Pitch Africa (Till, 2013; Wigglesworth, 2011; Wigglesworth & Till, 1998).

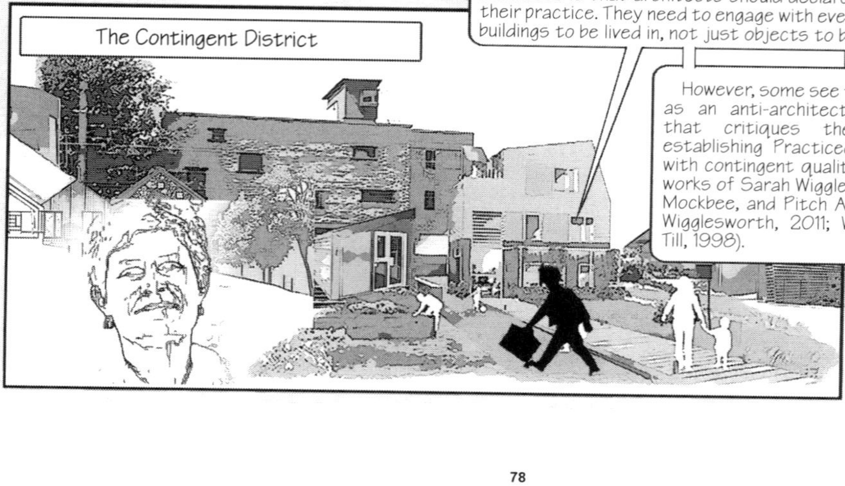

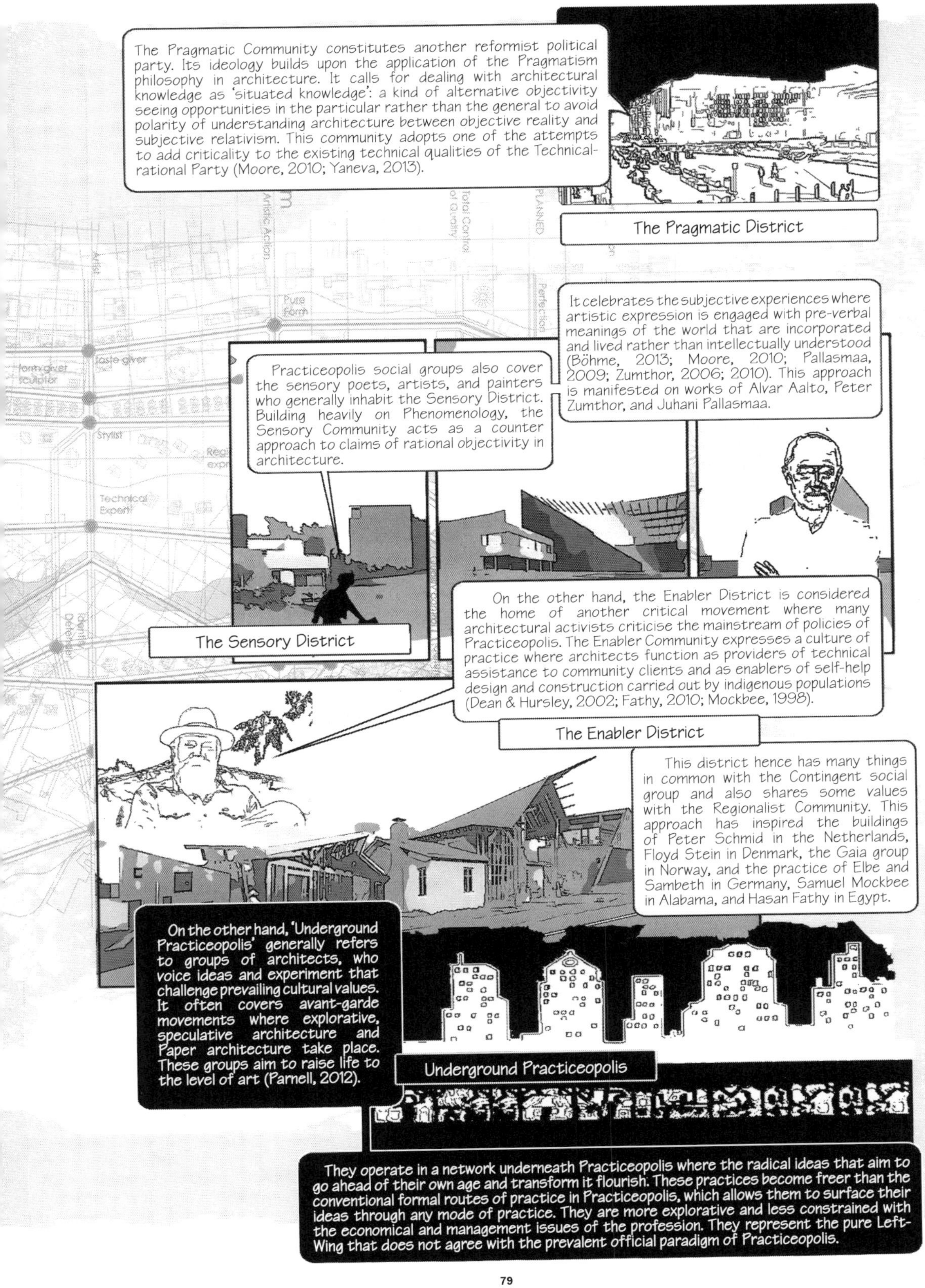
The Pragmatic Community constitutes another reformist political party. Its ideology builds upon the application of the Pragmatism philosophy in architecture. It calls for dealing with architectural knowledge as 'situated knowledge': a kind of alternative objectivity seeing opportunities in the particular rather than the general to avoid polarity of understanding architecture between objective reality and subjective relativism. This community adopts one of the attempts to add criticality to the existing technical qualities of the Technical-rational Party (Moore, 2010; Yaneva, 2013).
The Pragmatic District
Practiceopolis social groups also cover the sensory poets, artists, and painters who generally inhabit the Sensory District. Building heavily on Phenomenology, the Sensory Community acts as a counter approach to claims of rational objectivity in architecture.
It celebrates the subjective experiences where artistic expression is engaged with pre-verbal meanings of the world that are incorporated and lived rather than intellectually understood (Böhme, 2013; Moore, 2010; Pallasmaa, 2009; Zumthor, 2006; 2010). This approach is manifested on works of Alvar Aalto, Peter Zumthor, and Juhani Pallasmaa.
The Sensory District
On the other hand, the Enabler District is considered the home of another critical movement where many architectural activists criticise the mainstream of policies of Practiceopolis. The Enabler Community expresses a culture of practice where architects function as providers of technical assistance to community clients and as enablers of self-help design and construction carried out by indigenous populations (Dean & Hursley, 2002; Fathy, 2010; Mockbee, 1998).
The Enabler District
This district hence has many things in common with the Contingent social group and also shares some values with the Regionalist Community. This approach has inspired the buildings of Peter Schmid in the Netherlands, Floyd Stein in Denmark, the Gaia group in Norway, and the practice of Elbe and Sambeth in Germany, Samuel Mockbee in Alabama, and Hasan Fathy in Egypt.
On the other hand, 'Underground Practiceopolis' generally refers to groups of architects, who voice ideas and experiment that challenge prevailing cultural values. It often covers avant-garde movements where explorative, speculative architecture and Paper architecture take place. These groups aim to raise life to the level of art (Parnell, 2012).
Underground Practiceopolis
They operate in a network underneath Practiceopolis where the radical ideas that aim to go ahead of their own age and transform it flourish. These practices become freer than the conventional formal routes of practice in Practiceopolis, which allows them to surface their ideas through any mode of practice. They are more explorative and less constrained with the economical and management issues of the profession. They represent the pure Left-Wing that does not agree with the prevalent official paradigm of Practiceopolis.

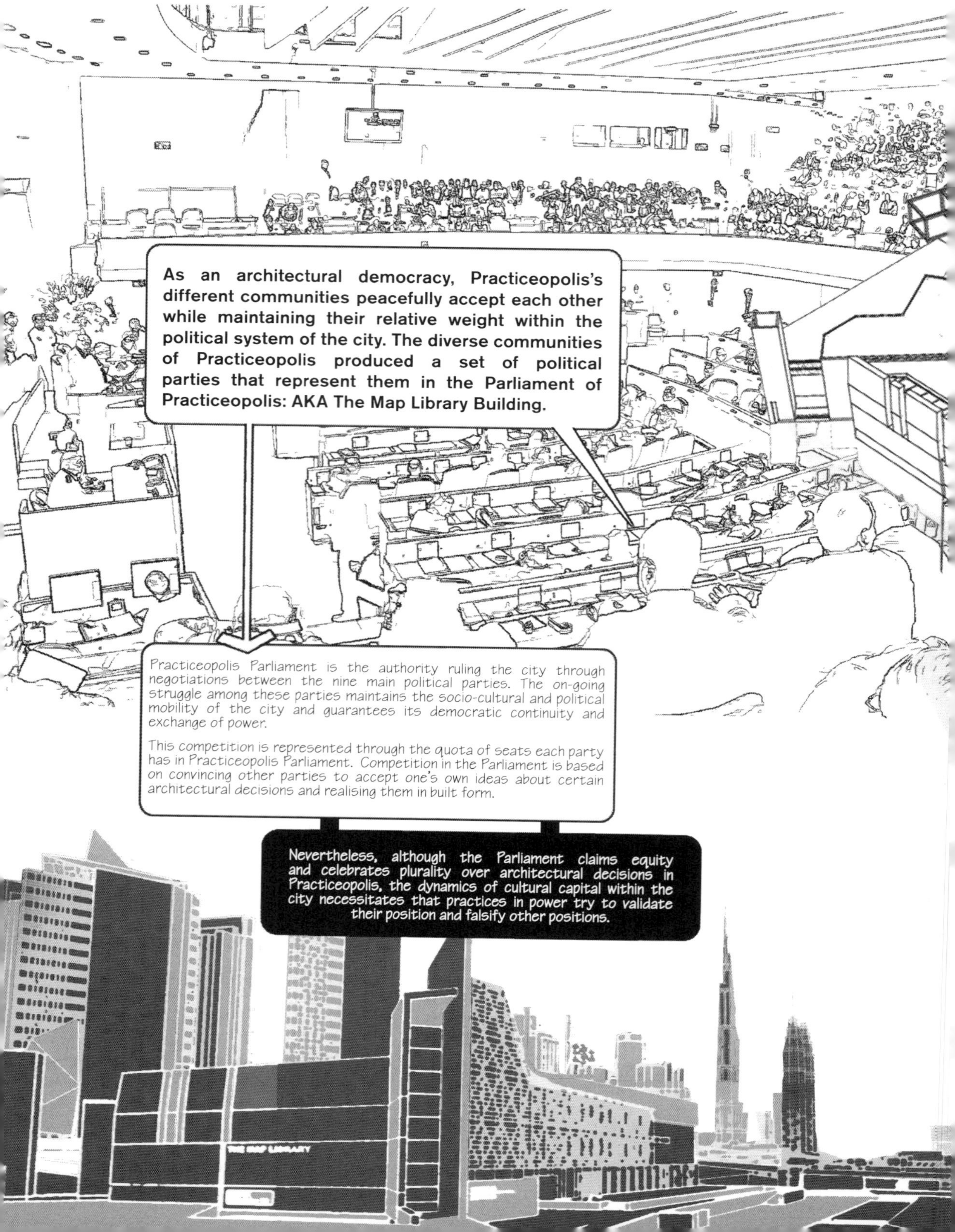
As an architectural democracy, Practiceopolis's different communities peacefully accept each other while maintaining their relative weight within the political system of the city. The diverse communities of Practiceopolis produced a set of political parties that represent them in the Parliament of Practiceopolis: AKA The Map Library Building.
Practiceopolis Parliament is the authority ruling the city through negotiations between the nine main political parties. The on-going struggle among these parties maintains the socio-cultural and political mobility of the city and guarantees its democratic continuity and exchange of power.
This competition is represented through the quota of seats each party has in Practiceopolis Parliament. Competition in the Parliament is based on convincing other parties to accept one's own ideas about certain architectural decisions and realising them in built form.
Nevertheless, although the Parliament claims equity and celebrates plurality over architectural decisions in Practiceopolis, the dynamics of cultural capital within the city necessitates that practices in power try to validate their position and falsify other positions.

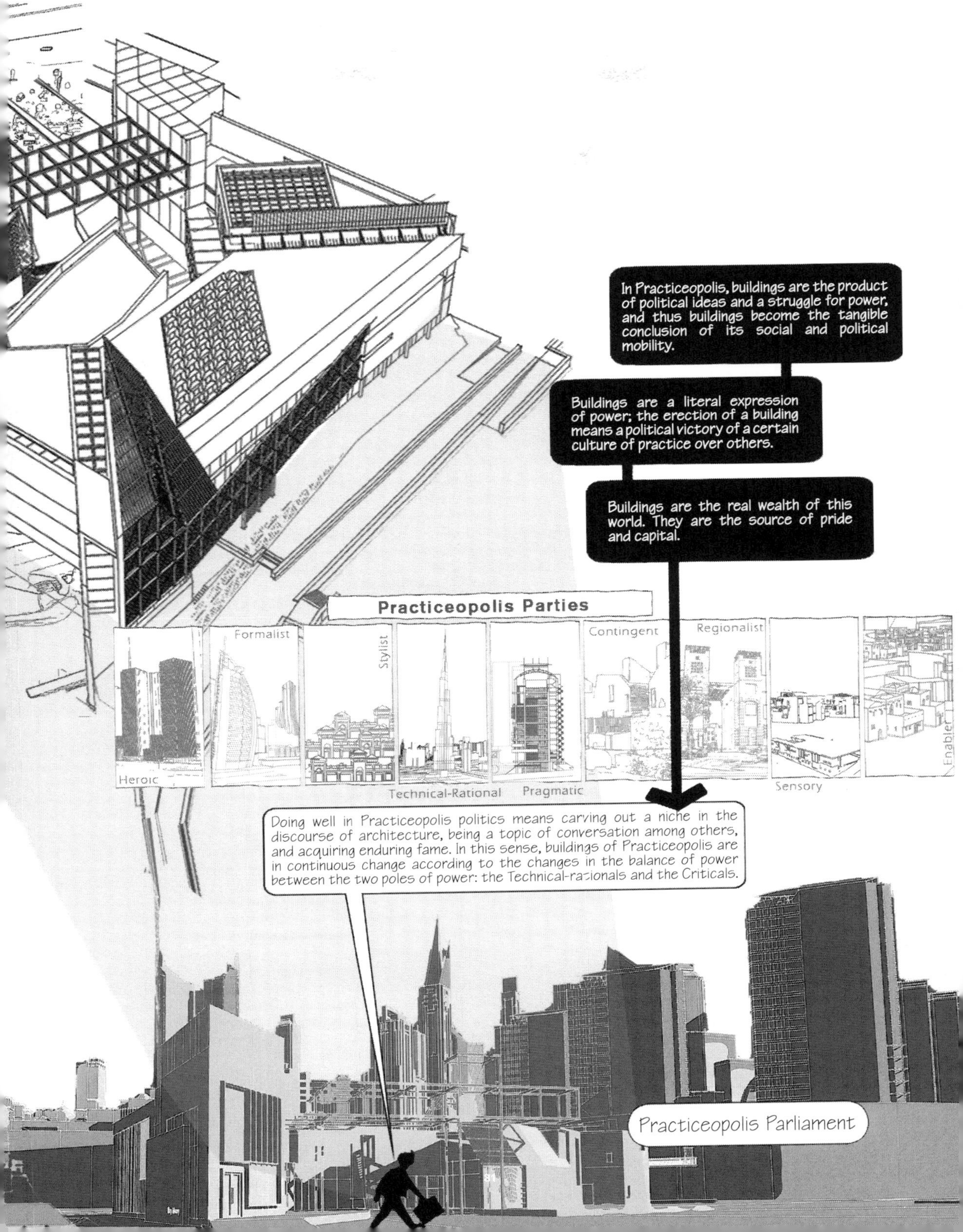
In Practiceopolis, buildings are the product of political ideas and a struggle for power, and thus buildings become the tangible conclusion of its social and political mobility.
Buildings are a literal expression of power; the erection of a building means a political victory of a certain culture of practice over others.
Buildings are the real wealth of this world. They are the source of pride and capital.
Practiceopolis Parties
Heroic
Formalist
Stylist
Technical-Rational
Pragmatic
Contingent
Regionalist
Sensory
Enabler
Doing well in Practiceopolis politics means carving out a niche in the discourse of architecture, being a topic of conversation among others, and acquiring enduring fame. In this sense, buildings of Practiceopolis are in continuous change according to the changes in the balance of power between the two poles of power: the Technical-rationals and the Criticals.
Practiceopolis Parliament

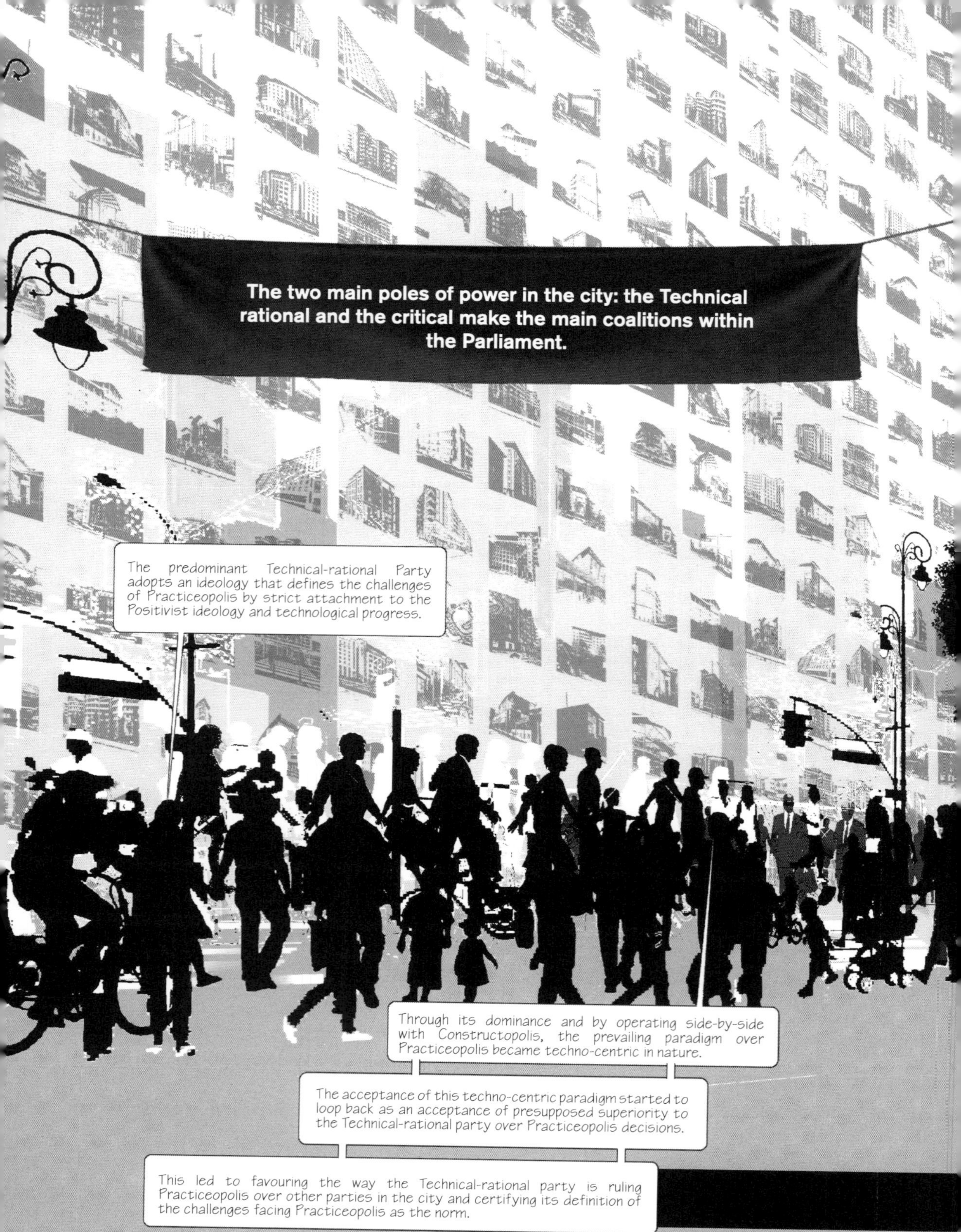
The two main poles of power in the city: the Technical rational and the critical make the main coalitions within the Parliament.
The predominant Technical-rational Party adopts an ideology that defines the challenges of Practiceopolis by strict attachment to the Positivist ideology and technological progress.
Through its dominance and by operating side-by-side with Constructopolis, the prevailing paradigm over Practiceopolis became techno-centric in nature.
The acceptance of this techno-centric paradigm started to loop back as an acceptance of presupposed superiority to the Technical-rational party over Practiceopolis decisions.
This led to favouring the way the Technical-rational party is ruling Practiceopolis over other parties in the city and certifying its definition of the challenges facing Practiceopolis as the norm.

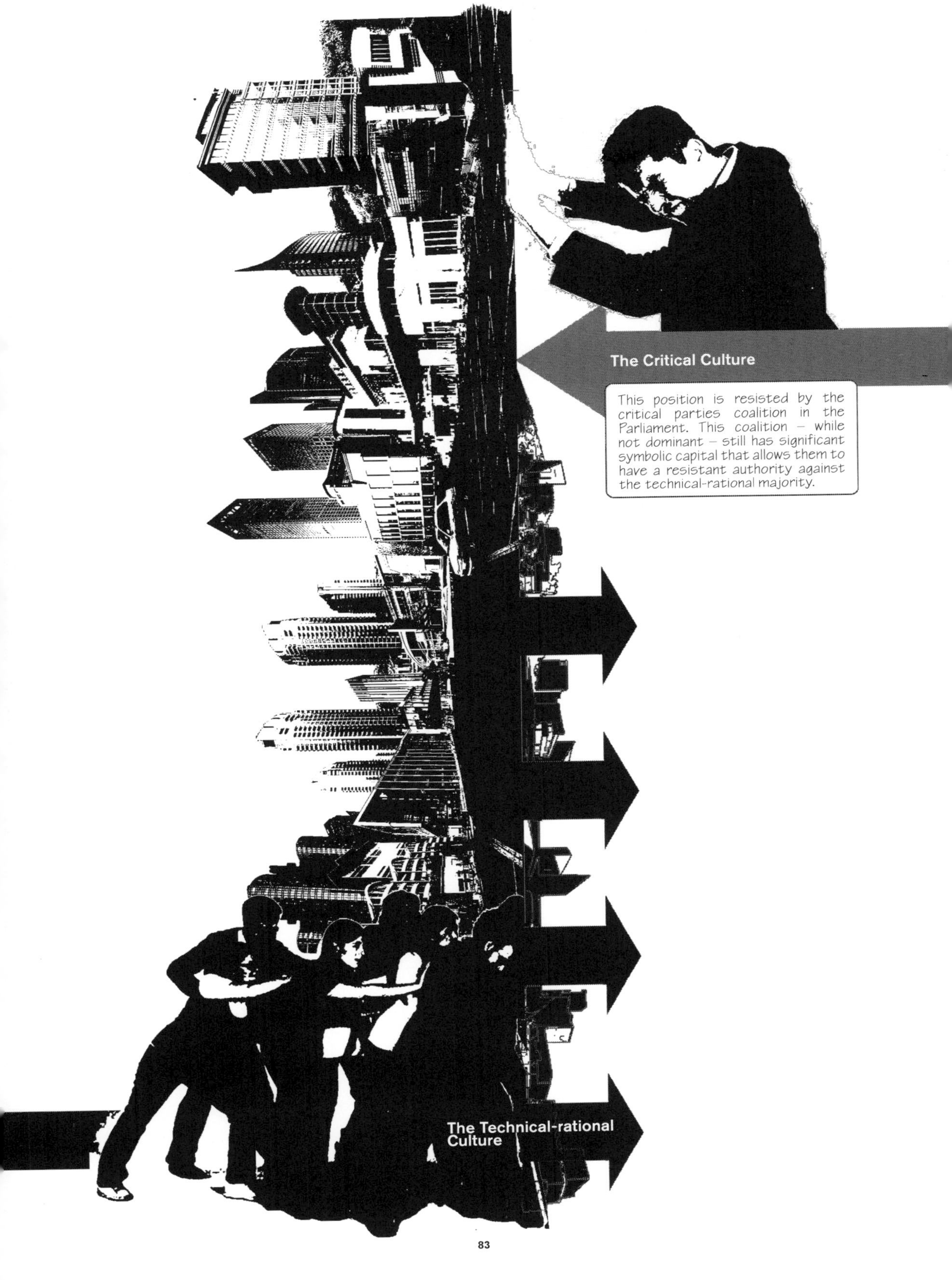
The Critical Culture
This position is resisted by the critical parties coalition in the Parliament. This coalition – while not dominant – still has significant symbolic capital that allows them to have a resistant authority against the technical-rational majority.
The Technical-rational Culture

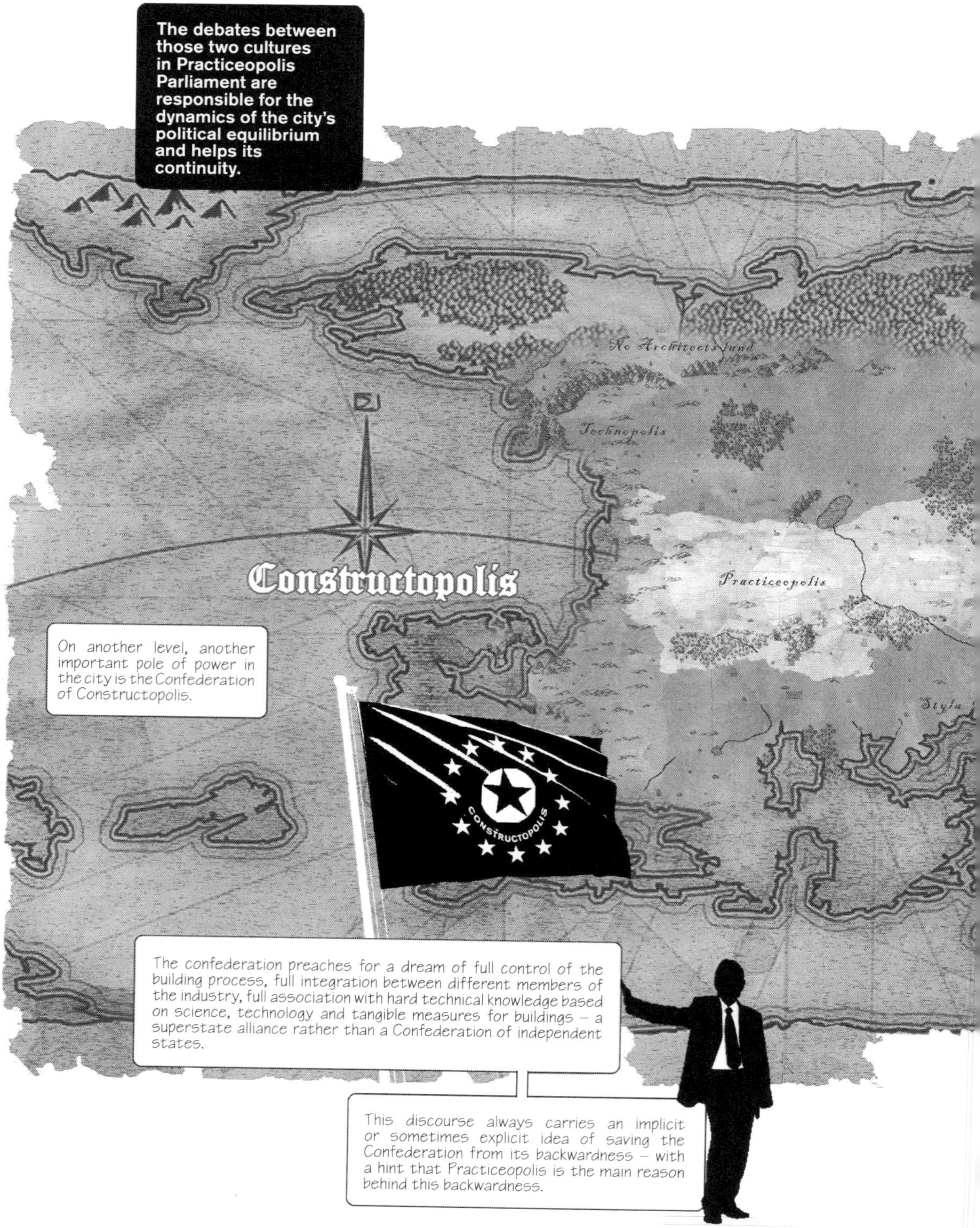
The debates between those two cultures in Practiceopolis Parliament are responsible for the dynamics of the city's political equilibrium and helps its continuity.
No Architects land
Technopolis
Constructopolis
Practiceopolis
On another level, another important pole of power in the city is the Confederation of Constructopolis.
CONSTRUCTOPOLIS
The confederation preaches for a dream of full control of the building process, full integration between different members of the industry, full association with hard technical knowledge based on science, technology and tangible measures for buildings – a superstate alliance rather than a Confederation of independent states.
This discourse always carries an implicit or sometimes explicit idea of saving the Confederation from its backwardness – with a hint that Practiceopolis is the main reason behind this backwardness.

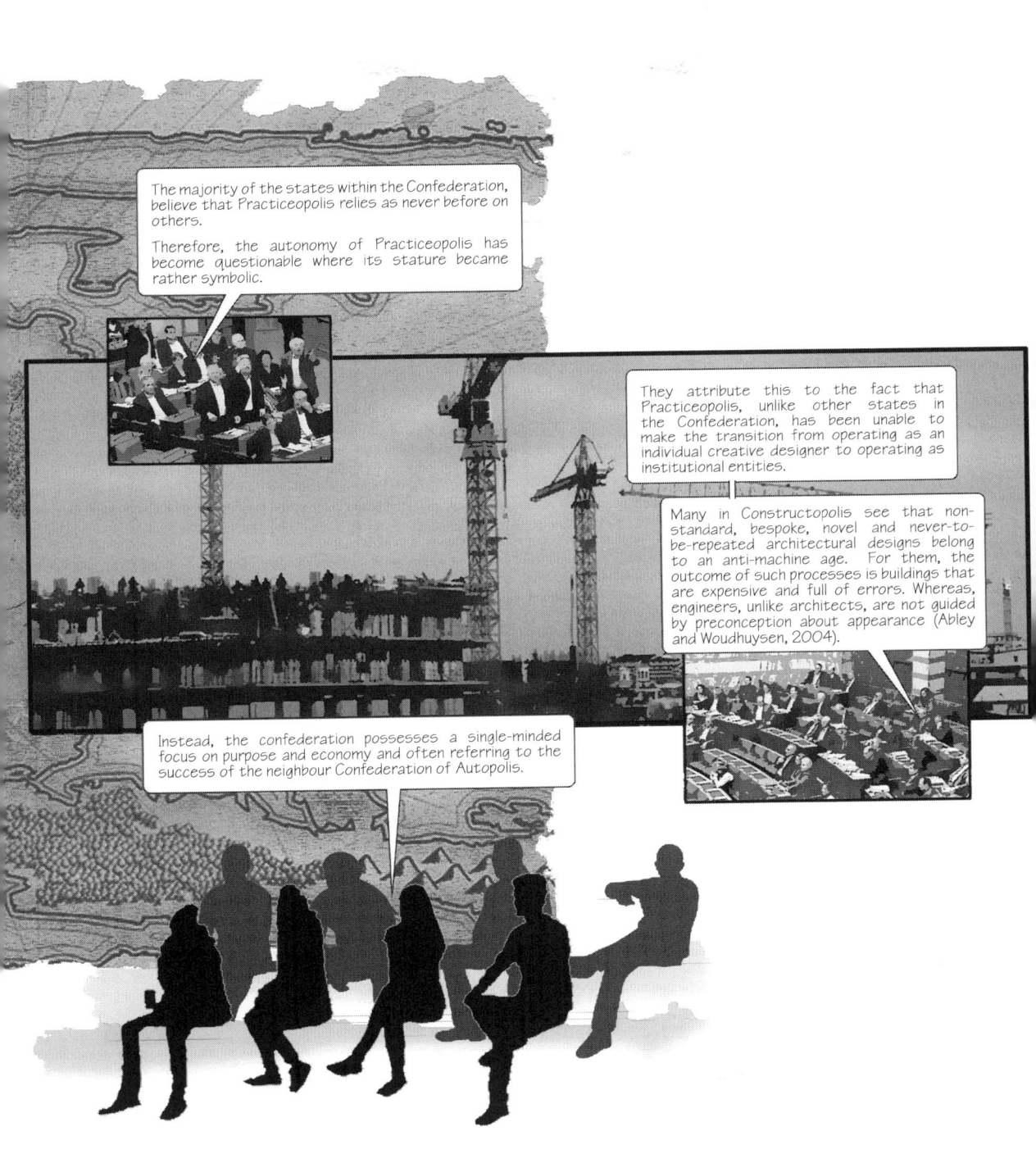

The majority of the states within the Confederation, believe that Practiceopolis relies as never before on others.

Therefore, the autonomy of Practiceopolis has become questionable where its stature became rather symbolic.

They attribute this to the fact that Practiceopolis, unlike other states in the Confederation, has been unable to make the transition from operating as an individual creative designer to operating as institutional entities.

Many in Constructopolis see that non-standard, bespoke, novel and never-to-be-repeated architectural designs belong to an anti-machine age. For them, the outcome of such processes is buildings that are expensive and full of errors. Whereas, engineers, unlike architects, are not guided by preconception about appearance (Abley and Woudhuysen, 2004).

Instead, the confederation possesses a single-minded focus on purpose and economy and often referring to the success of the neighbour Confederation of Autopolis.

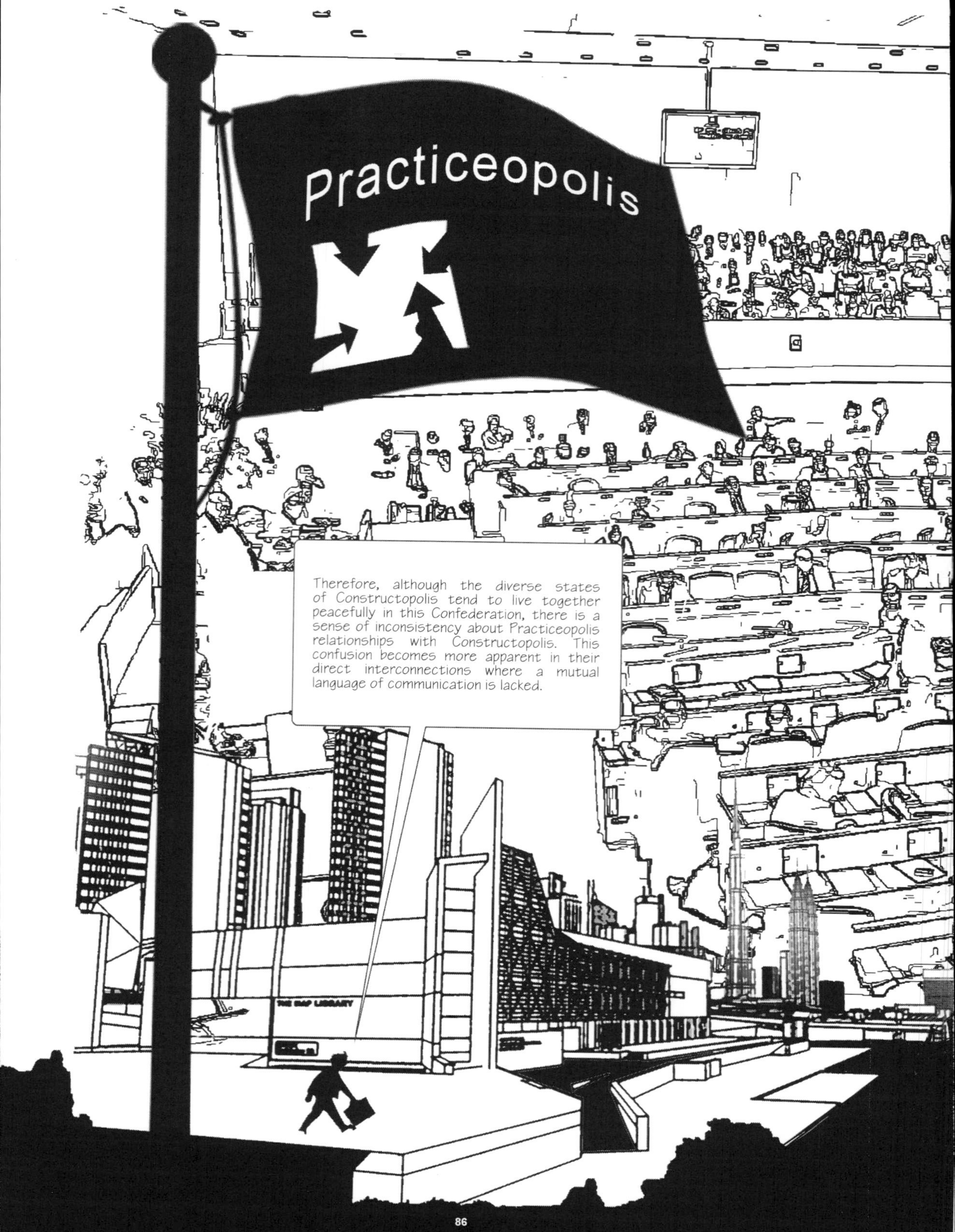
Practiceopolis
Therefore, although the diverse states of Constructopolis tend to live together peacefully in this Confederation, there is a sense of inconsistency about Practiceopolis relationships with Constructopolis. This confusion becomes more apparent in their direct interconnections where a mutual language of communication is lacked.

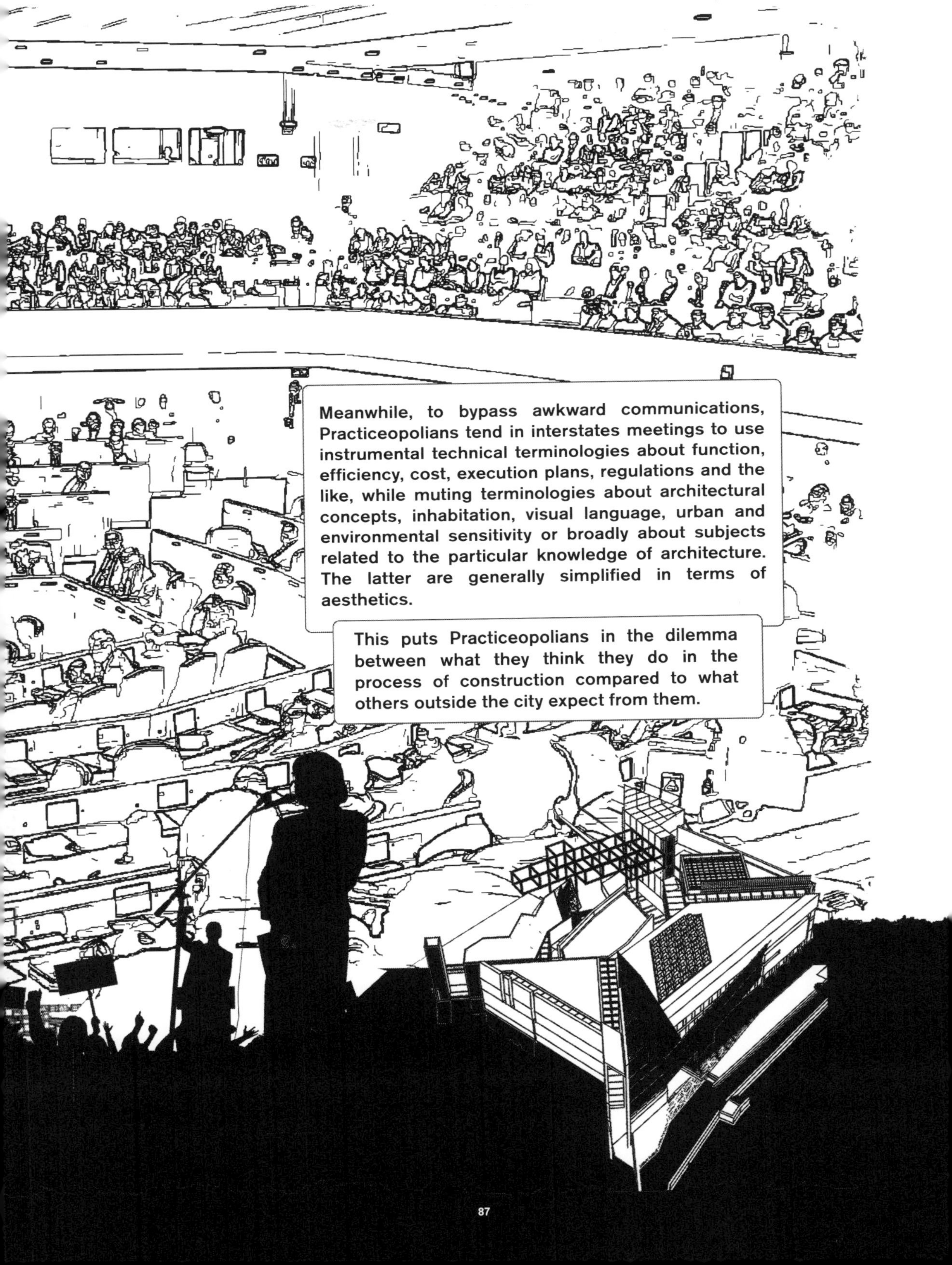
Meanwhile, to bypass awkward communications, Practiceopolians tend in interstates meetings to use instrumental technical terminologies about function, efficiency, cost, execution plans, regulations and the like, while muting terminologies about architectural concepts, inhabitation, visual language, urban and environmental sensitivity or broadly about subjects related to the particular knowledge of architecture. The latter are generally simplified in terms of aesthetics.
This puts Practiceopolians in the dilemma between what they think they do in the process of construction compared to what others outside the city expect from them.

In Practiceopolis Parliament, the argument about engaging more or siding less with the Confederation became an everyday topic in the Parliament agenda.

Interestingly!!,

the Technical-rational Party shares many values with other states in the Confederation.

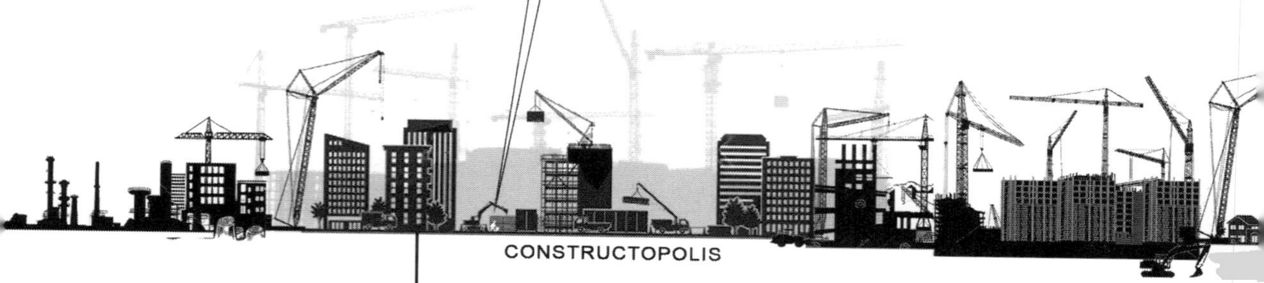
CONSTRUCTOPOLIS

Therefore, in inter-states meetings, the Technical-rational Party tends to support the Confederation's discourse and bases its arguments on the submission of the dominance of these values over the current status quo.

They believe that coping with this techno-centric status quo should the 'common sense' solution for the problems of Practiceopolis.

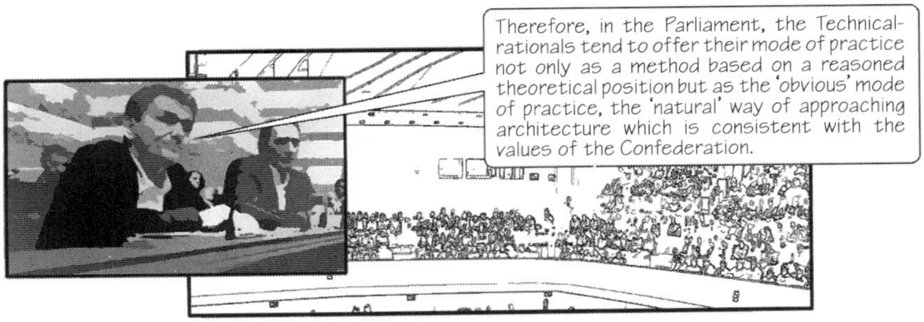
Therefore, in the Parliament, the Technical-rationals tend to offer their mode of practice not only as a method based on a reasoned theoretical position but as the 'obvious' mode of practice, the 'natural' way of approaching architecture which is consistent with the values of the Confederation.

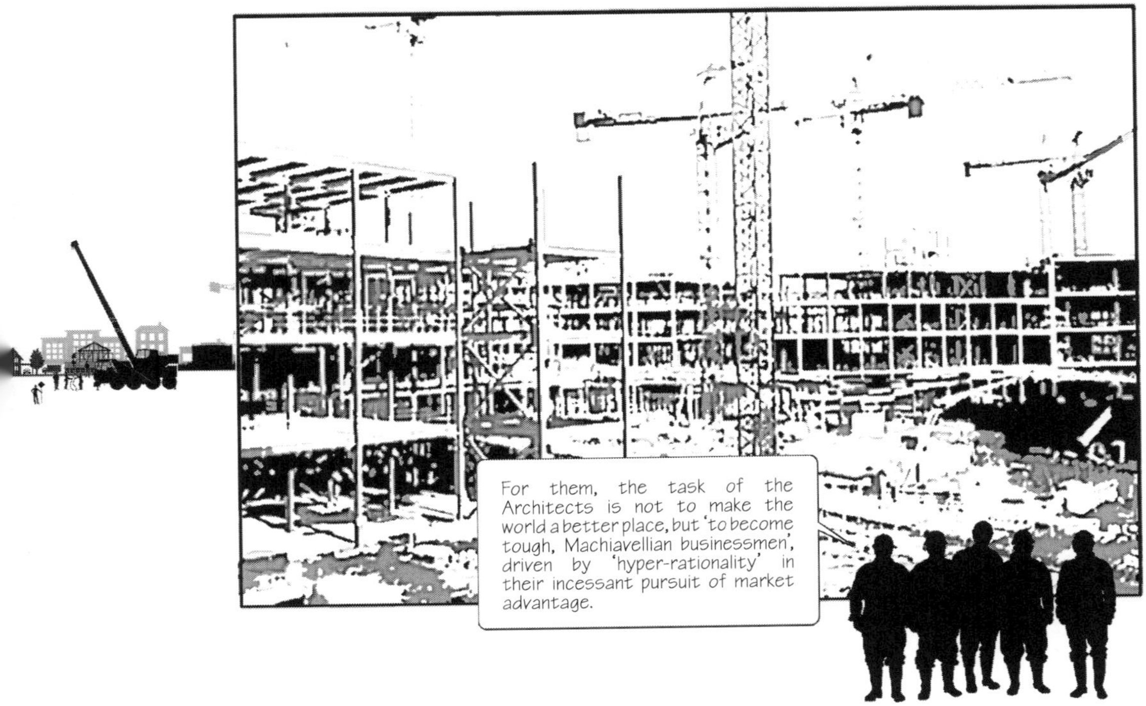
For them, the task of the Architects is not to make the world a better place, but 'to become tough, Machiavellian businessmen', driven by 'hyper-rationality' in their incessant pursuit of market advantage.

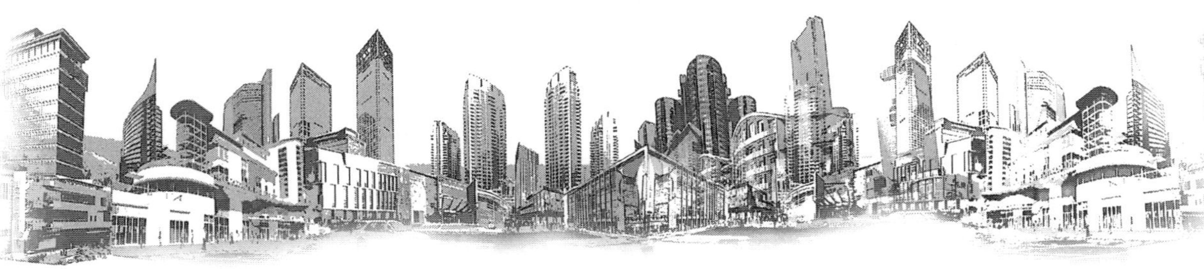

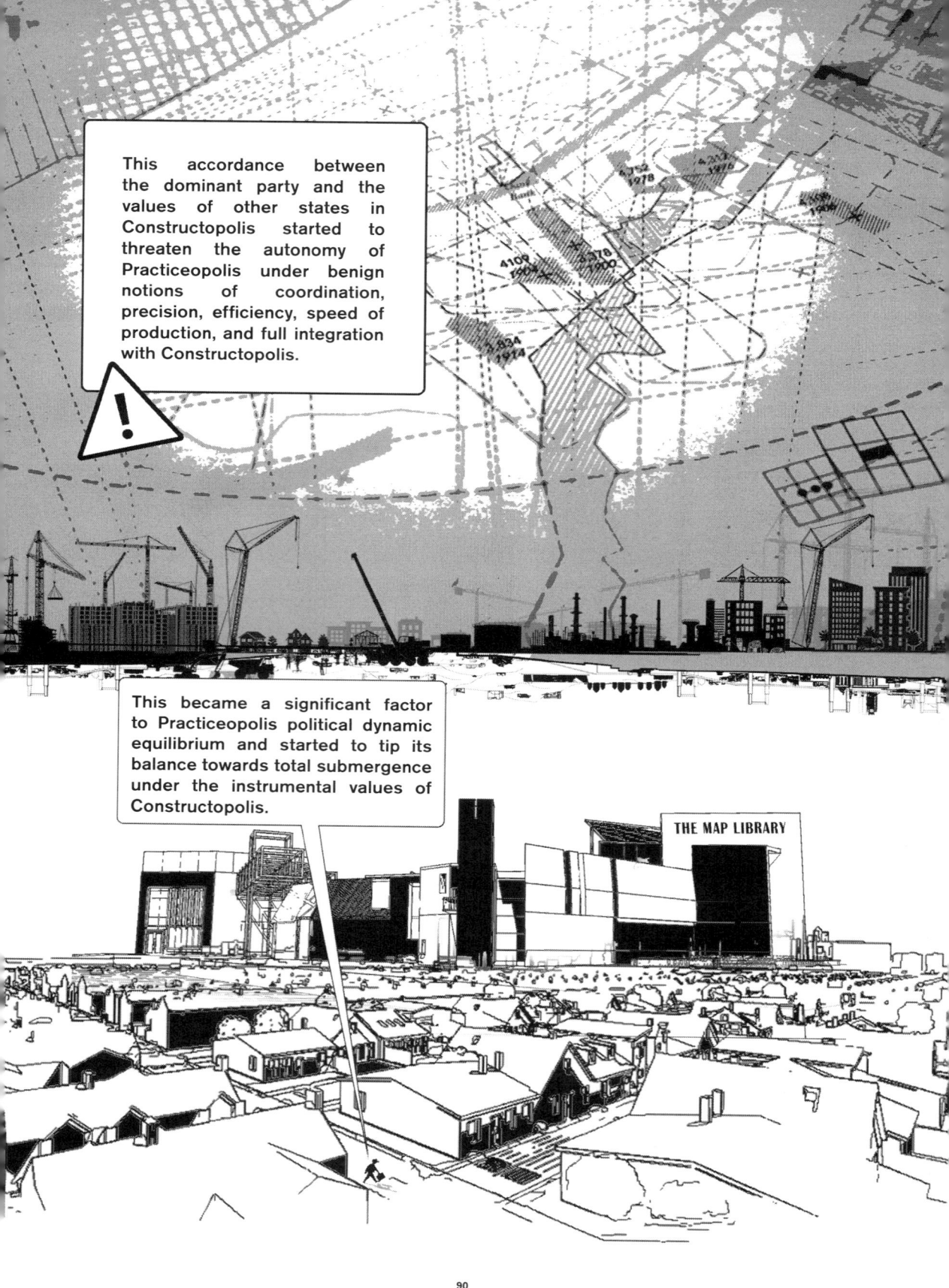

This accordance between the dominant party and the values of other states in Constructopolis started to threaten the autonomy of Practiceopolis under benign notions of coordination, precision, efficiency, speed of production, and full integration with Constructopolis.

This became a significant factor to Practiceopolis political dynamic equilibrium and started to tip its balance towards total submergence under the instrumental values of Constructopolis.

THE MAP LIBRARY

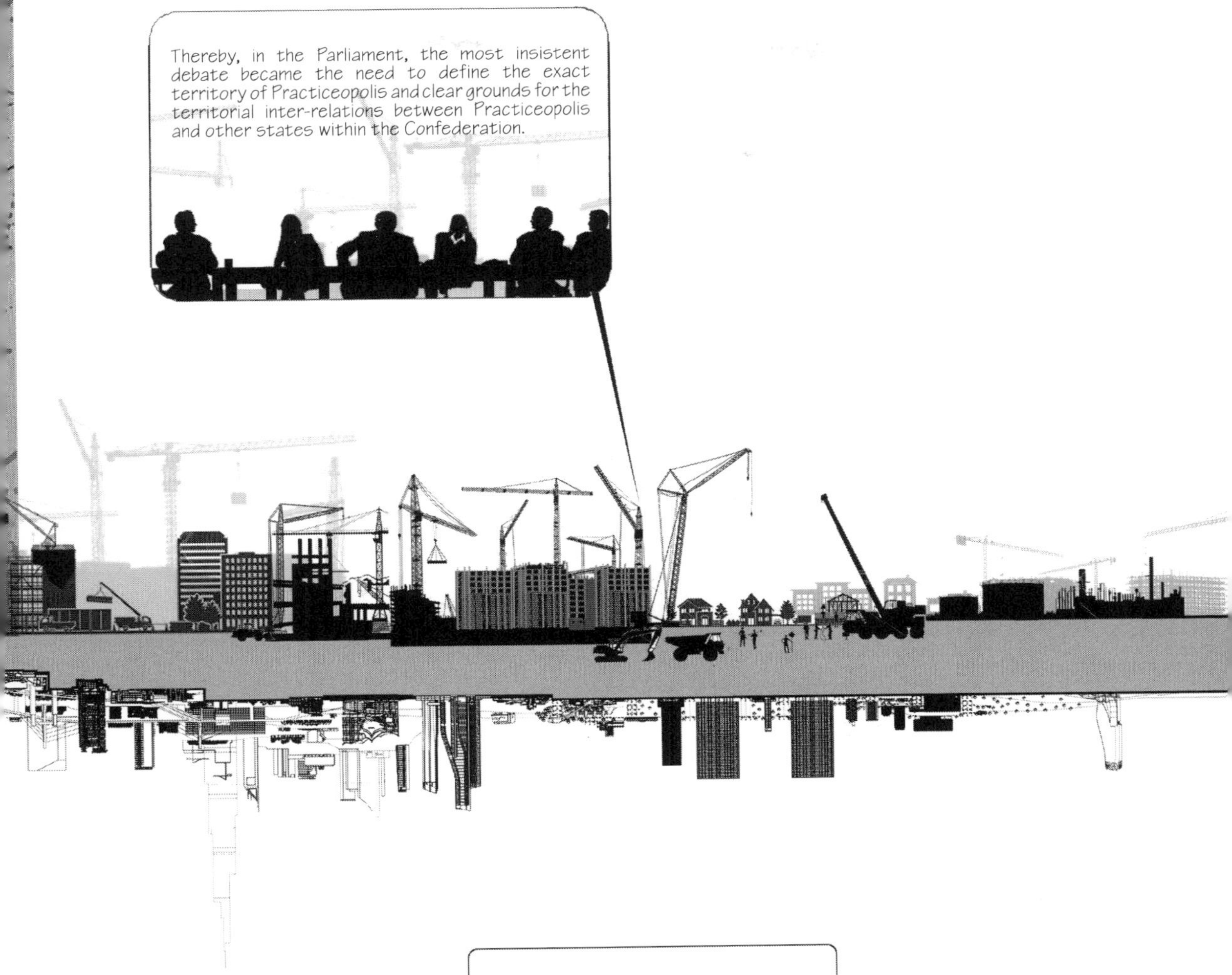
Thereby, in the Parliament, the most insistent debate became the need to define the exact territory of Practiceopolis and clear grounds for the territorial inter-relations between Practiceopolis and other states within the Confederation.

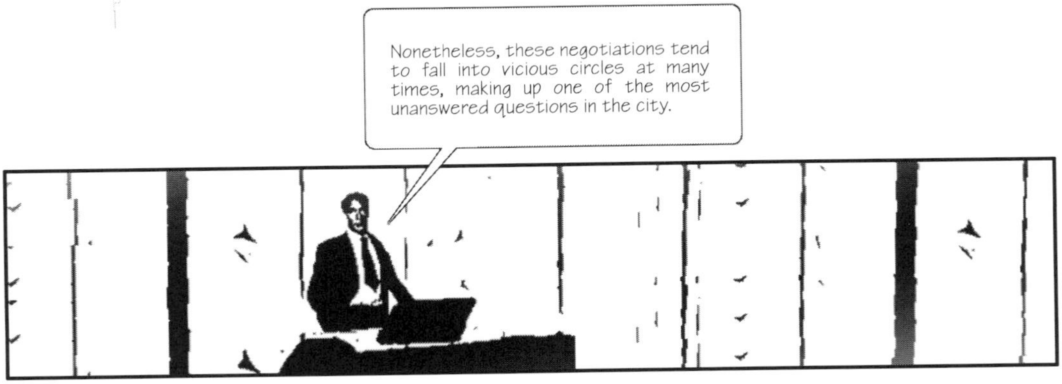
Nonetheless, these negotiations tend to fall into vicious circles at many times, making up one of the most unanswered questions in the city.

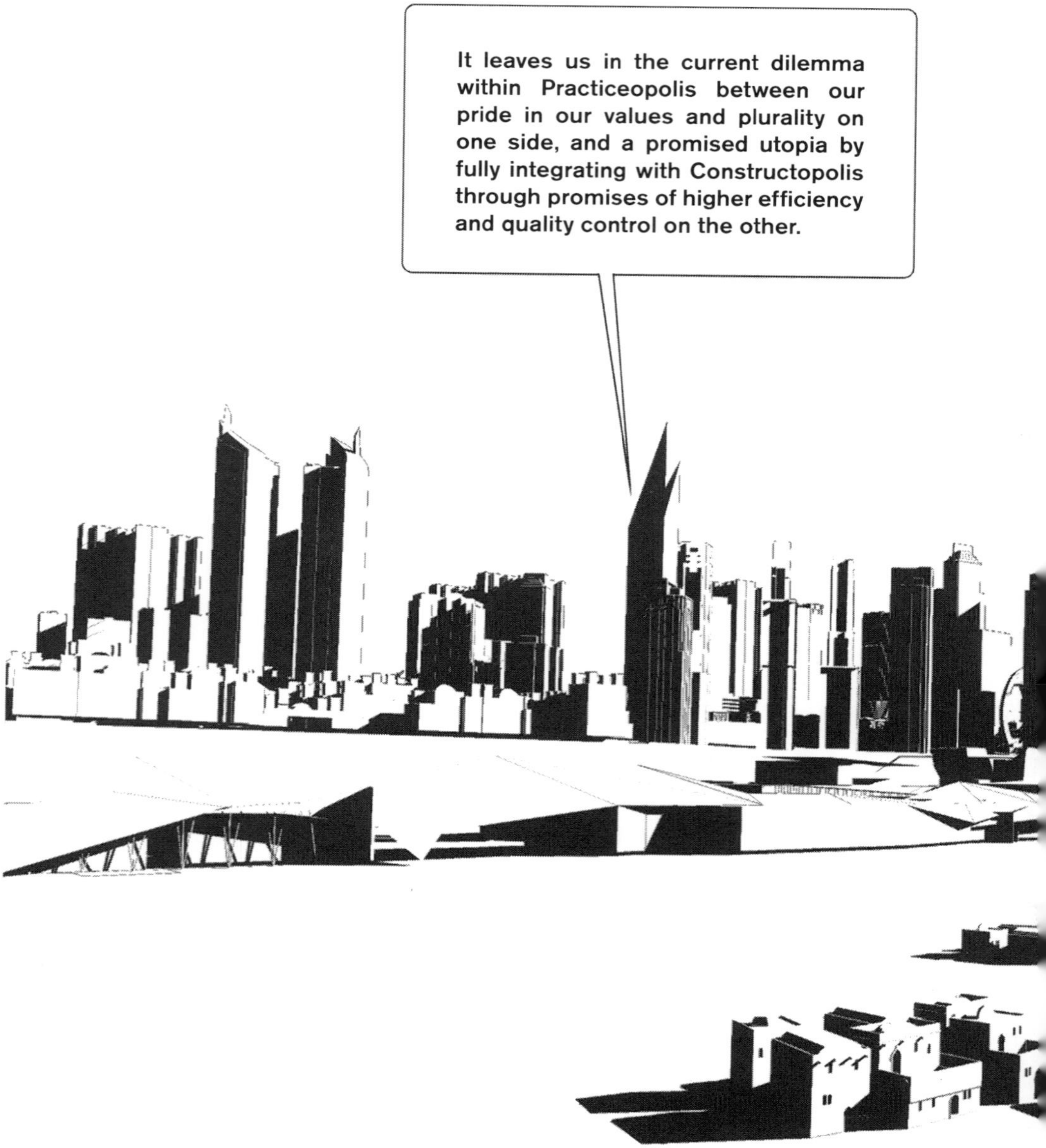
It leaves us in the current dilemma within Practiceopolis between our pride in our values and plurality on one side, and a promised utopia by fully integrating with Constructopolis through promises of higher efficiency and quality control on the other.

ON PRACTICEOPOLIS

The previous has drawn an overview of Practiceopolis, the imaginary representation of the contemporary architectural profession. It presented some glimpses of its history and social and political structure that shaped the architectural profession in the way it is at present. Here, it is important to mention that the Practiceopolis is not meant to be in any way exclusive, or frozen in time or space. The significance of Practiceopolis is that it offers an illustrated way of reading the profession from different angles. Nevertheless, Practiceopolis does not claim objectivity. It is not the only way of reading the contemporary architectural situation but it gives some helpful insights into the relations between different cultures of practice within the contemporary profession and their broader interaction with the construction industry.

There are multiple reasons for creating such a visual fictional metaphor. The particular setting of Practiceopolis reinforces certain political and socio-cultural struggles, where architecture is used literally as a mode for conveying ideologies, the structure of power, and political order. This fictional setting allows examining these ideologies and asking extreme questions about the values of the profession and the industry at large in a politically-correct way that otherwise may not be accepted. Practiceopolis employs cartoons' capacity to exaggerate reality and to put things to the extremity of fantasy. The imaginary setting allows the novel a temporary authority that enables it to interrogate the arguments about different cultures of practice, especially the dominant ones, which would not be potentially possible by other means. This temporary authority empowers the novel to dig into the informal implicit knowledge and preconceptions of the architectural profession, throwing out the constraints held by the architectural discipline and explore possible fictional logics to introduce new conceptions about it.

On the other hand, the nature of the city of Practiceopolis as a place between fantasy and reality echoes the significance of cities in cartoon. Cities in cartoon are as interesting as the stories that take place in them. They are one of the key characters affecting the plot of graphic stories. In order to follow the storyline, the reader needs to have a contextual and cultural background about the places where events of the story take place (Ahrens & Meteling, 2010). The metaphor of Practiceopolis hence brings together this significant nature of cities in cartoon with the extremity that this medium allows to go beyond the limitations of traditional research methodologies and riding the fine line between parody and criticism to help to raise broader lines of inquiry on the blurry area of the values of the architectural profession.

Besides, Practiceopolis resembles the stereotypical model of a contemporary metropolitan city, which it actually represents. It embodies a certain set of values, which are predominantly Western, indeed predominantly Anglo-American in origin, highlighting some of the latent prejudice in the contemporary architectural discourse. Practiceopolis hence looks globalised and Westernised, and therefore the ideas informing its morphology clearly have a history entwined with the global power relations of the last few centuries. It reflects our metropolis that became dominated by technical-rational architecture. It is an accurate but may be a disturbing reflection of the contemporary globalised city. This cannot go unacknowledged.

Additionally, while claimed as a democracy, it may be noticeable that the social and political world of Practiceopolis lacks a suitable representation of women both in the Parliament and in its casual everyday routines. This is – in a way – a reflection on the contemporary construction process as a whole, which is predominantly male-driven. While the discourse of the contemporary architectural profession has recently seen a major push toward inclusion of those who have been historically underrepresented in the field, this is still the exception rather than the norm and Practiceopolis naturally represents that.

Therefore, Practiceopolis must not be misread as a call for a perfect architectural world, an impossible totality that would inevitably fade into totalitarianism. Instead, Practiceopolis must be read as the 'non-place' not because it is ideal and inaccessible, but because it is 'everywhere' around us but we cannot see directly. Practiceopolis is a scattered mix of social, economic, and political factors distilled in a form of buildings. By recognising its political nature, we might begin to engage in a very different dialogue about the profession of architecture and its relation to other actors in the globalised building industry.

02: Stories from Practiceopolis

THE ATKINSON'S STORY

Lost between the Two Cultures

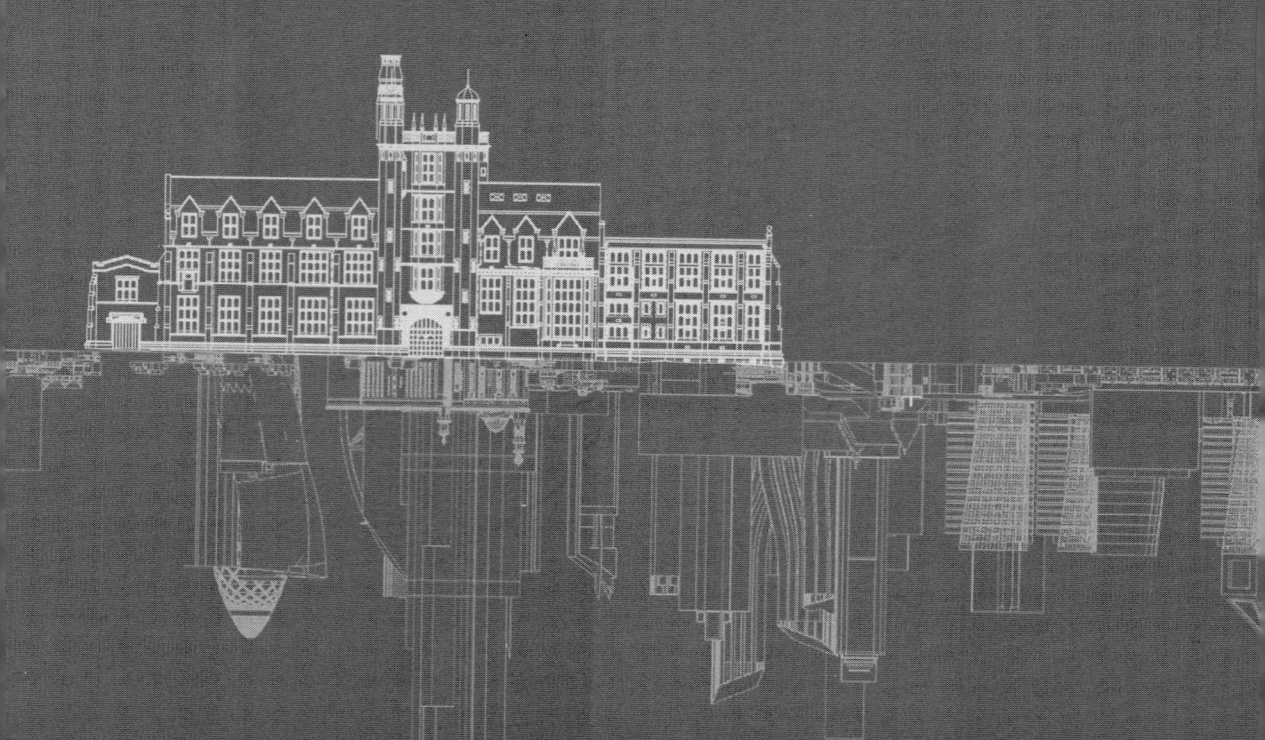

The following section will narrate some stories from within Practiceopolis – quasi-realistic stories that dramatise real-life architectural and extra-architectural exchanges from everyday architectural practice. The stories exaggerate the architectural profession's tacit everyday routines, in order to make it prominent and tangible. They are based on a series of project management and value engineering meetings held during the conduct of a live architectural project in the UK in which the author was part of the concept architects team (named in the novel as the Atkinson Building).

The building is portrayed as one of the most significant buildings of the city that witnessed many of the historical and ideological shifts that Practiceopolis has experienced. The following stories reflect upon the debates that occurred during the regeneration of this building, highlighting the interaction between the two prominent cultures of practice: the Critical and the Technical-rational. The Critical Culture is represented by Design House (DH), a research-led practice operating from Practiceopolis University and supervised by Alan, a professor of Architecture in the School of Political Science in the City and a critically-oriented concept architect with many years of experience. On the other hand, the Technical-rational Culture is represented by different actors from Practiceopolis and the broader Confederation. Practiceopolis Technical-rational Party is represented by EFM: The Estate Facility Management of Practiceopolis University. EFM is a technical-rational service that acts as the architectural representative of the client (Practiceopolis University). In addition, as substantially adopting the instrumental technical-rational ideology, Constructopolis is represented by many actors, different engineering consultants, contractors, quantity surveyors, in addition to a multinational Construction Design Management (CDM) coordinator called G&F.

Confused between the two prominent cultures of Practiceopolis, the author, a self-confessed technical-rational practitioner through training and experience, retells his experience as one of the team members of Design House (DH) and reflects upon the clash of values occurring in contemporary Constructopolis from a participant-observer seat.

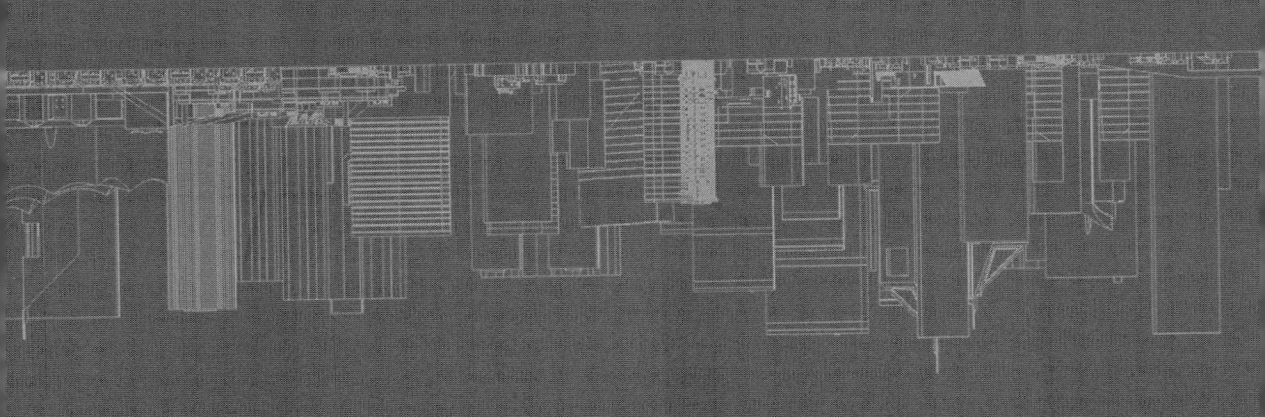

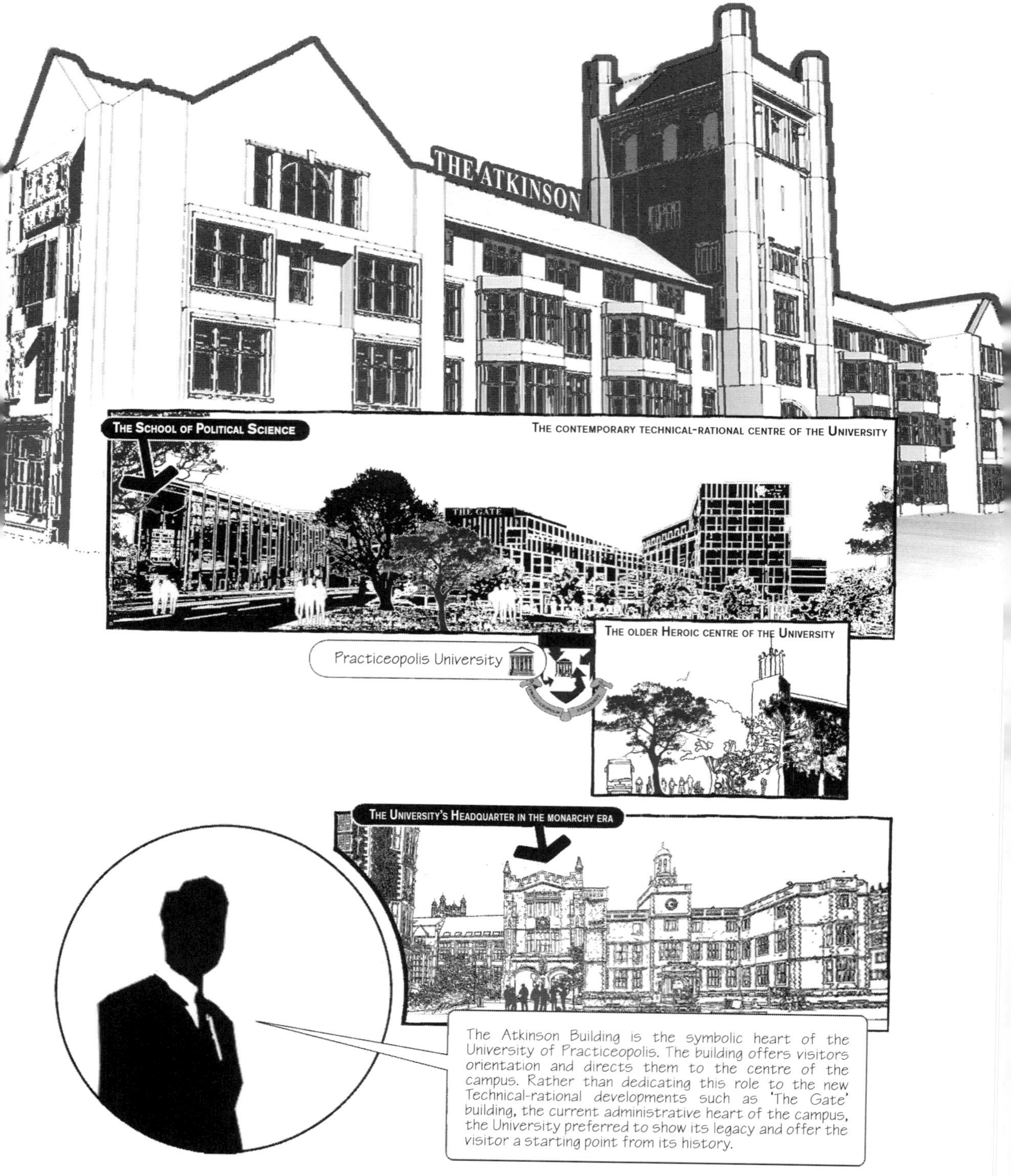
THE ATKINSON
THE SCHOOL OF POLITICAL SCIENCE
THE CONTEMPORARY TECHNICAL-RATIONAL CENTRE OF THE UNIVERSITY
THE GATE
Practiceopolis University
THE OLDER HEROIC CENTRE OF THE UNIVERSITY
THE UNIVERSITY'S HEADQUARTER IN THE MONARCHY ERA
The Atkinson Building is the symbolic heart of the University of Practiceopolis. The building offers visitors orientation and directs them to the centre of the campus. Rather than dedicating this role to the new Technical-rational developments such as 'The Gate' building, the current administrative heart of the campus, the University preferred to show its legacy and offer the visitor a starting point from its history.

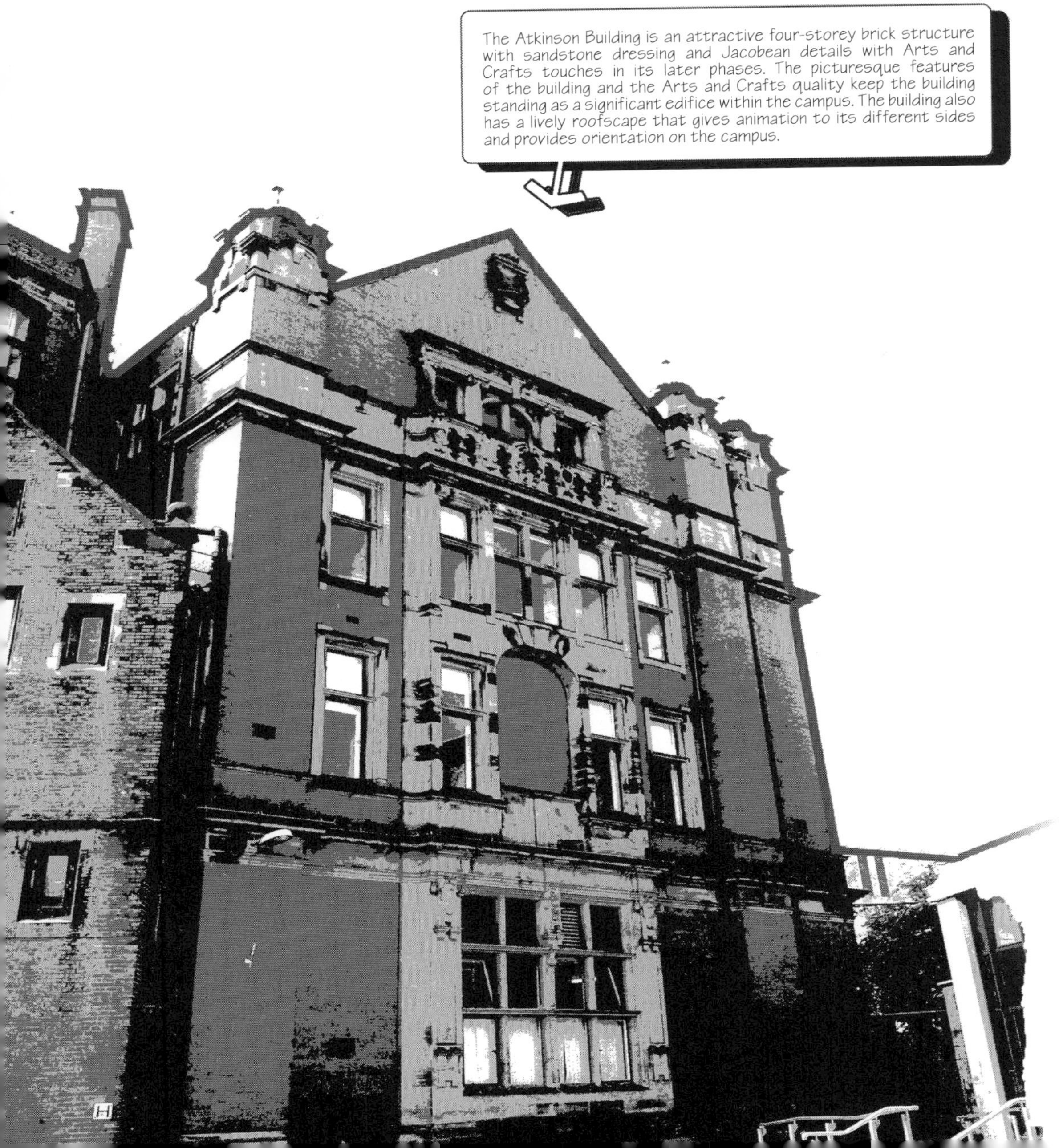
The Atkinson Building is an attractive four-storey brick structure with sandstone dressing and Jacobean details with Arts and Crafts touches in its later phases. The picturesque features of the building and the Arts and Crafts quality keep the building standing as a significant edifice within the campus. The building also has a lively roofscape that gives animation to its different sides and provides orientation on the campus.

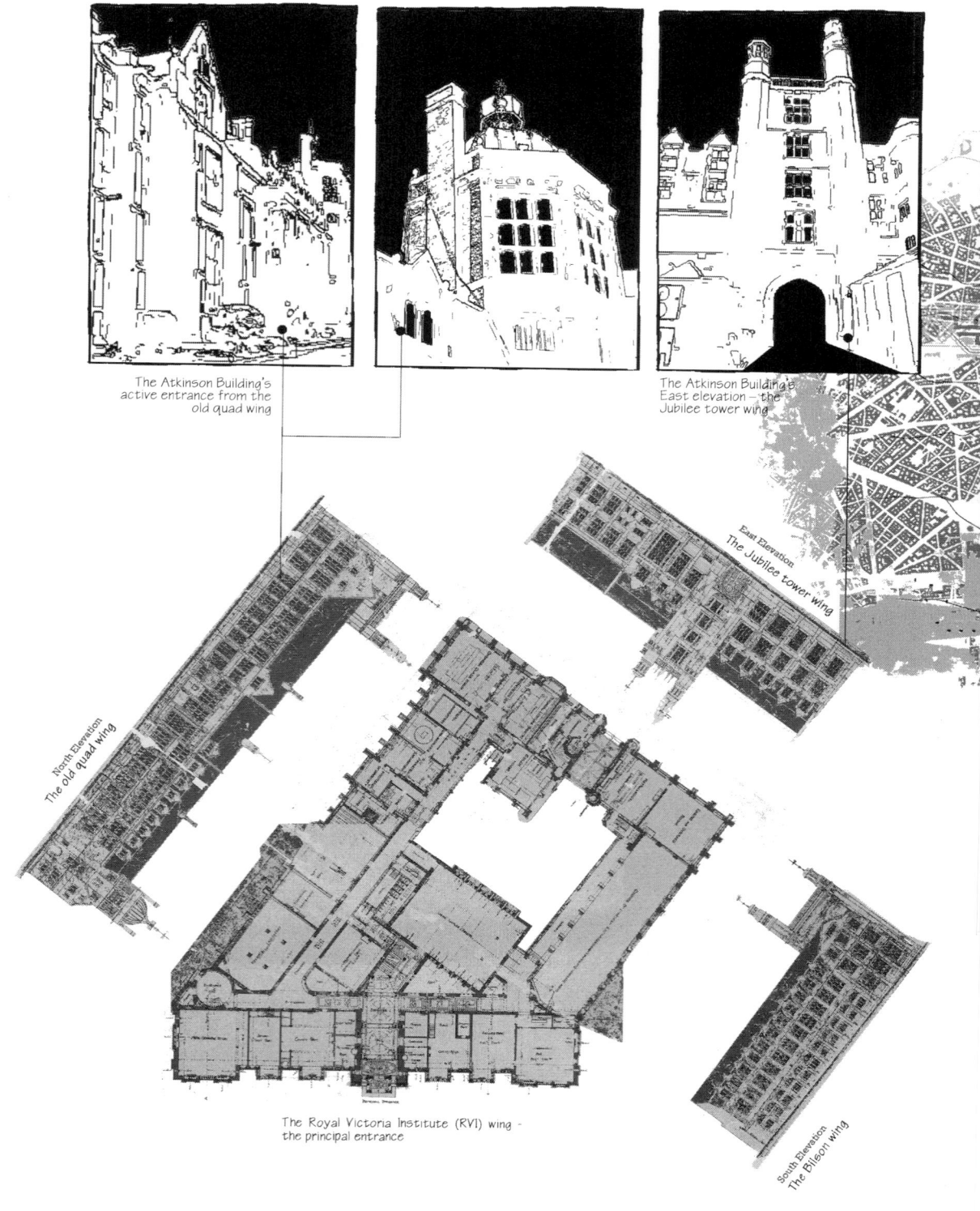

The Atkinson Building's
active entrance from the
old quad wing

The Atkinson Building's
East elevation – the
Jubilee tower wing

East Elevation
The Jubilee tower wing

North Elevation
The old quad wing

The Royal Victoria Institute (RVI) wing –
the principal entrance

South Elevation
The Bilson wing

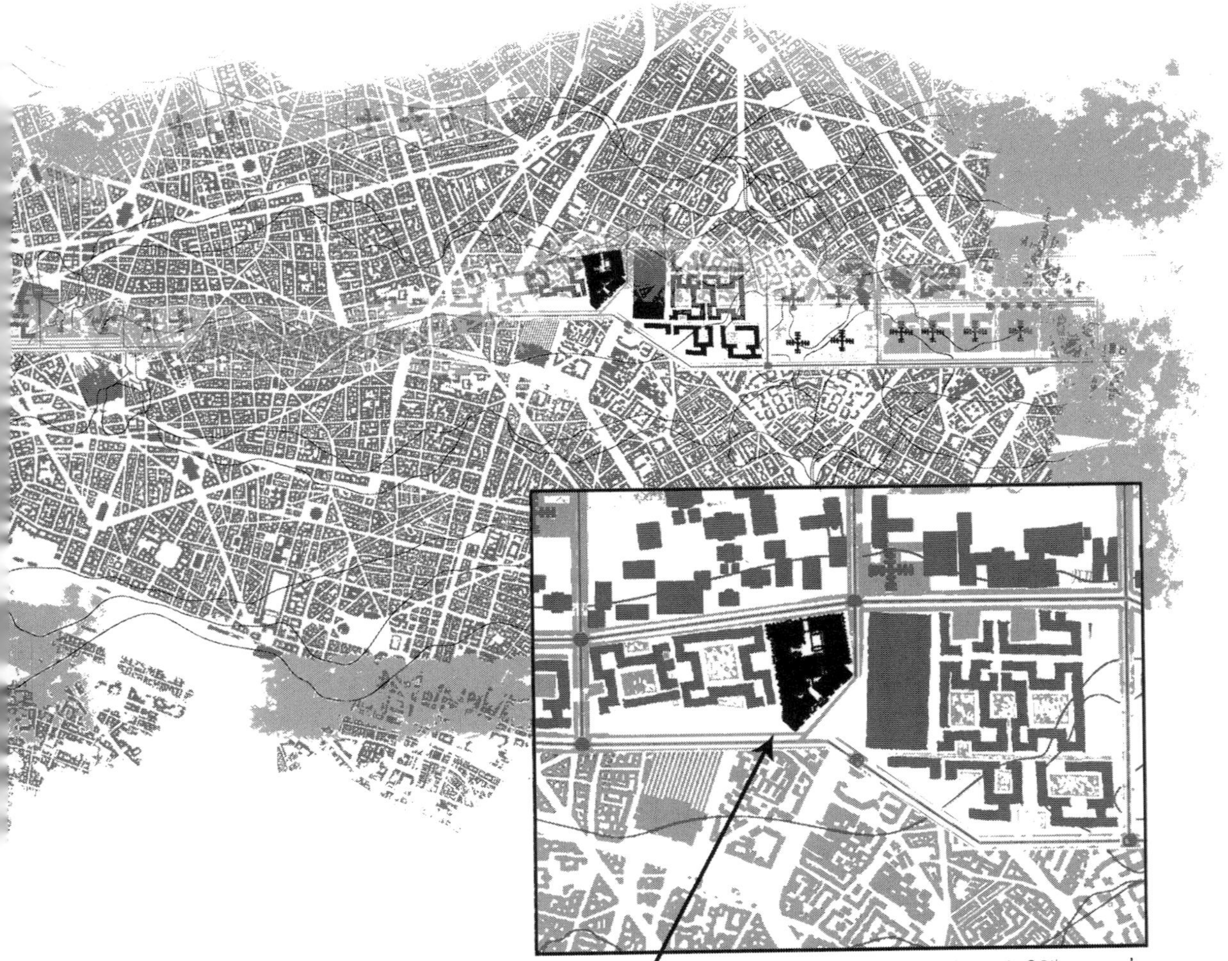

THE Atkinson Building in the early 20th century's ARCHITECTOPOLIS

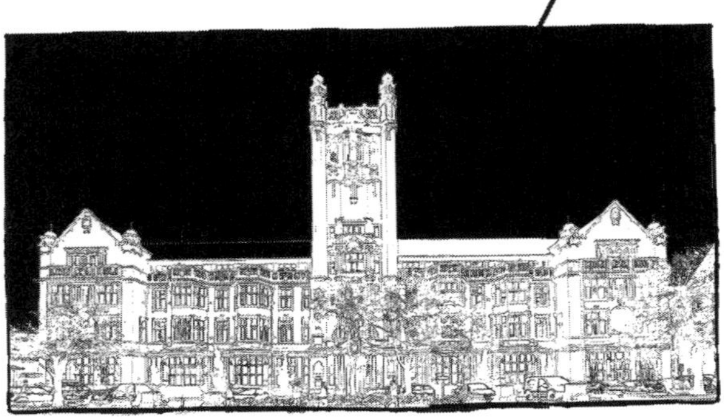

The Atkinson Building was built at the end of the new empire of Architectopolis. Its first three phases were finished by the first decade of the 20th century.

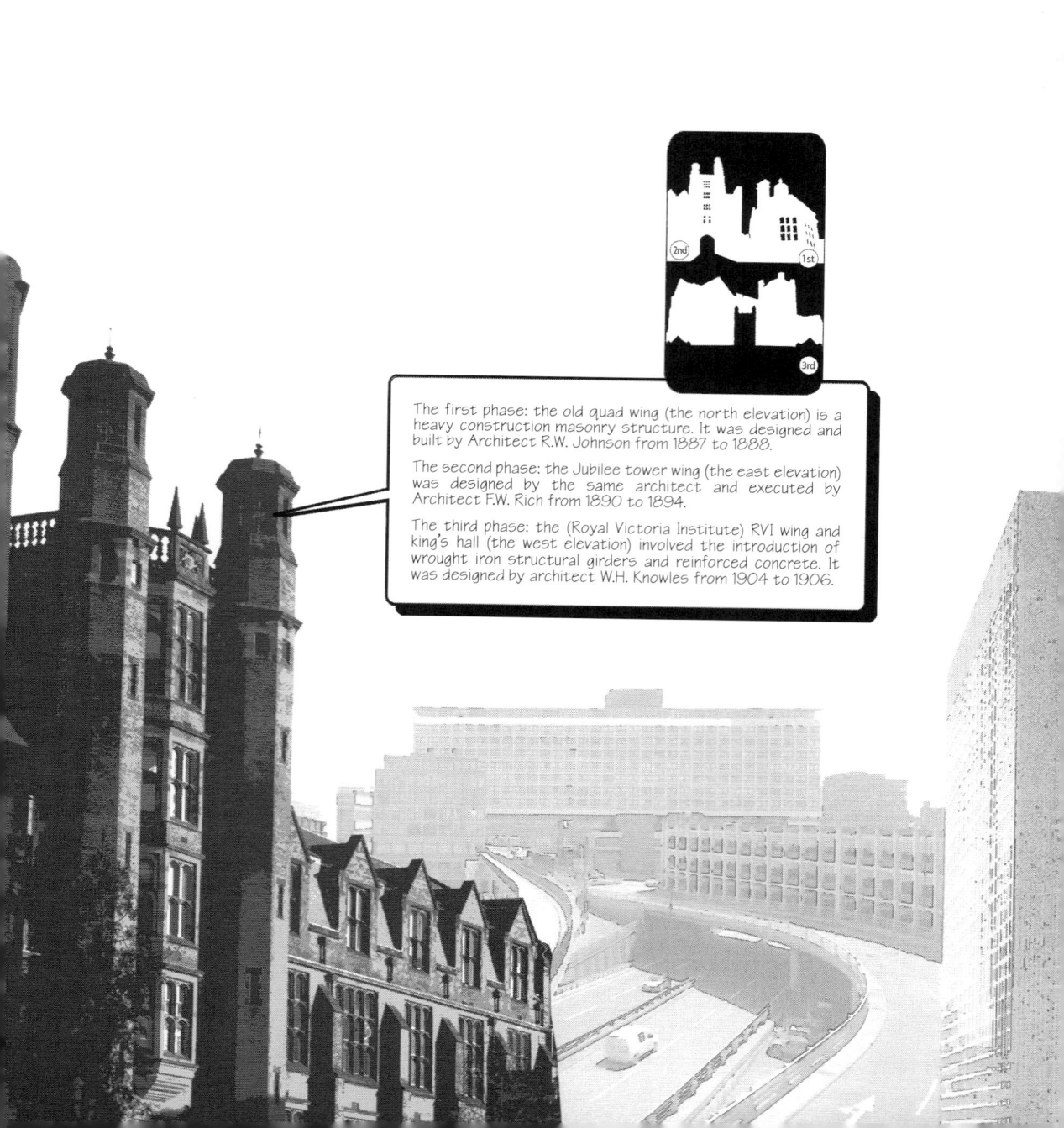

The first phase: the old quad wing (the north elevation) is a heavy construction masonry structure. It was designed and built by Architect R.W. Johnson from 1887 to 1888.

The second phase: the Jubilee tower wing (the east elevation) was designed by the same architect and executed by Architect F.W. Rich from 1890 to 1894.

The third phase: the (Royal Victoria Institute) RVI wing and king's hall (the west elevation) involved the introduction of wrought iron structural girders and reinforced concrete. It was designed by architect W.H. Knowles from 1904 to 1906.

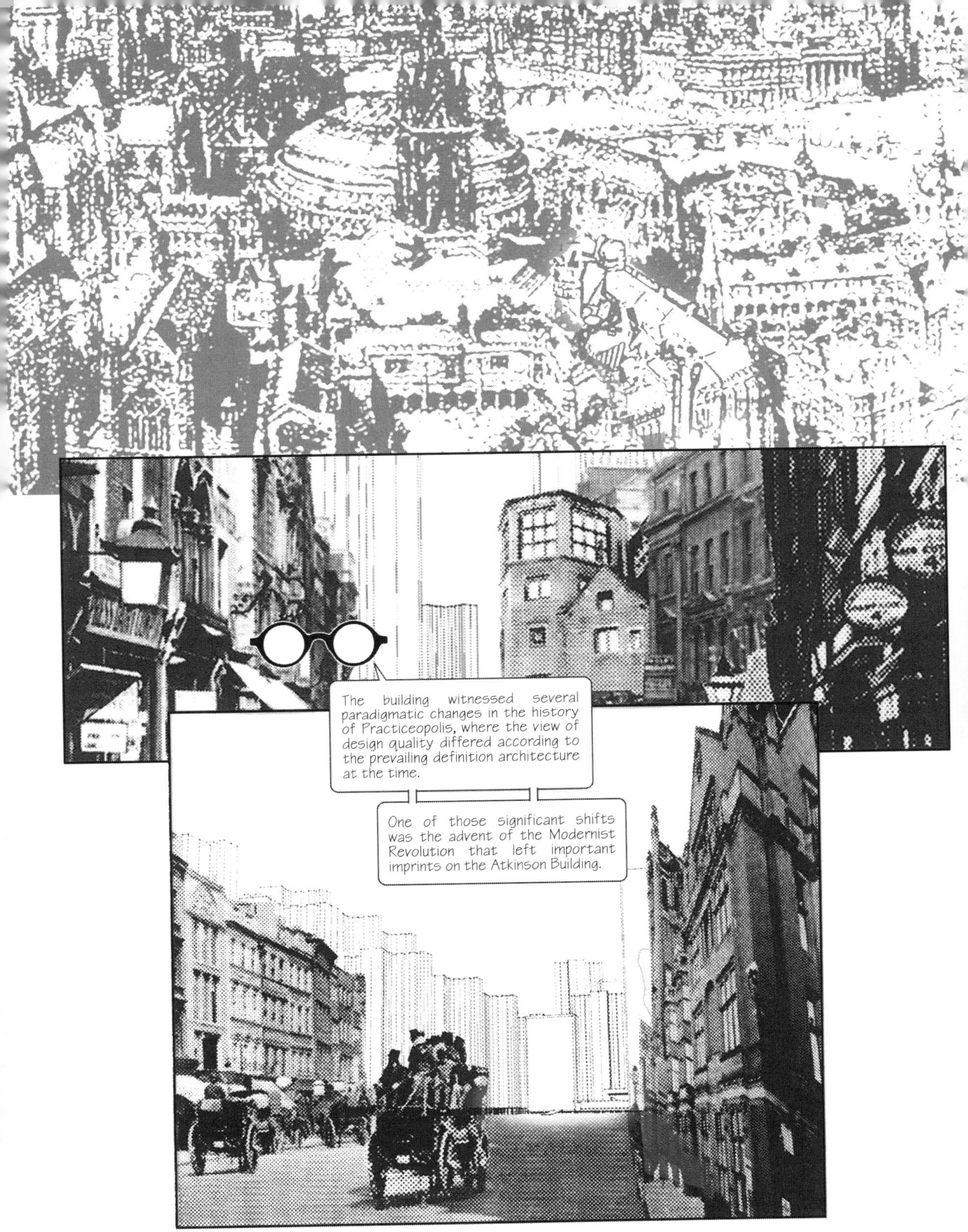
The building witnessed several paradigmatic changes in the history of Practiceopolis, where the view of design quality differed according to the prevailing definition architecture at the time.
One of those significant shifts was the advent of the Modernist Revolution that left important imprints on the Atkinson Building.

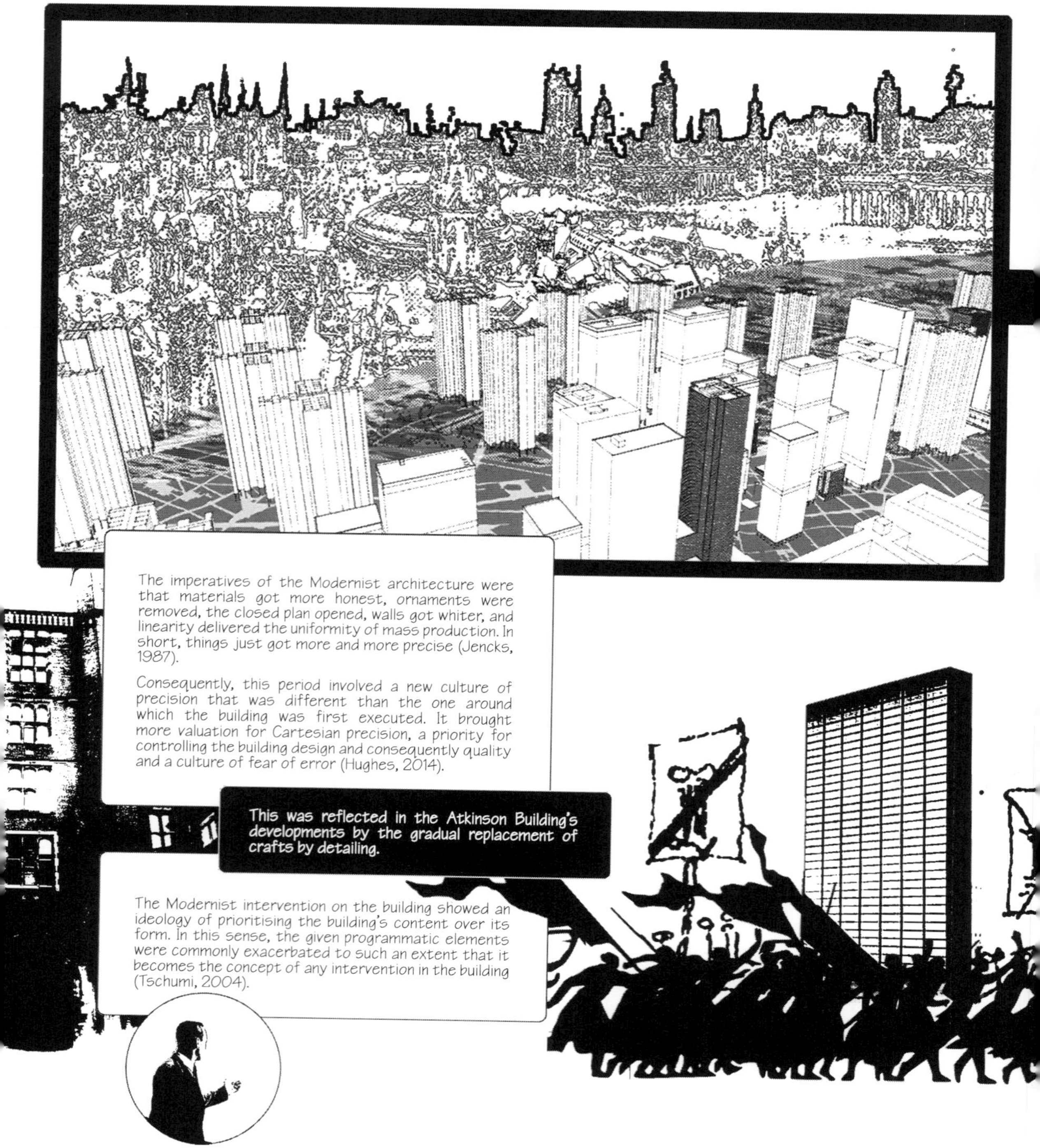
The imperatives of the Modernist architecture were that materials got more honest, ornaments were removed, the closed plan opened, walls got whiter, and linearity delivered the uniformity of mass production. In short, things just got more and more precise (Jencks, 1987).
Consequently, this period involved a new culture of precision that was different than the one around which the building was first executed. It brought more valuation for Cartesian precision, a priority for controlling the building design and consequently quality and a culture of fear of error (Hughes, 2014).
This was reflected in the Atkinson Building's developments by the gradual replacement of crafts by detailing.
The Modernist intervention on the building showed an ideology of prioritising the building's content over its form. In this sense, the given programmatic elements were commonly exacerbated to such an extent that it becomes the concept of any intervention in the building (Tschumi, 2004).

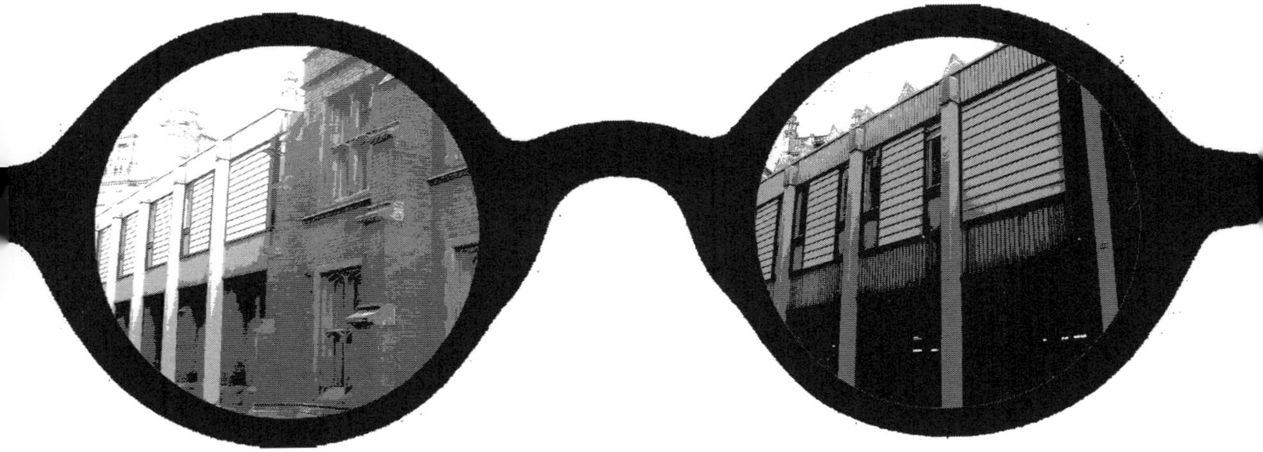

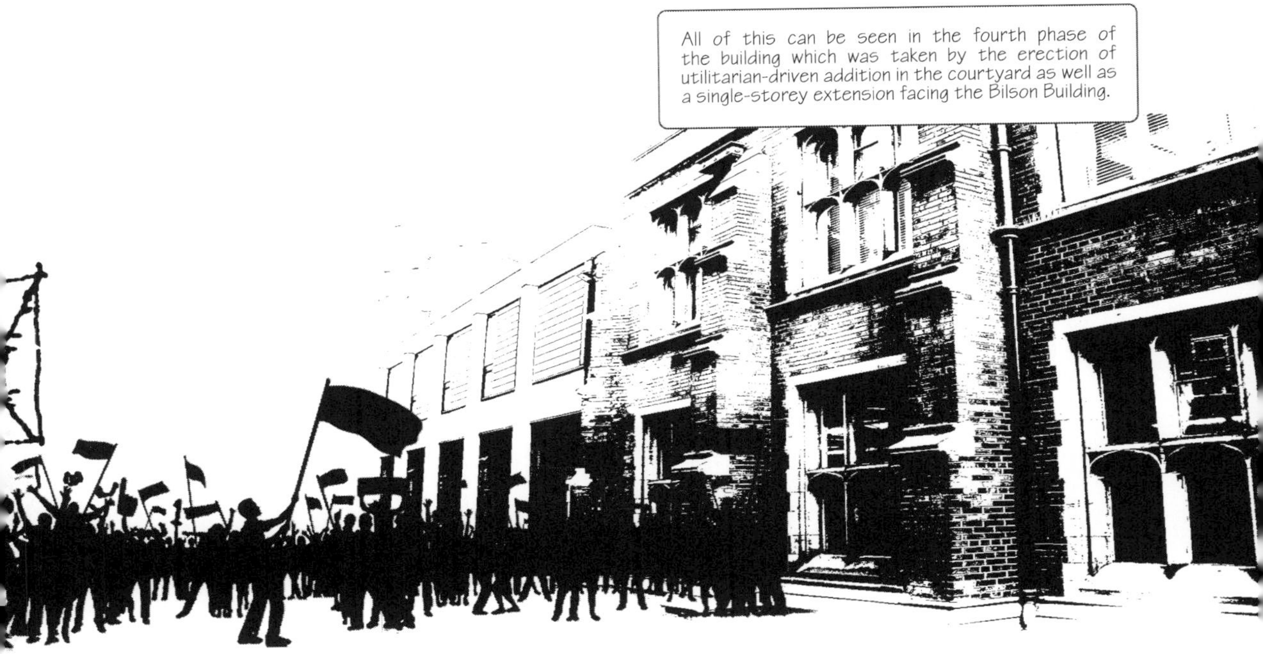
All of this can be seen in the fourth phase of the building which was taken by the erection of utilitarian-driven addition in the courtyard as well as a single-storey extension facing the Bilson Building.

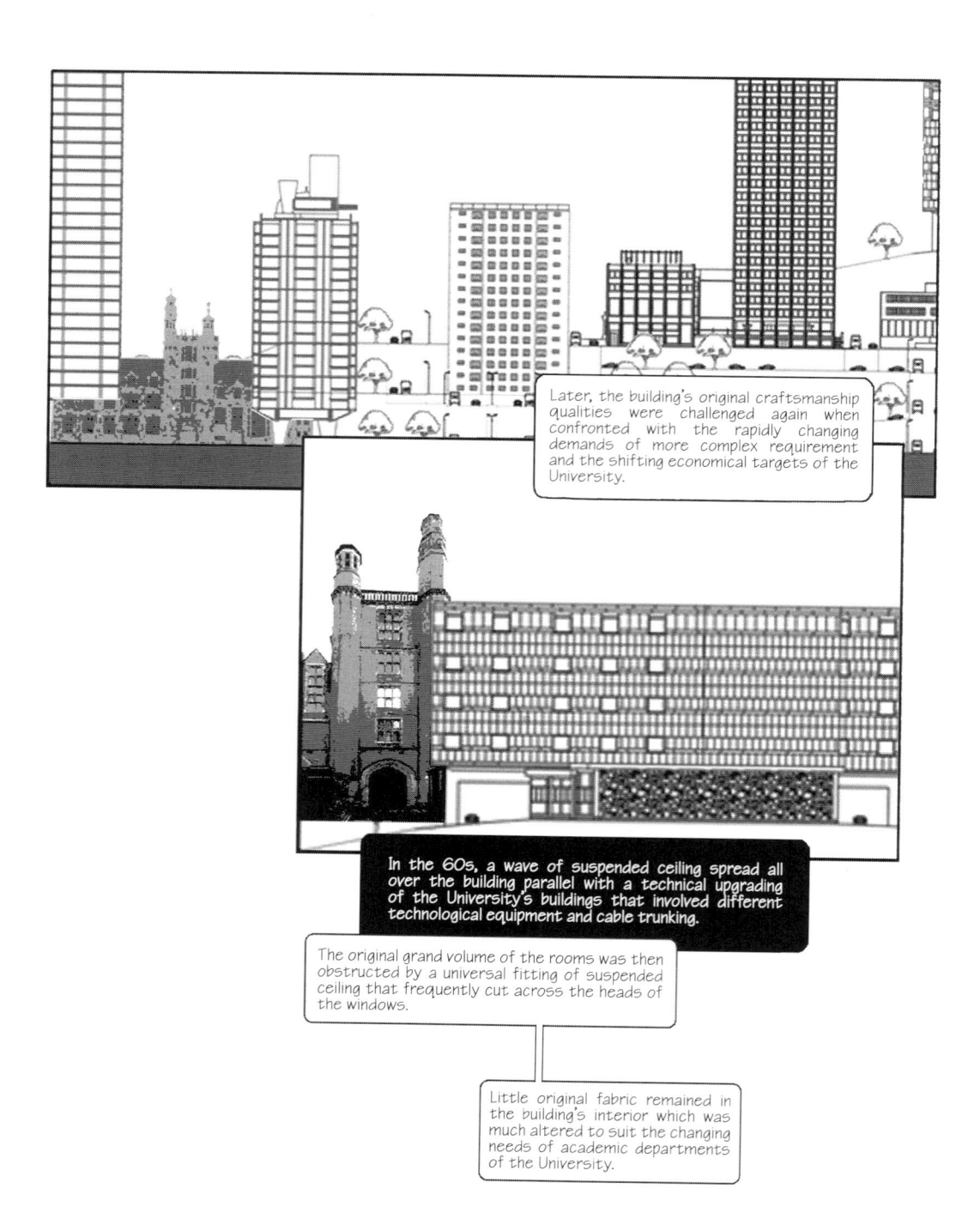

Later, the building's original craftsmanship qualities were challenged again when confronted with the rapidly changing demands of more complex requirement and the shifting economical targets of the University.

In the 60s, a wave of suspended ceiling spread all over the building parallel with a technical upgrading of the University's buildings that involved different technological equipment and cable trunking.

The original grand volume of the rooms was then obstructed by a universal fitting of suspended ceiling that frequently cut across the heads of the windows.

Little original fabric remained in the building's interior which was much altered to suit the changing needs of academic departments of the University.

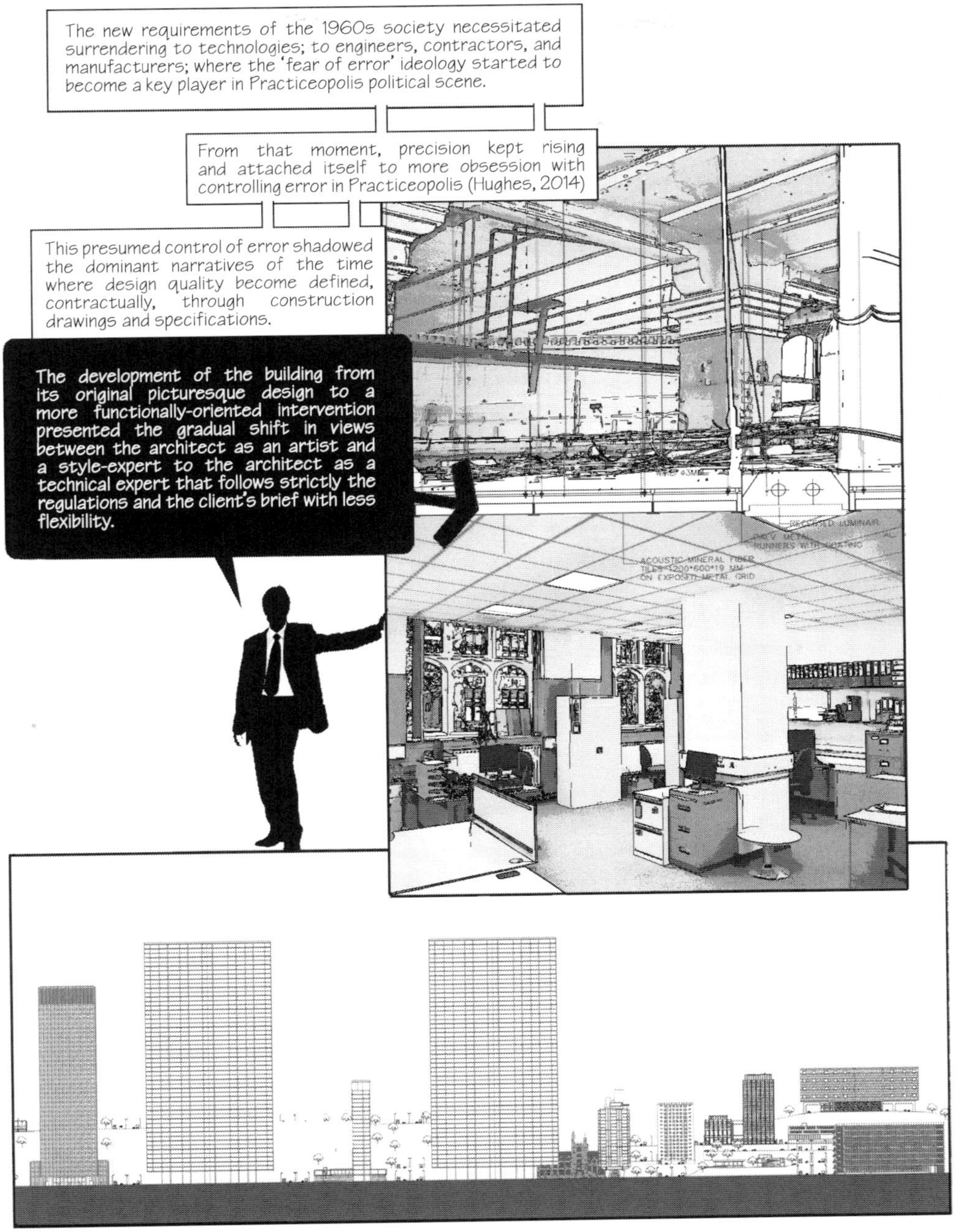
The new requirements of the 1960s society necessitated surrendering to technologies; to engineers, contractors, and manufacturers; where the 'fear of error' ideology started to become a key player in Practiceopolis political scene.
From that moment, precision kept rising and attached itself to more obsession with controlling error in Practiceopolis (Hughes, 2014)
This presumed control of error shadowed the dominant narratives of the time where design quality become defined, contractually, through construction drawings and specifications.
The development of the building from its original picturesque design to a more functionally-oriented intervention presented the gradual shift in views between the architect as an artist and a style-expert to the architect as a technical expert that follows strictly the regulations and the client's brief with less flexibility.

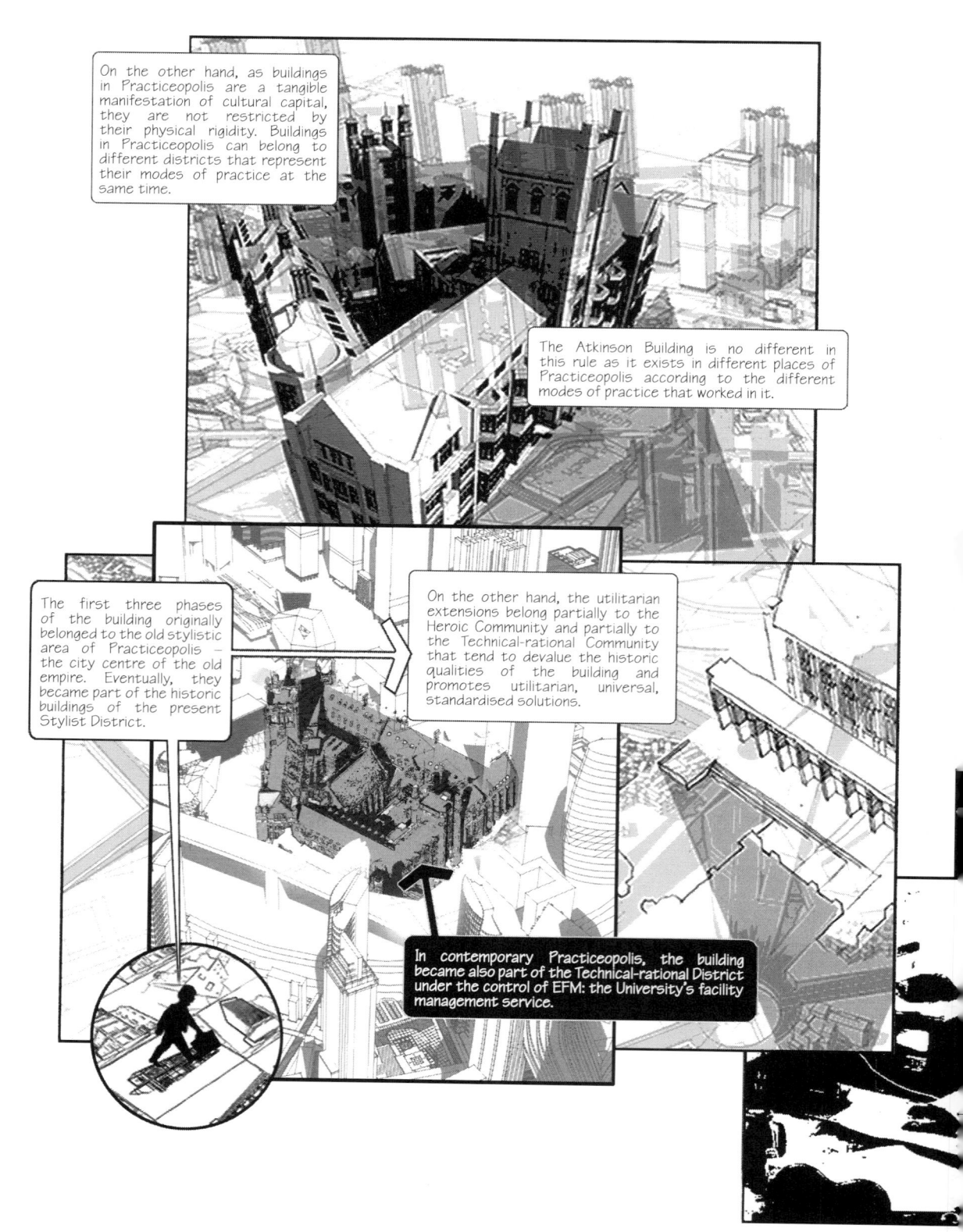

On the other hand, as buildings in Practiceopolis are a tangible manifestation of cultural capital, they are not restricted by their physical rigidity. Buildings in Practiceopolis can belong to different districts that represent their modes of practice at the same time.

The Atkinson Building is no different in this rule as it exists in different places of Practiceopolis according to the different modes of practice that worked in it.

The first three phases of the building originally belonged to the old stylistic area of Practiceopolis – the city centre of the old empire. Eventually, they became part of the historic buildings of the present Stylist District.

On the other hand, the utilitarian extensions belong partially to the Heroic Community and partially to the Technical-rational Community that tend to devalue the historic qualities of the building and promotes utilitarian, universal, standardised solutions.

In contemporary Practiceopolis, the building became also part of the Technical-rational District under the control of EFM: the University's facility management service.

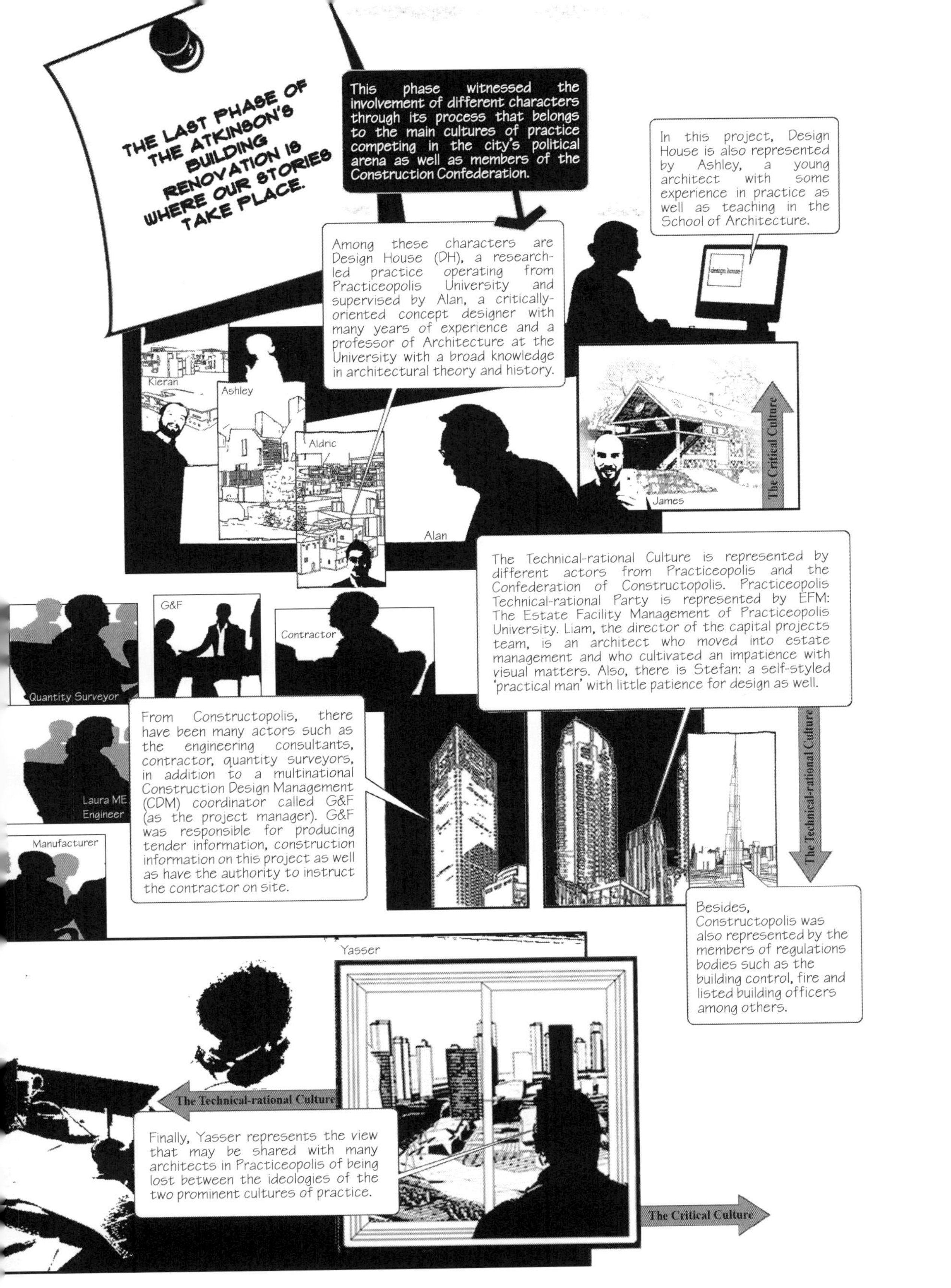
THE LAST PHASE OF THE ATKINSON'S BUILDING RENOVATION IS WHERE OUR STORIES TAKE PLACE.
This phase witnessed the involvement of different characters through its process that belongs to the main cultures of practice competing in the city's political arena as well as members of the Construction Confederation.
Among these characters are Design House (DH), a research-led practice operating from Practiceopolis University and supervised by Alan, a critically-oriented concept designer with many years of experience and a professor of Architecture at the University with a broad knowledge in architectural theory and history.
In this project, Design House is also represented by Ashley, a young architect with some experience in practice as well as teaching in the School of Architecture.
design house
Kieran
Ashley
Aldric
Alan
James
The Critical Culture
The Technical-rational Culture is represented by different actors from Practiceopolis and the Confederation of Constructopolis. Practiceopolis Technical-rational Party is represented by EFM: The Estate Facility Management of Practiceopolis University. Liam, the director of the capital projects team, is an architect who moved into estate management and who cultivated an impatience with visual matters. Also, there is Stefan: a self-styled 'practical man' with little patience for design as well.
G&F
Contractor
Quantity Surveyor
Laura ME Engineer
Manufacturer
From Constructopolis, there have been many actors such as the engineering consultants, contractor, quantity surveyors, in addition to a multinational Construction Design Management (CDM) coordinator called G&F (as the project manager). G&F was responsible for producing tender information, construction information on this project as well as have the authority to instruct the contractor on site.
The Technical-rational Culture
Besides, Constructopolis was also represented by the members of regulations bodies such as the building control, fire and listed building officers among others.
Yasser
The Technical-rational Culture
Finally, Yasser represents the view that may be shared with many architects in Practiceopolis of being lost between the ideologies of the two prominent cultures of practice.
The Critical Culture

THE TECHNICAL-RATIONALS

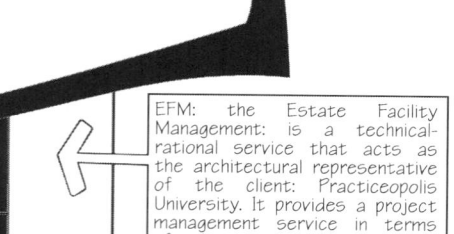

Liam

EFM: the Estate Facility Management: is a technical-rational service that acts as the architectural representative of the client: Practiceopolis University. It provides a project management service in terms of advice and management for major projects from the initial brief, through the design process, procurement and delivery on site.

Stefan

Also, there is Stefan: a self-styled 'practical man' with little patience for design but cares for buildability. He is assigned as the direct project manager of the Atkinson project.

Liam is the director of the Central Projects Team of EFM. He is an experienced architect who moved into estate management and has cultivated an impatience with visual and spatial matters.

BIM - THE FUTURE
THE ANSWER IS LEED
CONTRACTS

EFM

EFM HEADQUARTERS

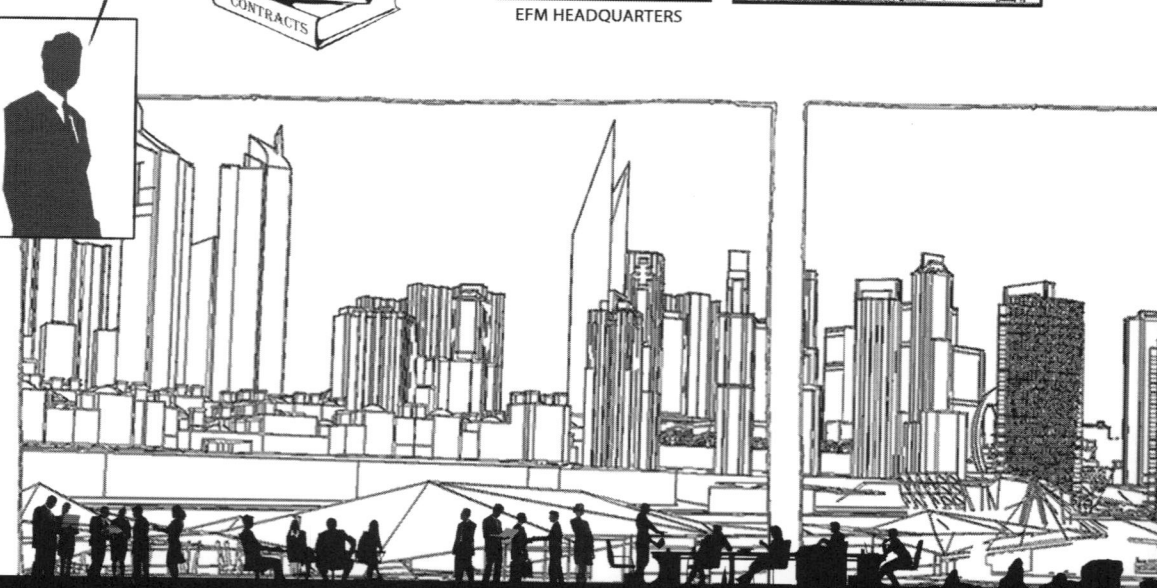

EFM is located in Practiceopolis in Technical-rational quarter overlooking one of the most prime areas in Practiceopolis city centre: the CAD/BIM square. It also belongs to the powerful political party of the Technical-rationals in Practiceopolis Parliament.

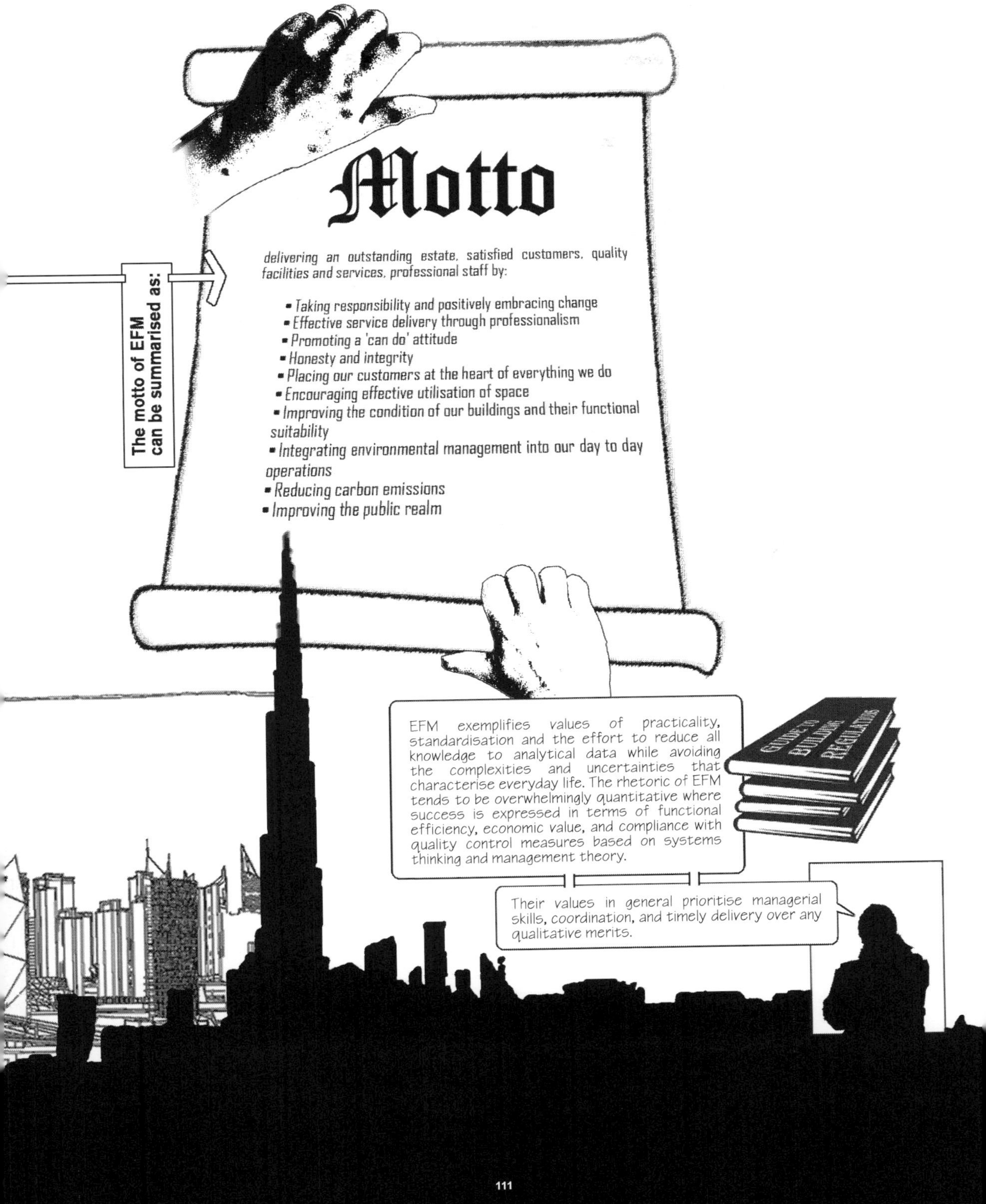
The motto of EFM can be summarised as:
Motto
delivering an outstanding estate, satisfied customers, quality facilities and services, professional staff by:
• Taking responsibility and positively embracing change
• Effective service delivery through professionalism
• Promoting a 'can do' attitude
• Honesty and integrity
• Placing our customers at the heart of everything we do
• Encouraging effective utilisation of space
• Improving the condition of our buildings and their functional suitability
• Integrating environmental management into our day to day operations
• Reducing carbon emissions
• Improving the public realm
EFM exemplifies values of practicality, standardisation and the effort to reduce all knowledge to analytical data while avoiding the complexities and uncertainties that characterise everyday life. The rhetoric of EFM tends to be overwhelmingly quantitative where success is expressed in terms of functional efficiency, economic value, and compliance with quality control measures based on systems thinking and management theory.
GUIDE TO BUILDING REGULATIONS
Their values in general prioritise managerial skills, coordination, and timely delivery over any qualitative merits.

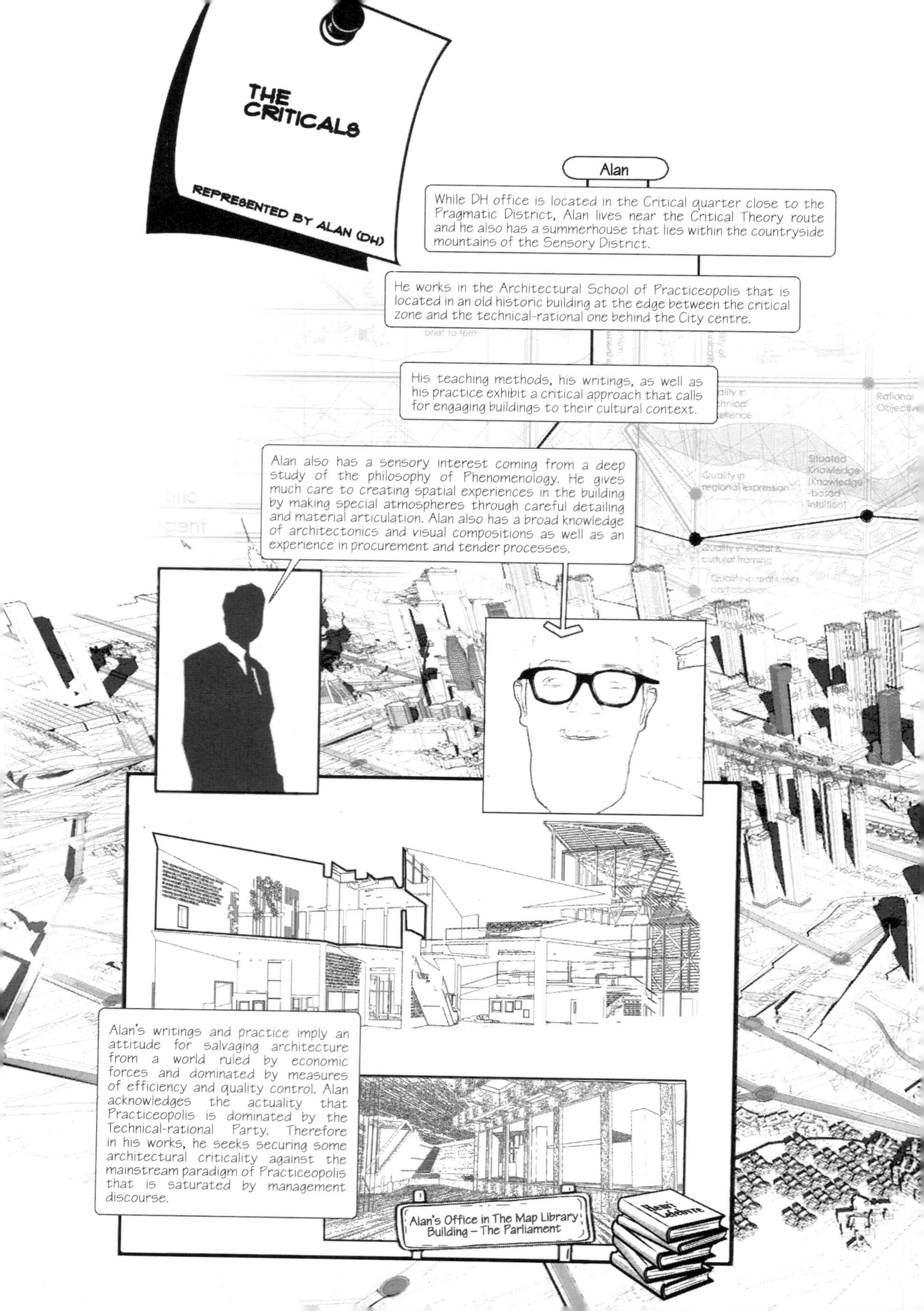
THE CRITICALS
REPRESENTED BY ALAN (DH)
Alan
While DH office is located in the Critical quarter close to the Pragmatic District, Alan lives near the Critical Theory route and he also has a summerhouse that lies within the countryside mountains of the Sensory District.
He works in the Architectural School of Practiceopolis that is located in an old historic building at the edge between the critical zone and the technical-rational one behind the City centre.
His teaching methods, his writings, as well as his practice exhibit a critical approach that calls for engaging buildings to their cultural context.
Alan also has a sensory interest coming from a deep study of the philosophy of Phenomenology. He gives much care to creating spatial experiences in the building by making special atmospheres through careful detailing and material articulation. Alan also has a broad knowledge of architectonics and visual compositions as well as an experience in procurement and tender processes.
Alan's writings and practice imply an attitude for salvaging architecture from a world ruled by economic forces and dominated by measures of efficiency and quality control. Alan acknowledges the actuality that Practiceopolis is dominated by the Technical-rational Party. Therefore in his works, he seeks securing some architectural criticality against the mainstream paradigm of Practiceopolis that is saturated by management discourse.
Alan's Office in The Map Library Building – The Parliament
Henri Lefebvre

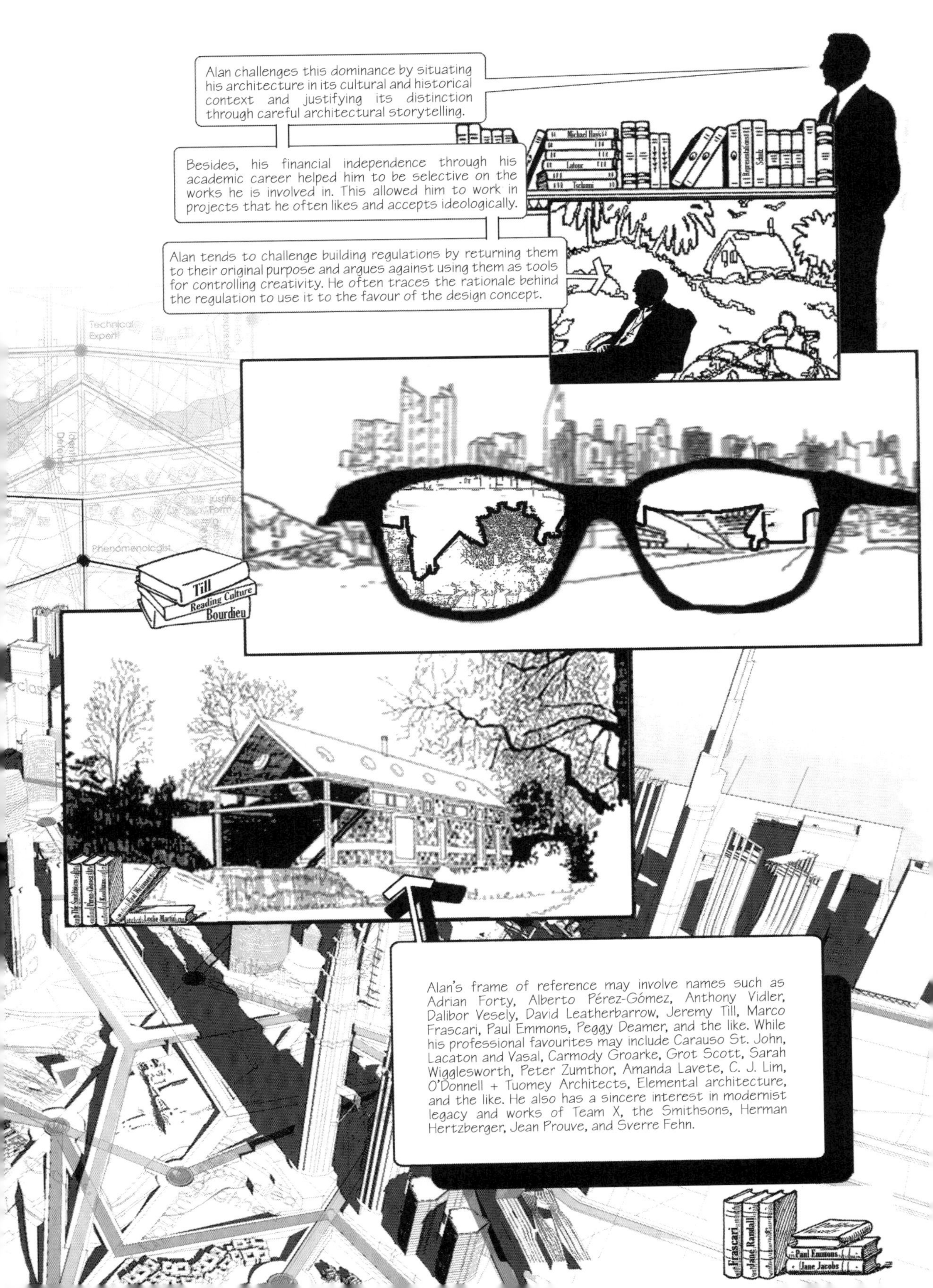
Alan challenges this dominance by situating his architecture in its cultural and historical context and justifying its distinction through careful architectural storytelling.
Besides, his financial independence through his academic career helped him to be selective on the works he is involved in. This allowed him to work in projects that he often likes and accepts ideologically.
Alan tends to challenge building regulations by returning them to their original purpose and argues against using them as tools for controlling creativity. He often traces the rationale behind the regulation to use it to the favour of the design concept.
Alan's frame of reference may involve names such as Adrian Forty, Alberto Pérez-Gómez, Anthony Vidler, Dalibor Vesely, David Leatherbarrow, Jeremy Till, Marco Frascari, Paul Emmons, Peggy Deamer, and the like. While his professional favourites may include Carauso St. John, Lacaton and Vasal, Carmody Groarke, Grot Scott, Sarah Wigglesworth, Peter Zumthor, Amanda Lavete, C. J. Lim, O'Donnell + Tuomey Architects, Elemental architecture, and the like. He also has a sincere interest in modernist legacy and works of Team X, the Smithsons, Herman Hertzberger, Jean Prouve, and Sverre Fehn.
Michael Hays
Latour
Tschumi
Schulz
Technical Expert
Phenomenologist
Till
Reading Culture
Bourdieu
Leslie Martin
Frascari
Paul Emmons
Jane Jacobs

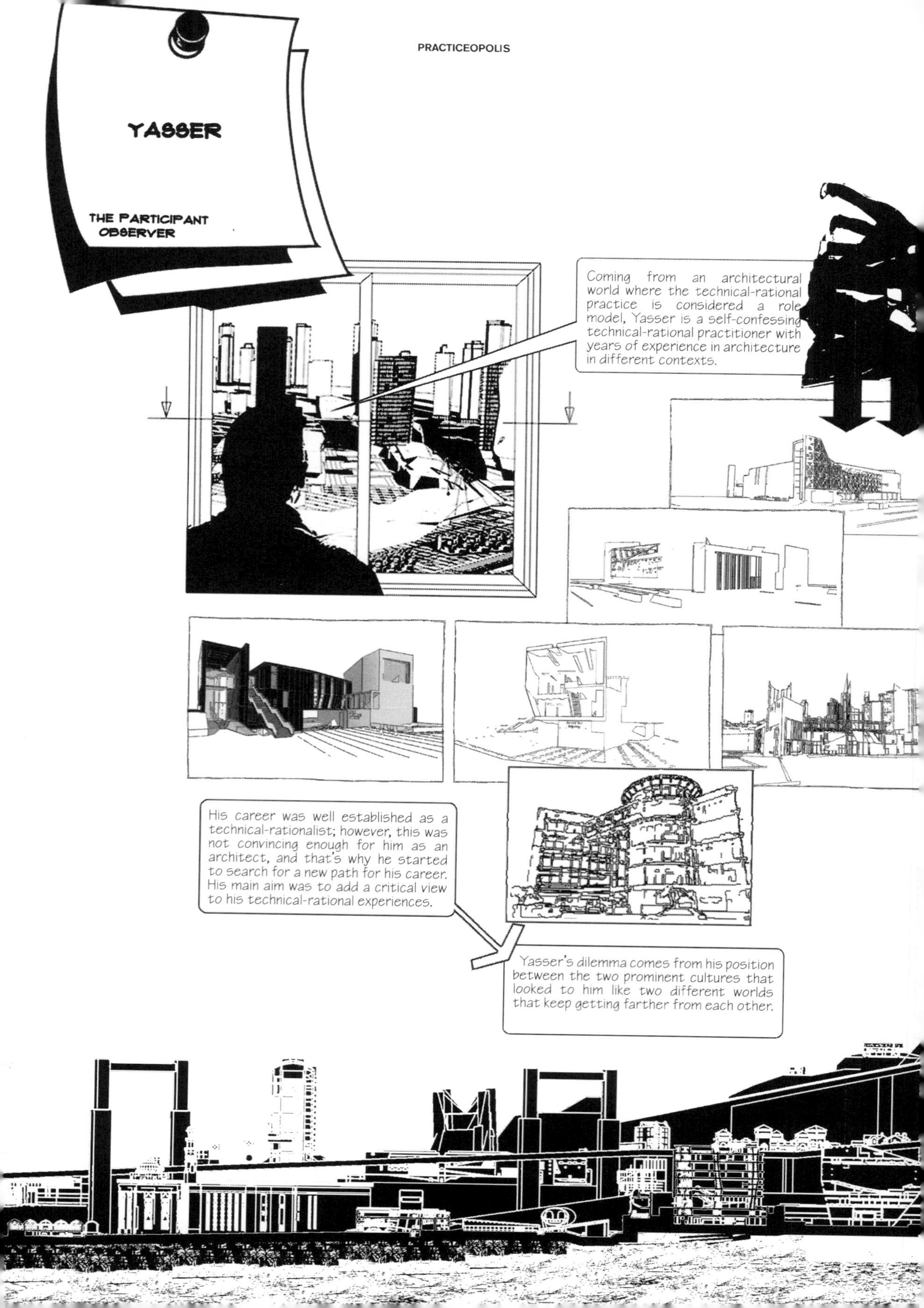
YASSER
THE PARTICIPANT OBSERVER
Coming from an architectural world where the technical-rational practice is considered a role model, Yasser is a self-confessing technical-rational practitioner with years of experience in architecture in different contexts.
His career was well established as a technical-rationalist; however, this was not convincing enough for him as an architect, and that's why he started to search for a new path for his career. His main aim was to add a critical view to his technical-rational experiences.
Yasser's dilemma comes from his position between the two prominent cultures that looked to him like two different worlds that keep getting farther from each other.

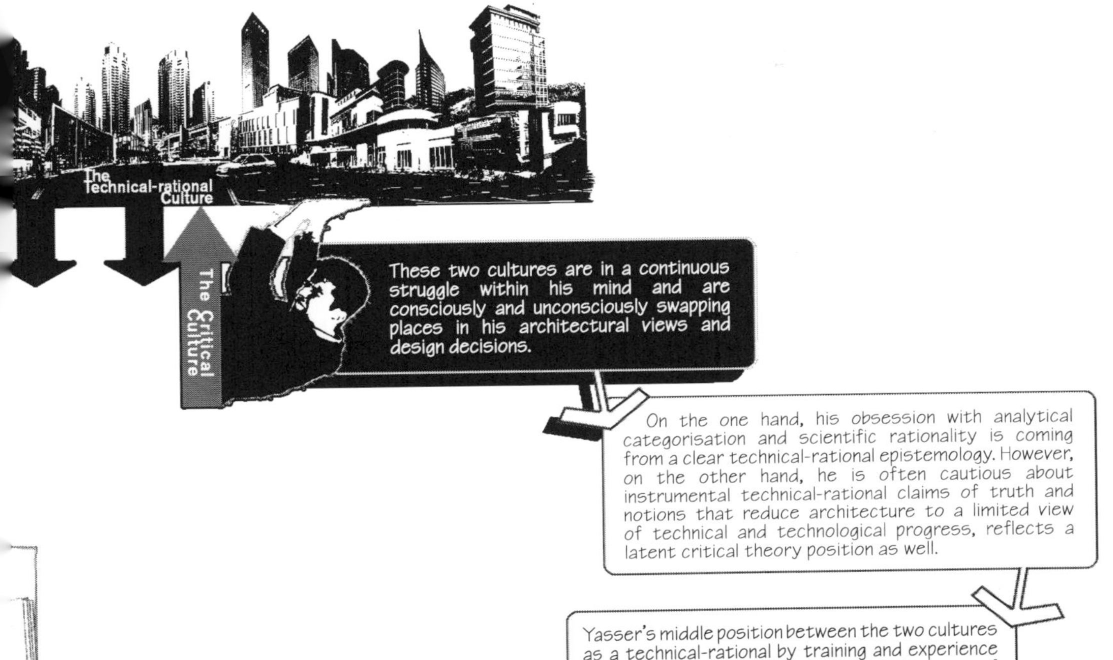
The Technical-rational Culture
The Critical Culture
These two cultures are in a continuous struggle within his mind and are consciously and unconsciously swapping places in his architectural views and design decisions.

On the one hand, his obsession with analytical categorisation and scientific rationality is coming from a clear technical-rational epistemology. However, on the other hand, he is often cautious about instrumental technical-rational claims of truth and notions that reduce architecture to a limited view of technical and technological progress, reflects a latent critical theory position as well.

Yasser's middle position between the two cultures as a technical-rational by training and experience and also as one of the members of the team of Design House gave him a semi-objective angle to his views on architecture and hence helped him to allocate himself in Practiceopolis more accurately.

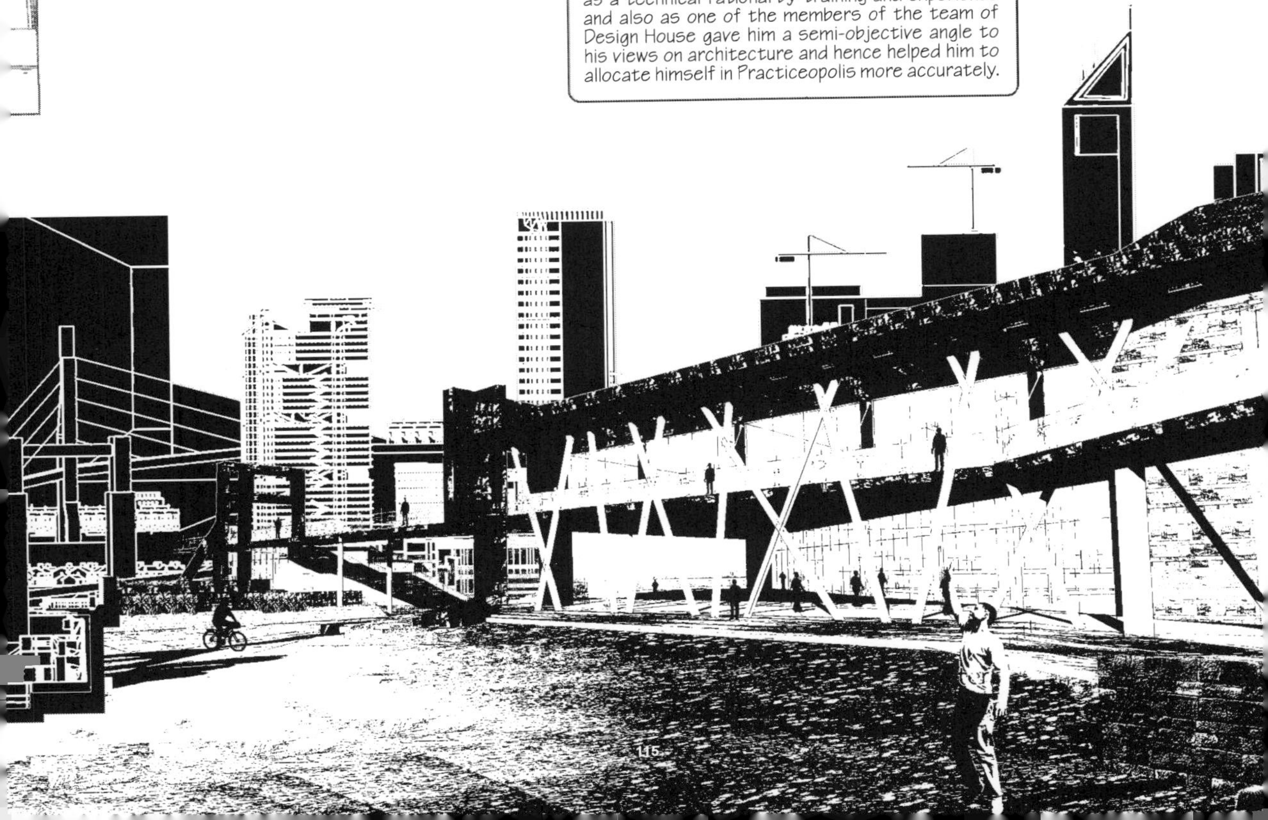

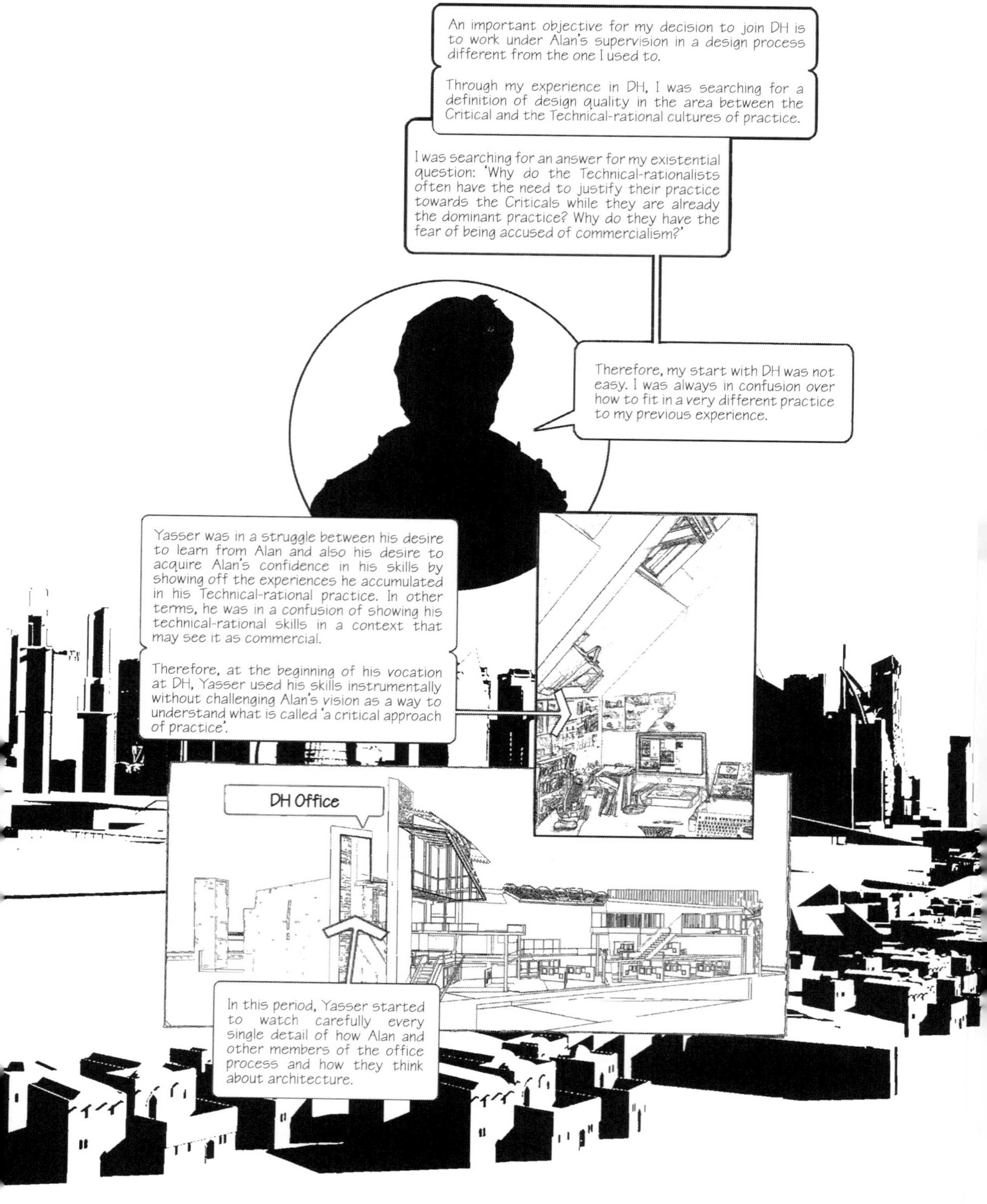
An important objective for my decision to join DH is to work under Alan's supervision in a design process different from the one I used to.
Through my experience in DH, I was searching for a definition of design quality in the area between the Critical and the Technical-rational cultures of practice.
I was searching for an answer for my existential question: 'Why do the Technical-rationalists often have the need to justify their practice towards the Criticals while they are already the dominant practice? Why do they have the fear of being accused of commercialism?'
Therefore, my start with DH was not easy. I was always in confusion over how to fit in a very different practice to my previous experience.
Yasser was in a struggle between his desire to learn from Alan and also his desire to acquire Alan's confidence in his skills by showing off the experiences he accumulated in his Technical-rational practice. In other terms, he was in a confusion of showing his technical-rational skills in a context that may see it as commercial.
Therefore, at the beginning of his vocation at DH, Yasser used his skills instrumentally without challenging Alan's vision as a way to understand what is called 'a critical approach of practice'.
DH Office
In this period, Yasser started to watch carefully every single detail of how Alan and other members of the office process and how they think about architecture.

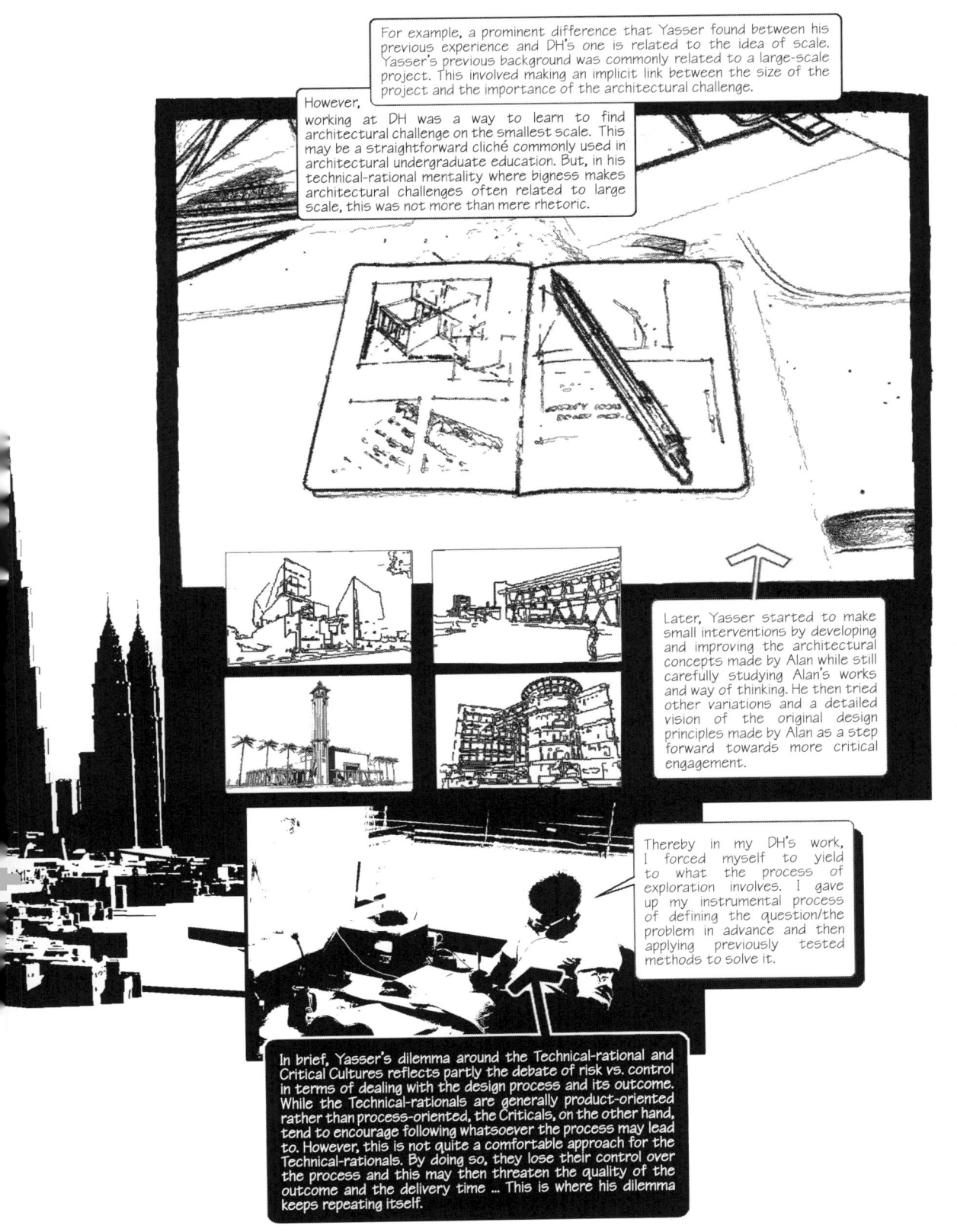

For example, a prominent difference that Yasser found between his previous experience and DH's one is related to the idea of scale. Yasser's previous background was commonly related to a large-scale project. This involved making an implicit link between the size of the project and the importance of the architectural challenge.

However, working at DH was a way to learn to find architectural challenge on the smallest scale. This may be a straightforward cliché commonly used in architectural undergraduate education. But, in his technical-rational mentality where bigness makes architectural challenges often related to large scale, this was not more than mere rhetoric.

Later, Yasser started to make small interventions by developing and improving the architectural concepts made by Alan while still carefully studying Alan's works and way of thinking. He then tried other variations and a detailed vision of the original design principles made by Alan as a step forward towards more critical engagement.

Thereby in my DH's work, I forced myself to yield to what the process of exploration involves. I gave up my instrumental process of defining the question/the problem in advance and then applying previously tested methods to solve it.

In brief, Yasser's dilemma around the Technical-rational and Critical Cultures reflects partly the debate of risk vs. control in terms of dealing with the design process and its outcome. While the Technical-rationals are generally product-oriented rather than process-oriented, the Criticals, on the other hand, tend to encourage following whatsoever the process may lead to. However, this is not quite a comfortable approach for the Technical-rationals. By doing so, they lose their control over the process and this may then threaten the quality of the outcome and the delivery time ... This is where his dilemma keeps repeating itself.

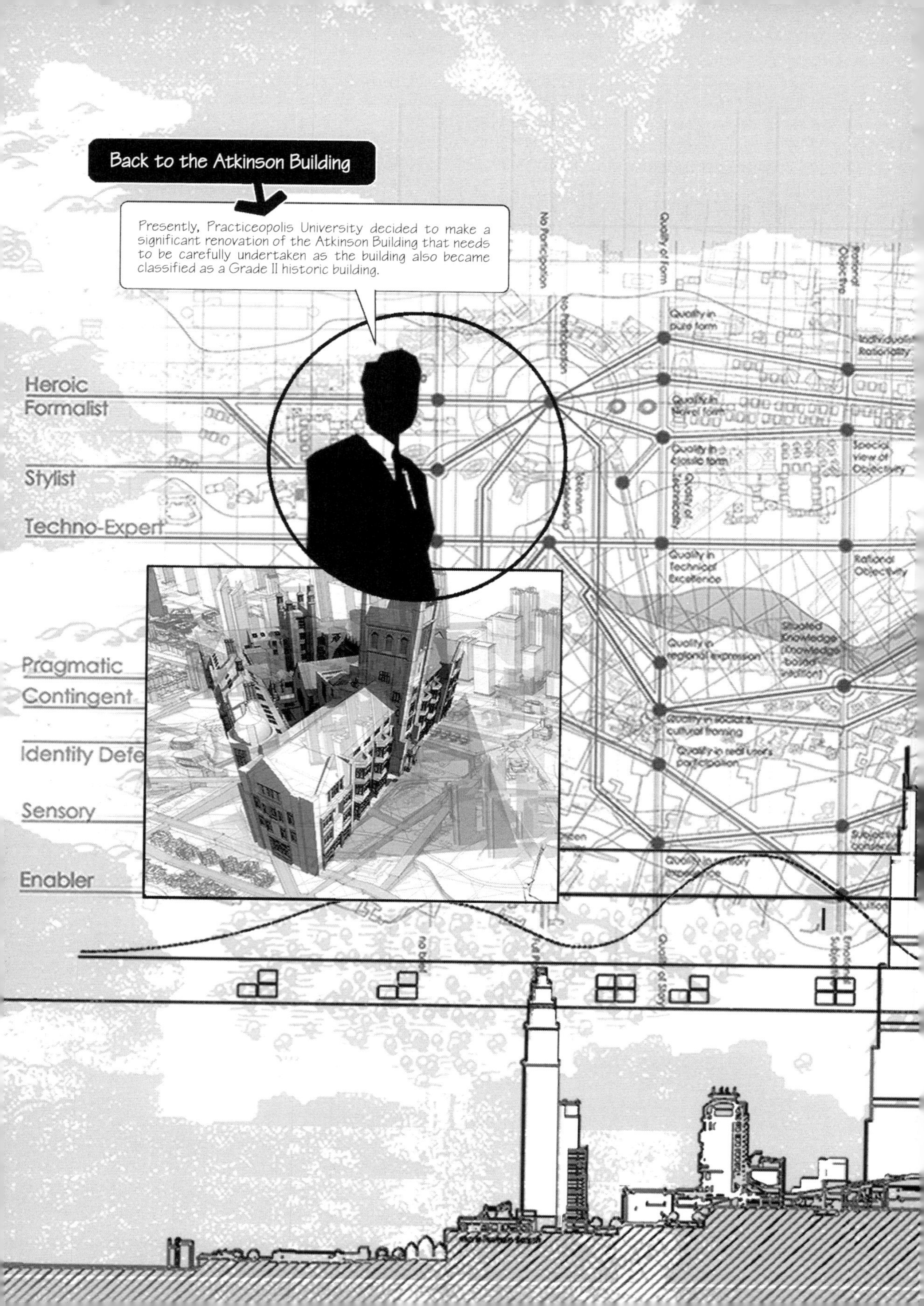

Back to the Atkinson Building
Presently, Practiceopolis University decided to make a significant renovation of the Atkinson Building that needs to be carefully undertaken as the building also became classified as a Grade II historic building.
Heroic
Formalist
Stylist
Techno-Expert
Pragmatic
Contingent
Sensory
Enabler
No Participation
Quality of form
Quality in pure form
Quality in classic form
Quality in Technical Excellence
Quality in regional expression
Quality in social & cultural framing
Quality in real user's participation
Rational Objectivity
Social view of Objectivity

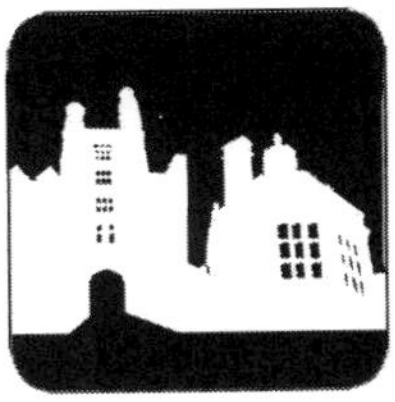

RENOVATING THE ATKINSON BUILDING

The Commission

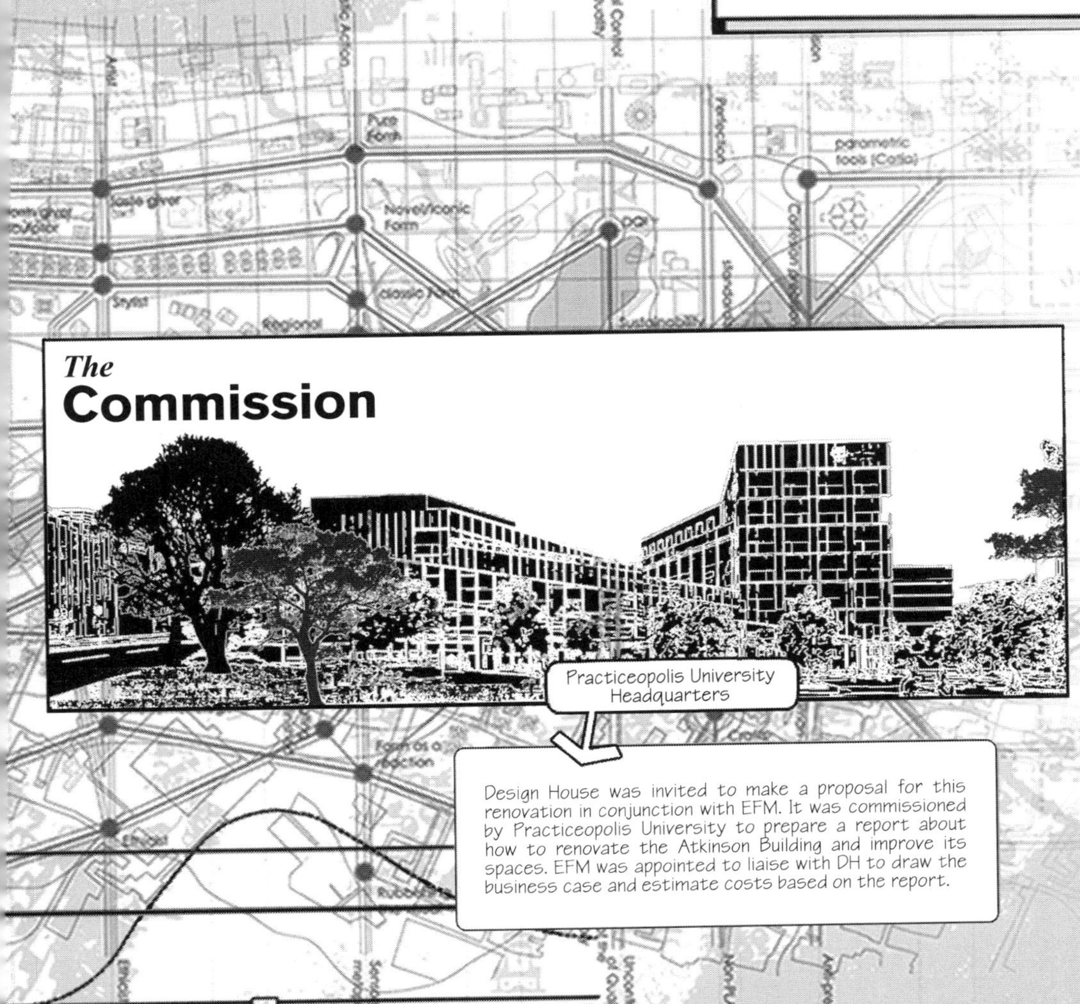
Practiceopolis University Headquarters

Design House was invited to make a proposal for this renovation in conjunction with EFM. It was commissioned by Practiceopolis University to prepare a report about how to renovate the Atkinson Building and improve its spaces. EFM was appointed to liaise with DH to draw the business case and estimate costs based on the report.

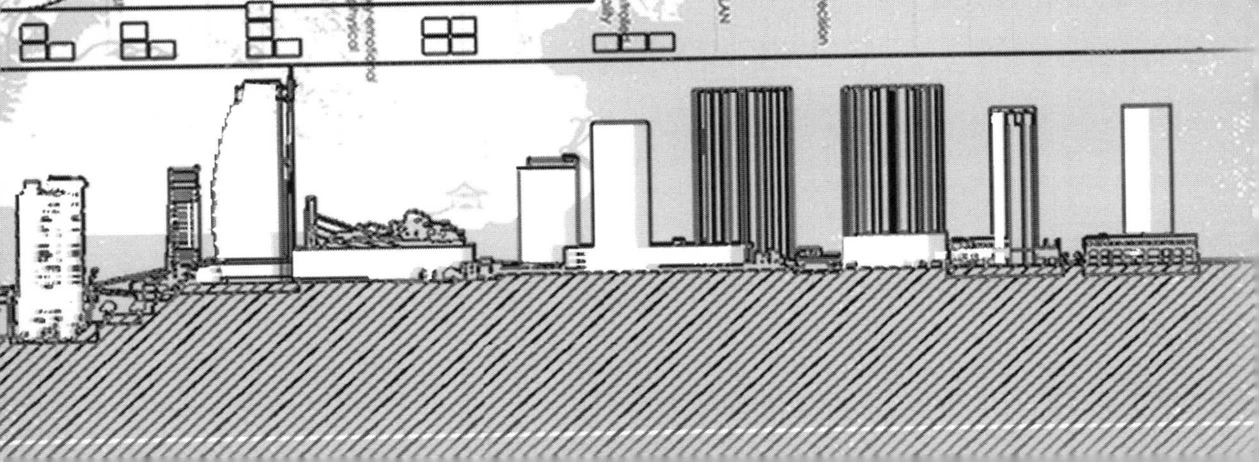

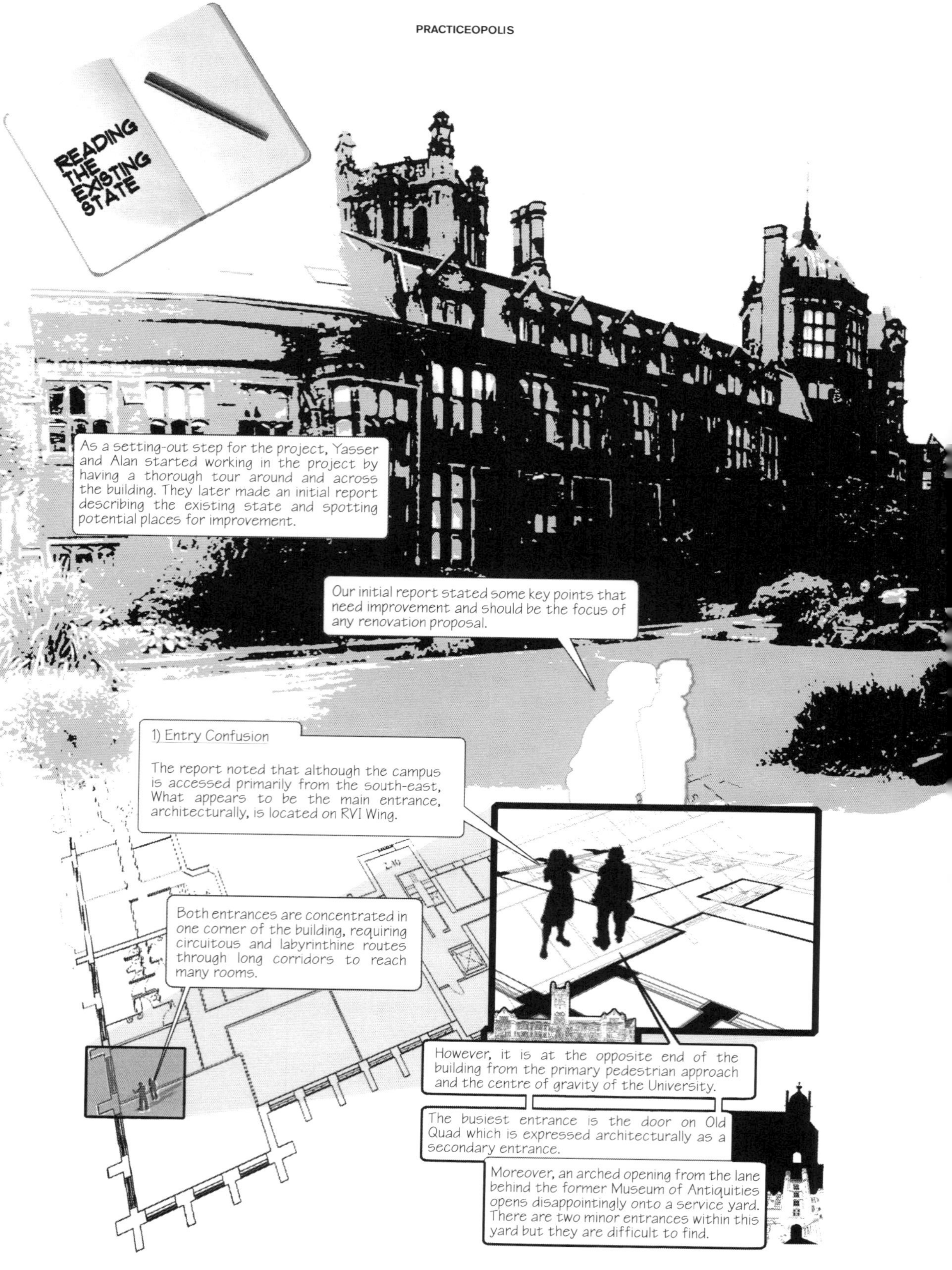

READING THE EXISTING STATE
As a setting-out step for the project, Yasser and Alan started working in the project by having a thorough tour around and across the building. They later made an initial report describing the existing state and spotting potential places for improvement.
Our initial report stated some key points that need improvement and should be the focus of any renovation proposal.
1) Entry Confusion
The report noted that although the campus is accessed primarily from the south-east, What appears to be the main entrance, architecturally, is located on RVI Wing.
Both entrances are concentrated in one corner of the building, requiring circuitous and labyrinthine routes through long corridors to reach many rooms.
However, it is at the opposite end of the building from the primary pedestrian approach and the centre of gravity of the University.
The busiest entrance is the door on Old Quad which is expressed architecturally as a secondary entrance.
Moreover, an arched opening from the lane behind the former Museum of Antiquities opens disappointingly onto a service yard. There are two minor entrances within this yard but they are difficult to find.

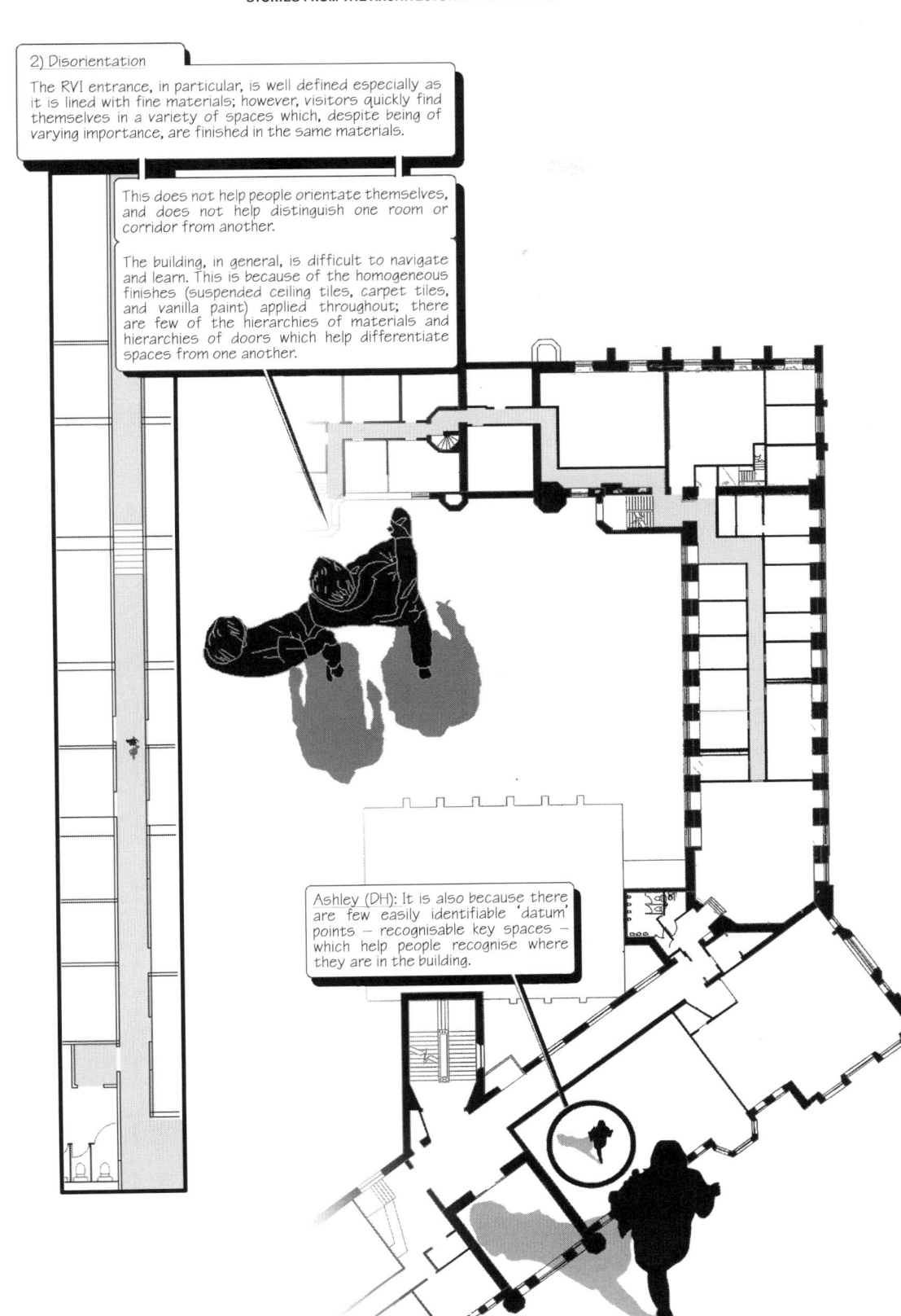

2) Disorientation

The RVI entrance, in particular, is well defined especially as it is lined with fine materials; however, visitors quickly find themselves in a variety of spaces which, despite being of varying importance, are finished in the same materials.

This does not help people orientate themselves, and does not help distinguish one room or corridor from another.

The building, in general, is difficult to navigate and learn. This is because of the homogeneous finishes (suspended ceiling tiles, carpet tiles, and vanilla paint) applied throughout; there are few of the hierarchies of materials and hierarchies of doors which help differentiate spaces from one another.

Ashley (DH): It is also because there are few easily identifiable 'datum' points — recognisable key spaces — which help people recognise where they are in the building.

3) The Courtyard

The service yard at the centre of the Atkinson Building is currently a 'back' rather than a 'front'. From the arched entrance, there is no sense of thoroughfare or destination. Although the yard contains two (minor) entrances to the building, they cannot be seen until the visitor is deep into the space. The yard is partially occupied by a corrugated-roofed service building which makes it hard to read the space as a 'quad'.

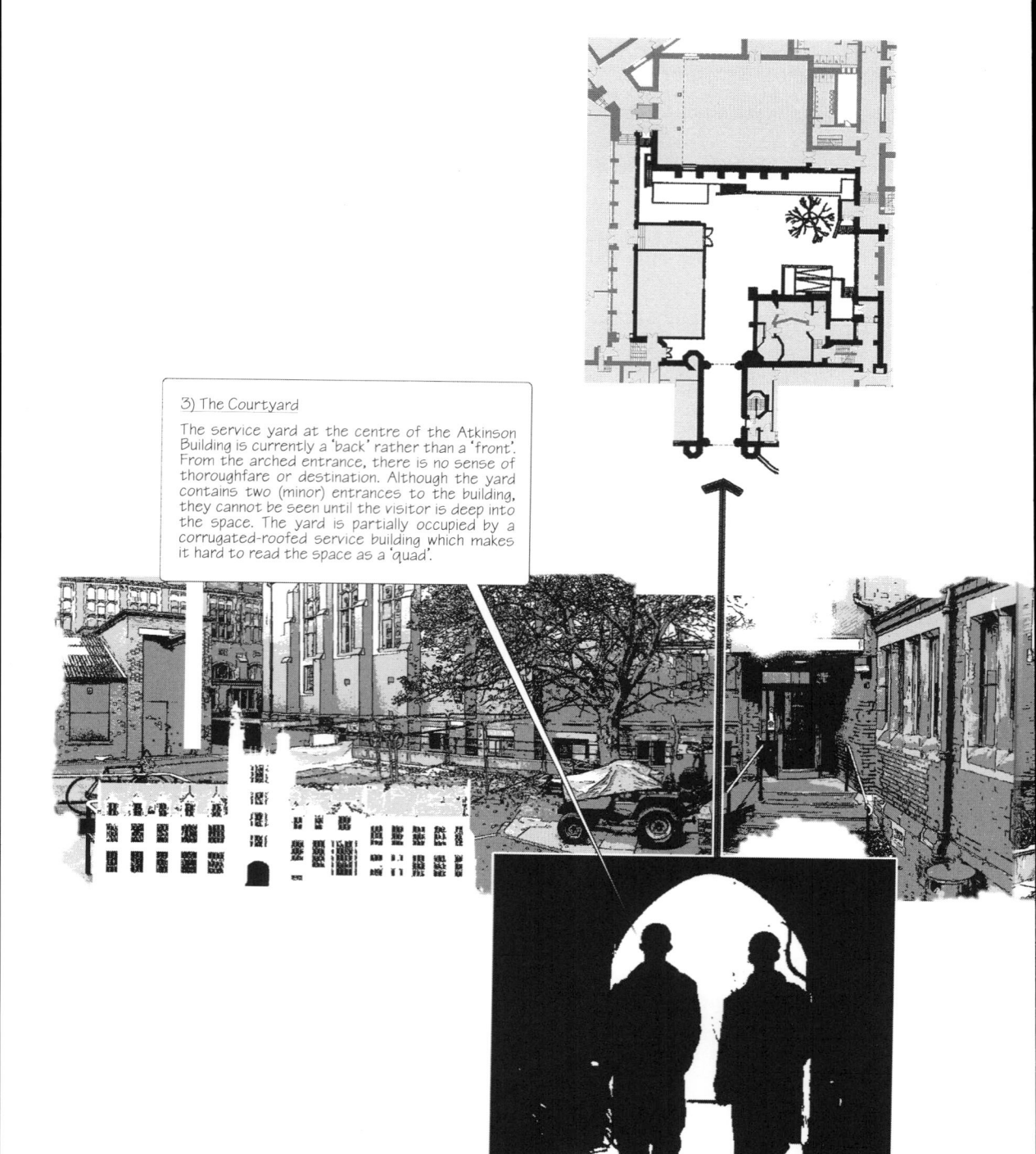

materials

The Queen Victoria Road entrance, in particular, is lined with fine materials.

However, visitors quickly find themselves in a variety of spaces which,

despite being of varying importance, are finished in the same mate...

carpet t... ...terboard painted in a vanilla colour; and suspended

ceilings. This ... help people orientate themselves, and does not help

distinguish one roo... ...rridor from another.

The building is difficult t... ...gate and learn. This is because of the homogenous finishe... ...spended ceiling tiles, carpet tiles,

vanilla paint) applied throughou... ...re are few of the heirarchies of materials and heirarchie... ...ors which help differentiate

spaces from one another. It is also because ... are few easily identifiable 'datum' points - recognisable key spaces - which help people understand where they are in the building.

While the original proportions of the rooms were generous - even grand - this is obscured by the almost universal fitting of suspended ceilings which frequently cut across the heads of windows. Consequently, much generosity and grandeur is lost. The building is not airconditioned so there are few services for the suspended ceilings to conceal.

Many larger rooms have been carvedup into smaller spaces with lightweight partitions. As with the suspended ceilings, this obscures the generosity and grandeur of the underlying spaces.

REPORT

4) The carved up spaces

The report also noted that while the original proportions of the rooms were generous — even grand — this is obscured by the almost universal fitting of suspended ceilings which frequently cut across the heads of windows.

Consequently, much of the space generosity and grandeur is lost. The building is not air-conditioned so there are few services for the suspended ceilings to conceal.

Many larger rooms have been carved up into smaller spaces with lightweight partitions.

As with the suspended ceilings, this obscures the generosity and grandeur of the underlying spaces.

The renovations of the Atkinson Building was a very important event in Practiceopolis because of the symbolic significance of this building within the University and within the city as a whole.

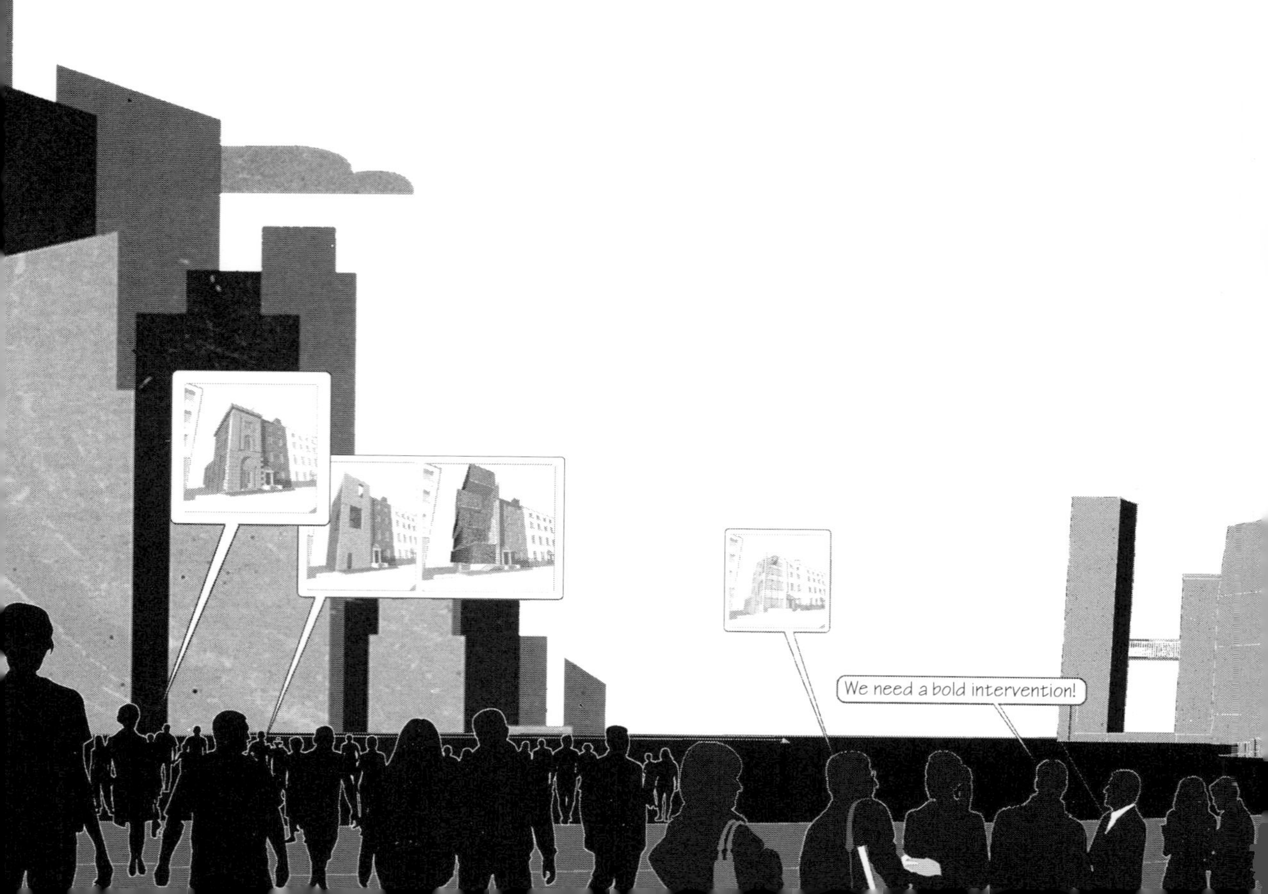
We need a bold intervention!

The
Proposal

Design House (DH) was going to present its proposal in the Map Library Building in front of representatives from different architectural communities as well as the MPs of the Parliament.

TODAY!
THE ATKINSON BUILDING
RENOVATION DESIGN
PROPOSAL
It really needs a 'make-good', technical upgrading!
I think some subtle changes will be enough!
No, just leave it as it is!

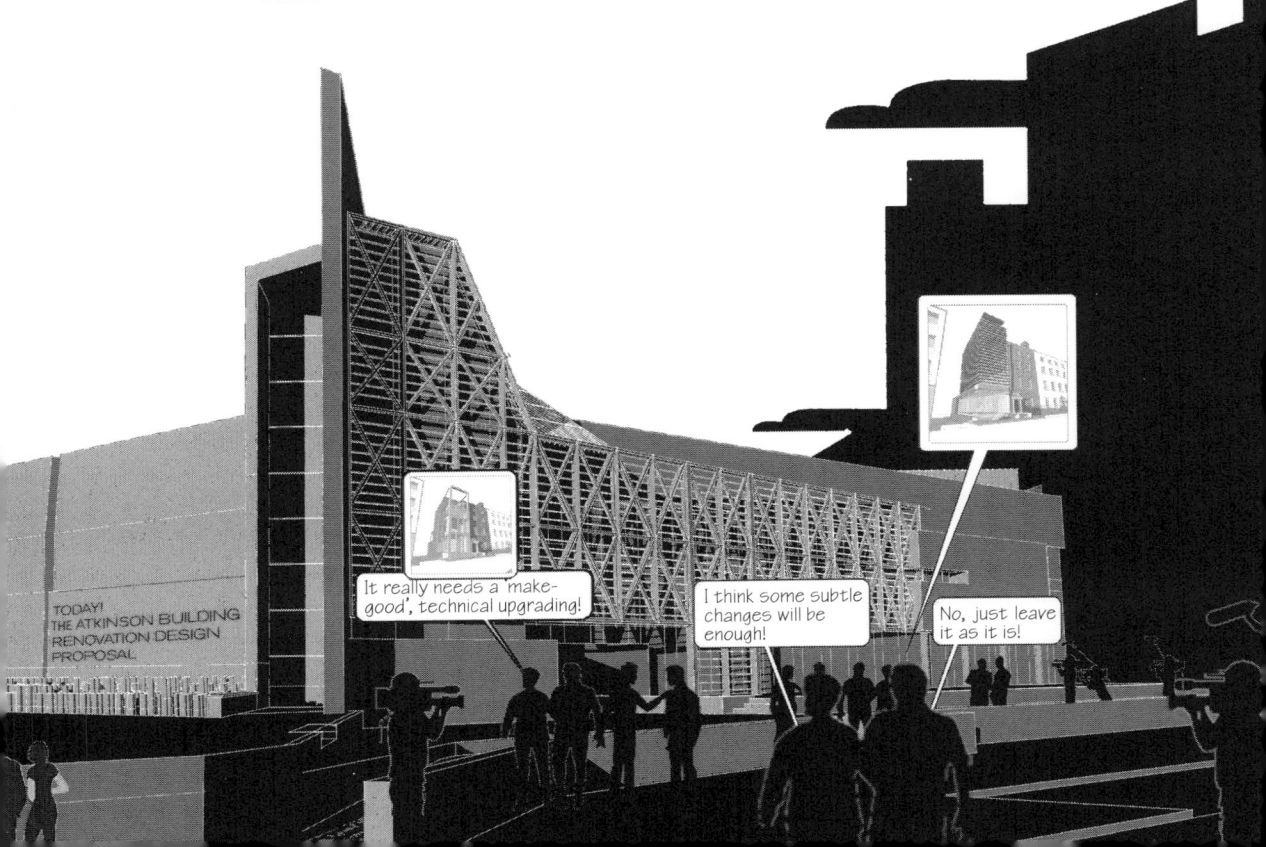

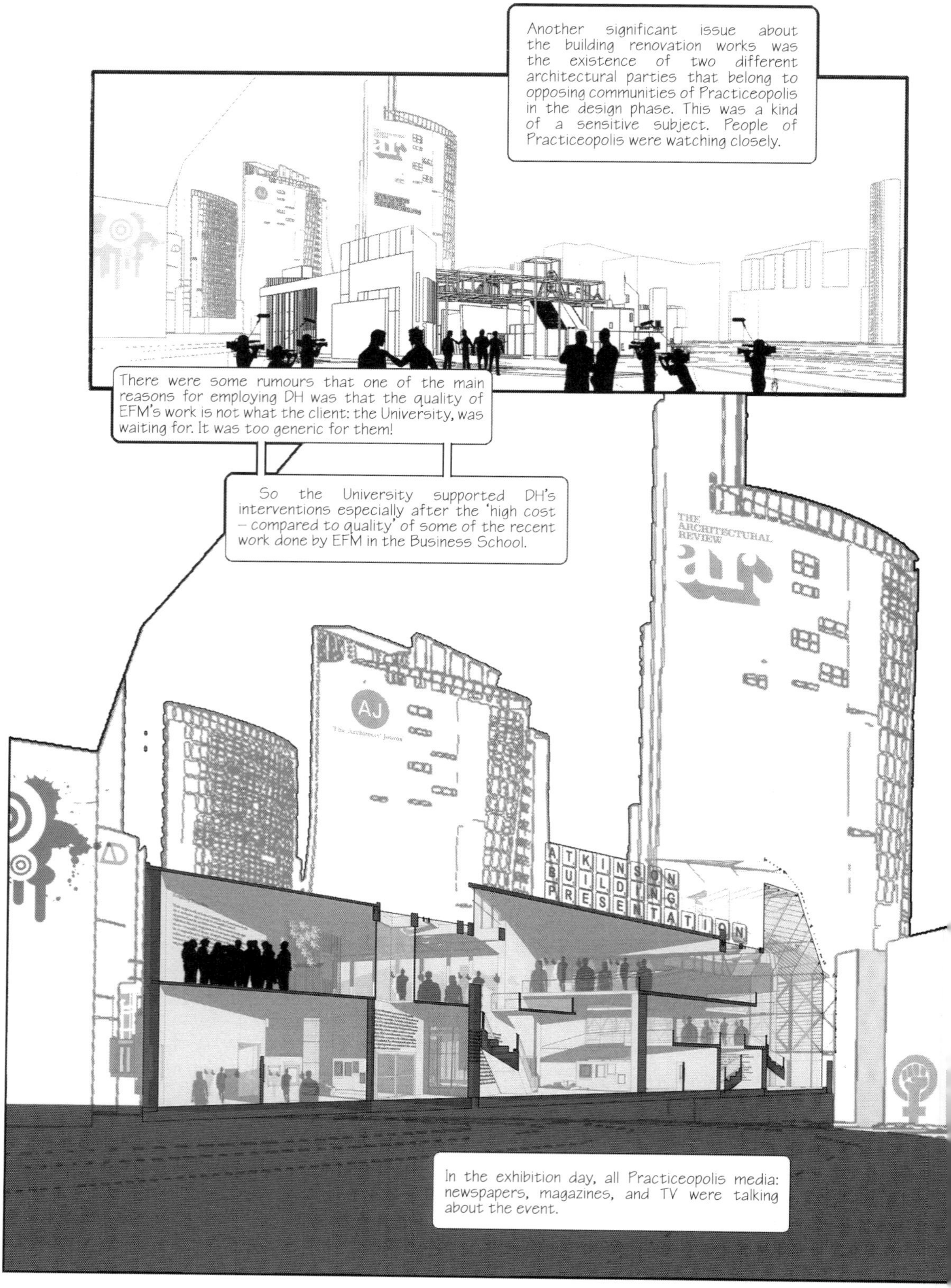
Another significant issue about the building renovation works was the existence of two different architectural parties that belong to opposing communities of Practiceopolis in the design phase. This was a kind of a sensitive subject. People of Practiceopolis were watching closely.
There were some rumours that one of the main reasons for employing DH was that the quality of EFM's work is not what the client: the University, was waiting for. It was too generic for them!
So the University supported DH's interventions especially after the 'high cost – compared to quality' of some of the recent work done by EFM in the Business School.
THE ARCHITECTURAL REVIEW
ar
AJ
ATKINSON
BUILDING
PRESENTATION
In the exhibition day, all Practiceopolis media: newspapers, magazines, and TV were talking about the event.

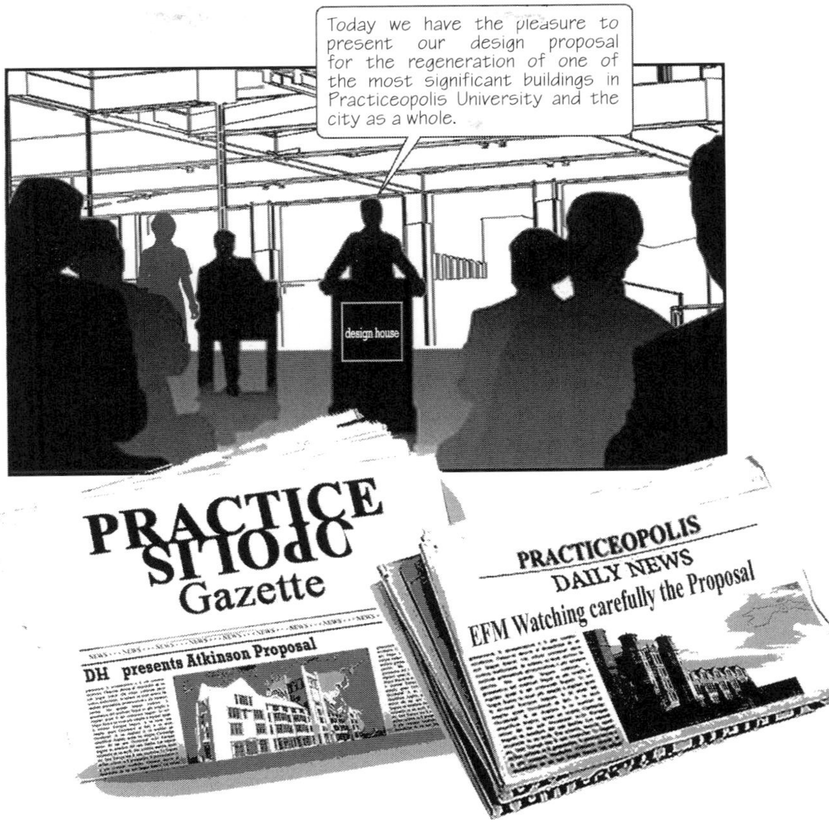
Today we have the pleasure to present our design proposal for the regeneration of one of the most significant buildings in Practiceopolis University and the city as a whole.
design house
PRACTICE POLIS Gazette
DH presents Atkinson Proposal
PRACTICEOPOLIS DAILY NEWS
EFM Watching carefully the Proposal

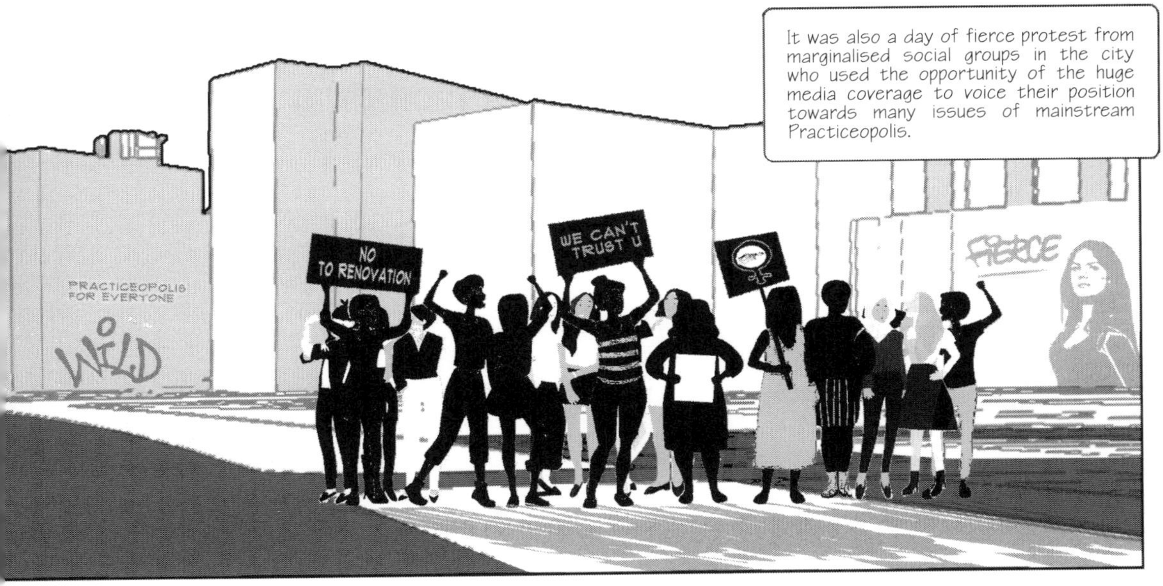
It was also a day of fierce protest from marginalised social groups in the city who used the opportunity of the huge media coverage to voice their position towards many issues of mainstream Practiceopolis.
PRACTICEOPOLIS FOR EVERYONE
WILD
NO TO RENOVATION
WE CAN'T TRUST U
FIERCE

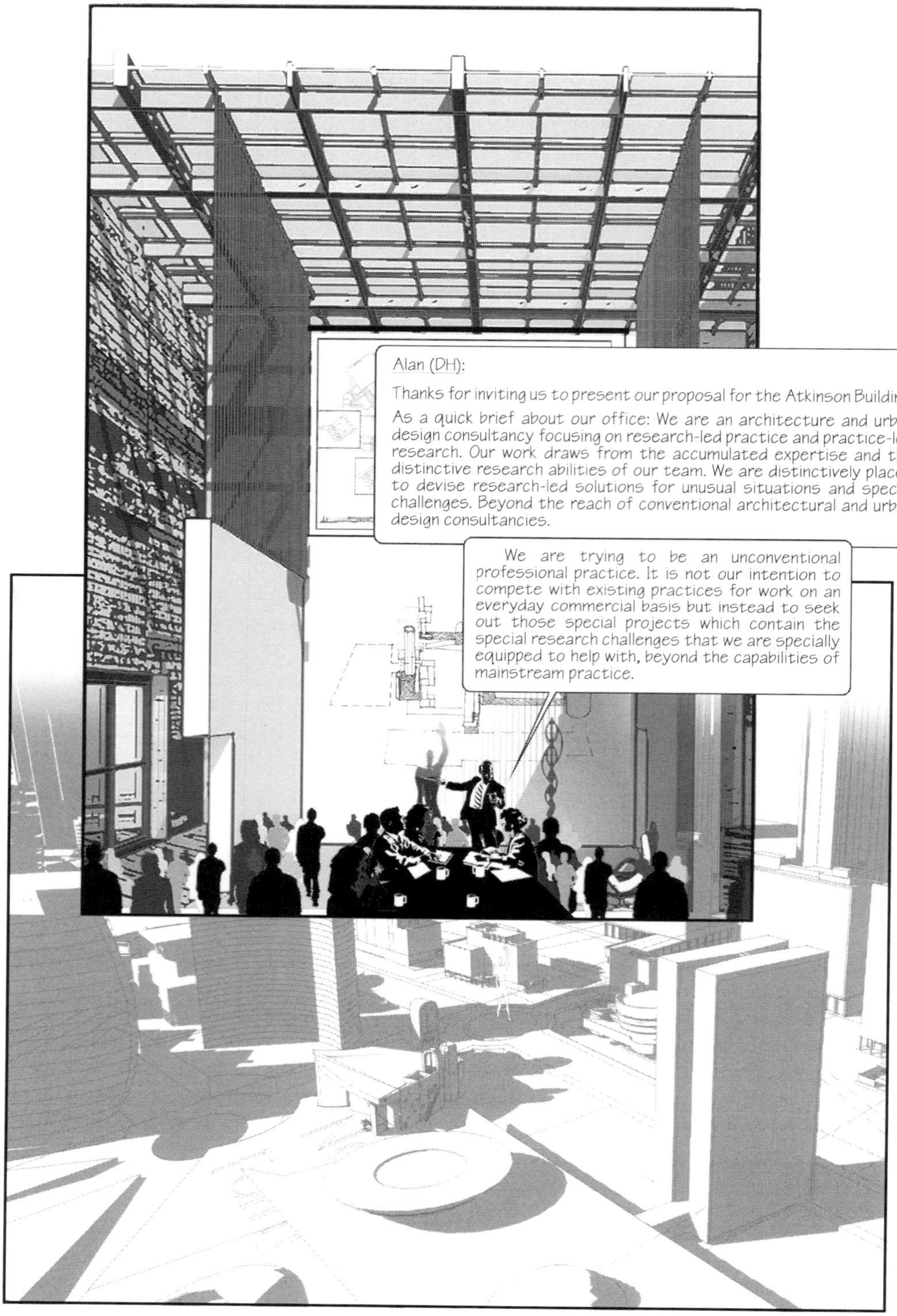
Alan (DH):
Thanks for inviting us to present our proposal for the Atkinson Building.
As a quick brief about our office: We are an architecture and urban design consultancy focusing on research-led practice and practice-led research. Our work draws from the accumulated expertise and the distinctive research abilities of our team. We are distinctively placed to devise research-led solutions for unusual situations and special challenges. Beyond the reach of conventional architectural and urban design consultancies.
We are trying to be an unconventional professional practice. It is not our intention to compete with existing practices for work on an everyday commercial basis but instead to seek out those special projects which contain the special research challenges that we are specially equipped to help with, beyond the capabilities of mainstream practice.

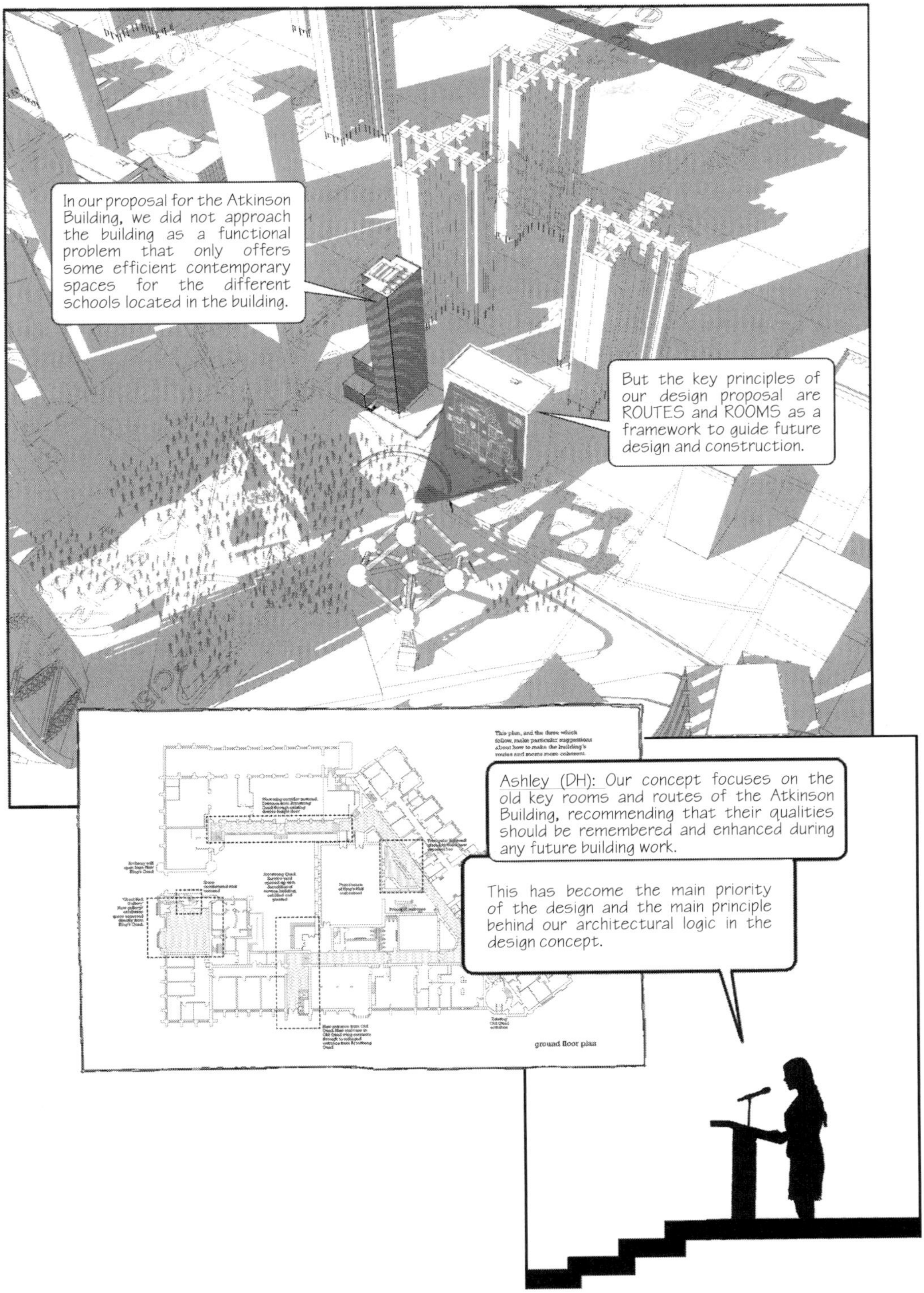
In our proposal for the Atkinson Building, we did not approach the building as a functional problem that only offers some efficient contemporary spaces for the different schools located in the building.
But the key principles of our design proposal are ROUTES and ROOMS as a framework to guide future design and construction.
Ashley (DH): Our concept focuses on the old key rooms and routes of the Atkinson Building, recommending that their qualities should be remembered and enhanced during any future building work.
This has become the main priority of the design and the main principle behind our architectural logic in the design concept.
ground floor plan

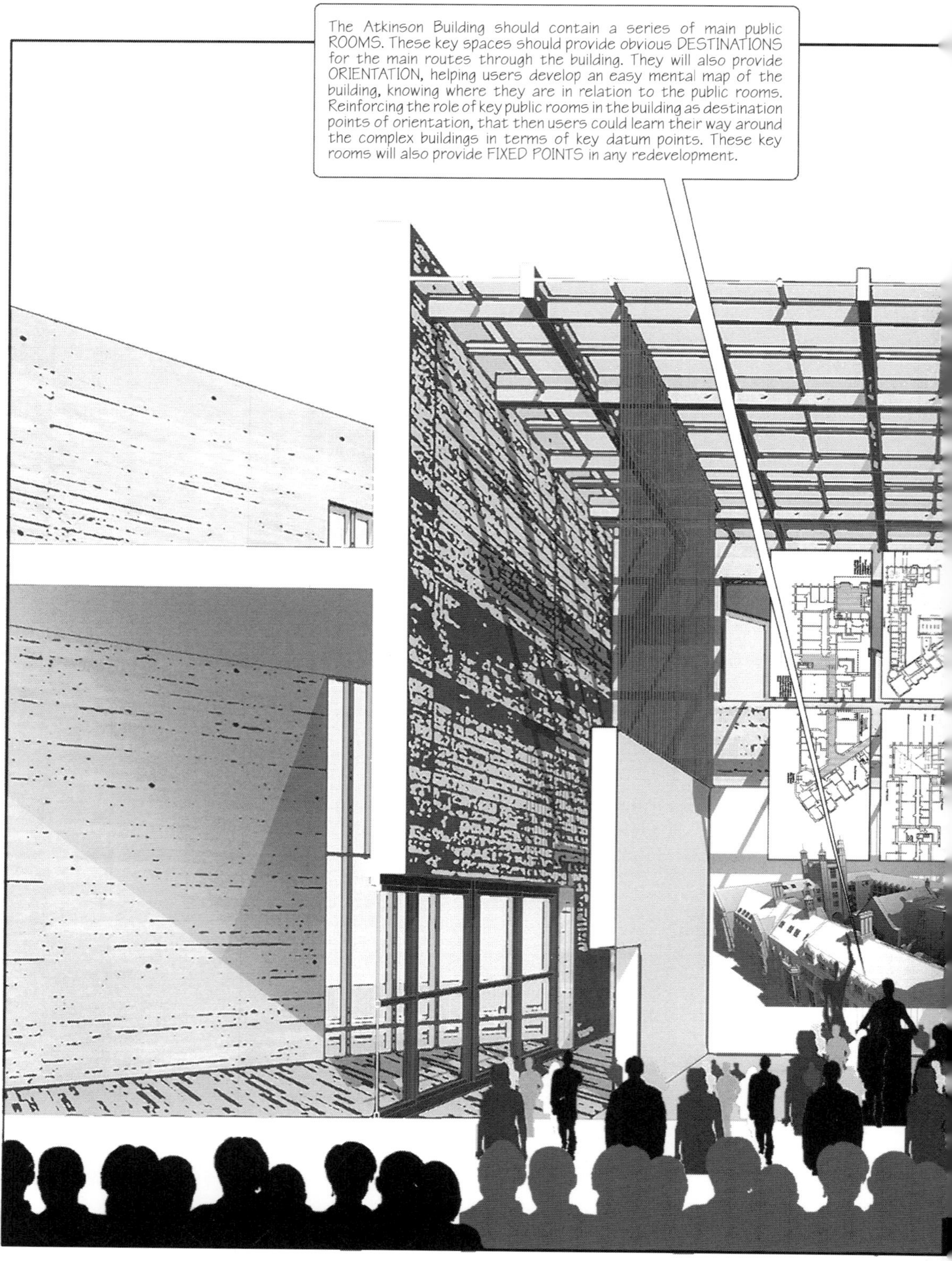
The Atkinson Building should contain a series of main public ROOMS. These key spaces should provide obvious DESTINATIONS for the main routes through the building. They will also provide ORIENTATION, helping users develop an easy mental map of the building, knowing where they are in relation to the public rooms. Reinforcing the role of key public rooms in the building as destination points of orientation, that then users could learn their way around the complex buildings in terms of key datum points. These key rooms will also provide FIXED POINTS in any redevelopment.

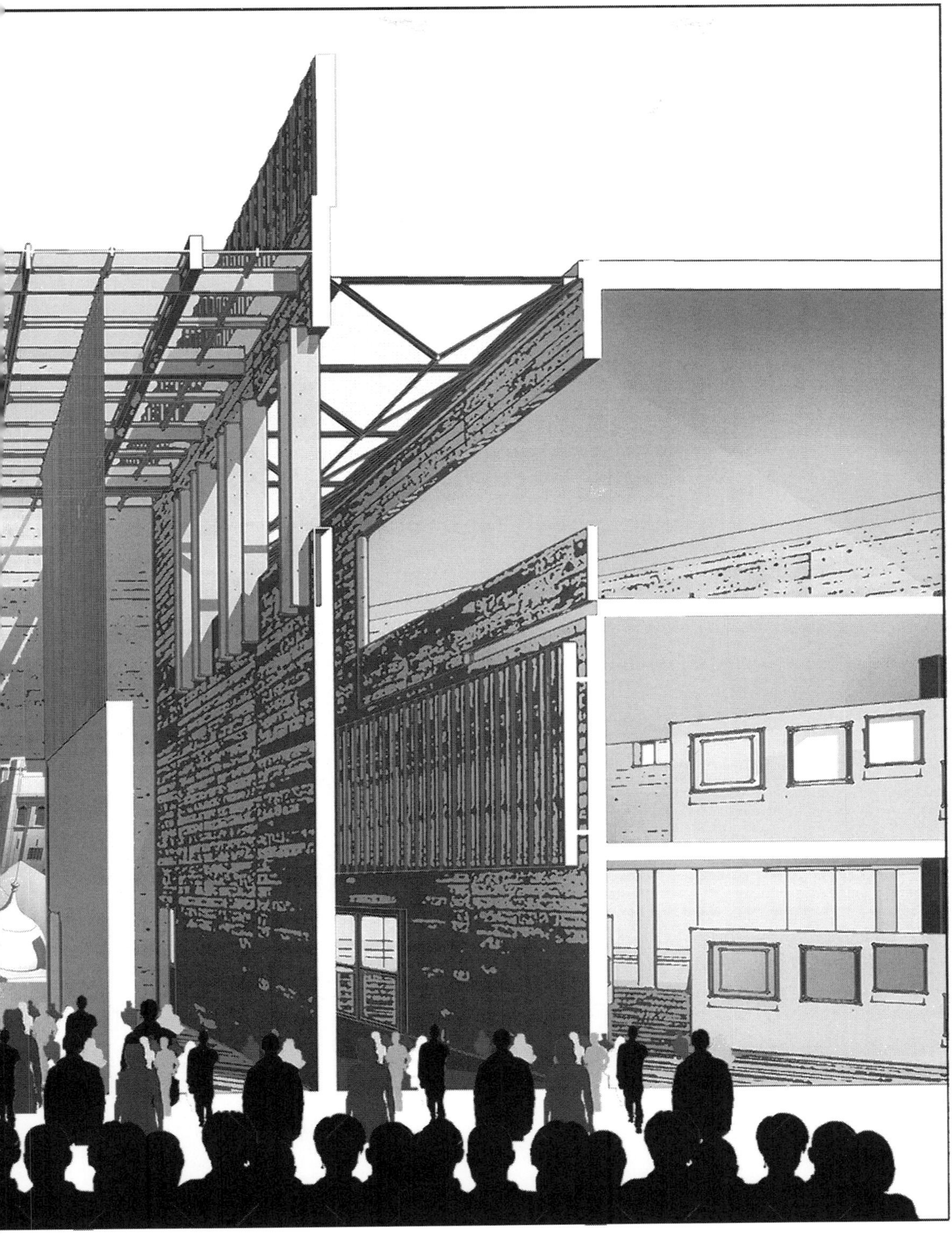

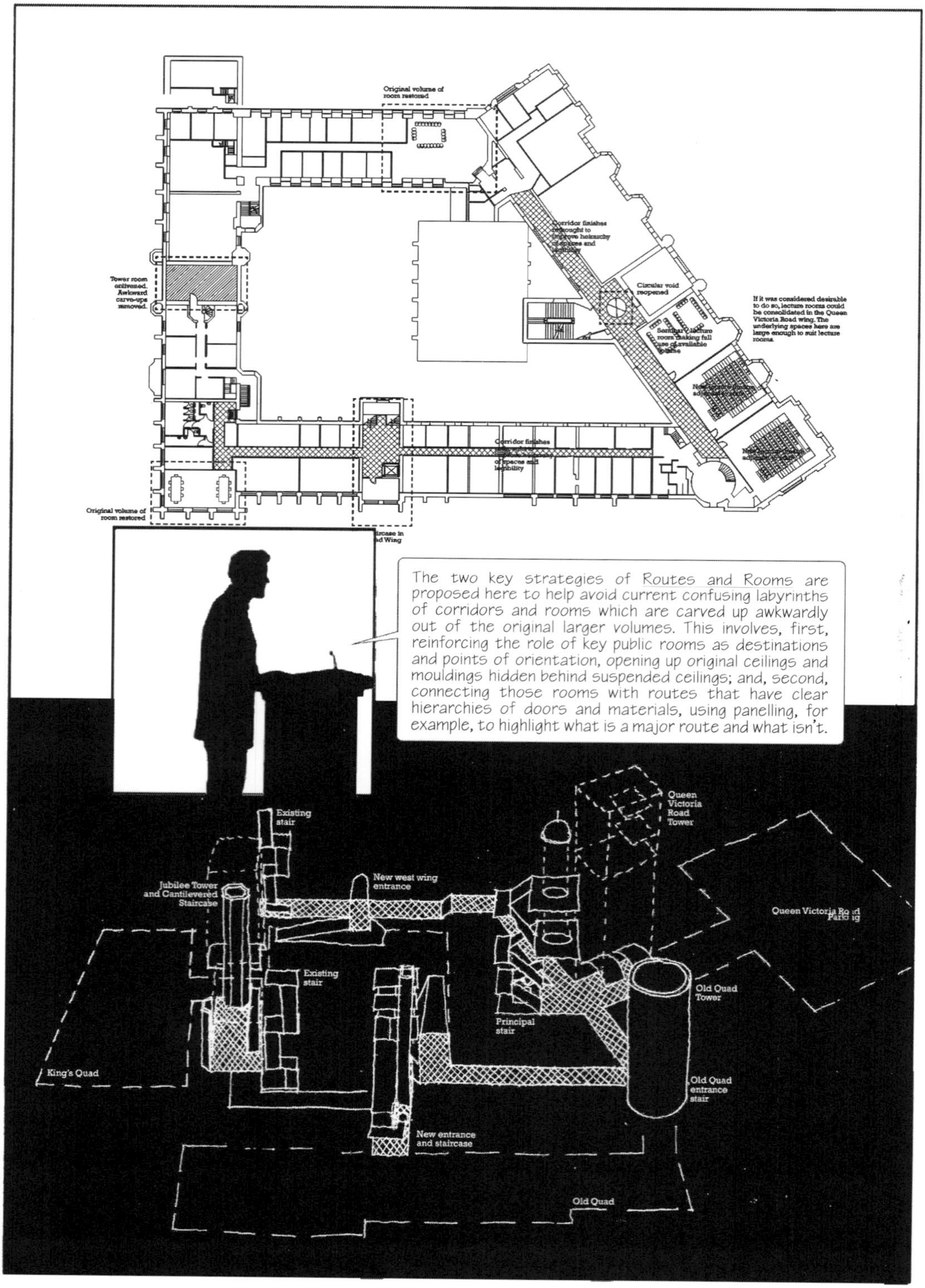
Original volume of room restored
Tower room enlivened. Awkward carve-ups removed.
Original volume of room restored
Circular void reopened
If it was considered desirable to do so, lecture rooms could be consolidated in the Queen Victoria Road wing. The underlying spaces here are large enough to suit lecture rooms.
The two key strategies of Routes and Rooms are proposed here to help avoid current confusing labyrinths of corridors and rooms which are carved up awkwardly out of the original larger volumes. This involves, first, reinforcing the role of key public rooms as destinations and points of orientation, opening up original ceilings and mouldings hidden behind suspended ceilings; and, second, connecting those rooms with routes that have clear hierarchies of doors and materials, using panelling, for example, to highlight what is a major route and what isn't.
Existing stair
Queen Victoria Road Tower
New west wing entrance
Jubilee Tower and Cantilevered Staircase
Queen Victoria Ro d
Existing stair
Old Quad Tower
Principal stair
King's Quad
Old Quad entrance stair
New entrance and staircase
Old Quad

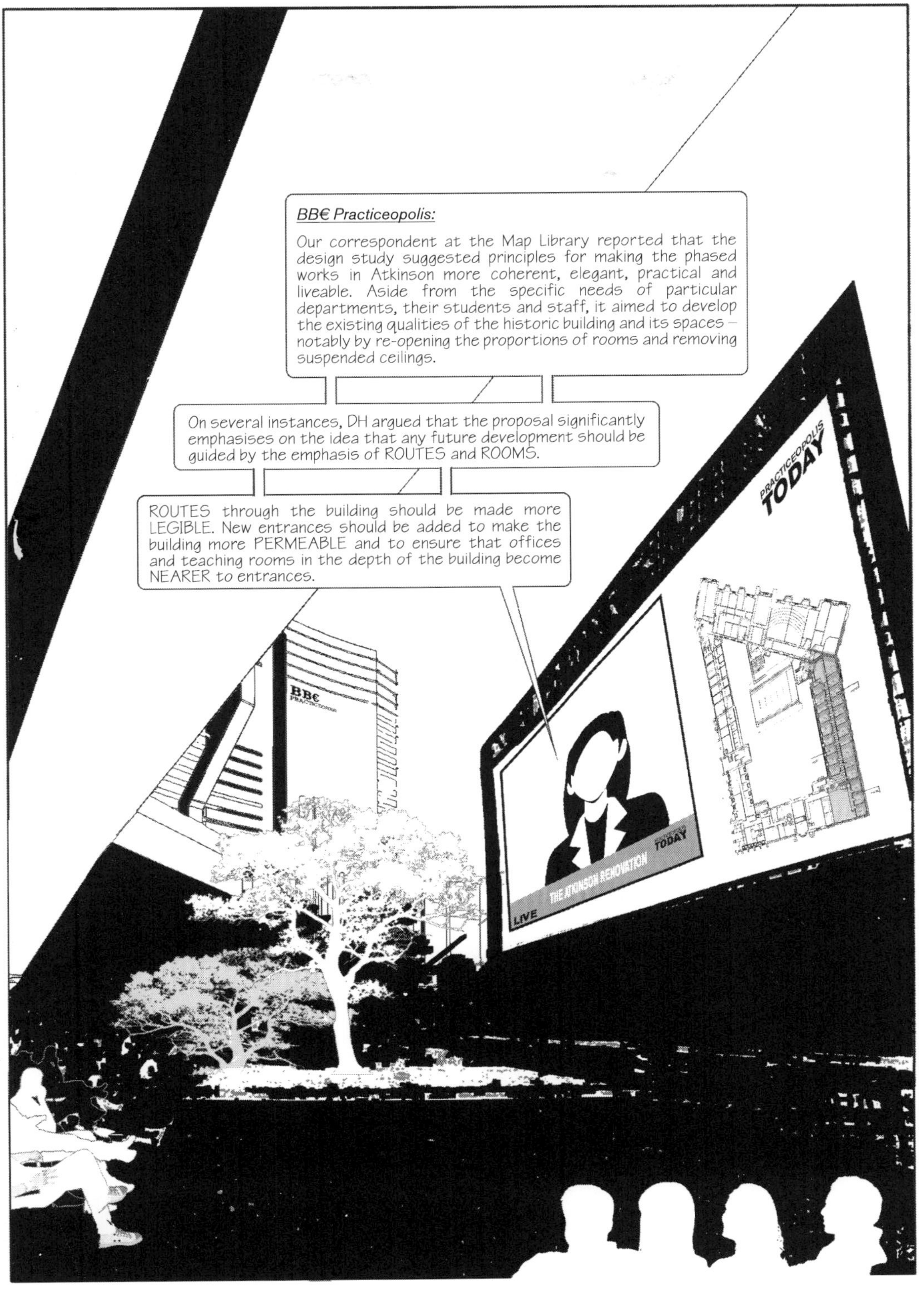
BB€ Practiceopolis:
Our correspondent at the Map Library reported that the design study suggested principles for making the phased works in Atkinson more coherent, elegant, practical and liveable. Aside from the specific needs of particular departments, their students and staff, it aimed to develop the existing qualities of the historic building and its spaces – notably by re-opening the proportions of rooms and removing suspended ceilings.
On several instances, DH argued that the proposal significantly emphasises on the idea that any future development should be guided by the emphasis of ROUTES and ROOMS.
ROUTES through the building should be made more LEGIBLE. New entrances should be added to make the building more PERMEABLE and to ensure that offices and teaching rooms in the depth of the building become NEARER to entrances.
BB€
PRACTICEOPOLIS TODAY
LIVE
THE ATKINSON RENOVATION
TODAY

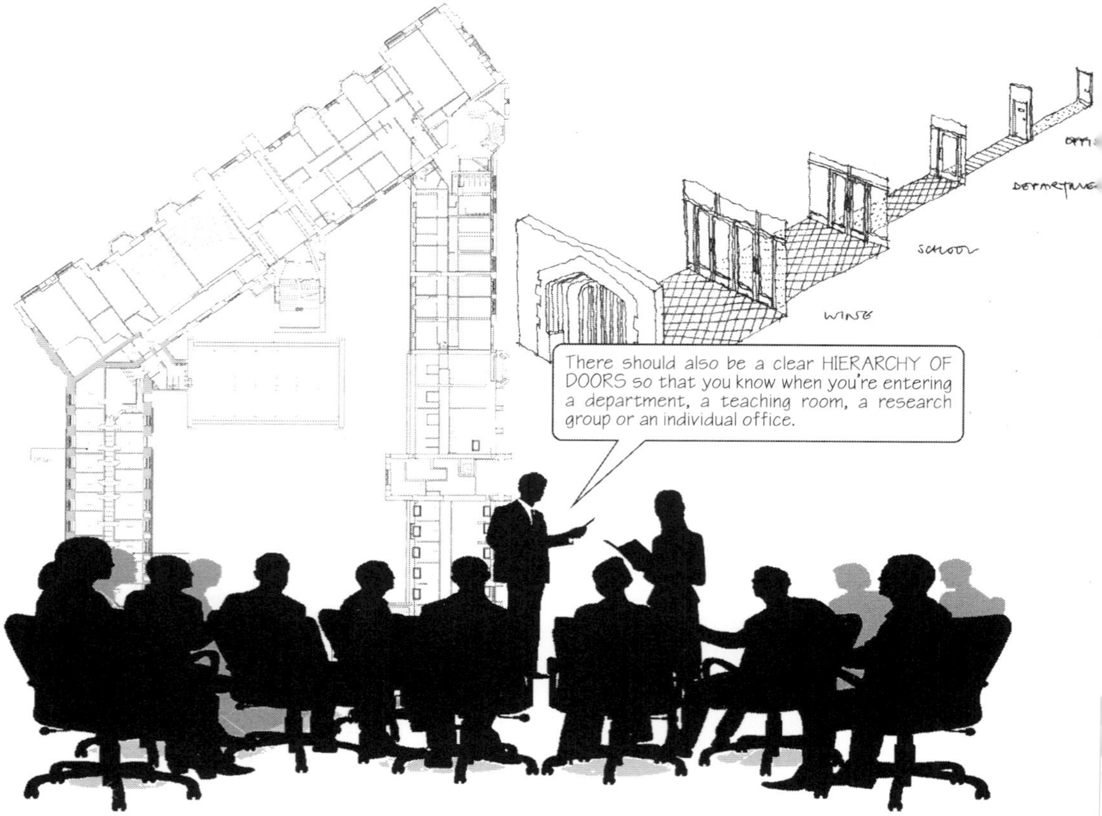
There should also be a clear HIERARCHY OF DOORS so that you know when you're entering a department, a teaching room, a research group or an individual office.

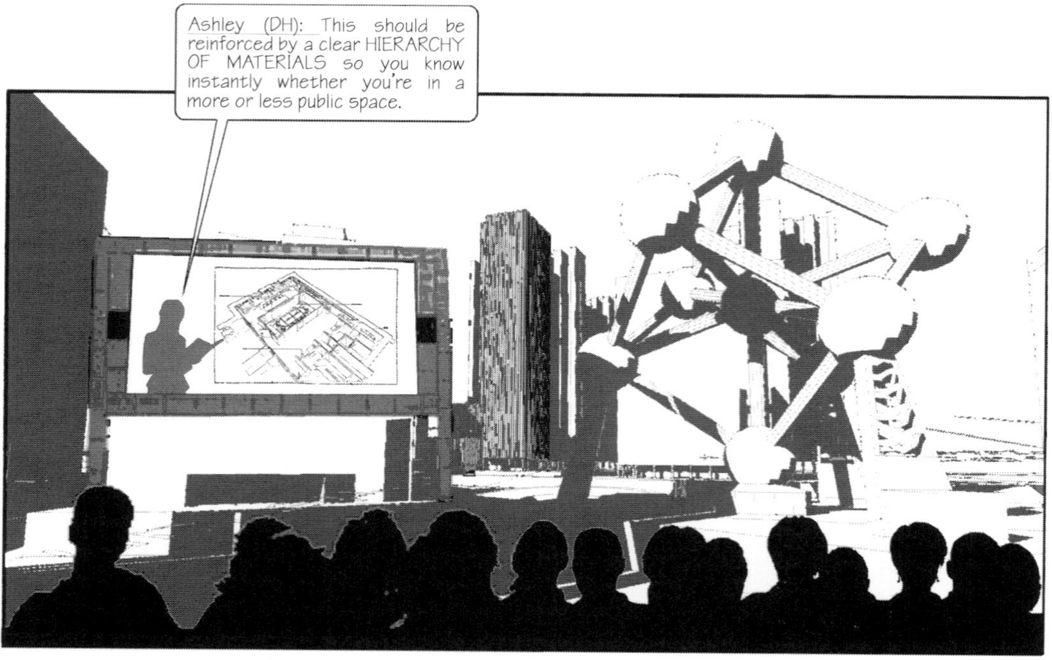
Ashley (DH): This should be reinforced by a clear HIERARCHY OF MATERIALS so you know instantly whether you're in a more or less public space.

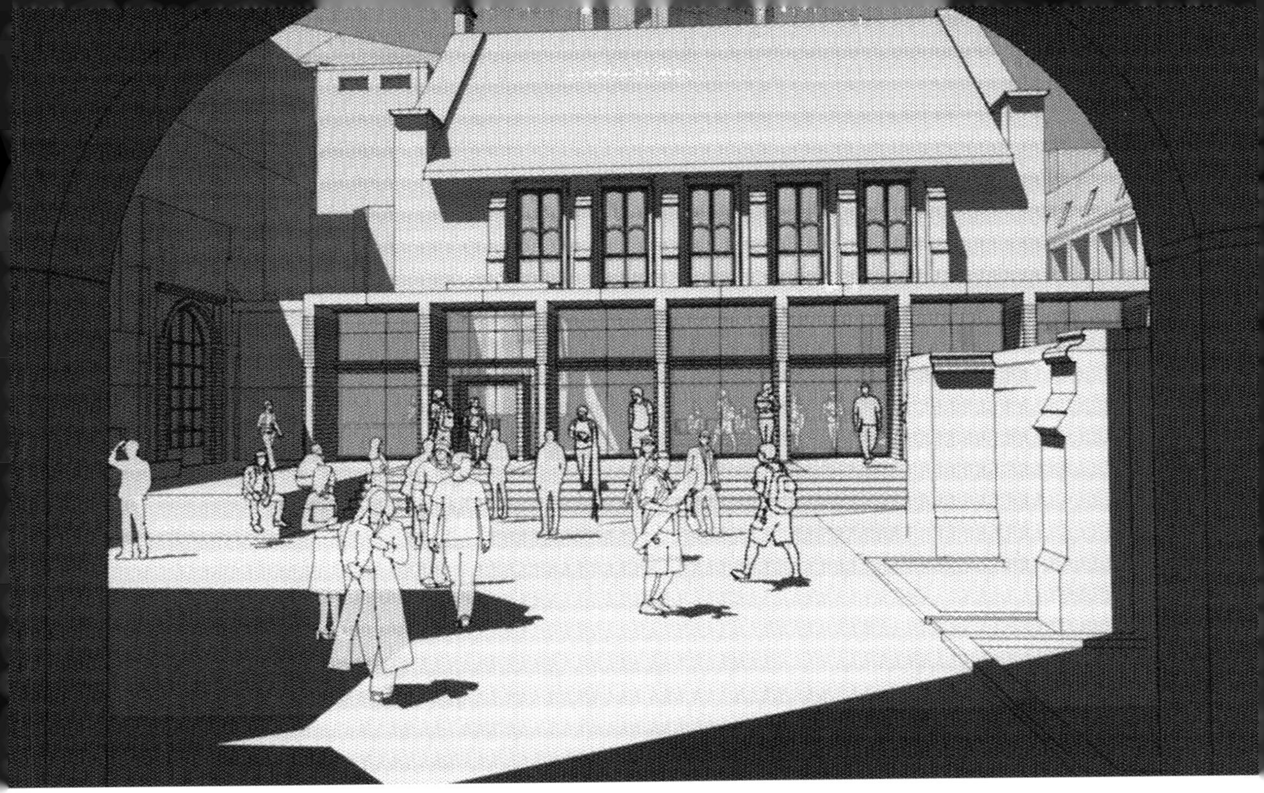

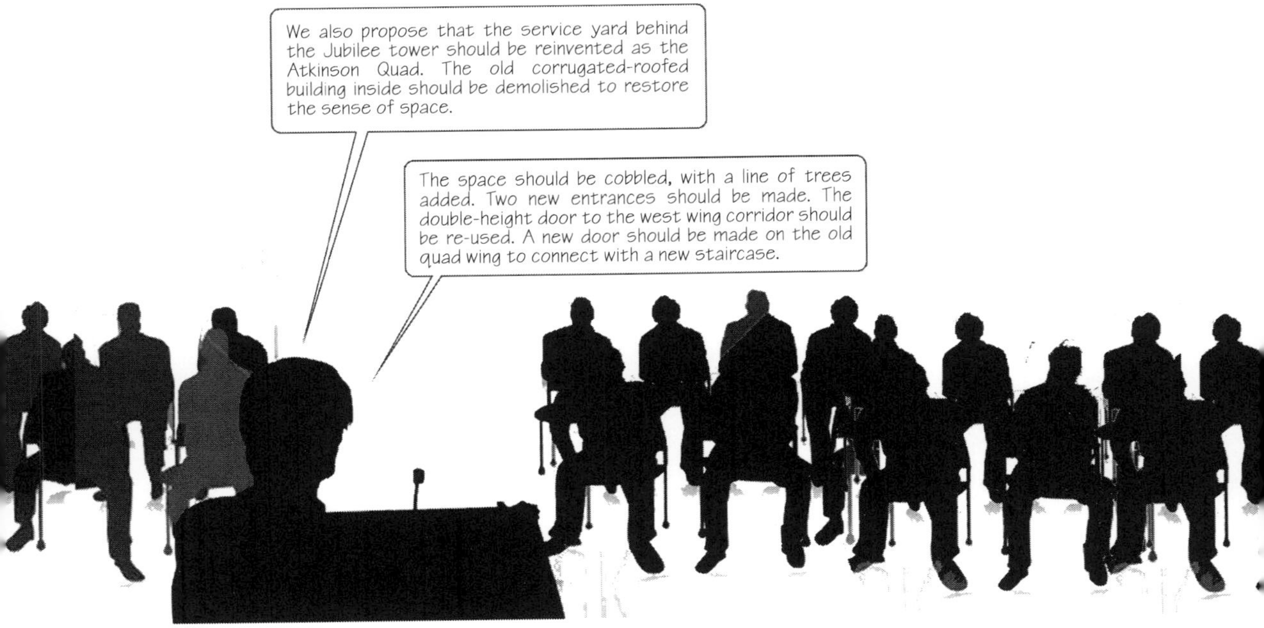
We also propose that the service yard behind the Jubilee tower should be reinvented as the Atkinson Quad. The old corrugated-roofed building inside should be demolished to restore the sense of space.
The space should be cobbled, with a line of trees added. Two new entrances should be made. The double-height door to the west wing corridor should be re-used. A new door should be made on the old quad wing to connect with a new staircase.

And DH named the key aspects of the design proposal for the second floor are as:

The object within the object

At the corner of the Atkinson Building, where the building turns from the Student Forum to the Old Quad, there was originally a double-height room with a vault which was open to the underside of a hipped roof. A mezzanine floor was subsequently inserted into this room at second floor level and the space was carved up into a series of rooms. The mezzanine has to stay here, but they propose re-opening a volume at second floor which exposes the hipped roof once again. This impressive, lofty volume should contain the library, a seminar space and a foyer, with clerestory glazing maintaining a view of the volume as a whole within the individual rooms.

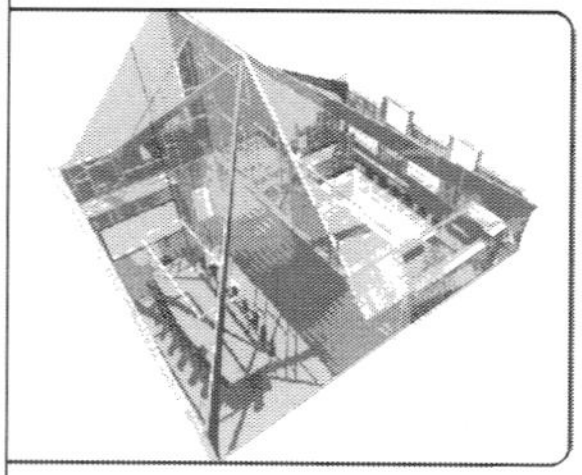

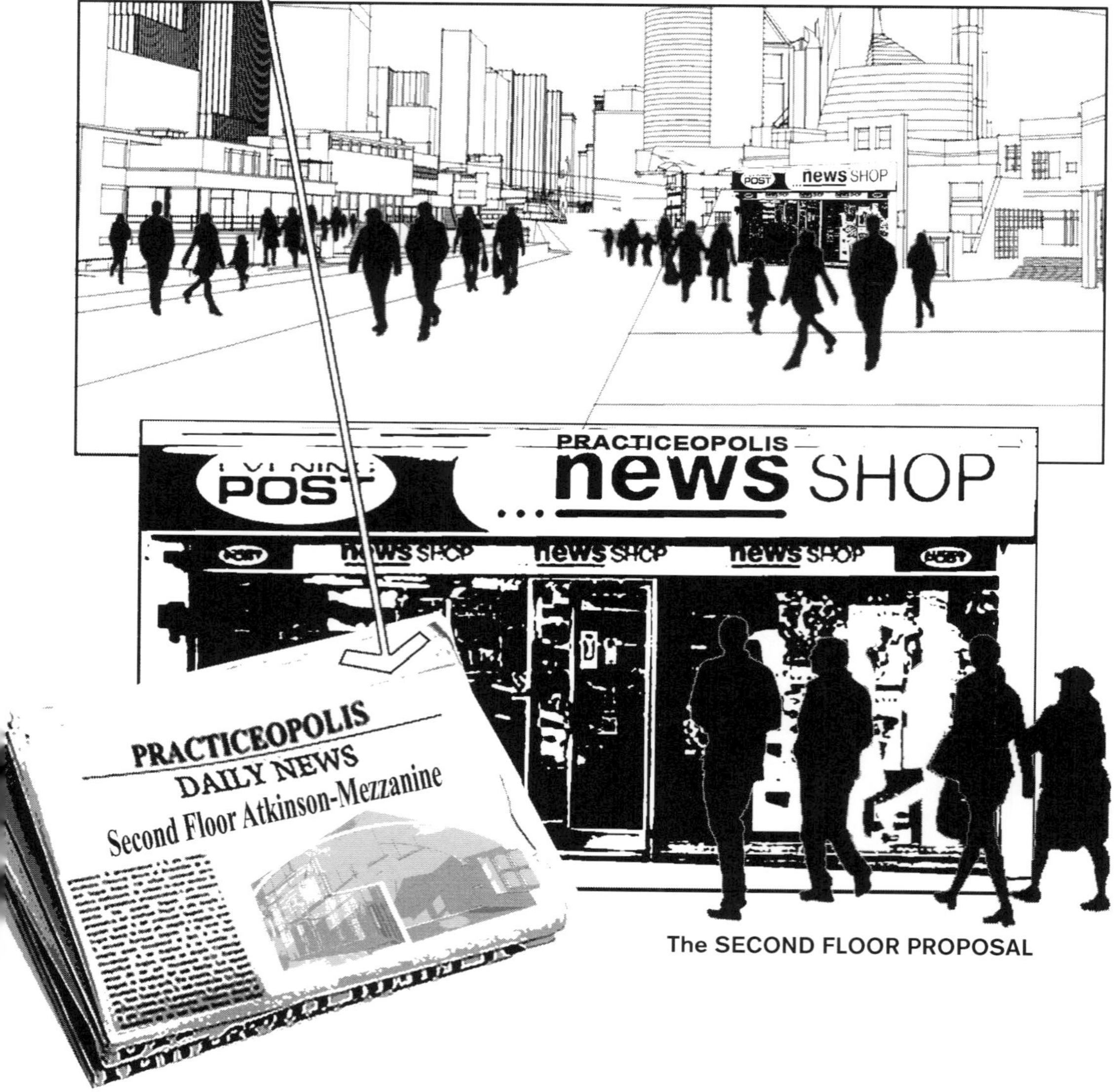

news SHOP
PRACTICEOPOLIS
POST
...news SHOP
PRACTICEOPOLIS
DAILY NEWS
Second Floor Atkinson-Mezzanine

The SECOND FLOOR PROPOSAL

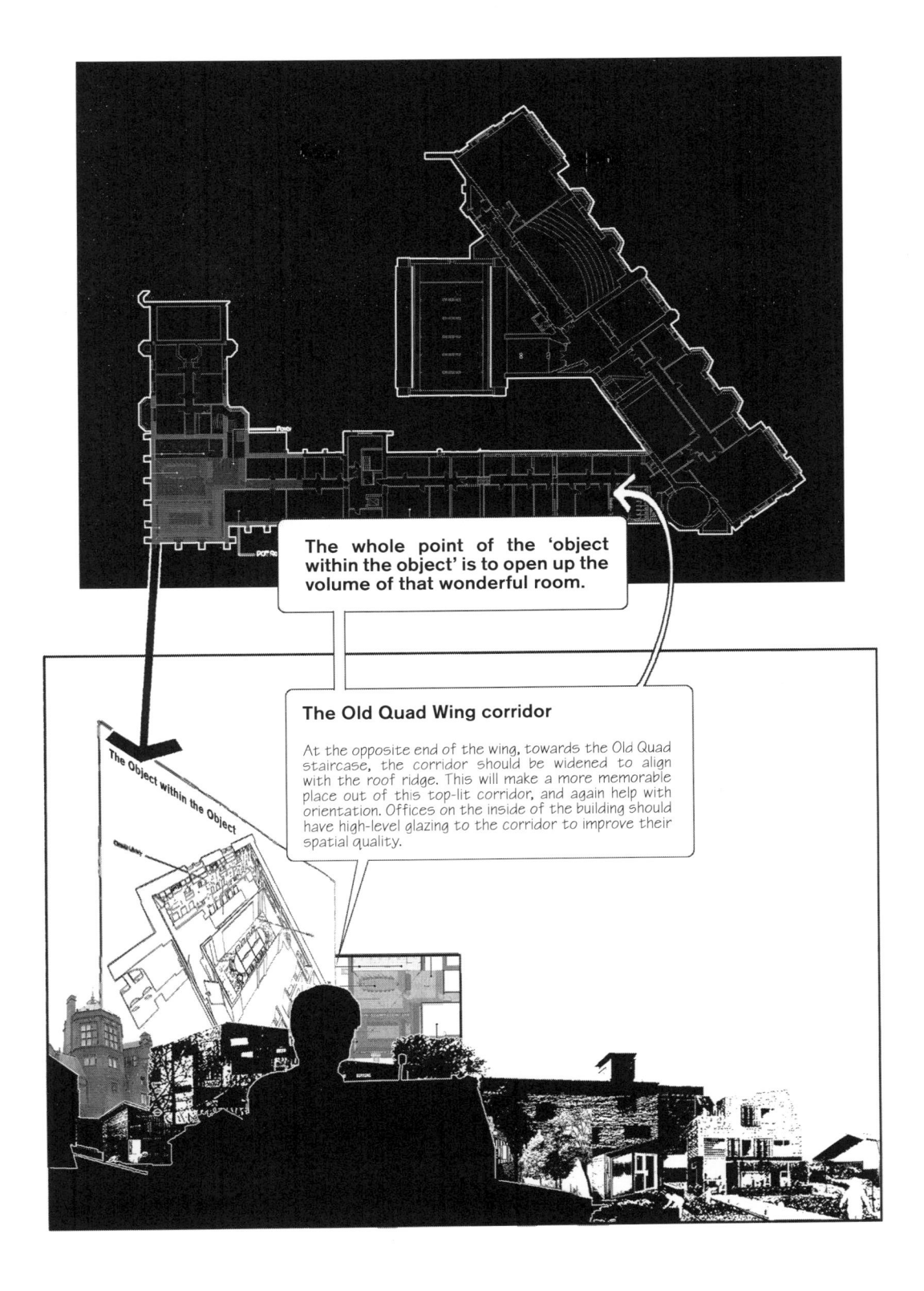

The whole point of the 'object within the object' is to open up the volume of that wonderful room.

The Old Quad Wing corridor

At the opposite end of the wing, towards the Old Quad staircase, the corridor should be widened to align with the roof ridge. This will make a more memorable place out of this top-lit corridor, and again help with orientation. Offices on the inside of the building should have high-level glazing to the corridor to improve their spatial quality.

The Object within the Object

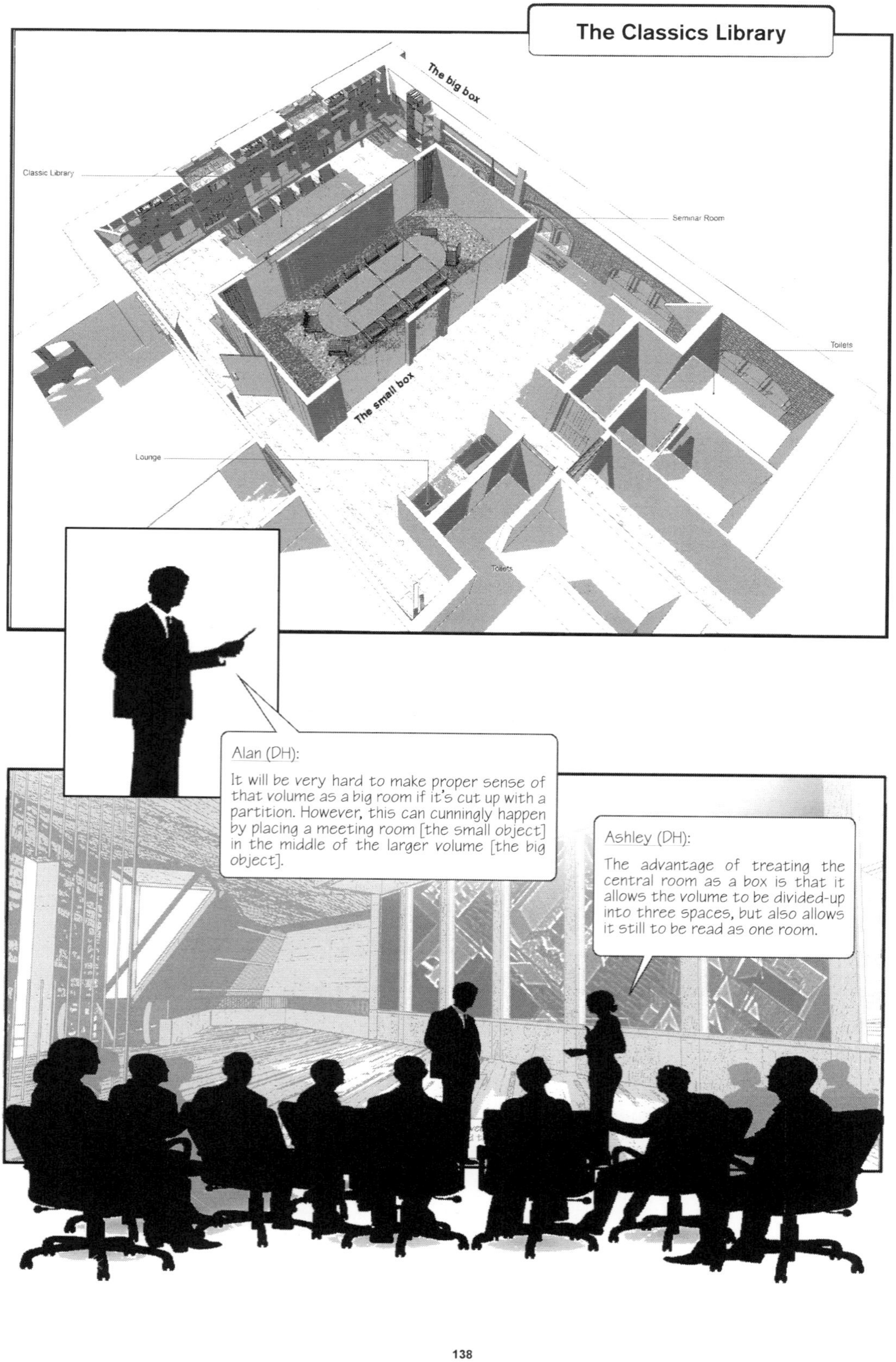
The Classics Library
The big box
Classic Library
Seminar Room
Toilets
The small box
Lounge
Toilets
Alan (DH):
It will be very hard to make proper sense of that volume as a big room if it's cut up with a partition. However, this can cunningly happen by placing a meeting room [the small object] in the middle of the larger volume [the big object].
Ashley (DH):
The advantage of treating the central room as a box is that it allows the volume to be divided-up into three spaces, but also allows it still to be read as one room.

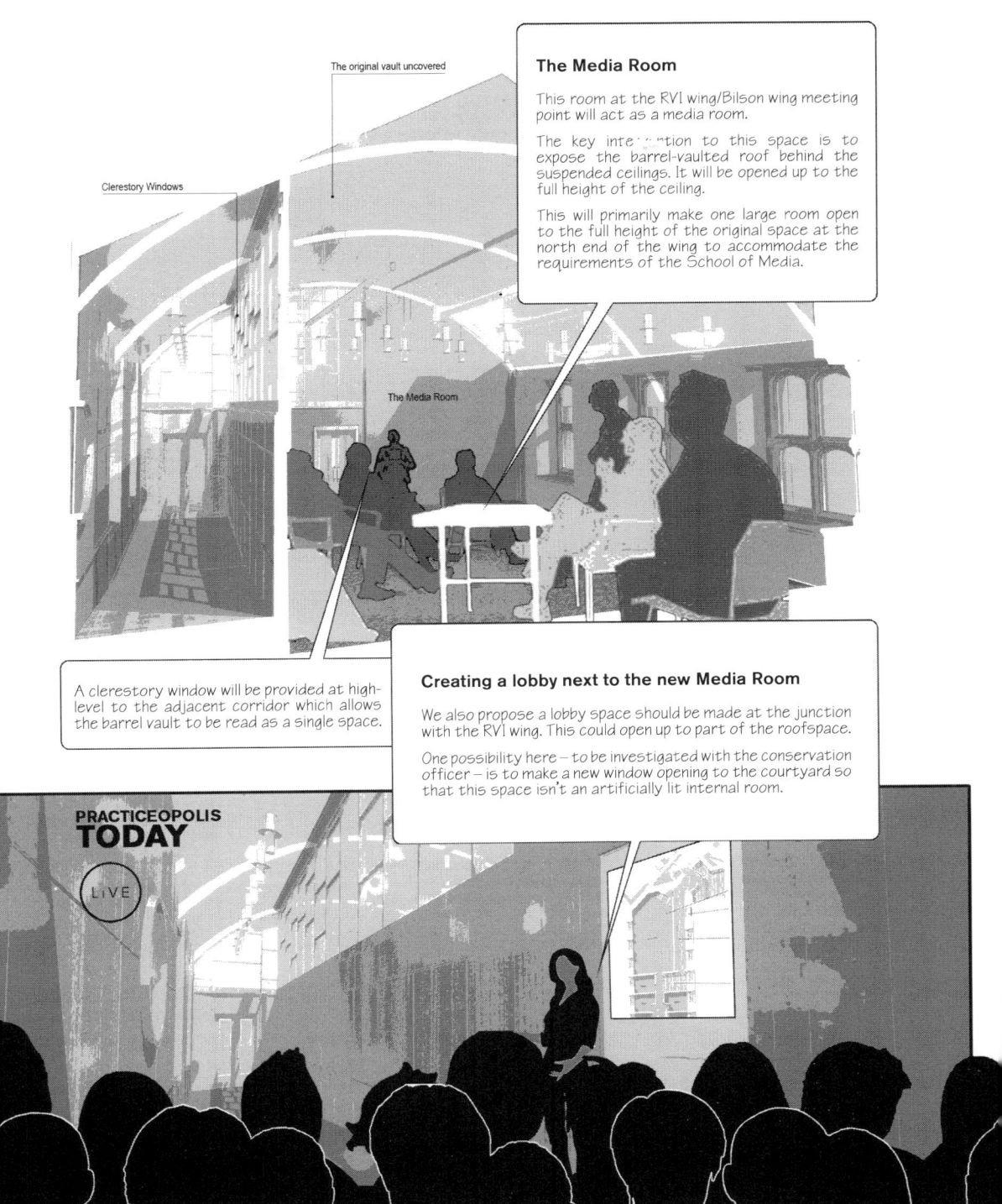

The original vault uncovered

Clerestory Windows

The Media Room

The Media Room

This room at the RVI wing/Bilson wing meeting point will act as a media room.

The key inte····tion to this space is to expose the barrel-vaulted roof behind the suspended ceilings. It will be opened up to the full height of the ceiling.

This will primarily make one large room open to the full height of the original space at the north end of the wing to accommodate the requirements of the School of Media.

A clerestory window will be provided at high-level to the adjacent corridor which allows the barrel vault to be read as a single space.

Creating a lobby next to the new Media Room

We also propose a lobby space should be made at the junction with the RVI wing. This could open up to part of the roofspace.

One possibility here – to be investigated with the conservation officer – is to make a new window opening to the courtyard so that this space isn't an artificially lit internal room.

PRACTICEOPOLIS
TODAY

LIVE

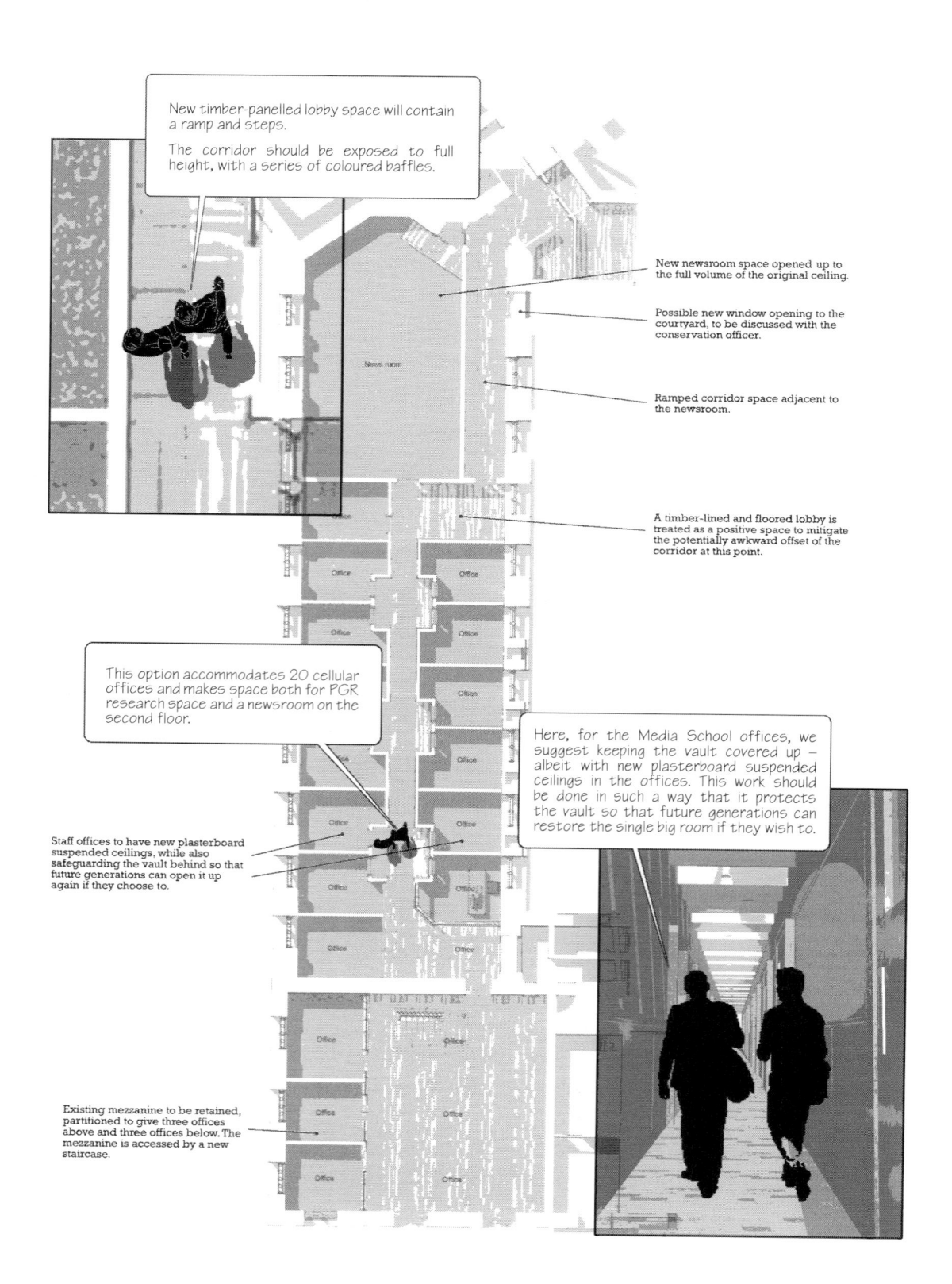

New timber-panelled lobby space will contain a ramp and steps.

The corridor should be exposed to full height, with a series of coloured baffles.

New newsroom space opened up to the full volume of the original ceiling.

Possible new window opening to the courtyard, to be discussed with the conservation officer.

Ramped corridor space adjacent to the newsroom.

A timber-lined and floored lobby is treated as a positive space to mitigate the potentially awkward offset of the corridor at this point.

This option accommodates 20 cellular offices and makes space both for PGR research space and a newsroom on the second floor.

Here, for the Media School offices, we suggest keeping the vault covered up – albeit with new plasterboard suspended ceilings in the offices. This work should be done in such a way that it protects the vault so that future generations can restore the single big room if they wish to.

Staff offices to have new plasterboard suspended ceilings, while also safeguarding the vault behind so that future generations can open it up again if they choose to.

Existing mezzanine to be retained, partitioned to give three offices above and three offices below. The mezzanine is accessed by a new staircase.

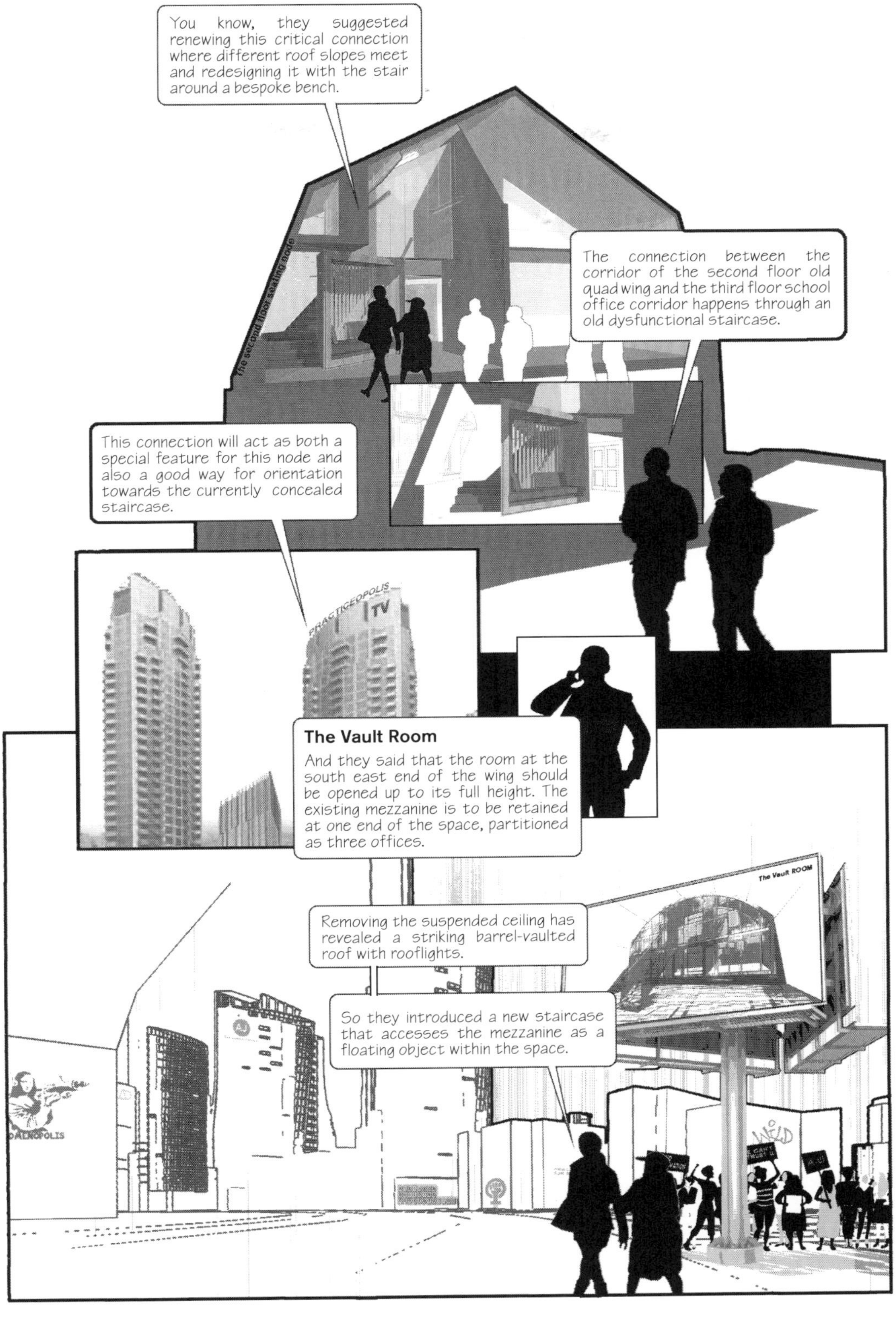
You know, they suggested renewing this critical connection where different roof slopes meet and redesigning it with the stair around a bespoke bench.
The second floor seating node
The connection between the corridor of the second floor old quad wing and the third floor school office corridor happens through an old dysfunctional staircase.
This connection will act as both a special feature for this node and also a good way for orientation towards the currently concealed staircase.
PRACTICEOPOLIS
TV
The Vault Room
And they said that the room at the south east end of the wing should be opened up to its full height. The existing mezzanine is to be retained at one end of the space, partitioned as three offices.
The Vault ROOM
Removing the suspended ceiling has revealed a striking barrel-vaulted roof with rooflights.
So they introduced a new staircase that accesses the mezzanine as a floating object within the space.

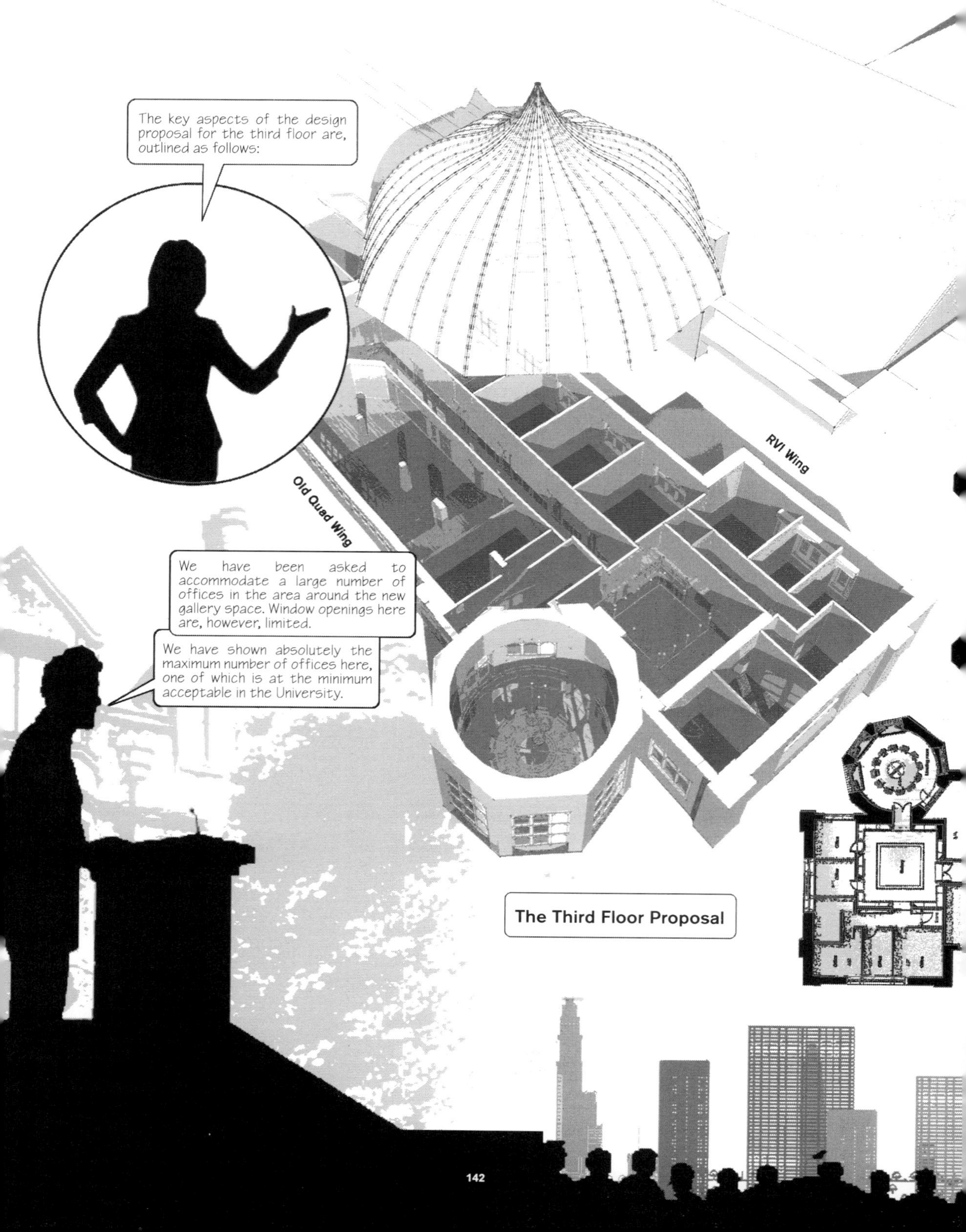
The key aspects of the design proposal for the third floor are, outlined as follows:
RVI Wing
Old Quad Wing
We have been asked to accommodate a large number of offices in the area around the new gallery space. Window openings here are, however, limited.
We have shown absolutely the maximum number of offices here, one of which is at the minimum acceptable in the University.
The Third Floor Proposal

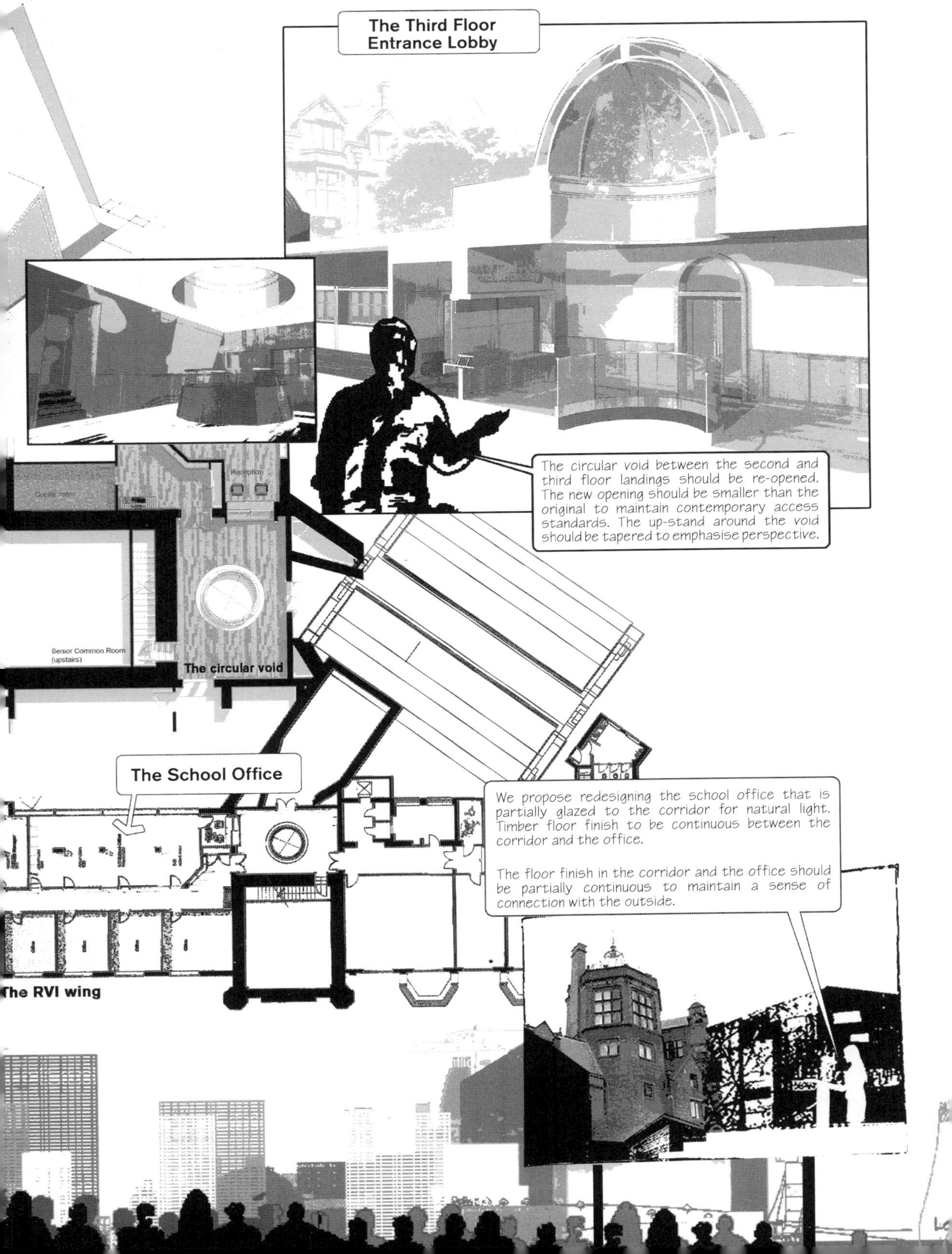
The Third Floor Entrance Lobby
The circular void between the second and third floor landings should be re-opened. The new opening should be smaller than the original to maintain contemporary access standards. The up-stand around the void should be tapered to emphasise perspective.
Reception
Copier room
Senior Common Room (upstairs)
The circular void
The School Office
We propose redesigning the school office that is partially glazed to the corridor for natural light. Timber floor finish to be continuous between the corridor and the office.
The floor finish in the corridor and the office should be partially continuous to maintain a sense of connection with the outside.
The RVI wing

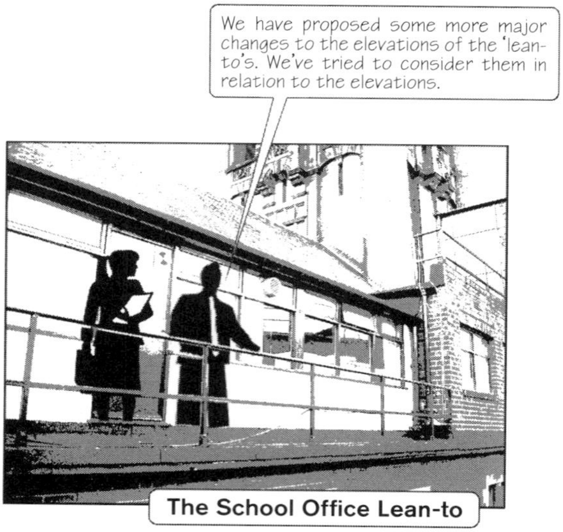
We have proposed some more major changes to the elevations of the 'lean-to's. We've tried to consider them in relation to the elevations.
The School Office Lean-to

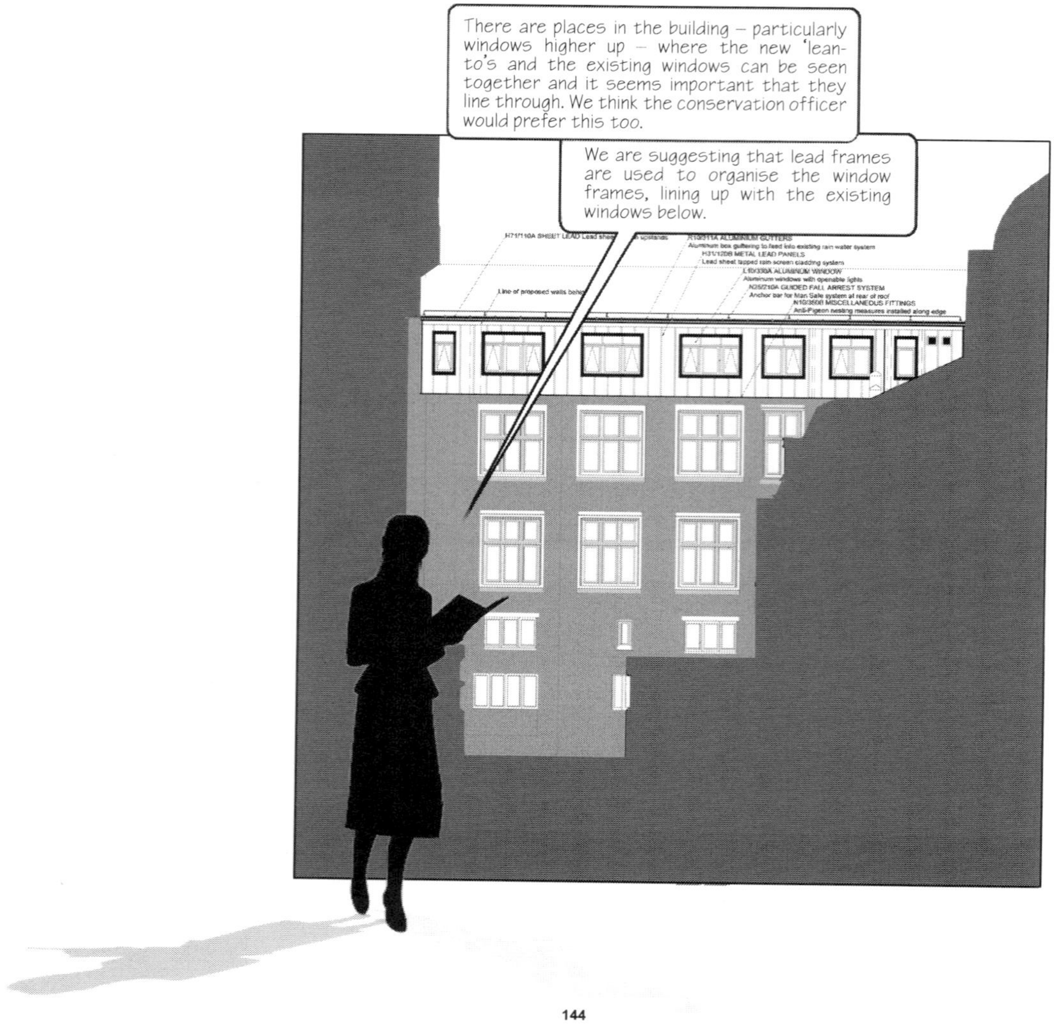
There are places in the building – particularly windows higher up – where the new 'lean-to's and the existing windows can be seen together and it seems important that they line through. We think the conservation officer would prefer this too.
We are suggesting that lead frames are used to organise the window frames, lining up with the existing windows below.
H31/12DB METAL LEAD PANELS
Lead sheet lapped rain screen cladding system
L10/330A ALUMINIUM WINDOW
Aluminium windows with openable lights
N25/210A GUIDED FALL ARREST SYSTEM
Anchor bar for Man Safe system at rear of roof
N10/350B MISCELLANEOUS FITTINGS
Anti-Pigeon nesting measures installed along edge

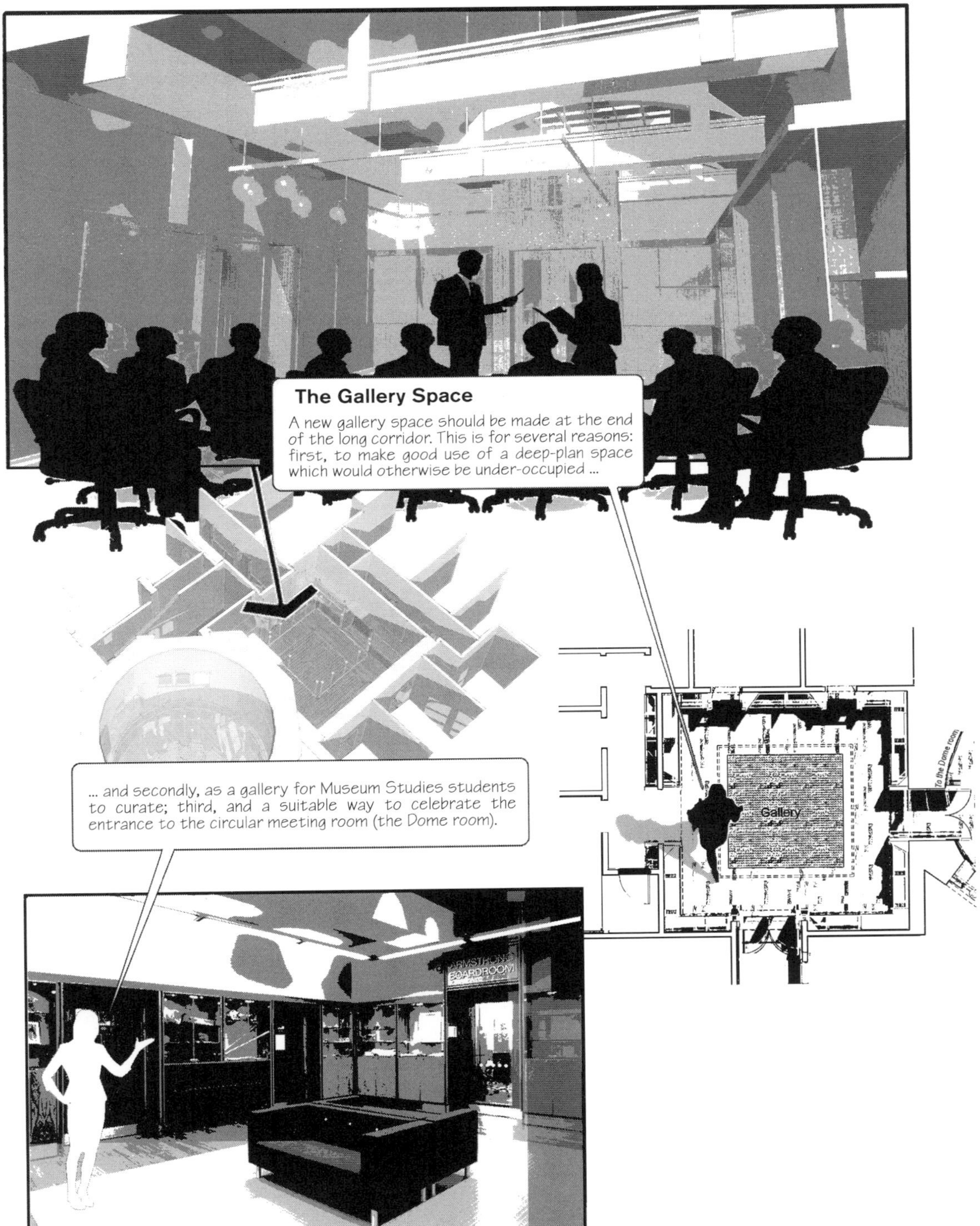
The Gallery Space
A new gallery space should be made at the end of the long corridor. This is for several reasons: first, to make good use of a deep-plan space which would otherwise be under-occupied ...
... and secondly, as a gallery for Museum Studies students to curate; third, and a suitable way to celebrate the entrance to the circular meeting room (the Dome room).
Gallery
To the Dome room
ARMSTRONG BOARDROOM

The Dome Room

Another of the building's most abused spaces is the fine room at the top of the tower which faces Old Quad. The view over the roofs towards the civic centre is delightful.

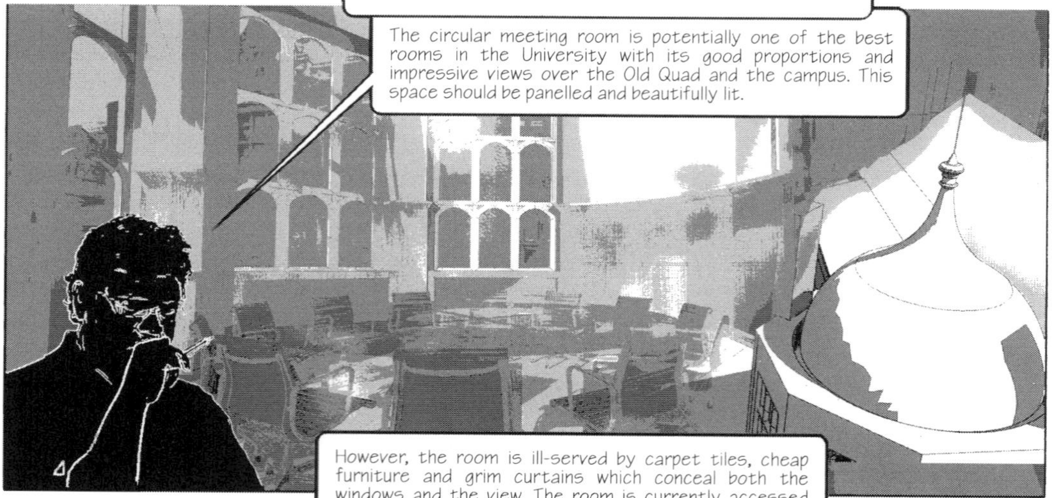

The circular meeting room is potentially one of the best rooms in the University with its good proportions and impressive views over the Old Quad and the campus. This space should be panelled and beautifully lit.

However, the room is ill-served by carpet tiles, cheap furniture and grim curtains which conceal both the windows and the view. The room is currently accessed by corridors carved up badly from a bigger space, filled with cheap shelves and dumped furniture. We recommend reconfiguring the entrance, painting the room sympathetically, fitting a timber floor, adding good furniture and perhaps panelling.

This could become one of the University's best meeting rooms, suitably impressive for important visitors and delightful for special meetings and seminars.

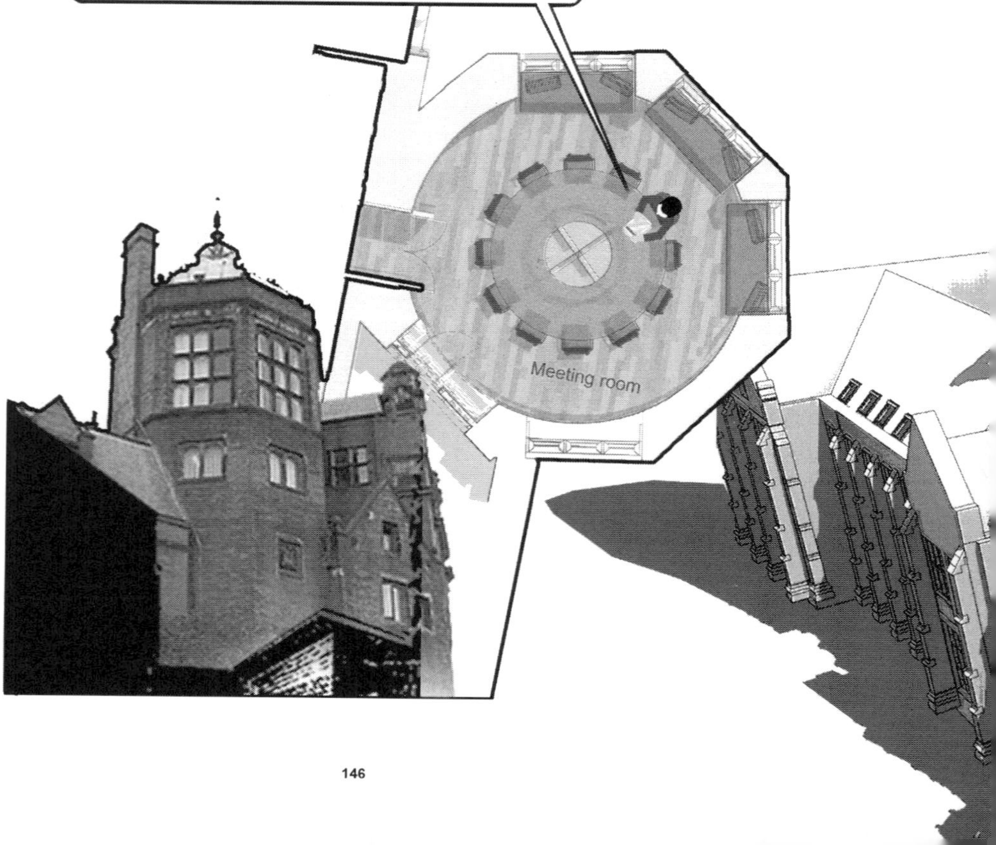
Meeting room

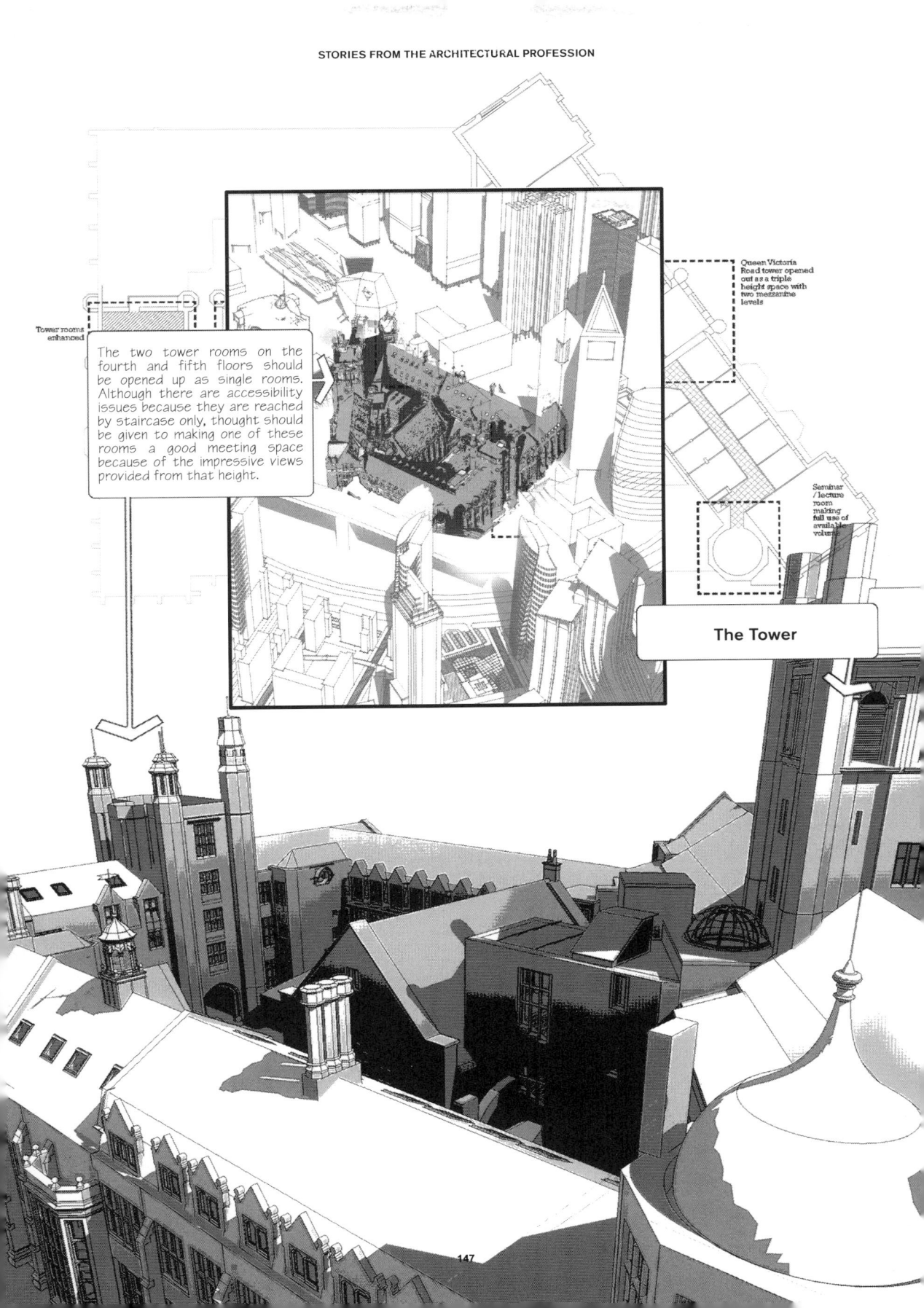

Tower rooms enhanced

The two tower rooms on the fourth and fifth floors should be opened up as single rooms. Although there are accessibility issues because they are reached by staircase only, thought should be given to making one of these rooms a good meeting space because of the impressive views provided from that height.

Queen Victoria Road tower opened out as a triple height space with two mezzanine levels

Seminar /lecture room making full use of available volume

The Tower

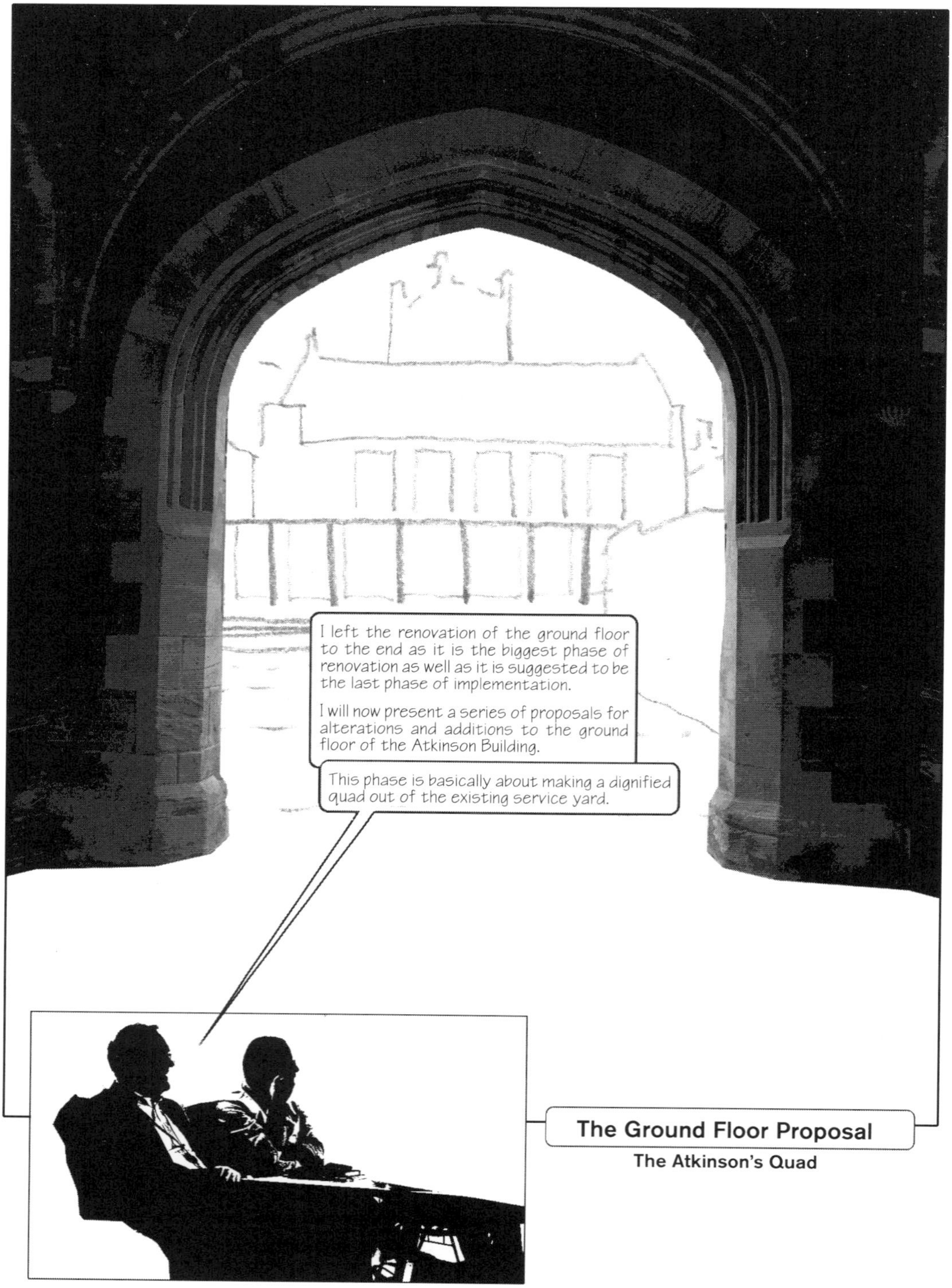
I left the renovation of the ground floor to the end as it is the biggest phase of renovation as well as it is suggested to be the last phase of implementation.
I will now present a series of proposals for alterations and additions to the ground floor of the Atkinson Building.
This phase is basically about making a dignified quad out of the existing service yard.
The Ground Floor Proposal
The Atkinson's Quad

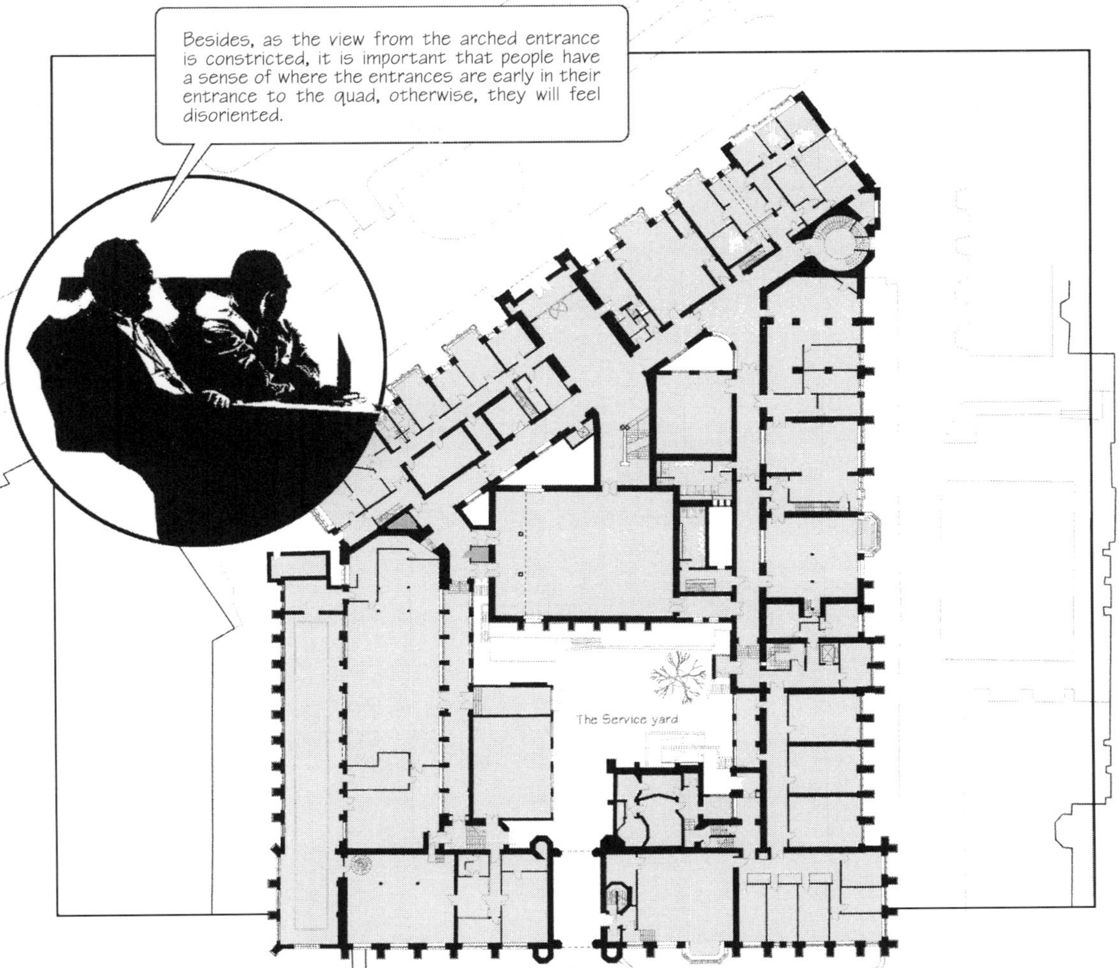
Besides, as the view from the arched entrance is constricted, it is important that people have a sense of where the entrances are early in their entrance to the quad, otherwise, they will feel disoriented.
The Service yard

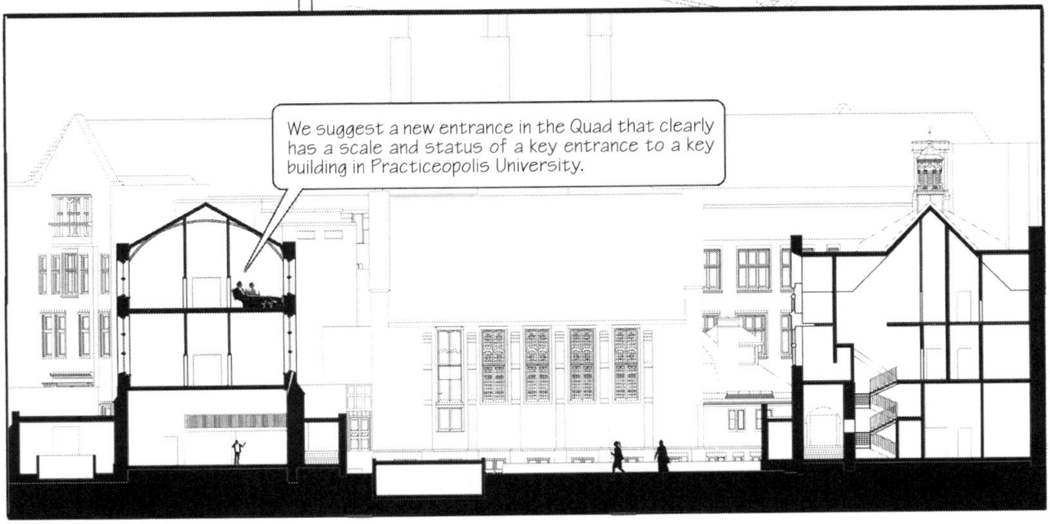
We suggest a new entrance in the Quad that clearly has a scale and status of a key entrance to a key building in Practiceopolis University.

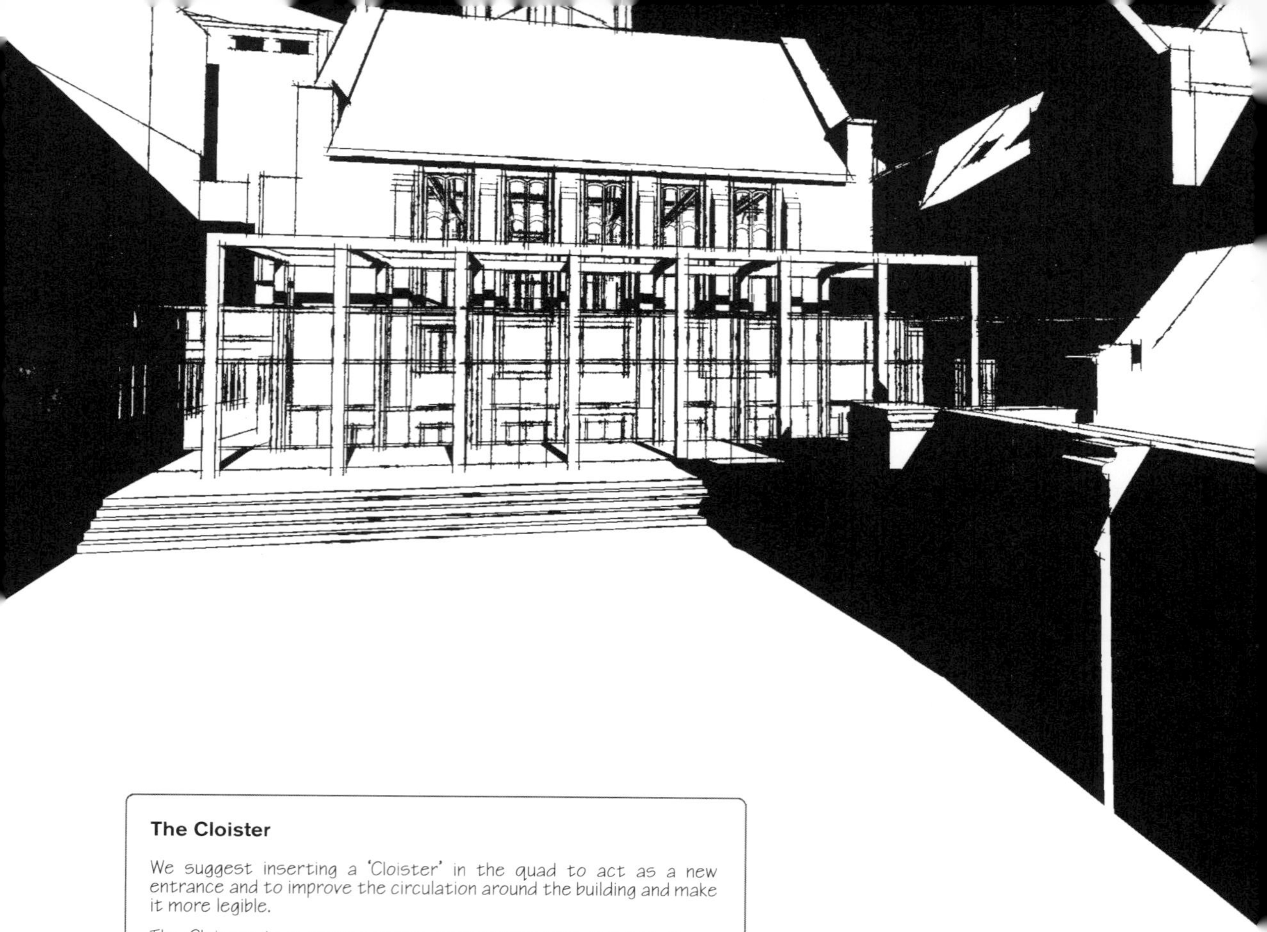

The Cloister

We suggest inserting a 'Cloister' in the quad to act as a new entrance and to improve the circulation around the building and make it more legible.

The Cloister is a contemporary intervention that will still rhyme with the historic qualities of the building while it will also act as a distinguishable architectural object that allows reading the quad as a formal entrance to building.

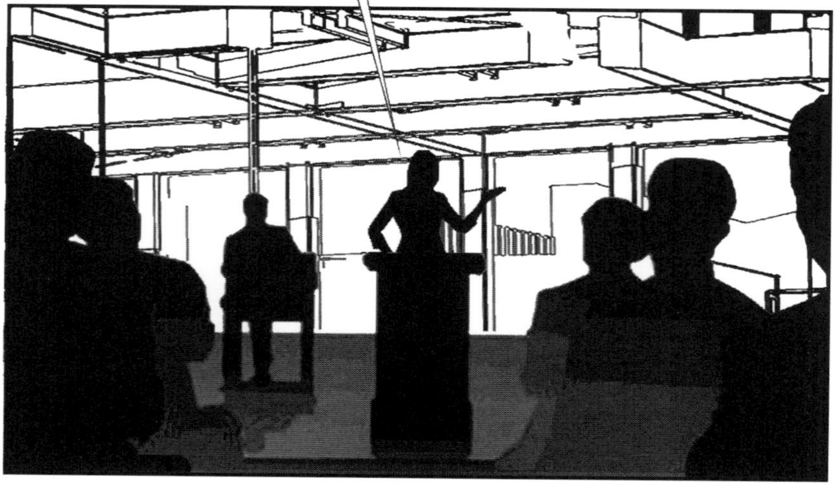

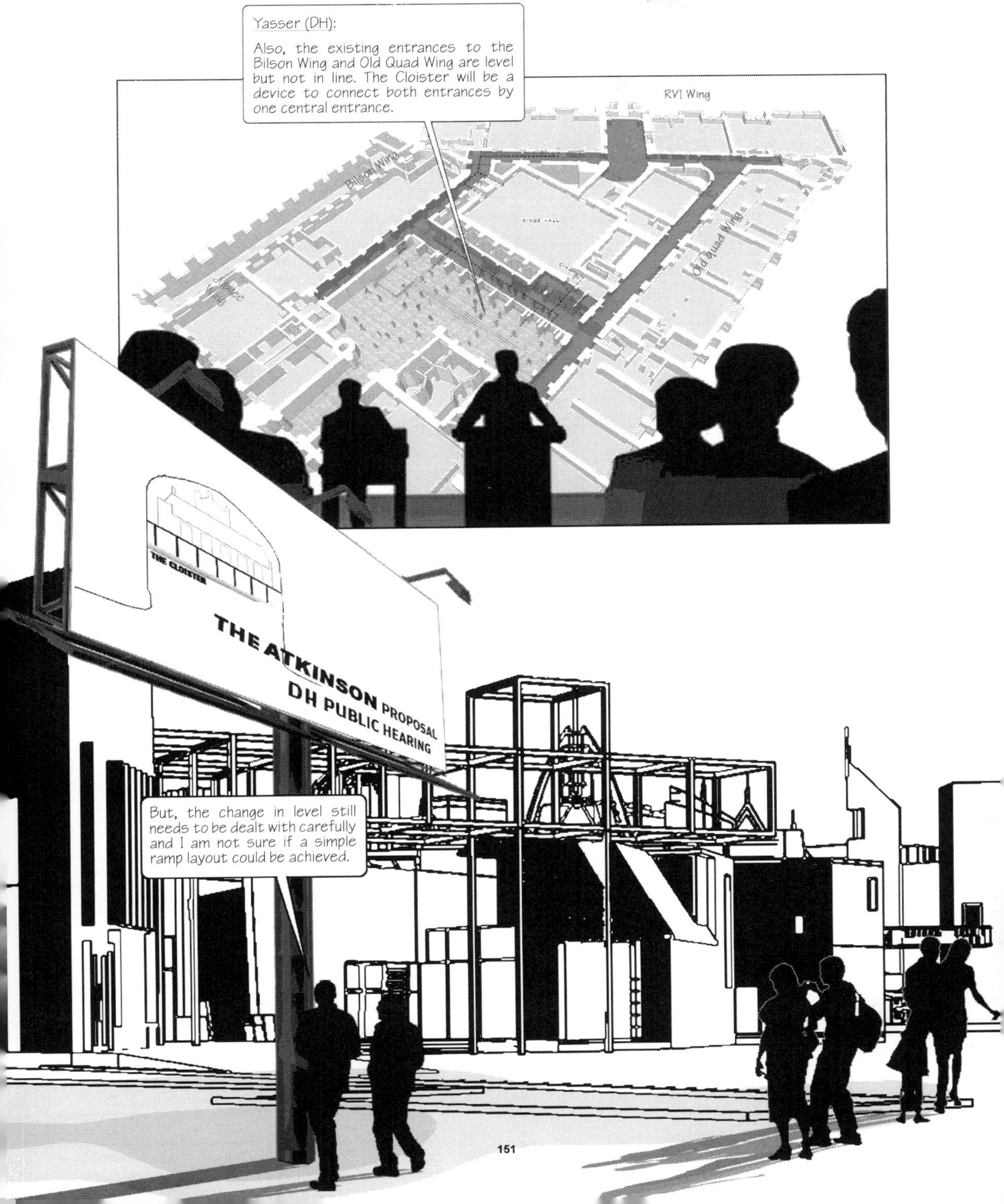
Yasser (DH):
Also, the existing entrances to the Bilson Wing and Old Quad Wing are level but not in line. The Cloister will be a device to connect both entrances by one central entrance.
RVI Wing
Bilson Wing
Old Quad Wing
THE CLOISTER
THE ATKINSON PROPOSAL
DH PUBLIC HEARING
But, the change in level still needs to be dealt with carefully and I am not sure if a simple ramp layout could be achieved.

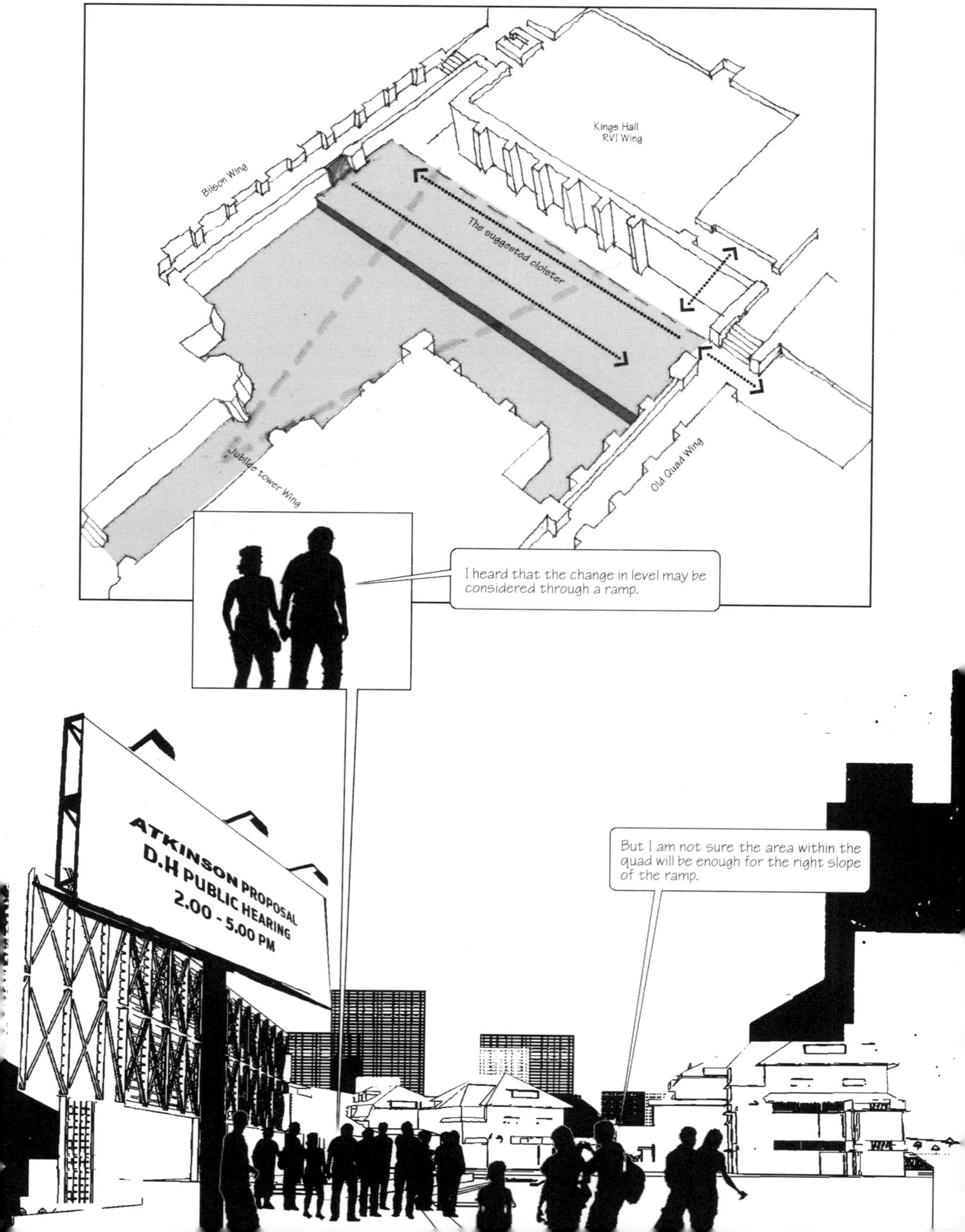
Kings Hall
RVI Wing
Bilson Wing
The suggested cloister
Jubilde tower Wing
Old Quad Wing
I heard that the change in level may be considered through a ramp.
ATKINSON PROPOSAL
D.H PUBLIC HEARING
2.00 - 5.00 PM
But I am not sure the area within the quad will be enough for the right slope of the ramp.

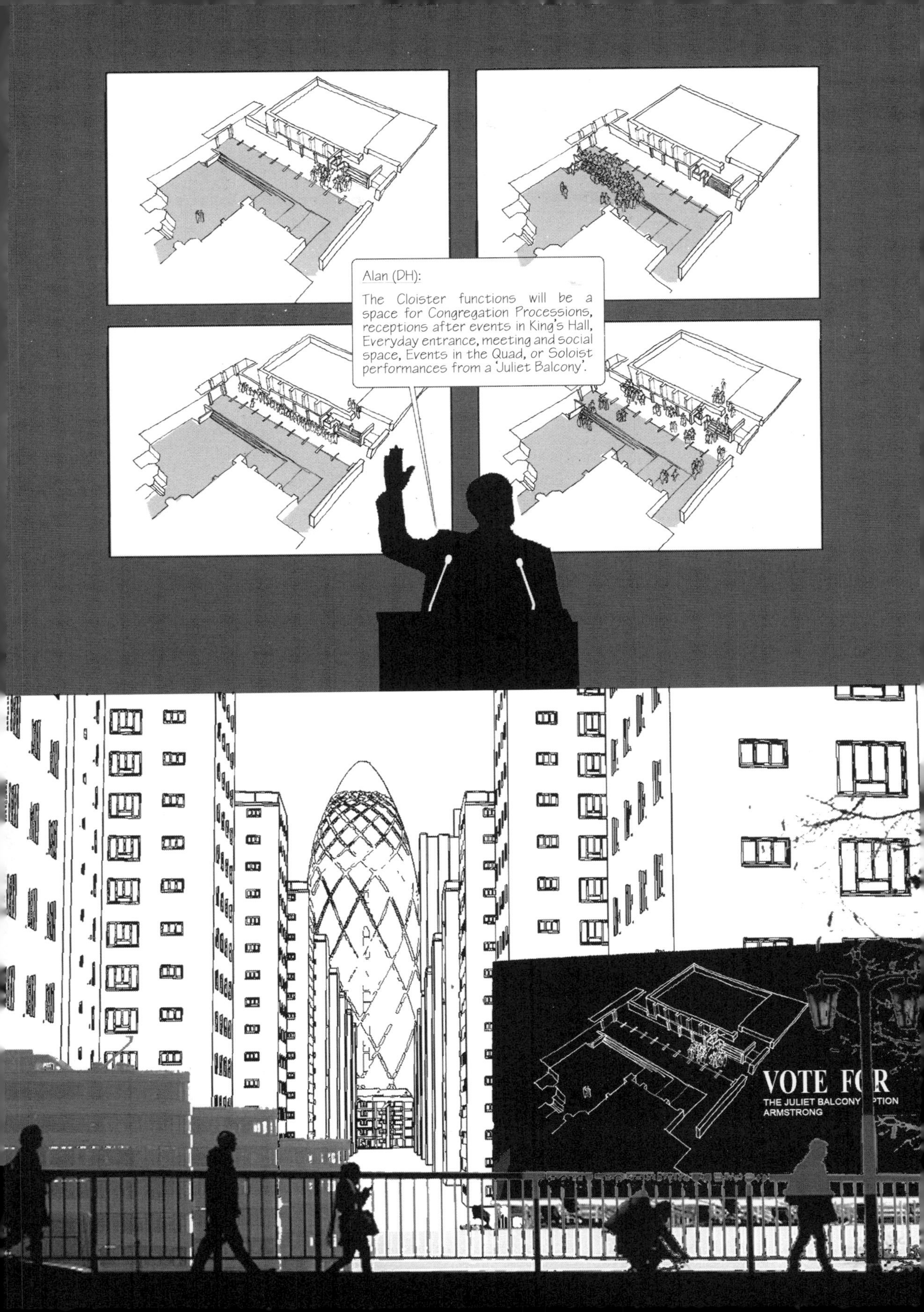
Alan (DH):
The Cloister functions will be a space for Congregation Processions, receptions after events in King's Hall, Everyday entrance, meeting and social space, Events in the Quad, or Soloist performances from a 'Juliet Balcony'.
VOTE F R
THE JULIET BALCONY PTION
ARMSTRONG

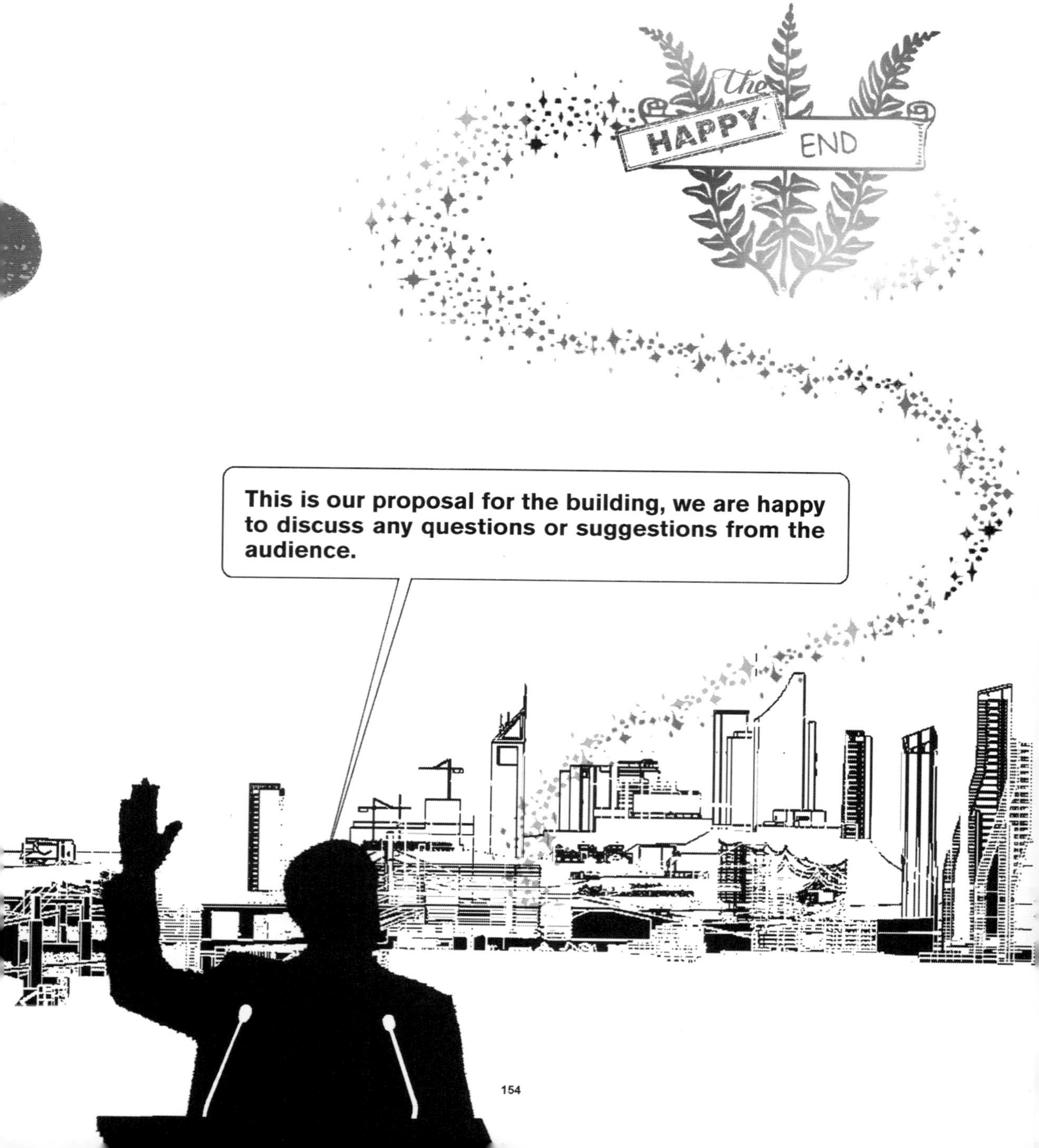
the
HAPPY
END
This is our proposal for the building, we are happy to discuss any questions or suggestions from the audience.

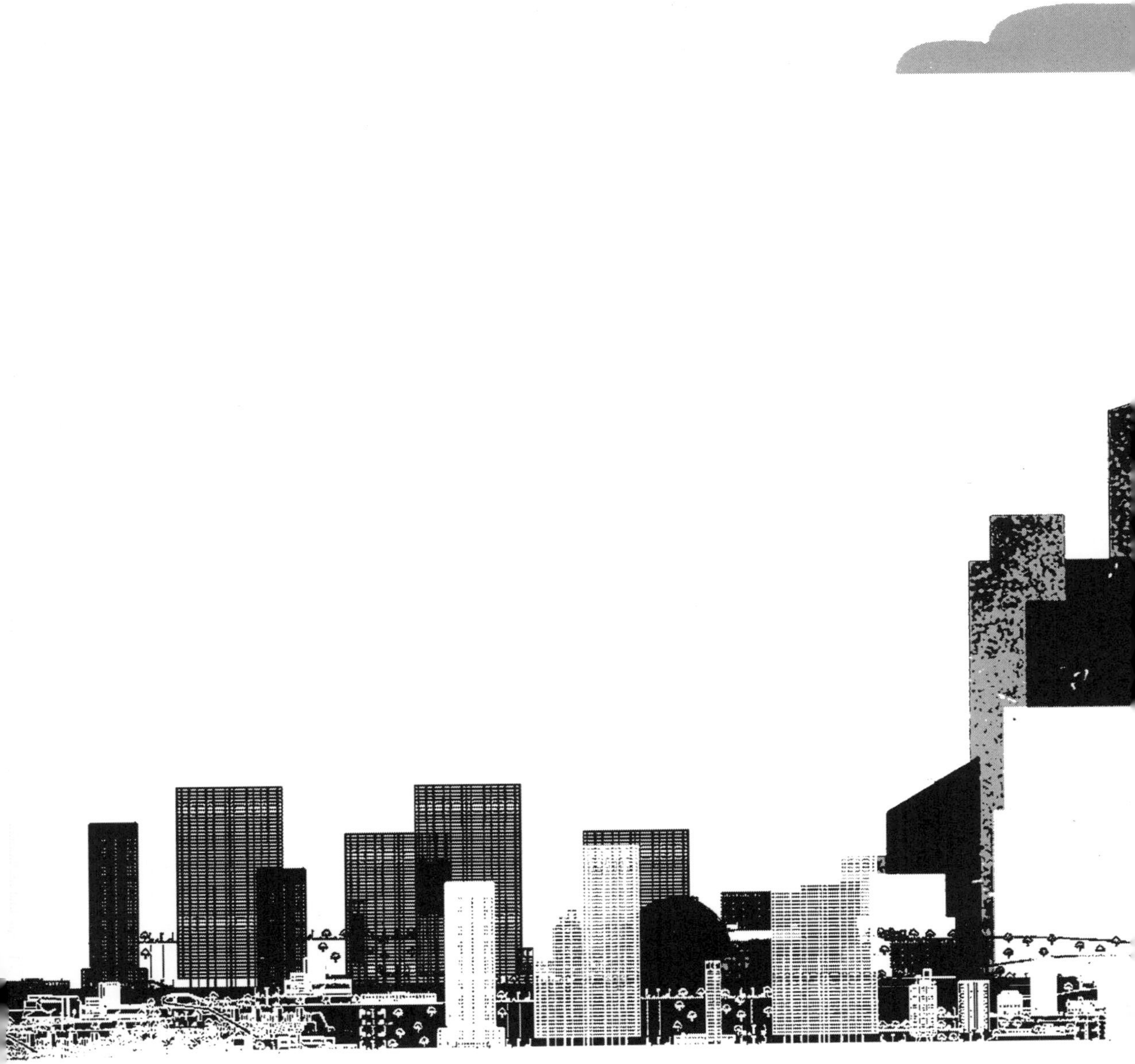

Later, the discussion went well with slight functional questions from the client and different stakeholders. The project was conceptually approved and moved to the next phase of design development and implementation.

STORIES FROM THE ARCHITECTURAL PROFESSION

The UNHAPPY TRUTH

The Clashes

After the presentation in the Parliament, EFM took the designs for comments and revisions. During the design development phase, several progress meetings took place at different places in Practiceopolis: some at EFM headquarters, some others at same halls in the Map Library, while also some meetings were in the Atkinson Building itself. These meetings were broadcasted live on TV, where people of Practiceopolis can follow the project development and can send their comments to the Parliament House.

The progress meetings of the Atkinson project displayed a semi-collaborative/ confrontational atmosphere among the team members. They showed clearly the disparate views between the Technical-rationals and the Criticals in the city. They also witnessed the hidden clashes of values and priorities between Practiceopolis and key actors of Constructopolis.

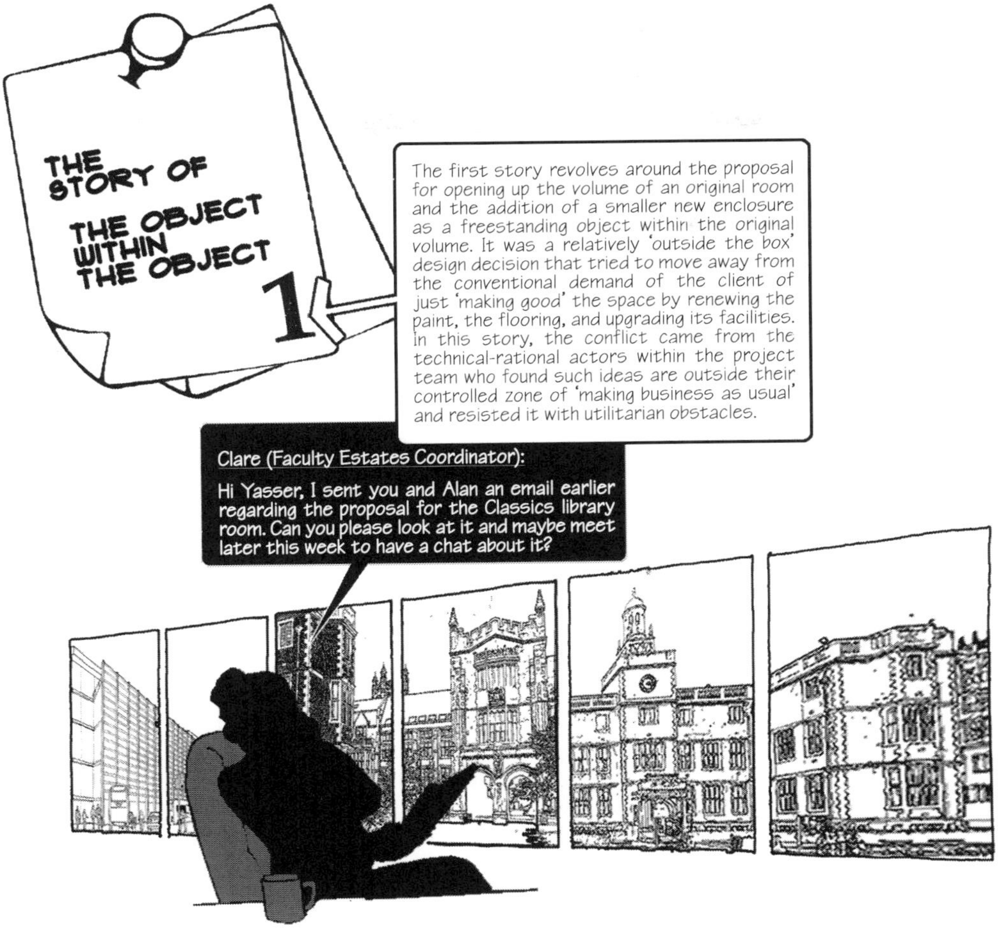
THE STORY OF
THE OBJECT WITHIN THE OBJECT
1
The first story revolves around the proposal for opening up the volume of an original room and the addition of a smaller new enclosure as a freestanding object within the original volume. It was a relatively 'outside the box' design decision that tried to move away from the conventional demand of the client of just 'making good' the space by renewing the paint, the flooring, and upgrading its facilities. In this story, the conflict came from the technical-rational actors within the project team who found such ideas are outside their controlled zone of 'making business as usual' and resisted it with utilitarian obstacles.
Clare (Faculty Estates Coordinator):
Hi Yasser, I sent you and Alan an email earlier regarding the proposal for the Classics library room. Can you please look at it and maybe meet later this week to have a chat about it?

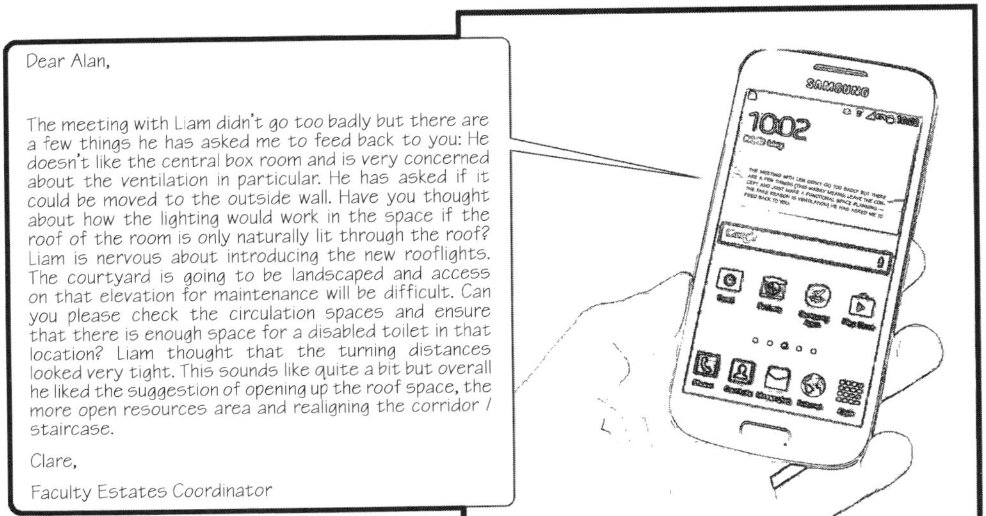
Dear Alan,
The meeting with Liam didn't go too badly but there are a few things he has asked me to feed back to you: He doesn't like the central box room and is very concerned about the ventilation in particular. He has asked if it could be moved to the outside wall. Have you thought about how the lighting would work in the space if the roof of the room is only naturally lit through the roof? Liam is nervous about introducing the new rooflights. The courtyard is going to be landscaped and access on that elevation for maintenance will be difficult. Can you please check the circulation spaces and ensure that there is enough space for a disabled toilet in that location? Liam thought that the turning distances looked very tight. This sounds like quite a bit but overall he liked the suggestion of opening up the roof space, the more open resources area and realigning the corridor / staircase.
Clare,
Faculty Estates Coordinator
SAMSUNG
10:02

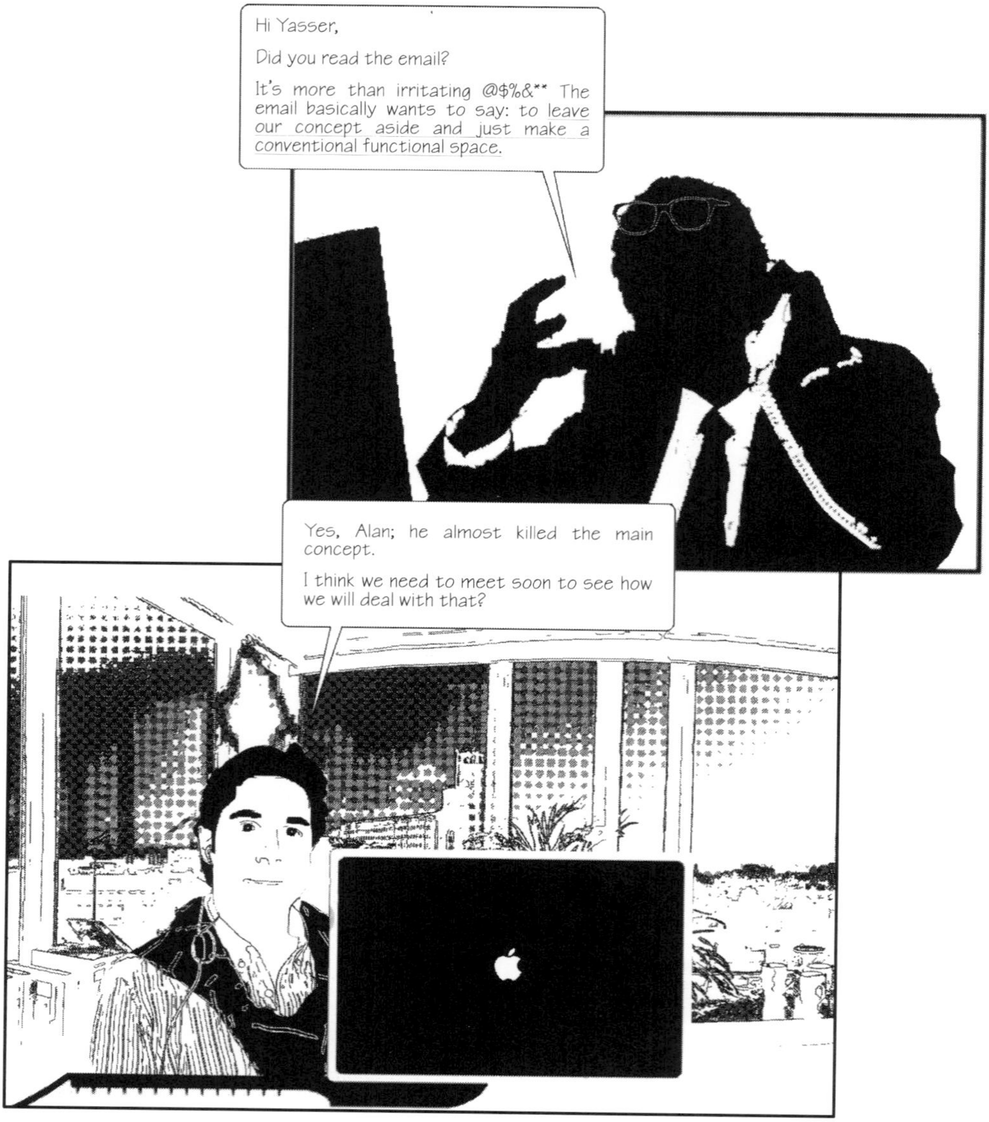
Hi Yasser,
Did you read the email?
It's more than irritating @$%&** The email basically wants to say: to leave our concept aside and just make a conventional functional space.
Yes, Alan; he almost killed the main concept.
I think we need to meet soon to see how we will deal with that?

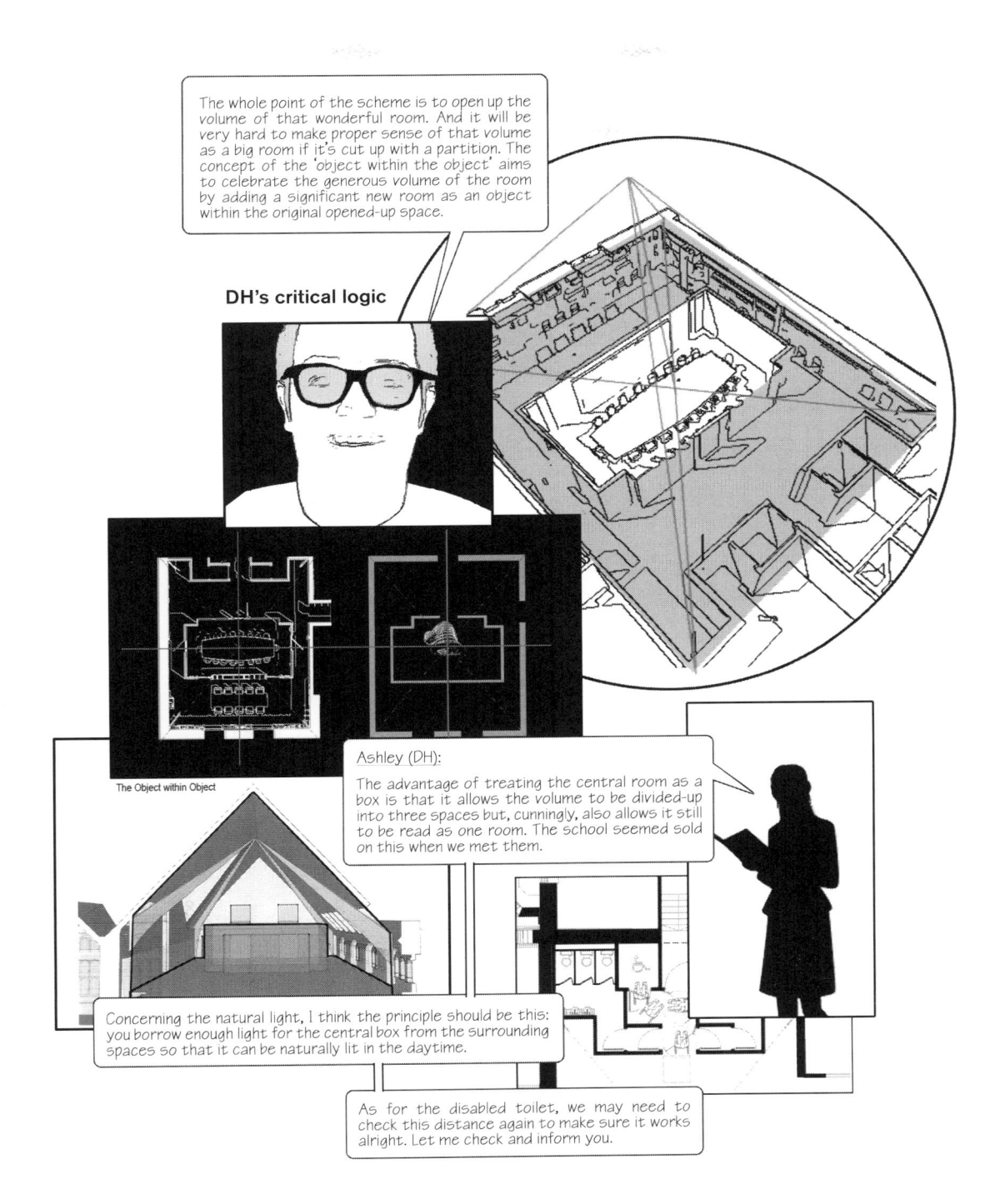

The whole point of the scheme is to open up the volume of that wonderful room. And it will be very hard to make proper sense of that volume as a big room if it's cut up with a partition. The concept of the 'object within the object' aims to celebrate the generous volume of the room by adding a significant new room as an object within the original opened-up space.

DH's critical logic

The Object within Object

Ashley (DH):

The advantage of treating the central room as a box is that it allows the volume to be divided-up into three spaces but, cunningly, also allows it still to be read as one room. The school seemed sold on this when we met them.

Concerning the natural light, I think the principle should be this: you borrow enough light for the central box from the surrounding spaces so that it can be naturally lit in the daytime.

As for the disabled toilet, we may need to check this distance again to make sure it works alright. Let me check and inform you.

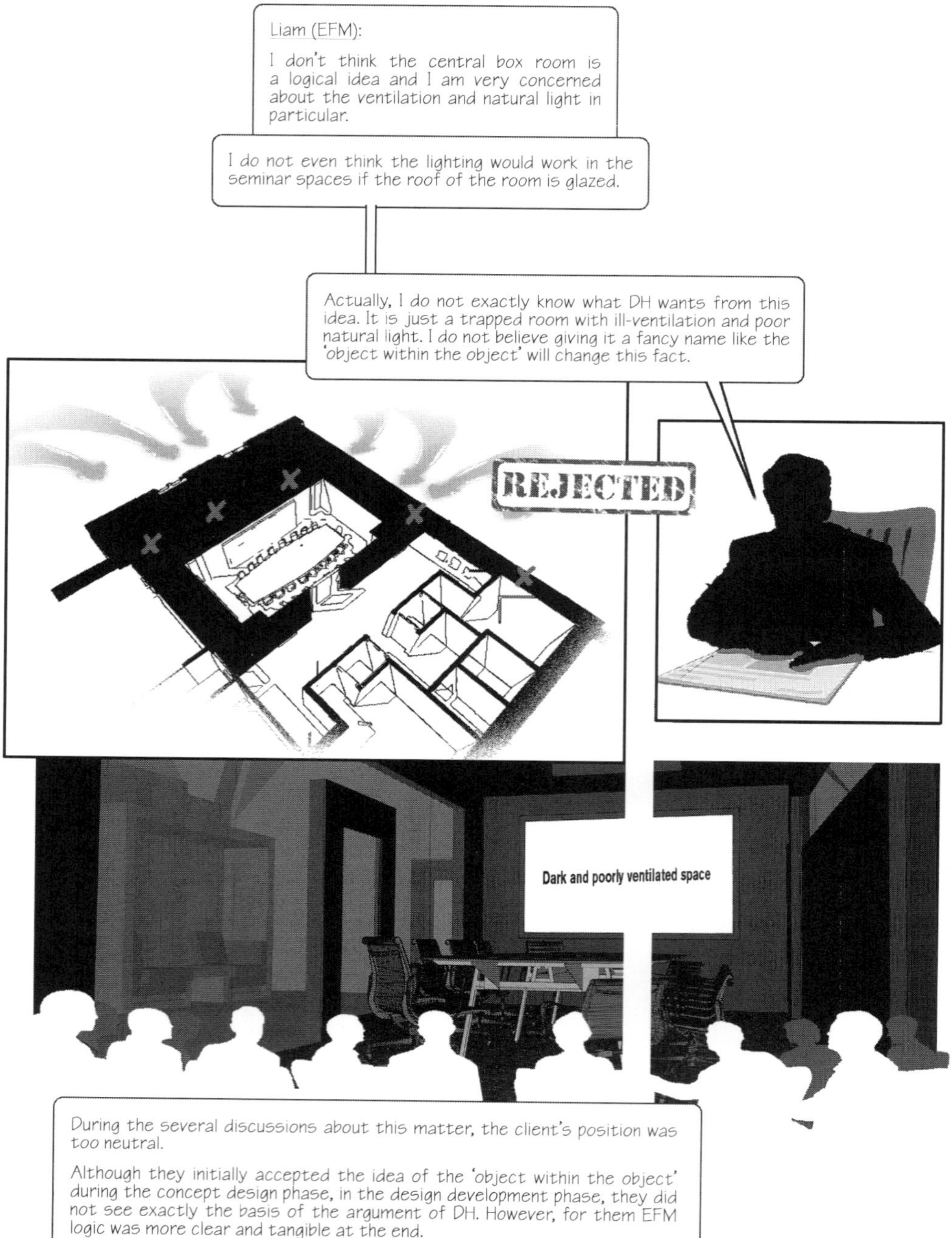
Liam (EFM):
I don't think the central box room is a logical idea and I am very concerned about the ventilation and natural light in particular.
I do not even think the lighting would work in the seminar spaces if the roof of the room is glazed.
Actually, I do not exactly know what DH wants from this idea. It is just a trapped room with ill-ventilation and poor natural light. I do not believe giving it a fancy name like the 'object within the object' will change this fact.
REJECTED
Dark and poorly ventilated space
During the several discussions about this matter, the client's position was too neutral.
Although they initially accepted the idea of the 'object within the object' during the concept design phase, in the design development phase, they did not see exactly the basis of the argument of DH. However, for them EFM logic was more clear and tangible at the end.

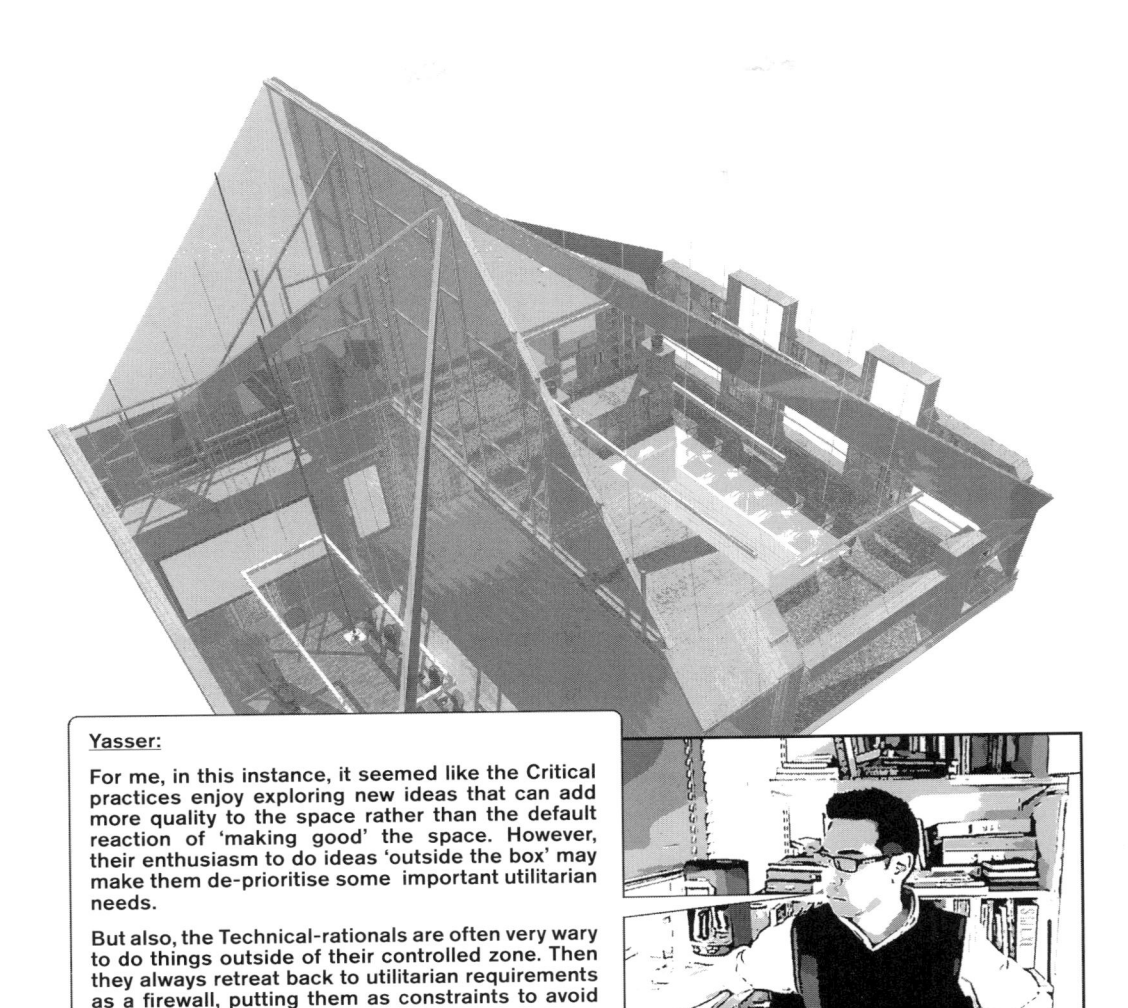

Yasser:

For me, in this instance, it seemed like the Critical practices enjoy exploring new ideas that can add more quality to the space rather than the default reaction of 'making good' the space. However, their enthusiasm to do ideas 'outside the box' may make them de-prioritise some important utilitarian needs.

But also, the Technical-rationals are often very wary to do things outside of their controlled zone. Then they always retreat back to utilitarian requirements as a firewall, putting them as constraints to avoid unusual ideas.

In the end, a compromise was achieved and the original volume was opened up but with a different room arrangement underneath but carrying the same spirit of the original concept of the 'object within the object'.

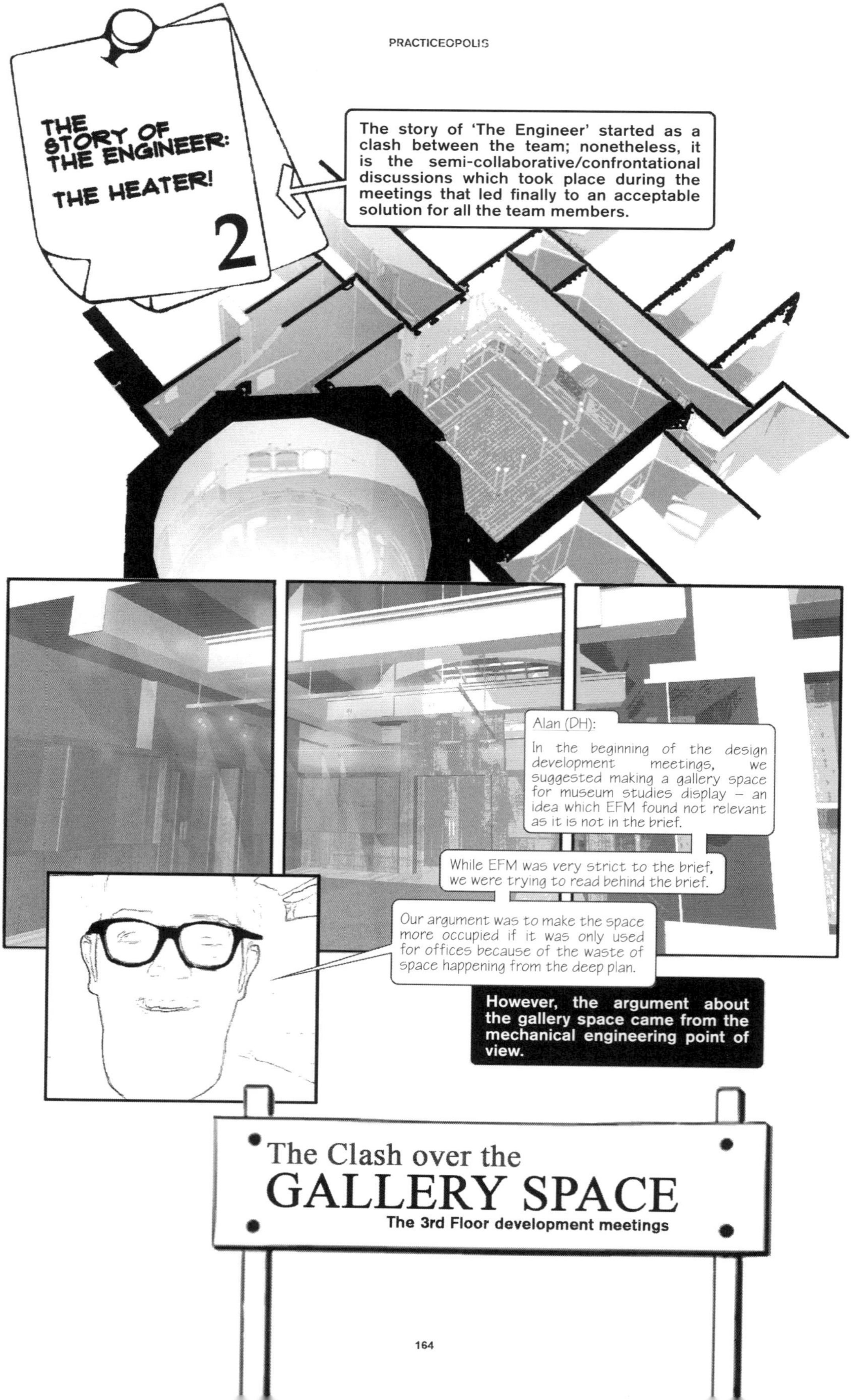
THE STORY OF THE ENGINEER: THE HEATER!
2
The story of 'The Engineer' started as a clash between the team; nonetheless, it is the semi-collaborative/confrontational discussions which took place during the meetings that led finally to an acceptable solution for all the team members.
Alan (DH):
In the beginning of the design development meetings, we suggested making a gallery space for museum studies display – an idea which EFM found not relevant as it is not in the brief.
While EFM was very strict to the brief, we were trying to read behind the brief.
Our argument was to make the space more occupied if it was only used for offices because of the waste of space happening from the deep plan.
However, the argument about the gallery space came from the mechanical engineering point of view.
The Clash over the
GALLERY SPACE
The 3rd Floor development meetings

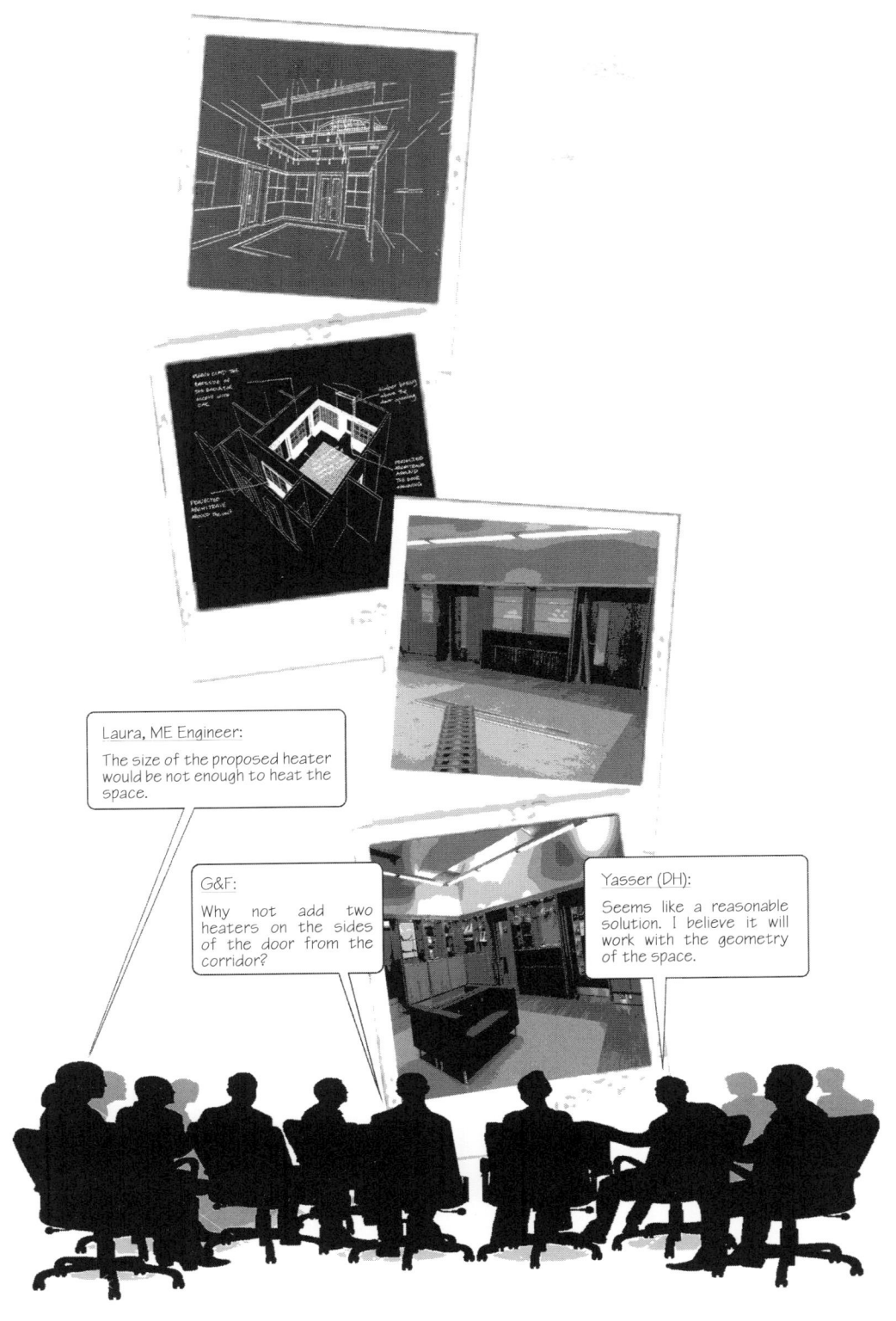

Laura, ME Engineer:
The size of the proposed heater would be not enough to heat the space.

G&F:
Why not add two heaters on the sides of the door from the corridor?

Yasser (DH):
Seems like a reasonable solution. I believe it will work with the geometry of the space.

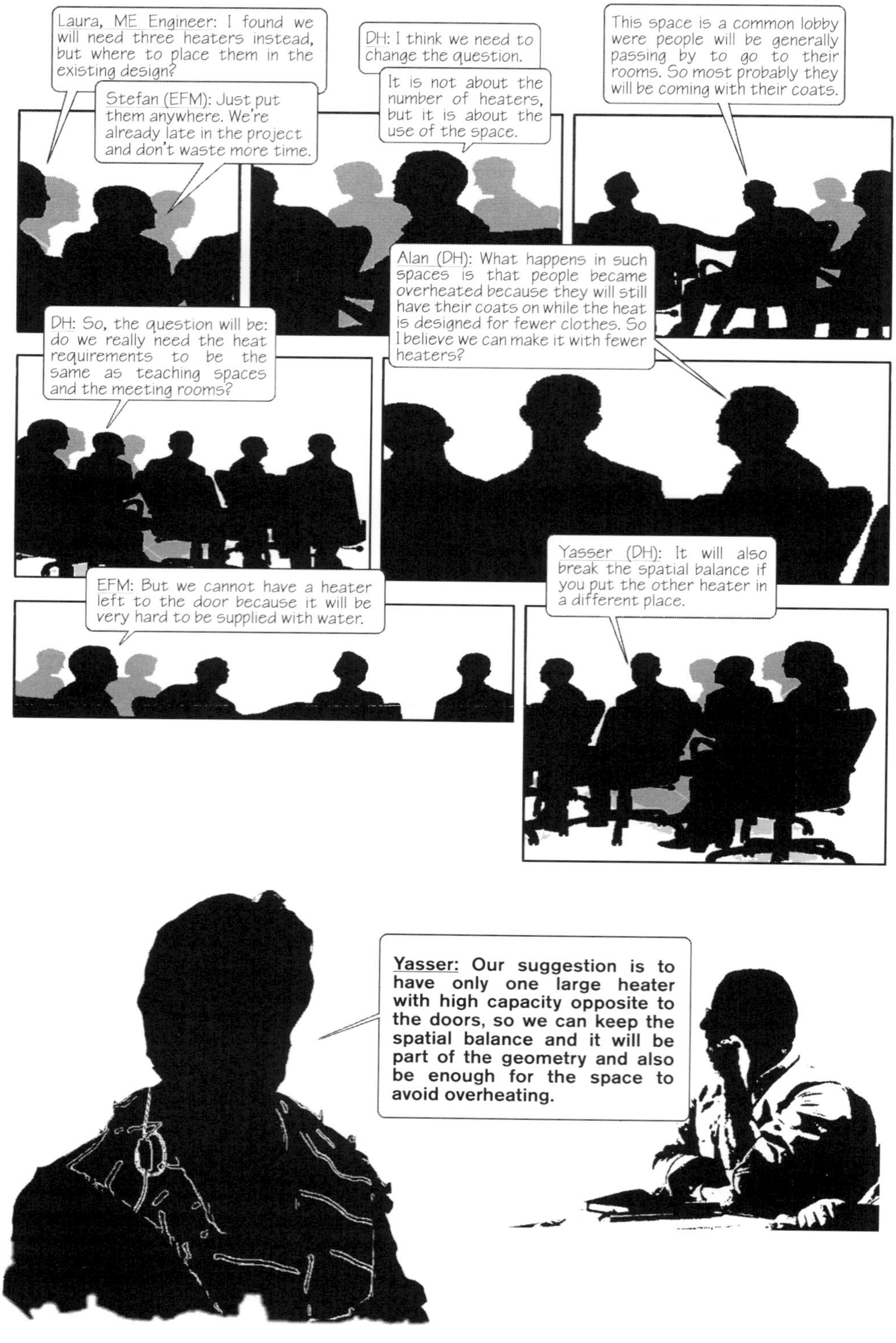

Laura, ME Engineer: I found we will need three heaters instead, but where to place them in the existing design?
Stefan (EFM): Just put them anywhere. We're already late in the project and don't waste more time.
DH: I think we need to change the question.
It is not about the number of heaters, but it is about the use of the space.
This space is a common lobby were people will be generally passing by to go to their rooms. So most probably they will be coming with their coats.
DH: So, the question will be: do we really need the heat requirements to be the same as teaching spaces and the meeting rooms?
Alan (DH): What happens in such spaces is that people became overheated because they will still have their coats on while the heat is designed for fewer clothes. So I believe we can make it with fewer heaters?
EFM: But we cannot have a heater left to the door because it will be very hard to be supplied with water.
Yasser (DH): It will also break the spatial balance if you put the other heater in a different place.
Yasser: Our suggestion is to have only one large heater with high capacity opposite to the doors, so we can keep the spatial balance and it will be part of the geometry and also be enough for the space to avoid overheating.

Laura, ME Engineer: I believe this can work;

I will *do* some revised calculations and produce new drawings.

We won this argument at the end!!

The issue here was clearly technical and it has a relatively straightforward technical solution.

Nevertheless, it showed how the technical actors in the building industry seem to be mostly focusing on solving certain defined problems without seeing the bigger picture around the problem or what their straightforward solution may do to the visual and spatial experience of the space.

When DH suggested a different solution for the issue in the hope of saving the qualities of the proposed space, the technical-rational actors skilfully and – also easily – tailored their original solution to the architectural suggestion.

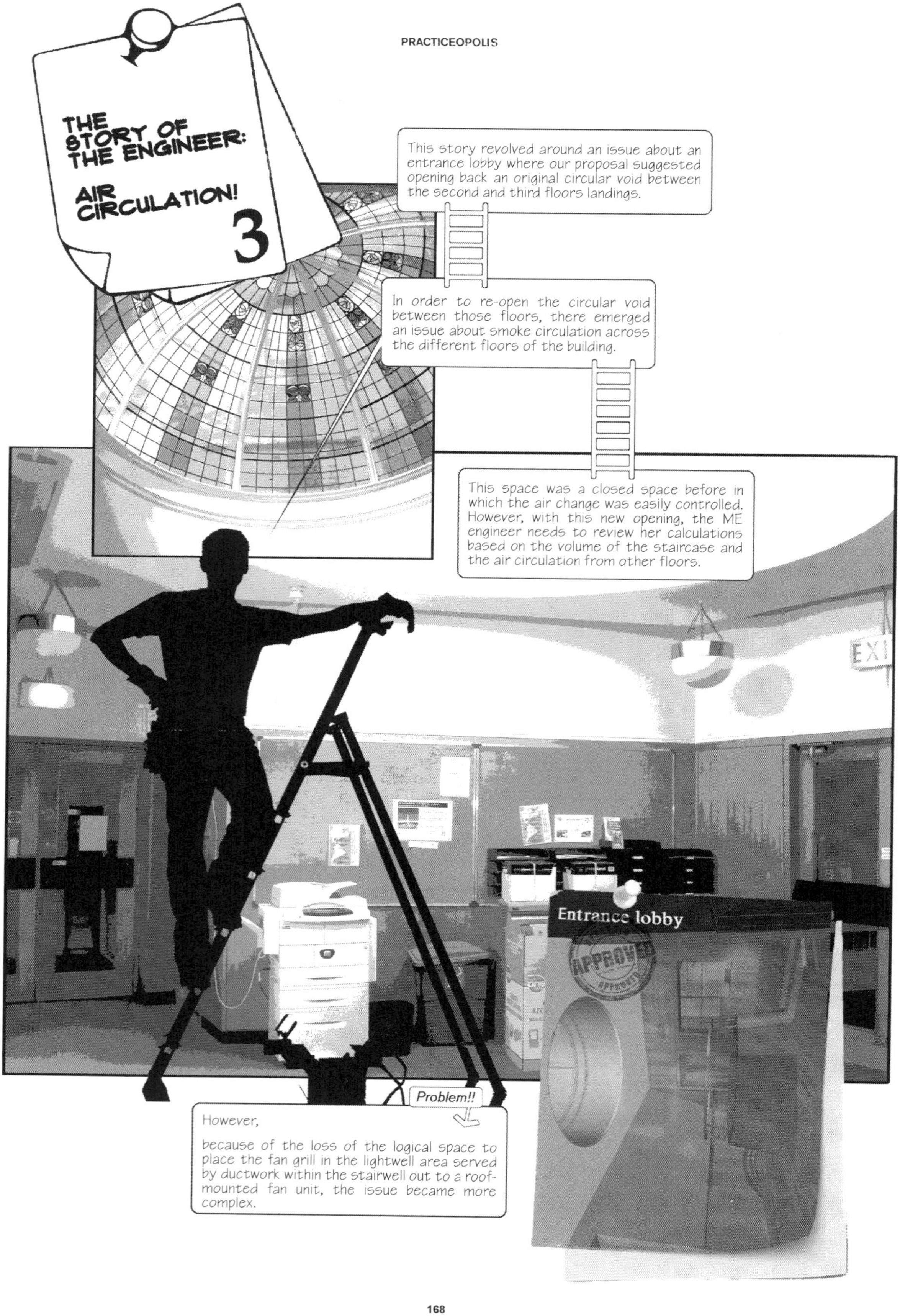
THE STORY OF THE ENGINEER:
AIR CIRCULATION!
3
This story revolved around an issue about an entrance lobby where our proposal suggested opening back an original circular void between the second and third floors landings.
In order to re-open the circular void between those floors, there emerged an issue about smoke circulation across the different floors of the building.
This space was a closed space before in which the air change was easily controlled. However, with this new opening, the ME engineer needs to review her calculations based on the volume of the staircase and the air circulation from other floors.
Problem!!
However,
because of the loss of the logical space to place the fan grill in the lightwell area served by ductwork within the stairwell out to a roof-mounted fan unit, the issue became more complex.
Entrance lobby
APPROVED

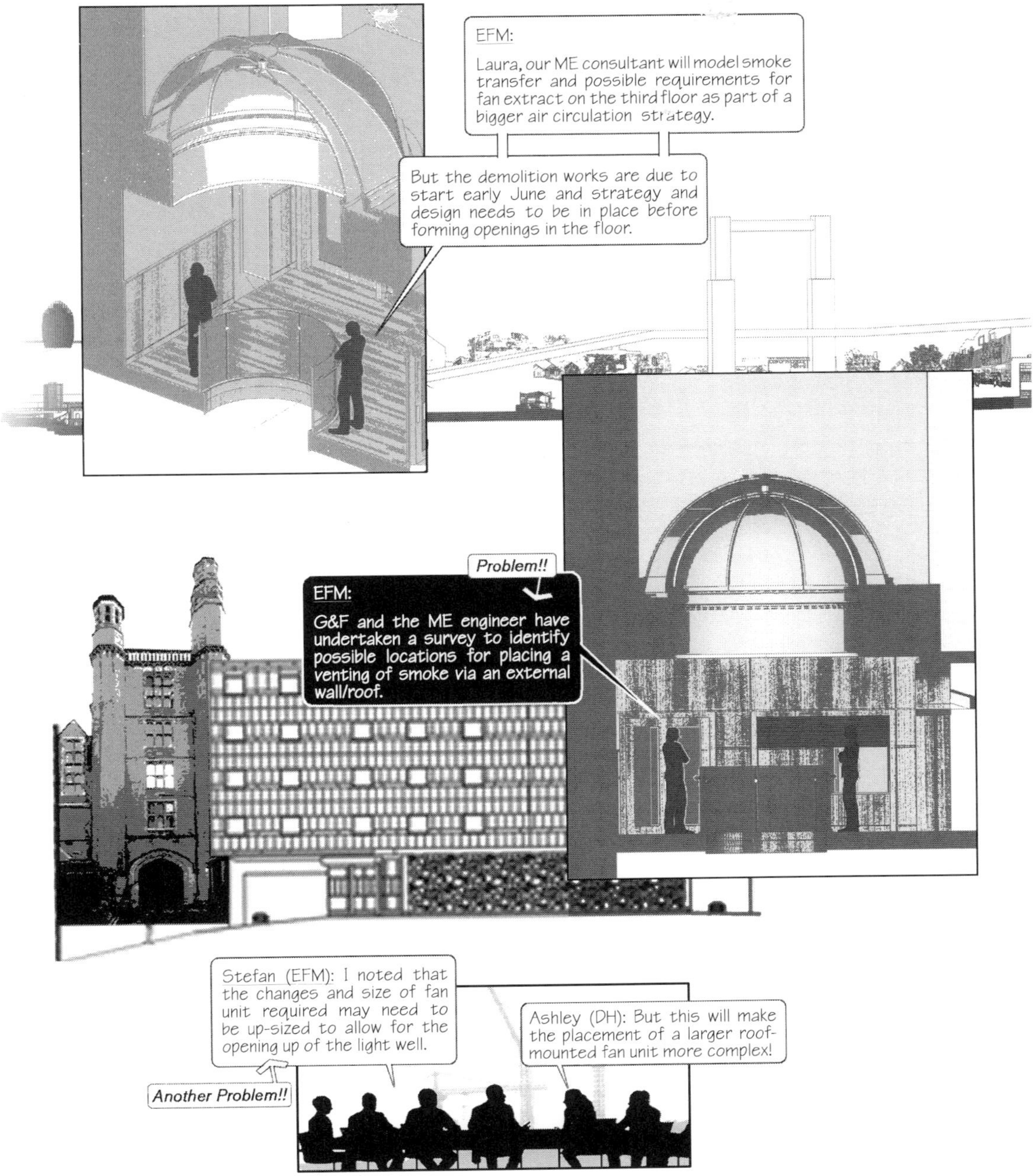
EFM:
Laura, our ME consultant will model smoke transfer and possible requirements for fan extract on the third floor as part of a bigger air circulation strategy.
But the demolition works are due to start early June and strategy and design needs to be in place before forming openings in the floor.
Problem!!
EFM:
G&F and the ME engineer have undertaken a survey to identify possible locations for placing a venting of smoke via an external wall/roof.
Stefan (EFM): I noted that the changes and size of fan unit required may need to be up-sized to allow for the opening up of the light well.
Another Problem!!
Ashley (DH): But this will make the placement of a larger roof-mounted fan unit more complex!

Stefan (EFM): Why not just close this void with a clear glass panel, so it will still look as an opening but without the headache of smoke calculation of the different floors?

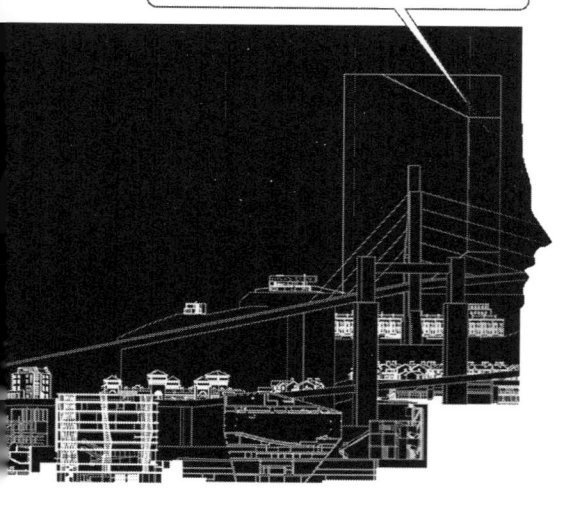

DH: Our position here is clearly against this suggestion. You are losing an important design quality to solve a utilitarian problem which is not acceptable to us.

If so, do not open it up at all!!

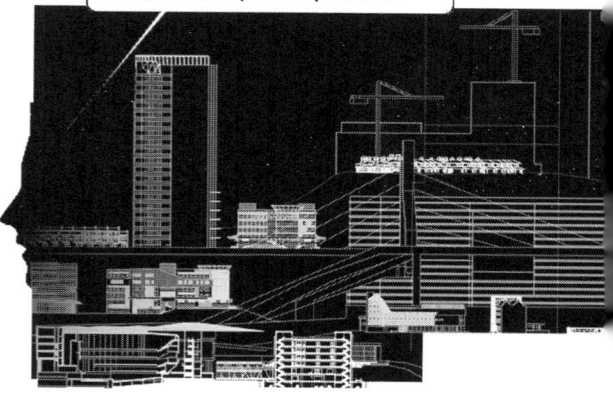

Yasser (DH):

However, in this case we were constrained with our limited knowledge about the technicality of mechanical air handling, therefore, we could not suggest a proper solution. Our only strategy to protect our proposal for opening up the circular void was just to critique whatever suggestion the ME engineer proposed until finding a suitable compromise.

This issue was finally solved when the team came to a solution of using an existing lift shaft to allocate the ductwork and directly link it to a large fan unit on the roof that fulfils the air circulation requirement.

In sum, this simple story shows how some bureaucratic exchanges in the building process may start as a pool for clashes, imposition, and control. However, they also can be turned into a collaborative impetus to find an acceptable compromise for all members of the construction team.

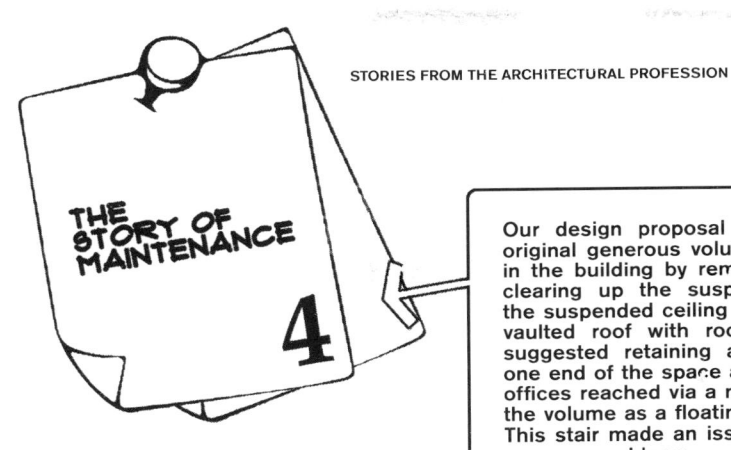

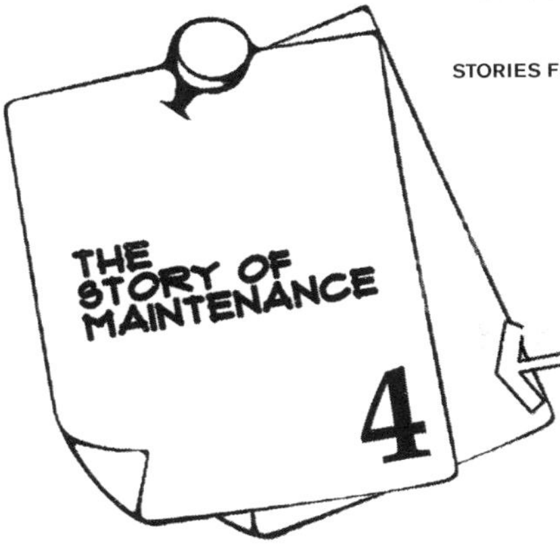
THE STORY OF MAINTENANCE
4

Our design proposal involved opening up an original generous volume of a certain key room in the building by removing later partitions and clearing up the suspended ceiling. Removing the suspended ceiling revealed a striking barrel-vaulted roof with rooflights. The design also suggested retaining an existing mezzanine at one end of the space and partitioning it as three offices reached via a new staircase inserted into the volume as a floating object within the space. This stair made an issue mainly with the facility management team.

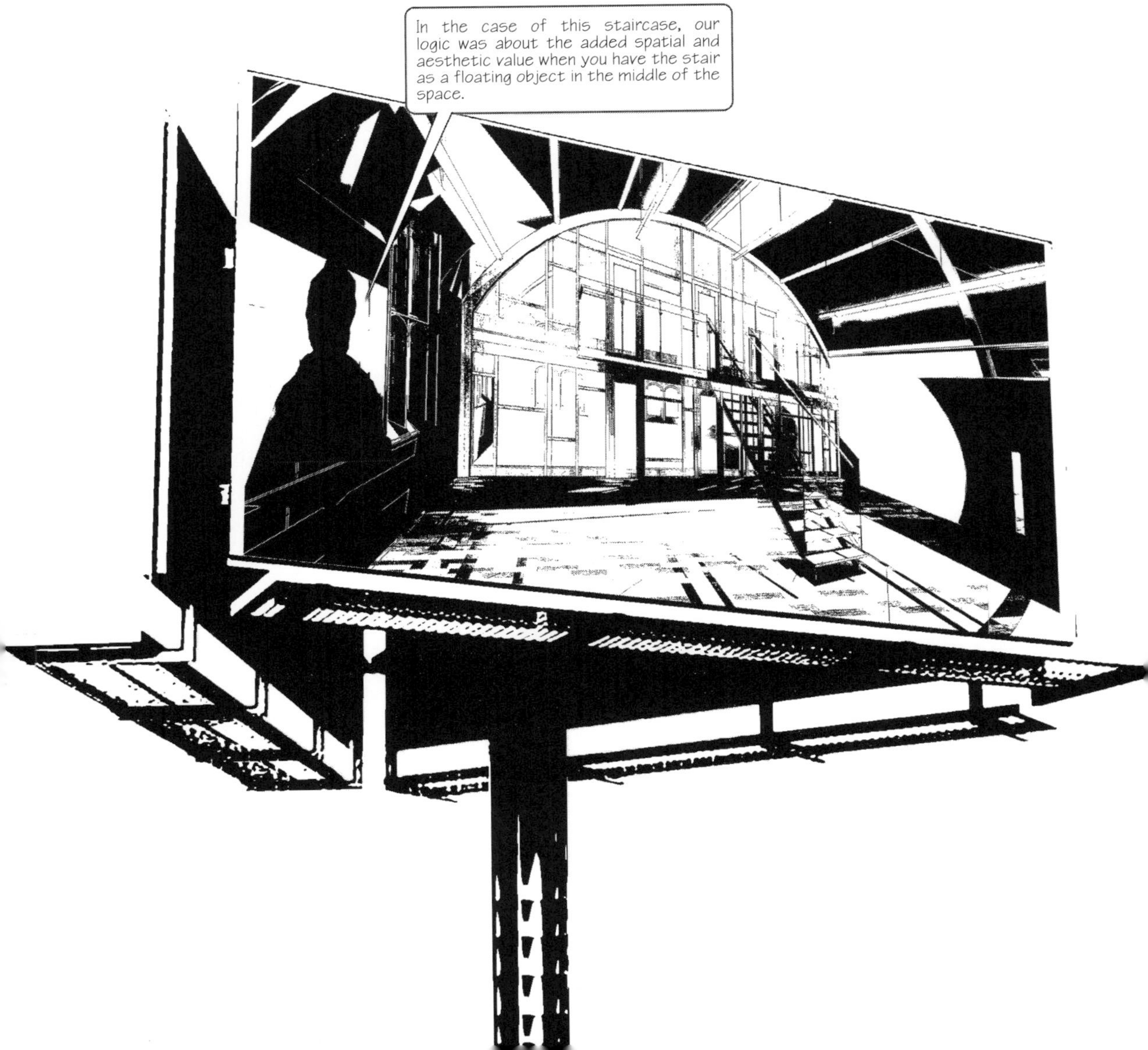
In the case of this staircase, our logic was about the added spatial and aesthetic value when you have the stair as a floating object in the middle of the space.

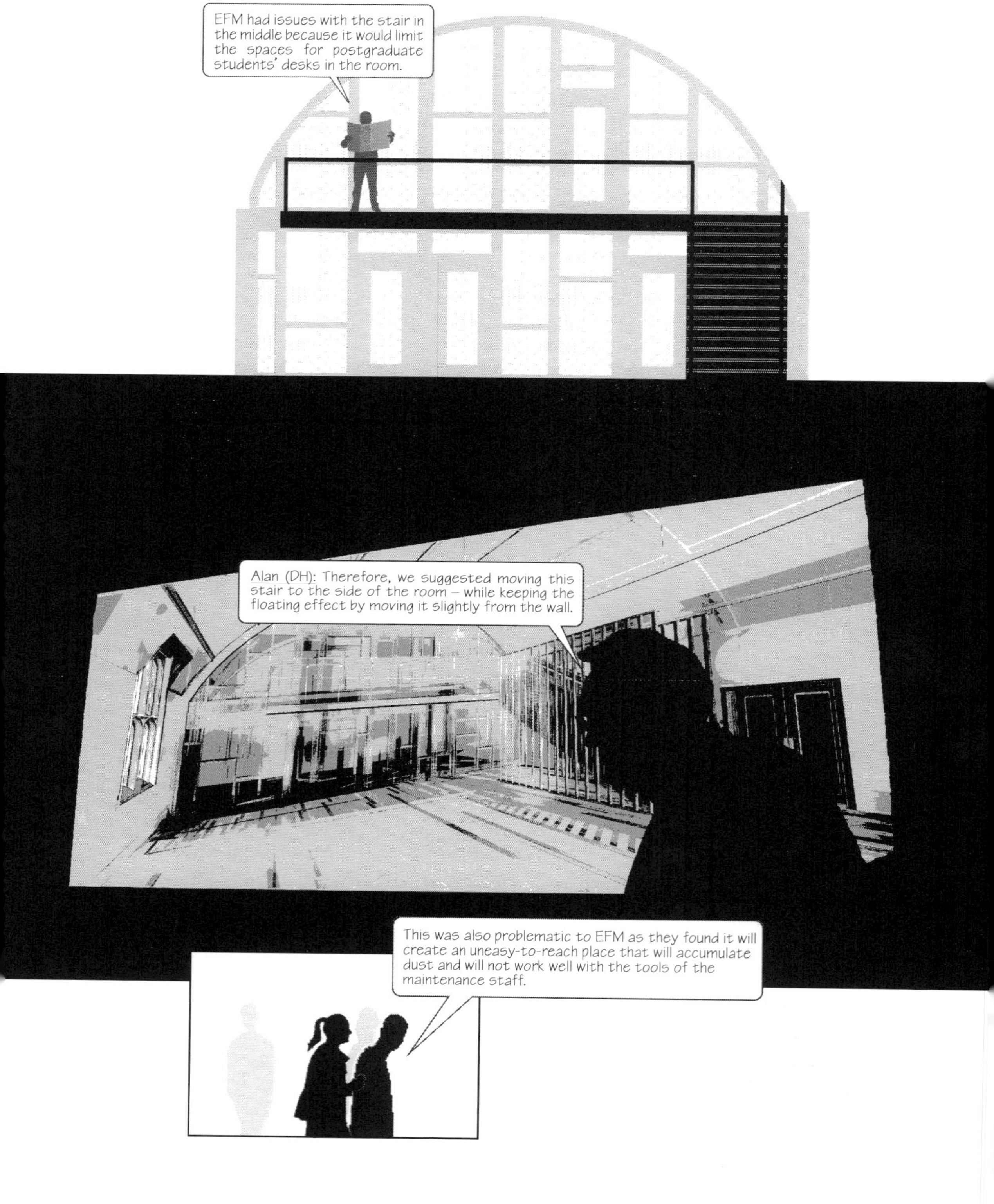
EFM had issues with the stair in the middle because it would limit the spaces for postgraduate students' desks in the room.
Alan (DH): Therefore, we suggested moving this stair to the side of the room – while keeping the floating effect by moving it slightly from the wall.
This was also problematic to EFM as they found it will create an uneasy-to-reach place that will accumulate dust and will not work well with the tools of the maintenance staff.

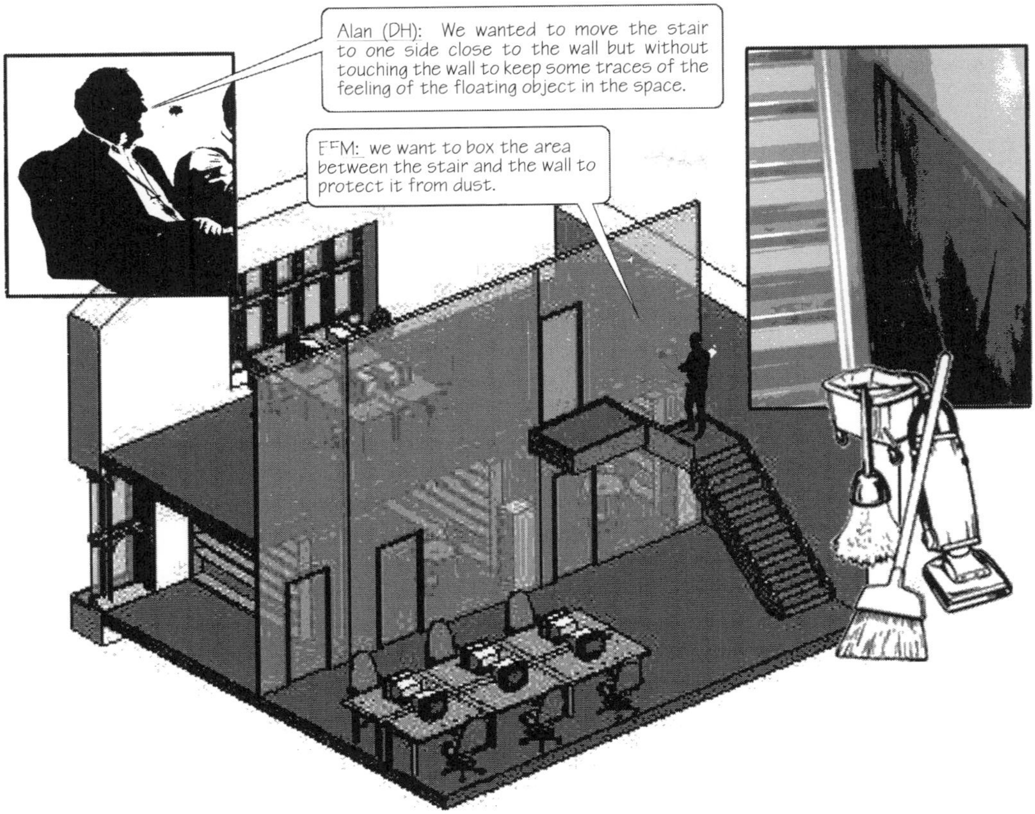
Alan (DH): We wanted to move the stair to one side close to the wall but without touching the wall to keep some traces of the feeling of the floating object in the space.
EFM: we want to box the area between the stair and the wall to protect it from dust.

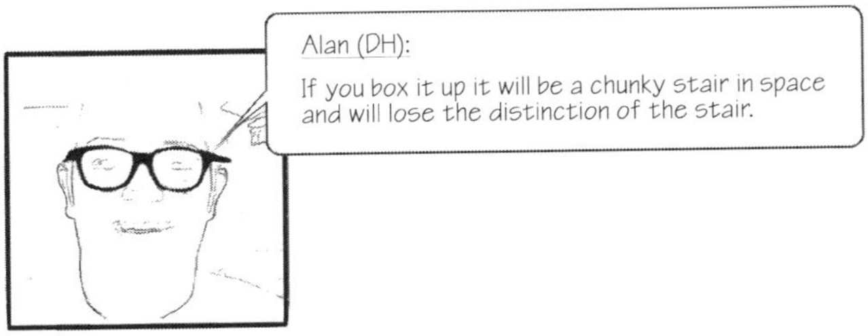
Alan (DH):
If you box it up it will be a chunky stair in space and will lose the distinction of the stair.

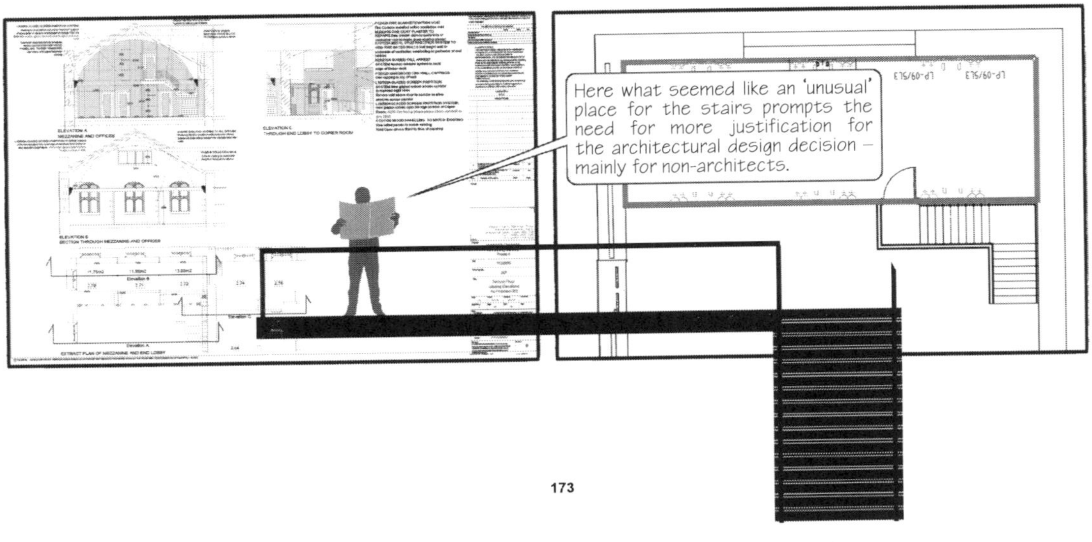
Here what seemed like an 'unusual' place for the stairs prompts the need for more justification for the architectural design decision – mainly for non-architects.

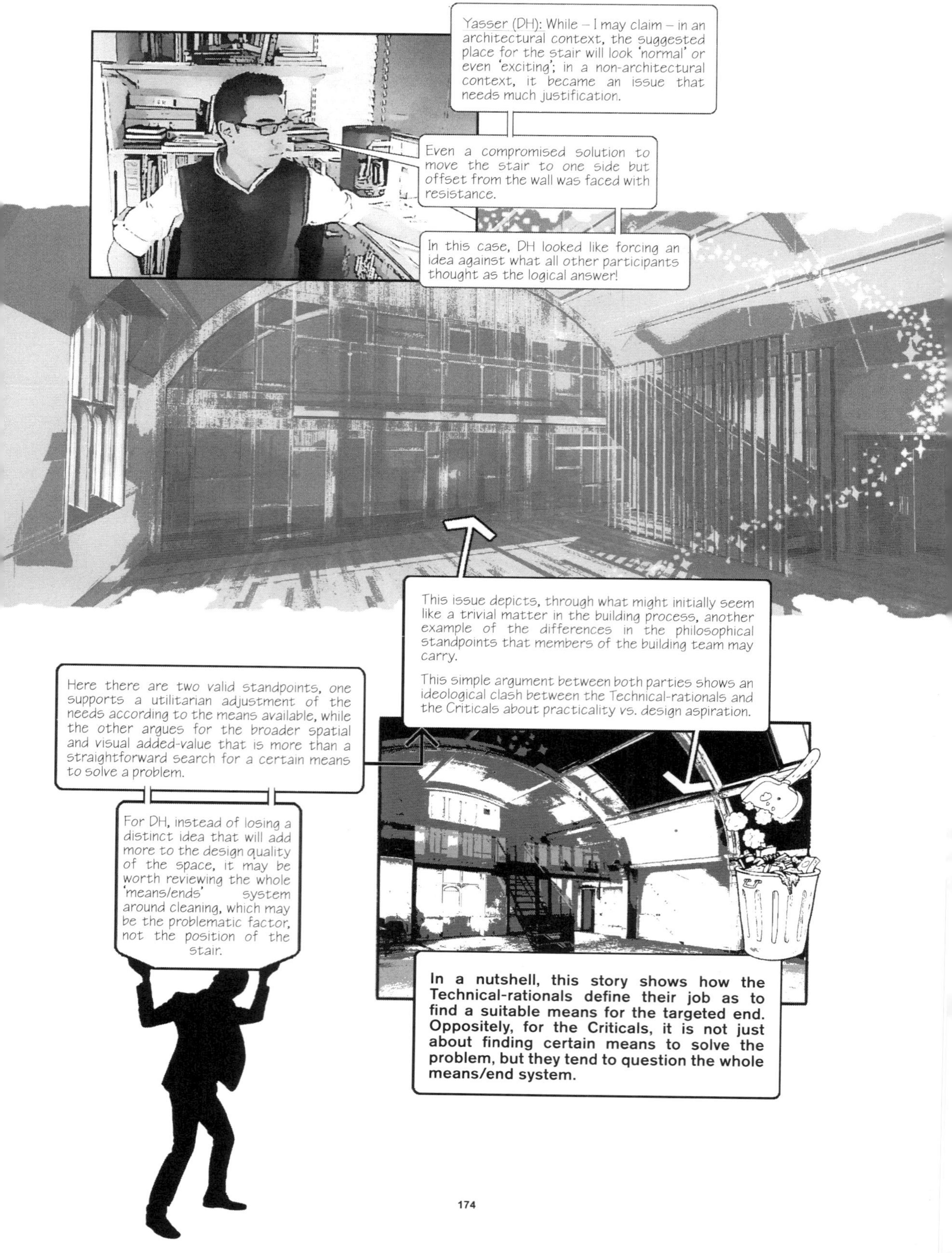
Yasser (DH): While – I may claim – in an architectural context, the suggested place for the stair will look 'normal' or even 'exciting'; in a non-architectural context, it became an issue that needs much justification.
Even a compromised solution to move the stair to one side but offset from the wall was faced with resistance.
In this case, DH looked like forcing an idea against what all other participants thought as the logical answer!
This issue depicts, through what might initially seem like a trivial matter in the building process, another example of the differences in the philosophical standpoints that members of the building team may carry.
This simple argument between both parties shows an ideological clash between the Technical-rationals and the Criticals about practicality vs. design aspiration.
Here there are two valid standpoints, one supports a utilitarian adjustment of the needs according to the means available, while the other argues for the broader spatial and visual added-value that is more than a straightforward search for a certain means to solve a problem.
For DH, instead of losing a distinct idea that will add more to the design quality of the space, it may be worth reviewing the whole 'means/ends' system around cleaning, which may be the problematic factor, not the position of the stair.
In a nutshell, this story shows how the Technical-rationals define their job as to find a suitable means for the targeted end. Oppositely, for the Criticals, it is not just about finding certain means to solve the problem, but they tend to question the whole means/end system.

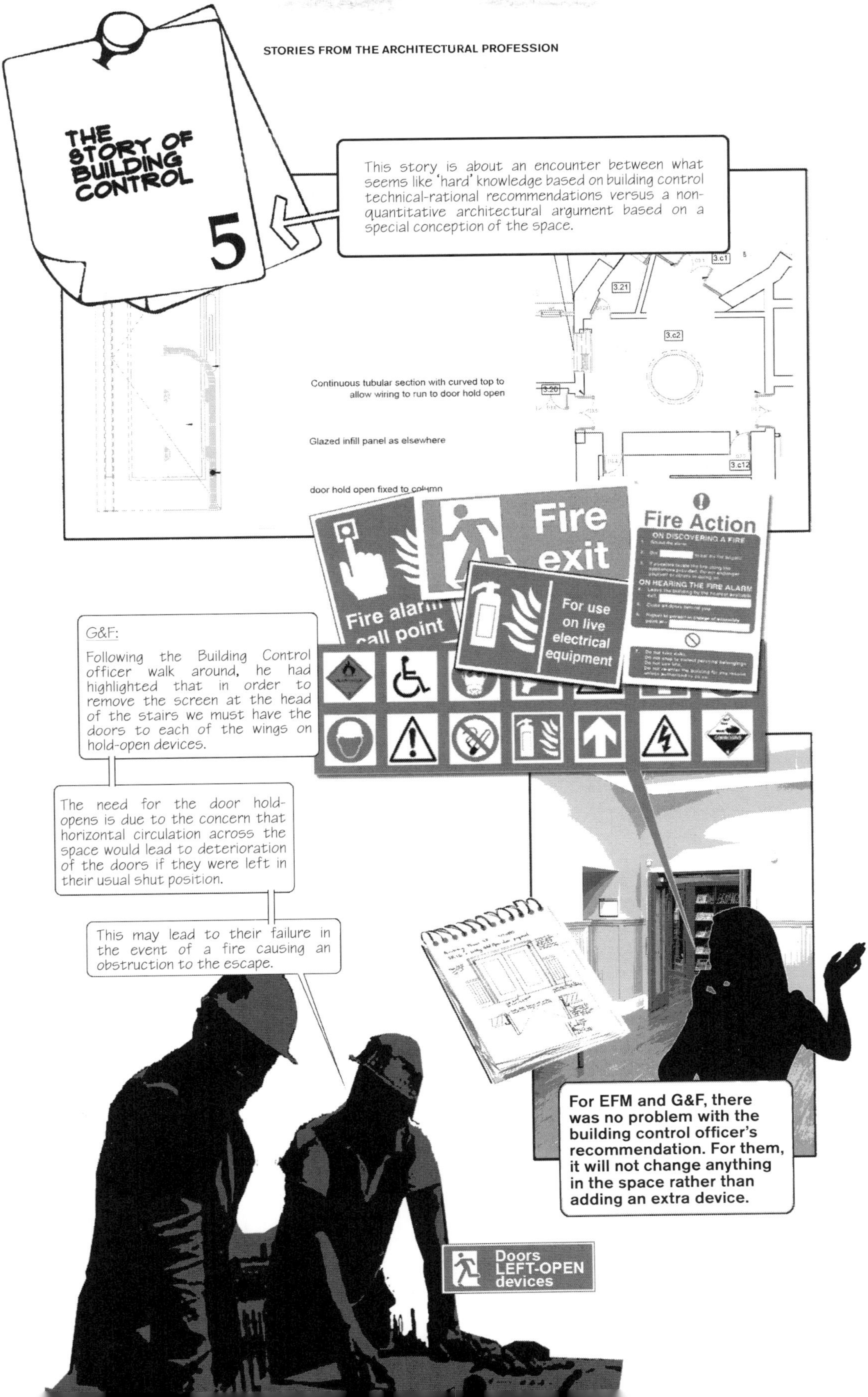
THE STORY OF BUILDING CONTROL
5
This story is about an encounter between what seems like 'hard' knowledge based on building control technical-rational recommendations versus a non-quantitative architectural argument based on a special conception of the space.
Continuous tubular section with curved top to allow wiring to run to door hold open
Glazed infill panel as elsewhere
door hold open fixed to column
Fire alarm call point
Fire exit
For use on live electrical equipment
Fire Action
G&F:
Following the Building Control officer walk around, he had highlighted that in order to remove the screen at the head of the stairs we must have the doors to each of the wings on hold-open devices.
The need for the door hold-opens is due to the concern that horizontal circulation across the space would lead to deterioration of the doors if they were left in their usual shut position.
This may lead to their failure in the event of a fire causing an obstruction to the escape.
For EFM and G&F, there was no problem with the building control officer's recommendation. For them, it will not change anything in the space rather than adding an extra device.
Doors LEFT-OPEN devices

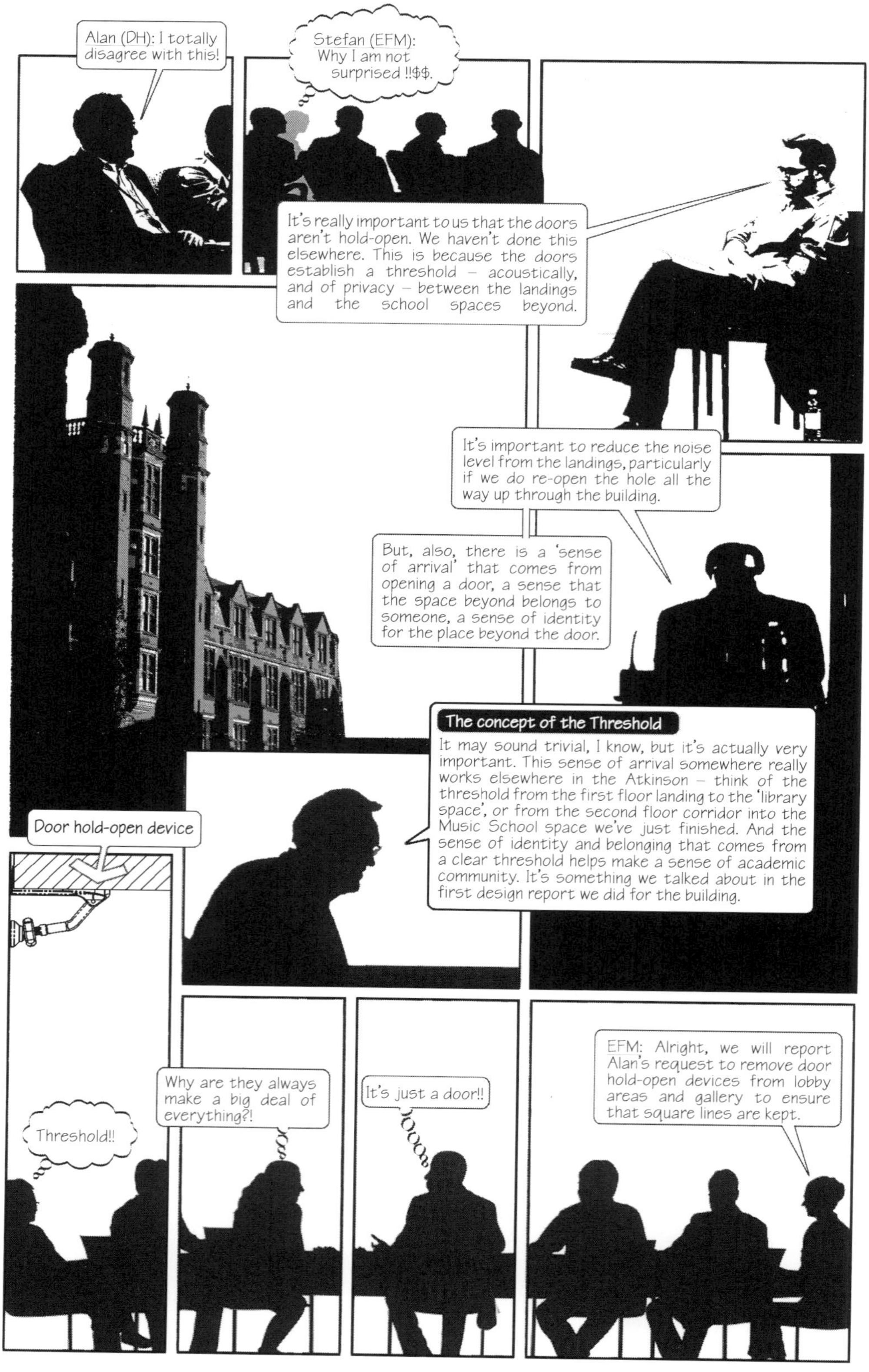
Alan (DH): I totally disagree with this!
Stefan (EFM): Why I am not surprised !!$$.
It's really important to us that the doors aren't hold-open. We haven't done this elsewhere. This is because the doors establish a threshold – acoustically, and of privacy – between the landings and the school spaces beyond.
It's important to reduce the noise level from the landings, particularly if we do re-open the hole all the way up through the building.
But, also, there is a 'sense of arrival' that comes from opening a door, a sense that the space beyond belongs to someone, a sense of identity for the place beyond the door.
The concept of the Threshold
It may sound trivial, I know, but it's actually very important. This sense of arrival somewhere really works elsewhere in the Atkinson – think of the threshold from the first floor landing to the 'library space', or from the second floor corridor into the Music School space we've just finished. And the sense of identity and belonging that comes from a clear threshold helps make a sense of academic community. It's something we talked about in the first design report we did for the building.
Door hold-open device
Threshold!!
Why are they always make a big deal of everything?!
It's just a door!!
EFM: Alright, we will report Alan's request to remove door hold-open devices from lobby areas and gallery to ensure that square lines are kept.

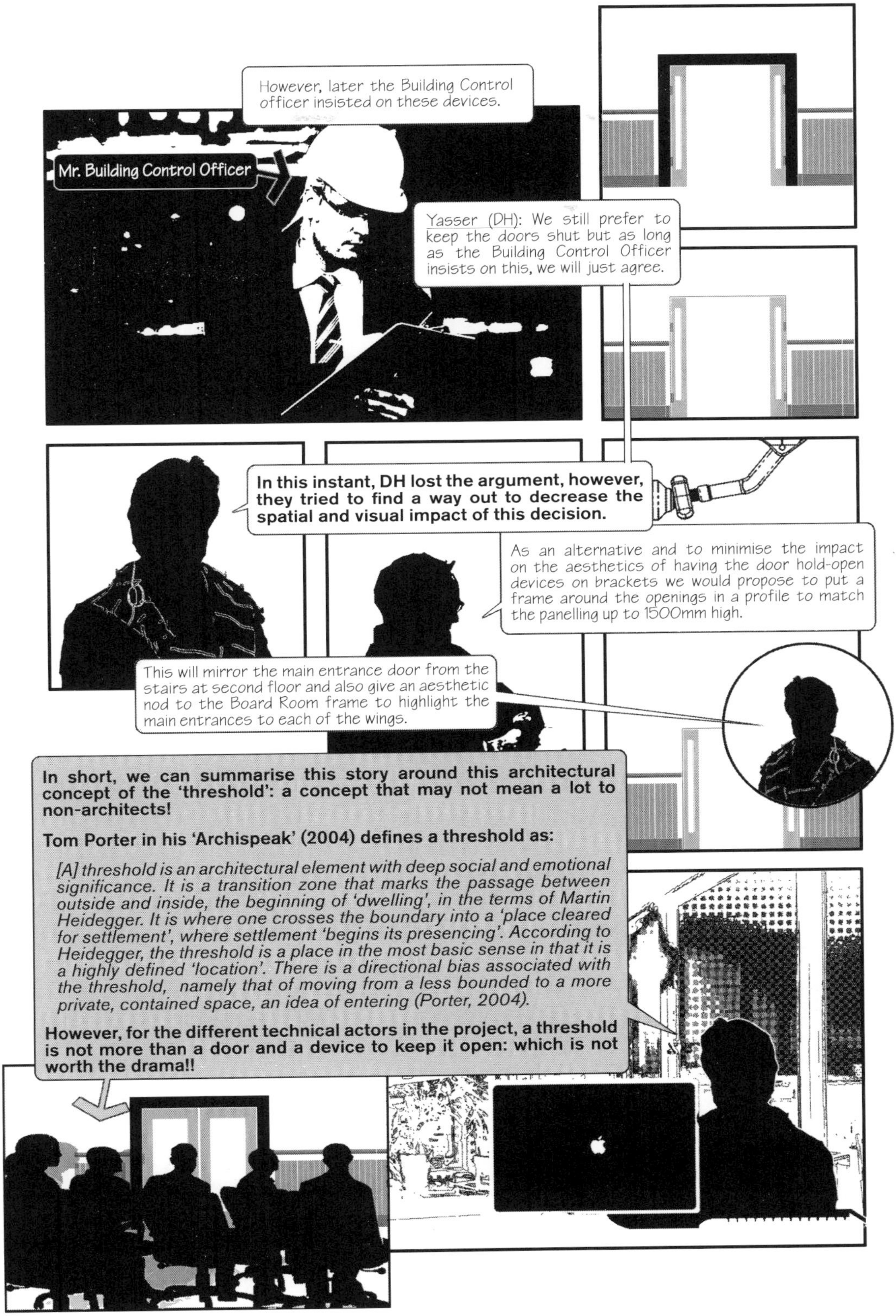
However, later the Building Control officer insisted on these devices.
Mr. Building Control Officer
Yasser (DH): We still prefer to keep the doors shut but as long as the Building Control Officer insists on this, we will just agree.
In this instant, DH lost the argument, however, they tried to find a way out to decrease the spatial and visual impact of this decision.
As an alternative and to minimise the impact on the aesthetics of having the door hold-open devices on brackets we would propose to put a frame around the openings in a profile to match the panelling up to 1500mm high.
This will mirror the main entrance door from the stairs at second floor and also give an aesthetic nod to the Board Room frame to highlight the main entrances to each of the wings.
In short, we can summarise this story around this architectural concept of the 'threshold': a concept that may not mean a lot to non-architects!
Tom Porter in his 'Archispeak' (2004) defines a threshold as:
[A] threshold is an architectural element with deep social and emotional significance. It is a transition zone that marks the passage between outside and inside, the beginning of 'dwelling', in the terms of Martin Heidegger. It is where one crosses the boundary into a 'place cleared for settlement', where settlement 'begins its presencing'. According to Heidegger, the threshold is a place in the most basic sense in that it is a highly defined 'location'. There is a directional bias associated with the threshold, namely that of moving from a less bounded to a more private, contained space, an idea of entering (Porter, 2004).
However, for the different technical actors in the project, a threshold is not more than a door and a device to keep it open: which is not worth the drama!!

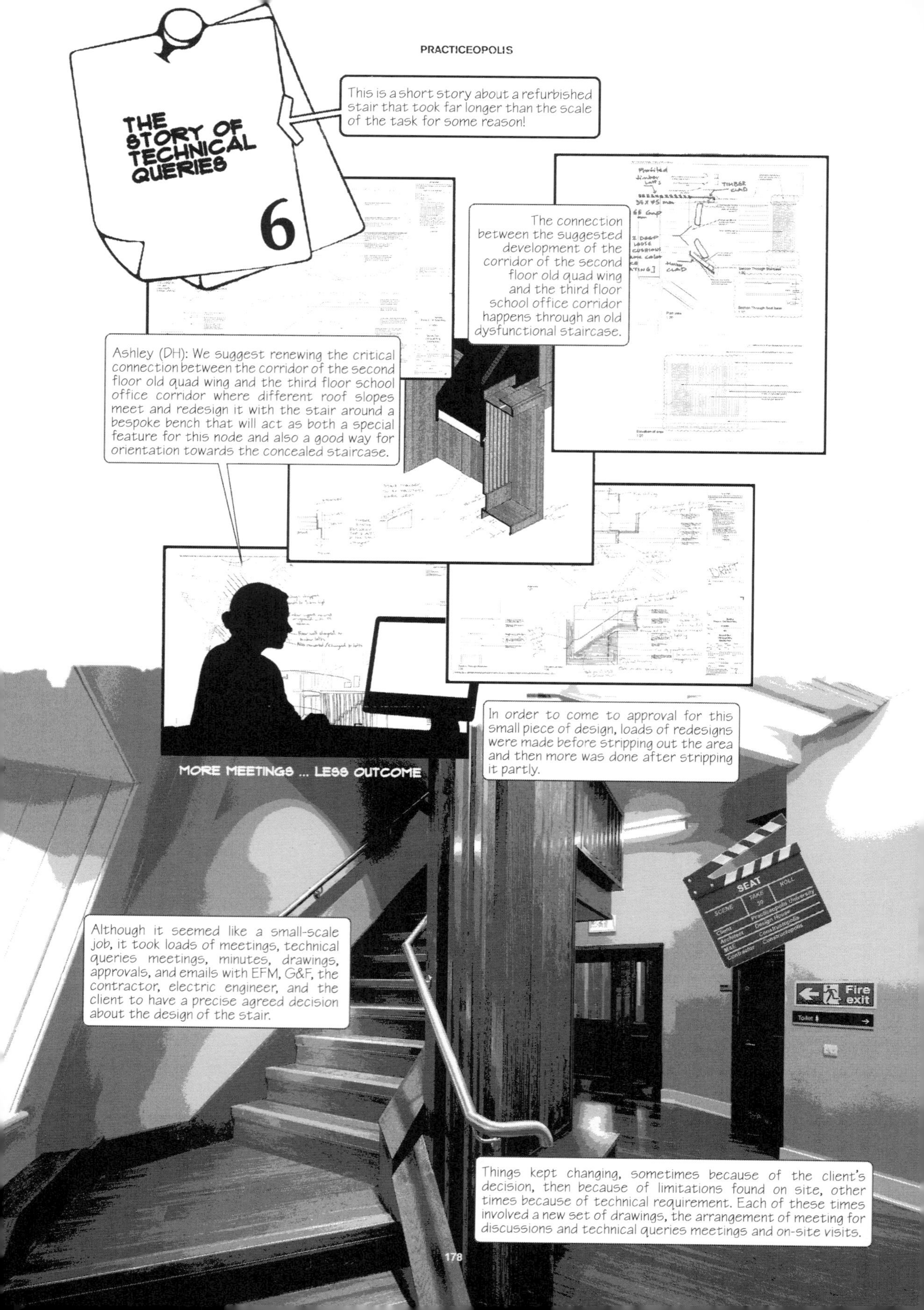
THE STORY OF TECHNICAL QUERIES
6
This is a short story about a refurbished stair that took far longer than the scale of the task for some reason!
The connection between the suggested development of the corridor of the second floor old quad wing and the third floor school office corridor happens through an old dysfunctional staircase.
Ashley (DH): We suggest renewing the critical connection between the corridor of the second floor old quad wing and the third floor school office corridor where different roof slopes meet and redesign it with the stair around a bespoke bench that will act as both a special feature for this node and also a good way for orientation towards the concealed staircase.
DRAFT
In order to come to approval for this small piece of design, loads of redesigns were made before stripping out the area and then more was done after stripping it partly.
MORE MEETINGS ... LESS OUTCOME
SEAT
Although it seemed like a small-scale job, it took loads of meetings, technical queries meetings, minutes, drawings, approvals, and emails with EFM, G&F, the contractor, electric engineer, and the client to have a precise agreed decision about the design of the stair.
Fire exit
Toilet
Things kept changing, sometimes because of the client's decision, then because of limitations found on site, other times because of technical requirement. Each of these times involved a new set of drawings, the arrangement of meeting for discussions and technical queries meetings and on-site visits.

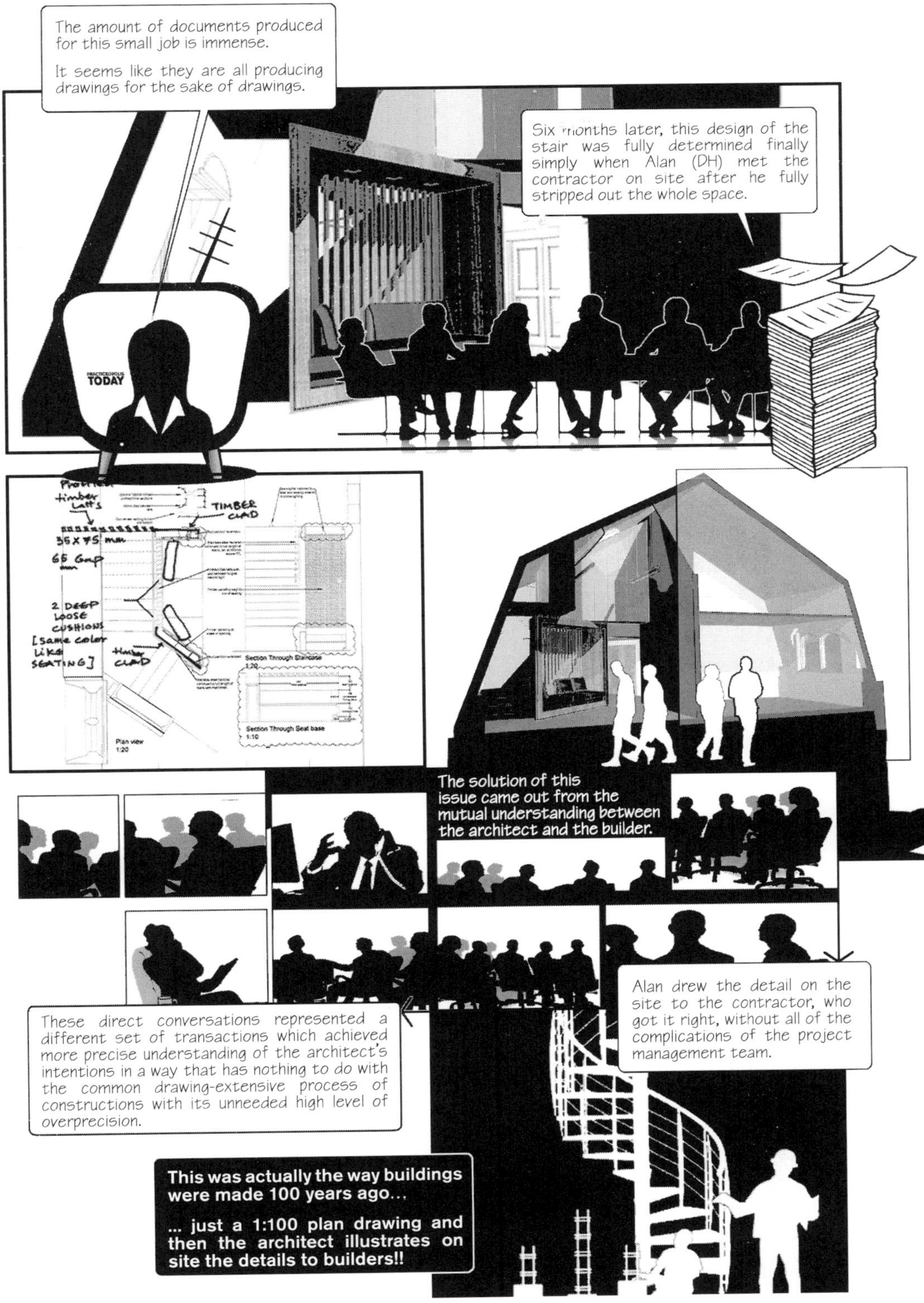
The amount of documents produced for this small job is immense.
It seems like they are all producing drawings for the sake of drawings.
Six months later, this design of the stair was fully determined finally simply when Alan (DH) met the contractor on site after he fully stripped out the whole space.
TODAY
TIMBER CLAD
35 X 75 mm
65 Gap
2 DEEP LOOSE CUSHIONS [same color like SEATING]
Section Through Staircase 1:20
Section Through Seat base 1:10
Plan view 1:20
The solution of this issue came out from the mutual understanding between the architect and the builder.
These direct conversations represented a different set of transactions which achieved more precise understanding of the architect's intentions in a way that has nothing to do with the common drawing-extensive process of constructions with its unneeded high level of overprecision.
Alan drew the detail on the site to the contractor, who got it right, without all of the complications of the project management team.
This was actually the way buildings were made 100 years ago...
... just a 1:100 plan drawing and then the architect illustrates on site the details to builders!!

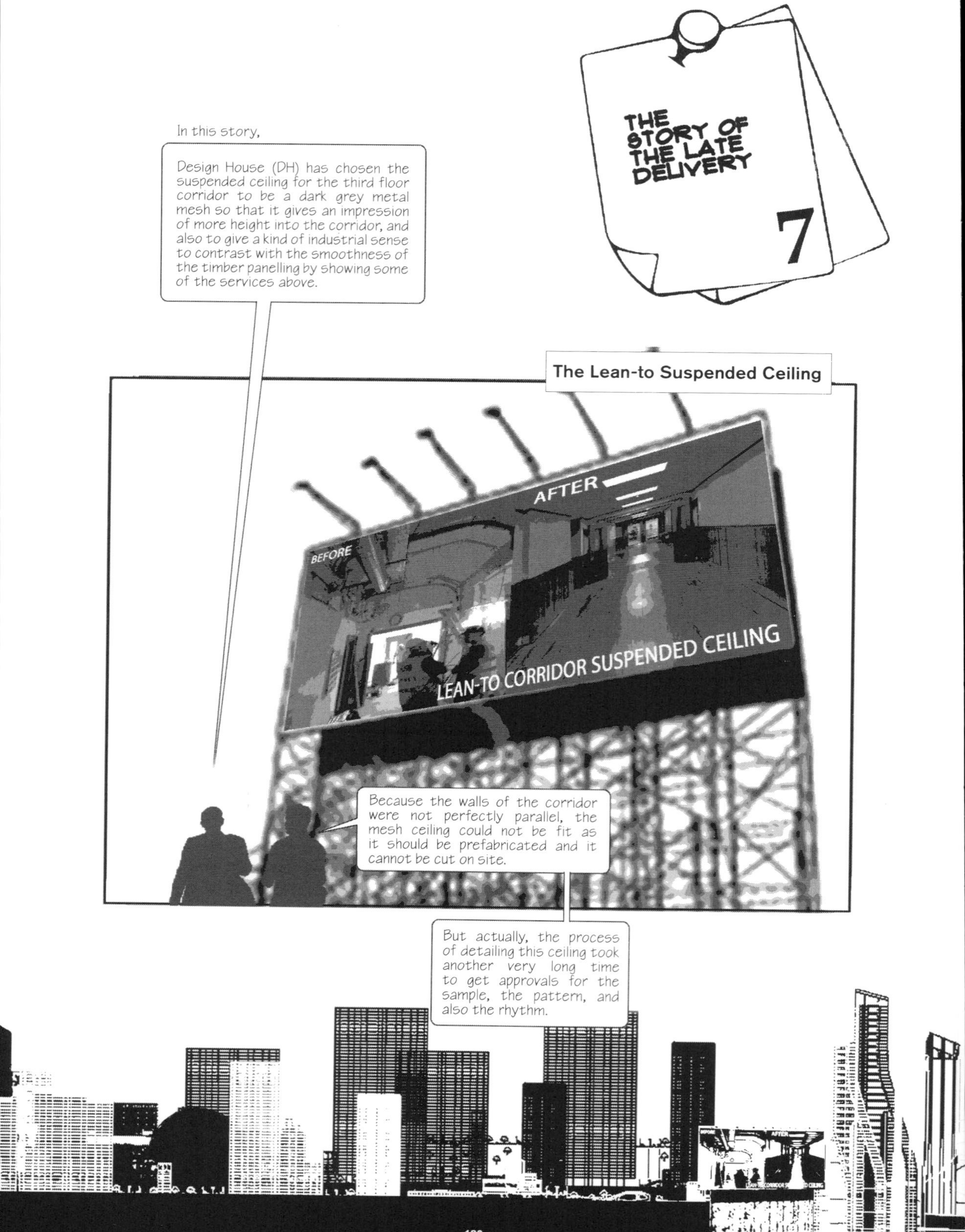
THE STORY OF THE LATE DELIVERY
7
In this story,
Design House (DH) has chosen the suspended ceiling for the third floor corridor to be a dark grey metal mesh so that it gives an impression of more height into the corridor, and also to give a kind of industrial sense to contrast with the smoothness of the timber panelling by showing some of the services above.
The Lean-to Suspended Ceiling
BEFORE
AFTER
LEAN-TO CORRIDOR SUSPENDED CEILING
Because the walls of the corridor were not perfectly parallel, the mesh ceiling could not be fit as it should be prefabricated and it cannot be cut on site.
But actually, the process of detailing this ceiling took another very long time to get approvals for the sample, the pattern, and also the rhythm.

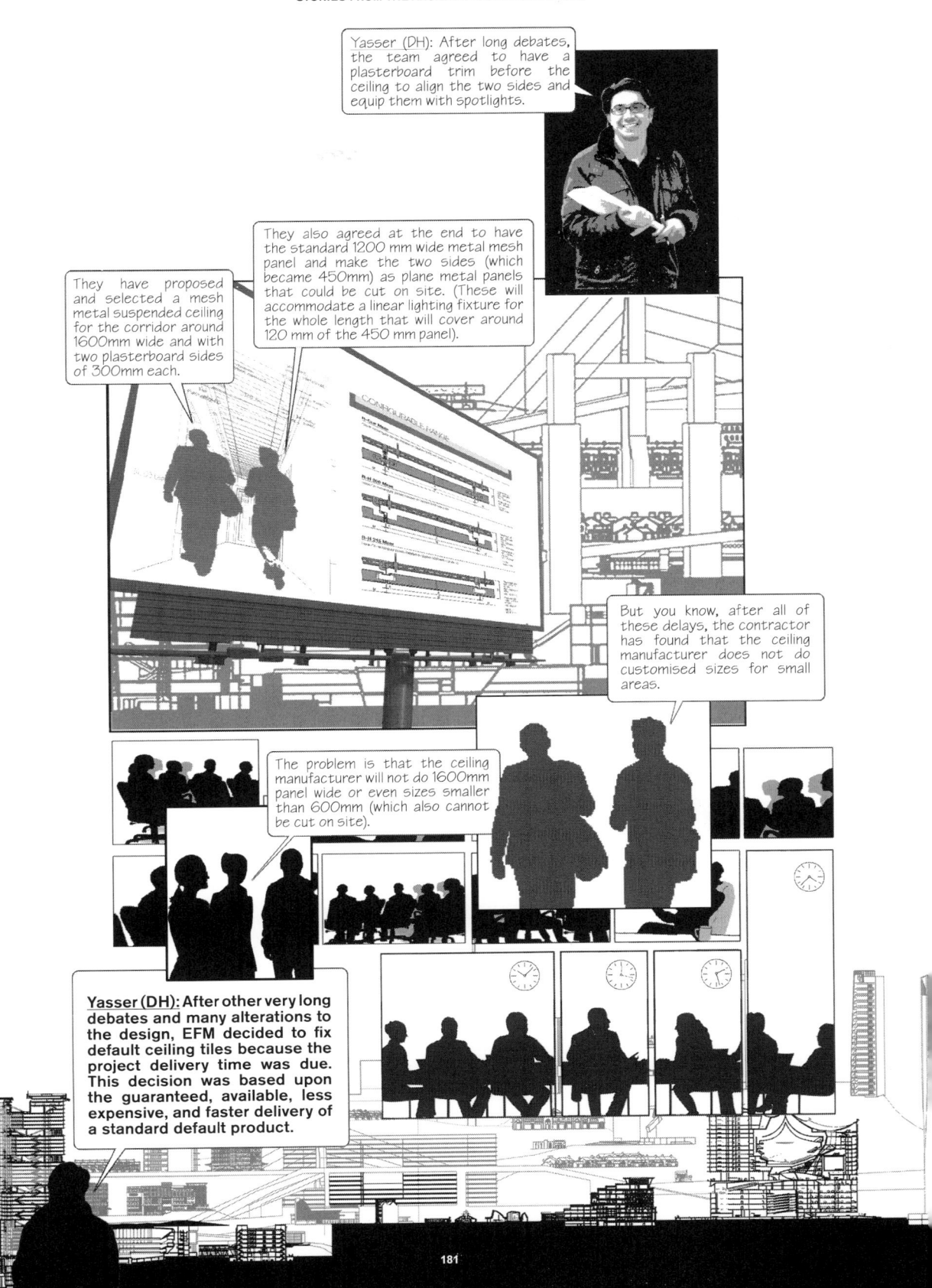

Yasser (DH): After long debates, the team agreed to have a plasterboard trim before the ceiling to align the two sides and equip them with spotlights.

They also agreed at the end to have the standard 1200 mm wide metal mesh panel and make the two sides (which became 450mm) as plane metal panels that could be cut on site. (These will accommodate a linear lighting fixture for the whole length that will cover around 120 mm of the 450 mm panel).

They have proposed and selected a mesh metal suspended ceiling for the corridor around 1600mm wide and with two plasterboard sides of 300mm each.

But you know, after all of these delays, the contractor has found that the ceiling manufacturer does not do customised sizes for small areas.

The problem is that the ceiling manufacturer will not do 1600mm panel wide or even sizes smaller than 600mm (which also cannot be cut on site).

Yasser (DH): After other very long debates and many alterations to the design, EFM decided to fix default ceiling tiles because the project delivery time was due. This decision was based upon the guaranteed, available, less expensive, and faster delivery of a standard default product.

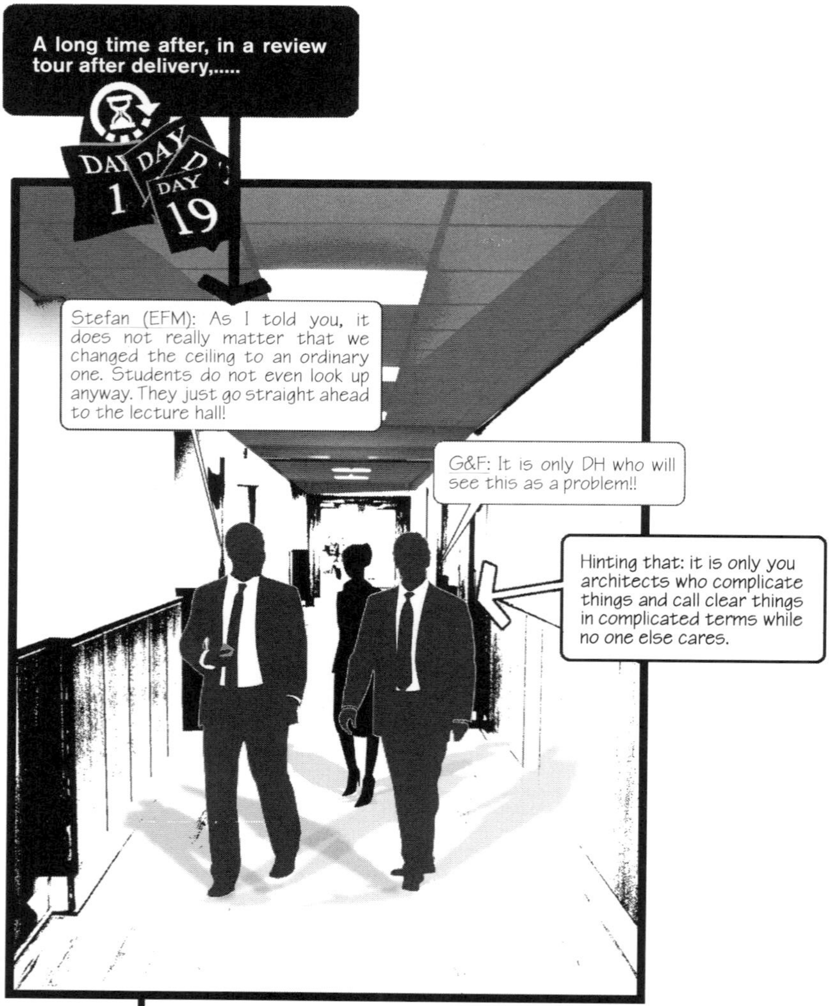
A long time after, in a review tour after delivery,.....
DAY 1
DAY 19
Stefan (EFM): As I told you, it does not really matter that we changed the ceiling to an ordinary one. Students do not even look up anyway. They just go straight ahead to the lecture hall!
G&F: It is only DH who will see this as a problem!!
Hinting that: it is only you architects who complicate things and call clear things in complicated terms while no one else cares.

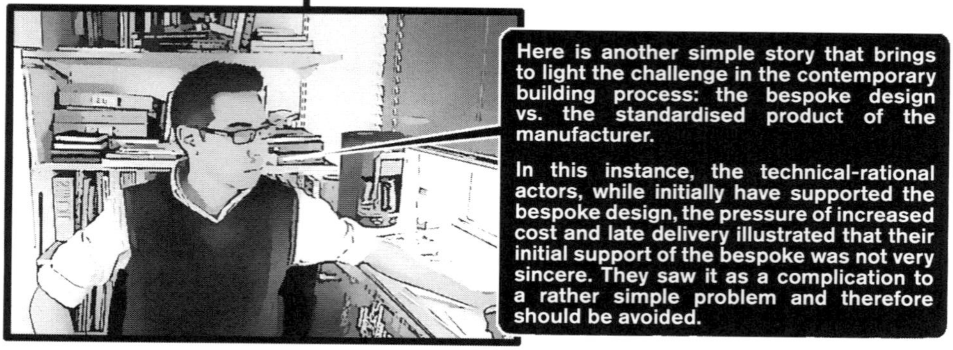
Here is another simple story that brings to light the challenge in the contemporary building process: the bespoke design vs. the standardised product of the manufacturer.
In this instance, the technical-rational actors, while initially have supported the bespoke design, the pressure of increased cost and late delivery illustrated that their initial support of the bespoke was not very sincere. They saw it as a complication to a rather simple problem and therefore should be avoided.

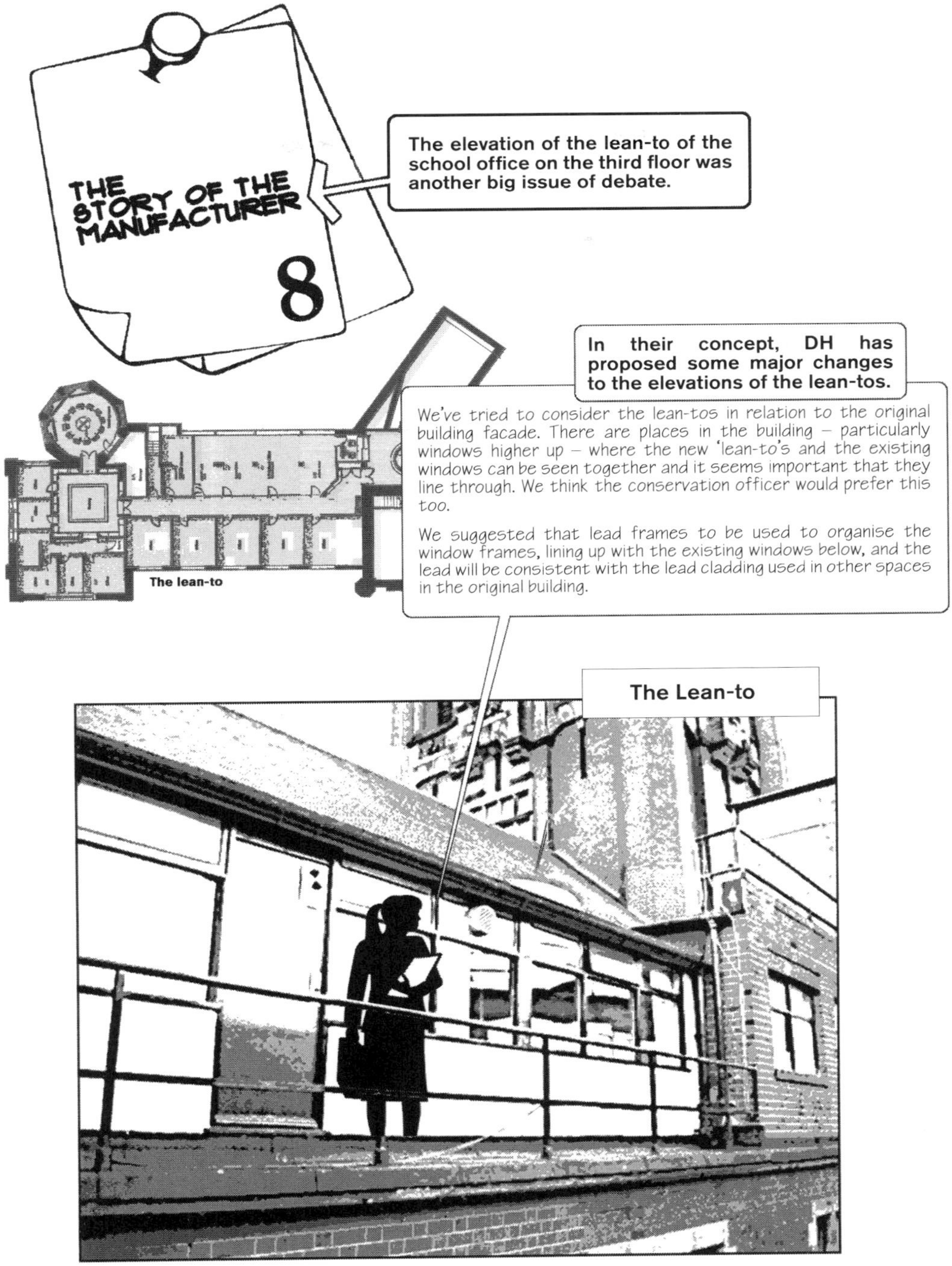
THE STORY OF THE MANUFACTURER
8
The elevation of the lean-to of the school office on the third floor was another big issue of debate.
In their concept, DH has proposed some major changes to the elevations of the lean-tos.
The lean-to
We've tried to consider the lean-tos in relation to the original building facade. There are places in the building – particularly windows higher up – where the new 'lean-to's and the existing windows can be seen together and it seems important that they line through. We think the conservation officer would prefer this too.
We suggested that lead frames to be used to organise the window frames, lining up with the existing windows below, and the lead will be consistent with the lead cladding used in other spaces in the original building.
The Lean-to

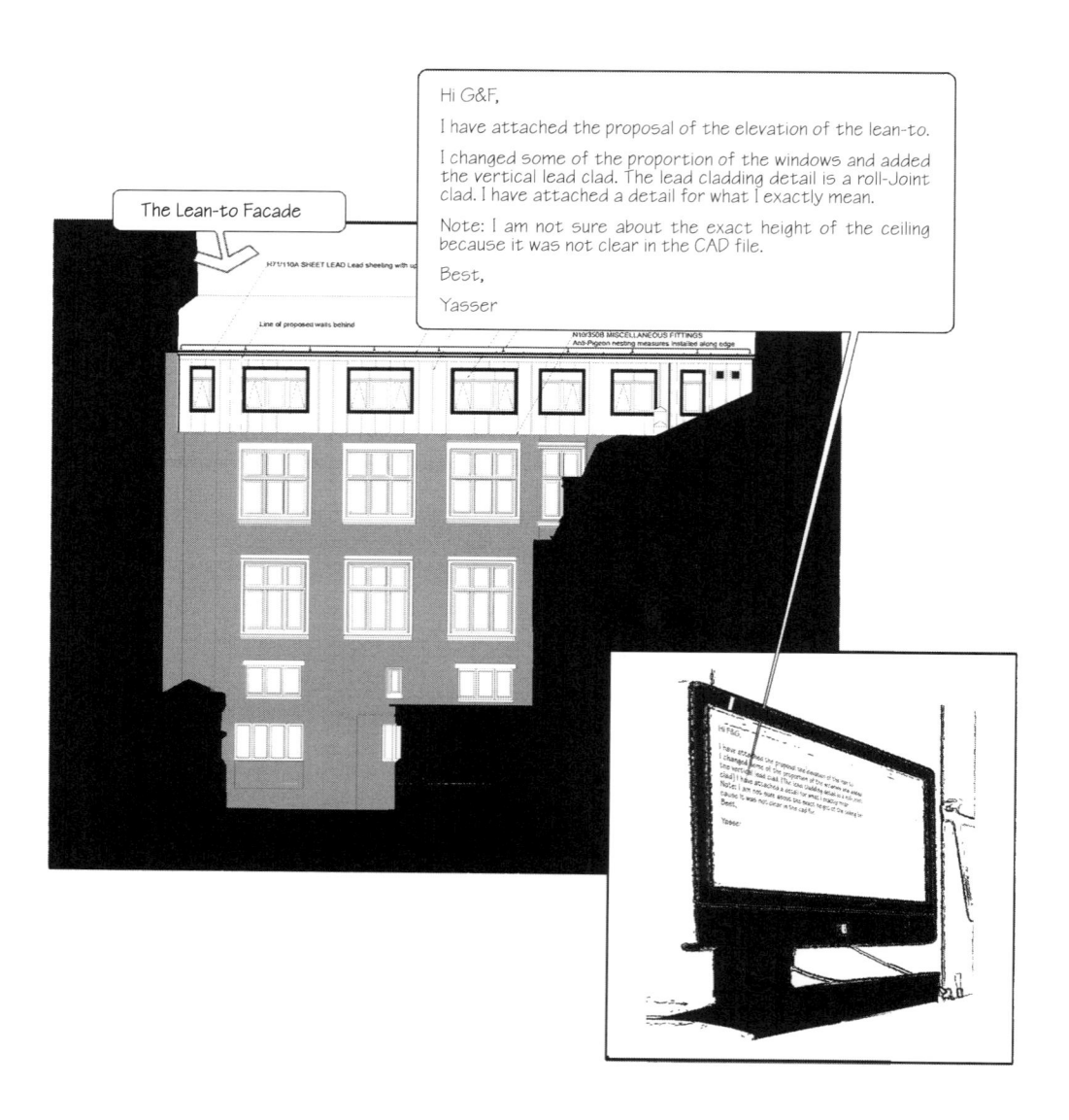

The Lean-to Facade
Hi G&F,
I have attached the proposal of the elevation of the lean-to.
I changed some of the proportion of the windows and added the vertical lead clad. The lead cladding detail is a roll-Joint clad. I have attached a detail for what I exactly mean.
Note: I am not sure about the exact height of the ceiling because it was not clear in the CAD file.
Best,
Yasser
Line of proposed walls behind
N10/350B MISCELLANEOUS FITTINGS
Anti-Pigeon nesting measures installed along edge

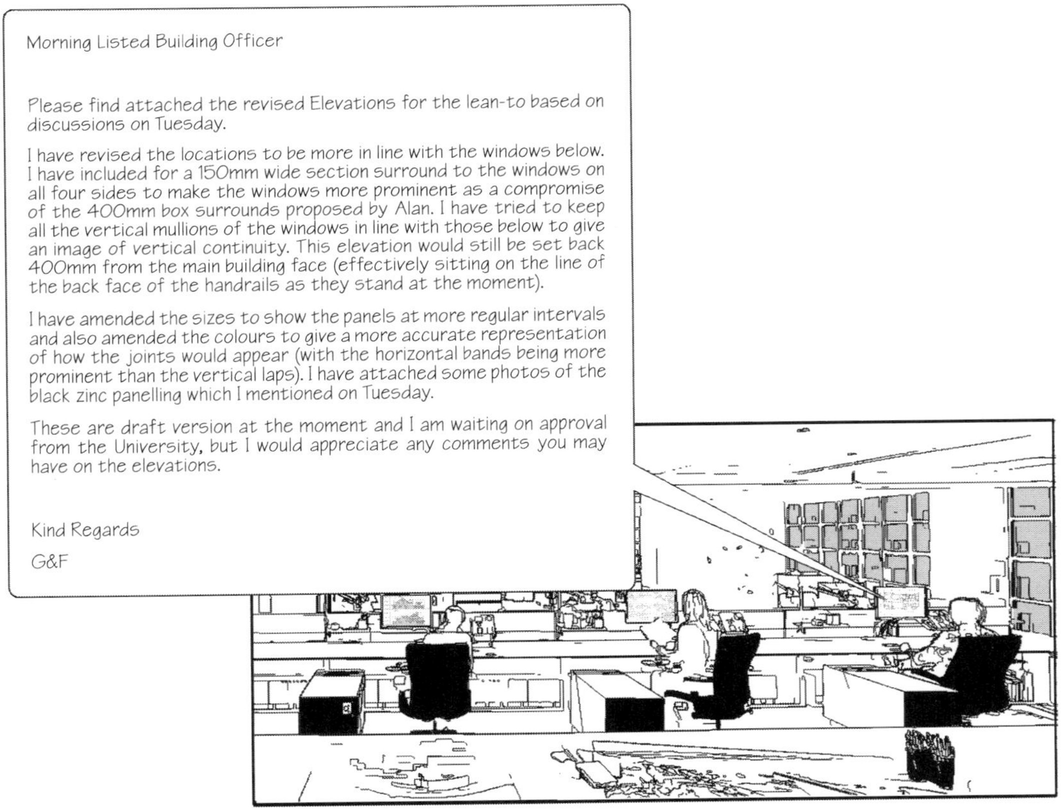

Morning Listed Building Officer

Please find attached the revised Elevations for the lean-to based on discussions on Tuesday.

I have revised the locations to be more in line with the windows below. I have included for a 150mm wide section surround to the windows on all four sides to make the windows more prominent as a compromise of the 400mm box surrounds proposed by Alan. I have tried to keep all the vertical mullions of the windows in line with those below to give an image of vertical continuity. This elevation would still be set back 400mm from the main building face (effectively sitting on the line of the back face of the handrails as they stand at the moment).

I have amended the sizes to show the panels at more regular intervals and also amended the colours to give a more accurate representation of how the joints would appear (with the horizontal bands being more prominent than the vertical laps). I have attached some photos of the black zinc panelling which I mentioned on Tuesday.

These are draft version at the moment and I am waiting on approval from the University, but I would appreciate any comments you may have on the elevations.

Kind Regards

G&F

Hi G&F,

Thanks for these amended drawings for comments. I have now had the chance to consider these.

The changes do respect the window line below much better and this is welcomed; however, I am still concerned that the extension has a strong horizontal emphasis which would detract from the rest of the elevation. It is considered that the windows in the extension should better respect the vertical emphasis and proportions of the rest of the elevation. The proposed cladding further emphasises the horizontal nature, are there any panels available with more vertical emphasis and proportions, possibly without the overlapping?

Could you look at amending the drawings to incorporate these suggestions as well? If you have any queries please just let me know.

Listed Building Officer

Alan,

Please find below comments from the Listed Building Officer. I issued out the drawings to them last week at the same time I issued them to yourselves for comment. I would appreciate it if you could bear these comments in mind when you make any proposed changes or comments.

Following last weeks meeting, Yasser was going to discuss the elevation with you and come back to me with your final comments following changes to the windows, their surrounds and the panelling above. Can you please give me an update on this as I am keen to get a finalised design so this can be submitted for Planning? There is now some urgency on this with the contractor already started on site.

Regards

G&F

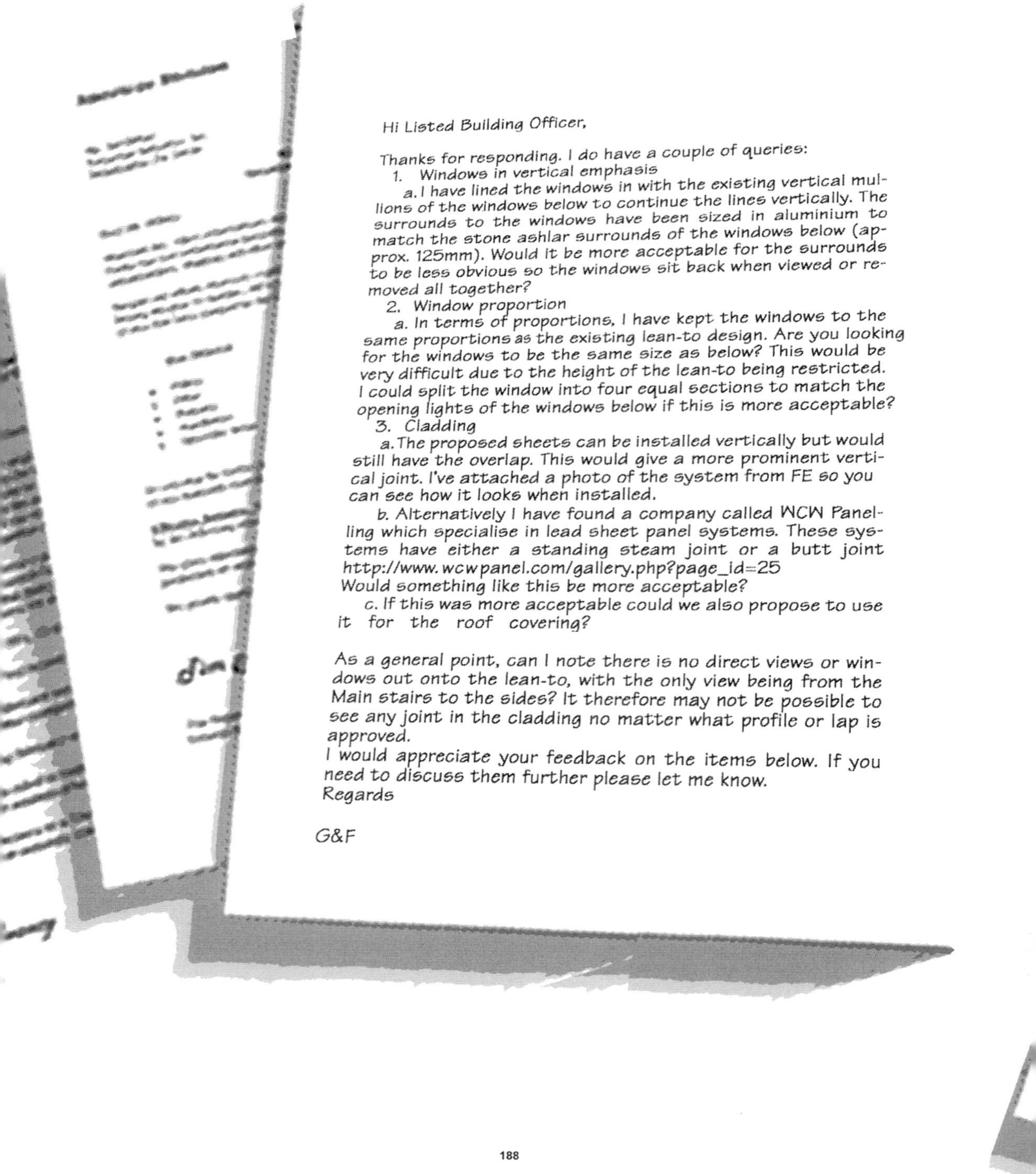

Hi Listed Building Officer,

Thanks for responding. I do have a couple of queries:

1. Windows in vertical emphasis

   a. I have lined the windows in with the existing vertical mullions of the windows below to continue the lines vertically. The surrounds to the windows have been sized in aluminium to match the stone ashlar surrounds of the windows below (approx. 125mm). Would it be more acceptable for the surrounds to be less obvious so the windows sit back when viewed or removed all together?

2. Window proportion

   a. In terms of proportions, I have kept the windows to the same proportions as the existing lean-to design. Are you looking for the windows to be the same size as below? This would be very difficult due to the height of the lean-to being restricted. I could split the window into four equal sections to match the opening lights of the windows below if this is more acceptable?

3. Cladding

   a. The proposed sheets can be installed vertically but would still have the overlap. This would give a more prominent vertical joint. I've attached a photo of the system from FE so you can see how it looks when installed.

   b. Alternatively I have found a company called WCW Panelling which specialise in lead sheet panel systems. These systems have either a standing steam joint or a butt joint http://www.wcwpanel.com/gallery.php?page_id=25
   Would something like this be more acceptable?

   c. If this was more acceptable could we also propose to use it for the roof covering?

As a general point, can I note there is no direct views or windows out onto the lean-to, with the only view being from the Main stairs to the sides? It therefore may not be possible to see any joint in the cladding no matter what profile or lap is approved.
I would appreciate your feedback on the items below. If you need to discuss them further please let me know.
Regards

G&F

Alan /Yasser,

Thanks for the comments/suggestions. I have picked up the comments to the external finish which mirrors an idea I have proposed to Listed Building last week to try and get feedback on. I have also looked at the proportions of the windows which I have edited to look closer to the windows lower down the building by removing the intermediate transom and having it as one panel. These would have to be on restrictors.

It has raised a concern with me over the section of lead above the windows within the surround. I know you were keen to keep it but I feel it may be better to drop it so that the surrounds mirror to the stone ashlar of the windows below. I would appreciate an answer so that I can go back to Listed Buildings with a definite proposal.

Regards

G&F

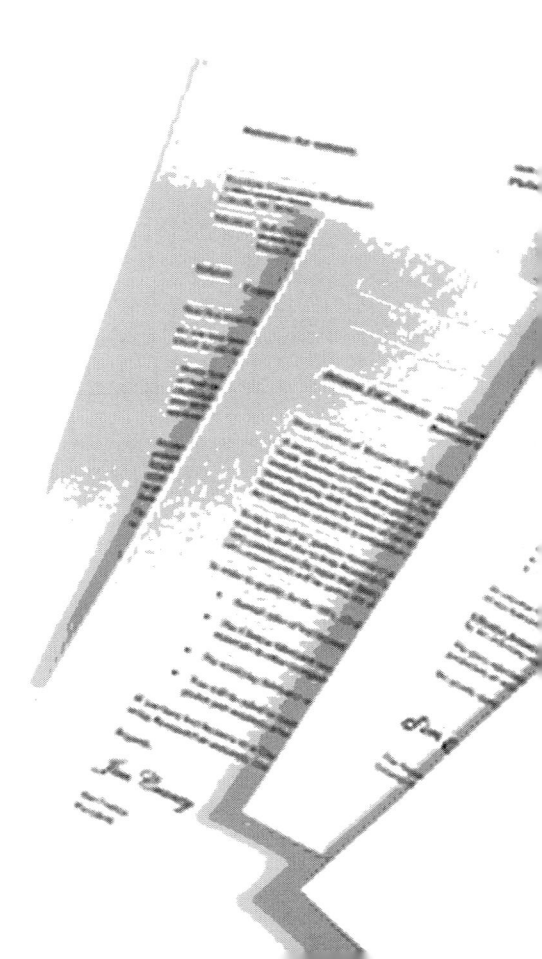

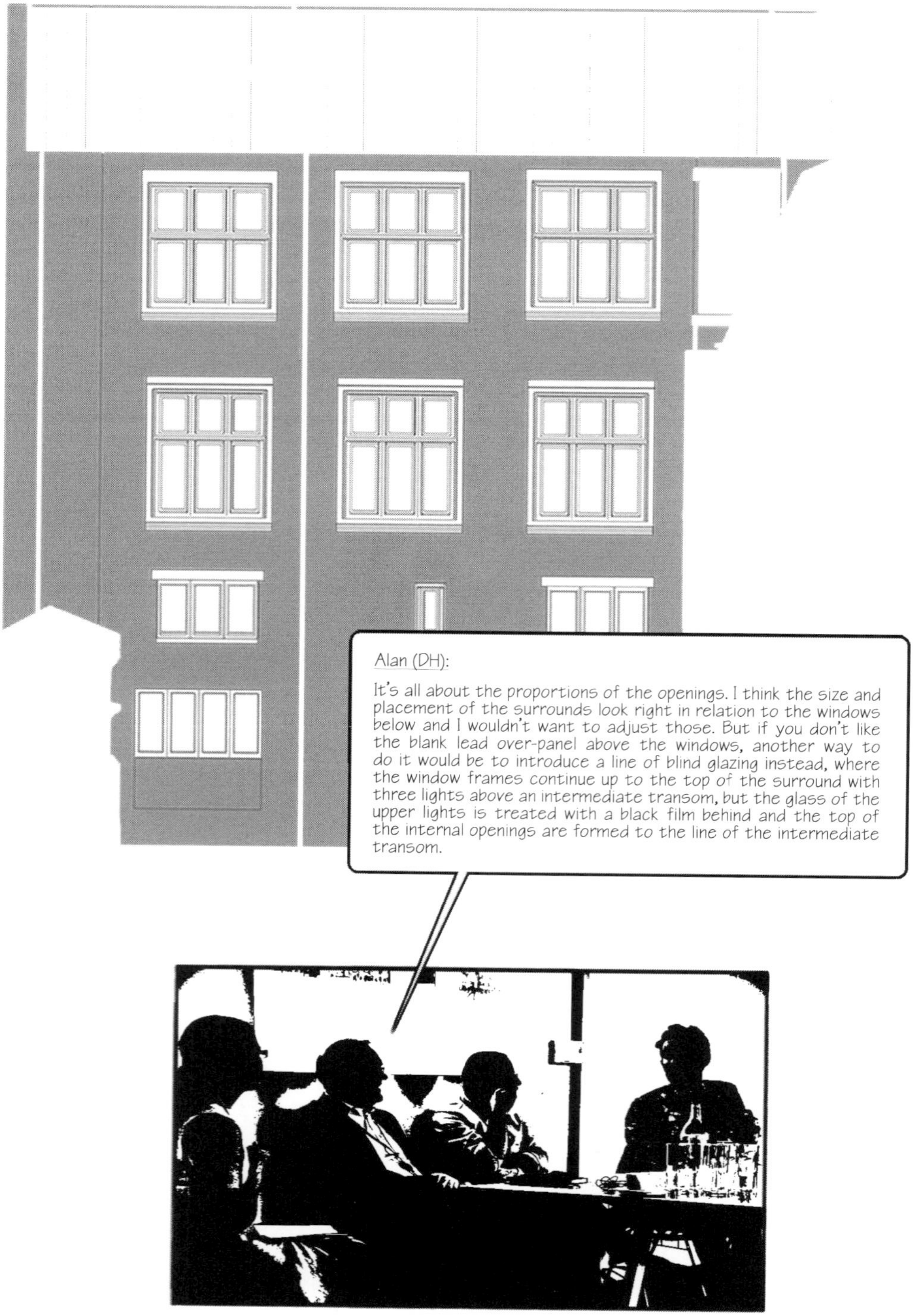
Alan (DH):
It's all about the proportions of the openings. I think the size and placement of the surrounds look right in relation to the windows below and I wouldn't want to adjust those. But if you don't like the blank lead over-panel above the windows, another way to do it would be to introduce a line of blind glazing instead, where the window frames continue up to the top of the surround with three lights above an intermediate transom, but the glass of the upper lights is treated with a black film behind and the top of the internal openings are formed to the line of the intermediate transom.

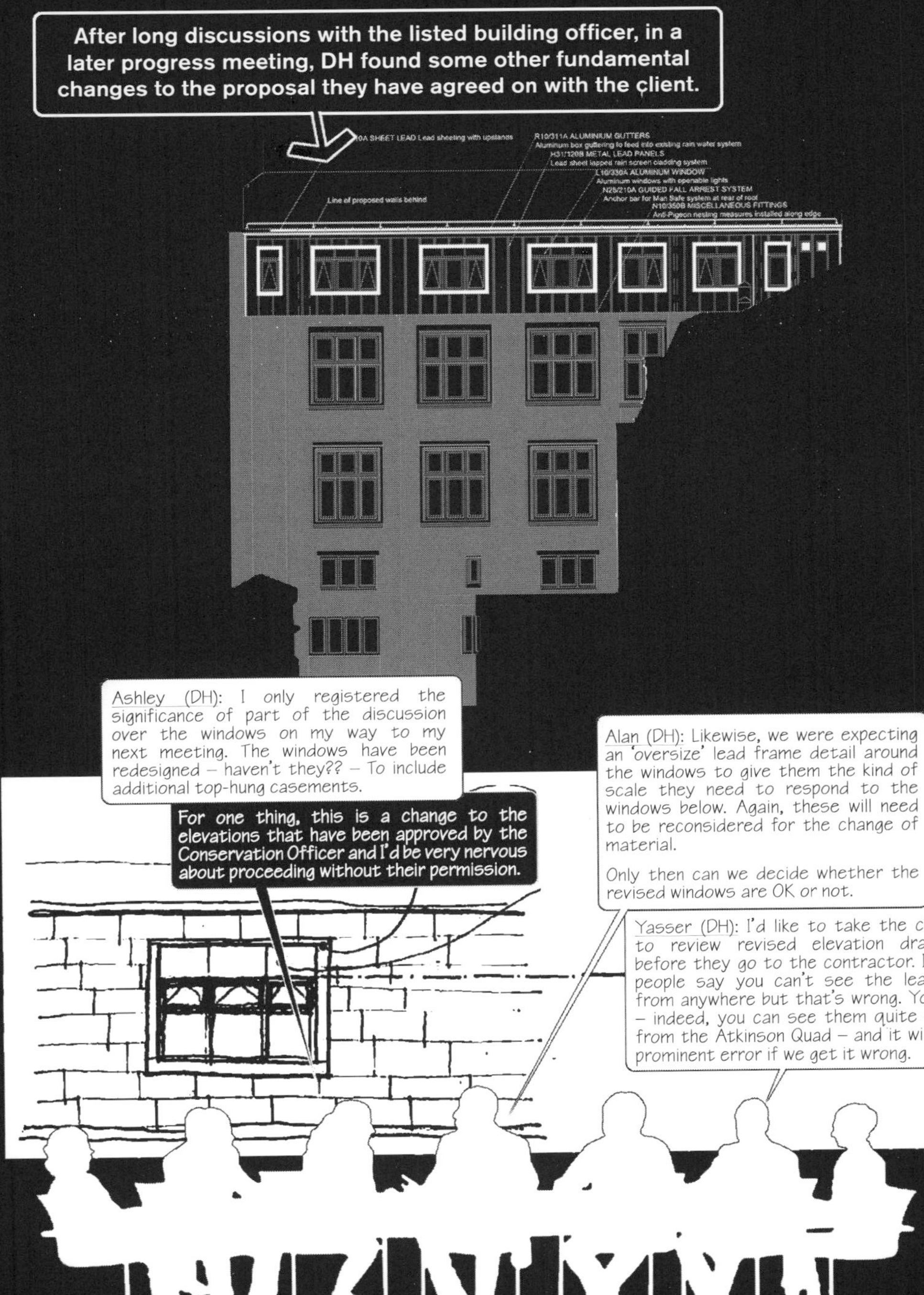
After long discussions with the listed building officer, in a later progress meeting, DH found some other fundamental changes to the proposal they have agreed on with the client.
R10/311A ALUMINIUM GUTTERS
Aluminum box guttering to feed into existing rain water system
H31/120B METAL LEAD PANELS
Lead sheet lapped rain screen cladding system
L10/330A ALUMINUM WINDOW
Aluminum windows with openable lights
N25/210A GUIDED FALL ARREST SYSTEM
Anchor bar for Man Safe system at rear of roof
N10/350B MISCELLANEOUS FITTINGS
Anti-Pigeon nesting measures installed along edge
Line of proposed walls behind
Ashley (DH): I only registered the significance of part of the discussion over the windows on my way to my next meeting. The windows have been redesigned – haven't they?? – To include additional top-hung casements.
For one thing, this is a change to the elevations that have been approved by the Conservation Officer and I'd be very nervous about proceeding without their permission.
Alan (DH): Likewise, we were expecting an 'oversize' lead frame detail around the windows to give them the kind of scale they need to respond to the windows below. Again, these will need to be reconsidered for the change of material.
Only then can we decide whether the revised windows are OK or not.
Yasser (DH): I'd like to take the chance to review revised elevation drawings before they go to the contractor. I know people say you can't see the lean-tos from anywhere but that's wrong. You can – indeed, you can see them quite easily from the Atkinson Quad – and it will be a prominent error if we get it wrong.

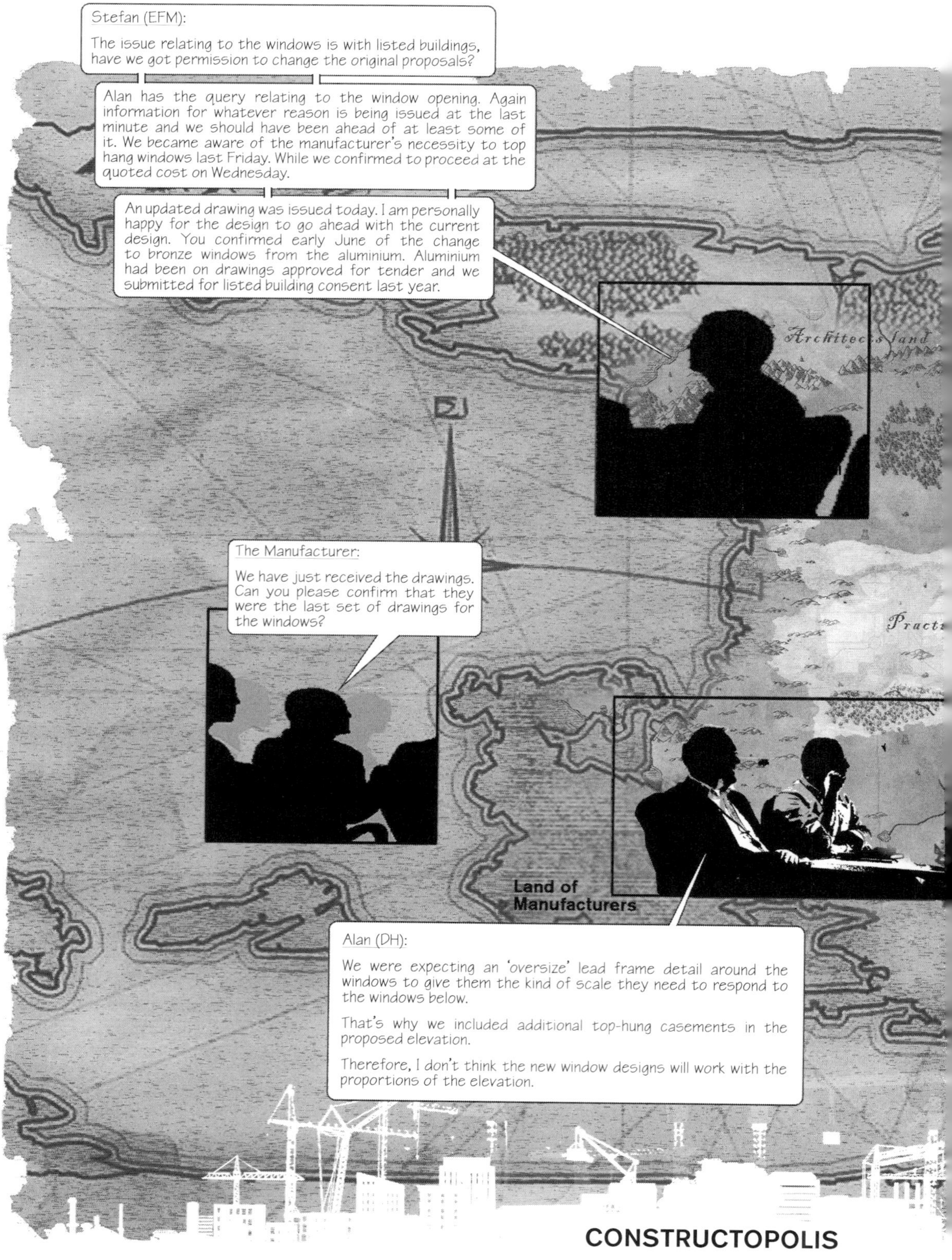
Stefan (EFM):
The issue relating to the windows is with listed buildings, have we got permission to change the original proposals?
Alan has the query relating to the window opening. Again information for whatever reason is being issued at the last minute and we should have been ahead of at least some of it. We became aware of the manufacturer's necessity to top hang windows last Friday. While we confirmed to proceed at the quoted cost on Wednesday.
An updated drawing was issued today. I am personally happy for the design to go ahead with the current design. You confirmed early June of the change to bronze windows from the aluminium. Aluminium had been on drawings approved for tender and we submitted for listed building consent last year.
The Manufacturer:
We have just received the drawings. Can you please confirm that they were the last set of drawings for the windows?
Land of Manufacturers
Alan (DH):
We were expecting an 'oversize' lead frame detail around the windows to give them the kind of scale they need to respond to the windows below.
That's why we included additional top-hung casements in the proposed elevation.
Therefore, I don't think the new window designs will work with the proportions of the elevation.
CONSTRUCTOPOLIS

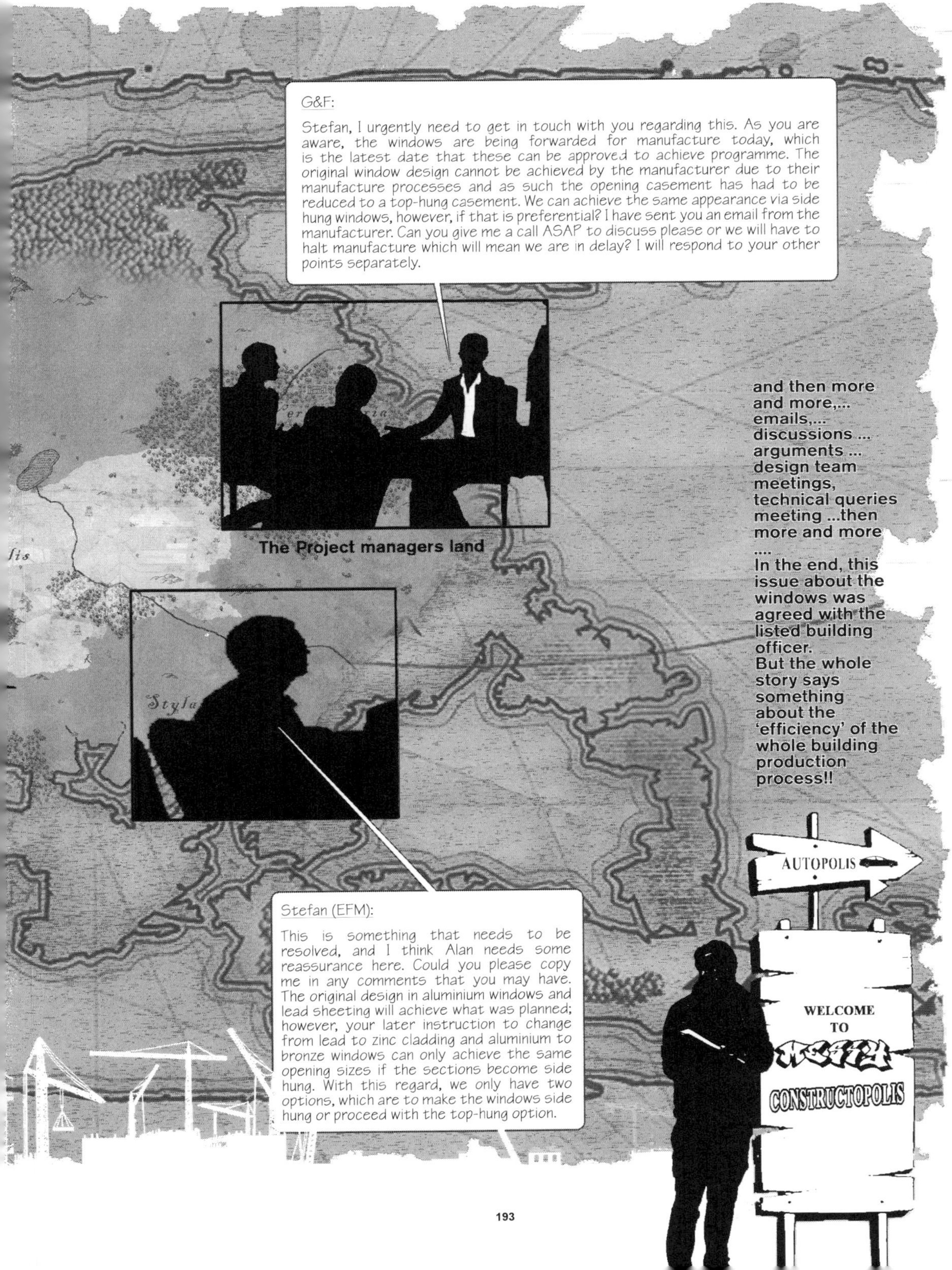
G&F:
Stefan, I urgently need to get in touch with you regarding this. As you are aware, the windows are being forwarded for manufacture today, which is the latest date that these can be approved to achieve programme. The original window design cannot be achieved by the manufacturer due to their manufacture processes and as such the opening casement has had to be reduced to a top-hung casement. We can achieve the same appearance via side hung windows, however, if that is preferential? I have sent you an email from the manufacturer. Can you give me a call ASAP to discuss please or we will have to halt manufacture which will mean we are in delay? I will respond to your other points separately.
The Project managers land
and then more and more,... emails,... discussions ... arguments ... design team meetings, technical queries meeting ...then more and more .... In the end, this issue about the windows was agreed with the listed building officer. But the whole story says something about the 'efficiency' of the whole building production process!!
Stefan (EFM):
This is something that needs to be resolved, and I think Alan needs some reassurance here. Could you please copy me in any comments that you may have. The original design in aluminium windows and lead sheeting will achieve what was planned; however, your later instruction to change from lead to zinc cladding and aluminium to bronze windows can only achieve the same opening sizes if the sections become side hung. With this regard, we only have two options, which are to make the windows side hung or proceed with the top-hung option.
AUTOPOLIS
WELCOME TO
CONSTRUCTOPOLIS

The story of 'The Warranty' presents another example of one bureaucratic encounter when two different standpoints about construction clash.

From: EFM

Good Morning Alan,

I realise that you are not in the office, but hope that I am not disturbing your break too much, as I know that you will probably be checking your mail.

There are a few things that have come up which I need to make you aware of and cannot wait until you get back.

The contractor has been looking at the proposals for the lean-to designs. G&F designs were somewhat contradicting in their specification, and now that the specification has been made clear the contractor has identified a fairly major problem. Short of hiring a tower crane, He has not been able to identify a suitable way of manhandling the lead onto the roof without putting operatives at risk. The weight of the rolled lead is excessive and extremely difficult to handle. As such they have made a request that the outer face of the building to be manufactured in Sarnafil* complete with the lead-roll details mimicking real lead.

There are several reasons for this possible switch. Firstly as explained is the safety concerns about the physical manhandling of such heavy objects, Secondly, this will reduce the time it takes to make the building reasonable watertight, a couple of days against a couple of weeks for the lead. Thirdly, the benefit to the programme of the faster installation, and lastly the fact that lead will come with a 12 month defect period whereas the Sarnafil comes with a 25 year guarantee. I know that in defence, the lead will be as good as the people who fit it, and whilst it should be good for 50+ years, the workmen available today do not have the levels of skill of those who worked lead in the past, and all resulting maintenance will fall back on the shoulders of EFM.

Please let me know your opinion?

Stefan

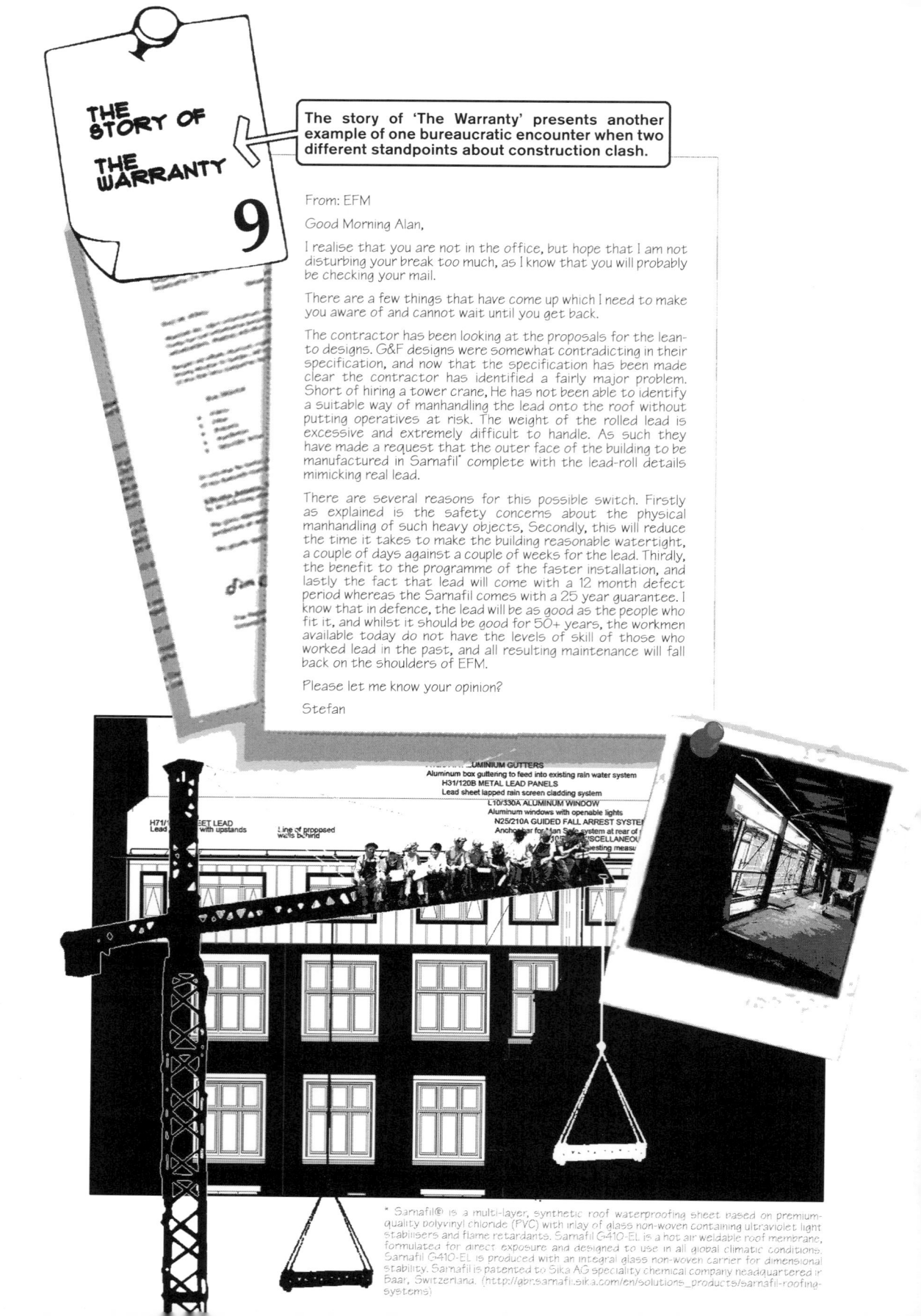

ALUMINIUM GUTTERS
Aluminum box guttering to feed into existing rain water system
H31/120B METAL LEAD PANELS
Lead sheet lapped rain screen cladding system
L10/330A ALUMINUM WINDOW
Aluminum windows with openable lights
N25/210A GUIDED FALL ARREST SYSTEM
Anchor bar for 'Man Safe' system at rear of

H71/ SHEET LEAD
Lead with upstands
Line of proposed walls behind

* Sarnafil© is a multi-layer, synthetic roof waterproofing sheet based on premium-quality polyvinyl chloride (PVC) with inlay of glass non-woven containing ultraviolet light stabilisers and flame retardants. Sarnafil G-410-EL is a hot air weldable roof membrane, formulated for direct exposure and designed to use in all global climatic conditions. Sarnafil G-410-EL is produced with an integral glass non-woven carrier for dimensional stability. Sarnafil is patented to Sika AG speciality chemical company headquartered in Baar, Switzerland. (http://gbr.sarnafil.sika.com/en/solutions_products/sarnafil-roofing-systems)

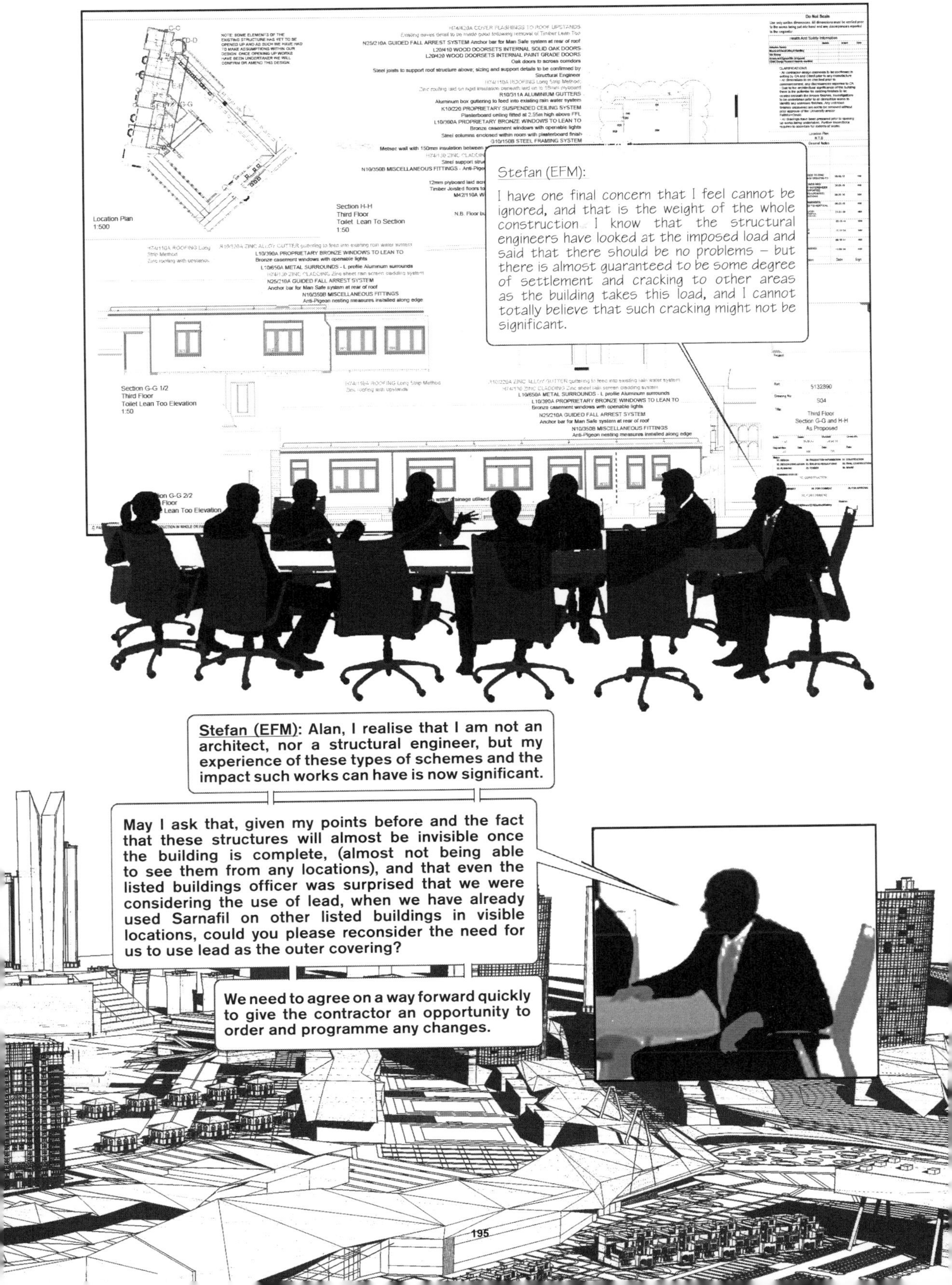
Location Plan
1:500
Section H-H
Third Floor
Toilet Lean To Section
1:50
Section G-G 1/2
Third Floor
Toilet Lean Too Elevation
1:50
Stefan (EFM):
I have one final concern that I feel cannot be ignored, and that is the weight of the whole construction. I know that the structural engineers have looked at the imposed load and said that there should be no problems – but there is almost guaranteed to be some degree of settlement and cracking to other areas as the building takes this load, and I cannot totally believe that such cracking might not be significant.
Stefan (EFM): Alan, I realise that I am not an architect, nor a structural engineer, but my experience of these types of schemes and the impact such works can have is now significant.
May I ask that, given my points before and the fact that these structures will almost be invisible once the building is complete, (almost not being able to see them from any locations), and that even the listed buildings officer was surprised that we were considering the use of lead, when we have already used Sarnafil on other listed buildings in visible locations, could you please reconsider the need for us to use lead as the outer covering?
We need to agree on a way forward quickly to give the contractor an opportunity to order and programme any changes.

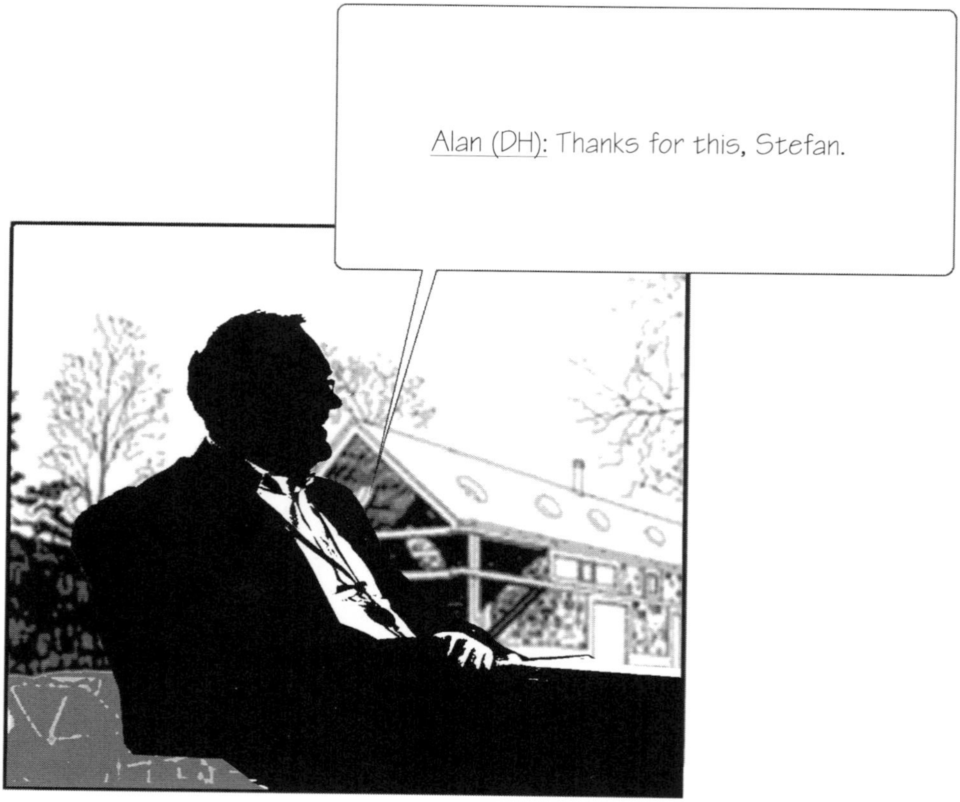
Alan (DH): Thanks for this, Stefan.

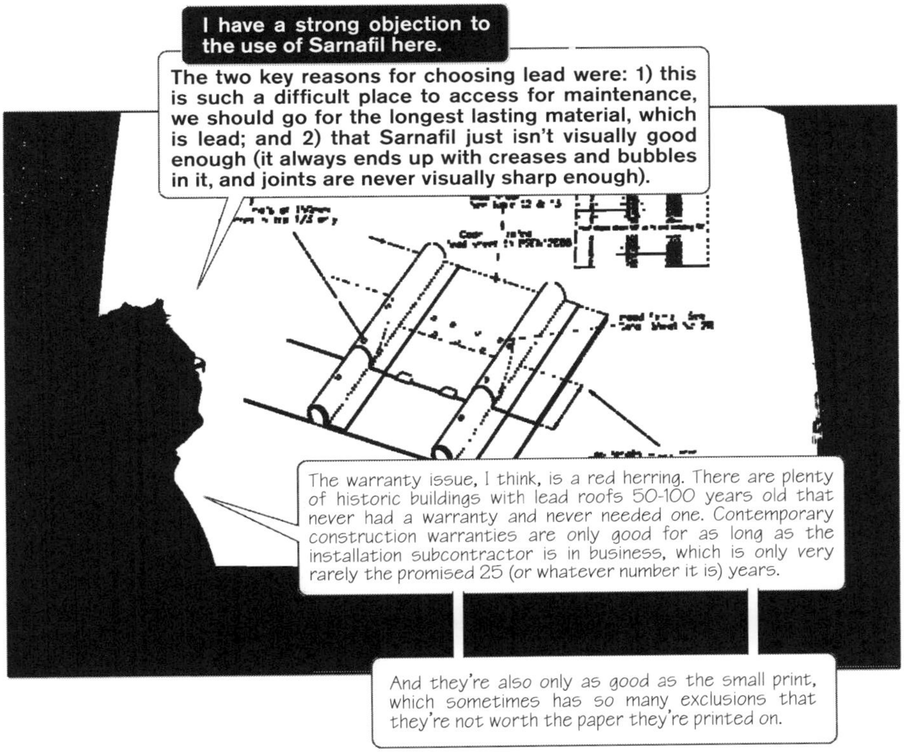
I have a strong objection to the use of Sarnafil here.
The two key reasons for choosing lead were: 1) this is such a difficult place to access for maintenance, we should go for the longest lasting material, which is lead; and 2) that Sarnafil just isn't visually good enough (it always ends up with creases and bubbles in it, and joints are never visually sharp enough).
The warranty issue, I think, is a red herring. There are plenty of historic buildings with lead roofs 50-100 years old that never had a warranty and never needed one. Contemporary construction warranties are only good for as long as the installation subcontractor is in business, which is only very rarely the promised 25 (or whatever number it is) years.
And they're also only as good as the small print, which sometimes has so many exclusions that they're not worth the paper they're printed on.

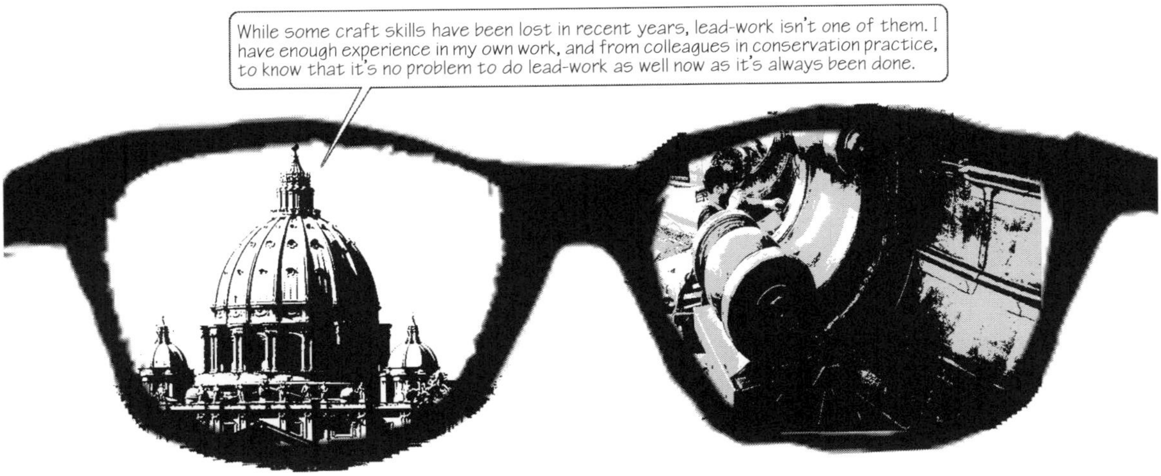
While some craft skills have been lost in recent years, lead-work isn't one of them. I have enough experience in my own work, and from colleagues in conservation practice, to know that it's no problem to do lead-work as well now as it's always been done.

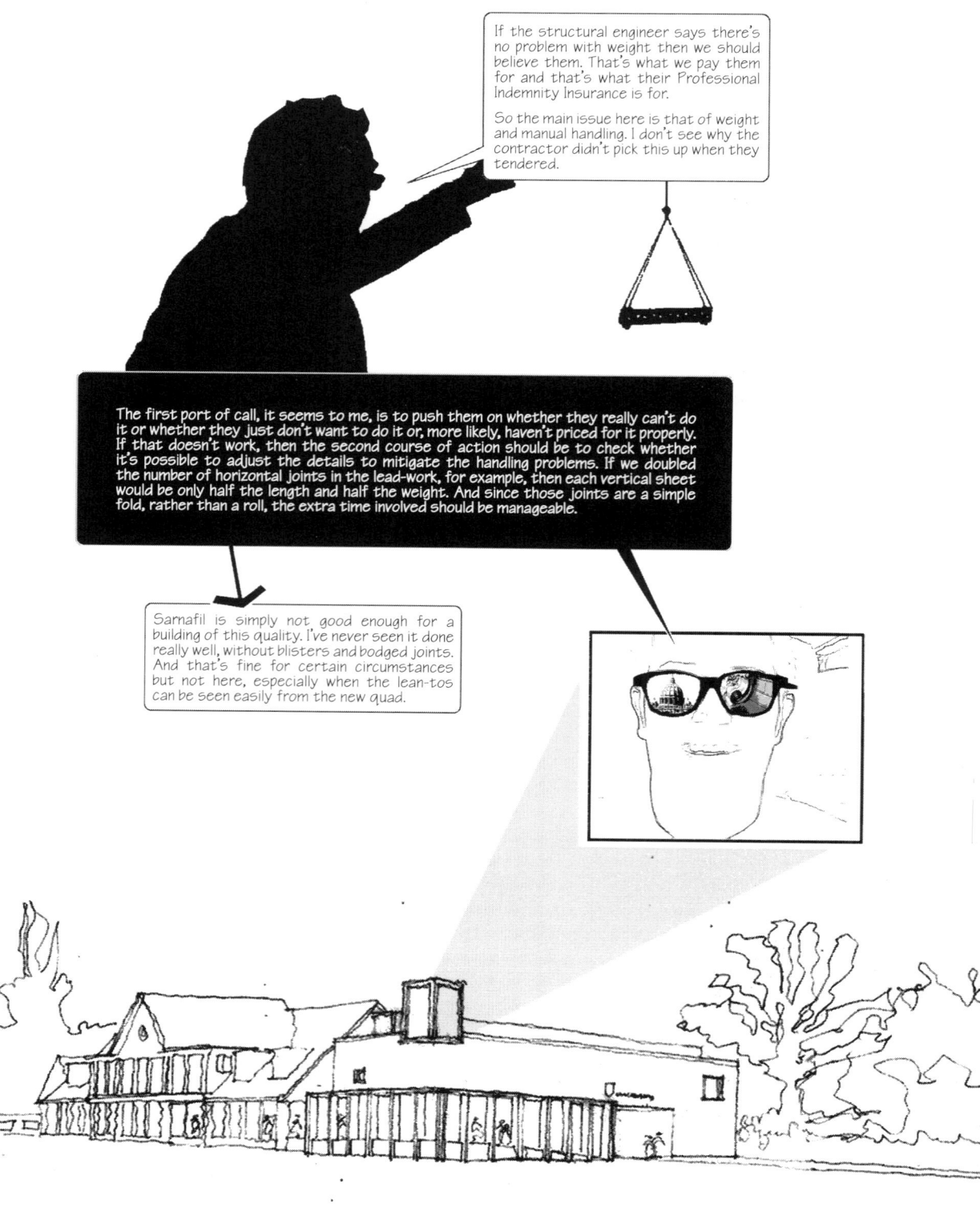

If the structural engineer says there's no problem with weight then we should believe them. That's what we pay them for and that's what their Professional Indemnity Insurance is for.

So the main issue here is that of weight and manual handling. I don't see why the contractor didn't pick this up when they tendered.

The first port of call, it seems to me, is to push them on whether they really can't do it or whether they just don't want to do it or, more likely, haven't priced for it properly. If that doesn't work, then the second course of action should be to check whether it's possible to adjust the details to mitigate the handling problems. If we doubled the number of horizontal joints in the lead-work, for example, then each vertical sheet would be only half the length and half the weight. And since those joints are a simple fold, rather than a roll, the extra time involved should be manageable.

Sarnafil is simply not good enough for a building of this quality. I've never seen it done really well, without blisters and bodged joints. And that's fine for certain circumstances but not here, especially when the lean-tos can be seen easily from the new quad.

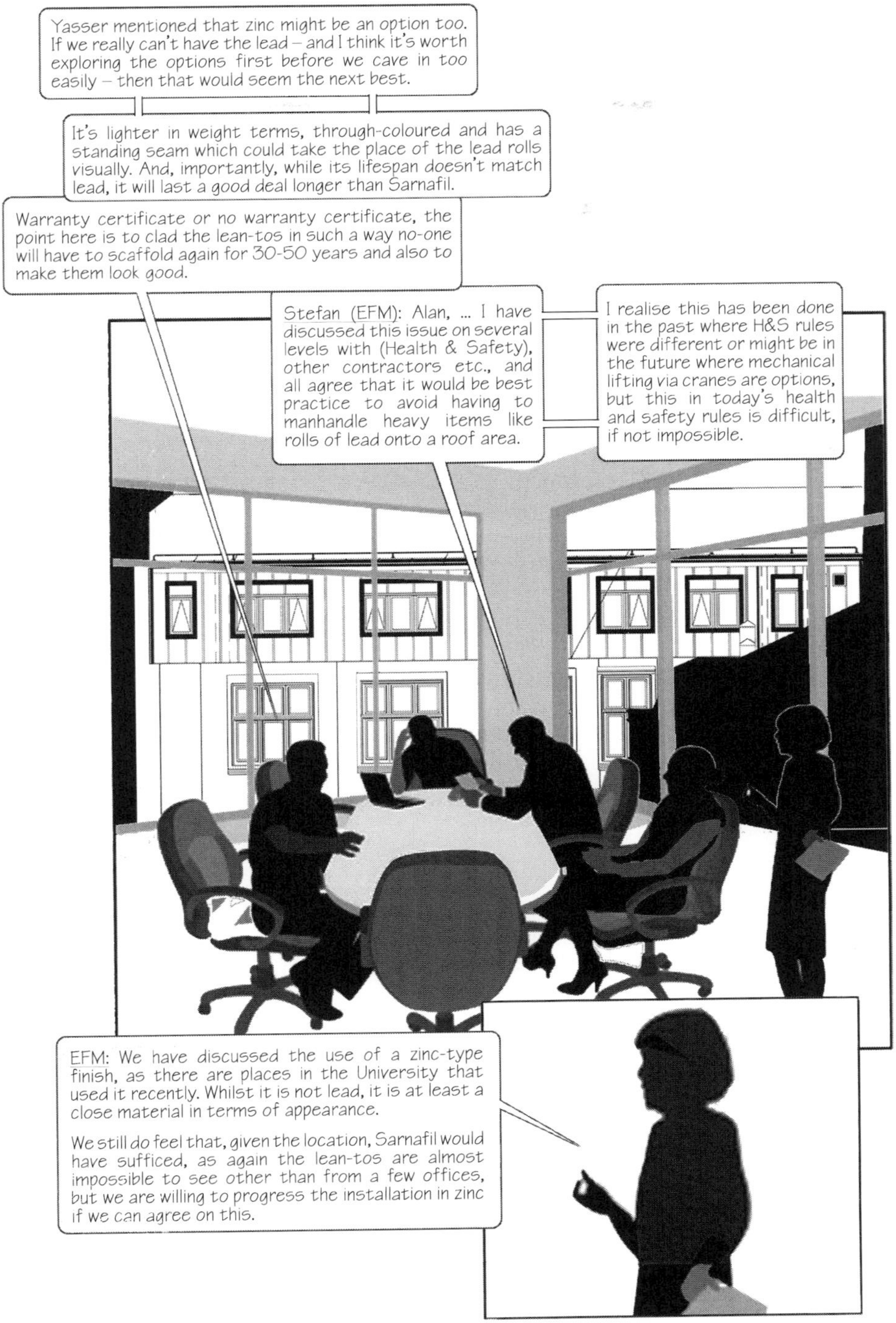
Yasser mentioned that zinc might be an option too. If we really can't have the lead – and I think it's worth exploring the options first before we cave in too easily – then that would seem the next best.
It's lighter in weight terms, through-coloured and has a standing seam which could take the place of the lead rolls visually. And, importantly, while its lifespan doesn't match lead, it will last a good deal longer than Sarnafil.
Warranty certificate or no warranty certificate, the point here is to clad the lean-tos in such a way no-one will have to scaffold again for 30-50 years and also to make them look good.
Stefan (EFM): Alan, ... I have discussed this issue on several levels with (Health & Safety), other contractors etc., and all agree that it would be best practice to avoid having to manhandle heavy items like rolls of lead onto a roof area.
I realise this has been done in the past where H&S rules were different or might be in the future where mechanical lifting via cranes are options, but this in today's health and safety rules is difficult, if not impossible.
EFM: We have discussed the use of a zinc-type finish, as there are places in the University that used it recently. Whilst it is not lead, it is at least a close material in terms of appearance.
We still do feel that, given the location, Sarnafil would have sufficed, as again the lean-tos are almost impossible to see other than from a few offices, but we are willing to progress the installation in zinc if we can agree on this.

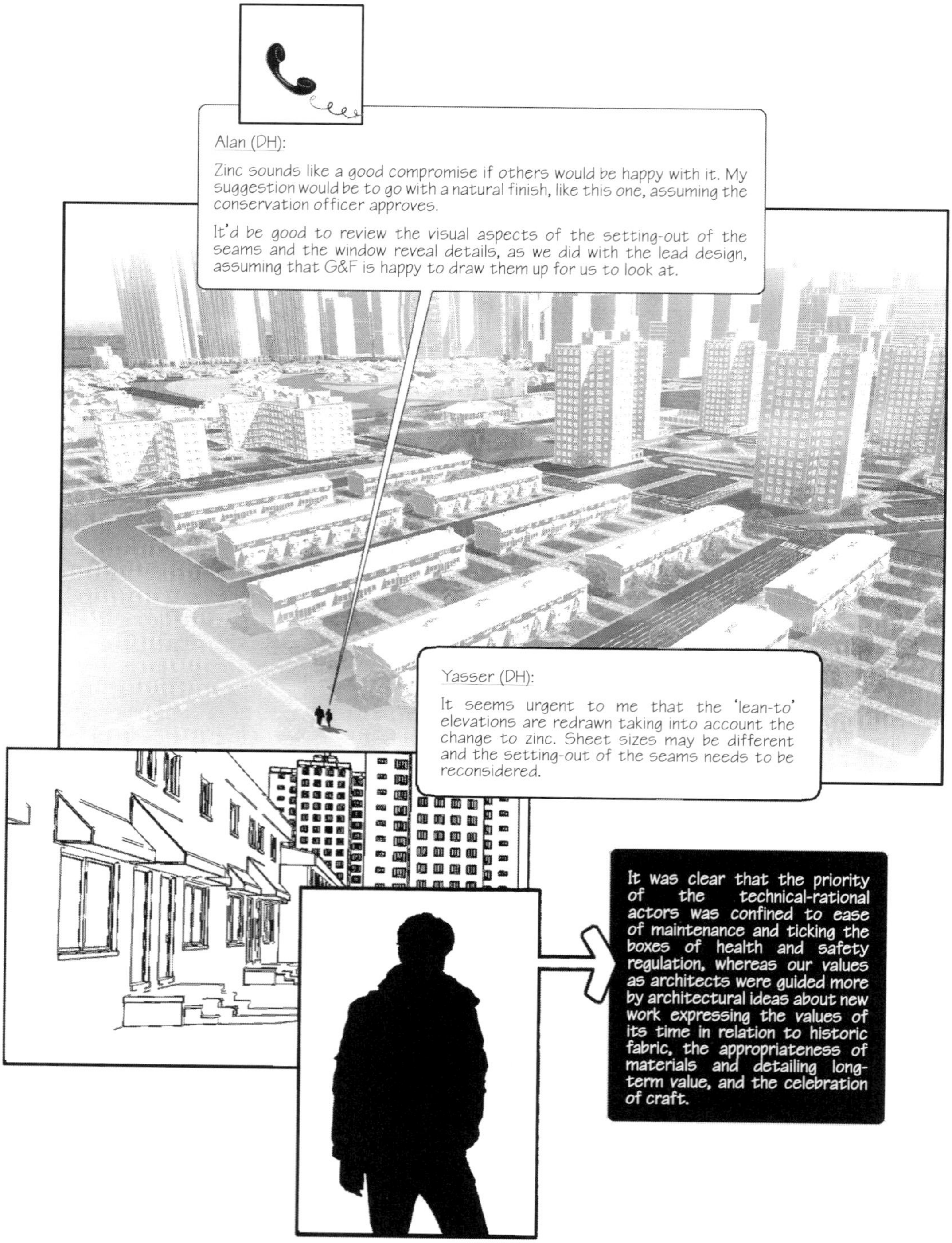
Alan (DH):
Zinc sounds like a good compromise if others would be happy with it. My suggestion would be to go with a natural finish, like this one, assuming the conservation officer approves.
It'd be good to review the visual aspects of the setting-out of the seams and the window reveal details, as we did with the lead design, assuming that G&F is happy to draw them up for us to look at.
Yasser (DH):
It seems urgent to me that the 'lean-to' elevations are redrawn taking into account the change to zinc. Sheet sizes may be different and the setting-out of the seams needs to be reconsidered.
It was clear that the priority of the technical-rational actors was confined to ease of maintenance and ticking the boxes of health and safety regulation, whereas our values as architects were guided more by architectural ideas about new work expressing the values of its time in relation to historic fabric, the appropriateness of materials and detailing long-term value, and the celebration of craft.

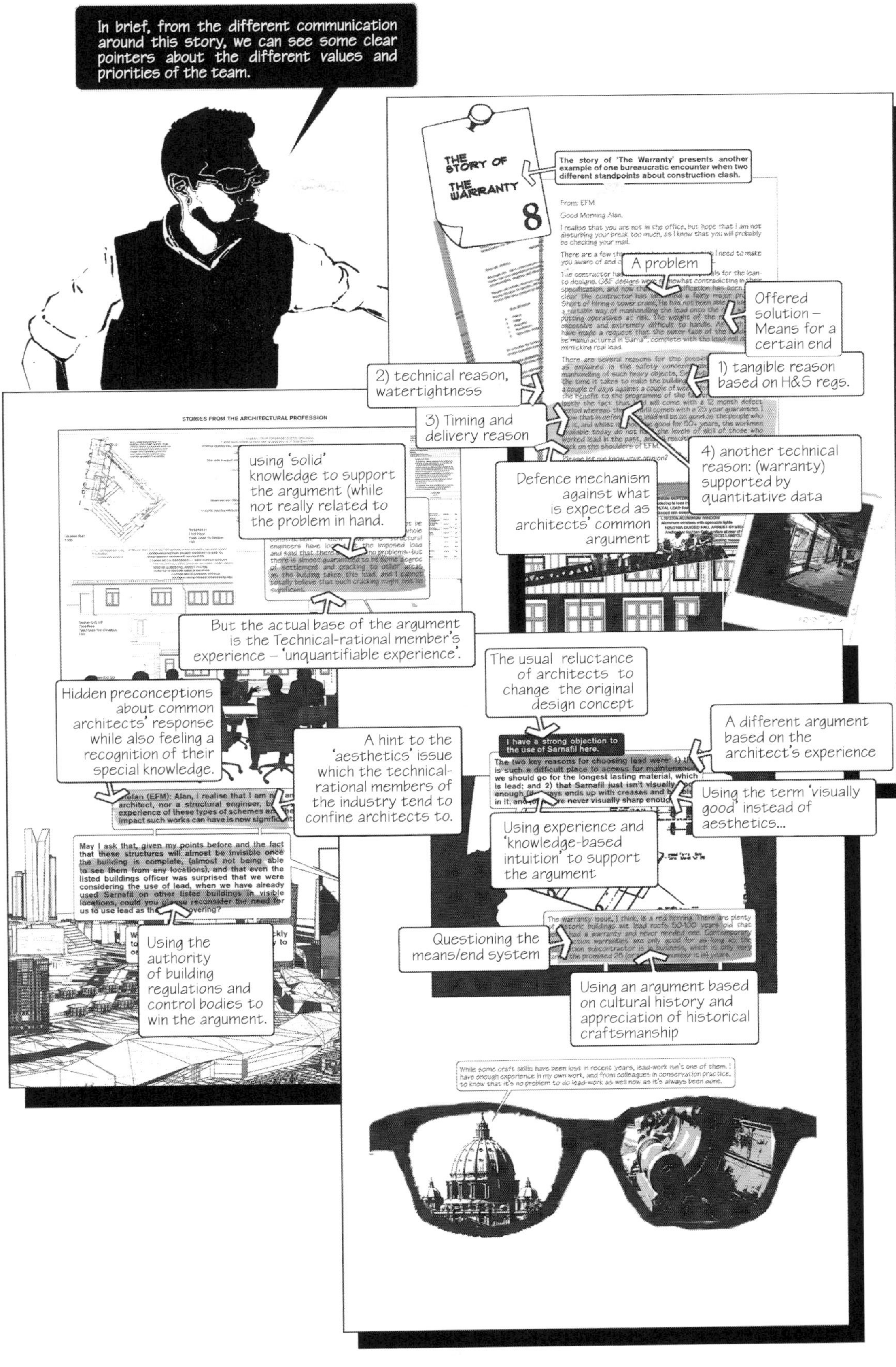
In brief, from the different communication around this story, we can see some clear pointers about the different values and priorities of the team.
THE STORY OF THE WARRANTY
8
The story of 'The Warranty' presents another example of one bureaucratic encounter when two different standpoints about construction clash.
From: EFM
Good Morning Alan.
A problem
Offered solution – Means for a certain end
1) tangible reason based on H&S regs.
2) technical reason, watertightness
3) Timing and delivery reason
4) another technical reason: (warranty) supported by quantitative data
Defence mechanism against what is expected as architects' common argument
STORIES FROM THE ARCHITECTURAL PROFESSION
using 'solid' knowledge to support the argument (while not really related to the problem in hand.
But the actual base of the argument is the Technical-rational member's experience – 'unquantifiable experience'.
Hidden preconceptions about common architects' response while also feeling a recognition of their special knowledge.
A hint to the 'aesthetics' issue which the technical-rational members of the industry tend to confine architects to.
May I ask that, given my points before and the fact that these structures will almost be invisible once the building is complete, (almost not being able to see them from any locations), and that even the listed buildings officer was surprised that we were considering the use of lead, when we have already used Sarnafil on other listed buildings in visible locations, could you please reconsider the need for us to use lead as the
Using the authority of building regulations and control bodies to win the argument.
The usual reluctance of architects to change the original design concept
I have a strong objection to the use of Sarnafil here.
A different argument based on the architect's experience
Using the term 'visually good' instead of aesthetics...
Using experience and 'knowledge-based intuition' to support the argument
Questioning the means/end system
Using an argument based on cultural history and appreciation of historical craftsmanship
While some craft skills have been lost in recent years, lead-work isn't one of them. I have enough experience in my own work, and from colleagues in conservation practice, to know that it's no problem to do lead-work as well now as it's always been done.

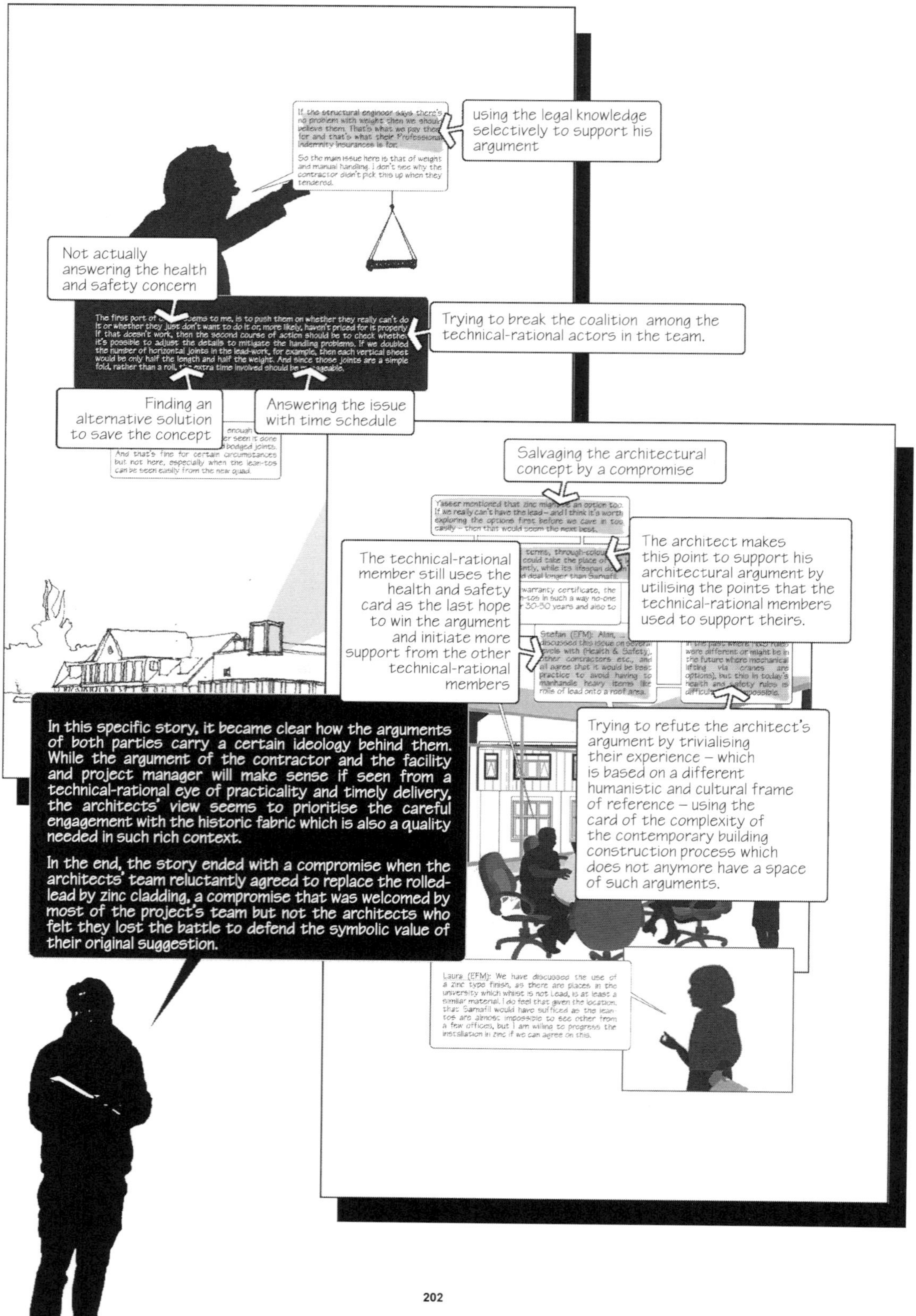
If the structural engineer says there's no problem with weight then we should believe them. That's what we pay them for and that's what their Professional Indemnity insurances is for.
So the main issue here is that of weight and manual handling. I don't see why the contractor didn't pick this up when they tendered.
using the legal knowledge selectively to support his argument
Not actually answering the health and safety concern
Trying to break the coalition among the technical-rational actors in the team.
Finding an alternative solution to save the concept
Answering the issue with time schedule
And that's fine for certain circumstances but not here, especially when the lean-tos can be seen easily from the new quad.
Salvaging the architectural concept by a compromise
If we really can't have the lead – and I think it's worth exploring the options first before we cave in too easily – then that would seem the next best.
The architect makes this point to support his architectural argument by utilising the points that the technical-rational members used to support theirs.
The technical-rational member still uses the health and safety card as the last hope to win the argument and initiate more support from the other technical-rational members
Trying to refute the architect's argument by trivialising their experience – which is based on a different humanistic and cultural frame of reference – using the card of the complexity of the contemporary building construction process which does not anymore have a space of such arguments.
In this specific story, it became clear how the arguments of both parties carry a certain ideology behind them. While the argument of the contractor and the facility and project manager will make sense if seen from a technical-rational eye of practicality and timely delivery, the architects' view seems to prioritise the careful engagement with the historic fabric which is also a quality needed in such rich context.
In the end, the story ended with a compromise when the architects' team reluctantly agreed to replace the rolled-lead by zinc cladding, a compromise that was welcomed by most of the project's team but not the architects who felt they lost the battle to defend the symbolic value of their original suggestion.
Laura (EFM): We have discussed the use of a zinc type finish, as there are places in the university which whilst is not Lead, is at least a similar material. I do feel that given the location, that Samafil would have sufficed as the lean-tos are almost impossible to see other from a few offices, but I am willing to progress the installation in zinc if we can agree on this.

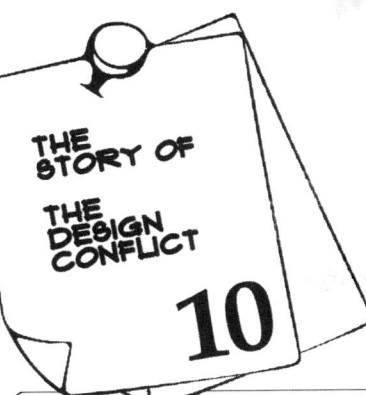

THE STORY OF THE DESIGN CONFLICT 10

The ground floor intervention was the biggest stage of our proposal. We have demolished the unoriginal buildings in the courtyard and we proposed turning the yard into an appropriate quad that will act as a new entrance to the building from the centre of gravity of the University campus.

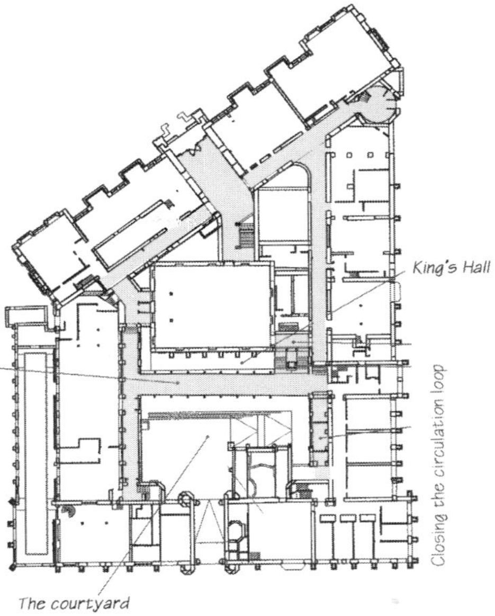

King's Hall
The Cloister
Closing the circulation loop
The courtyard

Our proposal suggested building a Cloister to link the two sides of the building and to function as a foyer for King's hall. The circulation in the ground floor would hence become far smoother by closing the loop of corridors and framing King's hall as the heart of the building.

This development also involves opening up previously partitioned rooms to their original volumes and providing more teaching space and an assembly room in order to reinstate original volumes, and comprising what was the use of the room chronologically as a lifetime of the space.

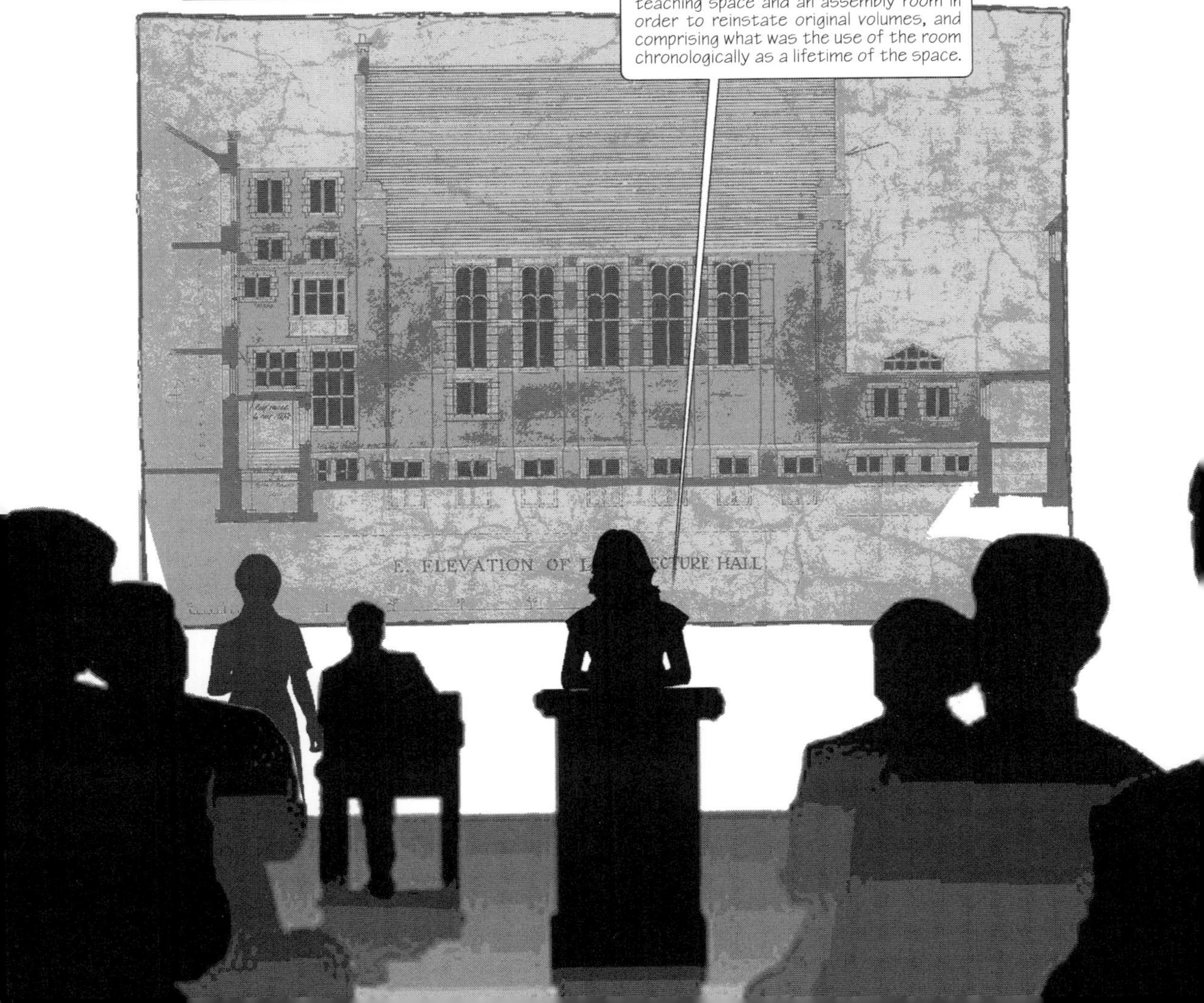

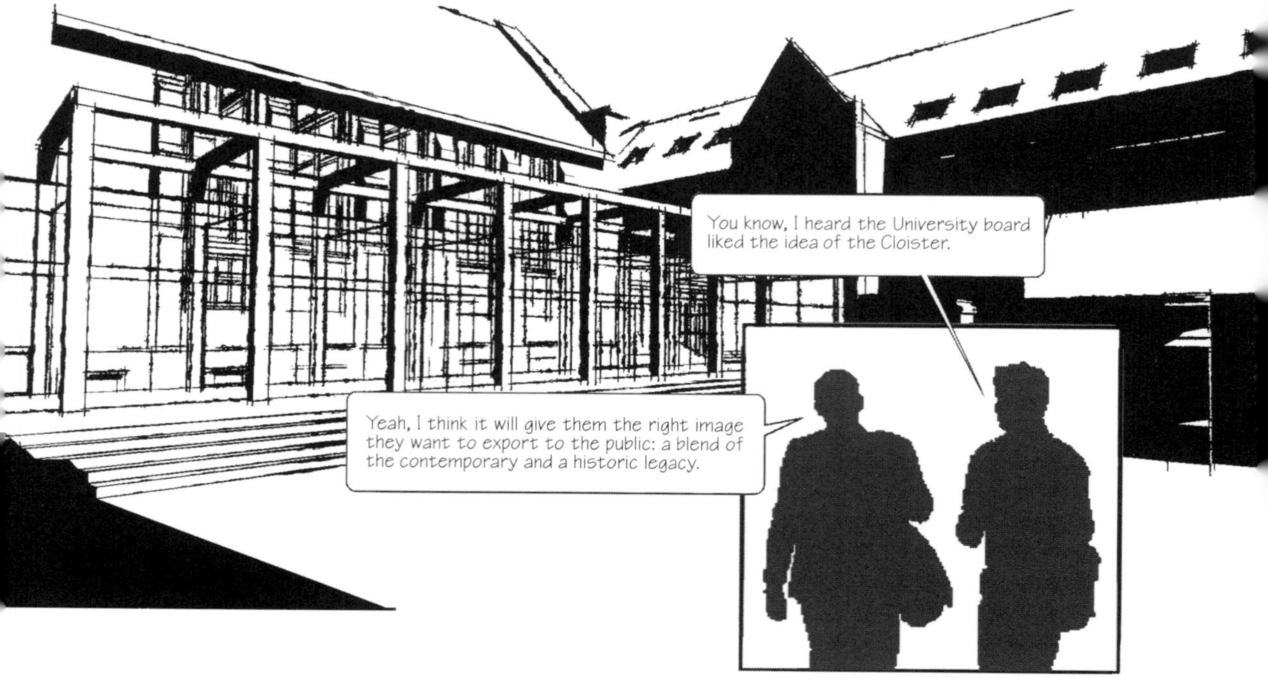
You know, I heard the University board liked the idea of the Cloister.
Yeah, I think it will give them the right image they want to export to the public: a blend of the contemporary and a historic legacy.

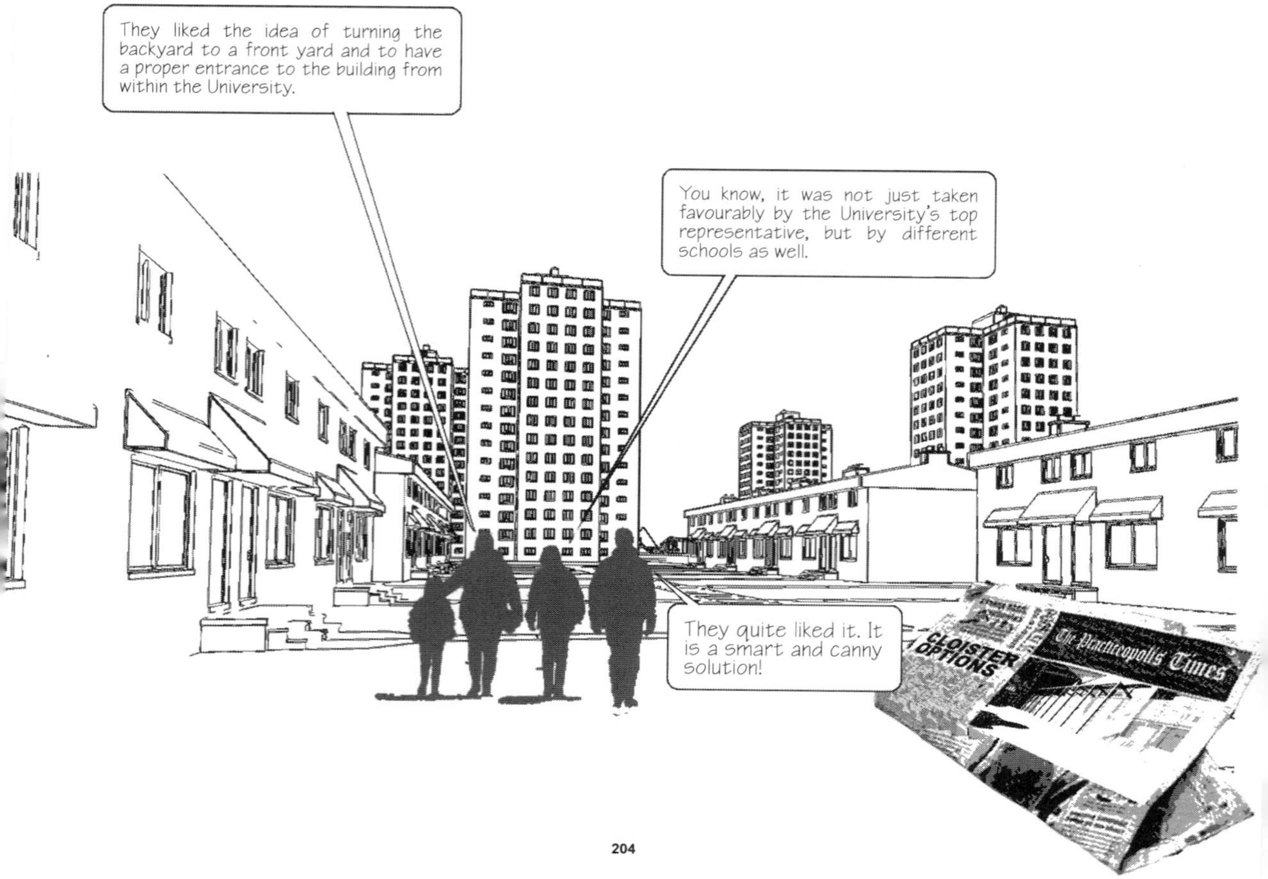
They liked the idea of turning the backyard to a front yard and to have a proper entrance to the building from within the University.
You know, it was not just taken favourably by the University's top representative, but by different schools as well.
They quite liked it. It is a smart and canny solution!
CLOISTER OPTIONS
The Practiceopolis Times

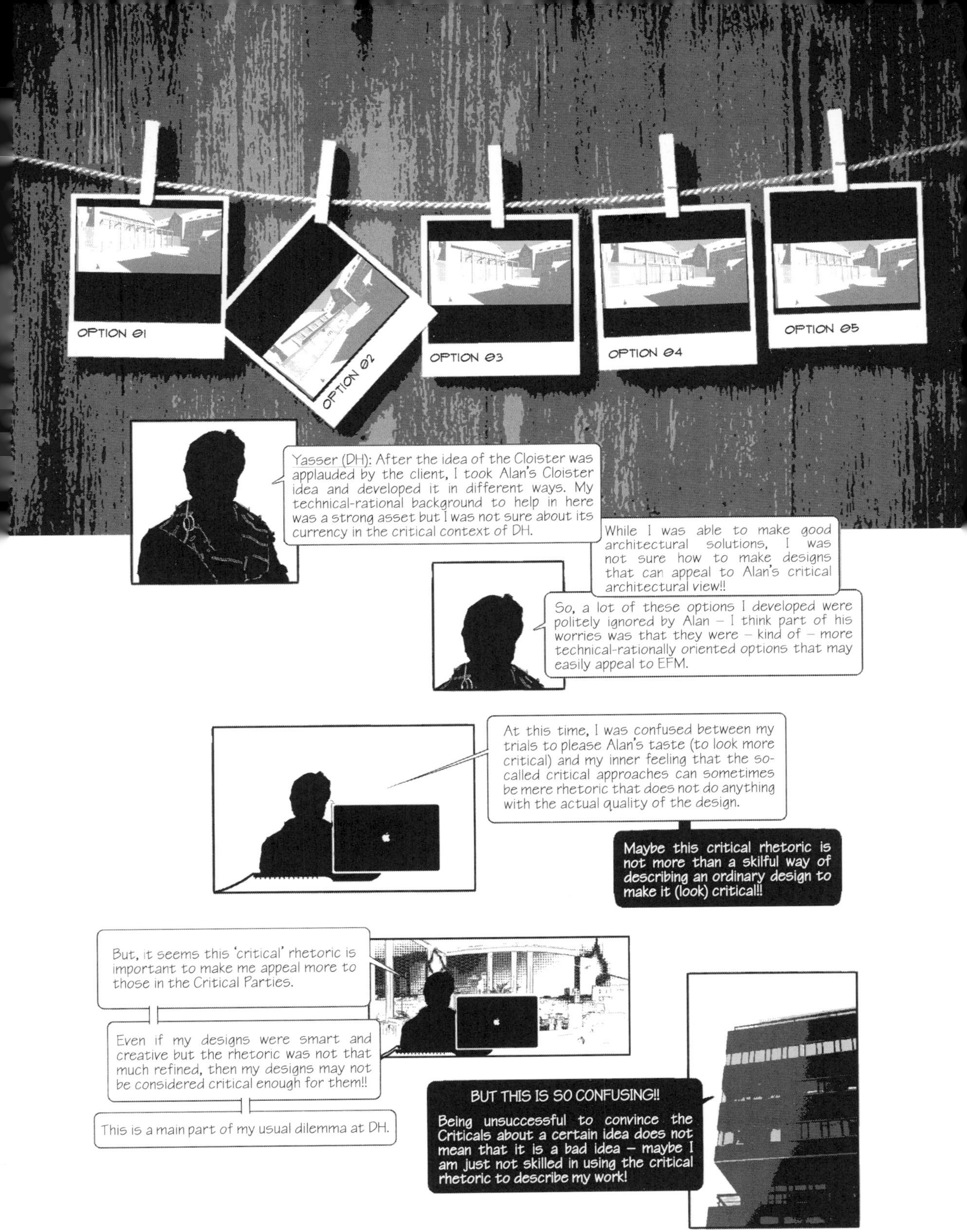
OPTION 01
OPTION 02
OPTION 03
OPTION 04
OPTION 05
Yasser (DH): After the idea of the Cloister was applauded by the client, I took Alan's Cloister idea and developed it in different ways. My technical-rational background to help in here was a strong asset but I was not sure about its currency in the critical context of DH.
While I was able to make good architectural solutions, I was not sure how to make designs that can appeal to Alan's critical architectural view!!
So, a lot of these options I developed were politely ignored by Alan – I think part of his worries was that they were – kind of – more technical-rationally oriented options that may easily appeal to EFM.
At this time, I was confused between my trials to please Alan's taste (to look more critical) and my inner feeling that the so-called critical approaches can sometimes be mere rhetoric that does not do anything with the actual quality of the design.
Maybe this critical rhetoric is not more than a skilful way of describing an ordinary design to make it (look) critical!!
But, it seems this 'critical' rhetoric is important to make me appeal more to those in the Critical Parties.
Even if my designs were smart and creative but the rhetoric was not that much refined, then my designs may not be considered critical enough for them!!
This is a main part of my usual dilemma at DH.
BUT THIS IS SO CONFUSING!!
Being unsuccessful to convince the Criticals about a certain idea does not mean that it is a bad idea – maybe I am just not skilled in using the critical rhetoric to describe my work!

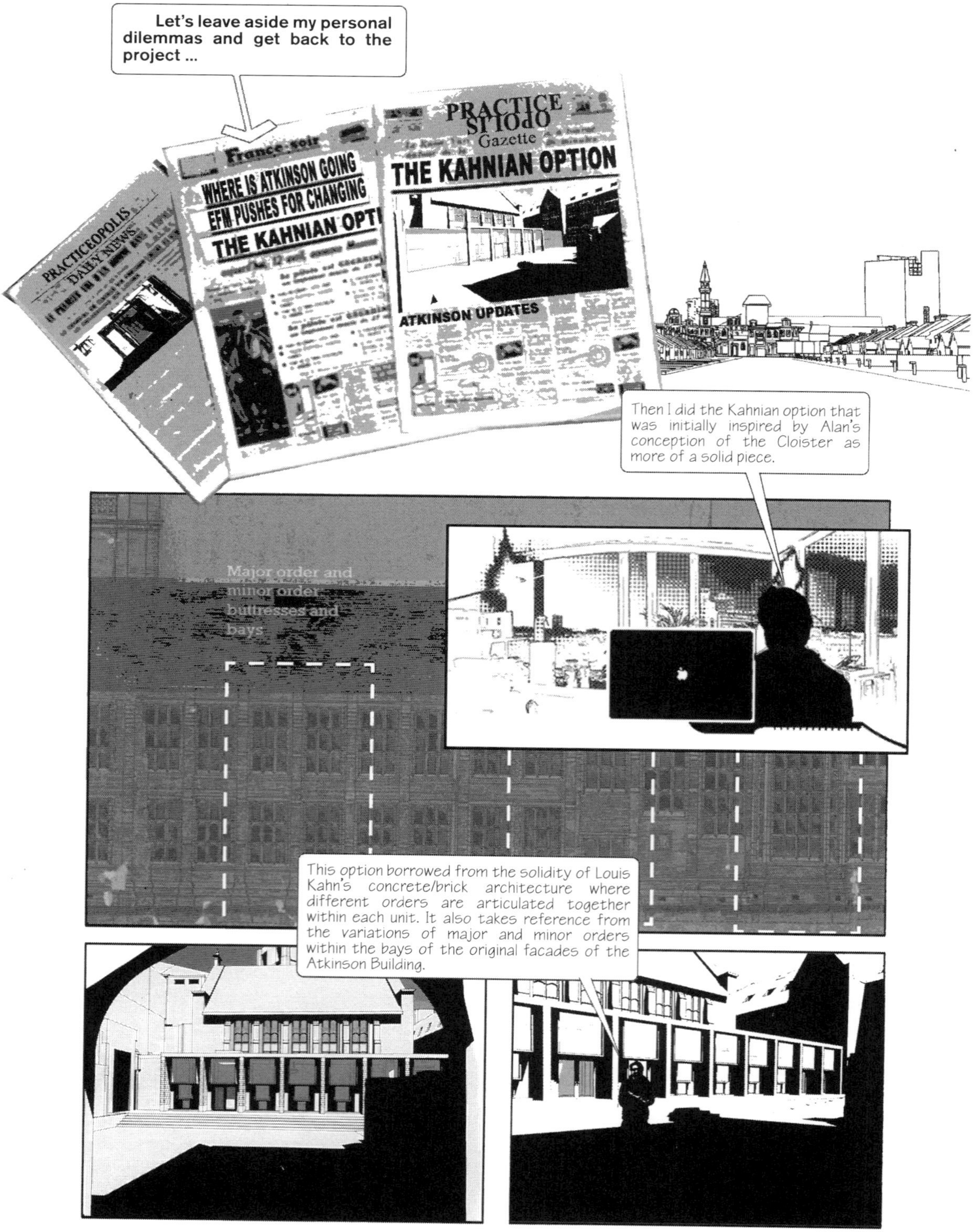
Let's leave aside my personal dilemmas and get back to the project ...
PRACTICEOPOLIS DAILY NEWS
France-soir
WHERE IS ATKINSON GOING
EFM PUSHES FOR CHANGING
THE KAHNIAN OPTI
PRACTICE
Gazette
THE KAHNIAN OPTION
ATKINSON UPDATES
Then I did the Kahnian option that was initially inspired by Alan's conception of the Cloister as more of a solid piece.
Major order and minor order buttresses and bays
This option borrowed from the solidity of Louis Kahn's concrete/brick architecture where different orders are articulated together within each unit. It also takes reference from the variations of major and minor orders within the bays of the original facades of the Atkinson Building.

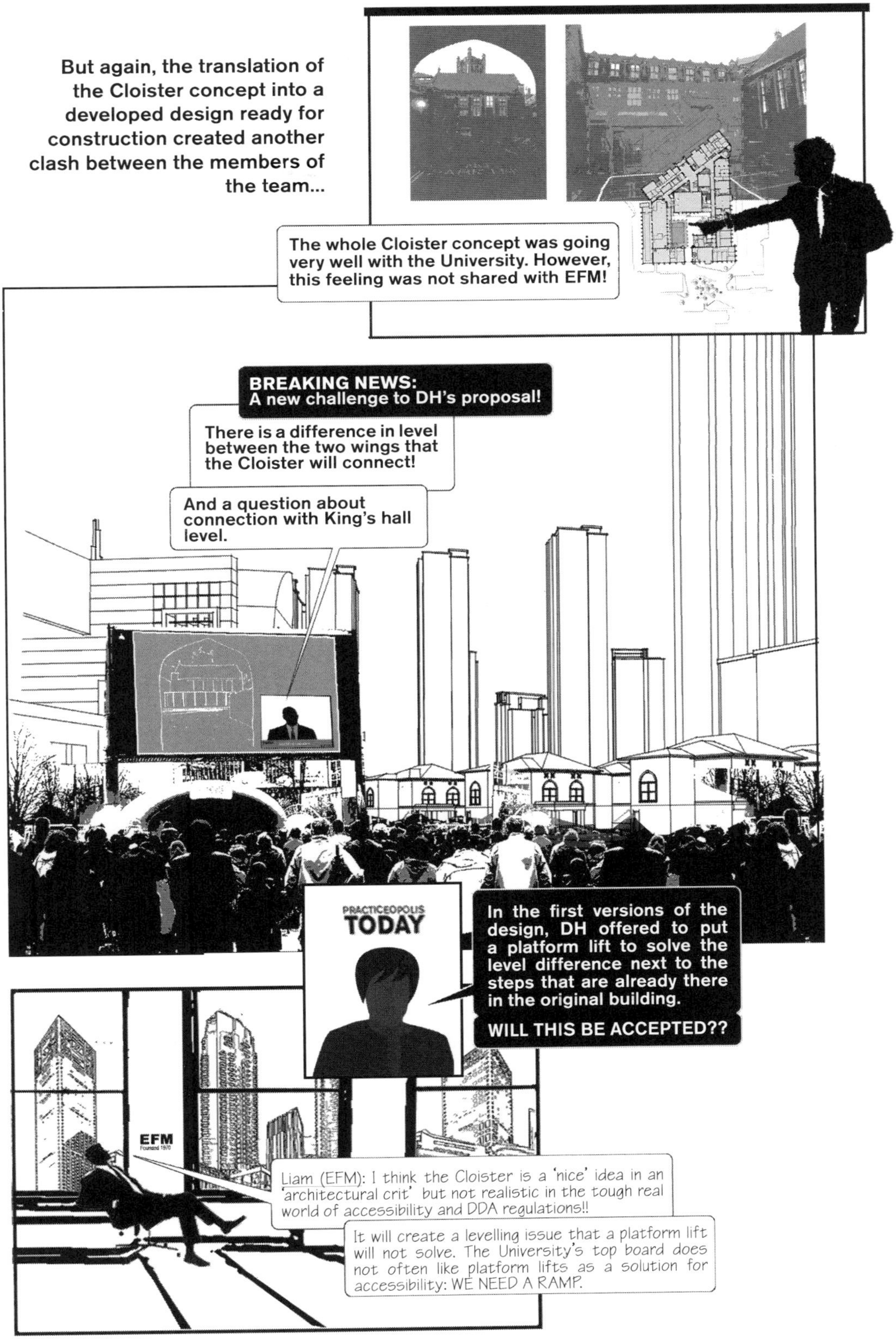
But again, the translation of the Cloister concept into a developed design ready for construction created another clash between the members of the team...
The whole Cloister concept was going very well with the University. However, this feeling was not shared with EFM!
BREAKING NEWS: A new challenge to DH's proposal!
There is a difference in level between the two wings that the Cloister will connect!
And a question about connection with King's hall level.
PRACTICEOPOLIS TODAY
In the first versions of the design, DH offered to put a platform lift to solve the level difference next to the steps that are already there in the original building.
WILL THIS BE ACCEPTED??
EFM
Liam (EFM): I think the Cloister is a 'nice' idea in an 'architectural crit' but not realistic in the tough real world of accessibility and DDA regulations!!
It will create a levelling issue that a platform lift will not solve. The University's top board does not often like platform lifts as a solution for accessibility: WE NEED A RAMP.

Yasser (DH): It was not clear if the need for omitting the proposed lift and replacing it by a ramp is really the University board's desire or it was EFM own understanding wrapped by the claim of the University's authority!!

But, this issue became an influential reason for changing the design proposal for the Cloister several times.

EFM: I don't know how the University agreed on the Cloister proposal from the beginning. I have not been at the initial meetings and I have many issues with this Cloister.

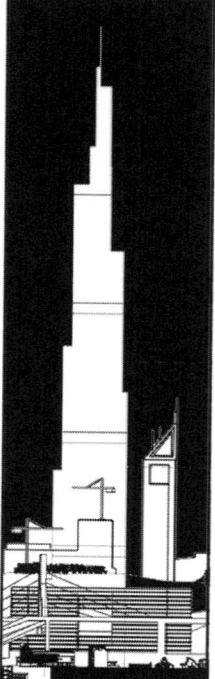

It is bulky and an excessive intervention that the brief did not ask for.

For us, the main objective of the ground floor intervention is to solve the accessibility issue in the old quad wing.

Therefore we find the whole idea of the Cloister is illogical, expensive and also would not solve the core problem that this intervention is supposed to offer – accessibility.

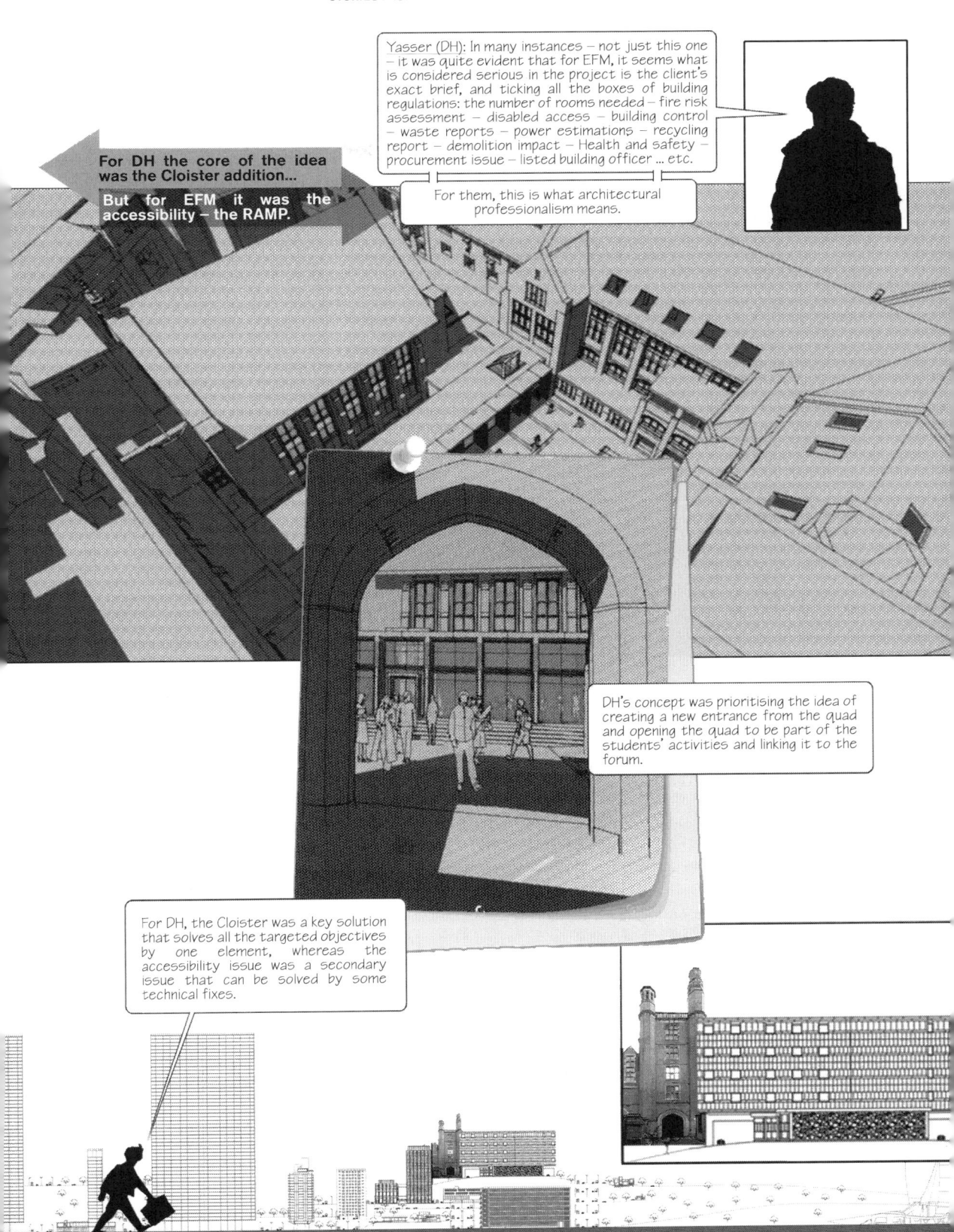

Yasser (DH): In many instances – not just this one – it was quite evident that for EFM, it seems what is considered serious in the project is the client's exact brief, and ticking all the boxes of building regulations: the number of rooms needed – fire risk assessment – disabled access – building control – waste reports – power estimations – recycling report – demolition impact – Health and safety – procurement issue – listed building officer … etc.

For them, this is what architectural professionalism means.

For DH the core of the idea was the Cloister addition...

But for EFM it was the accessibility – the RAMP.

DH's concept was prioritising the idea of creating a new entrance from the quad and opening the quad to be part of the students' activities and linking it to the forum.

For DH, the Cloister was a key solution that solves all the targeted objectives by one element, whereas the accessibility issue was a secondary issue that can be solved by some technical fixes.

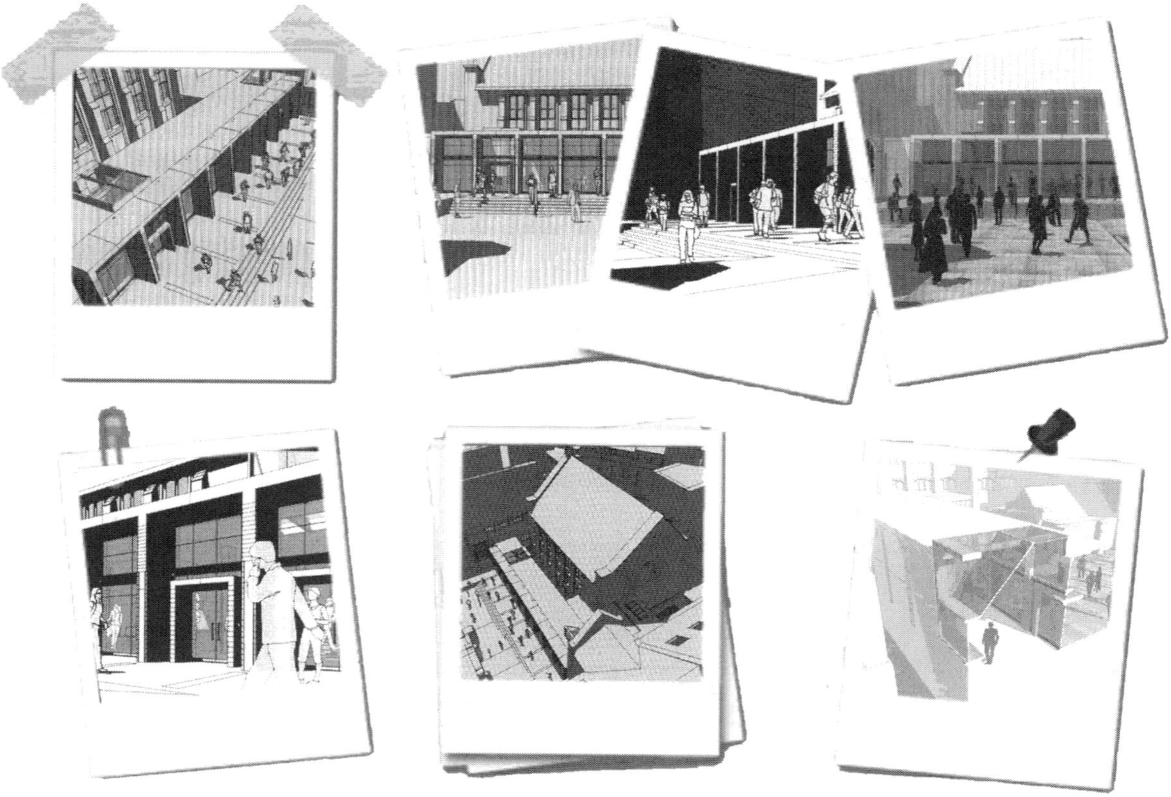

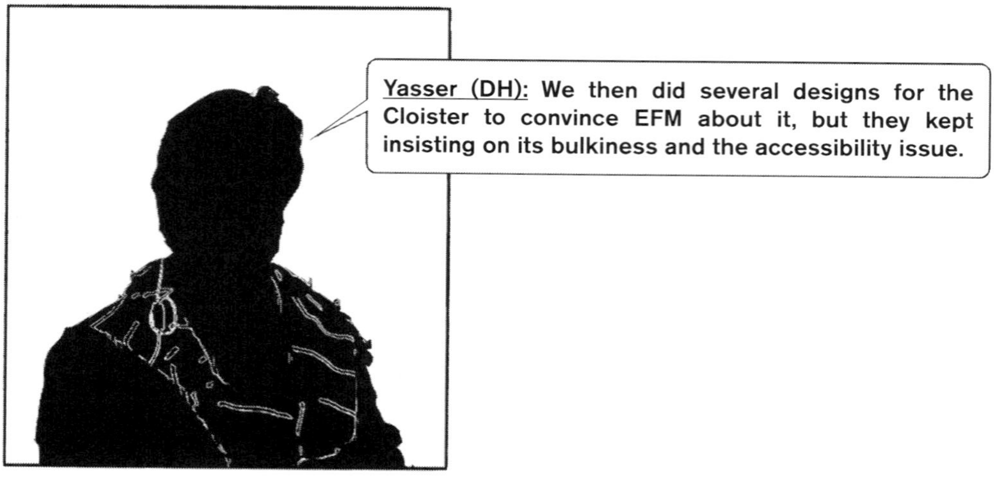
Yasser (DH): We then did several designs for the Cloister to convince EFM about it, but they kept insisting on its bulkiness and the accessibility issue.

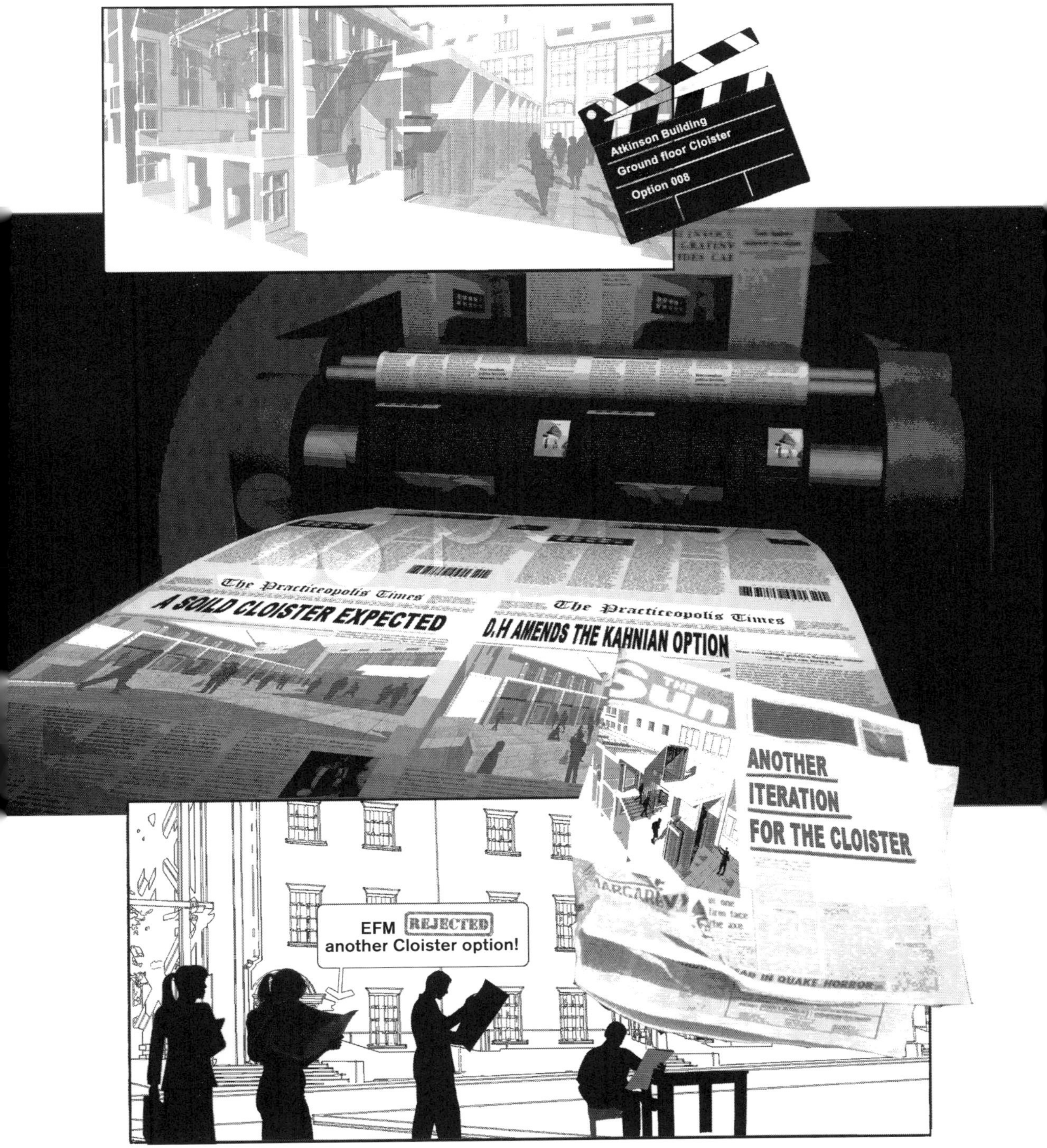
Atkinson Building
Ground floor Cloister
Option 008
The Practiceopolis Times
A SOILD CLOISTER EXPECTED
The Practiceopolis Times
D.H AMENDS THE KAHNIAN OPTION
THE Sun
ANOTHER ITERATION FOR THE CLOISTER
EFM REJECTED another Cloister option!

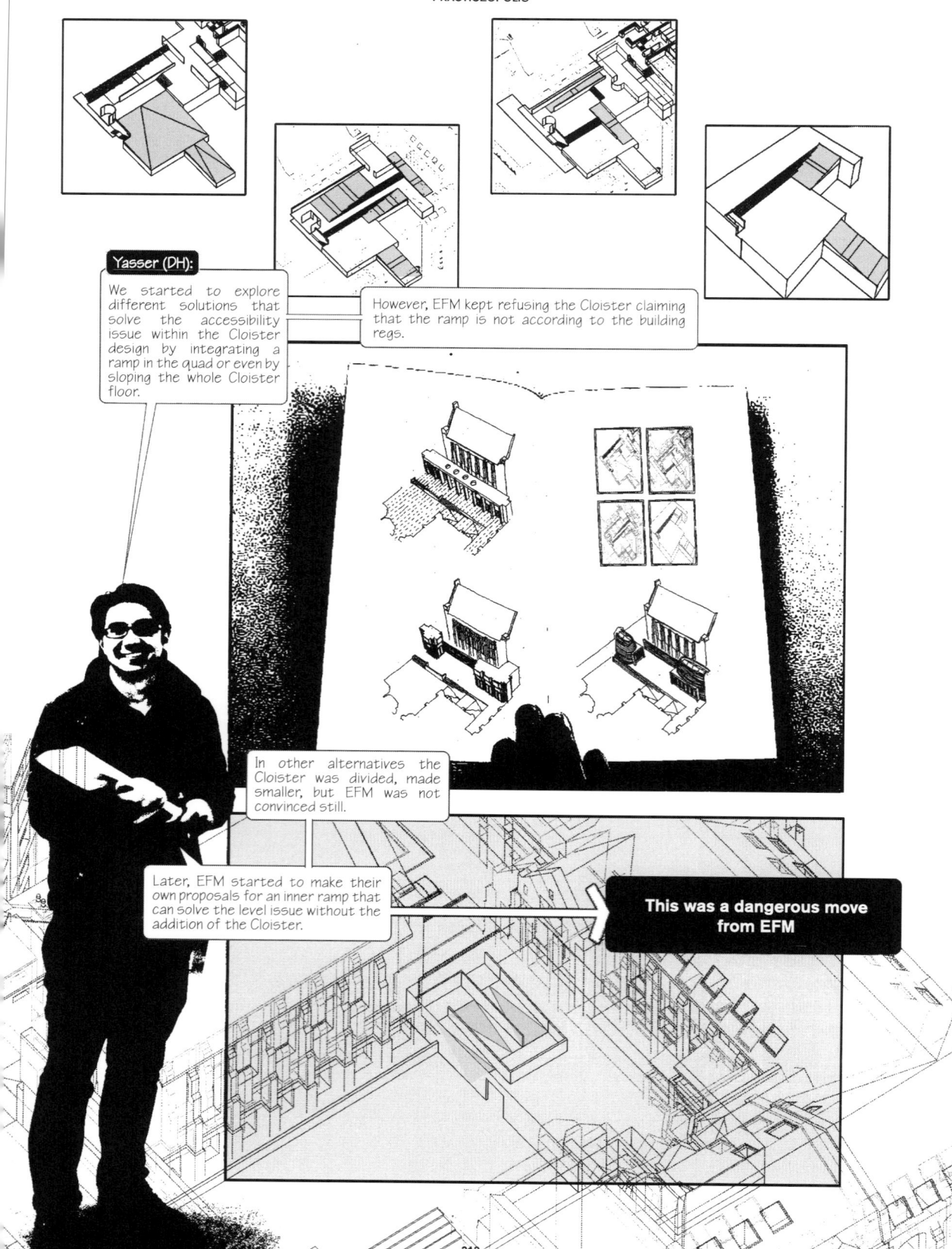

Yasser (DH):

We started to explore different solutions that solve the accessibility issue within the Cloister design by integrating a ramp in the quad or even by sloping the whole Cloister floor.

However, EFM kept refusing the Cloister claiming that the ramp is not according to the building regs.

In other alternatives the Cloister was divided, made smaller, but EFM was not convinced still.

Later, EFM started to make their own proposals for an inner ramp that can solve the level issue without the addition of the Cloister.

This was a dangerous move from EFM

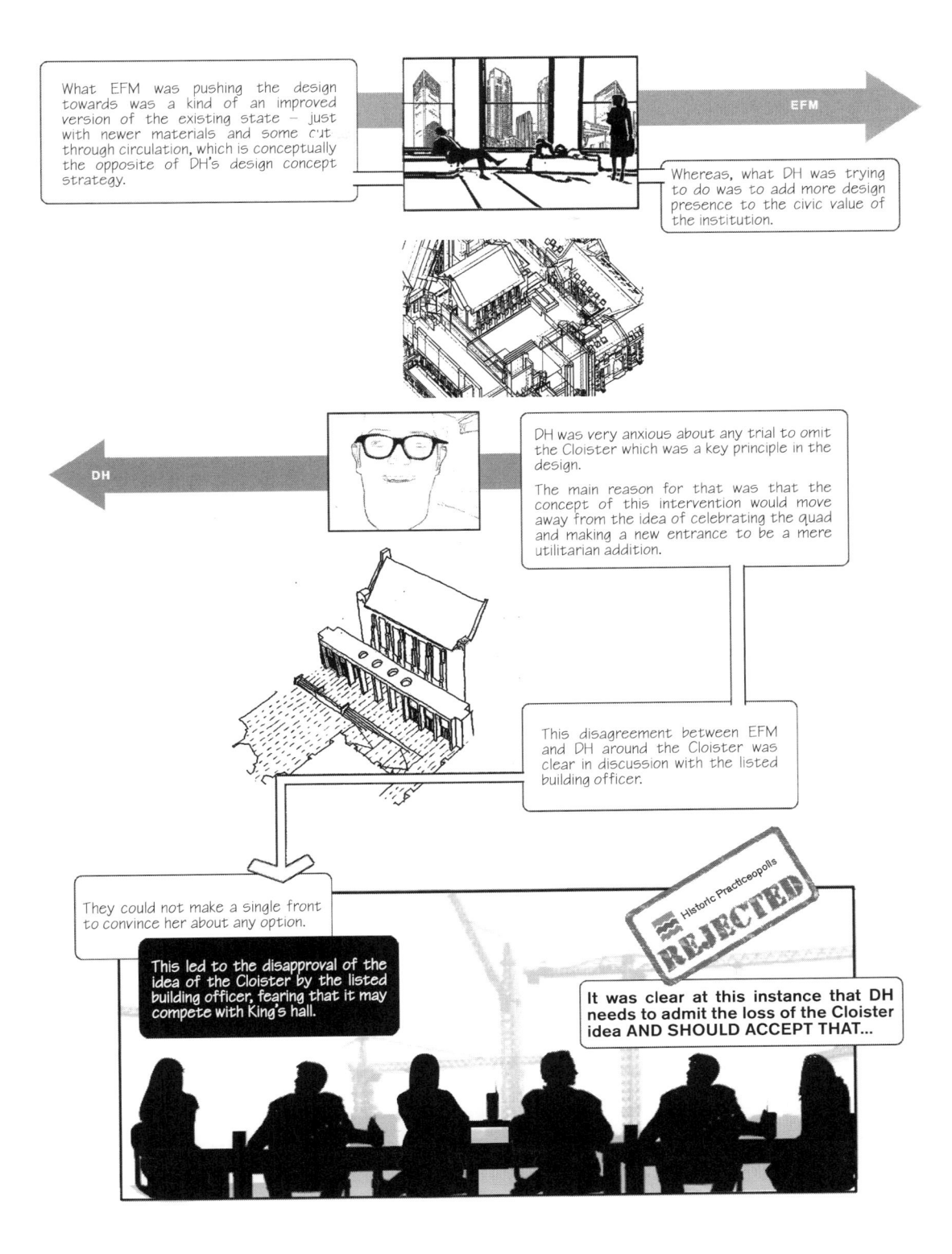

What EFM was pushing the design towards was a kind of an improved version of the existing state – just with newer materials and some cut through circulation, which is conceptually the opposite of DH's design concept strategy.

EFM

Whereas, what DH was trying to do was to add more design presence to the civic value of the institution.

DH

DH was very anxious about any trial to omit the Cloister which was a key principle in the design.

The main reason for that was that the concept of this intervention would move away from the idea of celebrating the quad and making a new entrance to be a mere utilitarian addition.

This disagreement between EFM and DH around the Cloister was clear in discussion with the listed building officer.

They could not make a single front to convince her about any option.

This led to the disapproval of the idea of the Cloister by the listed building officer, fearing that it may compete with King's hall.

Historic Practiceopolis
REJECTED

It was clear at this instance that DH needs to admit the loss of the Cloister idea AND SHOULD ACCEPT THAT...

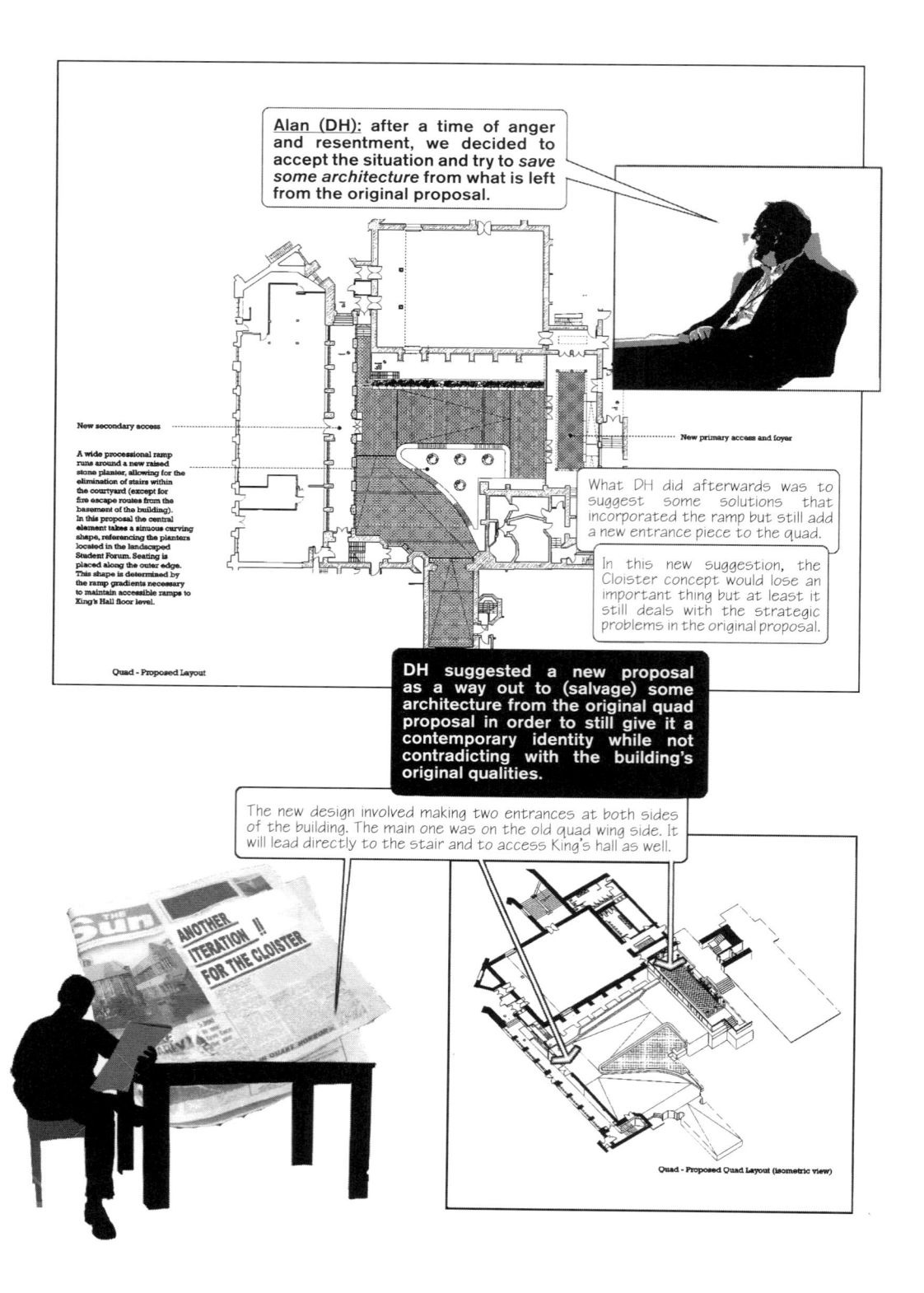

Alan (DH): after a time of anger and resentment, we decided to accept the situation and try to *save some architecture* from what is left from the original proposal.

New secondary access

A wide processional ramp runs around a new raised stone planter, allowing for the elimination of stairs within the courtyard (except for fire escape routes from the basement of the building). In this proposal the central element takes a sinuous curving shape, referencing the planters located in the landscaped Student Forum. Seating is placed along the outer edge. This shape is determined by the ramp gradients necessary to maintain accessible ramps to King's Hall floor level.

Quad - Proposed Layout

New primary access and foyer

What DH did afterwards was to suggest some solutions that incorporated the ramp but still add a new entrance piece to the quad.

In this new suggestion, the Cloister concept would lose an important thing but at least it still deals with the strategic problems in the original proposal.

DH suggested a new proposal as a way out to (salvage) some architecture from the original quad proposal in order to still give it a contemporary identity while not contradicting with the building's original qualities.

The new design involved making two entrances at both sides of the building. The main one was on the old quad wing side. It will lead directly to the stair and to access King's hall as well.

ANOTHER ITERATION !! FOR THE CLOISTER

Quad - Proposed Quad Layout (isometric view)

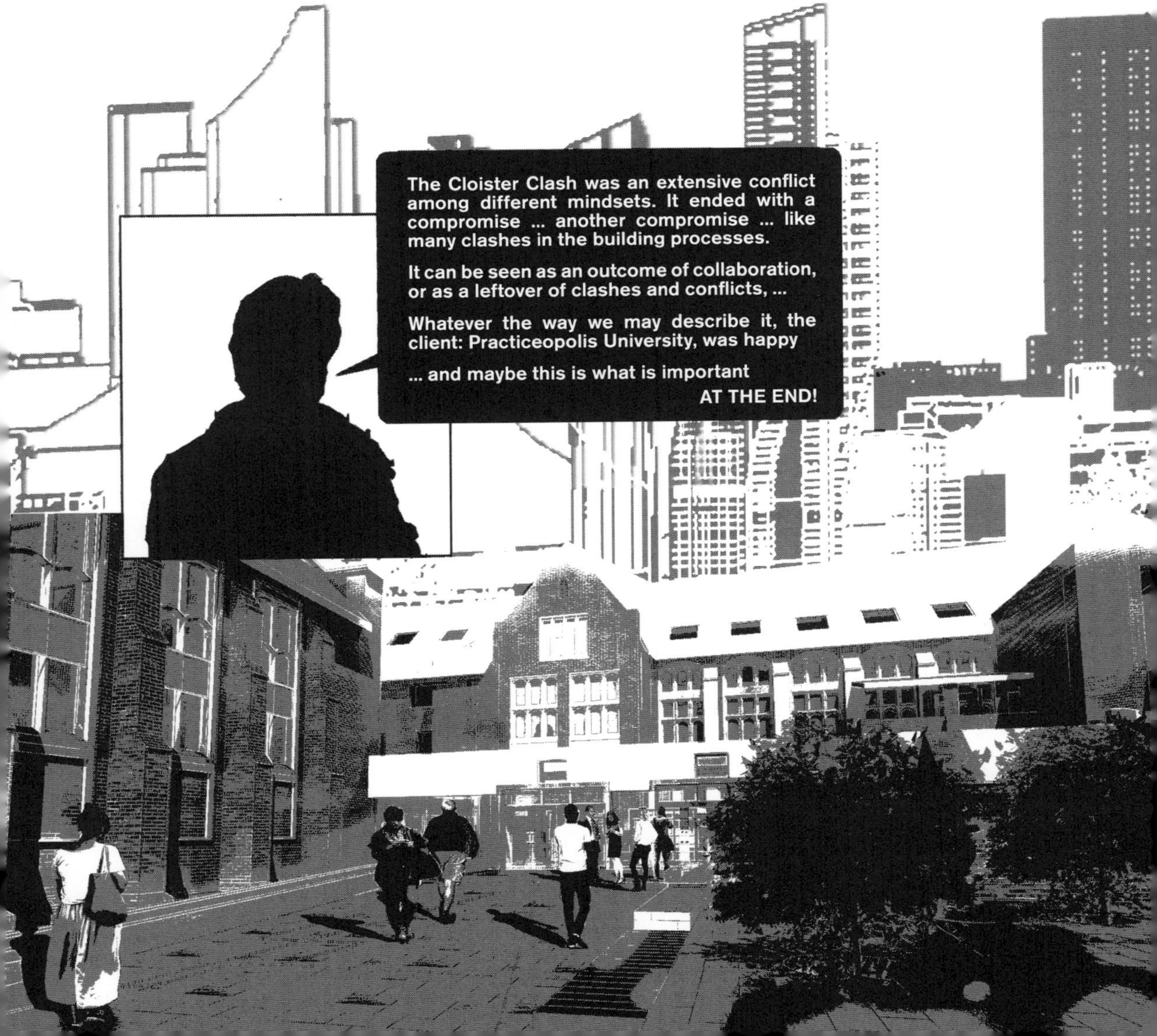
The Cloister Clash was an extensive conflict among different mindsets. It ended with a compromise ... another compromise ... like many clashes in the building processes.
It can be seen as an outcome of collaboration, or as a leftover of clashes and conflicts, ...
Whatever the way we may describe it, the client: Practiceopolis University, was happy
... and maybe this is what is important
AT THE END!

THE CRITICAL PARTY

THE TECHNICAL-RATIONAL PARTY

Sometime after, the Atkinson Building renovation was fully realised and appreciated by the client and users. However, the problems between DH and EFM escalated more after the ground floor conflicts. The clashes in the project opened up a lot of the hidden anger between the Technical-rationals and Criticals and raised to the surface many unspoken issues between Practiceopolis and the Confederation that were muted for long.

Because of the significance of the Atkinson Building, the issue was raised in the Parliament and both sides were invited to represent their arguments.

The
Debate
in Practiceopolis Parliament

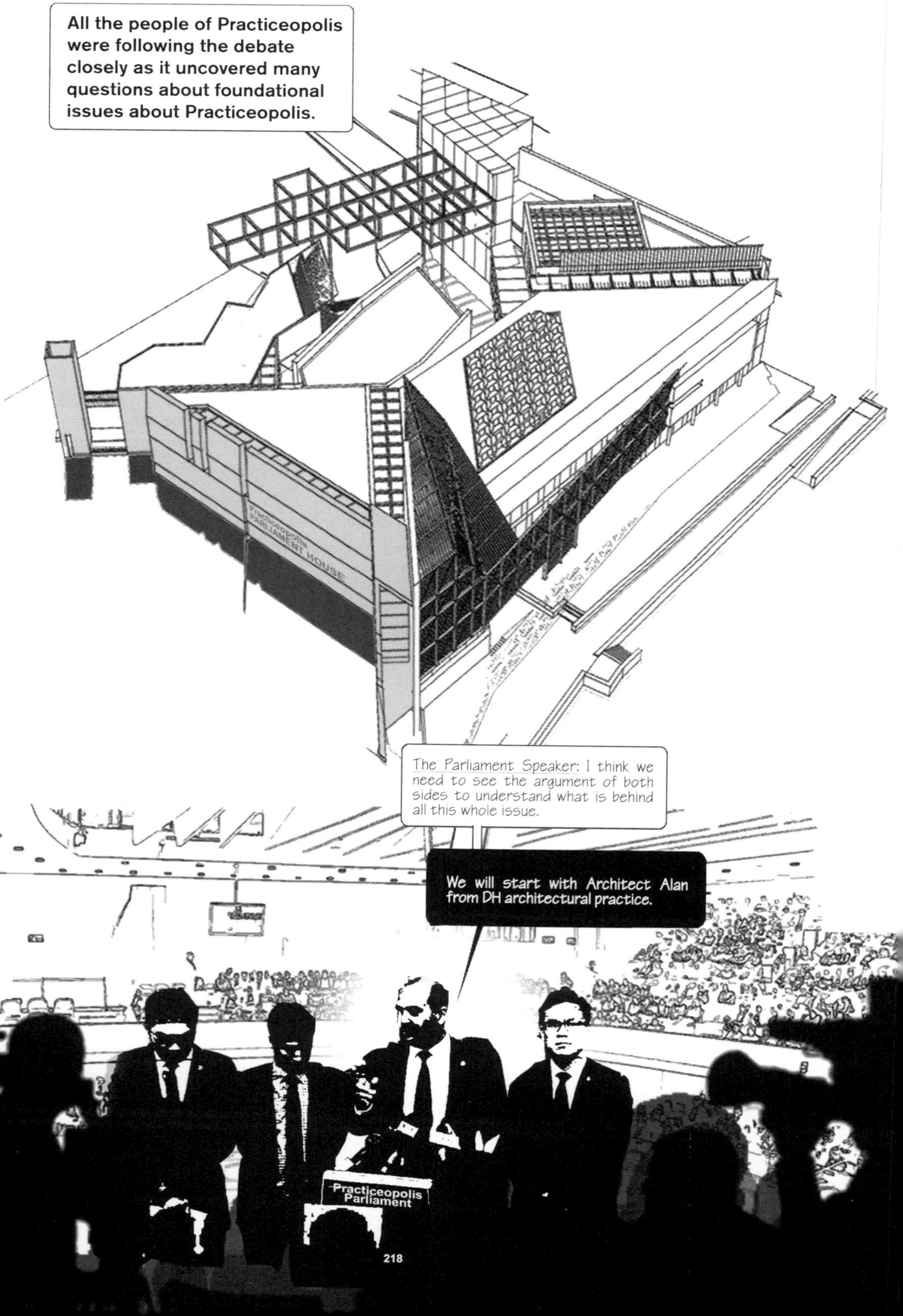
All the people of Practiceopolis were following the debate closely as it uncovered many questions about foundational issues about Practiceopolis.
Practiceopolis PARLIAMENT HOUSE
The Parliament Speaker: I think we need to see the argument of both sides to understand what is behind all this whole issue.
We will start with Architect Alan from DH architectural practice.
Practiceopolis Parliament

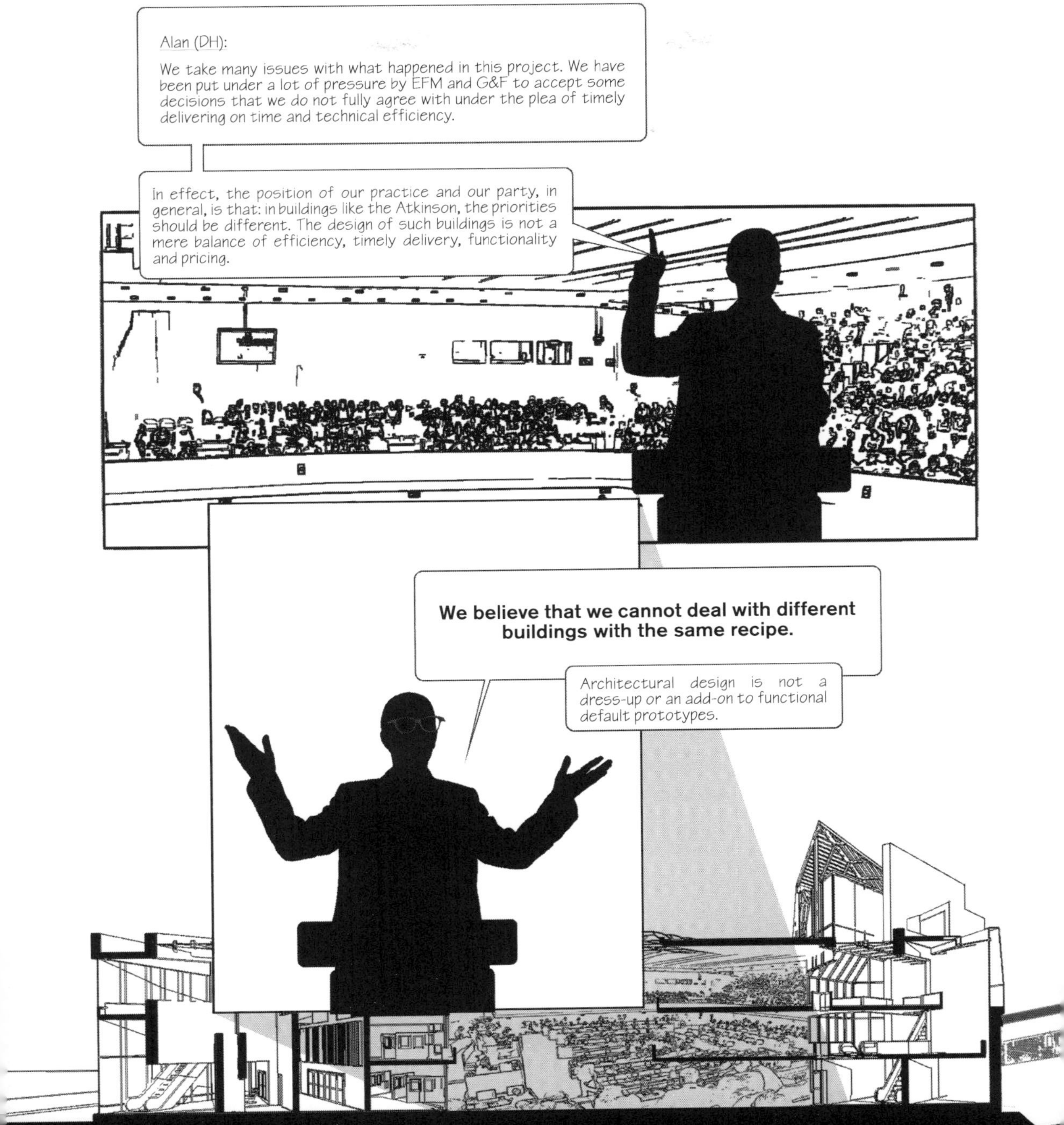
Alan (DH):
We take many issues with what happened in this project. We have been put under a lot of pressure by EFM and G&F to accept some decisions that we do not fully agree with under the plea of timely delivering on time and technical efficiency.
In effect, the position of our practice and our party, in general, is that: in buildings like the Atkinson, the priorities should be different. The design of such buildings is not a mere balance of efficiency, timely delivery, functionality and pricing.
We believe that we cannot deal with different buildings with the same recipe.
Architectural design is not a dress-up or an add-on to functional default prototypes.

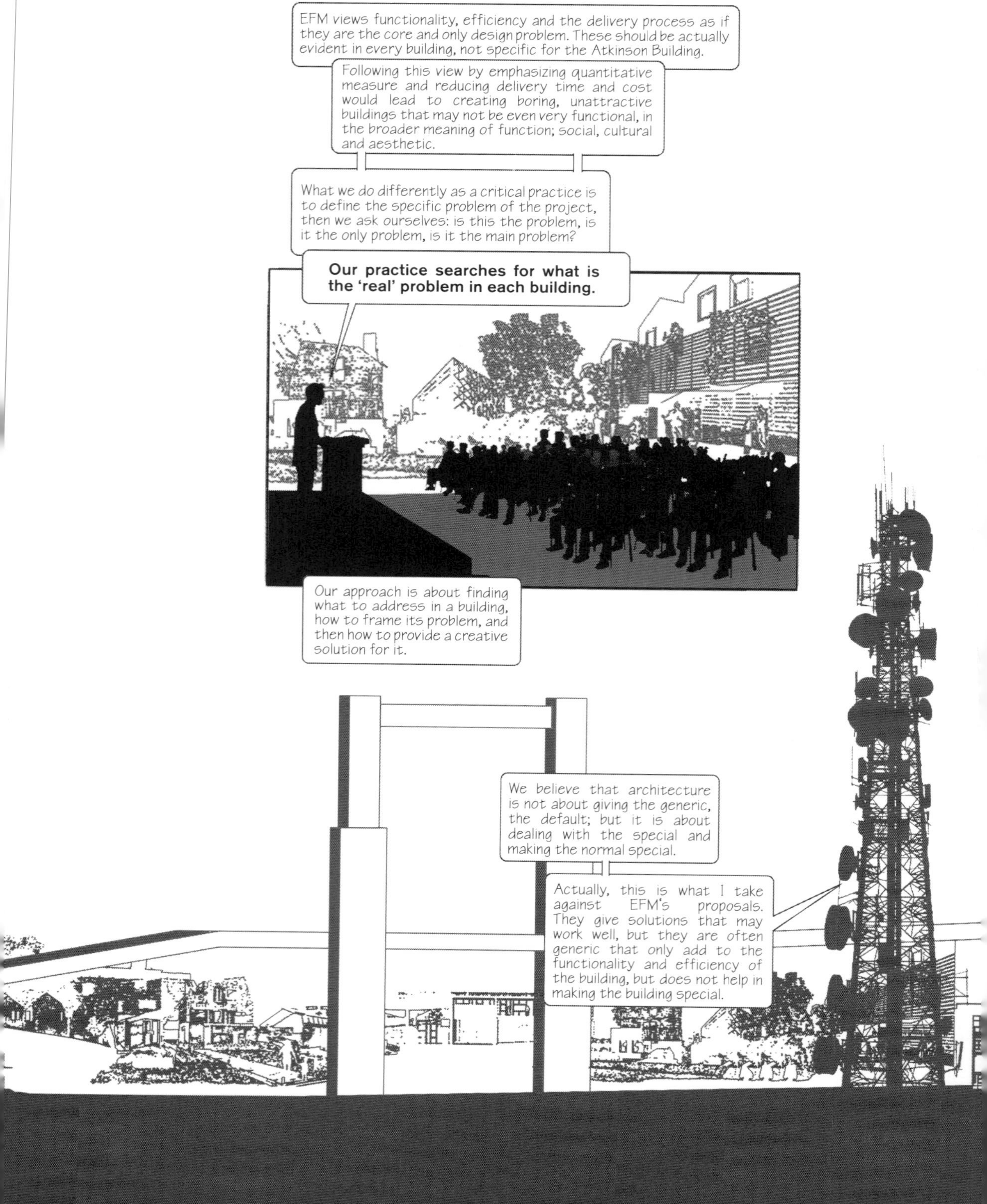
EFM views functionality, efficiency and the delivery process as if they are the core and only design problem. These should be actually evident in every building, not specific for the Atkinson Building.
Following this view by emphasizing quantitative measure and reducing delivery time and cost would lead to creating boring, unattractive buildings that may not be even very functional, in the broader meaning of function; social, cultural and aesthetic.
What we do differently as a critical practice is to define the specific problem of the project, then we ask ourselves: is this the problem, is it the only problem, is it the main problem?
Our practice searches for what is the 'real' problem in each building.
Our approach is about finding what to address in a building, how to frame its problem, and then how to provide a creative solution for it.
We believe that architecture is not about giving the generic, the default; but it is about dealing with the special and making the normal special.
Actually, this is what I take against EFM's proposals. They give solutions that may work well, but they are often generic that only add to the functionality and efficiency of the building, but does not help in making the building special.

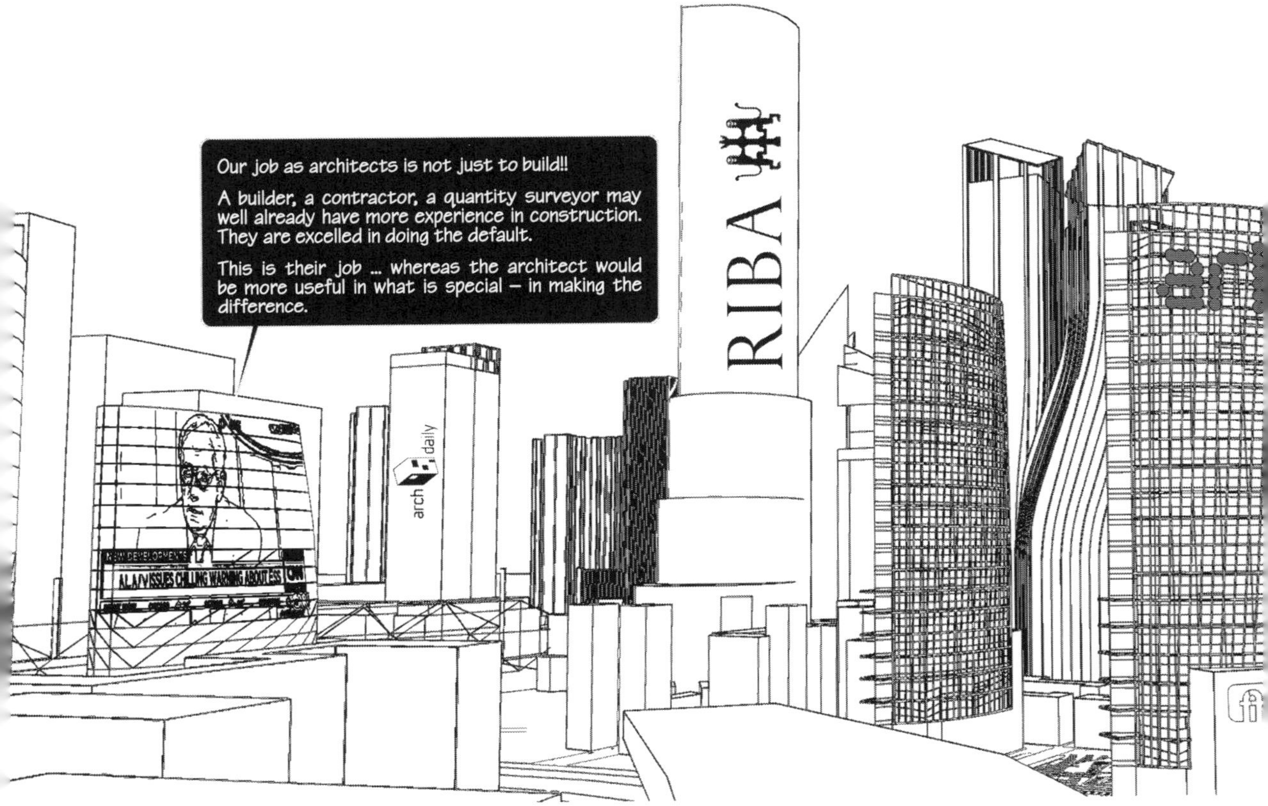
Our job as architects is not just to build!!
A builder, a contractor, a quantity surveyor may well already have more experience in construction. They are excelled in doing the default.
This is their job ... whereas the architect would be more useful in what is special – in making the difference.
RIBA
arch daily

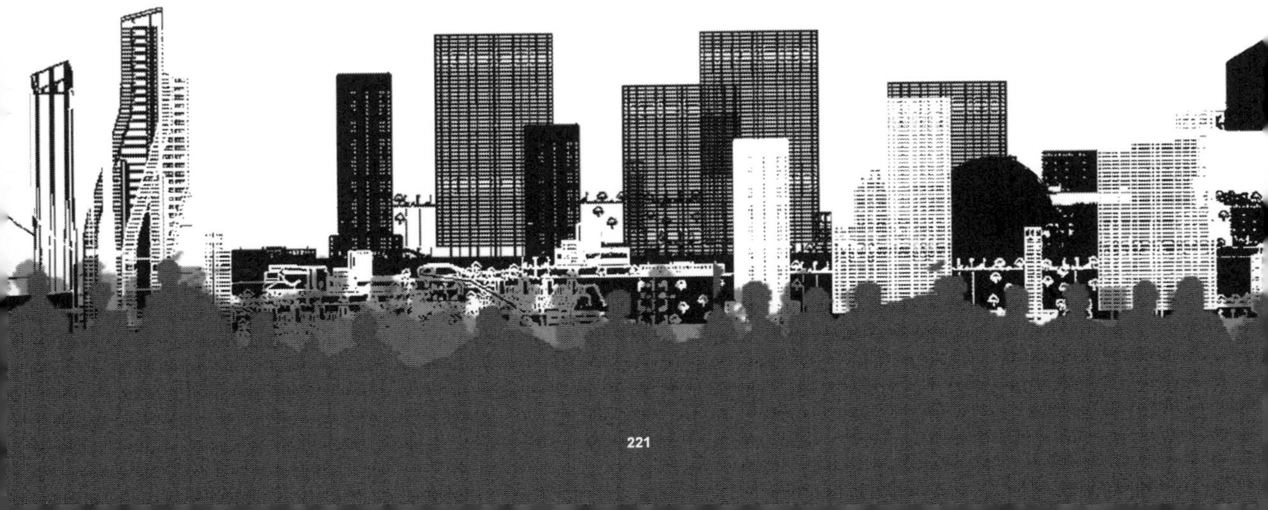

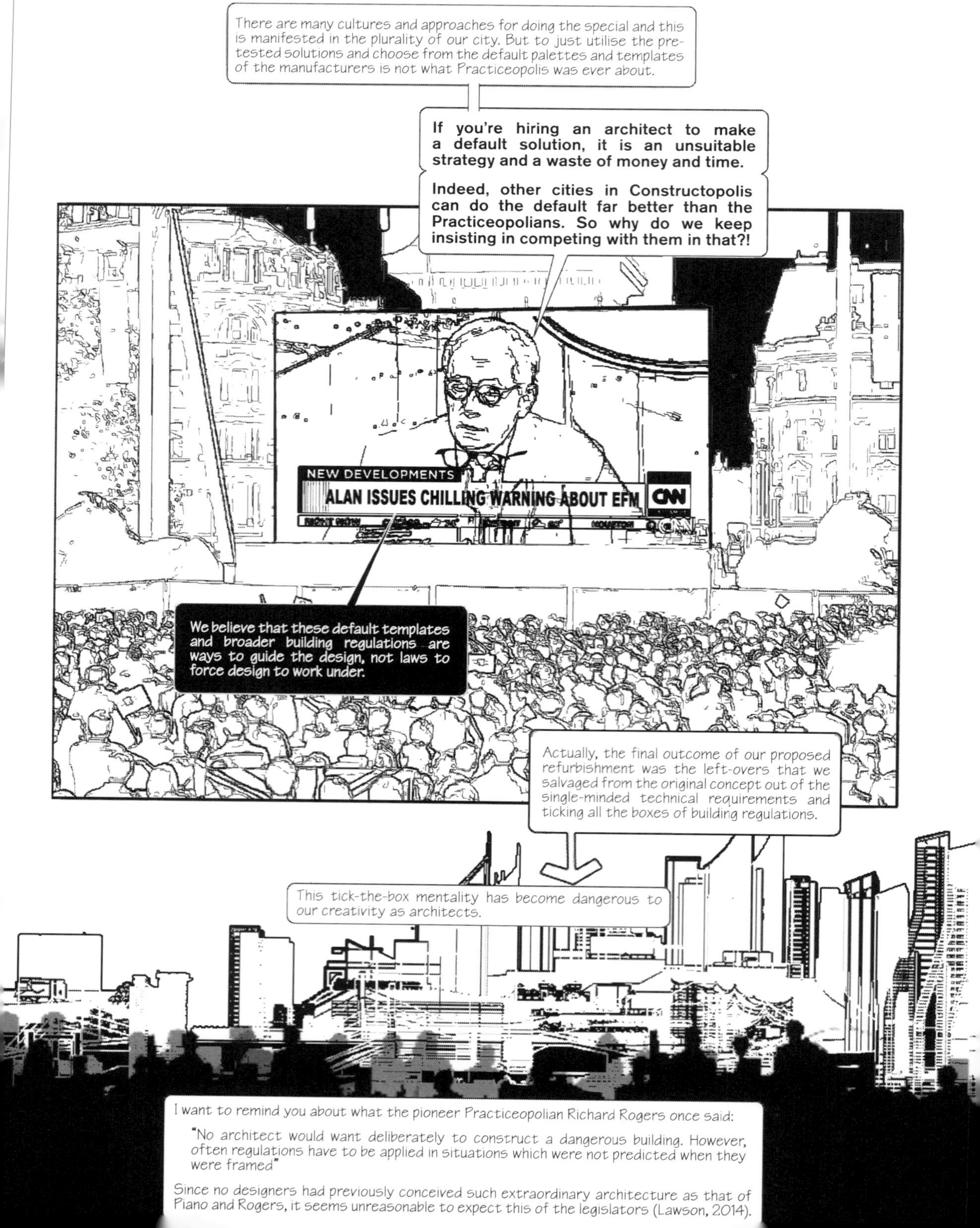
There are many cultures and approaches for doing the special and this is manifested in the plurality of our city. But to just utilise the pre-tested solutions and choose from the default palettes and templates of the manufacturers is not what Practiceopolis was ever about.
If you're hiring an architect to make a default solution, it is an unsuitable strategy and a waste of money and time.
Indeed, other cities in Constructopolis can do the default far better than the Practiceopolians. So why do we keep insisting in competing with them in that?!
NEW DEVELOPMENTS
ALAN ISSUES CHILLING WARNING ABOUT EFM
CNN
We believe that these default templates and broader building regulations are ways to guide the design, not laws to force design to work under.
Actually, the final outcome of our proposed refurbishment was the left-overs that we salvaged from the original concept out of the single-minded technical requirements and ticking all the boxes of building regulations.
This tick-the-box mentality has become dangerous to our creativity as architects.
I want to remind you about what the pioneer Practiceopolian Richard Rogers once said:
"No architect would want deliberately to construct a dangerous building. However, often regulations have to be applied in situations which were not predicted when they were framed"
Since no designers had previously conceived such extraordinary architecture as that of Piano and Rogers, it seems unreasonable to expect this of the legislators (Lawson, 2014).

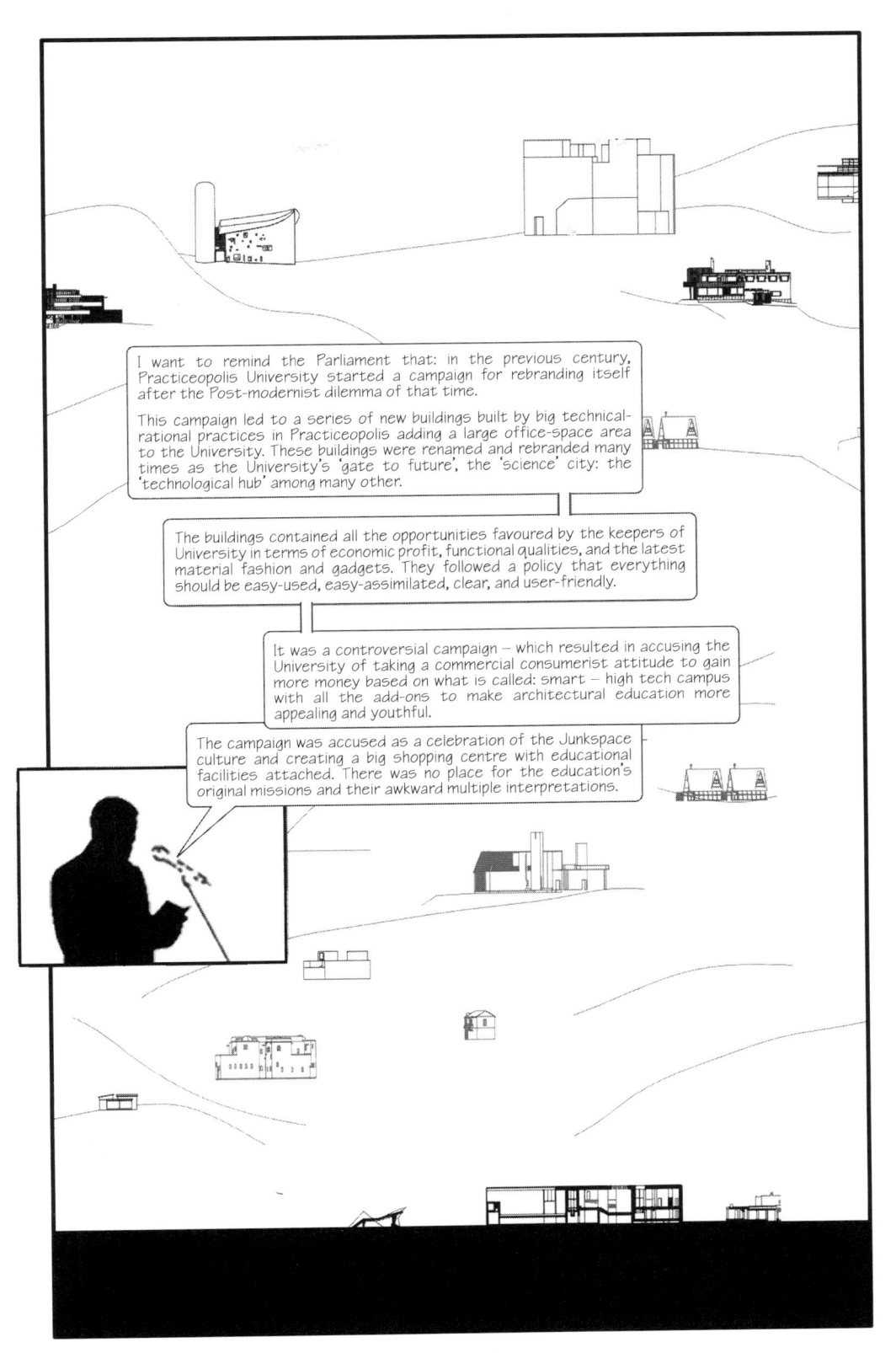

I want to remind the Parliament that: in the previous century, Practiceopolis University started a campaign for rebranding itself after the Post-modernist dilemma of that time.

This campaign led to a series of new buildings built by big technical-rational practices in Practiceopolis adding a large office-space area to the University. These buildings were renamed and rebranded many times as the University's 'gate to future', the 'science' city: the 'technological hub' among many other.

The buildings contained all the opportunities favoured by the keepers of University in terms of economic profit, functional qualities, and the latest material fashion and gadgets. They followed a policy that everything should be easy-used, easy-assimilated, clear, and user-friendly.

It was a controversial campaign – which resulted in accusing the University of taking a commercial consumerist attitude to gain more money based on what is called: smart – high tech campus with all the add-ons to make architectural education more appealing and youthful.

The campaign was accused as a celebration of the Junkspace culture and creating a big shopping centre with educational facilities attached. There was no place for the education's original missions and their awkward multiple interpretations.

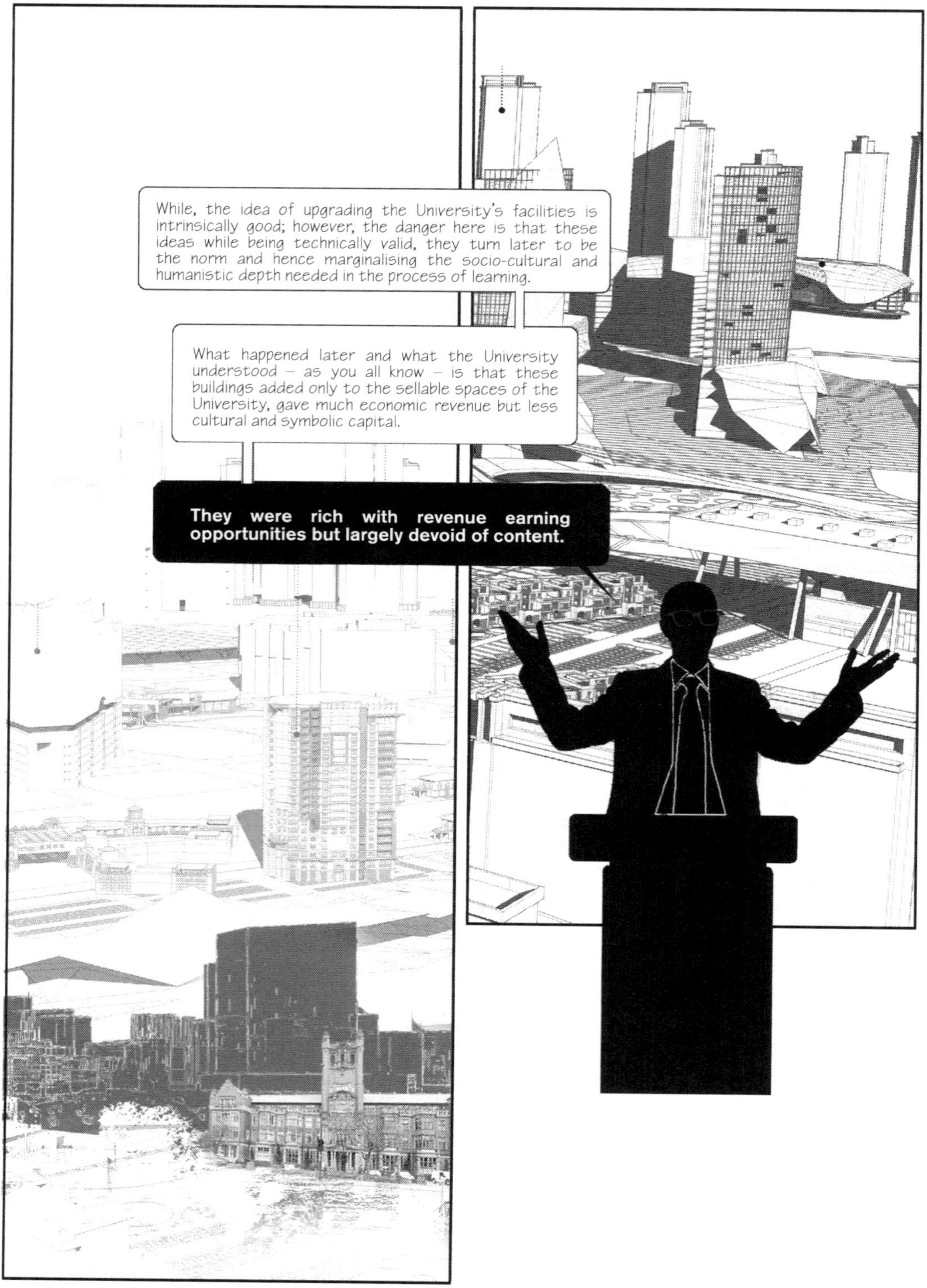
While, the idea of upgrading the University's facilities is intrinsically good; however, the danger here is that these ideas while being technically valid, they turn later to be the norm and hence marginalising the socio-cultural and humanistic depth needed in the process of learning.
What happened later and what the University understood – as you all know – is that these buildings added only to the sellable spaces of the University, gave much economic revenue but less cultural and symbolic capital.
They were rich with revenue earning opportunities but largely devoid of content.

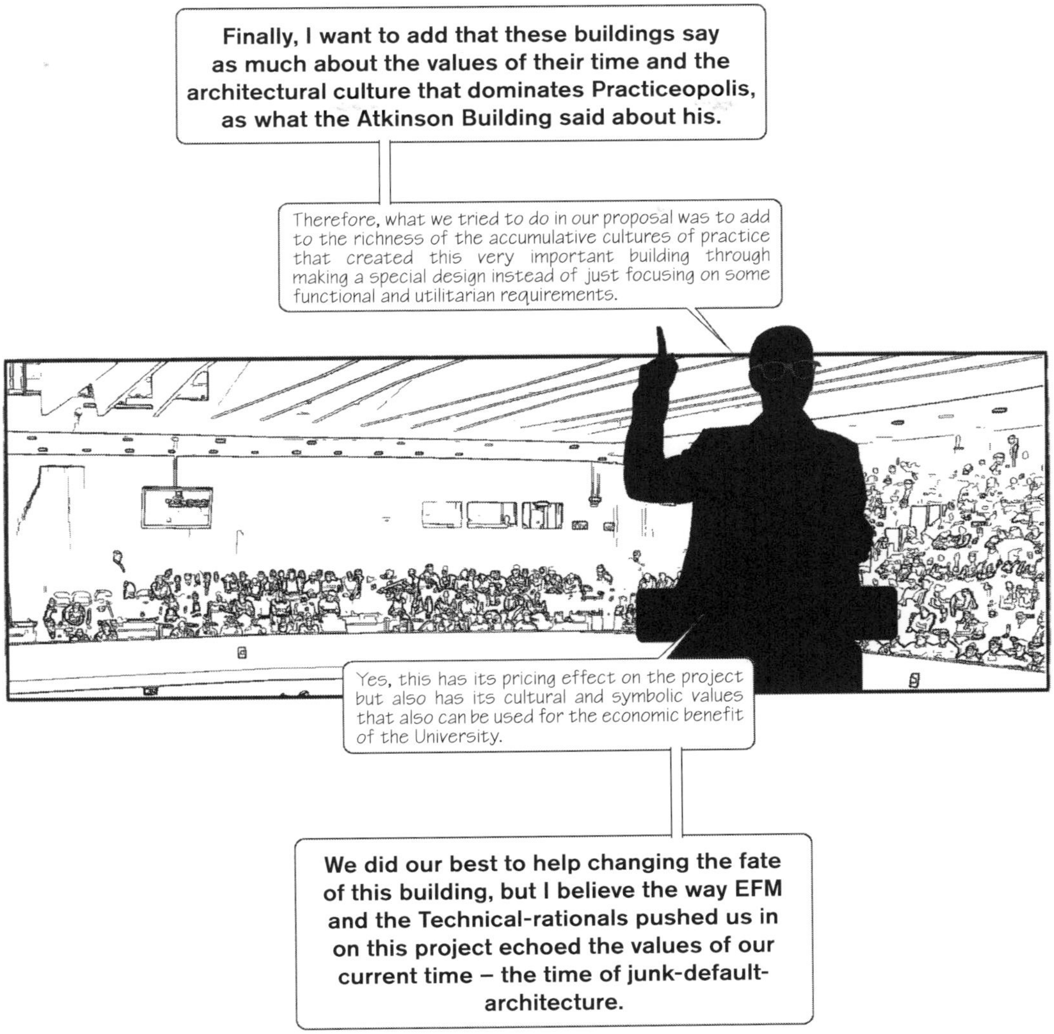
Finally, I want to add that these buildings say as much about the values of their time and the architectural culture that dominates Practiceopolis, as what the Atkinson Building said about his.
Therefore, what we tried to do in our proposal was to add to the richness of the accumulative cultures of practice that created this very important building through making a special design instead of just focusing on some functional and utilitarian requirements.
Yes, this has its pricing effect on the project but also has its cultural and symbolic values that also can be used for the economic benefit of the University.
We did our best to help changing the fate of this building, but I believe the way EFM and the Technical-rationals pushed us in on this project echoed the values of our current time – the time of junk-default-architecture.

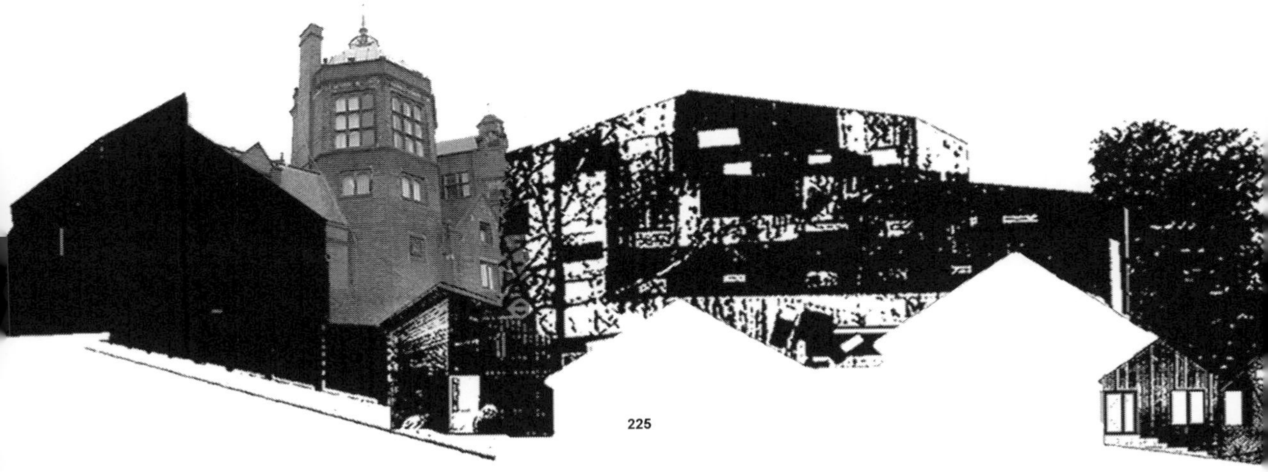

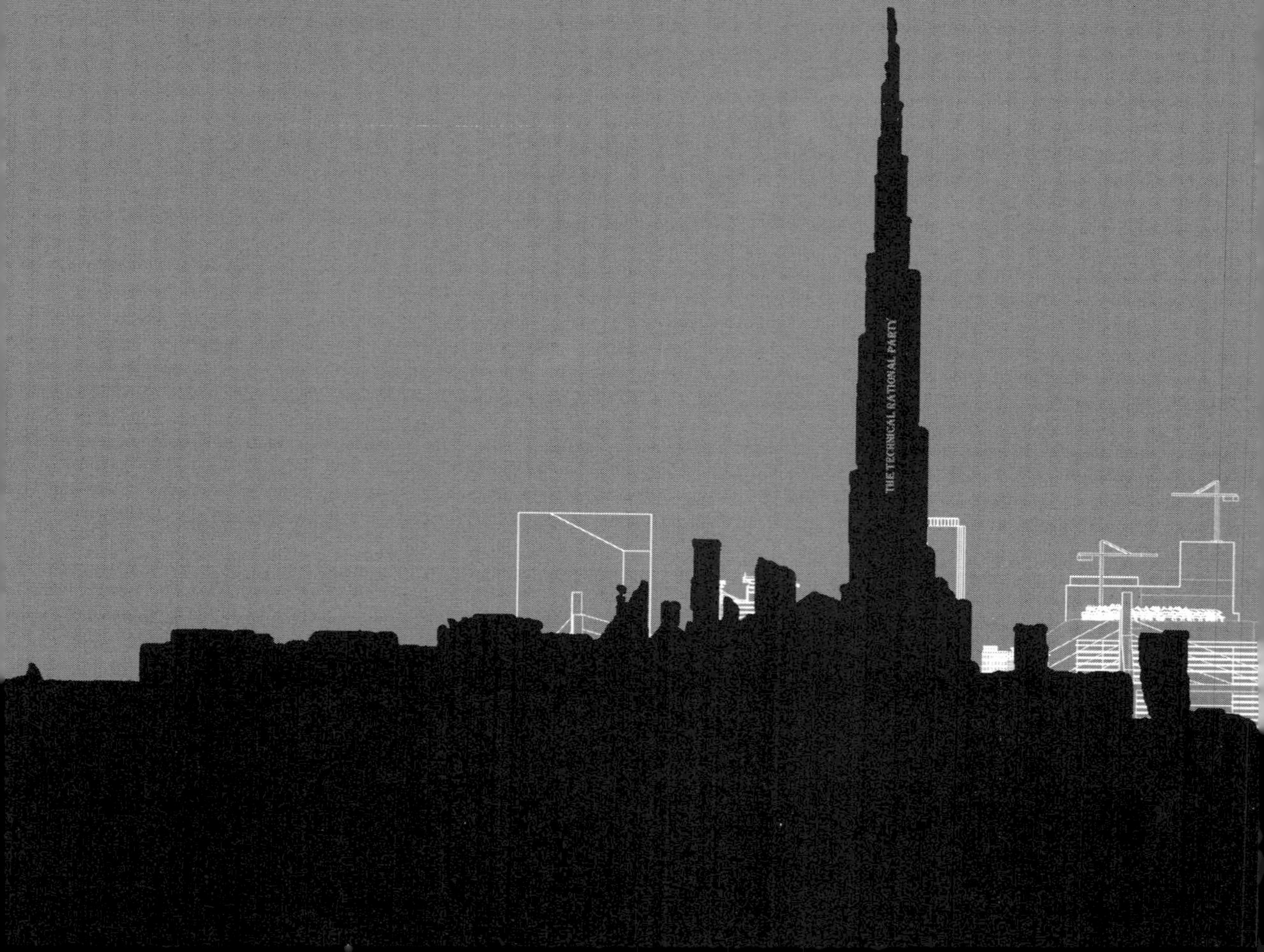
THE TECHNICAL NATIONAL PARTY

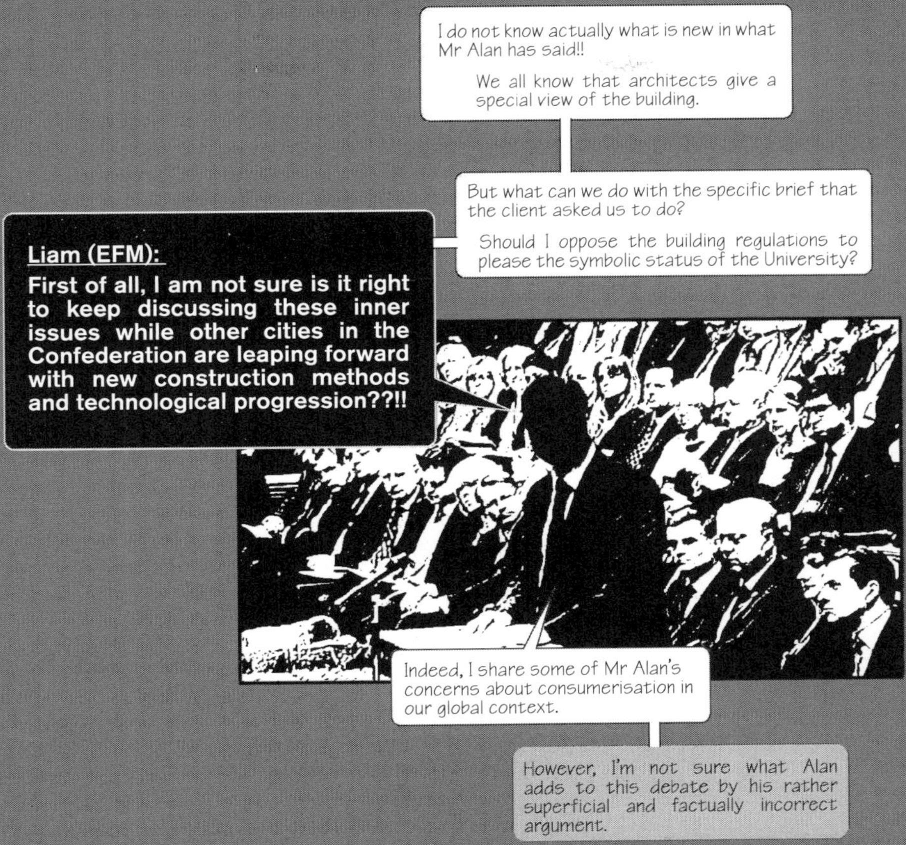
I do not know actually what is new in what Mr Alan has said!!
We all know that architects give a special view of the building.
But what can we do with the specific brief that the client asked us to do?
Should I oppose the building regulations to please the symbolic status of the University?
Liam (EFM):
First of all, I am not sure is it right to keep discussing these inner issues while other cities in the Confederation are leaping forward with new construction methods and technological progression??!!
Indeed, I share some of Mr Alan's concerns about consumerisation in our global context.
However, I'm not sure what Alan adds to this debate by his rather superficial and factually incorrect argument.

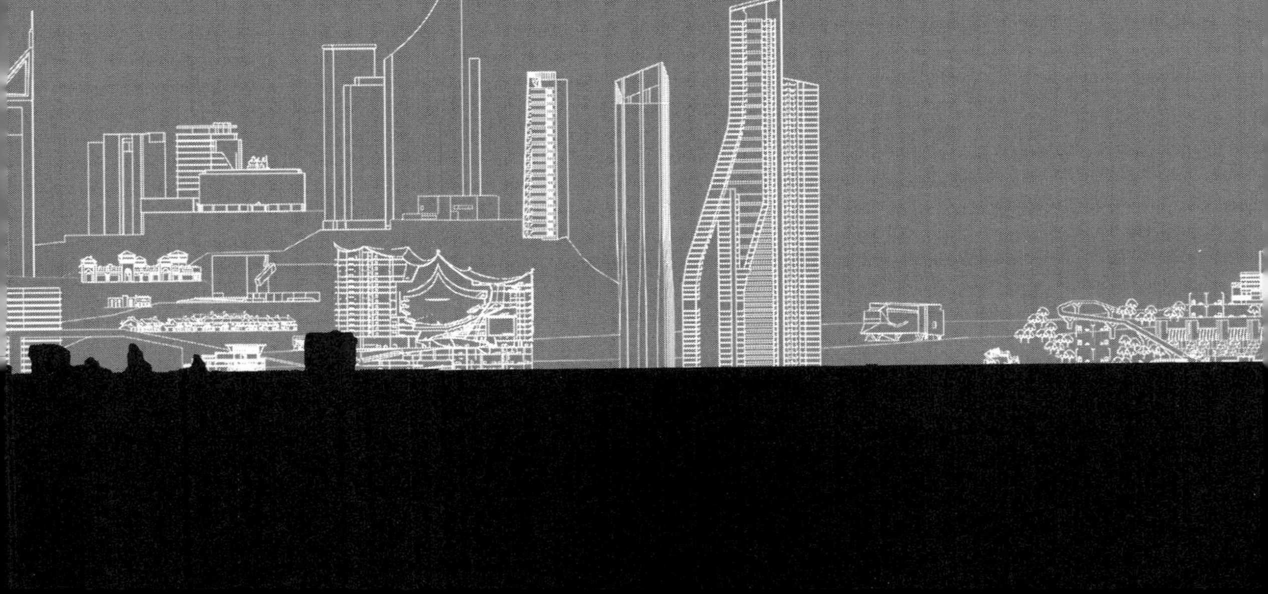

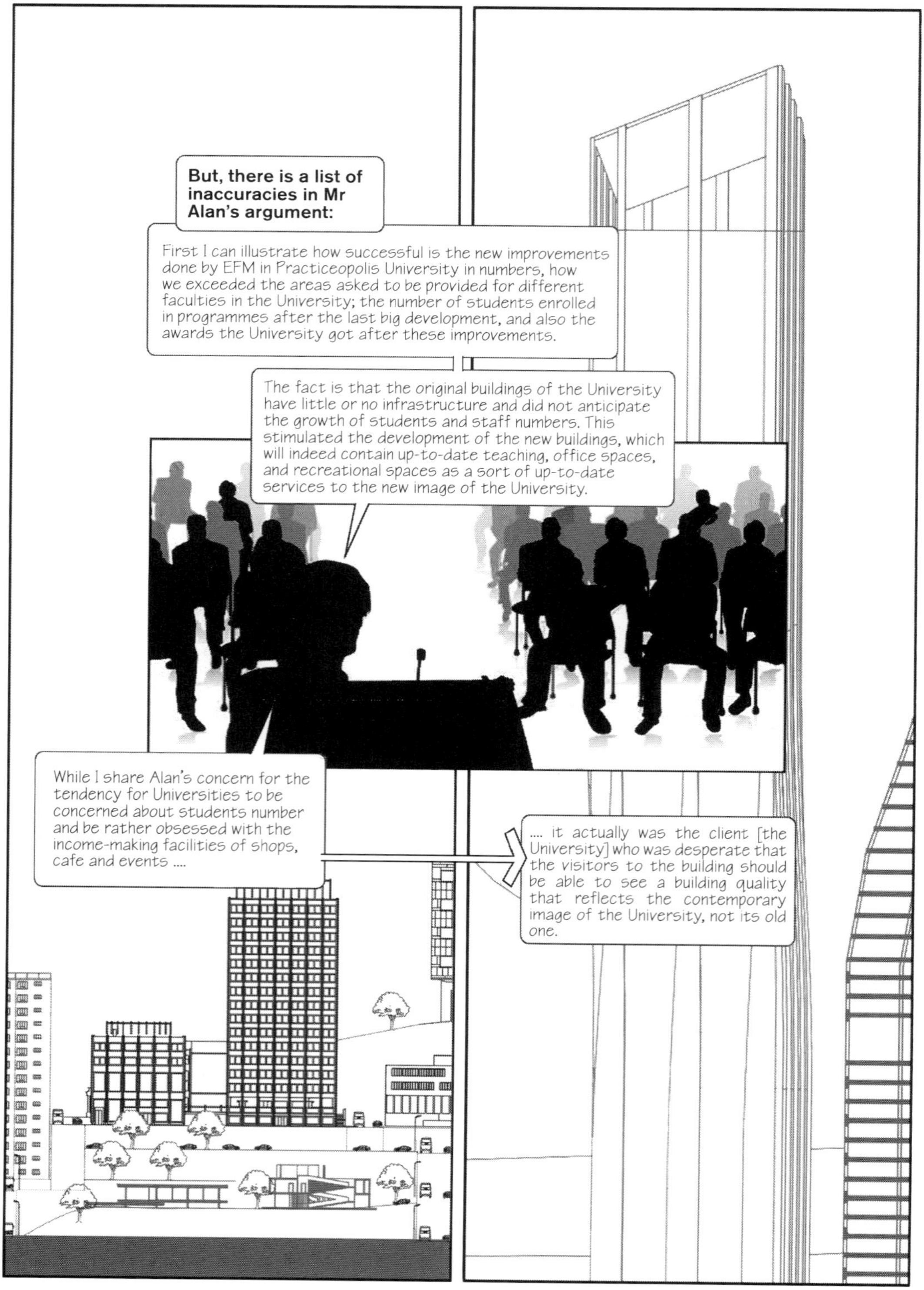

But, there is a list of inaccuracies in Mr Alan's argument:
First I can illustrate how successful is the new improvements done by EFM in Practiceopolis University in numbers, how we exceeded the areas asked to be provided for different faculties in the University; the number of students enrolled in programmes after the last big development, and also the awards the University got after these improvements.
The fact is that the original buildings of the University have little or no infrastructure and did not anticipate the growth of students and staff numbers. This stimulated the development of the new buildings, which will indeed contain up-to-date teaching, office spaces, and recreational spaces as a sort of up-to-date services to the new image of the University.
While I share Alan's concern for the tendency for Universities to be concerned about students number and be rather obsessed with the income-making facilities of shops, cafe and events ....
.... it actually was the client [the University] who was desperate that the visitors to the building should be able to see a building quality that reflects the contemporary image of the University, not its old one.

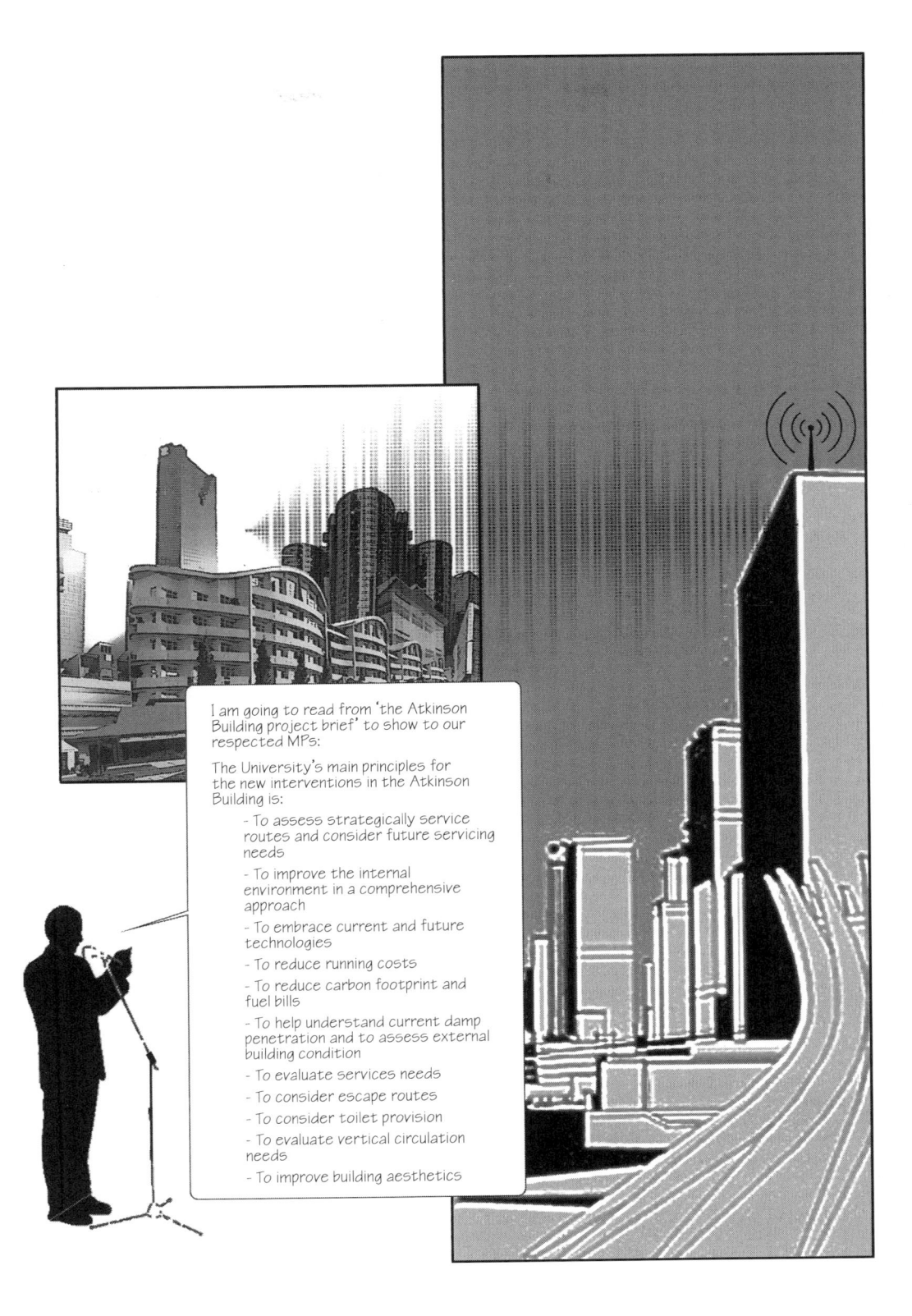

I am going to read from 'the Atkinson Building project brief' to show to our respected MPs:

The University's main principles for the new interventions in the Atkinson Building is:

- To assess strategically service routes and consider future servicing needs

- To improve the internal environment in a comprehensive approach

- To embrace current and future technologies

- To reduce running costs

- To reduce carbon footprint and fuel bills

- To help understand current damp penetration and to assess external building condition

- To evaluate services needs

- To consider escape routes

- To consider toilet provision

- To evaluate vertical circulation needs

- To improve building aesthetics

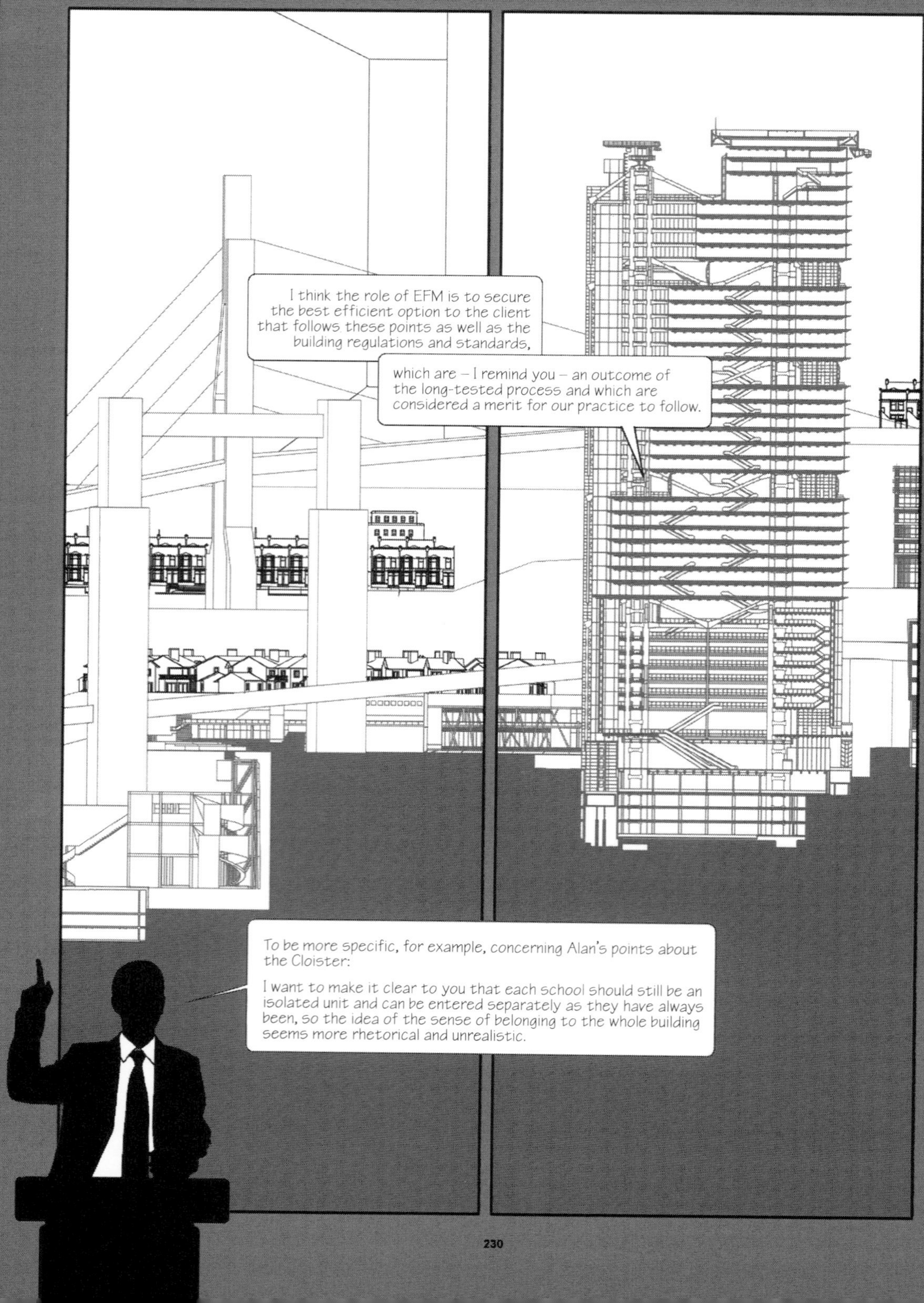
I think the role of EFM is to secure the best efficient option to the client that follows these points as well as the building regulations and standards,
which are – I remind you – an outcome of the long-tested process and which are considered a merit for our practice to follow.
To be more specific, for example, concerning Alan's points about the Cloister:
I want to make it clear to you that each school should still be an isolated unit and can be entered separately as they have always been, so the idea of the sense of belonging to the whole building seems more rhetorical and unrealistic.

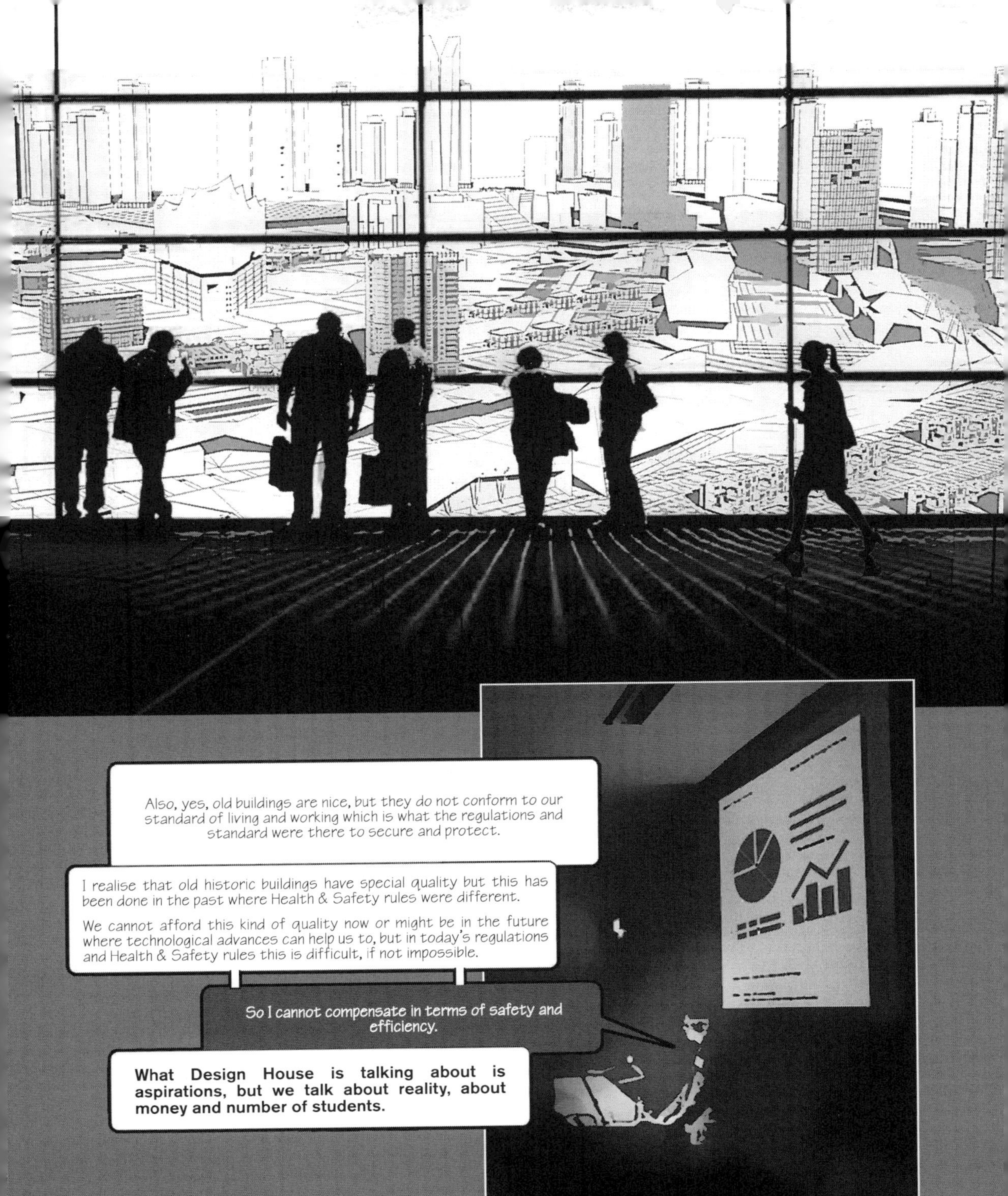
Also, yes, old buildings are nice, but they do not conform to our standard of living and working which is what the regulations and standard were there to secure and protect.
I realise that old historic buildings have special quality but this has been done in the past where Health & Safety rules were different.
We cannot afford this kind of quality now or might be in the future where technological advances can help us to, but in today's regulations and Health & Safety rules this is difficult, if not impossible.
So I cannot compensate in terms of safety and efficiency.
What Design House is talking about is aspirations, but we talk about reality, about money and number of students.

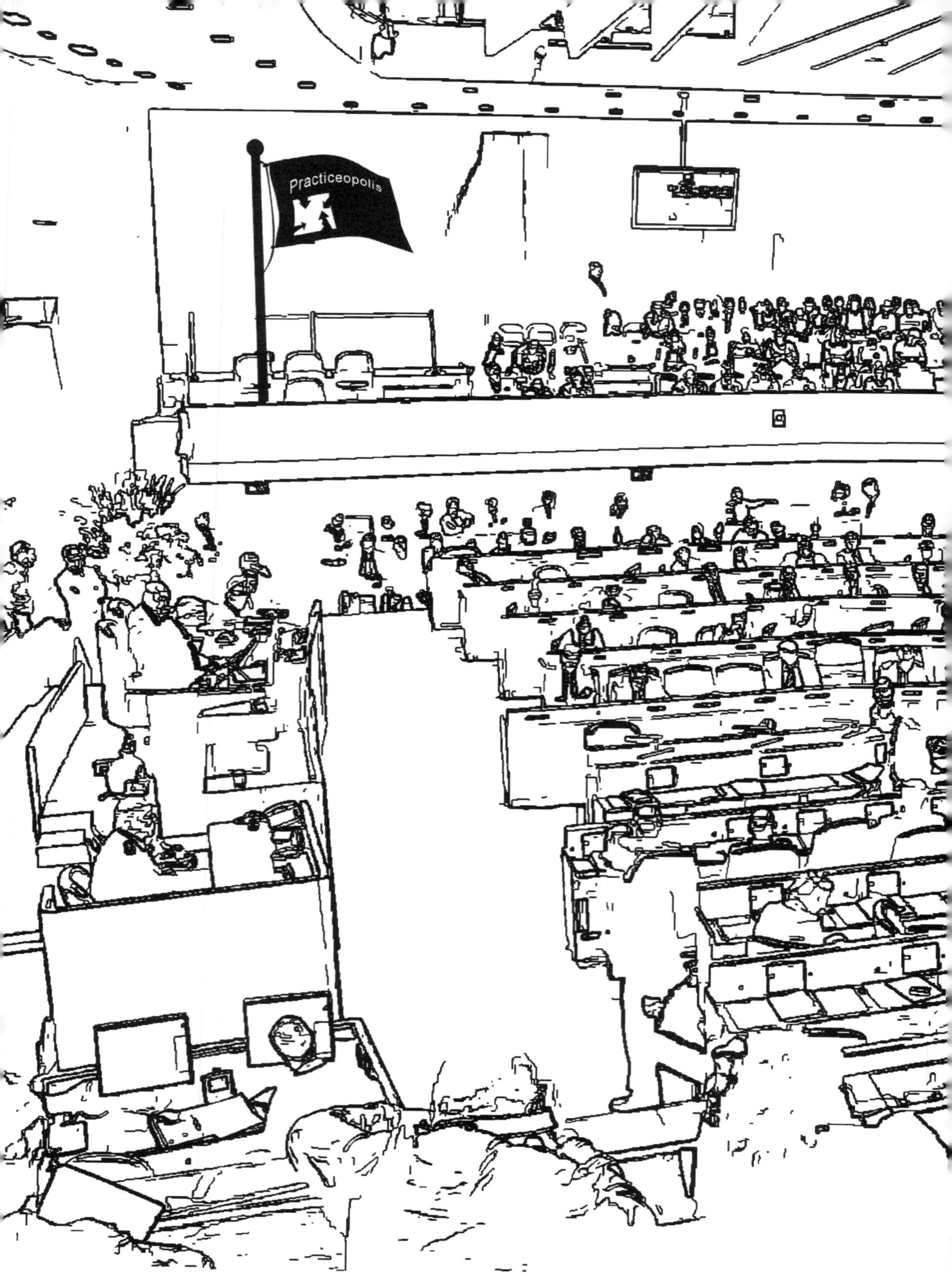
Practiceopolis

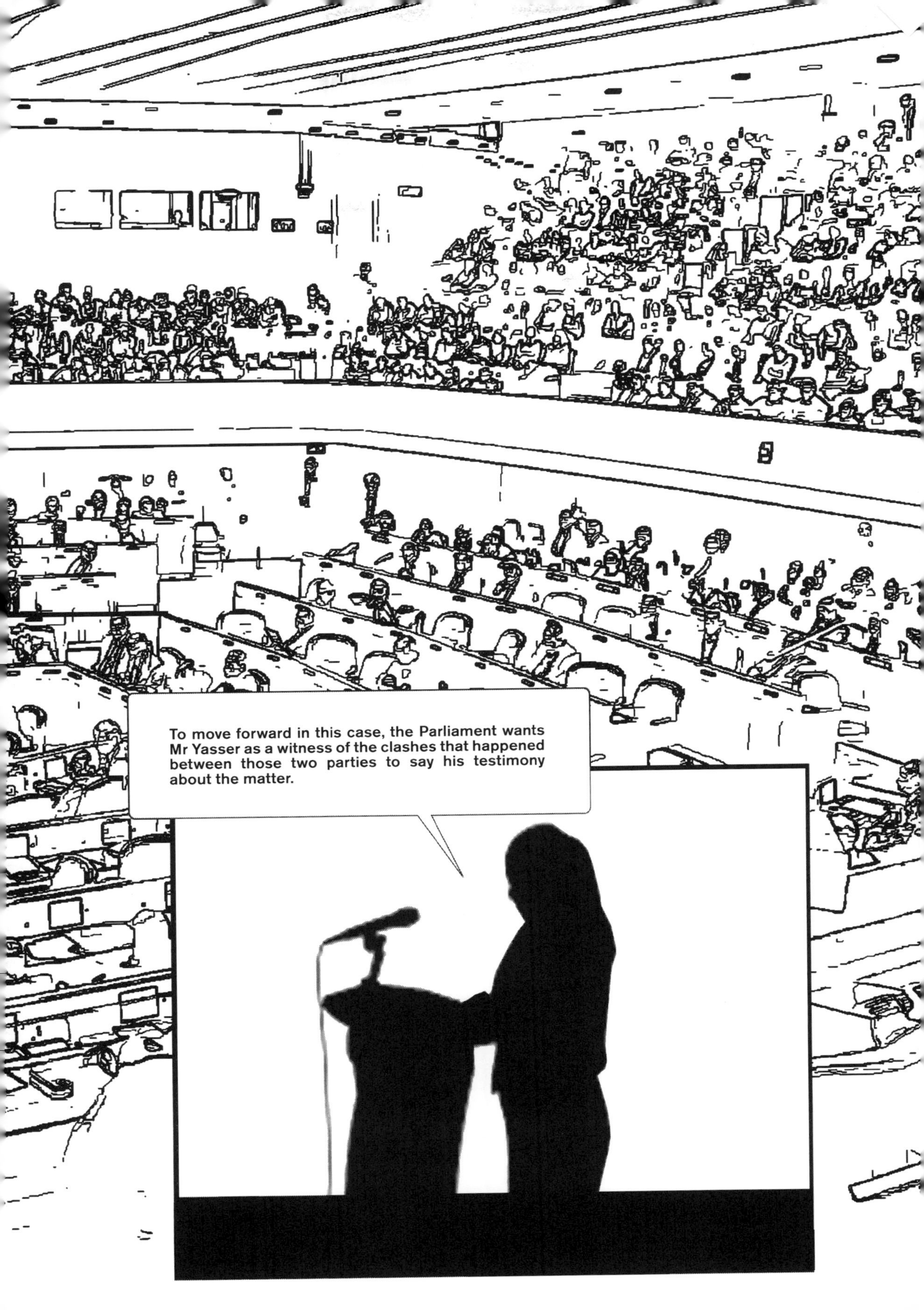
To move forward in this case, the Parliament wants Mr Yasser as a witness of the clashes that happened between those two parties to say his testimony about the matter.

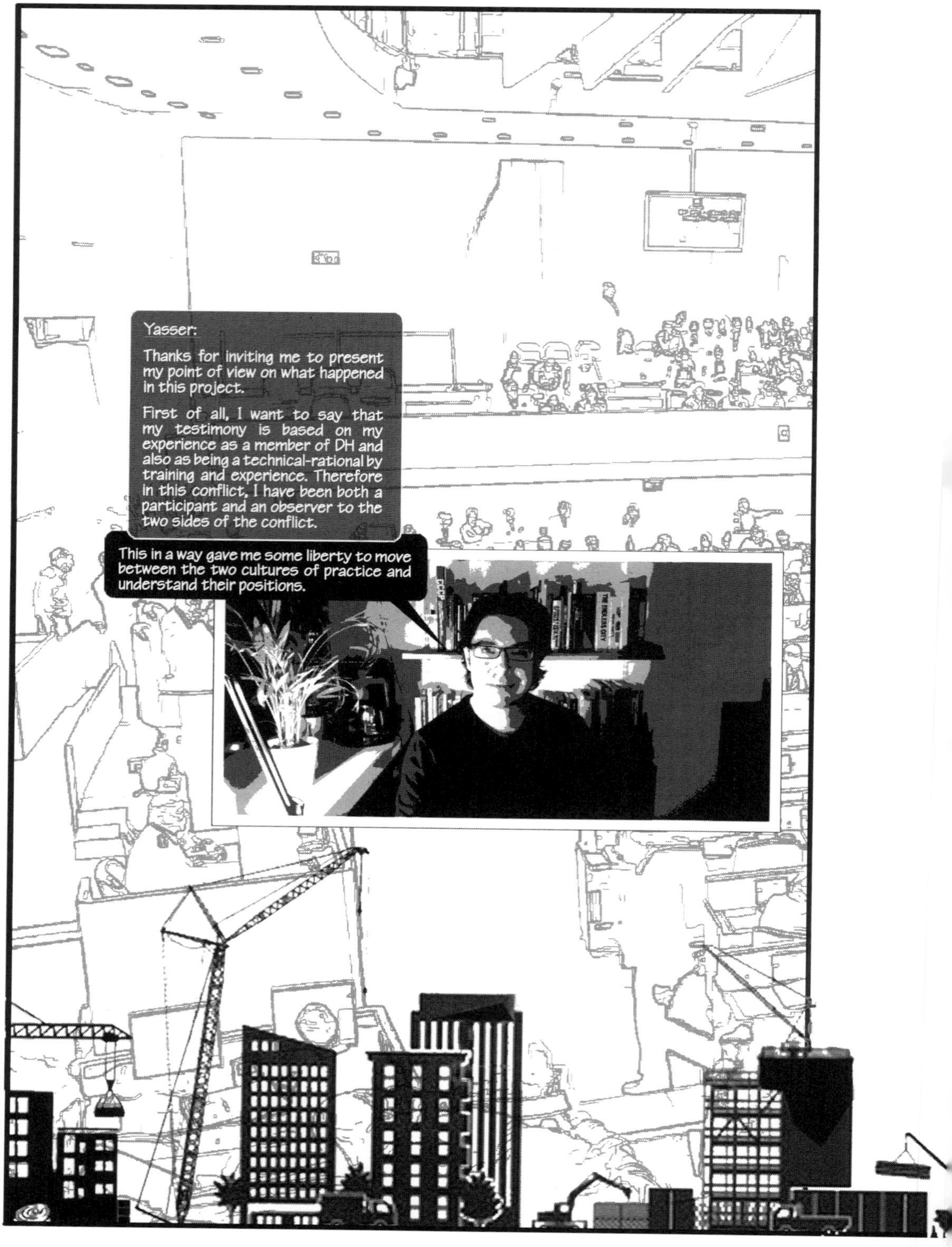
Yasser:
Thanks for inviting me to present my point of view on what happened in this project.
First of all, I want to say that my testimony is based on my experience as a member of DH and also as being a technical-rational by training and experience. Therefore in this conflict, I have been both a participant and an observer to the two sides of the conflict.
This in a way gave me some liberty to move between the two cultures of practice and understand their positions.

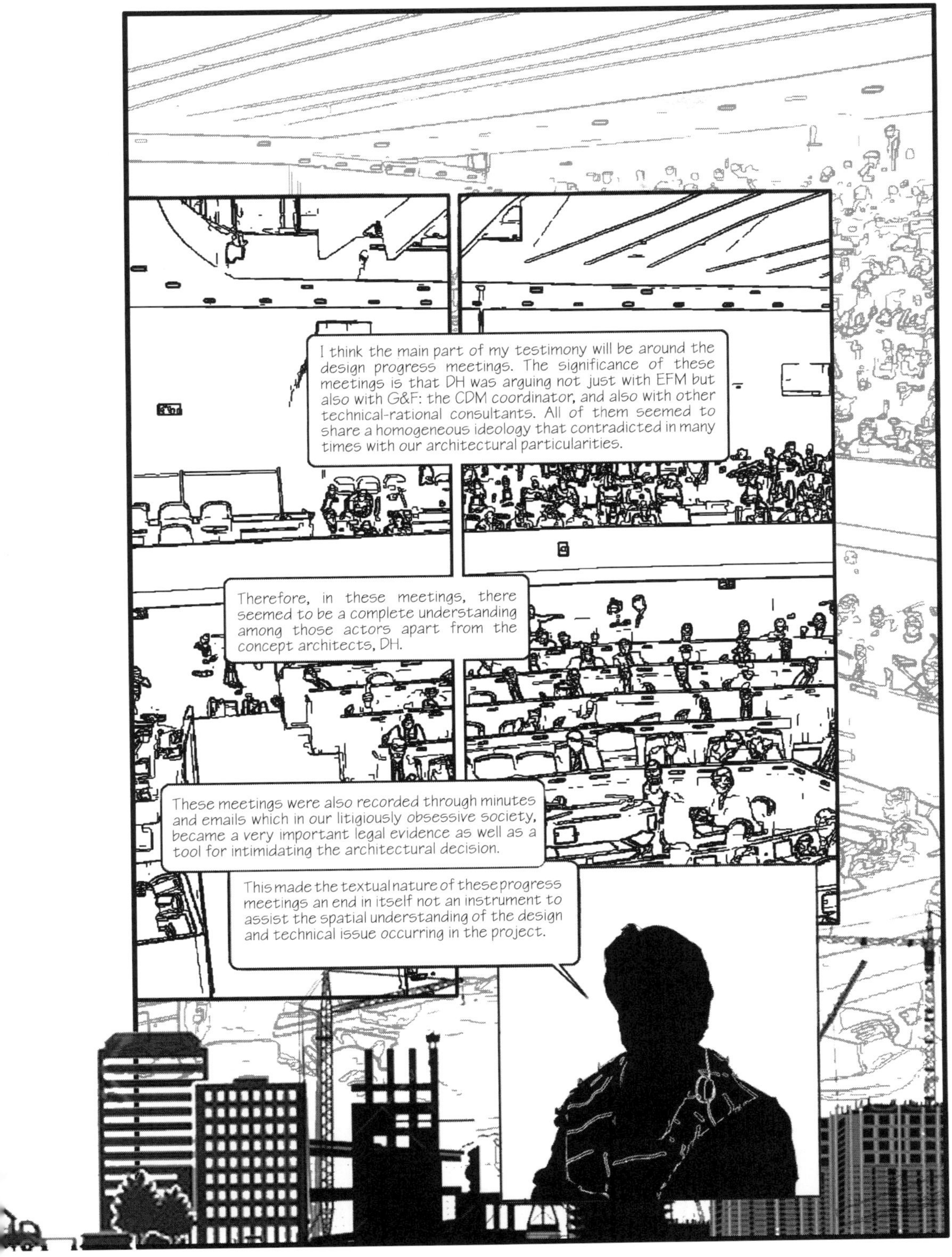
I think the main part of my testimony will be around the design progress meetings. The significance of these meetings is that DH was arguing not just with EFM but also with G&F: the CDM coordinator, and also with other technical-rational consultants. All of them seemed to share a homogeneous ideology that contradicted in many times with our architectural particularities.
Therefore, in these meetings, there seemed to be a complete understanding among those actors apart from the concept architects, DH.
These meetings were also recorded through minutes and emails which in our litigiously obsessive society, became a very important legal evidence as well as a tool for intimidating the architectural decision.
This made the textual nature of these progress meetings an end in itself not an instrument to assist the spatial understanding of the design and technical issue occurring in the project.

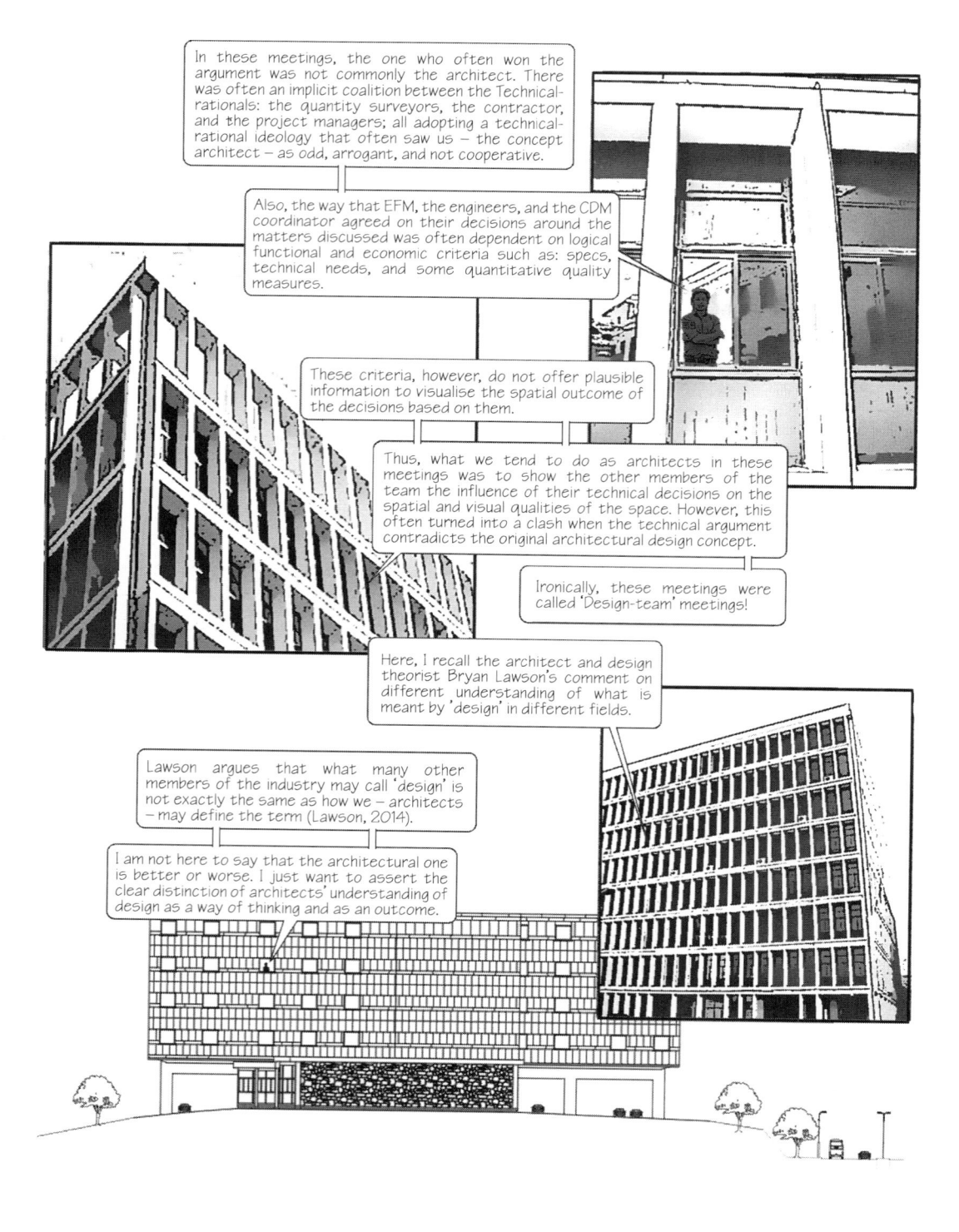

In these meetings, the one who often won the argument was not commonly the architect. There was often an implicit coalition between the Technical-rationals: the quantity surveyors, the contractor, and the project managers; all adopting a technical-rational ideology that often saw us — the concept architect — as odd, arrogant, and not cooperative.

Also, the way that EFM, the engineers, and the CDM coordinator agreed on their decisions around the matters discussed was often dependent on logical functional and economic criteria such as: specs, technical needs, and some quantitative quality measures.

These criteria, however, do not offer plausible information to visualise the spatial outcome of the decisions based on them.

Thus, what we tend to do as architects in these meetings was to show the other members of the team the influence of their technical decisions on the spatial and visual qualities of the space. However, this often turned into a clash when the technical argument contradicts the original architectural design concept.

Ironically, these meetings were called 'Design-team' meetings!

Here, I recall the architect and design theorist Bryan Lawson's comment on different understanding of what is meant by 'design' in different fields.

Lawson argues that what many other members of the industry may call 'design' is not exactly the same as how we — architects — may define the term (Lawson, 2014).

I am not here to say that the architectural one is better or worse. I just want to assert the clear distinction of architects' understanding of design as a way of thinking and as an outcome.

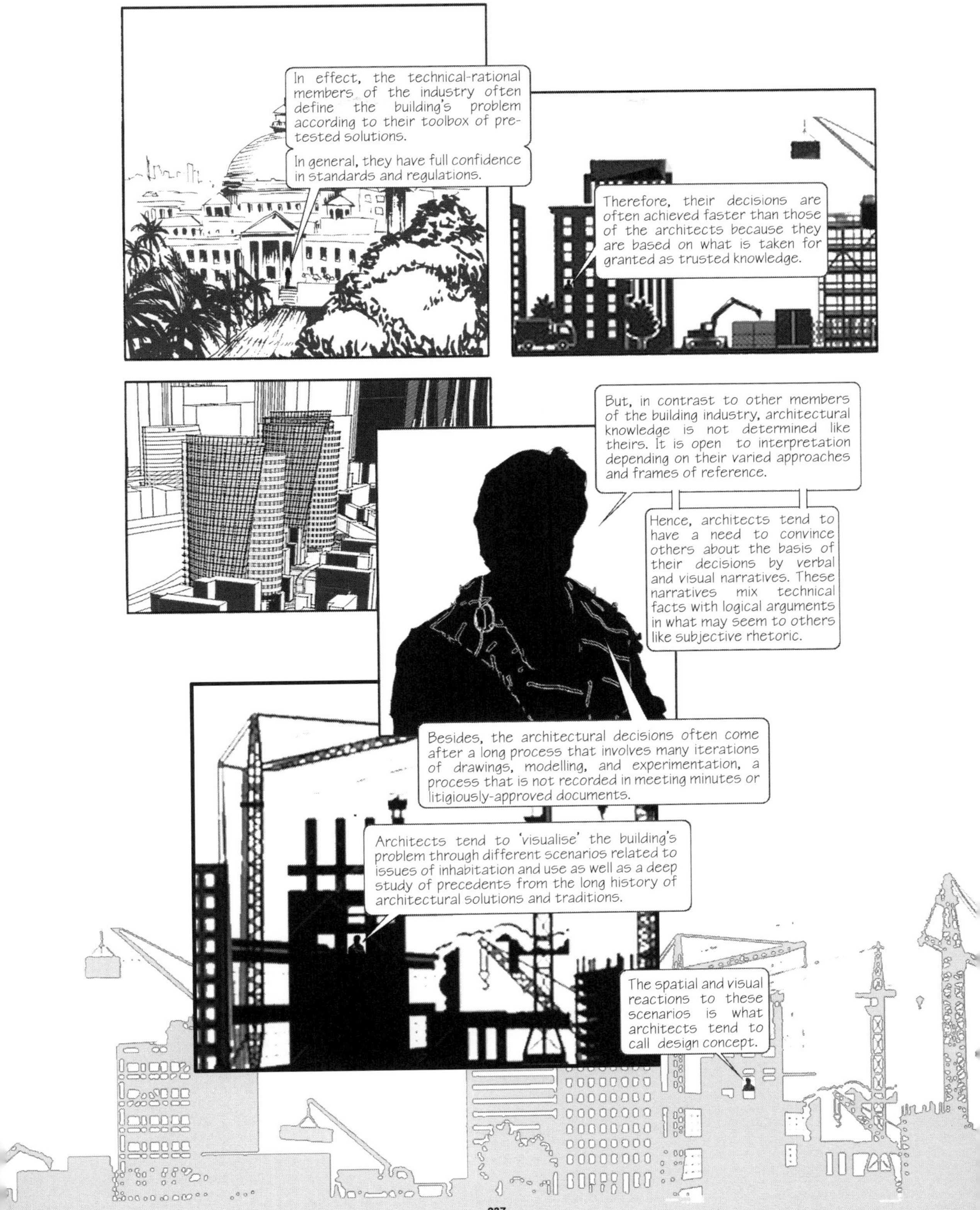
In effect, the technical-rational members of the industry often define the building's problem according to their toolbox of pre-tested solutions.
In general, they have full confidence in standards and regulations.
Therefore, their decisions are often achieved faster than those of the architects because they are based on what is taken for granted as trusted knowledge.
But, in contrast to other members of the building industry, architectural knowledge is not determined like theirs. It is open to interpretation depending on their varied approaches and frames of reference.
Hence, architects tend to have a need to convince others about the basis of their decisions by verbal and visual narratives. These narratives mix technical facts with logical arguments in what may seem to others like subjective rhetoric.
Besides, the architectural decisions often come after a long process that involves many iterations of drawings, modelling, and experimentation, a process that is not recorded in meeting minutes or litigiously-approved documents.
Architects tend to 'visualise' the building's problem through different scenarios related to issues of inhabitation and use as well as a deep study of precedents from the long history of architectural solutions and traditions.
The spatial and visual reactions to these scenarios is what architects tend to call design concept.

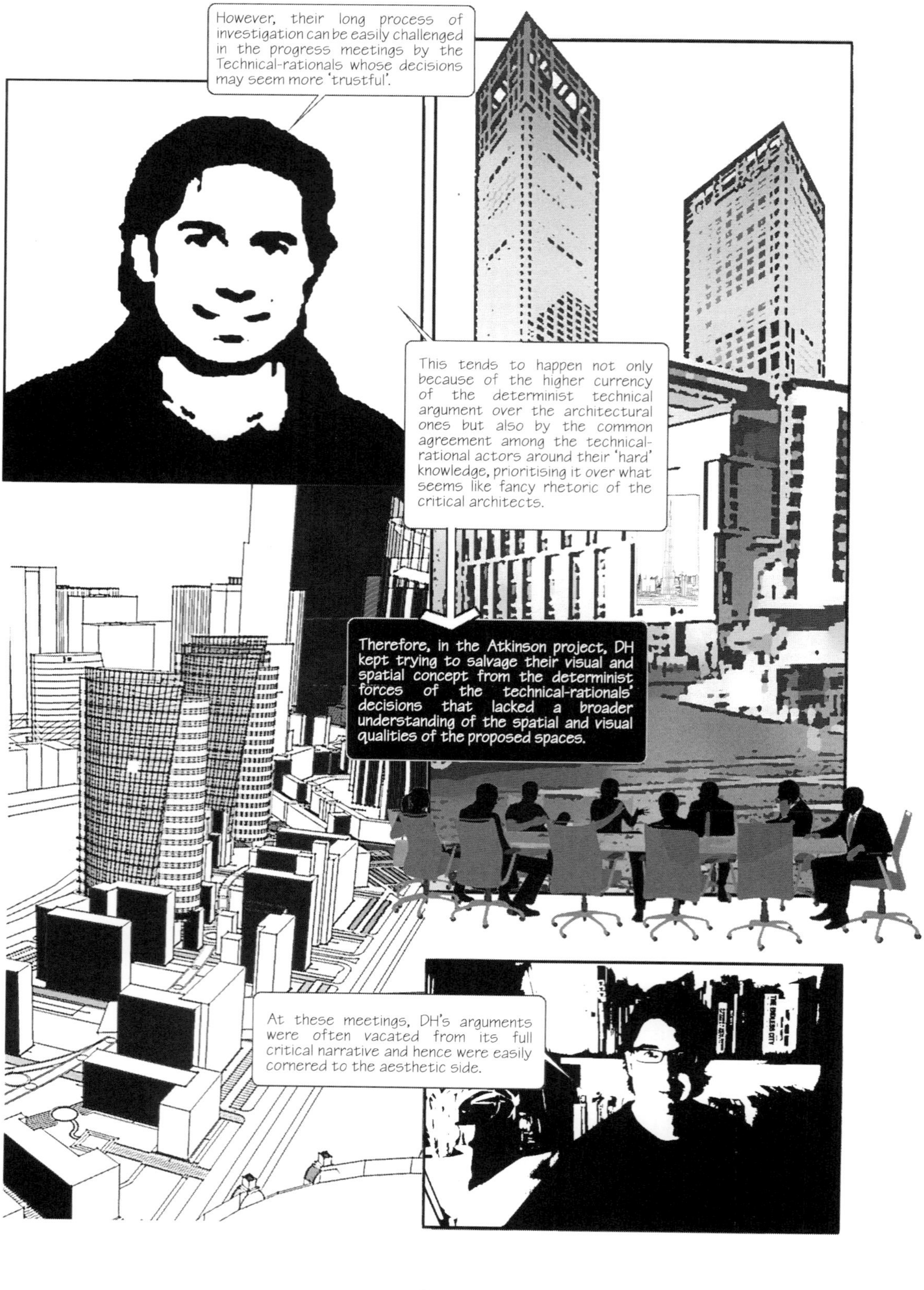
However, their long process of investigation can be easily challenged in the progress meetings by the Technical-rationals whose decisions may seem more 'trustful'.
This tends to happen not only because of the higher currency of the determinist technical argument over the architectural ones but also by the common agreement among the technical-rational actors around their 'hard' knowledge, prioritising it over what seems like fancy rhetoric of the critical architects.
Therefore, in the Atkinson project, DH kept trying to salvage their visual and spatial concept from the determinist forces of the technical-rationals' decisions that lacked a broader understanding of the spatial and visual qualities of the proposed spaces.
At these meetings, DH's arguments were often vacated from its full critical narrative and hence were easily cornered to the aesthetic side.

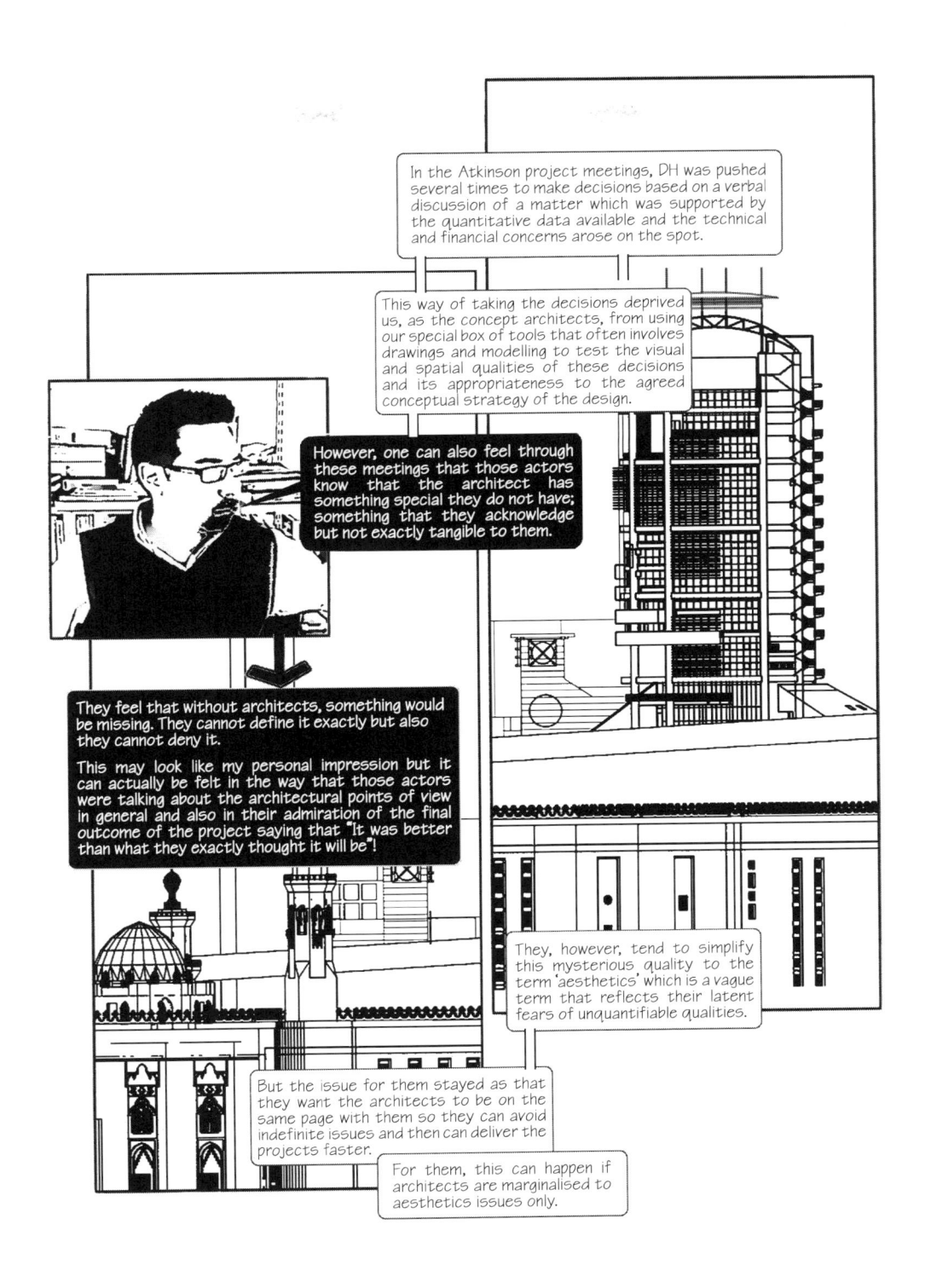

In the Atkinson project meetings, DH was pushed several times to make decisions based on a verbal discussion of a matter which was supported by the quantitative data available and the technical and financial concerns arose on the spot.

This way of taking the decisions deprived us, as the concept architects, from using our special box of tools that often involves drawings and modelling to test the visual and spatial qualities of these decisions and its appropriateness to the agreed conceptual strategy of the design.

However, one can also feel through these meetings that those actors know that the architect has something special they do not have; something that they acknowledge but not exactly tangible to them.

They feel that without architects, something would be missing. They cannot define it exactly but also they cannot deny it.

This may look like my personal impression but it can actually be felt in the way that those actors were talking about the architectural points of view in general and also in their admiration of the final outcome of the project saying that "It was better than what they exactly thought it will be"!

They, however, tend to simplify this mysterious quality to the term 'aesthetics' which is a vague term that reflects their latent fears of unquantifiable qualities.

But the issue for them stayed as that they want the architects to be on the same page with them so they can avoid indefinite issues and then can deliver the projects faster.

For them, this can happen if architects are marginalised to aesthetics issues only.

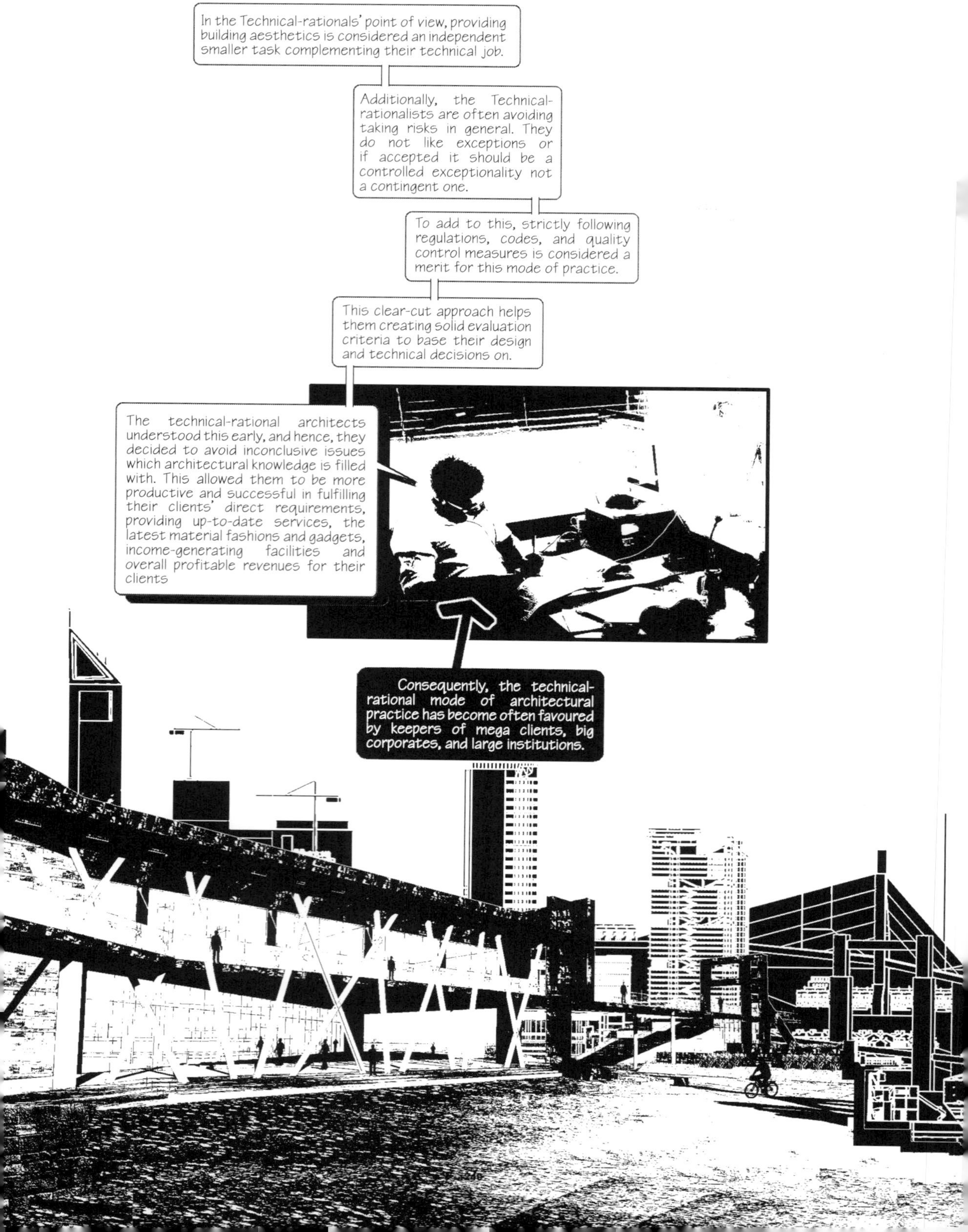
In the Technical-rationals' point of view, providing building aesthetics is considered an independent smaller task complementing their technical job.
Additionally, the Technical-rationalists are often avoiding taking risks in general. They do not like exceptions or if accepted it should be a controlled exceptionality not a contingent one.
To add to this, strictly following regulations, codes, and quality control measures is considered a merit for this mode of practice.
This clear-cut approach helps them creating solid evaluation criteria to base their design and technical decisions on.
The technical-rational architects understood this early, and hence, they decided to avoid inconclusive issues which architectural knowledge is filled with. This allowed them to be more productive and successful in fulfilling their clients' direct requirements, providing up-to-date services, the latest material fashions and gadgets, income-generating facilities and overall profitable revenues for their clients
Consequently, the technical-rational mode of architectural practice has become often favoured by keepers of mega clients, big corporates, and large institutions.

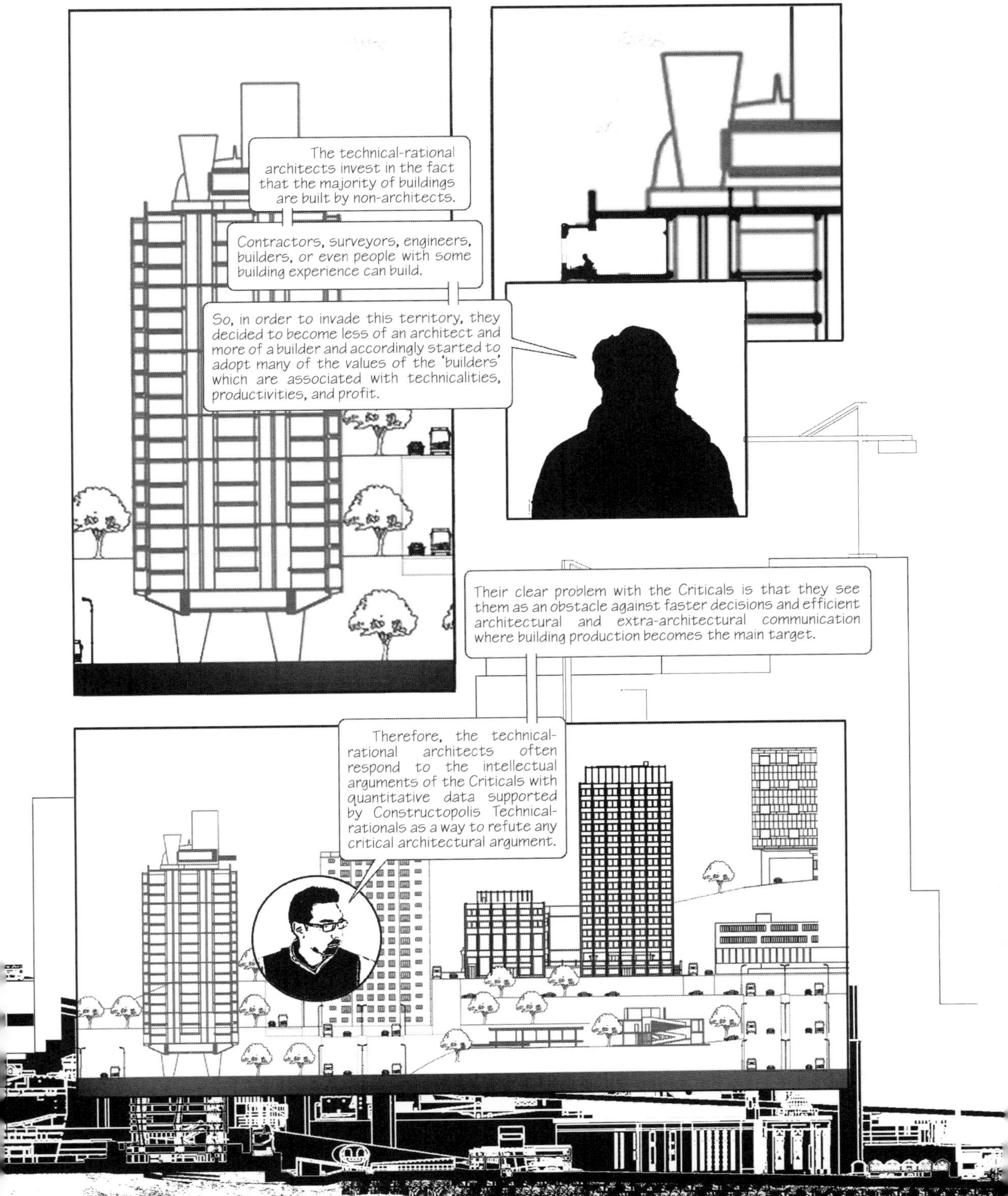
The technical-rational architects invest in the fact that the majority of buildings are built by non-architects.
Contractors, surveyors, engineers, builders, or even people with some building experience can build.
So, in order to invade this territory, they decided to become less of an architect and more of a builder and accordingly started to adopt many of the values of the 'builders' which are associated with technicalities, productivities, and profit.
Their clear problem with the Criticals is that they see them as an obstacle against faster decisions and efficient architectural and extra-architectural communication where building production becomes the main target.
Therefore, the technical-rational architects often respond to the intellectual arguments of the Criticals with quantitative data supported by Constructopolis Technical-rationals as a way to refute any critical architectural argument.

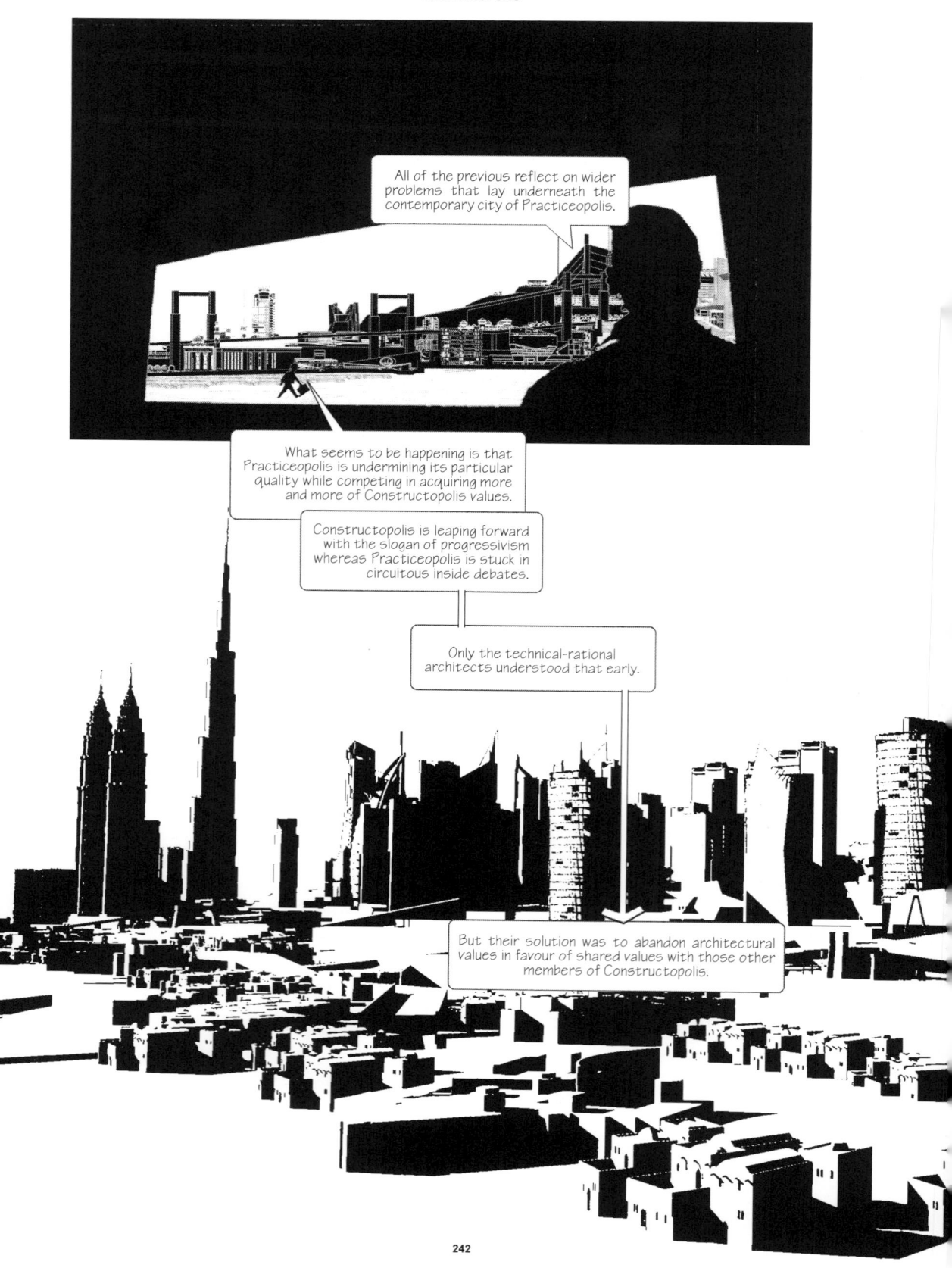

All of the previous reflect on wider problems that lay underneath the contemporary city of Practiceopolis.

What seems to be happening is that Practiceopolis is undermining its particular quality while competing in acquiring more and more of Constructopolis values.

Constructopolis is leaping forward with the slogan of progressivism whereas Practiceopolis is stuck in circuitous inside debates.

Only the technical-rational architects understood that early.

But their solution was to abandon architectural values in favour of shared values with those other members of Constructopolis.

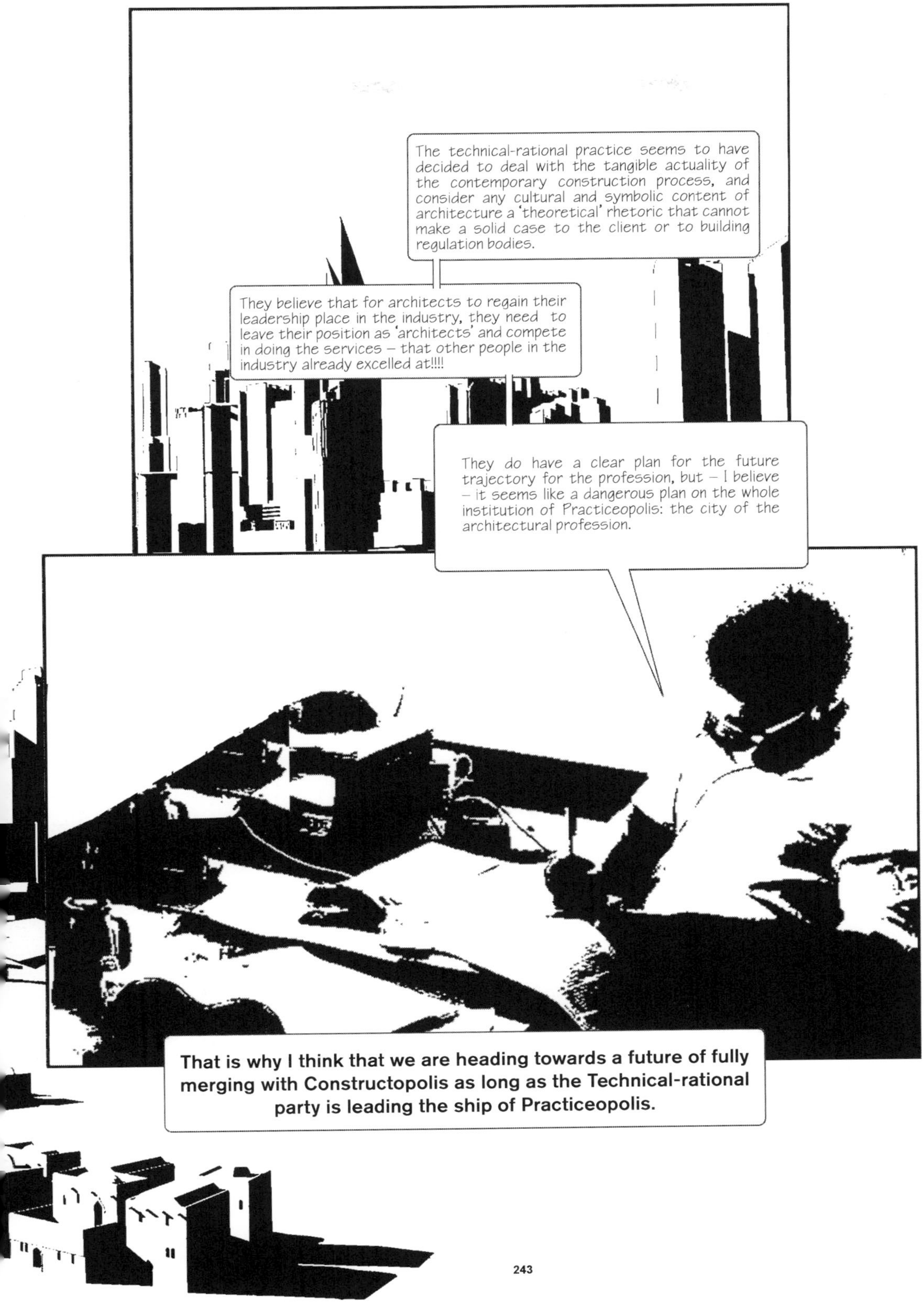
The technical-rational practice seems to have decided to deal with the tangible actuality of the contemporary construction process, and consider any cultural and symbolic content of architecture a 'theoretical' rhetoric that cannot make a solid case to the client or to building regulation bodies.
They believe that for architects to regain their leadership place in the industry, they need to leave their position as 'architects' and compete in doing the services – that other people in the industry already excelled at!!!!
They do have a clear plan for the future trajectory for the profession, but – I believe – it seems like a dangerous plan on the whole institution of Practiceopolis: the city of the architectural profession.
That is why I think that we are heading towards a future of fully merging with Constructopolis as long as the Technical-rational party is leading the ship of Practiceopolis.

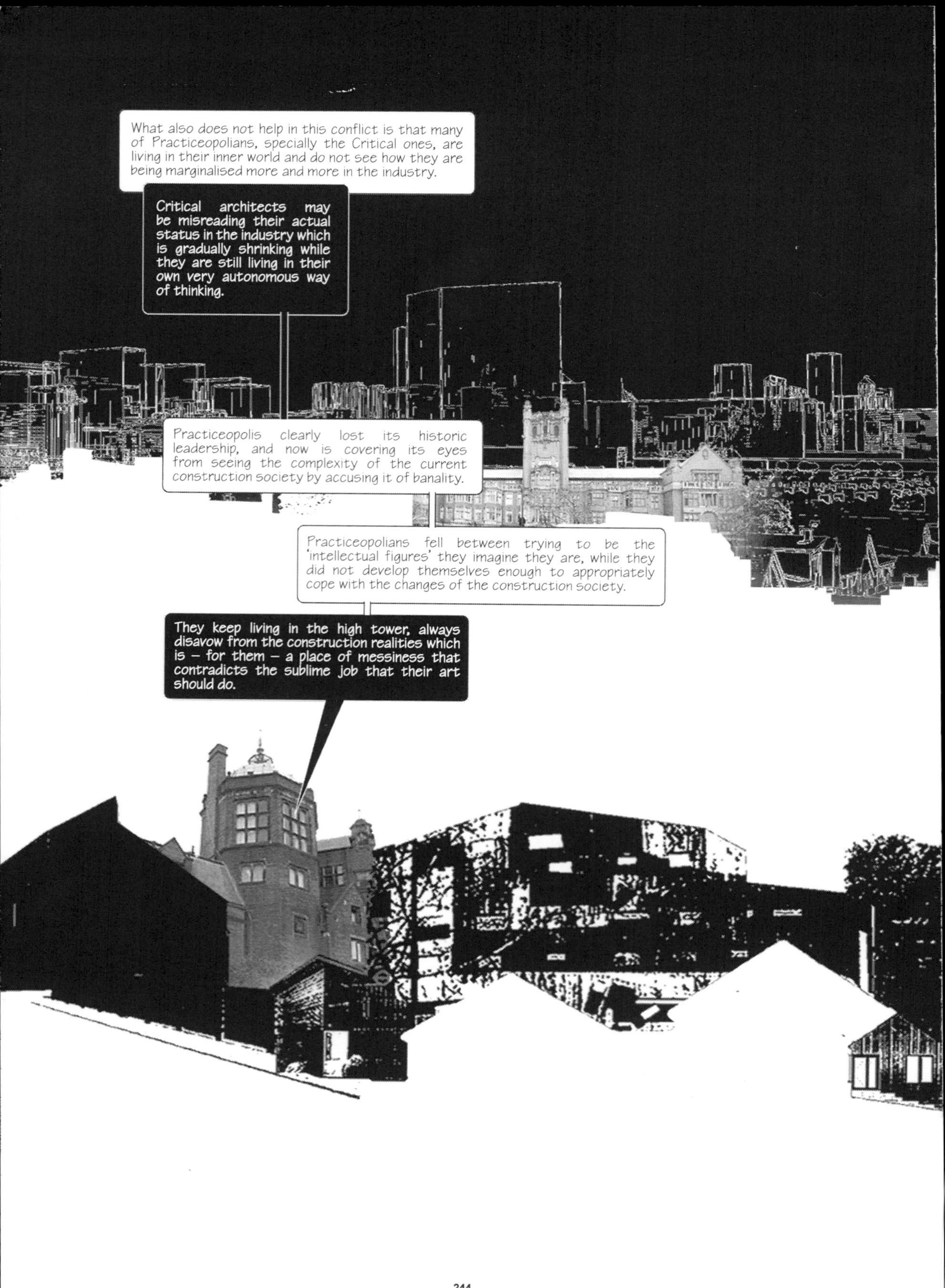
What also does not help in this conflict is that many of Practiceopolians, specially the Critical ones, are living in their inner world and do not see how they are being marginalised more and more in the industry.
Critical architects may be misreading their actual status in the industry which is gradually shrinking while they are still living in their own very autonomous way of thinking.
Practiceopolis clearly lost its historic leadership, and now is covering its eyes from seeing the complexity of the current construction society by accusing it of banality.
Practiceopolians fell between trying to be the 'intellectual figures' they imagine they are, while they did not develop themselves enough to appropriately cope with the changes of the construction society.
They keep living in the high tower, always disavow from the construction realities which is – for them – a place of messiness that contradicts the sublime job that their art should do.

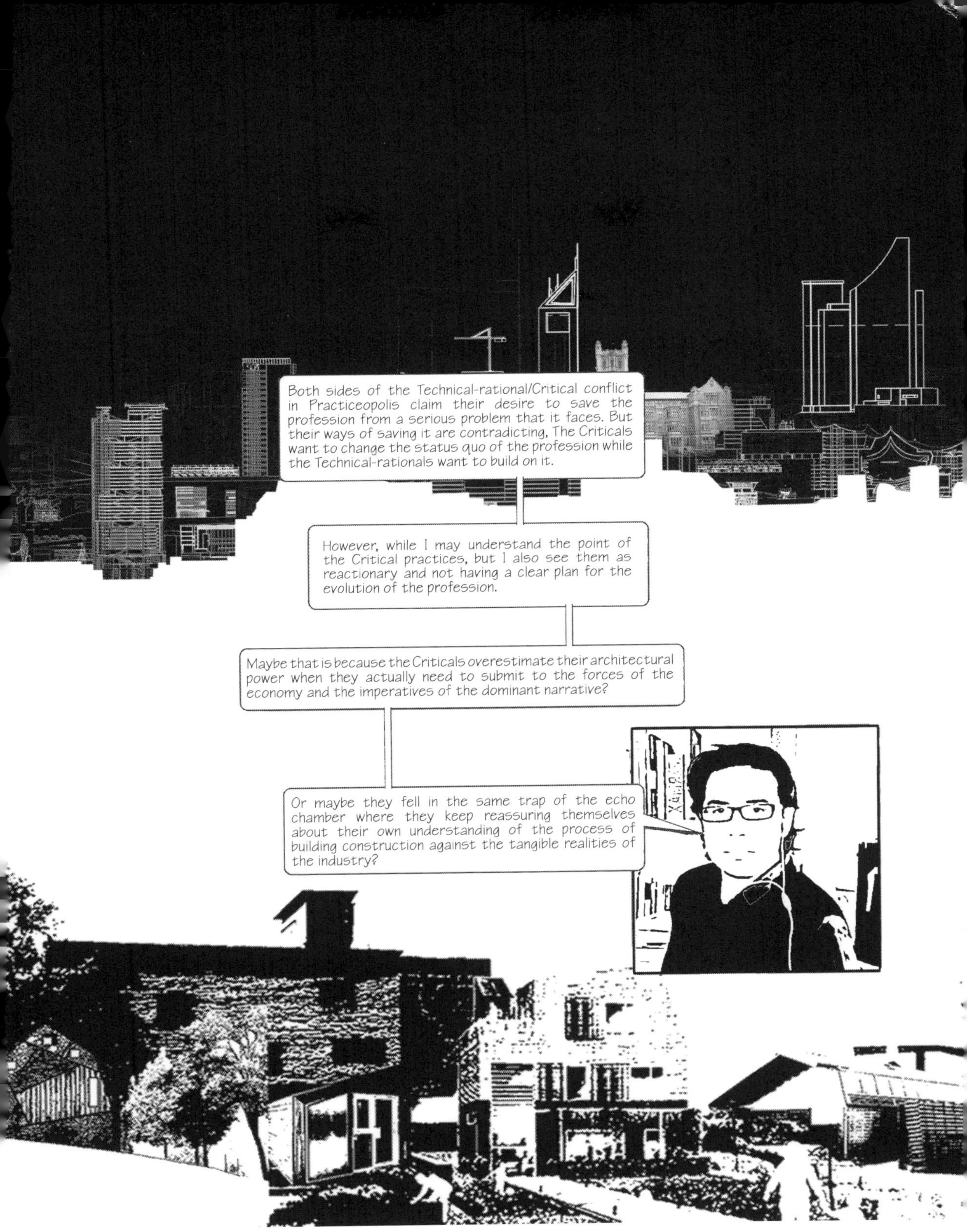
Both sides of the Technical-rational/Critical conflict in Practiceopolis claim their desire to save the profession from a serious problem that it faces. But their ways of saving it are contradicting, The Criticals want to change the status quo of the profession while the Technical-rationals want to build on it.
However, while I may understand the point of the Critical practices, but I also see them as reactionary and not having a clear plan for the evolution of the profession.
Maybe that is because the Criticals overestimate their architectural power when they actually need to submit to the forces of the economy and the imperatives of the dominant narrative?
Or maybe they fell in the same trap of the echo chamber where they keep reassuring themselves about their own understanding of the process of building construction against the tangible realities of the industry?

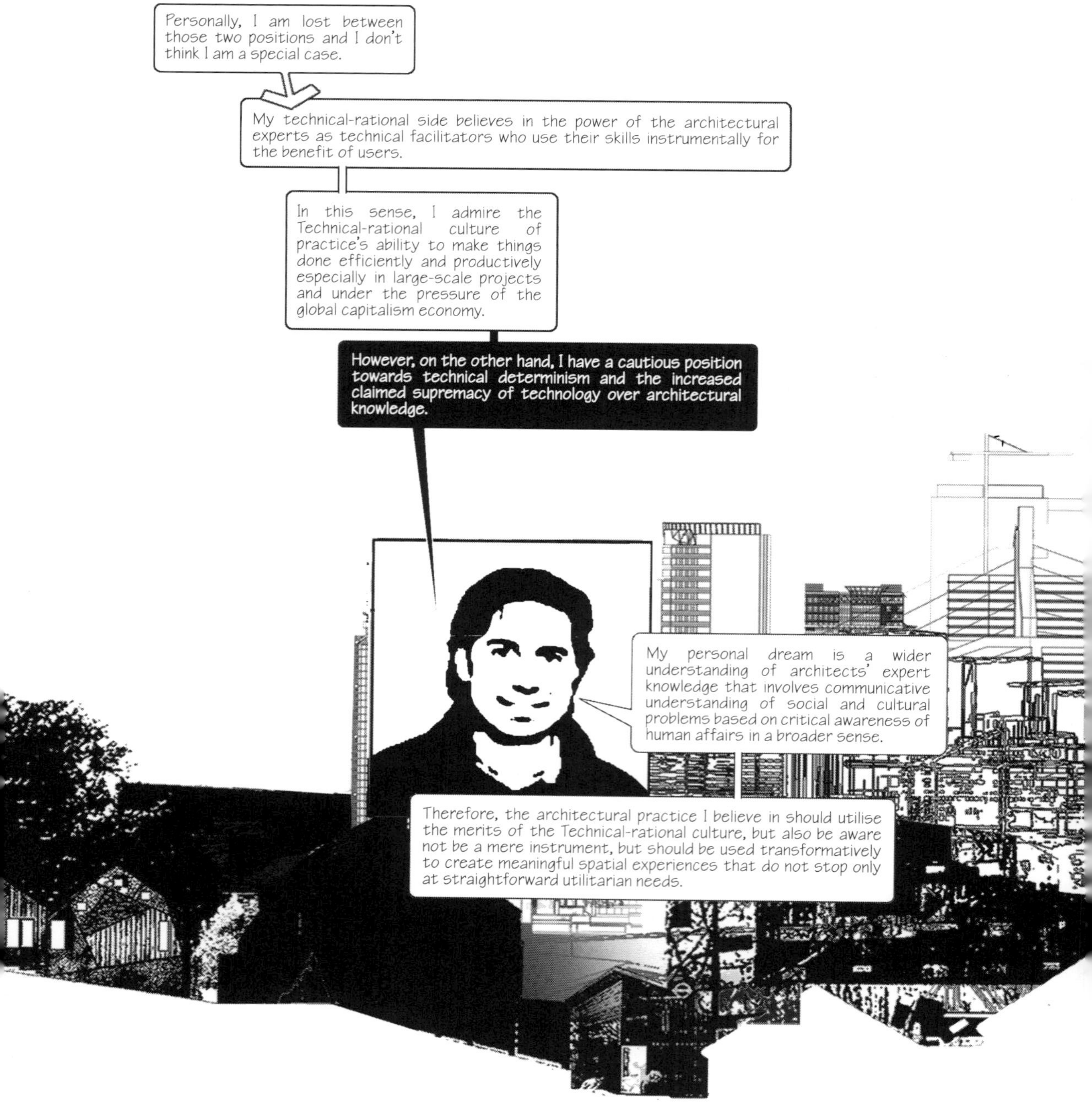
Personally, I am lost between those two positions and I don't think I am a special case.
My technical-rational side believes in the power of the architectural experts as technical facilitators who use their skills instrumentally for the benefit of users.
In this sense, I admire the Technical-rational culture of practice's ability to make things done efficiently and productively especially in large-scale projects and under the pressure of the global capitalism economy.
However, on the other hand, I have a cautious position towards technical determinism and the increased claimed supremacy of technology over architectural knowledge.
My personal dream is a wider understanding of architects' expert knowledge that involves communicative understanding of social and cultural problems based on critical awareness of human affairs in a broader sense.
Therefore, the architectural practice I believe in should utilise the merits of the Technical-rational culture, but also be aware not be a mere instrument, but should be used transformatively to create meaningful spatial experiences that do not stop only at straightforward utilitarian needs.

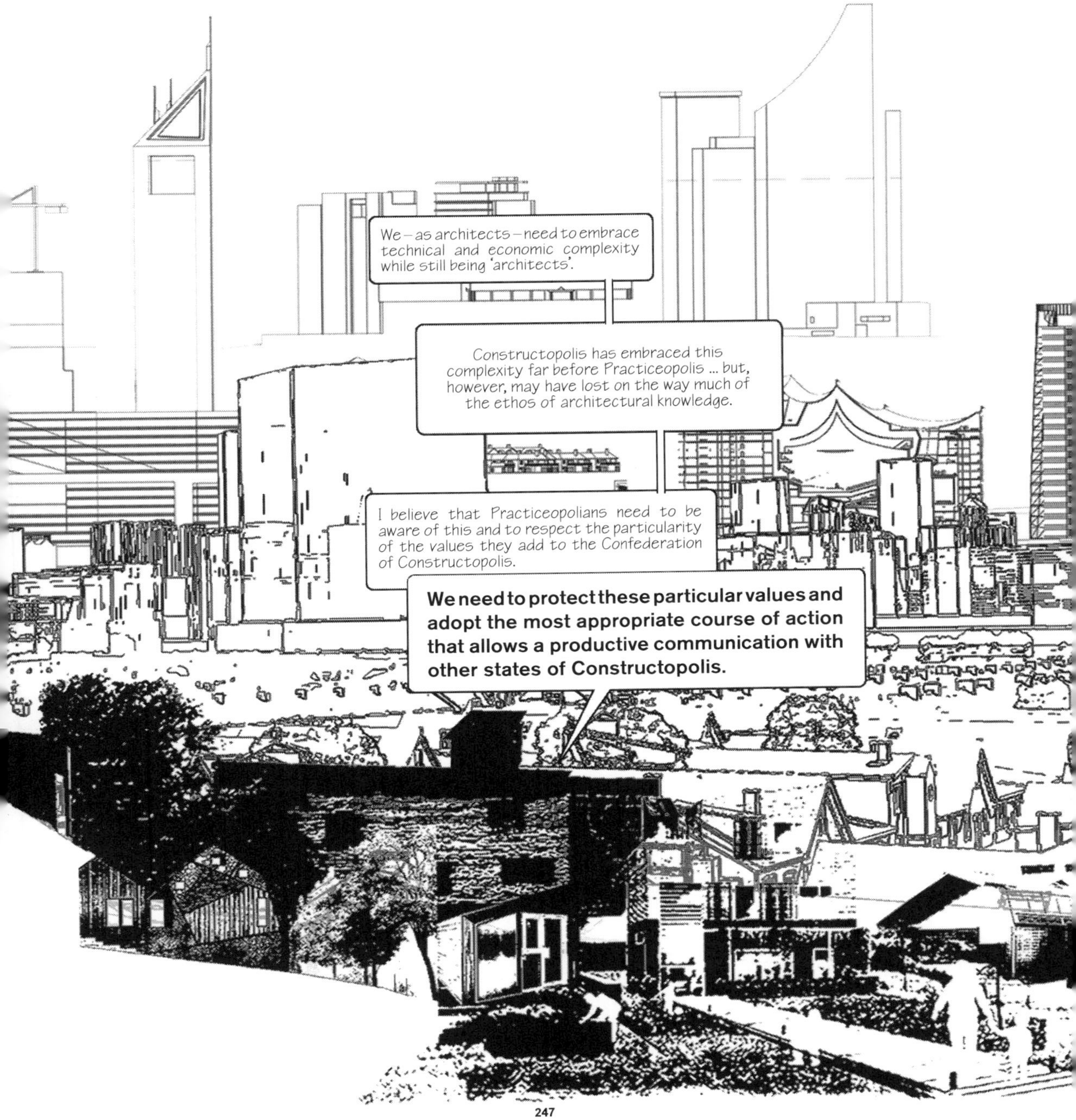
We – as architects – need to embrace technical and economic complexity while still being 'architects'.
Constructopolis has embraced this complexity far before Practiceopolis ... but, however, may have lost on the way much of the ethos of architectural knowledge.
I believe that Practiceopolians need to be aware of this and to respect the particularity of the values they add to the Confederation of Constructopolis.
We need to protect these particular values and adopt the most appropriate course of action that allows a productive communication with other states of Constructopolis.

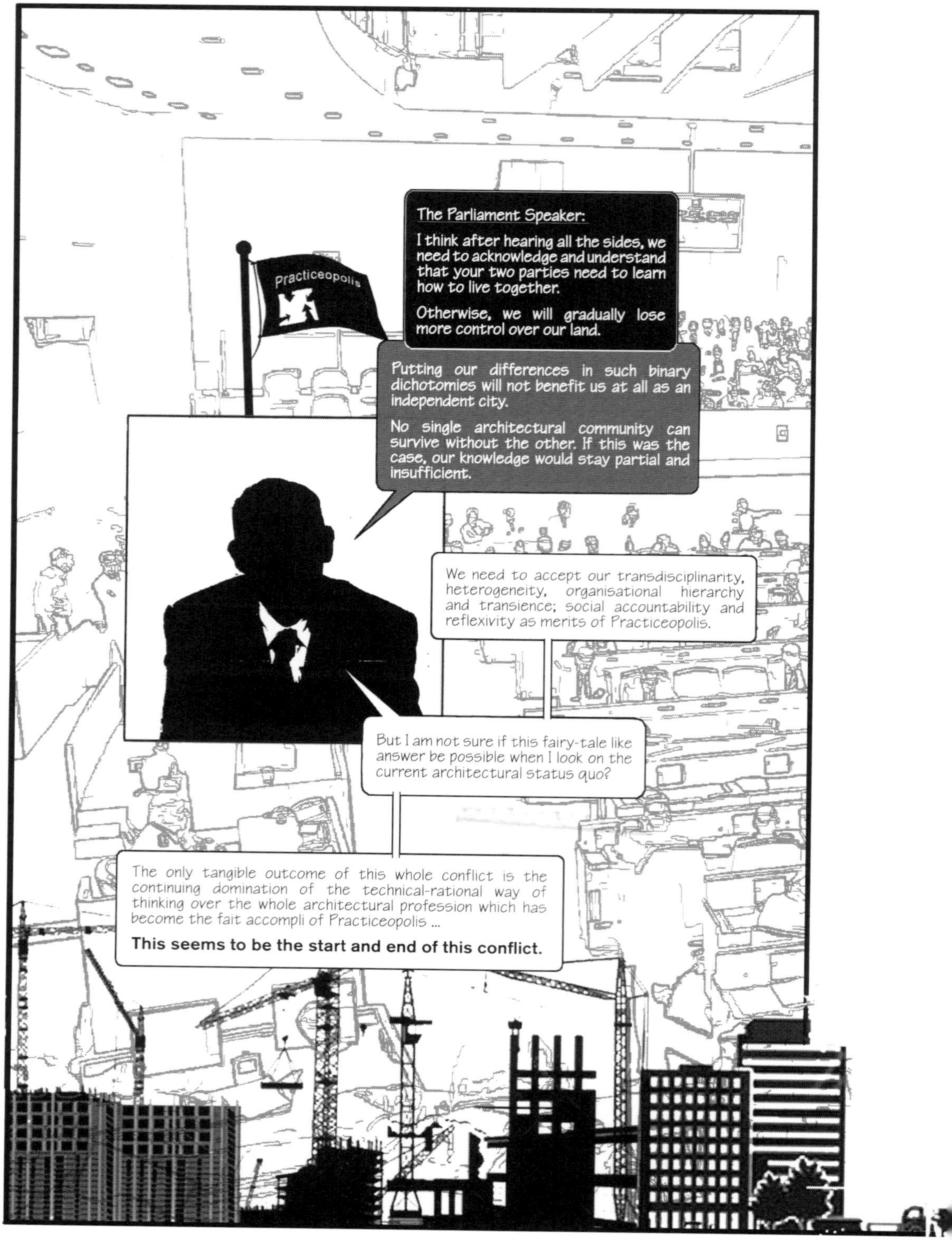
Practiceopolis
The Parliament Speaker:
I think after hearing all the sides, we need to acknowledge and understand that your two parties need to learn how to live together.
Otherwise, we will gradually lose more control over our land.
Putting our differences in such binary dichotomies will not benefit us at all as an independent city.
No single architectural community can survive without the other. If this was the case, our knowledge would stay partial and insufficient.
We need to accept our transdisciplinarity, heterogeneity, organisational hierarchy and transience; social accountability and reflexivity as merits of Practiceopolis.
But I am not sure if this fairy-tale like answer be possible when I look on the current architectural status quo?
The only tangible outcome of this whole conflict is the continuing domination of the technical-rational way of thinking over the whole architectural profession which has become the fait accompli of Practiceopolis ...
This seems to be the start and end of this conflict.

The continuing domination of the technical-rational way of thinking over Practiceopolis ...

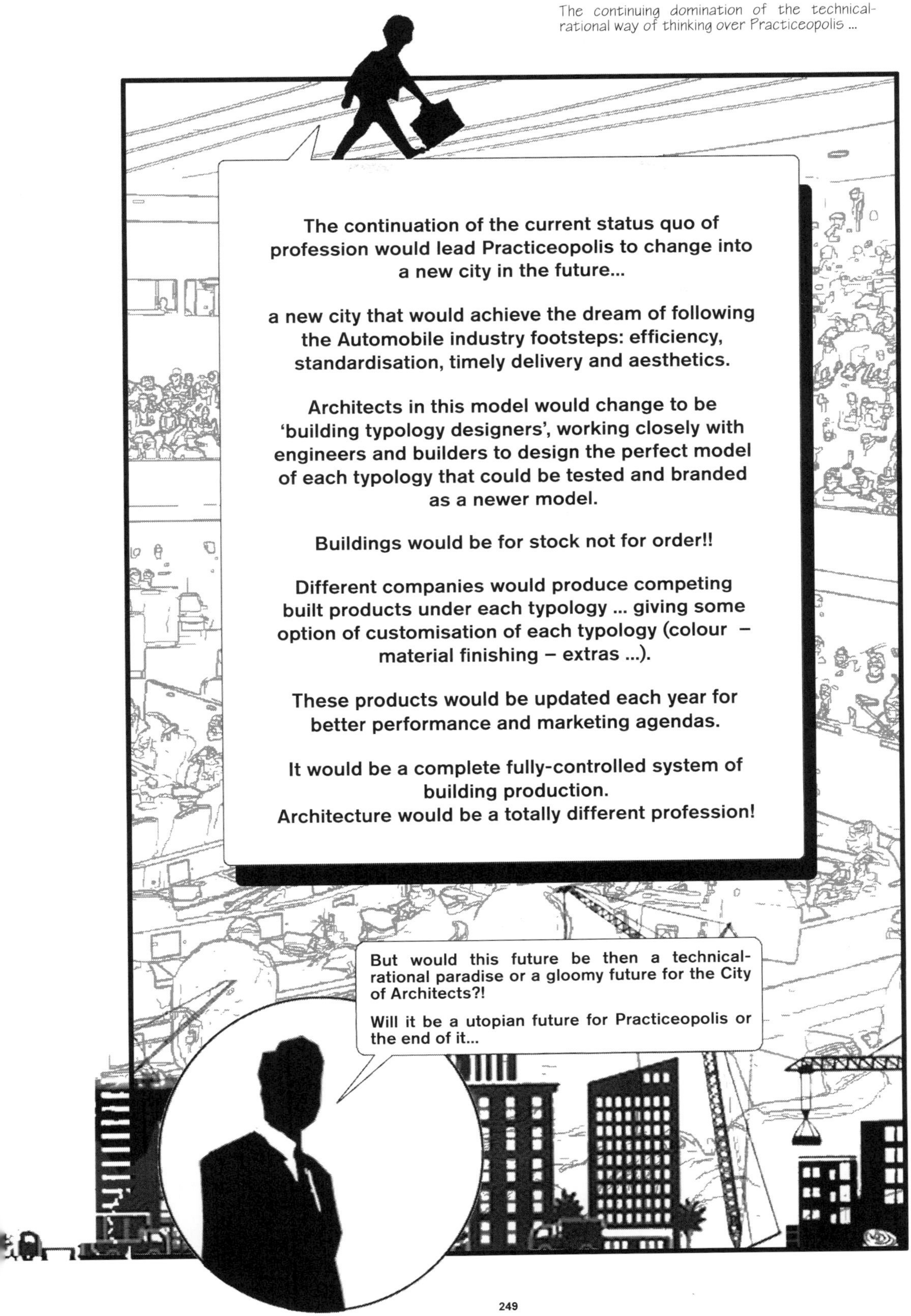
The continuation of the current status quo of profession would lead Practiceopolis to change into a new city in the future...
a new city that would achieve the dream of following the Automobile industry footsteps: efficiency, standardisation, timely delivery and aesthetics.
Architects in this model would change to be 'building typology designers', working closely with engineers and builders to design the perfect model of each typology that could be tested and branded as a newer model.
Buildings would be for stock not for order!!
Different companies would produce competing built products under each typology ... giving some option of customisation of each typology (colour – material finishing – extras ...).
These products would be updated each year for better performance and marketing agendas.
It would be a complete fully-controlled system of building production.
Architecture would be a totally different profession!
But would this future be then a technical-rational paradise or a gloomy future for the City of Architects?!
Will it be a utopian future for Practiceopolis or the end of it...

Some years later, ...

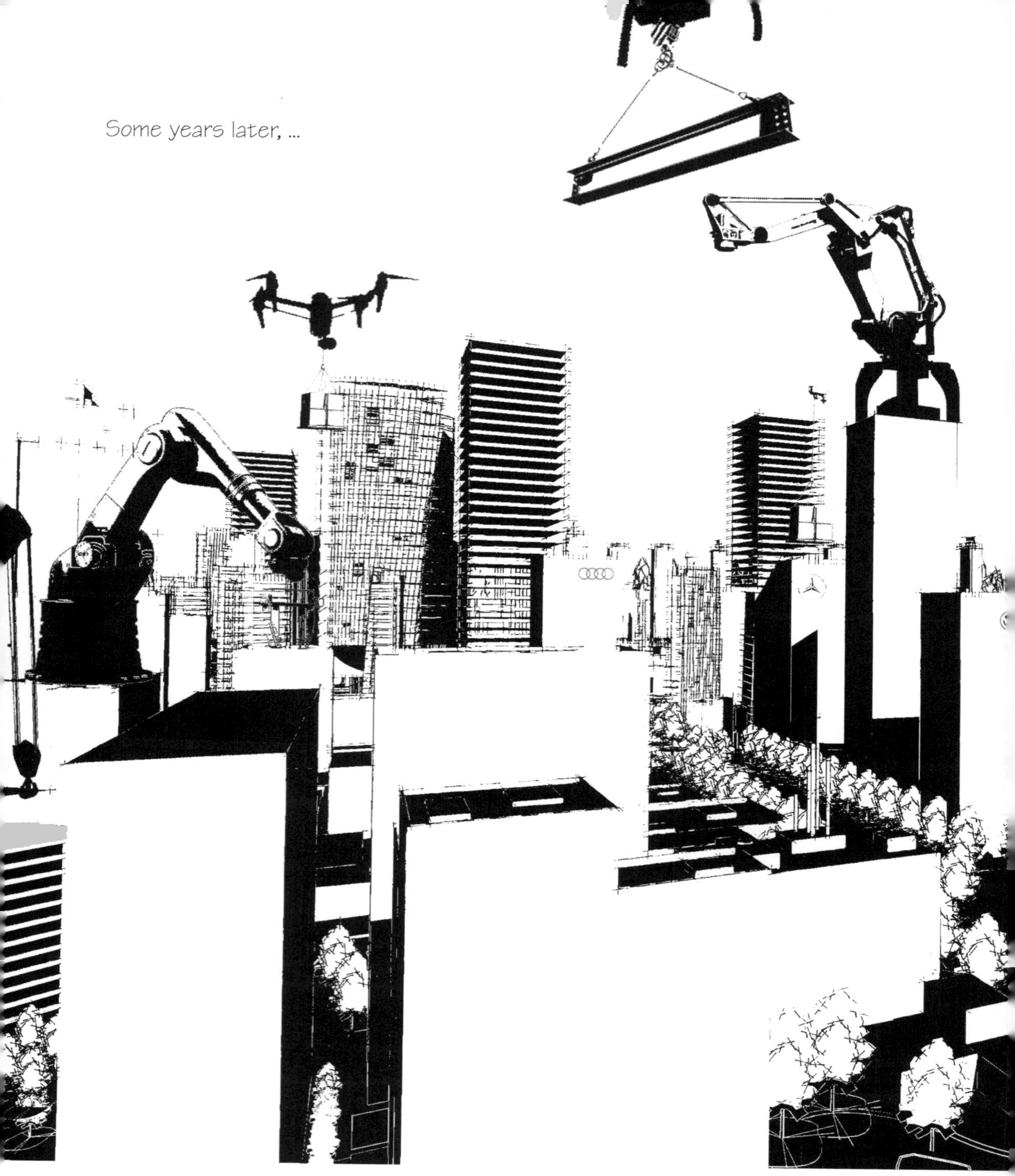

BUILDING
OPOLIS

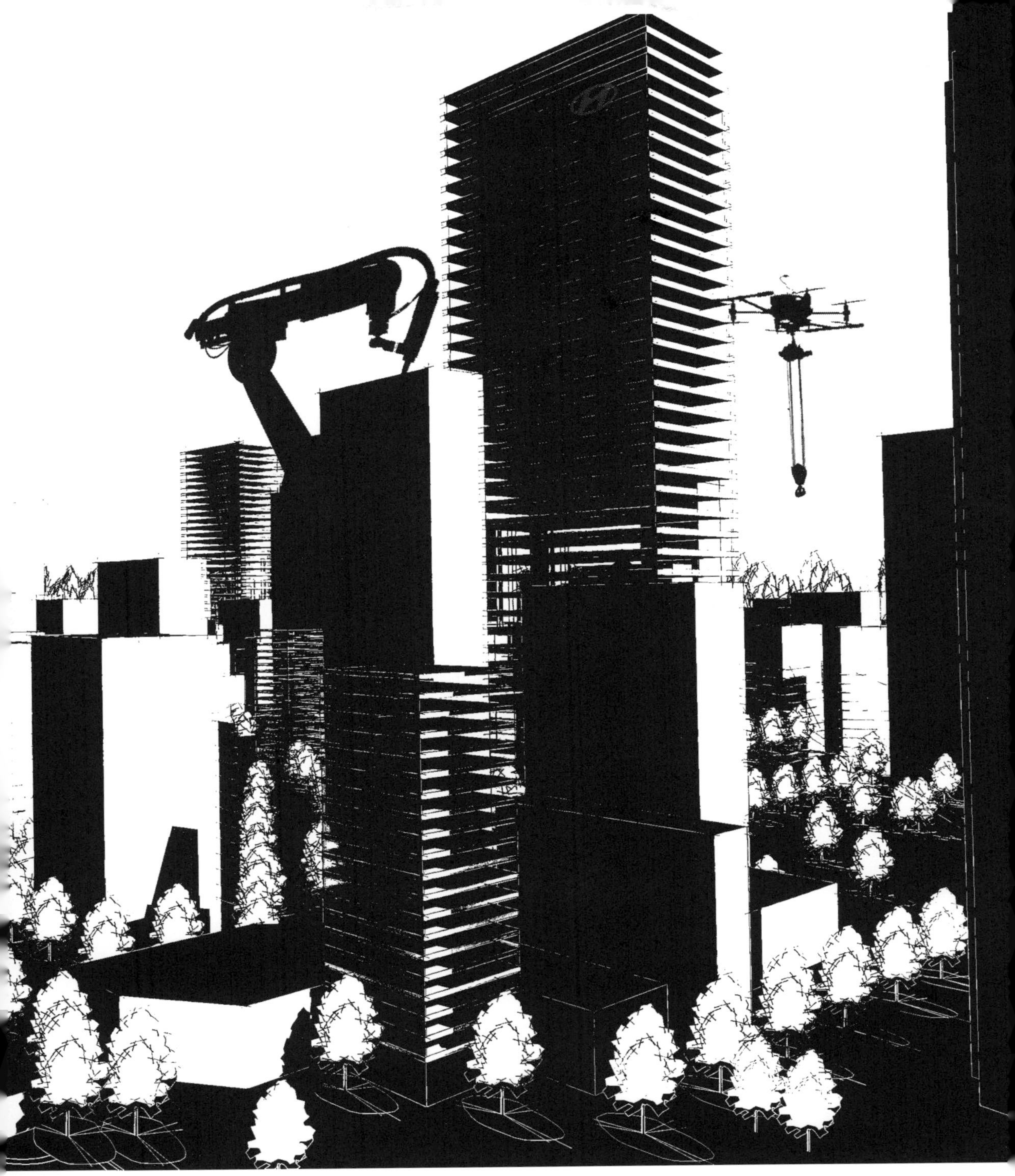

The following generations, who were not so fond of the study of architecture as their forebears had been, saw that the vast City of Practiceopolis was useless, and not without some pitilessness was it. In the deserts of the island of Constructopolis, still today, there are tattered ruins of that Practiceopolis, inhabited by old 'has-been' architects; in all the land there is no other relic of the disciplines of architecture.

A reimagination of J. L. Borges (1975) 'On Exactitude in Science'

EPILOGUE

These were some of the many stories of Practiceopolis. They displayed an exaggerated confrontation between the prominent cultures of practice within the contemporary architectural profession. They depicted the competition between the two cultures as a healthy phenomenon that allows the mobility of the profession. However, they also showed how the nature of the inherent value-conflict accompanied by the domination of one of these cultures of practice may have threatened the balance of the contemporary profession. The novel presented how this value-conflict has stemmed from the existence of different frames of reference, priorities, and preferences among the actors involved in the construction process. It raised critical questions about mundane routines in the architectural profession that practitioners may have taken for granted, reflecting upon the largely tacit assumptions which inform these routines. They noted how decisions typically paired to the specialist knowledge of the architect have become progressively implicated by the values and agendas of collaborating actors in a way that may not always agree with the priorities of architectural repertoire. While these stories may seem almost trivial in the everyday world outside the novel, nevertheless, they depicted the difference of values and priorities manifest between the actors of the industry that influence the arguments they provide and, consequently, their conclusions.

SPECULATION ON THE FUTURE OF THE ARCHITECTURAL PROFESSION

Aside from the dramatic exaggeration of the novel, the current status quo of the architectural profession may indicate certain scenarios about its future trajectory. One scenario – which may be promoted by those adopting the technical-rational ideology – envisions an architectural 'utopia' where integration and coordination, timely delivery, and elimination of errors would be achieved through technical and technological progress. A more pessimistic scenario may see this future as an end of the historical legacy of the architectural profession and its rhetorical repertoire under a technical-rational autocracy. This scenario anticipates the marginalisation of any particular values of the architectural field; limiting them to issues related to aesthetics and style; and replacing them by technical, quantifiable, and profit-based values. Nevertheless, as suggested in the novel, it is perhaps more probable that the future of the profession would be an extension of the current domination of the technical-rational values. This future, whilst carrying some benign benefits, however, it would lead to naturalising more the 'normative' generic technical-rational architecture as the expected and accepted mode of practice. It may then lead to marginalising many of the unique values that architectural knowledge can add to the process of building production. Such dominance would push the architectural profession further towards a disempowered role in the building process that only facilitates the production of precise, efficient, and quality-controlled built environment in line with the technical-rational values of the industry.

In turn, the technical-rational ideology's control over the profession would prompt it to maintain its dominant status by prioritising the factors and mediums that have enabled its control, mainly notions of integrated building processes, quality control, precision, and control of risk. This would induce technical-rational practices to keep defining architectural challenges according to the terms of these notions – which they would often excel at compared to any other mode of practice. Intentionally or unintentionally, this would lead to creating a closed loop of self-benefit based on reproducing the necessity of the mediums that have allowed the dominance of the technical-rational ideology in the first place and that also could be best applied in a technical-rational environment.

This loop of reproducing the dominance of the technical-rational perspective would consequently lead the architectural profession towards an unquestioned alignment with the values of the broader building industry. These values would become gradually the norm and the default for practising architecture, where any other approach to architectural practice would be the exception and often viewed pejoratively. This alignment would not just endanger the dynamic equilibrium of the architectural profession but also the whole institution of the architectural field. This situation can be described – in Koolhaas's terms – as that the Technical-rational Culture of practice would manage to impose its 'generic' architecture and mass-market it by its bigness that can no longer accommodate architectural values. As such, the art of architecture would become useless in that 'Bigness' while forcing to the margins the multiplicity of intellectual dialogues within the architectural field and a significant part of what the architecture knowledge allows. By associating the challenges of the architectural profession with precision, efficiency, and quality control, architects' responsibilities would be firmly confined to the operation of quantitative technical knowledge and by extension bypassing pressing issues of cultural and humanistic relevance to be someone else's problem.[1]

The prevalence of this technical-rational discourse over the profession would also lead to unquestioned censorship of what is deemed important and worthy and what is not in the scope of the profession's remit. This discourse would create patterns and constructs about the proper way of practising architecture and reinforce them through the supposed authority of the 'hard numbers' of its quantitative technical agenda of quality and delivery control. Like all devices for reducing the unmeasurable to concrete numbers and substituting the arithmetic for judgement, it is an appealing idea – at least to people who employ architects such as big contractors, real estate companies or multi-disciplined consultancy firms, even if not always to architects themselves. These numbers, however, are not actually neutral as they help to promote a version of reality that favours a certain idea about the profession over others. The prevalence of this discourse would allow technical-rational practices to suppress the resistance of the more critically-oriented modes of practice for the sake of the preservation of the existing forms of its dominance. It would create an emotional reaction that serves the technical-rational claims of architectural rightness. Thereby, the idea that the technical-rational mode of practice could be the right way of practising architecture is not just uncritical but also problematic. By defining rightness where there is only partial right, this makes it a game of dominance that prioritises assumptions that only satisfy the preferences of the dominant practice.

For those reasons, the novel adopted a pessimistic view about the future of the profession, informed by concerns from the current outcome of the domination of the Technical-rational Culture. The novel predicts that the claimed technical-rational utopia would not take place. Instead, it may be an end of architecture as a distinct profession, its historical body of knowledge and its rhetorical tropes. In effect, this pessimistic future for the profession is not just an outcome of external forces from different technical-rational members of the industry, nor a reaction to the critical practices' defeat against the overwhelming imperatives of the values of the globalised capitalist economy. It also may happen because of certain qualities displayed by Critical Culture of practice.

Following a critical architectural path means to be sceptical and 'critical' even to your own narrative. Practitioners who follow a critical path would not often make decisions and promises before they scrutinise their own attitude to be consistent with their architectural values and principles. They believe that every claim of truth carries its own biases and intellectual baggage, which in turn confuses any effort to search for truth. Hence, all what they can aspire to is to reach an acceptable consistent relative version of the truth. Accordingly, critical practitioners tend to start their resistance against the forces of domination and claims of truth by first fighting against their own biases. Consequently, they tend to pre-use part of their defence strategies against the domination of the Technical-rational Culture towards themselves which in turn limit their chances to stop the domination of the overwhelming technical-rational discourse.

On the opposite side, the technical-rational actors of the industry tend not to rely much on philosophical self-critique. This is based on an assumption that what is based on technology and science is broadly true. So, in any disputes, they use all their measurable quantitative troops to support their arguments against any 'critical' attack. The technical-rational actors in the industry, in general, tend to use the past and present to serve their arguments. They often have a selective memory that chooses what to remember and what to hide about their recurrent promises of the future architectural technical utopia. They also know when and where to exaggerate success and what failures to forget to serve their arguments. Those actors are often light and fast in claiming victory with simple fact, while critical practitioners are slow, loaded with their different understandings of the truth. In this sense, the technical-rational actors enter their fight armed with solid numbers and tested technologies whereas the critical practices are already wounded with hard 'critical' questions to their own arguments.

Regardless, while the current conditions of the architectural profession imply one of the two scenarios: the technical-rational utopia or autocracy, there is a still a chance to find an alternative route for the future of the architectural profession; a route that is realistic about acknowledging the inevitable change happening to the profession and also the benefits of utilising the capabilities of the technical-rational approach to architecture. However, this route should have an informed position that understands the uniqueness of the architectural profession's particular values and hence must promote and market the diverse and rich modes of thinking available in the architectural field as indispensable to the improvement of the process of building production. There are recent calls starting to touch upon this position in the works of Flora Samuel, Simon Foxell, Fredrik Nilsson, and Michael Hensel, among a few others. Still, more needs to be done to strengthen this new position and to encourage architects to ride the tide of change while appreciating the value and uniqueness of the architectural knowledge for the benefit of both the construction industry and the built environment as a whole.

PRACTICEOPOLIS

Finally, Practiceopolis can be seen as a useful tool for design and practice-based research in architecture. It allows representing, visualising, and documenting research and design through an accessible and transferable format which can be comparable to formal academic research. It is a special creative space, a mix of facts, design, and science fiction that encourages human imagination by combining the traditions of writing and storytelling with the crafting of cartoon drawings. Practiceopolis utilises what Simon Grand (2011) calls: 'The Design Fiction Method Toolbox': projection, materialisations, processes, systems, and multitude. It allows projection: making possible the creation and construction of possible future worlds, in relation to the actual world. It also gives a space for materialisations: making it possible to materialise those future worlds in terms of images, artefacts, interfaces, and usages. Practiceopolis provides a process and a system for experimentation and the exploration of hypotheses. It offers a medium for challenging the taken-for-granted, unquestioned, self-evident nature of the world as it is, while at the same time emphasising and mapping the multitude of possible alternative world-views that go beyond one-sided ideological premises.[2]

By doing so, the world of Practiceopolis opens up some blind spots that the architectural profession conceals about its foundational confusions and its conflicting relations within the building industry. It emphasises the importance of entering into the controversies between different perspectives, methods, and strategies of members of the construction process to help extend architectural discussions to acknowledge different ideological positions and to allow these ideologies to be seen from outside its supporting contexts. To be clear, Practiceopolis is a 'world' not because it contains everything in the architectural field, but because it contains enough to encourage architects' imaginations, which, could be a much better way to explore questions, activities, logics, and practices about the architectural profession. It is an easy-to-imagine place that enables architects to reference their debates in a tangible, concrete – yet still metaphorical – way. It creates a medium for architects to provoke the imagination, open a discussion to explore possibilities and new considerations that words by themselves are not able to express. Practiceopolis allows new ways of thinking about the near future, optimistic or pessimistic futures, to support a critical perspective for the architects' future.

ACKNOWLEDGEMENTS

I would like to express my deep appreciation to my loving family for their continuous prayers, caring support and for always providing me with encouragement. Words are inadequate to express how I am grateful to all of you; for the faithful and untiring support of my wife Amira, the immense support of my father and mother, and the prayers of my brother and sister. Thank you all for your long patience and empathy, your prayers and blessings kept me going through a challenging and testing process.

I would like also to express my sincere gratitude to Prof. Adam Sharr for his continued and consistent support through the formulation and writing of this book. He has provided me with motivation, a wealth of knowledge and originality of thoughts. Thank you for meaningful and regular feedback and – above all – for your patience and encouragement through many challenging times. To Adam who believed in me, and helped me to discover myself and revivify my architectural skills. To Adam who coined the term: Practiceopolis!

I want to express a special note of thanks to the Design Office who partially funded my research, has been both a vital distraction and an imminent catalyst for establishing the direction of my research. Special thanks to the Design Office team: James, Kieran, and Aldric who made this research journey possible and whose valuable comments and thought-provoking discussions informed my research trajectory at key moments.

My sincere thanks also go to Professor Katie Lloyd-Thomas, Professor Graham Farmer and Dr Peter Kellett, Newcastle University for their valuable input to key areas of my research. Also a special thanks to Dr Ahmed Oaf, Cairo University for facilitating some obstacles that challenged this research.

Many thanks to the team at the Newcastle University Research Reserve for their sincere support while searching through the extensive 1980s archive of Architectural Record. I also want to express my appreciation to Architecture Research Collective (ARC) and the Institute for Creative Arts Practice, Newcastle University as well as Leicester School of Architecture, De Montfort University for their support in making this book possible.

Last but not least, I would like to thank my friends: Mohamed Bahgaat, Amr Abdullah, Momen, Mohamed Islam, Mohamed Essayed, and Rehab for standing by me in many hard times through the creation of this book.

BIBLIOGRAPHY

Prologue

1. Cartwright, N. (1983) *How the laws of physics lie*. Oxford University Press; Dynamic equilibrium (2006). In *Oxford dictionary of sports science & medicine*, 3rd edn. New York: Oxford University Press.
2. Pollio, V. (1914) *Vitruvius: the ten books on architecture*. Cambridge, Massachusetts: Harvard University press.
3. Crinson, M. and Lubbock, J. (1994) *Architecture, art or profession? Three hundred years of architectural education in Britain*. Manchester: Manchester University Press.
4. Foxell, S. (2018) *Professionalism for the built environment*. London: Routledge.
5. Lawson, B. (2014) *How designers think: the design process demystified*. Oxford: Elsevier.
6. Capelin, J. (1985) Practice: why are architects on the defensive?, *Architectural Record*, 173(4), pp. 41-43; Cole-Colander, C. (2003) Designing the customer experience, *Building Research & Information*, 31(5), pp. 357-366; Cuff, D. (1992) *Architecture: the story of practice*. Cambridge, Massachusetts: MIT Press; Foxell, *Professionalism for the built environment*; Gutman, R. (1988) *Architectural practice: a critical view*. New York: Princeton Architectural Press; Olson, S. (1995) End of the pure design firm?, *Architectural Record*, 183(3), pp. 36-39; Wagner, W. (1985) Round table: the fast-growing and fast-changing role of the corporate architect, *Architectural Record*, 173(1), pp. 35-47.
7. Cuff, *The story of practice*; Rand, A. (2007) *The fountainhead*. London: Penguin.
8. Abley, I. and Woudhuysen, J. (2004) *Why is construction so backward?* Chichester: Wiley; Glendinning, M. (2010) *Architecture's evil empire? Triumph and tragedy of global modernism*. London: Reaktion; Sebastian, R. (2011) Changing roles of the clients, architects and contractors through BIM, *Engineering, Construction and Architectural Management*, 18(2), pp. 176-187; Wagner, Round table
9. Robinson, D., Jamieson, C., Worthington, J. and Cole, C. (2010) *The future for architects?* London: Building Futures, RIBA, p. 3.
10. Abley and Woudhuysen, *Why is construction so backward?*; Capelin, 'Practice: why are architects on the defensive?'; Dutoit, A., Odgers, J. and Sharr, A. (2010) *Quality out of control: standards for measuring architecture*. London: Routledge; Glendinning, *Architecture's evil empire?*; Vesely, D. (2004) *Architecture in the age of divided representation: the question of creativity in the shadow of production*. Cambridge, Massachusetts: MIT Press.
11. Kieran, S. and Timberlake, J. (2003) *Refabricating architecture: how manufacturing methodologies are poised to transform building construction*. London: McGraw Hill; Thomson, D.S., Austin, S.A., Devine-Wright, H. and Mills, G.R. (2003) Managing Value and Quality in Design, *Building Research & Information*, 31(5), pp. 334-345.
12. Samuel, F. (2018) *Why architects matter: evidencing and communicating the value of architects*. London: Routledge.
13. Gerardi, N. (1983) Round table: the architect's role in built-for-sale housing, *Architectural Record*, 171.

14. Frascari, M. (2011) *Eleven exercises in the art of architectural drawing slow food for the architect's imagination*. London: Routledge.
15. Capelin, Practice: why are architects on the defensive?; Cole-Colander, Designing the customer experience; Cuff, *The story of practice*; Markus, T.A. (2003) Lessons from the design quality indicator, *Building Research & Information*, 31(5), pp. 399-405; Tombesi, P. (2004) 'Architectural feasts or professional fausts? A double perspective on the bargains of globalization', *Architecture Australia*, 93(4), pp. 48-50.
16. Frampton, K. (2007) *Modern architecture: a critical history*. London: Thames & Hudson; Glusberg, J. (1988) *Vision of the modern*. London: Academy Editions.
17. Hughes, F. (2014) *The architecture of error: matter, measure, and the misadventures of precision*. Cambridge, Massachusetts: MIT Press.
18. Jencks, C. (1987) *Le Corbusier and the tragic view of architecture*. Middlesex: Penguin; Jencks, C. (2002) *The new paradigm in architecture: the language of post-modernism*. London: Yale University Press.
19. McVicar, M. (2012) 'God is in the details'/'the detail is moot': a meeting between Mies and Koolhaas', in Sharr, A. (ed.) *Reading architecture and culture: researching buildings, spaces, and documents*. London: Routledge, pp. 165-178.
20. Schön, D.A. (1985) *The design studio: an exploration of its traditions and potentials*. London: RIBA Publications for RIBA Building Industry; Schön, D.A. (2017) *The reflective practitioner: how professionals think in action*. London: Routledge.
21. Megahed Y. and Sharr A. (2018) Practiceopolis: from an imaginary city to a graphic novel, *JAE: Journal of Architectural Education*, 72, pp. 146-166.
22. Schön, *The reflective practitioner*.
23. Pérez-Gómez, A. (1983) *Architecture and the crisis of modern science*. Cambridge, Massachusetts: MIT Press.
24. Ibid.
25. Vesely, *Architecture in the age of divided representation*.
26. Koolhaas, R. (2002) Junkspace, *Obsolescence*, (100) October, pp. 175-190; McVicar, 'God is in the details'/'the detail is moot'.
27. Cuff, D. (1999) The political paradoxes of practice: political economy of local and global architecture, *arq: Architectural Research Quarterly*, 3(1), pp. 77-88; Robinson et al, *The future for architects?*
28. Ibid; Hughes, *The architecture of error*; Murphy, D. (2016) *Last futures: nature, technology and the end of architecture*. London: Verso Books; Koolhaas, 'Junkspace'; McVicar, 'God is in the details'/'The detail is moot'.
29. Abley and Woudhuysen, *Why is construction so backward?*; Glendinning, *Architecture's evil empire?*; Government Construction Strategy (2012), London: Cabinet Office. [Online]. Available at: https://www.gov.uk/government/publications/government-construction-strategy; Ostime, N. (2013) *RIBA job book*. 9th edn. London: RIBA Publications.
30. Norberg-Schulz, C. (1968) *Intentions in architecture*. Cambridge, Massachusetts: MIT press.
31. Cole-Colander, C. (2003) *Designing the customer experience*.
32. Abley and Woudhuysen, *Why is construction so backward?*; Glendinning, *architecture's evil empire?*; Kieran and Timberlake, *Refabricating architecture*.
33. Cole-Colander, C. (2003) Designing the customer experience, *Building Research & Information*, 31(5), pp. 357-366; Sharr, A. (2010) Leslie Martin and the science of architectural form, in Dutoit, A., Odgers, J. and Sharr, A. (eds.) *Quality out of control: standards for measuring architecture*. London, New York: Routledge.
34. Hughes, *The architecture of error*; Murphy, *Last futures*.

35. Cuff, *The story of practice*; McElroy, M. (1984) Marketing: how big corporations choose design firms, *Architectural Record*, 172(7), p. 45; Tombesi, Architectural feasts or professional fausts?

36. Quirk, V. (2013) The 100 Largest Architecture Firms In the World, *ArchDaily*, [Online]. Available at: http://www.archdaily.com/330759/the-100-largest-architecture-firms-in-the-world; Sklair, L. (2017) *The icon project: architecture, cities, and capitalist globalization*. Oxford: Oxford University Press: pp. 83, 87, 88.

37. Hays, K.M. (1984) Critical architecture: between culture and form, *Perspecta* 21, pp. 15-29; Yaneva, A. (2013) *Mapping controversies in architecture*. Burlington: Ashgate Publishing.

38. Forty, A. (2004) *Words and buildings: a vocabulary of modern architecture*. New York: Thames & Hudson; Sharr, A. (2003) Can architecture lie? On truth, knowledge and contemporary architectural theory, *Architectural Theory Review*, 8(2), pp. 164-172; Sharr, A. (2012) *Reading architecture and culture: researching buildings, spaces, and documents*. London: Routledge.

39. Frascari, *Eleven exercises in the art of architectural drawing*; Vesely, *Architecture in the age of divided representation*.

40. Foster, H. and Koolhaas, R., (2013) *Junkspace with running room*. London: Notting Hill Editions Ltd.; Koolhaas, Junkspace.

41. Belsey, C. (2003) *Critical practice*. London: Routledge.

42. Bourdieu, P. (1996) *The rules of art: genesis and structure of the literary field*. Cambridge: Polity Press.; Stevens, G. (2002) *The favored circle: the social foundations of architectural distinction*. Cambridge, Massachusetts: MIT Press.

43. Wacquant, L. (2017) Pierre Bourdieu, in Stones, R. (ed.) *Key sociological thinkers*. London: Macmillan Education, pp. 229-239.

44. Yaneva, *Mapping controversies in architecture*.

45. Abley and Woudhuysen, *Why is construction so backward?*; Kieran and Timberlake, *Refabricating architecture*; Vesely, *Architecture in the age of divided representation*.

46. Snow, C.P. (1969) *The two cultures: and a second look*. Cambridge: Cambridge University Press.

47. Broshar, M., Strong, M., & Friedman, D. S. (2006) Report on integrated practice, *American Institute of Architects*; Robinson et al, *The future for architects?*

48. Feenberg, A. (2012) *Questioning technology*. New York: Routledge; Grabow, P. (2008) An alternative to instrumentalism: technology as a form of transcendence, *International Journal of Technology, Knowledge and Society: Annual Review*, 4(3).

49. Bleecker, J. (2009) *Design fiction: a short essay on design, science, fact and fiction*. London: Near Future Laboratory. [online] Available at: https://drbfw5wfjlxon.cloudfront.net/writing/DesignFiction_WebEdition.pdf; Bleecker, J. (2011) Design fiction, in Grand, S. and Jonas, W. (eds.) *Mapping design research: positions and perspectives*. Basel: Birkhäuser.

50. Snow, *The two cultures*.

Practiceopolis

Abley, I. and Woudhuysen, J. (2004) *Why is construction so backward?* Chichester: Wiley;

Ahrens, J. and Meteling, A. (2010) *Comics and the city: urban space in print, picture and sequence.* New York: The Continuum International Publishing Group Inc.

AIA (2011) *The architecture student's handbook of professional practice.* 14th edn. Somerset: John Wiley & Sons, Inc.

Berkel, B.V. and Bos, C. (2002) *UN studio UN fold.* Rotterdam: nai010 Publishers.

Böhme, G. (2013) The art of the stage set as a paradigm for an aesthetics of atmospheres, *Ambiances,* [Online]. Available at: http://ambiances.revues.org/315 (Accessed: March 2020).

Borges, J.L. (1975) On exactitude in science, in *A universal history of infamy.* Harmondsworth: Penguin.

Cohen, J.L. (1996) *Mies van der Rohe.* London: E & FN Spon.

Crinson, M. and Lubbock, J. (1994) *Architecture, art or profession? Three hundred years of architectural education in Britain.* Manchester: Manchester University Press.

Crook, J.M. (1989) *The dilemma of style: architectural ideas from the picturesque to the post-modern.* London: John Murray.

Cuff, D. (1992) *Architecture: the story of practice.* Cambridge, Massachusetts: MIT Press;

Cuff, D. (1999) The political paradoxes of practice: political economy of local and global architecture, *arq: Architectural Research Quarterly*, 3(1), pp. 77-88.

Dean, A.O. and Hursley, T. (2002) *Rural studio: Samuel Mockbee and an architecture of decency.* New York: Princeton Architectural Press.

Farmer, G., and Guy, S. (2010) Making morality: sustainable architecture and the pragmatic imagination, *Building Research & Information, 38*(4), pp. 368-378.

Fathy, H. (2010) *Architecture for the poor: an experiment in rural Egypt.* Chicago: University of Chicago Press.

Feenberg, A. (2012) *Questioning technology.* New York: Routledge.

Feinstein, C.H. (1998) Pessimism perpetuated: real wages and the standard of living in Britain during and after the industrial revolution. *The Journal of Economic History*, *58*(3), pp. 625-658.

Foster, H. and Koolhaas, R., (2013). *Junkspace with running room.* London: Notting Hill Editions Ltd.

Foxell, S. (2018) *Professionalism for the built environment.* London: Routledge.

Frampton, K. (2016) Toward a critical regionalism: six points for an architecture of resistance, in Docherty, T. (ed.) *Postmodernism: a reader.* New York: Routledge.

Glusberg, J. (1988) *Vision of the modern.* London: Academy Editions.

Glusberg, J. (1991) *Deconstruction: a student guide.* London: Academy Editions.

Grabow, P. (2008) An alternative to instrumentalism: technology as a form of transcendence, *International Journal of Technology, Knowledge and Society: Annual Review*, 4(3).

Guiton, J. (1981) *The ideas of Le Corbusier on architecture and urban planning*. New York: G. Braziller.

Guy, S. and Farmer, G. (2001) Reinterpreting sustainable architecture: the place of technology, *Journal of Architectural Education*, 54(3), pp. 140-148.

Hensel, M.U. and Nilsson, F., eds. (2016) *The changing shape of practice: integrating research and design in architecture*. London: Routledge.

Hensel, M.U. and Nilsson, F., (2019) *The changing shape of architecture: further cases of integrating research and design in practice*. London: Routledge.

Horn, J., Rosenband, L.N. and Smith, M.R., eds. (2010) *Reconceptualizing the industrial revolution*. Cambridge, Massachusetts: MIT press.

Hughes, F. (2014) *The architecture of error: matter, measure, and the misadventures of precision*. Cambridge, Massachusetts: MIT Press.

Hvattum, M. (2013) Crisis and correspondence: style in the nineteenth century. *Architectural Histories*, 1(1), p. 21. DOI: http://doi.org/10.5334/ah.an

Jencks, C. (1987) *Le Corbusier and the tragic view of architecture*. Middlesex: Penguin.

Kieran, S. and Timberlake, J. (2003) *Refabricating architecture: how manufacturing methodologies are poised to transform building construction*. London: McGraw Hill.

Koolhaas, R. (2002) Junkspace, *Obsolescence*, 100 (October), pp. 175-190.

Kostof, S. (1977) *The architect: chapters in the history of the profession*. USA: Oxford University Press.

Kubler, G. (1987) Toward a reductive theory of visual style. in Lang, B. (ed.), *The concept of style*. New York and London: Cornell University Press. pp. 163-173. [Online]. Available at: https://monoskop.org/File:Kubler_George_1979_1987_Toward_a_Reductive_Theory_of_Visual_Style.pdf (Accessed: March 2020).

Kuhn, T.S. and Hacking, I. (2012) *The Structure of scientific revolutions: 50th anniversary edition*. 4th edn. Chicago: University of Chicago Press.

Landes, D.S. (2015) *Wealth and poverty of nations*. London: Hachette.

Lawson, B. (2014) *How designers think: the design process demystified*. Oxford: Elsevier.

Loureiro, F. (2015) The image in power: Vilém Flusser and the craft of architecture, *Architecture Philosophy*, 1(2), pp. 214-230.

McVicar, M. (2012) 'God is in the details'/'the detail is moot': a meeting between Mies and Koolhaas', in Sharr, A. (ed.) *Reading architecture and culture: researching buildings, spaces, and documents*. London: Routledge, pp. 165-178.

Milward, A.S. & Economic History Society (1984) *The economic effects of the two world wars on Britain,* 2nd edn. London: Macmillan.

Mockbee, S. (1998) The Rural Studio, in Till, J. and Wigglesworth, S. (eds.) *The Everyday and Architecture*. London: Architectural Design.

Moore, K. (2010) *Overlooking the visual: demystifying the art of design*. London: Routledge.

Murphy, D. (2016) *Last futures: nature, technology and the end of architecture*. London: Verso Books.

Nisbet, R.A. (1980) *History of the idea of progress*. New York: Basic Books.

Norberg-Schulz, C. (1968) *Intentions in architecture*. Cambridge, Massachusetts: MIT press.

Pallasmaa, J. (2009) *The thinking hand: existential and embodied wisdom in architecture*. Chichester, UK: Wiley.

Parnell, S. (2012) AR's and AD's post-war editorial policies: the making of modern architecture in Britain. *The Journal of Architecture*, 17(5), pp.763-775.

Pérez-Gómez, A. (1983) *Architecture and the crisis of modern science*. Cambridge, Massachusetts: MIT Press.

Porter, T. (2004) *Archispeak: an illustrated guide to architectural terms*. London: Routledge.

Porter, T. (2011) *Will Alsop: the noise*. Abingdon: Routledge.

Saint, A. (2007) *Architect and engineer: a study in sibling rivalry*. London: Yale University Press.

Schön, D.A. (2017) *The reflective practitioner: how professionals think in action*. London: Routledge.

Sharr, A. (2018) *Modern architecture: a very short introduction*. Oxford: Oxford University Press.

Steele, J. (2005) *The architecture of Rasem Badran: narratives on people and place*. New York: Thames & Hudson.

Steele, J. (2019) *Abdelhalim Ibrahim Abdelhalim: an architecture of collective memory*. Cairo: American University in Cairo Press.

Stevens, G. (2002) *The favored circle: the social foundations of architectural distinction*. Cambridge, Massachusetts: MIT press.

Szreter, S. and Mooney, G. (1998) Urbanization, mortality, and the standard of living debate: new estimates of the expectation of life at birth in nineteenth-century British cities. *The Economic History Review*, 51(1), pp. 84-112.

Terry, Q. (1993) *Quinlan Terry: selected works*. London: Academy Editions.

Till, J. (2013) *Architecture depends*. Cambridge, Massachusetts: MIT Press.

Tschumi, B. (2004) *Event-cities 3: concept vs. context vs. content*. Cambridge, Massachusetts: MIT Press.

Wagner, W. (1985) Round table: the fast-growing and fast-changing role of the corporate architect, *Architectural Record*, 173(1), pp. 35-47.

Webster, H. (2011) *Bourdieu for architects*. New York: Routledge.

Wigglesworth, S. and Till, J. (1998) *The everyday and architecture*. Somerset: John Wiley & Sons.

Wigglesworth, S. (2011) *Around and about Stock Orchard Street*. London: Routledge.

Womersley, S. and Portman, J. (2002) *John Portman and associates: selected and current works*. Melbourne: Images Publishing Group.

Wright, R. (2010) *An illustrated short history of progress*. New York: Canongate Books.

Yaneva, A. (2013) *Mapping controversies in architecture*. Burlington: Ashgate Publishing.

Zumthor, P. (2006) *Atmospheres: architectural environments, surrounding objects*. Basel: Birkhäuser.

Zumthor, P. (2010) *Thinking architecture*. Basel: Birkhäuser.

Epilogue

1. Foster, H. and Koolhaas, R. (2013) *Junkspace with running room*. London: Notting Hill Editions Ltd.; Koolhaas, R. (2002) Junkspace, *Obsolescence*, 100 (October), pp. 175-190.

2. Grand, S. (2011) Research as design: promising strategies and possible futures, in Grand, S. and Jonas, W. (eds.) *Mapping design research: positions and perspectives*. Basel: Birkhäuser.